BOOKS BY ROBIN HOBB

THE FARSEER TRILOGY
Assassin's Apprentice
Royal Assassin
Assassin's Quest

THE LIVESHIP TRADERS TRILOGY
Ship of Magic
Mad Ship
Ship of Destiny

THE TAWNY MAN TRILOGY
Fool's Errand
Golden Fool
Fool's Fate

THE SOLDIER SON TRILOGY
Shaman's Crossing
Forest Mage
Renegade's Magic

THE RAIN WILDS CHRONICLES
Dragon Keeper
Dragon Haven
City of Dragons
Blood of Dragons

* AVAILABLE FROM RANDOM HOUSE

Fool's Assassin

Fool's Assassin

BOOK ONE OF THE
FITZ AND THE FOOL TRILOGY

ROBIN HOBB

 DEL REY ⬥ NEW YORK

Published in the United States by Del Rey, an imprint of Random House, a division of Random House LLC, a Penguin Random House Company, New York.

DEL REY and the HOUSE colophon are registered trademarks of Random House LLC.

ISBN 978-0-553-39242-5
eBook ISBN 978-0-553-39243-2

Printed in the United States of America on acid-free paper

www.delreybooks.com

9 8 7 6 5 4 3 2 1

First Edition

Book design by Christopher M. Zucker

This one is for the guys.
To Soren, Felix, and Blake.

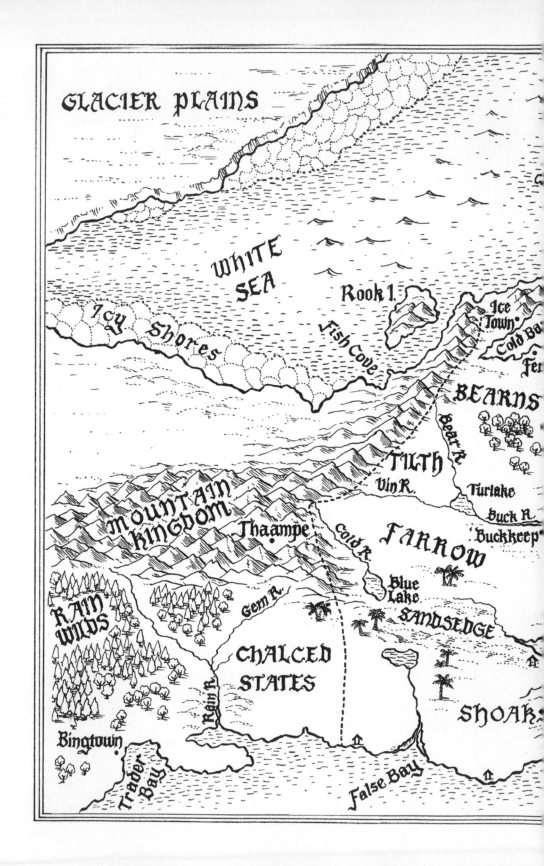

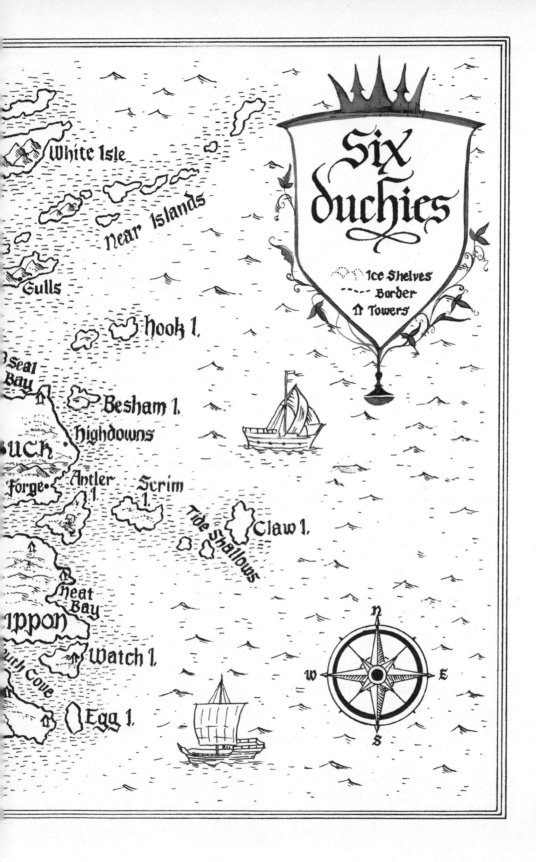

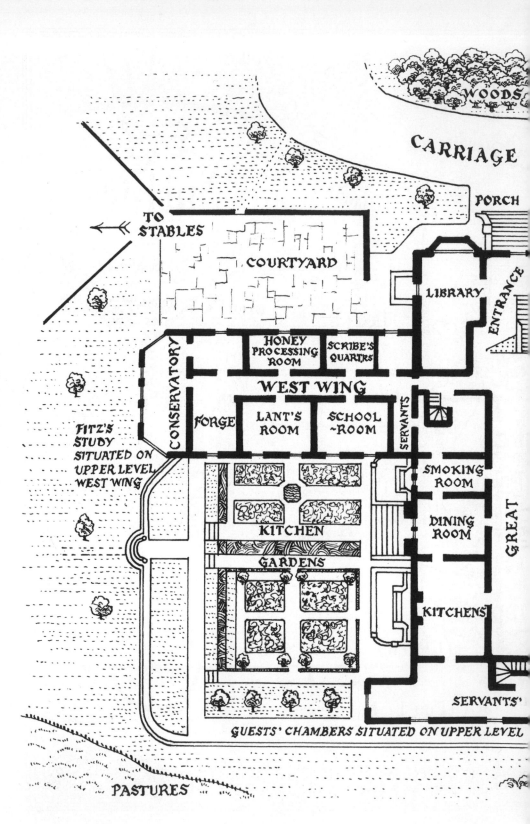

WOODS

CARRIAGE

PORCH

TO STABLES

COURTYARD

LIBRARY

ENTRANCE

HONEY PROCESSING ROOM

SCRIBE'S QUARTRS

CONSERVATORY

WEST WING

FORGE

LANT'S ROOM

SCHOOL ~ROOM

SERVANTS

FITZ'S STUDY SITUATED ON UPPER LEVEL WEST WING

SMOKING ROOM

DINING ROOM

GREAT

KITCHEN GARDENS

KITCHENS

SERVANTS'

GUESTS' CHAMBERS SITUATED ON UPPER LEVEL

PASTURES

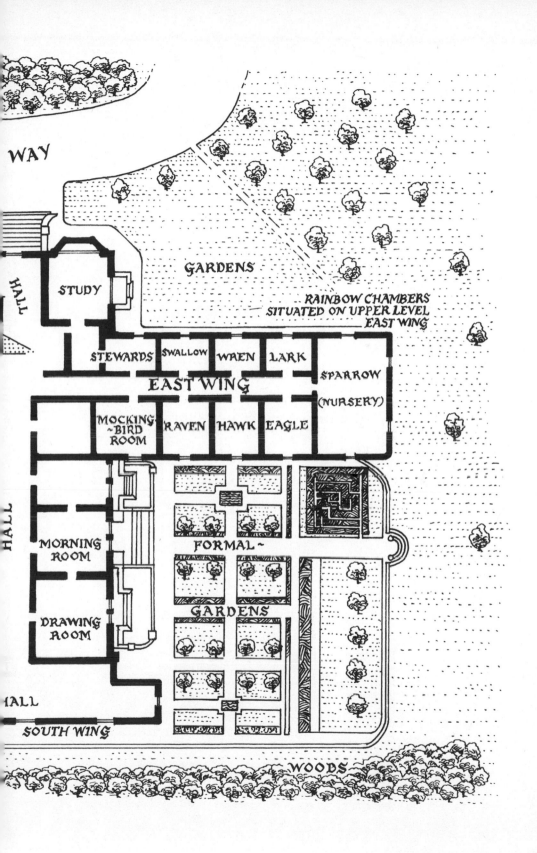

WAY

HALL

STUDY

GARDENS

RAINBOW CHAMBERS
SITUATED ON UPPER LEVEL
EAST WING

STEWARDS SWALLOW WREN LARK

EAST WING

SPARROW

(NURSERY)

MOCKING ~BIRD ROOM RAVEN HAWK EAGLE

HALL

MORNING ROOM

FORMAL ~

DRAWING ROOM

GARDENS

HALL

SOUTH WING

WOODS

Fool's Assassin

PROLOGUE

My dear Lady Fennis,

We have been friends far too long for me to be circumspect. As you so delicately hinted, yes, there has been shattering news delivered to me. My stepson, Prince Chivalry, has exposed himself as the crude fellow I have always known him to be. His bastard child, fathered on a Mountain whore, has been revealed.

As shameful as that is, it could have been handled far more discreetly if his clever-as-a-stone brother Prince Verity had taken swift and decisive action to eliminate the disgrace. Instead he has announced the child in an indiscreet message to my husband.

And so, in the face of this base behavior, what does my lord do? Why, not only does he insist the bastard must be brought to Buckkeep Castle, he then bestows on Chivalry the title to Withywoods, and sends him out to pasture there with his awkward, barren wife. Withywoods! A fine estate that any number of my friends would be

pleased to occupy, and he rewards it to his son for fathering a bas-
tard with a foreign commoner! Nor does King Shrewd find it dis-
tasteful that said bastard has been brought back here to Buckkeep
Castle where any member of my court may see the little Mountain
savage.

And the final insult to me and my son? He has decreed that
Prince Verity will now take up the title of king-in-waiting, and be
the next presumed heir to the throne. When Chivalry had the de-
cency to secede his claim in the face of this disgrace, I secretly re-
joiced, believing that Regal would immediately be recognized as the
next king. While he may be younger than both his half-brothers, no
one can dispute that his bloodlines are more noble, and his bearing
as lordly as his name.

Truly, I am wasted here. As wasted as my son, Regal. When I
gave up my own reign and titles to be Shrewd's queen, it was in the
belief that any child I bore him would be seen as possessing far bet-
ter lineage than the two reckless boys his former queen gave him,
and would reign after Shrewd. But does he now look at Chivalry
and admit his mistake in naming him heir? No. Instead he sets him
aside only to install his doltish younger brother as king-in-waiting.
Verity. Hulking, square-faced Verity, with all the grace of an ox.

It is too much, my dear. Too much for me to bear. I would leave
court, save that Regal would then be without a defender here.

MISSIVE FROM QUEEN DESIRE TO LADY FENNIS OF TILTH

I hated her when I was a boy. I recall the first time I found that missive, unfinished and never sent. I read it, confirming for myself that
the queen I had never formally met had, indeed, hated me from the
moment she knew of me. I made it mutual. I never asked Chade
how he came by that letter. A bastard himself and half-brother to
King Shrewd, Chade had never hesitated in pursuing the best interests of the Farseer throne. He had purloined it from Queen Desire's desk, perhaps. Perhaps it had been his ploy to make it appear
that the queen snubbed Lady Fennis by not responding to her letter. Does it matter now? I do not know, for I do not know what effect my old mentor gained with his theft.

Yet I do wonder, sometimes, if it was an accident that I found and read Queen Desire's letter to Lady Fennis, or if it was a deliberate revelation on Chade's part. He was my mentor in those days, teaching me the assassin's arts. Chade served his king ruthlessly, as assassin, spy, and manipulator of the court at Buckkeep Castle, and taught me to do the same. A royal bastard, he told me, is safe in a court only so long as he is useful. Ostensibly I was a lowly bastard, ignored or reviled as I navigated the dangerous currents of politics in the castle. But both King Shrewd and I knew that I was protected by the king's hand and his assassin. It was not only poisons and knife-work and subterfuge that he taught me, but what one must do to survive as a bastard of royal lineage. Did he seek to give me warning, or teach me to hate that I might be more firmly his? Even those questions come to me too late.

Over the years I have seen Queen Desire in so many guises. First she was the horrid woman who hated my father and hated me even more, the woman with the power to snatch the crown from my father's head and condemn me to a life where even my name was the mark of my bastardy. I recall a time in my life when I feared to let her see me.

Years after I arrived at Buckkeep, when my father was murdered at Withywoods, hers was the hand most likely behind it. And yet there was nothing I or Chade could do about it, no justice we could demand. I remember wondering if King Shrewd did not know or if he did not care. I remember knowing with absolute certainty that if Queen Desire wished my death, she could ask for it. I even wondered then if Chade would protect me or if he would bow to his duty and allow it to happen. Such things for a child to wonder.

Withywoods was an idea to me, a harsh place of banishment and humiliation. When I was a boy and I lived in Buckkeep, I was told that was where my father had gone, to hide from the shame that was me. He had abdicated his throne and crown; bowed his head to the hurt and anger of his lawful wife, Patience; apologized to king and court for his failure of virtue and judgment; and fled from the bastard he had sired.

And so I imagined that place based on the only places I had ever lived, as a fortified castle on a hill. I had thought of it as a place like the stockade fortress at Moonseye in the Mountain Kingdom, or the steep walls of Buckkeep Castle perched on top of sheer and forbidding black cliffs overlooking the sea. I had imagined my father, brooding alone in a chill stone hall hung with battle pennants and ancient arms. I imagined stony fields that gave onto gray-fogged marshes.

Later I would discover that Withywoods was a grand manor, a large and comfortable home built in a wide and generous valley. Its walls were not of stone, but of golden oak and rich maple, and though the floors of the halls were flagged with flat river stone, the walls were paneled in warm wood. The gentle sunlight of the farming valley fell in broad stripes into the rooms through the tall, narrow windows. The carriageway to the front door was wide, and graceful white birches lined it. In autumn they shed a carpet of gold on the road, and in winter, burdened with snow, they arched over it, a frosted white tunnel paned with glimpses of blue sky.

Withywoods was not a fortress banishment, not an exile, but a tolerant pasturing-out for my father and his barren wife. I think my grandfather had loved my father as much as his stepmother hated him. King Shrewd sent him to that distant estate to be safe.

And when my time came to go there, with the woman I loved and her lively boys and the woman who had always wanted to be my mother, it became for a time a haven of rest and peace for us.

Time is an unkind teacher, delivering lessons that we learn far too late for them to be useful. Years after I could have benefited from them, the insights come to me. Now I look back on "old" King Shrewd and see him as a man beset by a long and wasting illness that stole from him the comfort of his own body and the sharpness of his mind. But worse, I see Queen Desire for what she was: not an evil woman intent on making my little life miserable, but a mother full of ruthless love for her only son, intent that he should never be slighted in any way. She would stop at nothing to put him on a throne.

What would I not have done to protect my little daughter? What action would have been too extreme? If I say, "I would have killed them all, with no regrets," does that make me a monster?

Or just a father?

But it is all hindsight. All these lessons, learned too late. When I was still a young man, I felt in my flesh like a bent old gaffer, full of pains and sighs. Oh, how I pitied myself, and justified every wild decision I had ever made! And then, when it came time for me to be the wise elder of my household, I was trapped in the body of a man of middle years, still subject to those passions and impulses, still relying on the strength of my right arm when I would have been wiser to stop and employ my powers of reason.

Lessons learned too late. Insights discovered decades later.

And so much lost as a result.

Chapter 1

WITHYWOODS

Burrich, old friend,

Well, we are settled here, I suppose. It has not been a pleasant time for me, or for you if your somewhat terse message conceals as much as I suspect it does. The house is immense, far too large for the two of us. It is so like you to ask after our mounts before inquiring after my own health. I will answer that query first. I'm pleased to tell you that Silk has taken the change in stable quite calmly, as the well-mannered palfrey she has always been. Tallfellow, in contrast, has made a new hobby out of bullying the resident stallion, but we have taken steps to be sure their stalls and paddocks are well separated now. I've reduced his grain and there is a young stableman here named, oddly enough, Tallman, who was absolutely ecstatic to receive my request that he take the horse out and run him hard at least once a day. With such a regimen, I am sure he will soon settle.

My lady wife. You did not ask after her, but I know you well, my *friend. So I will tell you that Patience has been furious, wounded, melancholy, hysterical, and altogether of a hundred different minds about the situation. She berates me that I was unfaithful to her before we met, and in the next instant forgives me and blames herself that she has not furnished me an heir, given that "it is evident that the problem is entirely with me." Somehow, we two will weather this.*

I appreciate that you have taken command of my other responsibilities there. My brother has told me enough of your charge's temperament that I send my sympathy to both of you and my deepest thanks. On whom else could I rely at a time such as this, for a favor so extreme?

I trust you to understand why I remain circumspect in this regard. Give Vixen a pat, a hug, and a large bone from me. I am confident that I owe as much to her vigilance as to yours. My wife is calling for me down the halls. I must end this and send it on its way. My brother may have words for you from me when next your paths cross.

UNSIGNED LETTER FROM
CHIVALRY TO STABLEMASTER BURRICH

Fresh snowfall perched in white ramparts on the bare black birch limbs that lined the drive. White gleamed against black, like a fool's winter motley. The snow came down in loose clumps of flakes, adding a fresh layer of glistening white to the banked snow in the courtyard. It was softening the hard ridges of fresh wheel tracks in the carriageway, erasing the boys' footprints in the snow and smoothing the rutted pathways to mere suggestions of themselves. As I watched, another carriage arrived, drawn by a dapple-gray team. The driver's red-cloaked shoulders were dusted with snow. A page in green and yellow darted from the steps of Withywoods to open the carriage door and gesture a welcome to our guests. From my vantage I could not tell who they were, save that their garb bespoke Withy merchants rather than gentry from one of the neighboring estates. As they passed out of my view and their driver moved the carriage off to our stables, I looked up at the afternoon sky. Definitely more to come. I suspected it would snow all night. Well, that was fitting. I let the curtain fall and turned as Molly entered our bedchamber.

"Fitz! You aren't ready yet?"

I glanced down at myself. "I thought I was . . ."

My wife clicked her tongue at me. "Oh, Fitz. It's Winterfest. The halls are festooned with greenery, Patience had Cook create a feast that will probably sustain the whole household for three days, all three sets of minstrels that she invited are tuning up, and half our guests have already arrived. You should be down there, greeting them as they enter. And you're not even dressed yet."

I thought of asking her what was wrong with what I was wearing, but she was already digging through my clothing chest, lifting garments, considering them, and discarding them. I waited. "This," she said, pulling out a white linen shirt with ridges of lace down the sleeves. "And this jerkin over it. Everyone knows that wearing green at Winterfest is good luck. With your silver chain to match the buttons. These leggings. They're old-fashioned enough to make you look like an old man, but at least they're not as saggy as those you have on. I know better than to ask you to wear your new trousers."

"I *am* an old man. At forty-seven, surely I'm allowed to dress as I please."

She lowered her brows and gave me a mock glare. She set her hands to her hips. "Are you calling me an old woman, sirrah? For I seem to recall I have three years on you."

"Of course not!" I hastily amended my words. But I could not resist grumbling, "But I have no idea why everyone wishes to dress as if they are Jamaillian nobility. The fabric on those trousers is so thin, the slightest bramble would tear them, and . . ."

She looked up at me with an exasperated sigh. "Yes. I've heard it from you a hundred times. Let's ignore that there are few brambles inside Withywoods, shall we? So. Take these clean leggings. The ones you have on are a disgrace; didn't you wear them yesterday when you were helping with that horse that had a cracked hoof? And put on your house shoes, not those worn boots. You'll be expected to dance, you know."

She straightened from her excavation of my clothing chest. Conceding to the inevitable, I'd already begun shedding garments. As I thrust my head out of the shirt, my gaze met hers. She was smiling in a familiar way, and as I considered her holly crown, the cascading lace on her blouse and gaily embroidered kirtle, I found a smile to answer hers. Her smile broadened even as she took a step back from me. "Now, Fitz. We've guests below, waiting for us."

"They've waited this long, they can wait a bit longer. Our daughter can mind them."

I advanced a step. She retreated to the door and set her hand to the knob, all the while shaking her head so that her black ringlets danced on her brow and shoulders. She lowered her head and looked up at me through her lashes, and suddenly she seemed just a girl to me again. A wild Buckkeep Town girl, to be pursued down a sandy beach. Did she remember? Perhaps, for she caught her lower lip between her teeth and I saw her resolve almost weaken. Then, "No. Our guests can't wait, and while Nettle can welcome them, a greeting from the daughter of the house is not the same as an acknowledgment from you and me. Riddle may stand at her shoulder as our steward and help her, but until the king gives his permission for them to wed, we should not present them as a couple. So it is you and I who must wait. Because I'm not going to be content with 'a bit' of your time tonight. I expect better effort than that from you."

"Really?" I challenged her. I took two swift steps toward her, but with a girlish shriek she was out the door. As she pulled it almost shut, she added through the crack, "Hurry up! You know how quickly Patience's parties can get out of hand. I've left Nettle in charge of things, but you know, Riddle is very nearly as bad as Patience." A pause. "And do not dare to be late and leave me with no dancing partner!"

She shut the door just as I reached it. I halted and then, with a small sigh, went back for my clean leggings and soft shoes. She would expect me to dance, and I would do my best. I did know that Riddle was apt to enjoy himself at any sort of festivity at Withywoods with an abandon that was very unlike the reserved fellow he showed himself at Buckkeep, and perhaps not precisely correct for a man who was ostensibly just our former household steward. I found myself smiling. Where he led, sometimes Nettle followed, showing a merry side of herself that she, too, seldom revealed at the king's court. Hearth and Just, the two of Molly's six grown sons who were still at home, would need very little encouragement to join in. As Patience had invited half of Withy and far more musicians than could perform in one evening, I fully expected that our Winterfest revelry would last at least three days.

With some reluctance, I removed my leggings and pulled on the trousers. They were a dark green that was nearly black, thin linen, and almost as voluminous as a skirt. They tied at my waist with ribbons. A broad silk sash completed the ridiculous garment. I told myself that my wearing them would please Molly. I suspected that Riddle would have been bothered into donning similar garb. I sighed again, wondering why we must all emulate Jamaillian fashions, and then resigned myself to it. I finished dressing, badgered my hair into a warrior's tail, and left our bedchamber. I paused at the top of the grand oak staircase; the sounds of merriment drifted up to me. I took a breath as if I were about to dive into deep water. I had nothing to fear, no reason to hesitate, and yet the ingrained habits of my distant boyhood still clutched at me. I had every right to descend this stair, to walk among the glad company below as master of the house and husband to the lady who owned it. Now I was known as Holder Tom Badgerlock, common-born perhaps but elevated alongside Lady Molly to gentry status. The bastard Fitz-Chivalry Farseer—grandson and nephew and cousin to kings—had been laid to rest twoscore years ago. To the folk below, I was Holder Tom and the founder of the feast they would enjoy.

Even if I was wearing silly Jamaillian trousers.

I paused a moment longer, listening. I could hear two distinct groups of minstrels vying to tune their instruments. Riddle's laugh rang suddenly clear and loud, making me smile. The hum of voices from the Great Hall lifted in volume and then fell again. One set of minstrels gained ascendancy, for a lively drumbeat suddenly broke through the voices to dominate all. The dancing would soon begin. Truly, I was late, and had best descend. Yet there was sweetness to

standing here, above it all, imagining Nettle's flashing feet and sparkling eyes as Riddle led her through the dance steps. Oh, and Molly!
She would be waiting for me! I had become a passable dancer over
the years, for her sake, as she loved it so. She would not easily forgive me if I left her standing.

I hurried down the polished oak steps two at a time, reached the
hall foyer, and was there suddenly ambushed by Revel. Our new
young steward was looking very fine indeed in a white shirt, black
jacket, and black trousers in the Jamaillian fashion. His green house
shoes were startling, as was the yellow scarf at his throat. Green
and yellow were the Withywoods colors, and I suspected these ac-
coutrements were Patience's idea. I did not let the smile curve my
mouth but I think he read it in my eyes. He stood even taller and
looked down at me as he soberly informed me, "Sir, there are minstrels at the door."

I gave him a puzzled glance. "Well, let them in, man. It's Winterfest."

He stood still, his lips folded in disapproval. "Sir, I do not think
they were invited."

"It's Winterfest," I repeated, beginning to be annoyed. Molly
would not be pleased at being kept waiting. "Patience invites every
minstrel, puppeteer, tumbler, tinker, or blacksmith she meets to
come and sojourn with us for a time. She probably invited them
months ago and forgot all about it."

I did not think his back could get stiffer, but it did. "Sir, they
were outside the stable, trying to peer in through a crack in the
planking. Tallman heard the dogs barking and went to see what it
was about and found them. That is when they said they were minstrels, invited for Winterfest."

"And?"

He took a short breath. "Sir, I do not think they are minstrels.
They have no instruments. And while one said they were minstrels,
another said, no, they were tumblers. But when Tallman said he
would walk them up to the front door, they said that he needn't,
they only wished to beg shelter for the night, and the stable would
be fine." He shook his head. "Tallman spoke to me privately when

he brought them up. He thinks they're none of what they claim to be. And so do I."

I gave him a look. Revel folded his arms. He did not meet my glance, but his mouth was stubborn. I found a bit of patience for him. He was young and fairly new to the household. Cravit Soft-hands, our ancient steward, had died last year. Riddle had stepped up to shoulder many of the old man's duties, but insisted that Withywoods needed a new steward trained. I'd casually replied that I did not have time to find one, and within three days Riddle had brought Revel to us. After two months, Revel was still learning his place, I told myself, and considered that perhaps Riddle had infused him with a bit too much caution. Riddle was, after all, Chade's man, insinuated into our household to watch my back and probably spy on me. Despite his current merriness and devotion to my daughter, he was a man steeped in carefulness. Given his way, we'd have had a guard contingent at Withywoods to rival the Queen's Own. I reined my mind back to the question at hand.

"Revel, I appreciate your care. But it's Winterfest. And be they minstrels or wandering beggars, no man should be turned from our door on such a holiday, or on such a snowy evening. While there's room in the house, they need not sleep in the stable. Bring them in. I'm sure all will be well."

"Sir." He was not agreeing, but he was obeying. I suppressed a sigh. That would do for now. I turned to join the throng in the Great Hall.

"Sir?"

I turned back to him. My voice was stern as I asked him, "Is there something else, Revel? Something pressing?" I could hear the tentative notes of musicians bringing their instruments into harmony, and then the music suddenly opened into blossom. I'd missed the start of the first dance. I gritted my teeth as I thought of Molly standing alone, watching the dancers whirl.

I saw his teeth catch for an instant on his lower lip. He decided to press on. "Sir, the messenger still waits for you in your study."

"Messenger?"

Revel gave a martyred sigh. "Hours ago, I sent one of our temporary pages looking for you with a message. He said he shouted it at you through the door of the steams. I have to inform you, sir, this is what comes of us using untrained boys and girls as pages. We should have a few here permanently, if only to train them for future need."

At my wearied look, Revel cleared his throat and changed tactics. "My apologies, sir. I should have sent him back to confirm you'd heard him."

"I didn't. Revel, would you mind dealing with it for me?" I took a hesitant step toward the hall. The music was rising.

Revel gave a minute shake of his head. "I am very sorry, sir. But the messenger says the message is specifically for you. I have asked twice if I could be of any help, and offered to write the message for you." He shook his head. "The messenger insists that only you can receive the words."

I guessed the message, then. Holder Barit had been trying to wrangle me into agreeing that he could pasture some of his flock with our sheep. Our shepherd had adamantly insisted that this would be too many beasts for our winter pasturage. I intended to listen to Shepherd Lin, even if Barit was now willing to offer a decent amount of money. Winterfest eve was no time to be doing business. It would keep. "It's fine, Revel. And don't be too stern with our pages. You are right. We should have one or two on staff. But most of them will grow up to work in the orchards or follow their mothers' trades. It's rare that we need them here at Withy." I didn't want to be thinking about this right now. Molly was waiting! I took a breath and made my decision. "Thoughtless as it is for me to have left a messenger waiting so long, it would be ruder by far if I leave my lady unpartnered for the second dance as well as the first. Please extend my apology to the messenger for my unfortunate delay and see that he is made comfortable with food and drink. Tell him that I'll come to the study directly after the second dance." I had no wish to do so. The festivities beckoned tonight. A better idea came to me. "No! Invite him to join the festivities. Tell him to enjoy himself, and that we will sit down together before noon tomorrow." I could think of nothing in my life that could possibly be so pressing as to demand my attention tonight.

"Her, sir."

"Revel?"

"Her. The messenger is a girl, sir. Scarcely a woman, by the look of her. Of course, I have already offered her food and drink. I would not so neglect anyone who came to your door. Let alone one who seems to have come a long and weary way."

Music was playing and Molly was waiting. Better the messenger wait than Molly. "Then offer her a room, and ask if she would like a hot bath drawn or a quiet meal alone before we meet tomorrow. Do your best to see she is comfortable, Revel, and I will give her as much of my time as she wishes tomorrow."

"I shall, sir."

He turned to go back to the entrance hall, and I hastened to the Great Hall of Withywoods. The two tall doors stood open, the golden oak planks gleaming in firelight and candlelight. Music and the tap and slap of dancing feet spilled into the paneled corridor, but just as I drew near the musicians played the last refrain and with a shout the first dance was over. I rolled my eyes at my ill luck.

But as I stepped into the hall, breasting the wave of applause for the minstrels, I saw that Molly's dance partner was bowing gravely to her. My stepson had rescued his mother and taken her to the floor. Young Hearth had been growing like a weed for the past year. He was as darkly handsome as his father, Burrich, had been, but his brow and smiling mouth were Molly's. At seventeen he could look down at the top of his mother's head. His cheeks were flushed with the lively dance, and Molly did not appear to have missed me even a tiny bit. As she looked up and her eyes met mine across the hall, she smiled. I blessed Hearth and resolved that I would find a substantial way to convey my thanks to him. Across the room, his older brother, Just, lounged against the hearth. Nettle and Riddle stood nearby; Nettle's cheeks were pink and I knew Just was teasing his older sister, and Riddle was in on it.

I made my way across the room to Molly, pausing often to bow and return greetings to our many guests who hailed me. Every rank and walk of life was reflected there. The gentry and minor nobility of our area were there, finely dressed in lace and linen trousers; Tinker John and the village seamstress and a local cheesemaker were there as well. Their festive garments might be a bit more dated, and some were well worn, but they had been freshly brushed for the occasion and the shining holly crowns and sprigs that many wore were newly harvested. Molly had put out her best scented candles, so the fragrances of lavender and honeysuckle filled the air even as the dancing flames painted the walls with gold and honey. Grand fires blazed in all three hearths, with spitted meats tended by red-faced village lads employed for the occasion. Several maids were busy at the ale keg in the corner, topping mugs on the trays they would offer to the breathless dancers when the music paused.

At one end of the room, tables were laden with breads, apples, dishes of raisins and nuts, pastries and creams, platters of smoked meats and fish, and many another dish I didn't recognize. Dripping slices of fresh-cut meat from the roasts on the spits supplied all that any man could ask for, and added their rich fragrance to the festive air. Benches were filled with guests already enjoying food and drink, for there was also beer and wine in plenty.

At the other end of the room the first minstrels were yielding the stage to the second group. The floor had been strewn with sand for the dancers. Undoubtedly it had been swept into elegant patterns when the guests first arrived, but it now showed the busy tread of the merrymakers. I reached Molly's side just as the musicians swept into their opening notes. This tune was as pensive as the first had been jolly, so as Molly seized my hand and led me to the dance floor, I was able to keep possession of both her hands and hear her voice through the melody. "You look very fine tonight, Holder Badgerlock." She drew me into line with the other men.

I bowed gravely over our joined hands. "If you are pleased, then I am content," I replied. I ignored the flapping of fabric against my calves as we turned, parted briefly, and then clasped hands again. I caught a glimpse of Riddle and Nettle. Yes, Riddle wore the same sort of flapping trousers, in blue, and he held my daughter not by her fingertips but by her hands. Nettle was smiling. When I glanced back at Molly, she was smiling, too. She had noted the direction of my glance.

"Were we ever that young?" she asked me.

I shook my head. "I think not," I said. "Life was harsher for us when we were that age."

I saw her cast her thoughts back through the years. "When I was Nettle's age, I was already the mother of three children and carrying a fourth. And you were . . ." She let the thought trail away, and I did not speak. I had been living in a little cabin near Forge with my wolf. Was that the year I had taken in Hap? The orphan had been glad of a home, and Nighteyes had been glad of livelier company. I had thought myself resigned, then, to losing her to Burrich. Nineteen long years ago. I pushed the long shadow of those days aside. I stepped closer, put my hands to her waist, and lifted her as we turned. She set her hands to my shoulders, her mouth opening in surprise and delight. Around us, the other dancers gawked briefly. As I put her back on her feet, I observed, "And that is why we should be young now."

"You, perhaps." Her cheeks were pink and she seemed a bit breathless as we made another promenade and turned, parted then rejoined. Or almost rejoined. No, I should have turned again and then . . . I'd hopelessly muddled it, just as I'd been taking great pride that I recalled every step from the last time we had danced this. The other dancers avoided me, parting to flow past me as if I were a stubborn rock in a creek. I spun in a circle, looking for Molly, and found her standing behind me, her hands lifted in a useless attempt to contain her laughter. I reached for her, intending to insert us back into the dance, but she seized both my hands and pulled me from the floor, laughing breathlessly. I rolled my eyes and tried to apologize but, "It's all right, dear. A bit of rest and something to drink would be welcome. Hearth wore me out earlier with his prancing. I need to sit down." She caught her breath suddenly and swayed against me. Her brow glistened with perspiration. She set her hand to the back of her neck and rubbed it as if to relieve a cramp.

"And I the same," I lied to her. Her face flushed, she smiled faintly at me as she pressed her hand to her breast as if to calm her fluttering heart. I smiled back at her and took her to her chair by the hearth. I had scarcely seated her before a page was at my elbow, offering to bring her wine. She nodded and sent him scampering.

"What was that, stitched all round his cap?" I asked distractedly.

"Feathers. And locks of hair from horse tails." She was still breathless.

I looked askance at her.

"It was Patience's fancy this year. All the boys she hired from Withy to act as pages for the holiday are dressed so. Feathers to bid all our troubles take flight, and horse tail hairs, which is what we will show to our problems as we flee them."

"I . . . see." My second lie of the evening.

"Well, it's good that you do, as I certainly don't. But every Winterfest, it's something, isn't it? Do you remember the year that Patience handed out greenwood staffs to every unmarried man who came to the festival? With the length based on her assessment of his masculinity?"

I bit down on the laugh that threatened to escape. "I do. Apparently she thought the young ladies needed a clear indication of which men would make the best mates."

Molly lifted her brows. "Perhaps they did. There were six weddings at Springfest that year."

My wife looked across the room. Patience, my stepmother, was dressed in a grand old gown of pale-blue velvet trimmed with black lace at the cuffs and throat. Her long gray hair had been braided and pinned to her head in a coronet. She had a single sprig of holly in it, and several dozen bright-blue feathers stuck in at all angles. A fan dangled from a bracelet at her wrist; it was blue to match her gown and feathers, and also edged with stiffened black lace. She looked both lovely and eccentric to me, as she always had. She was wagging a finger at Molly's youngest, warning him about something. Hearth stood straight, looking solemnly down at her, but his clasped fingers fidgeted behind his back. His brother Just stood at a distance, concealing his grin and waiting for him to be released. I took pity on them both. Patience seemed to think they were still ten and twelve, despite how they towered over her. Just was barely short of his twentieth birthday, and Hearth was Molly's youngest at seventeen. Yet he stood like a scolded boy and tolerantly accepted Patience's rebuke.

"I want to let Lady Patience know that more of her minstrels have arrived. I hope this is the last batch of them. Any more and I suspect they'll be coming to blows over who gets to perform and for how long." Any minstrels invited to perform at Withywoods were assured of meals and a warm place to sleep, and a small purse for their efforts. The rest of their rewards were won from the guests, and often the musicians who performed the most reaped the greatest gain. Three sets of musicians were more than ample for a Winterfest at our holding. Four would be a challenge.

Molly nodded. She lifted her hands to her rosy cheeks. "I think I'll just sit here a bit longer. Oh, here's the lad with my wine!"

There was a lull in the music, and I took the opportunity to cross the dance floor quickly. Patience saw me coming and first smiled and then scowled at me. By the time I reached her side, she had completely forgotten Hearth and he had escaped with his brother. She snapped her fan shut, pointed it at me, and asked me accusingly, "What has become of your leggings? Those skirts are flapping about your legs like a ship with storm-torn canvas!"

I looked down at them, and up at her. "The new style from Jamaillia." As her disapproval deepened, I added, "Molly chose them."

Lady Patience stared down as if perhaps I had a litter of kittens concealed in them. Then she lifted her eyes to mine, smiled, and said, "A lovely color. And I am sure she is pleased that you wore them."

"She is."

Patience lifted her hand, I extended my arm, she placed her hand on my forearm, and we began a slow perambulation of the Great Hall. Folk parted for her, bowing and curtsying. Lady Patience, for so she was this evening, gravely inclined her head or warmly greeted or embraced as each person merited. I was content simply to be her escort, to see her enjoying herself, and to endeavor to keep a straight face through her whispered asides about Lord Durden's breath or her pity for how quickly Tinker Dan was losing his hair. Some of the older guests remembered when she was not only the lady of Withywoods but wife to Prince Chivalry. In many ways, she still reigned here, for Nettle spent a good portion of her time at Buckkeep Castle as Skillmistress to King Dutiful, and Molly was content to let Patience have her way in most things.

"There are times in a woman's life when only the company of other women can suffice," Patience had explained to me when she had summarily moved in with us at Withywoods five years previously. "Girls need an older woman in the house as they become women, to explain those changes to them. And when that other change comes early to women, especially women who hoped to bear more children, it is good to have the guidance of a woman who has also known that disappointment. Men are simply not helpful at this time." And while I had known trepidation about the arrangement when Patience first arrived with her baggage train of animals, seeds, and plants, she had proven the wisdom of her words. I knew it was rare for two women to exist so contentedly under one roof and blessed my good fortune.

When we reached her favorite chair by the hearth, I deposited her there, fetched her a cup of mulled cider, and then confided to her, "The last of your musicians arrived just as I came down the stairs. I haven't seen them enter yet, but I thought you'd want to know that they are here."

She raised her brows at me and then turned to peer the length of the room. The third set of musicians were moving to take over the dais there. She looked back at me, "No, they're all here. I was most careful in my selection this year. For Winterfest, I thought to myself, we must have some warm-tempered folk to keep the chill away. And so, if you look, there is a redhead in every group that I've invited. There, see the woman warming her voice? Look at that cascade of auburn hair. Don't tell me that she won't warm this fest with her spirit alone." She did indeed appear to be a very warmnatured woman. She let the dancers rest by launching into a long story song, more fit for listening than dancing, sung in a rich and throaty voice. Her audience, old and young, drew closer to her as she sang the old tale of the maiden seduced by the Old Man of winter and carried off to his distant ice fortress in the far south.

All were rapt by the tale, and so it was that my eye caught the motion as two men and a woman entered the hall. They looked around as if dazzled, and perhaps they were after their long hike through an evening of falling snow. It was obvious they had come on foot, for their rough leather trousers were soaked to the knee. Their garb was odd, as minstrels were wont to wear, but unlike any that I had ever seen. Their knee-boots were yellow mottled brown from the wet, their leather trousers short, barely hanging past the tops of their boots. Their jackets were of the same leather, tanned to the same pale brown, with shirts of heavy-knit wool beneath them. They looked uncomfortable, as if the wool was too snug a fit under the leathers. "There they are now," I told her.

Patience stared at them from across the room. "I did not hire them," she declared with an offended sniff. "Look at that woman, pale as a ghost. There's no heat to her at all. And the men are just as wintry, with hair the color of an ice bear's hide. Brr. They chill me just looking at them." Then the lines smoothed from her brow. "So. I shall not allow them to sing tonight. But let's invite them back for high summer, when a chilly tale or a cool wind would be welcome on a muggy evening."

But before I could move to do her bidding, I heard a roar of "Tom! There you are! So good to see you, old friend!"

I turned with that mixture of elation and dismay that surprise visits from unconventional and loving friends stir in one. Web was crossing the room in long strides, with Swift but a step or two behind. I lifted my arms wide and went to greet them. The burly Witmaster had grown in girth these last few years. As always, his cheeks were as red as if he had just stepped in from the wind. Molly's son Swift was a couple of steps behind him, but as I watched, Nettle emerged from the crowd of guests and ambushed her brother in a hug. He stopped to lift her and whirl her in a joyous circle. Then Web engulfed me in a spine-cracking hug, followed by several solid thumps to my back. "You're looking well!" he told me as I tried to catch my breath. "Almost whole again, aren't you? Ah, and Lady Patience!" Having released me from his exuberant greeting, he bowed gracefully over the hand that Patience extended to him. "Such a rich blue gown! You put me in mind of a jay's bright feathers! But please tell me the feathers in your hair did not come from a live bird!"

"Of course not!" Patience looked properly horrified at the thought. "I found him dead on the garden path last summer. And I thought, now here is a time for me to see just what is beneath those lovely blue feathers. But I saved those feathers, of course, plucking them carefully before I boiled him down to bones. And then, once I had discarded the jay broth, my task was before me: to assemble his little bones into a skeleton. Did you know that a bird's wing is as close to a man's hand as is a frog's flipper? All those tiny bones! Well, doubtless you know the task is somewhere on my workbench, half-done as are so many of my projects. But yesterday, when I was thinking of feathers to take flight from our troubles, I remembered that I had a whole box full! And luckily for me, the beetles had not found and eaten them down to the quill, as they did when I tried to save the gull feathers. Oh! Gull! Have I been thoughtless? I beg pardon!"

She had obviously suddenly recalled that he was bonded with a gull. But Web smiled at her kindly and said, "We of the Wit know that when life is done, what remains is empty. None, I think, know better than we do. We sense the presence of all life, with some burning brighter than others. A plant is not as vital in our senses as is a tree. And of course a deer outshines both, and a bird most of all."

I opened my mouth to object to that. With my Wit I could sense birds, but had never found them particularly brimming with life. I recalled something that Burrich—the man who had all but raised me—had said to me, many years ago, when he had declared that I would not work with the hawks at Buckkeep Castle. "They don't like you; you are too warm." And I had thought he meant my flesh, but now I wondered if he had sensed something about my Wit that he could not then have explained to me. For the Wit had then been a despised magic, and if either of us had admitted to possessing it, we would have been hanged, quartered, and burned over water.

"Why do you sigh?" Patience abruptly demanded of me.

"Your pardon. I was not aware I had done so."

"Well, you did! Witmaster Web was just telling me the most fascinating things about a bat's wing and suddenly you sigh as if you find us the most boring old things in the world!" She punctuated her words with a tap of her fan on my shoulder.

Web laughed. "Lady Patience, doubtless his thoughts were elsewhere. I know Tom of old, and recall his melancholy streak well! Ah, but I have been keeping you to myself, and here are others of your guests, come to claim you!"

Was Patience deceived? I think not, but it pleased her to allow herself to be drawn away from us by the charming young man that doubtless Nettle had dispatched to allow Web to speak to me privately. Almost I wished she had not done so; Web had sent me several letters and I was sure I knew the current of the conversation he wished to draw me into. It had been long since I had been bonded with an animal through my Wit. But what Web seemed to equate with a sulking child I felt was more like the solitude of a long-married man who is suddenly widowed. No one could replace Nighteyes in my heart; nor could I imagine such a connection with any other creature. Gone was gone, as he had just said. The echoes of my wolf within me were enough to sustain me now. Those vivid memories, so strong that sometimes I felt I still heard his thoughts in my mind, would always be preferable to any other joining.

So now, as Web ventured past banalities about how I had been, and if Molly had been keeping well, and had the harvest been good this year, I deliberately diverted a conversation that would lead us, inevitably, to the importance he placed on my learning more of the Wit and on discussing my solitary status. My considered opinion was that as I was unpartnered and intended to remain so for the rest of my life, I needed no more knowledge of the Wit-magic than what I had now.

So I tipped my head toward the "musicians" still standing by the door and told him, "I fear they've come a long way for nothing. Patience has told me that redheaded singers are for Winterfest, and she will save the blonds for summer." I expected Web to share my amusement at Lady Patience's eccentricities. The strangers had not ventured into the hall to join the merriment, but remained by the door, speaking only to one another. They stood as longtime companions do, closer together than one stands near an acquaintance. The tallest man had a weathered, craggy face. The woman at his side, with her face tilted toward him, had broad cheekbones and a high, lined forehead. "Blonds?" Web asked me, staring round.

I smiled. "The strangely dressed trio by the door. See them? In yellow boots and coats?"

He swept his eyes past them twice and then, with a start, stared at them. His eyes grew wider.

"Do you know them?" I asked at his look of dread.

"Are they Forged?" he asked in a hoarse whisper.

"Forged? How could they be?" I stared at them, wondering what had alarmed Web. Forging stripped a man's humanity from him, tore him from the network of life and connection that enabled all of us to care and be cared about. Forged ones loved only themselves. Once, there had been many of them in the Six Duchies, preying on their families and neighbors, tearing the kingdom apart from within as the Red-Ship Raiders released our own people as a foe among us. Forging had been the dark magic of the Pale Woman and her captain Kebal Rawbread. But we had prevailed and driven the raiders from our shores. Years after the Red-Ship Wars had ended, we had taken ships to her last stronghold on Aslevjal Island, where we made an end of them forever. The Forged ones they had created were long gone to their graves. No one had practiced that evil magic for years.

"They feel Forged to me. My Wit cannot find them. I can barely sense them except with my eyes. Where did they come from?"

As a Witmaster, Web relied on that beast-magic far more keenly than I did. Perhaps it had become his dominant sense, for the Wit gives one a tingle of awareness for any living creature. Now, alerted by Web, I deliberately extended my own Wit toward the newcomers. I did not have his level of awareness, and the crowded room muddled my senses even more. I could feel almost nothing from them. I dismissed that with a shrug.

"Not Forged," I decided. "They huddle together too companionably. If they were Forged, each would be immediately seeking what they most needed, food, drink, or warmth. They hesitate, not wishing to be seen as intruders here, but uncomfortable not knowing our ways. So not Forged. Forged ones never care for such niceties."

I suddenly realized I sounded far too much like Chade's apprentice assassin in how I analyzed them. They were guests, not targets. I cleared my throat. "I do not know where they came from. Revel told me they came to the door as musicians for the feast. Or perhaps tumblers."

Web was still staring at them. "They are neither," he said decisively. Curiosity blossomed in his voice as he announced, "So. Let us speak to them and find out who and what they are."

I watched as the three conferred with one another. The woman and the younger man nodded brusquely at what the taller man was saying. Then, as if they were herd dogs set to bringing in sheep, they abruptly left his side and began to move purposefully through the crowd. The woman kept her hand at her hip, as if her fingers sought a sword that was not there. Their heads turned and their eyes roved as they went. Seeking something? No. Someone. The woman stood on tiptoe, trying to peer over the heads of the gathered folk who were watching the change of musicians. Their leader faded back toward the door. Did he guard it lest their prey escape? Or was I imagining things? "Who do they hunt?" I heard myself ask softly.

Web didn't respond. He'd already started moving toward where they had been. But as he turned from me, a lively drumbeat was suddenly joined by uplifted voices and a trilling pipe, and dancers surged back onto the floor. Couples spun and hopped like spinning tops to the lively tune, and blocked our path and my view. I put my hand on Web's broad shoulder and tugged him back from the hazards of the dance floor. "We'll go around," I told him, and led the way. But even that path was fraught with delays, for there were guests to greet, and one could not hurry through those conversations without seeming rude. Web, ever engaging and garrulous, seemed to lose his interest in the odd strangers. He focused his attention strongly on each person he was introduced to, and convinced them of his charm simply by his intense interest in who they were and what they did for a living and if they were having an enjoyable time tonight. I watched the room but could no longer locate the strangers.

They were not warming themselves at the big hearth as we passed it. Nor did I see them enjoying food or drink, or dancing, or watching the fest from the benches. When the music ended and the tide of dancers retreated, I firmly excused myself from Web and Lady Essence's conversation and strode across the room to where I had last seen them. I was convinced now that they were not musicians and this was not a random stopping place for them. I tried not to let my suspicions escalate; my early training did not always serve me well in social situations.

I didn't find any of them. I slipped out of the Great Hall into the relative quiet of the corridor outside it and looked for them in vain. Gone. I took a breath and resolutely let my curiosity go. Doubtless they were somewhere in Withywoods, changing into dry clothing or having a glass of wine or perhaps lost in the crowd of dancers. I would see them again. For now, I was the host of the gathering, and my Molly had been left alone too long. I had guests to attend to and a pretty wife to dance with and a lovely feast. If they were musicians or tumblers, they would soon make themselves known, for doubtless they would hope to win the favor and the largesse of the gathered guests. It was even possible that I was the person they were looking for, as I controlled the purse that paid the entertainers. If I waited long enough, they would approach me. And if they were beggars or travelers, then still they were welcome here. Why must I always imagine danger to my loved ones?

I plunged myself back into the maelstrom of merriment, danced again with Molly, invited Nettle to join me in a jig but lost her to Riddle, interrupted Hearth seeing how many honey-cakes he could stack into a tower on a single plate for the amusement of a pretty Withy maiden, overindulged myself in ginger cookies, and was ultimately trapped by Web near the ale keg. He filled his mug after me, and then nudged us toward a bench not far from the hearth. I looked for Molly, but she and Nettle had their heads together, and as I watched they moved as one to stir Patience from where she was dozing in a chair. She was protesting feebly as they gathered her up to take her to her chambers.

Web spoke without beating about the bush. "It's not natural, Tom," he chided me, heedless of who might overhear us. "You are so alone, you echo to my Wit. You should open yourself to the possibility of bonding again. For one of Old Blood to go so long unpartnered is not healthy."

"I don't feel the need," I told him honestly. "I've a good life here, with Molly and Patience and the boys. There's honest work to keep me busy, and my idle time is enjoyed with those I love. Web, I don't doubt your wisdom and experience, but I also don't doubt my own heart. I don't need anything more than what I have right now."

He looked into my eyes. I met his gaze. My last utterance was almost true. If I could have had my wolf back again, then, yes, life would have been much sweeter. If I could have opened my door, and found the Fool grinning on my doorstep, then my life would have been full indeed. But there was no point in sighing after what I could not have. It only distracted me from what I did have, and that was more than I'd ever had in my life. A home, my lady, youngsters growing to manhood under my roof, and the comforts of my own bed at night. Just enough consultations from Buckkeep Castle that I could feel I was still needed in the greater world, yet few enough that I knew, truly, they could get by without me and let me have a measure of peace. I had anniversaries I could be proud of. It was nearly eight years that Molly had been my wife. It was almost ten years since I'd killed anyone.

Almost ten years since I'd last seen the Fool.

And there it was, that stone-dropping-into-a-well plunge of my heart. I kept it from showing on my face or in my eyes. That gulf, after all, had nothing to do with how long I'd gone with no animal companion. That was a different sort of loneliness entirely. Wasn't it?

Perhaps not. The loneliness that can never be filled by anyone except the one whose loss created the absence; well, then, perhaps it was the same.

Web was still watching me. I realized that I'd been staring past his shoulder at the dancers, but now the floor was empty. I shifted my gaze back to meet his. "I'm fine as I am, old friend. Content. Why should I tamper with that? Would you prefer I long for more when I have so much already?"

It was the perfect question to stop Web's well-meaning pestering. I saw him think over my words, and then a deep smile rose onto his face, one that came from his heart. "No, Tom, I wouldn't wish that on you, truly. I'm a man who can admit when he's wrong, and perhaps I've been measuring your wheat with my bushel."

The discussion suddenly tipped upside-down for me. The words burst from me. "Your gull, Risk, she is well, still?"

He smiled crookedly. "As well as might be expected. She's old, Fitz. Twenty-three years with me, and she was probably two or three when we met."

I was silent; I'd never stopped to wonder how long a gull might live, and I didn't ask him now. All the questions that were too cruel to ask left me silent. He shook his head and looked away from me. "Eventually I'll lose her, unless accident or disease takes me first. And I'll mourn her. Or she will mourn me. But I also know that if I am left alone, eventually I'll look about for another partner. Not because Risk and I do not have something wonderful together, but because I am Old Blood. And we are not meant to be solitary souls."

"I'll think well on what you have said to me," I promised. Web deserved that courtesy from me. Time to leave this topic. "Did you ever manage to have words with our odd guests?"

He nodded slowly. "I did. But not many, and with the woman only. Tom, she made me uneasy. She rang oddly against my senses, as muted as muffled bells. She claimed that they were traveling jugglers and hoped to entertain us later. She was stingy in speaking of herself, but full of questions for me. She was looking for a friend of hers, who might also have come this way recently. Had I heard of any other travelers or visitors to the area? And when I told them that while I was a friend of the household, I had but arrived this night as well, then she asked me if I had met any other strangers on the road."

"I wonder if a member of their party became separated from them."

Web shook his head. "I think not." He frowned slightly. "It was passing strange, Tom. When I asked who . . ."

And then Just touched my elbow. "Mother would like your help," he said quietly. A simple request, yet something in the way he said it alarmed me.

"Where is she?"

"She and Nettle are in Lady Patience's chambers."

"At once," I said, and Web nodded as I set off.

Chapter 2

SPILLED BLOOD

Of all the magics known to be possessed by men, the highest and noblest is that collection of talents known as the Skill. Surely it is no coincidence that through generations of Farseer rule, it often manifests in those destined to become our kings and queens. Strength of character and generosity of spirit, the blessings of both El and Eda, often accompany this hereditary magic of the Farseer line. It conveys to the user the ability to send his thoughts afar, to influence gently the thinking of his dukes and duchesses, or to strike fear in the heart of his enemies. Tradition tells us that many a Farseer ruler, his strength supplemented by the courage and talent of his Skill-coterie, could work wondrous cures on both body and mind as well as commanding both his ships at sea and our defenders upon the land. Queen Efficacious established six coteries for herself, placing one Skill-talented group in each duchy, and thus making the magic of the Skill available to each of her trusted dukes and duch-

esses during her enlightened reign, to the great benefit of all her
people.

At the other end of the magical spectrum is the Wit, a base and
corrupting magic that most often afflicts the lowborn who live and
breed alongside the animals they cherish. This magic, once thought
to be useful to goose girls and shepherds and stable boys, is now
known to be dangerous not only to those who succumb to its influ-
ence but to all those around them as well. The mind-to-mind con-
tamination of communicating with beasts leads to animalistic
behaviors and appetites. While this writer laments that even nobly
born youth have been known to fall prey to the attractions of beast-
magic, I cannot sympathize beyond wishing that they be quickly dis-
covered and eliminated before they can infect the innocent with
their loathsome appetites.

ON THE NATURAL MAGICS OF THE SIX DUCHIES,
SCRIBE SWEET-TONGUE

I all but forgot our strange visitors as I hurried through the halls of
Withywoods. My immediate fear was for Patience. She had fallen
twice in the last month, but blamed it on the room "suddenly
whirling all about me." I did not run but my stride was as long as I
could make it, and I did not knock when I reached her chambers
but darted straight in.

Molly was sitting on the floor. Nettle knelt beside her and Patience stood, flapping a cloth at her. There was a pungent smell of
sharp herbs in the room, and a little glass vial rolled on its side on
the floor. Two serving women stood in a corner, obviously bullied
away from her by Patience's sharp tongue. "What happened?" I
demanded.

"I fainted." Molly sounded both annoyed and ashamed. "So
silly of me. Help me up, Tom."

"Of course," I said, trying to hide my dismay. I reached down for
her, and she leaned on me heavily as I drew her to her feet. She
swayed slightly, but hid it by clutching my arm.

"I'm fine now. A bit too much whirling about on the dance floor,
and perhaps too many glasses."

Patience and Nettle exchanged glances, undeceived.

"Perhaps you and I should let our evening end. Nettle and the lads can perform the duties of the house."

"Nonsense!" Molly exclaimed. Then she looked up at me, her eyes still a bit unfocused, and added, "Unless you are weary?"

"I am," I lied expertly, concealing my rising alarm. "So many folk all in one place! And we have three more days of this, at least. There will be plenty of time for conversation and food and music."

"Well. If you are tired, then, my love, I shall give way to you."

Patience gave me the tiniest nod and added, "I'm going to do the same, my dears. Bed for these old bones, but tomorrow I shall wear my dancing slippers!"

"I am warned, then!" I agreed, and submitted to a slap from her fan. As I turned her mother toward the door, Nettle shot me a grateful look. I knew she would draw me aside for a quiet talk the next day, and knew also that I had no answers for her, other than that her mother and I were both getting older.

Molly leaned on my arm as we walked sedately through the halls. Our path led us past the merrymaking, where guests delayed us with brief bits of conversation, compliments on the food and music, and wishes for a good night. I could feel Molly's exhaustion in her dragging steps and slow replies, but as ever she was Lady Molly to our guests. Finally I managed to pull her free of them. We limped slowly up the stairs with Molly leaning on me, and when we reached the door of our bedchamber she breathed an audible sigh of relief. "I don't know why I'm so tired," she complained. "I didn't have that much to drink. And now I've spoiled everything."

"You've spoiled nothing," I protested, and opened the door to find our bedroom had been transformed. Draperies of ivy confined our bed, and evergreen boughs graced the mantel and perfumed the air. The fat yellow candles that burned about the room gave off scents of wintergreen and bayberry. There was a new coverlet on the bed and matching hangings, all done in the green and golden-yellow of Withywoods, with twining willow leaves as a motif. I was astonished. "When did you find time to arrange all this?"

"Our new house steward is a man of many talents," she replied, smiling, but then she sighed and said, "I thought we would be com-ing here after midnight, drunk with dance and music and wine. I planned on seducing you."

Before I could respond, she added, "I know that of late, I have not been as ardent as once I was. Sometimes I feel I am the dried husk of a woman now that there is no chance of ever giving you another child. I thought tonight we might regain, for a time . . . But now I feel light-headed, and not in a pleasant way. Fitz, I think I will do no more in that bed than sleep beside you tonight." She let go of me and tottered a few steps to sink down on the edge of the bed. Her fingers fumbled at the laces of her kirtle.

"Let me do that for you," I offered. She raised an eyebrow at me. "With no thought of more than that!" I assured her. "Molly, just to have you sleep beside me every night is the fulfillment of my dream of years. Time enough for more when you are not exhausted." I loosened the confining laces, and she sighed as I eased her out of the garment. The buttons on her blouse were tiny things made from mother-of-pearl. She brushed my clumsy fingers aside to undo them, then stood. She was very unlike her tidy self as she let her skirts fall on top of the discarded clothing. I'd found and brought to her a soft nightgown. She pulled it on over her head, and it tangled on the holly crown in her hair. I lifted it gently free and smiled as I beheld the woman my lovely Molly Redskirts had become. A long-ago Winterfest came to my mind, as I'm sure it did for her. But as she sank down to sit on the edge of the bed again, I saw the furrows in her brow. She lifted a hand to rub her forehead. "Fitz, I'm so sorry. I've ruined all I planned."

"Nonsense. Here. Let me tuck you in."

She gripped my shoulder to stand and swayed as I opened the bed to the linens for her. "In you go," I told her, and she made no saucy reply, but only sighed heavily as she sat, then eased over onto the bed and lifted her feet after her. She closed her eyes. "The room is spinning. And it's not wine."

I sat down on the edge of the bed and took her hand. She frowned. "Be still. Any movement makes the room spin faster."

"It will pass," I told her, hoping it would, and sat very still. I watched her. The candles burned steadily, releasing the fragrances she had imbued in them over the summer past. The fire on the hearth crackled, flames consuming the carefully stacked logs. Slowly the lines of discomfort in her face eased. Her breathing steadied. The stealth and patience of my youthful training sustained me. I very gradually eased my weight from the bedside and when I finally stood beside the bed, I doubted that she had felt any motion at all, for she slept on.

I ghosted about the room, extinguishing all but two of her candles. I poked at the fire, added another log, and set the fire screen before it. I was not sleepy, or even weary. I had no desire to return to the festivities and explain why I was there while Molly was not. For a time longer I stood, the fire warming my back. Molly was a shape behind the mostly drawn bed curtains. The flames crackled, and my ears could almost sort the kiss of the driven snow against the windows from the sounds of the merrymaking down below. Slowly I took off my festive garments and resumed the comforts of my familiar leggings and tunic. Then silently I left the room, drawing the door slowly closed behind me.

I did not descend by the main stairs. Instead I took a roundabout path, down a servants' back staircase and through a mostly deserted corridor until finally I reached my private den. I unlocked the tall doors and slipped inside. The remains of the hearth fire were a few winking coals. I woke them with a few twists of paper from my desk, burning the useless musings of that morning and then adding more fuel. I went to my desk, sat, and drew a blank sheet of paper toward me. I stared at it and wondered: Why not just burn it now? Why write on it, stare at the words, and then burn it? Was there really anything left in me that I could trust only to paper? I had the life I had dreamed of: the home, the loving wife, the children grown. Buckkeep Castle respected me. This was the quiet backwater I'd always dreamed of. It was over a decade since I'd even thought of killing anyone. I set down the quill and leaned back in my chair.

A tap at the door startled me. I sat up straight and instinctively looked about the room, wondering if there was anything I should hastily conceal. Silly. "Who is it?" Who but Molly, Nettle, or Riddle would know I was here? And none of them would have tapped first.

"It's Revel, sir!" His voice sounded shaky.

I stood. "Come in! What is it?"

He was out of breath and pale as he pushed open the door and stood framed in it. "I don't know. Riddle sent me running. He says, 'Come, come right now, to your estate study.' Where I left the messenger. Oh, sir. There's blood on the floor there, and no sign of her." He gasped in a shuddering breath. "Oh, sir, I'm so sorry. I offered a room, but she said no and—"

"With me, Revel," I said, as if he were a guardsman and mine to command. He went paler at my snapped command but then stood a bit straighter, glad to cede all decisions to me. My hands moved instinctively, confirming a few small concealed weapons that never left my person. Then we were off at a run through the corridors of Withywoods. Blood spilled in my home. Blood spilled by someone besides me—and not Riddle, or he would have quietly cleaned it away, not summoned me. Violence in my home, against a guest. I fought the blind fury that rose in me, quenched it with icy anger. They would die. Whoever had done this would die.

I led him by a roundabout path that avoided passages where we might encounter guests and reached the estate study after interrupting only one indiscreet young couple and scaring one drunken youngster looking for a place to doze. I berated myself for how many people I had let into my home, how many I knew only by face or name.

And Molly was sleeping alone and unguarded.

I skidded to a halt by the study door. My voice was hoarse with anger as I took a nasty knife that had been strapped to my forearm and shoved it at Revel. He staggered back a step in fear. "Take it," I barked at him. "Go to my bedchamber. Look in on my lady, be sure she sleeps undisturbed. Then stand outside the door and kill anyone who seeks to come in. Do you understand me?"

"Sir." He coughed and then gulped, "I have a knife already, sir.

Riddle made me take it." Awkwardly he drew it from inside his immaculate jacket. It was twice the length of the one I'd offered, an honorable weapon rather than an assassin's little friend.

"Go, then," I told him, and he did.

I drummed on the door with my fingertips, knowing Riddle would recognize me by that, and then slipped in. Riddle straightened slowly from where he had crouched. "Nettle sent me to find a bottle of the good brandy she said you had here. She wanted to offer some to Lord Canterby. When I saw the papers on the floor, and then the blood, I sent Revel for you. Look here."

Revel had brought the messenger food and wine and served them at my desk. Why had she declined to go to a guest room or join us in the Great Hall? Had she known she was in danger? She'd eaten at least some of the food, I judged, before the tray had been dashed to the floor along with a few papers from my desk. The falling wineglass had not shattered but had left a half-moon of spilled wine on the polished dark stone of the floor. And around that moon was a constellation of blood stars. A swung blade had flung those scattered red drops.

I stood up and swept my gaze across the study. And that was all. No rifled drawers, nothing moved or taken. Not a thing out of place at all. Not enough blood for her to have died here, but there was no sign of any further struggle. We exchanged a silent look, and as one moved to the heavily curtained doors. In summers I sometimes opened them wide to look out onto a garden of heathers for Molly's bees. Riddle started to sweep the curtain to one side, but it caught. "A fold of it is shut in the door. They went this way."

Knives drawn, we opened the doors and peered out into the snow and darkness. Half of one footprint remained where the eaves had partially sheltered it. The other tracks were barely dimples in the windblown snow. As we stood there, another gust swept past us, as if the wind itself sought to help them escape us. Riddle and I stared into the storm. "Two or more," he said, surveying what remained of the trail.

"Let's go before it's gone completely," I suggested.

He looked down woefully at his thin, flapping skirt-trousers. "Very well."

"No. Wait. Do a wander through the festivities. See what you see, and bid Nettle and the boys be wary." I paused. "Some odd folk came to the door tonight, professing to be minstrels. But Patience said she had not hired them. Web spoke briefly with one of the strangers. He started to tell me what she said, but I was called away. They were looking for someone. That much was obvious."

His face grew darker. He turned to go and then turned back. "Molly?"

"I put Revel on her door."

He made a face. "I'll check them first. Revel has potential, but for now it's only potential." He stepped toward the door.

"Riddle." My voice stopped him. I took the bottle of brandy from the shelf and handed it to him. "Let no one think anything is amiss. Tell Nettle if you think it wise."

He nodded. I nodded back and as he left, I took down a sword that had hung on the mantel. Decoration now, but it had once been a weapon and would be again. It had a nice heft. No time for a cloak or boots. No time to go for a lantern or torch. I waded out into the snow, sword in hand, the light from the opened doors behind me. In twenty paces I knew all I needed to know. The wind had erased their tracks completely. I stood, staring off into the darkness, flinging myself wide-Witted into the night. No humans. Two small creatures, rabbits probably, had hunkered down in the shelter of some snow-draped bushes. But that was all. No tracks, and whoever had done this was already both out of my eyesight and beyond the range of my Wit. And if they were the strangers, it seemed my Wit might not have found them even if they were close.

I went back into the den, shaking the snow from my wet shoes before I entered. I shut the door behind me and let the curtain fall. My messenger and her message were gone. Dead? Or fled? Had someone gone out the door, or had she let someone in? Was it her blood on the floor, or someone else's? The fury I had felt earlier at the idea that someone might do violence to a guest in my home flared in me again. I suppressed it. Later, I might indulge it. When I had a target.

Find the target.

I left the study, closing the door behind me. I moved swiftly and silently, years and dignity and present social standing swept aside and erased. I made no sound and carried no light with me. I kept the sword at my side. First, to my own bedchamber. I built castles of thoughts as I ran. The messenger had sought me. Regardless of whether she was attacker or attacked, I might be the intended target for the violence. I flowed up the stair like a hunting cat, every sense burning and raw. I was aware of Revel keeping his vigil by the door long before he knew I was coming. I lifted a finger to my lips as I drew near. He startled when he saw me, but kept silent. I drew close. "All is well here?" I breathed the question.

He nodded and as softly replied, "Riddle was here not that long ago, sir, and insisted I admit him to be sure that all was well with the lady." He stared at the sword.

"And it was?"

His gaze snapped back to me. "Of course, sir! Would I stand here so calmly were it not so?"

"Of course not. Forgive my asking. Revel, please remain here until I come back to relieve you, or I send Riddle or one of Molly's sons." I offered him the sword. He took it, holding it like a poker. He looked from it to me.

"But our guests . . ." he began feebly.

"Are never as important as our lady. Guard this door, Revel."

"I will, sir."

I reflected that he deserved more than an order. "We still do not know whose blood was shed. Someone used the doors in the study that go out to the garden. To enter or to leave, I do not know. Tell me a bit more of the messenger's appearance."

He bit his upper lip, worrying the information from his memory. "She was a girl, sir. That is, more girl than woman. Slight and slender. Her hair was blond and she wore it loose. Her clothing looked as if it had been of good quality but had seen hard use. It was a foreign style, the cape tapered in at the waist and then belling out, with sleeves belled as well. It was green and looked heavy but did not appear to be wool. There was fur on the edging of the hood, of a kind I do not know. I offered to take her cloak and hood but she did not wish to give them up to me. She wore loose trousers, perhaps of the same fabric, but black with white flowers figured on them. Her boots did not reach her knee and seemed thin and were laced tight to her calf."

So much detail about her garments! "But what did she herself look like?"

"She was young. She looked white with cold and seemed grateful when I built up the fire for her and offered her hot tea. Her fingers were pale as ice against the mug when she took it from me . . ." His voice trailed away. He looked up at me suddenly. "She didn't want to leave the study, sir. Or to give up her cloak. Should I have known she was frightened?"

Had Riddle truly thought he could make more of this man than a house steward? Tears stood in his brown eyes. "Revel, you did all that you should have done. If anyone is at fault, it is I. I should have gone to the study as soon as I heard there was a messenger. Please. Just keep watch here for a short time longer until I send someone to relieve you. Then you should go back to what you do best. Tend to our guests. Let no one suspect that anything is amiss."

"I can do that, sir." He spoke softly. Was the reproach in his dog's eyes for me or himself? No time to wonder.

"Thank you, Revel," I told him and left him with a clap on his shoulder. I moved swiftly down the corridor, already reaching for Nettle with my Skill-magic. The moment our thoughts touched, my daughter's outrage blasted into my mind. *Riddle told me. How dare anyone do this in our home! Is Mother safe?*

She is. I'm on my way down. Revel is on watch on her door, but I'd like you or one of the boys to take his place.

Me. I'll make my excuses and be right up. A heartbeat's pause, then, fiercely, *Find who did this!*

I intend to.

I think she took satisfaction in my cold assurance.

I moved swiftly through the corridors of Withywoods, every

sense alert. I was not surprised when I rounded a corner and found Riddle waiting for me. "Anything?" I asked him.

"Nettle's gone up to her mother's room." He glanced past me. "You know that you were probably the target in some way."

"Perhaps. Or the messenger herself, or the message she bore, or someone seeking to do injury to whoever sent the message by delaying or destroying it."

We were moving swiftly together, trotting side by side like wolves on a trail.

I loved this.

The thought ambushed me and I almost stumbled. I loved this? Hunting someone who had attacked someone else in the sanctity of my own home? Why would I love that?

We always loved the hunt. An ancient echo of the wolf I had been and the wolf who was still with me. *The hunt for meat is best, but any hunt is always the hunt, and one is never more alive than during the hunt.*

"And I am alive."

Riddle shot me a questioning glance, but instead of asking a question he gave me information. "Revel himself took the food and tea to the messenger. The two pages who were on the front door recall admitting her. She came on foot, and one says that she seemed to come from behind the stable rather than up the carriage-way. No one else saw her, though of course the kitchen staff recall making up a tray for her. I haven't had a chance to go out to the stables and see what they know there."

I glanced down at myself. I was scarcely dressed to appear before our guests. "I'll do that now," I said. "Alert the boys."

"Are you sure?"

"It's their home, Riddle. And they are not really boys anymore. They've been talking of leaving for the last three months. In spring I think they'll fly."

"And you have no one else to trust. Tom, when this is over, we are going to talk again. You need a few house soldiers, a few men who can be brutes when the situation calls for it, but can open a door and serve wine to a guest as well."

"We'll talk later," I agreed, but grudgingly. It wasn't the first time he had pointed out to me that I should have some sort of house guard for Withywoods. I resisted the idea. I was no longer an assassin, living to guard my king and carry out his quiet work. I was a respectable landholder, a man of grapes and sheep now, a man of plows and shears, not knives and swords. And there was, I had to admit, my conceit that I could always protect my own household against whatever limited threats might find their way to my door.

But I hadn't tonight.

I left Riddle and trotted through the halls on my way to the stables. There was, I told myself, truly no indication that whatever bloodshed there had been was deadly. Nor did it have to be related to me or to my own. Perhaps the messenger had enemies of her own who had followed her. I reached a servants' entrance, pushed open the heavy door, and dashed across the snowy courtyard to the stable door. Even in that brief run, I had snow down the back of my neck and in my mouth. I slid back the bar on the stable doors and pushed one open just enough to slip in.

Inside was the warmth of stabled animals, the pleasant smell of horses and soft light from a shielded lantern on a hook. In response to my entrance, Tallman was already hobbling toward me. His son, Tallerman, supervised most of the work of the stables now, but Tallman still considered himself in charge. On days when there was a great deal of coming and going, as there was tonight, he rigorously controlled which animals were stabled where. He had strong feelings about teams left standing all evening in harness. He peered at me through the gloom of the stable and then gave a start as he recognized me. "Holder Tom!" he cried in his cracking voice. "Shouldn't you be dancing with the fine folk in the Great Hall?"

Like many another oldster, his years had diminished his regard for the differences in our status. Or perhaps it was that he'd seen that I could shovel out a stall with the best of men, and he therefore respected me as an equal. "Soon enough," I replied. "The dancing will go on till dawn, you know. But I thought I would wander out here and be sure all is well in the stable in such a storm."

"All's well here. This barn was built sturdy two decades ago, and it'll stand for a dozen more, I reckon."

I nodded. "Steward Revel tells me that you had visitors here to-night, ones that made you uneasy."

His querying look changed to a scowl. "Yes. If you act like a horse thief, I'll speak to you like you're a horse thief. Don't come prying and peeking around my stables and then tell me you're a minstrel. They were no more minstrels than Copper there is a pony. They didn't smell right to me, and I took them directly up to the door." He peered at me. "That Revel fellow was supposed to warn you. You didn't let them in, did you?"

Hard to admit it. I nodded once. "It's Winterfest. I let everyone in." I cleared my throat at his lowering stare. "Before that. Did you notice anyone else here at the stables, anyone odd?"

"You mean that foreign girl?"

I nodded.

"Only her. She came in here like she thought it was the house. 'I need to speak to the master,' she told one of the hands, so he brought her to me, thinking she wanted me. But she looked at me and said, 'No, the master with the crooked nose and the badger's hair.' So, begging your pardon, we knew she meant you and sent her up to the house."

I dropped my hand from where I'd touched the bridge of my nose and the old break there. This was just getting odder and odder. A vanished messenger who had come seeking me with only a de-scription rather than my name. "That's all?" I asked.

He frowned thoughtfully. "Yes. Unless you want to hear about Merchant Cottleby trying to get me to stable his horses here when both have signs of mange. Poor creatures. I put them under shelter in the woodshed, but they're not getting anywhere near our stock. And if his driver wants to complain, I'll tell him what I think of his horsemanship." He looked at me fiercely, as if I might challenge his wisdom.

I smiled at him. "A small kindness, Tallman, for the horses' sake. Pack them up some of the liniment you make."

He stared at me a moment, then gave a short nod. "Could do that. Not the beasts' fault they're ill cared for."

I started to leave, then turned back. "Tallman. How long between the time the girl arrived and the three you took for horse thieves?"

He lifted his gaunt shoulders and then let them fall. "She came before Caul Toely arrived. Then came that tailor fellow, and the Willow sisters on those matched ponies of theirs. Those ladies never ride in a carriage, do they? Then the Cooper boys and their mother, and—"

I dared to interrupt him. "Tallman. Do you think they were following her?"

He stopped. I waited impatiently as he weighed what he knew. Then he nodded, his mouth tight. "I should have puzzled that out for myself. Same sort of boots, and they came right to the barn and were trying to peek in. Not looking for horses to steal, but following that girl." His eyes met mine angrily. "They hurt her?"

"I don't know, Tallman. She's gone. I'm going to go see if those three are still here."

"You do that. If they aren't there, they can't be far, in this weather. You want I should send a lad to Stocker's Holding, ask to borrow their tracking dogs?" He shook his head and added sourly, "I've said many a time, it wouldn't hurt us to have our own hunting pack."

"Thank you, Tallman, but no dogs. The way the snow is coming down, I doubt there's any trail to follow."

"You change your mind, Tom, you let me know. I can have my son go fetch those hounds in a heartbeat. And"—and now he was calling after me as I beat a retreat—"if you come to your senses about keeping our own dogs, you let me know! I know a great bitch, will have her pups by spring! You just let me know!"

"Later, Tallman!" I shouted the words back to him, and got a mouthful of snow for my trouble. The snow was still coming down, and the wind was rising. I suddenly felt certain that those I sought were still within Withywoods. No one would be desperate enough to try to flee during this storm. I reached for Nettle. *Is all still well with your mother?*

I left her sleeping, with Hearth sitting in a chair by her fire. I told him to latch the door behind me, and I heard him do it. *I'm with Riddle and Just, and our guests. We have discovered nothing out of the ordinary. There is no sign of the messenger.*

Dead? Fled? Hiding within Withywoods? It had to be one of the three. *There were three minstrels who came late. Two men and a woman. Web seemed unsettled by them. Are they still among our guests?* I pictured them for her in my mind.

I saw them earlier. But they did not look like musicians to me, nor behave like them. They gave no indication of wanting a turn on the dais.

Send Just to me, please. We're going to do a quick search of the unoccupied wings. And let me know if you and Riddle find the three strangers.

Just and I divided Withywoods and went room-to-room, looking for any sign of intrusion in the unoccupied areas of the manor. It was not an easy task in the rambling old place, and I relied on my Wit as much as my eyes to tell me if a room was truly empty. Nettle and Riddle found no sign of the three strangers, and when she asked our other guests if they had seen them, the responses were so conflicting as to be useless. Even our servants, who sometimes irritated me with the close attention they paid to family doings, had nothing to report. The three and the messenger were as gone as if they had never visited us at all.

Toward the small hours of the morning, when our guests were sated with food and music and were departing for their homes or seeking the chambers we had offered them, I called off the search. Riddle and the lads joined Revel in seeing that all the outside doors were secured for the night, and then made a quiet patrol of the south wing, where we had housed our guests. While they were doing that, I resolved to slip off to my private den in the west wing. From there I could access a spy-network that only Patience, Molly, and I knew existed. It was my low intention that I would wander it tonight and peer in on our sleeping guests to see if anyone had offered the strangers shelter in their rooms.

Such was my intent. But when I reached the doors of my study, the hackles on my neck arose. Even before I touched the door handle, I knew it was not quite latched. And yet I recalled clearly that I had shut the door behind me before I had followed Revel to join Riddle. Someone had been here since I last left it.

I drew my knife before I eased the door open. The interior of the room was dim, the candles guttering out and the fire subsiding. I stood for a time, exploring the room with my senses. There was no one inside, my Wit said, but I recalled that earlier the strangers had been almost transparent to Web, a man with a much more finely tuned magic than I possessed. And so I stood, ears pricked, and waited. But it was what I smelled that made me angry. Blood. In my den.

My knife led the way as I advanced. With my free hand I kindled a fresh candle and poked up the fire. Then I stood still, looking around my room. They had been here. They had come here, to my den, someone's blood still wet on them.

If Chade had not trained me through a thousand exercises to recall a room exactly as I had left it, their passage might have been unnoticeable. I smelled a brush of blood on the corner of my desk, and there was a small smear of browning red where my papers had been shifted. But even without the scent of blood and its tiny traces, they had been here, touching my papers, moving the scroll I'd been translating. They'd tried to open the drawer of my desk, but had not found the hidden catch. Someone had picked up the memory-stone carving the Fool had made for me decades before and put it back on the mantel with the facet that showed my face looking out into the room. When I picked it up to correct it, my lip lifted in a snarl. On the Fool's image, a clumsy thumb had left blood smeared down his cheek. The surge of fury I felt was not rational.

When I lifted the stone, I felt the tide of the memories stored in it. The Fool's last words to me, stored in the stone, tugged at my recollection. "I have never been wise," he had said. A reminder of the recklessness of our youths, or a promise that someday he would ignore caution and return? I closed my mind against that message. Not now.

And foolishly, I tried to swipe the blood from his face with my thumb.

Memory stone is peculiar stuff. Of old, Skill-coteries had traveled to a distant quarry in the Mountain Kingdom where they carved dragons from it, imbuing the stone with their memories before being absorbed into their creations to give them a semblance of life. I'd seen it happen, once. Verity, my king, had given himself to a stone dragon, and then risen in that guise to bring terror and war to the enemies of the Six Duchies. On Aslevjal Island I'd discovered that small cubes of the gleaming black stuff had been used by the Elderlings to store songs and poetry.

I myself had wakened the slumbering dragons of previous generations with an offering of blood and a call to arms that was both Wit- and Skill-wrapped into one magic.

Blood on memory stone, and my touch. The Skill and the Wit both boiling inside me. The smear of blood sank into the stone.

The Fool opened wide his mouth and screamed. I saw his lips stretch, his bared teeth and stiffened tongue. It was a screech of unremitting agony.

No sound reached my ears. It was more intimate than that. Sourceless and enduring, the endless, hopeless, merciless agony of systematic torture engulfed me. It filled my entire body and burned my skin as if I were a glass brimming with black despair. It was too familiar, for it was not the keen pain of any one physical torment but the overwhelming drowning of the mind and soul in the knowledge that nothing could prevent this agony. My own memories rose up in a shrieking chorus. Once more I sprawled on the cold stone floor of Prince Regal's dungeons, my battered body suffocating my tormented mind. I tore my awareness free of that memory, denying that bond. The Fool's carved eyes stared at me blindly. For a moment our gazes met, and then all went dark and my eyes burned. My enervated hands fumbled the carving, nearly dropping it but instead hugging it to me as I collapsed to my knees. I held it to my chest, feeling a far-distant wolf lift his muzzle and snarl in fury. "I'm sorry, I'm sorry, I'm sorry!" I babbled blindly, as if it were the Fool himself I had injured. Sweat burst from every pore on my body, drenching me. Still clutching the carving to me, I sank onto my side. Slowly, vision came back to my open, tearing eyes. I stared into the dying fire, haunted by images of dull-red instruments soaking in the flames, smelling blood both old and new mixed with the acrid stench of terror. I remembered how to close my eyes. I felt the wolf move to stand over me, threatening to rend any who came near. Slowly, the echoes of the pain passed. I drew breath.

Blood had the power to waken memory stone, whether it was an Elderling-carved dragon or the bust the Fool had shaped. And in that brief linking, I knew that the girl was dead. I'd felt her terror at being hunted and cornered, her memory of past torments, and the agony of her death. By that, I knew her for Revel's girlish messenger rather than the soldier-schooled woman I'd seen with the two men. They'd followed her, they'd hunted her through my home, and they'd killed her. I did not know why or what message they had foiled, but I would find them and I would find out.

I rolled to my belly, still holding the carving to my chest. My head swam. I got my knees under me, knelt, and managed to stand by holding on to the desktop. Staggering to my chair, I sat down. I set the carving on the desk before me and looked at it. It had not changed. Had I imagined that movement, the Fool's soundless scream and staring eyes? Had I shared some distant experience of the Fool's, or had the carving expressed the terror and pain the messenger had felt at her death?

I started to lift the carving, to set it to my brow to view again the simple memories he had stored in it for me. But my hands shook and I set it back on the desk. Not now. If somehow I'd merged the girl's pain into the stone, I did not want to know that now, or share that agony again. Right now I needed to hunt.

I tugged my sleeves down over my hands, and restored the carving to its place on the mantel. Still a bit shaky, I explored my den, looking for other signs of their presence, but found nothing.

Someone had come here, to my private den, forced the doors, and disturbed some very private possessions. There were few things that touched to the heart of me as that carving did, precious few things that tied me to a past when I had served my king with the two dearest friends I had ever known. That someone, a stranger, had dared to handle it and had profaned it with blood he had shed brought me to the edge of a killing fury, and when I considered that it might easily have been stolen, my vision went red for a moment.

I shook my head angrily, forcing cold on myself. *Think.* How had they found this place? It was obvious. When Revel had been sent to find me, they had followed. But if finding me was the true objective, why hadn't they attacked then? And how had I missed being aware of them? Were they Forged, as Web had first suspected, humans with every connection to humanity torn from them? I doubted it; they had moved as a group in the ballroom, with trepidation and self-control such as I had never seen in the Forged. Had they, then, had some way of masking their life signatures? I knew of no magic that could do that. When my wolf had been alive we had, with difficulty, learned to keep our communication private. But that was scarcely the same as being able to completely conceal myself from the awareness of other Witted.

I pushed that concern aside for a moment. I reached for Nettle with the Skill, and swiftly shared most of what I knew with her. I made no mention of the blood or the carving. That was private.

I'm with Mother. Riddle took Hearth and Just with him. He has told Just that he must guard Patience's door while Riddle and Hearth are checking every unoccupied room in the manor.

Excellent. How is your mother?

Still sleeping. She looks as she always does and I can detect nothing wrong with her. But I was very alarmed when she fainted earlier. Much more worried than I wished her to see. Her father died when he was only two years older than she is now.

He had ruined his health with drink, and the brawling and stupid accidents that go with it.

Her mother died very young.

I pressed my palms to my eyes and pushed on my brow with my fingers. It was too frightening. I could not think about it. *Stay there with her, please. I've just a few more places that I wish to search, and then I'll come take your place.*

I'm fine here. You needn't hurry.

Did she suspect what I was about to do? I doubted it. Only Patience and Molly and I knew of the concealed labyrinth of secret passages in Withywoods. While the peepholes within the passage did not give me a view of every single bedchamber, they would allow me to look in on many of them, to see if any harbored more guests than we had invited.

It was closer to dawn than midnight when I emerged from the passageways. I was festooned with cobwebs, chilled to the bone, and weary. I had discovered nothing save that at least two of the housemaids were willing, for luck, fancy, or perhaps some coin, to spend the night in beds not their own. I'd seen one young wife weeping into her hands while her husband snored drunkenly halfway into their bed, and one old couple indulging in Smoke so potent that the slight drift of it into my secret passageway had dizzied me.

But of the peculiar minstrels or the messenger's body, there was no sign.

I returned to my room and released Nettle to go to hers. I did not sleep that night or even lie down, but sat in a chair by the hearth and watched over Molly and pondered. Had the intruders been insane enough to flee into the snowstorm, taking the messenger's body with them? At least one had remained in Withywoods long enough to follow Revel and enter my den. Why? To what end? Nothing had been taken from there, no member of my household injured. I was determined to get to the bottom of it.

But over the next few days it was as if we had dreamed the stray minstrels and the messenger. Molly recovered to feast, dance, and laugh with our guests for the rest of Winterfest with no sign of illness or weakness. I felt dirty that I kept my bloody knowledge hidden from her, and even worse that I bound her sons to silence, but both Nettle and Riddle agreed with me. She did not need the extra worry right now.

Snow continued to fall for another day and a night, obscuring all signs of anyone who might have come or gone. Once the blood was cleaned from the floor, no trace remained of our foreign visitors. Revel surprised me by being able to keep a still tongue on the peculiar events, for Riddle, Nettle, and I had decided that discreet inquiries might win us more information than trumpeting our concerns

about. But other than a few guests who commented on the foreign-
ers who had arrived and departed from the feast without sharing
any of the merriment, we discovered nothing. Web had little to say
that he had not already told me. He had thought it odd that the
woman would not tell him the name of the "friend" she was seeking. And that was all.

Nettle, Riddle, and I debated telling Chade of the incident. I did
not want to, but in the end they persuaded me. On the first quiet
evening after Winterfest, when our guests had departed and Withywoods was comparatively quiet, I went to my study. Nettle accompanied me, and Riddle with her. We sat, she joined her thoughts to
mine, and together we Skilled our tale to Chade. Nettle was a quiet
presence as I presented my detailed report. I had thought she might
offer more detail, but all I felt from her was a quiet confirmation of
my telling. Chade asked few questions, but I sensed him storing
every detail. I knew he would glean whatever information he could
from his far-flung spy-network and share it with me. I was still surprised when he said, "I advise you to wait. Someone sent the messenger, and that one may reach out to you again when she does not
return. Let Riddle go to Withy and spend some time in the taverns
there for a few nights. If there is anything to hear, he will hear it.
And I will make a few discreet inquiries. Other than that, I think
you've done as much as you can. Except, of course, as before, I advise you to consider adding a few house soldiers to your staff. Ones
who can serve a cup of tea or cut a throat with equal skill."

"I scarcely think that's necessary," I said firmly, and sensed his
distant sigh.

"As you think best," he finished and withdrew his mind from
ours.

I did as he suggested, sending Riddle to the taverns, but he heard
nothing. No message arrived asking what had become of a messenger. For a time I walked with my hackles up, alert to anything that
might be the slightest bit out of the ordinary. But as days and then
months passed, the incident faded from the foreground of my
mind. Riddle's premise that perhaps none of them were what they

had claimed to be, and that we had been passing witnesses to some-one settling an old debt, was as valid as any I could imagine.

Years later, I would marvel at my stupidity. How could I not have known? For years I had waited and longed for a message from the Fool. And when finally it came, I had not received it.

Chapter 3

THE FELLING OF FALLSTAR

A secret is only yours so long as you don't share it. Tell it to one person, and it's a secret no more.

CHADE FALLSTAR

Chickens squawked, kids bleated, and the savory smell of sizzling meat floated in the summer air. Blue summer sky arched over the market stalls at Oaksbywater, the largest market town within an easy journey of Withywoods Manor. Oaksbywater was a cross-roads town, with good access to the surrounding farms in the valley and a well-tended King's Road that led to a port on the Buck River. Goods came from both up and down the river, and in from outly-ing villages. The tenth-day markets were the most crowded; farm-ers' carts filled the market circle while smaller vendors had set up stalls or spread blankets on the village green under the spreading oaks by the lively creek that gave the town its name. The humbler

merchants had no more than fresh vegetables or home crafts arranged on mats on the ground, while the farmers with larger holdings set up temporary benches to hold baskets of dyed woolens or
rounds of cheese or slabs of smoked pork.

Behind the tenth-day market stalls were the resident merchants
of Oaksbywater. There was a cobbler's shop, a weavers' mercantile,
a tinker, and a large smithy. The King's Dogs Inn had set out benches
and tables outside in the shade. The cloth merchant displayed racks
of fabric and twisted hanks of dyed yarn for sale, the smith's shop
offered wares of tin and iron and copper, and the cobbler had
brought his bench outside his shop and sat sewing a lady's soft red
slipper. The pleasant din of folks bargaining and gossiping ebbed
and flowed in waves against my ears.

I was seated at one of the tavern's benches under the oak, a mug
of cider at my elbow. My errands were completed. We'd had a message from Just, the first to reach us in many a month. He and Hearth
had left home almost three years ago. With youth's fine disregard
for the concerns of their elders, they'd sent messages only sporadi-
cally. Just had finished the first year of his apprenticeship with a
wainwright in Highdowns, and his master was very pleased with
him indeed. He wrote that Hearth had taken work on a river ferry
and seemed content at that occupation. Molly and I had both re-
joiced at the news that he was finally settled and doing well. But Just
had added that he had lost his favorite belt-knife, a bone-handled
one with a thin, slightly curved blade that the smith in Oaksbywater had made for him when he was thirteen. I'd put in the order for
a replacement two weeks ago and picked it up today. That single
small package was at my feet beside a huddle of Molly's purchases.

I was watching the cobbler and wondering if Molly would like a
pair of red slippers. But evidently that pair was spoken for; as I
watched, a slender young woman with a mop of unruly dark curls
sauntered from the market crowd to stand before the cobbler. I
could not hear the words they spoke, but the man took three more
stitches and a knot, bit off his thread, and offered the slipper and its
mate to her. Her face alight with a saucy grin, she set her stacked
coppers on his bench and sat down immediately to try on her new

shoes. Freshly shod, she stood up, lifted her skirts almost to her knees, and tried a few dancing steps there in the dusty street.

I grinned and looked around for someone to share my enjoyment of her unabashed pleasure. But the two old plowmen on the other end of my bench were complaining to each other about the prospect of rain or the lack thereof, and my Molly was out among the other shoppers enjoying a day of haggling with merchants. In the past, when the boys were younger and Patience alive, market days had been far more complicated trips. But in the space of little more than a year we'd lost my stepmother and seen the lads venture out on their own. For most of a year, I think we were both stunned by the abrupt change in our lives. For almost two years after that, we had floundered about in a home that suddenly seemed much too large. Only recently had we cautiously begun to explore our new latitude. Today we had escaped the confines of our life as lady and holder of the estate to take a day to ourselves. We'd planned it well. Molly had a short list of items she wished to buy. I needed no list to remind me that this was my day for idleness. I was anticipating music during an evening meal at the inn. If we lingered too late, we might even stay the night and begin our journey back to Withywoods the next morning. I wondered idly why the idea of Molly and me alone overnight in an inn raised thoughts more worthy of a boy of fifteen than a man of fifty years. It made me smile.

FitzChivalry!

The Skill-reaching was a shout inside my mind, an anxious cry that was inaudible to anyone else in the market. I knew in an instant that it was Nettle and that she was full of worry. The Skill was like that: so much information conveyed in an instant. A part of my mind noted that she called me FitzChivalry, not Tom Badgerlock or Tom or even Shadow Wolf. She never called me Father or Papa. I'd lost the right to those titles years ago. But "FitzChivalry" spoke of matters that had more to do with the Farseer crown than with our family ties.

What's wrong? I settled myself on the bench and fixed an empty smile on my face as I Skill-reached across the distance to Buckkeep

Castle on the coast. I saw the uplifted branches of the oak against the blue sky, but was also aware of a darkened room around Nettle.

It's Chade. We think he took a fall and perhaps struck his head. He was found sprawled on the steps to the Queen's Garden this morning. We don't know how long he had been there, and we've been unable to rouse him. King Dutiful wishes you to come at once.

I'm here, I assured her. *Let me see him.*

I'm touching him now. You can't feel him? I couldn't and Dutiful couldn't, and Thick was completely flummoxed. "I see him but he's not there," he said to us.

Fear sent cold tendrils from my belly up to my heart. An old memory of Verity's queen, Kettricken, falling down those same steps—victim of a plot to kill her unborn child in the fall—filled my mind. I immediately wondered if Chade's fall had been an accident at all. I tried to hide the thought from Nettle as I reached through her to grope for Chade. Nothing. *I can't sense him. Does he live?* I asked, scrabbling for some semblance of calm. I pushed my Skill, and became more aware of the room where Nettle sat beside a draped bed. The curtained windows made it dim. There was a small brazier burning somewhere; I smelled the piercing smoke of restorative herbs. I sat out in the fresh air but felt the stuffiness of the closed room all around me. Nettle drew a breath and showed me Chade through her eyes. My old mentor was laid out as straight beneath his blankets as if he were stretched on a funeral pyre. His face was pale, his eyes sunken, and a bruise darkened one temple and swelled his brow on that side. I could see King Dutiful's councilor through my daughter's eyes, but had no fuller sense of him.

He breathes. But he will not wake and none of us has any sense of him being here. It's as if I'm touching—

Dirt. I finished the thought for her. That was how Thick had expressed it years ago, when I had begged him and Dutiful to reach out with the Skill and help me heal the Fool. He had been dead to them. Dead and already turning back into earth. *But he's breathing?*

I already told you he was! Frantic impatience bordering on anger tinged her words. *Fitz, we would not have reached for you if this was a*

*simple healing. And if he were dead, I'd tell you that. Dutiful wants you
to come right now, as soon as possible. Even with Thick lending strength
to them, the Skill-coterie has not been able to reach him. If we can't reach
him, we can't heal him. You are our last hope.*

I'm at Oaksbywater market. I'll need to go back to Withywoods, pack
a few things, and get a saddle horse. I'll be there in three days, or less.

*That won't do. Dutiful knows that you won't like the idea, but he
wants you to come by the stone portals.*

I don't do that. I asserted it strongly, already knowing that for
Chade, I would risk it, as I had not in all the years since I had been
lost in the stones. The thought of entering that gleaming blackness
raised the hair on the back of my neck and my arms. I was terrified
to the point of illness just thinking of it. Terrified. And tempted.

*Fitz. You have to. It's the only hope we have. The healers we have
called in are completely useless, but on one thing they agree. Chade is
sinking. We cannot reach him with the Skill, and they say that all their
experience tells them that within a few days he will die, his eyes bulging
from his face from the blow to his head. If you arrive here in three days,
it will be to watch him burn on a pyre.*

I will come. I formed the thought dully. Could I make myself do
it? I had to.

*Through the stones, she pressed me. If you are at Oaksbywater, you
are not far from their Judgment Stone on Gallows Hill. The charts we
have show that it has the glyph for our Witness Stones. You could be here
easily before nightfall.*

Through the stones. I tried to keep both bitterness and fear from
my thought. *Your mother is here at the market with me. We came in the
high-wheeled cart. I will have to send her home alone.* Parted yet again
by Farseer business, the simple pleasure of a shared meal and an
evening of a tavern minstrel's songs snatched away from us.

She will understand, Nettle tried to comfort me.

She will. But she won't be pleased by it. I broke my thoughts free of
Nettle. I had not closed my eyes, but I felt as if I opened them. The
fresh air and the clamor of the summer market, the bright sunlight
dappling down through the oak's leaves, even the girl in the red
slippers seemed like sudden intrusions into my grimmer reality. I

realized that while I had been Skilling, my unseeing gaze had been resting on her. She was now returning my stare with a querying smile. I lowered my eyes hastily. Time to go.

I drained the last of my cider, thudded my empty mug back on the board, and stood, searching the milling market for Molly. I spotted her at the same time she saw me. Once she had been as slender as the girl in the red slippers. Now Molly was a woman easing past the middle years of her life. She was moving steadily if not swiftly through the crowd, a small, sturdy woman with bright dark eyes and a determined set to her mouth. She carried a fold of soft gray fabric over her arm as if it were a hard-won war trophy. For a moment the sight of her drove all other considerations from my mind. I simply stood and watched her coming toward me. She smiled at me and patted her merchandise. I pitied the merchant who had been the victim of her bargaining. She had ever been a thrifty woman; becoming Lady Molly of Withywoods had changed none of that. The sunlight glinted on the silver that threaded her once-dark curls.

I stooped to retrieve her earlier purchases. There was a crock of a particular soft cheese that she enjoyed, a pouch of culkey leaves for scenting candles, and a carefully wrapped parcel of bright-red peppers that she had cautioned me not to touch with my bare hands. They were for our gardener's granny: She claimed to know a potion formula that could ease the knots in old knuckles. Molly wanted to try it. Of late she suffered from an aching lower back. Beside it was a stoppered pot that held a blood-strengthening tea.

I loaded my arms and as I turned, I bumped into the red-slippers girl. "Beg pardon," I said, stepping back from her, but she looked up at me with a merry smile.

"No harm done," she assured me, cocking her head. Then the curve of her smile deepened as she added, "But if you'd like to make up for nearly treading on my very new slippers, you might buy a mug of cider to share with me."

I stared at her dumbfounded. She'd thought I'd been watching her when I was Skilling. Well, actually, yes, I had been staring at her, but she had mistaken it for a man's interest in a pretty girl. Which she was. Pretty, and young, much younger than I'd realized when I first noticed her. Just as I was much older than her interested gaze assumed. Her request was both flattering and unnerving. "You'll have to settle for accepting an apology from me. I'm on my way to meet my lady wife." I nodded toward Molly.

The girl turned, looked directly at Molly, and turned back to me. "Your lady wife? Or did you mean to say your mother?"

I stared down at the girl. Any charm her youth and prettiness had held for me had vanished from my heart. "Excuse me," I said coldly and stepped away from her and toward my Molly. A familiar ache squeezed my heart. It was a fear I fought against every day. Molly was aging away from me, the years carrying her further and further from me in a slow and inexorable current. I was nearing fifty years, but my body stubbornly persisted in holding the lines of a man of thirty-five. A Skill-enhanced healing from years before still had the power to waken and rage through me whenever I injured myself. Under its control, I was seldom ill, and cuts or bruises healed rapidly. Last spring I'd fallen from a hayloft and broken my forearm. I'd gone to sleep that night with it splinted firmly, and wakened ravenously hungry and thin as a winter wolf. My arm had been sore but I could use it. The undesired magic had kept me fit and youthful, a terrible blessing as I watched Molly slowly stoop under the burden of the stacked years she bore. The Skill refused to allow my body to keep pace with hers. The remorseless current of time bore her steadily away from me. Since her fainting spell at that Winterfest, her aging had seemed to accelerate. She tired more easily, and had occasional spells of dizziness and blurred vision. It saddened me, for her choice was to dismiss such things and refuse to discuss them afterward.

As I advanced toward Molly, I noticed that her smile had become fixed. She had not missed the interplay between the girl and me. I spoke before she could, pitching my words for her ears only amid the market's din. "Nettle Skilled to me. It's Chade. He's badly injured. They want me to come to Buckkeep Castle."

"You have to leave tonight?"

"No. Immediately."

She looked at me. Emotions played over her face. Annoyance. Anger. And then, terribly, resignation. "You must go," she told me.

"I'm afraid I must."

She nodded tightly, and took several of her purchases from my laden arms. Together we walked through the market toward the inn. Our little two-wheeled cart was drawn up outside. I'd stabled our horse, rather hoping that we'd spend the night there. As I put the rest of her purchases under the seat, I said, "You don't have to rush back home, you know. You can stay and enjoy the rest of the market day."

She sighed. "No. I'll call the ostler to have our horse brought out. I didn't come for the market, Fitz. I came for a day with you. And that's over. If we go home now, you can be on your way before evening."

I cleared my throat and broke the news to her. "It's too urgent for that. I'll have to use the stone on Gallows Hill."

She stared at me, her mouth ajar. I met that gaze, trying to hide my own fear. "I wish you wouldn't," she said breathlessly.

"I wish I didn't have to."

A time longer, her eyes searched my face. For an instant she folded her faded lips and I thought she would argue with me. Then she said stiffly, "Fetch the horse. I'll drive you there."

It was an easy walk, but I didn't argue. She wanted to be there. She wanted to watch me enter the stone and disappear from her sight. She had never seen me do it, and had never wanted to see me do it. But if I must, she would watch me go. I knew her thoughts. It might be the last time she'd ever see me, if my Skill went awry. I offered her the only comfort I could. "I'll have Nettle send a bird from Buckkeep as soon as I'm safely there. So you needn't worry."

"Oh, I'll worry. For a day and a half, until the bird reaches me. It's what I'm best at."

The shadows had just begun to lengthen when I handed her down from the cart at the top of Gallows Hill. She held my hand as we walked the steep trail to the top. Oaksbywater didn't boast a circle of standing stones as Buckkeep did. There was only the old gallows, the splintery gray wood baking in the summer sunlight with daisies growing incongruously and cheerfully all round the legs of it. And behind it, on the very crest of the hill, the single standing stone, gleaming black and veined with silver: memory stone. It was easily the height of three men. It had five faces, and each had a single glyph chiseled into it. Since we had discovered the true use of the standing stones, King Dutiful had sent out teams of men to clean each stone and record its glyphs and orientation. Each glyph signified a destination. Some we now knew; most we did not. Even after a decade of studying scrolls about the forgotten Skill-magic, most practitioners regarded travel via the portal stones as dangerous and debilitating.

Molly and I circled the stone together, looking up at it. The sun was shining into my eyes when I saw the glyph that would take me to the Witness Stones near Buckkeep. I stared at it, feeling fear form cold in my belly. I did not want to do this. I had to.

The stone stood black and still, beckoning me like a pond of water on a hot summer day. And like a deep pool, it could pull me into its depths and drown me forever.

"Come back to me as soon as you can," Molly whispered. And then she flung her arms around me and held me in a fierce hug. She spoke into my chest. "I hate the days when we must be parted. I hate the duties that still tug at you, and I hate how always they seem to tear us apart. I hate your dashing off at a moment's notice to do them." She spoke the words savagely and each was a small knife plunged into me. Then she added, "But I love that you are the kind of man who still does what he must do. Our daughter calls, and you go to her. As we both know you must." She took a deep breath and shook her head at her flash of temper. "Fitz, Fitz, I am still so jealous of every minute of your time. And as I age, it seems that I wish to cling to you more, not less. But go. Go do what you must and come back to me as quickly as ever you can. But not by the stones. Come back to me safely, my dear."

Simple words, and to this day, I do not know why they bolstered my courage as they did. I held her closer to me and stiffened my own spine. "I'll be fine," I assured her. "The time I was lost in the stones, it was only because I'd used them so often in the days before. This will be easy. I'll step in here and stumble out by the Witness Stones above Buckkeep Town. And first thing I'll have a bird sent to Withywoods to tell you I'm there."

"And it will take at least a day to get here. But I'll be watching for it."

I kissed her again, and then stepped free of her. My knees were shaking and abruptly I wished I had pissed earlier. Facing a sudden and unknown danger is different from deliberately plunging oneself into a previously experienced and known to be life-threatening task. Imagine deliberately walking into a bonfire. Or stepping over the railing of a ship in a storm. I could die. Or worse, not die, forever, in that cool black stillness.

Only four steps away. I could not faint. I could not let my terror show. I had to do this. The stone was only two steps away. I lifted a hand and gave Molly a final wave, but dared not look back at her. My mouth had gone dry in purest fear. With the same hand, I set my palm to the face of the standing stone, right under the glyph that would carry me to Buckkeep.

The stone's face was cool. The Skill infused me in an indescribable way. I didn't step into the stone; it engulfed me. A moment of black and sparkling nothing. An indefinable sense of well-being caressed and tempted me. I was on the cusp of understanding something wonderful; in a moment I would grasp it fully. I would not just comprehend it. I would be it. Complete. Unheeding of anything, or anyone, ever again. Fulfilled.

Then I tumbled out. The first coherent thought I had on falling out of the stone onto the wet and grassy hillside above Buckkeep was the same as my last thought before I entered. I wondered what Molly had seen as I left her.

I had dropped to my quivering knees as I emerged. I didn't try to move. I looked out, breathing air that carried a hint of brine from Buckkeep Bay. It was cooler here, and the air was moister. Rain had fallen recently. Sheep grazed the hillside before me. One had lifted its head to regard me; now it dropped it back to the grass. I could see the back walls of Buckkeep Castle across a rumpled distance of stony pasture and wind-gnarled trees. The fortress of black stone stood as it seemed it always had, its towers giving it a sweeping view of the sea. I could not see it, but I knew that on the steep cliffs below it Buckkeep Town clung like a creeping lichen of people and structures. Home. I was home.

Slowly my heartbeat returned to normal. A creaking cart crested the hill and made its way toward the castle gates. With a critical eye, I approved the slow pace of a sentry along the castle walls above it. We were at peace now, but still Dutiful maintained the watch. Good. Chalced might seem to be preoccupied with its own civil war, but rumor said the duchess now controlled most of her wayward provinces. And as soon as it was at peace with itself, doubtless Chalced would once more seek war with its neighbors.

I looked back at the Skill-pillar. The sudden desire to reenter it, to bathe again in that unsettling pleasure of sparkling darkness, seized me. There was something there that was immense and wonderful, something that I longed to join. I could step back inside and find it. It waited for me.

I drew a deep breath and reached out with the Skill to Nettle. *Let fly a bird to Withywoods. Let Molly know I am here and safe. Choose the swiftest bird that will home there.*

Done. And why didn't you let me know before you entered the stone? I heard her speak to someone in the room. "He's here. Send a lad with a horse for him, now." Then she focused on me again. *What if you had emerged senseless and without words as you did all those years ago?*

I let her rebuke flow past me. She was right, of course, and Chade would be furious with me. No. The thought came with freezing dismay. Chade might never be furious with me again. I started walking toward the keep, and then could not prevent myself from breaking into a trot. I Skilled to Nettle again. *Do the guards on the gate know I'm coming?*

King Dutiful himself ordered them to expect Holder Badgerlock, with an important message for me from my mother. No one will delay you. I'll send a boy with a horse.

I'll be there before he clears the stables. I broke into a run.

Chade's bedchamber was grand. And still as death. It was on the same floor as Dutiful's royal apartments, and I doubted that my king's chambers were as indulgent as those of the old assassin-turned-advisor. My feet sank into the thick moss-green rugs. The heavy hangings over the windows admitted not a ray of daylight. Instead flickering candles filled the room with the scent of melting beeswax. In a gleaming brass brazier beside his bed a smoke of restorative herbs thickened the air. I coughed and groped my way to the bedside. There was a pitcher there and a filled cup. "Only water?" I asked of the hovering healers, and someone assented. I drained the cup, and coughed again. I was still trying to catch my breath from my dash up the wide stairways of the castle.

King Dutiful was coming somewhere behind me, as was Nettle. Thick sat on a stool in the corner, the tip of his tongue resting on his lower lip and his simpleton's face welling sadness and tears. His Skilled music was a muted dirge. He squinted at me for a long moment, and then his froggy mouth spread in a smile of welcome. "I know you," he told me.

And I know you, old friend, I Skilled to him. I pushed from my thoughts that he had not aged well; those of his kind seldom did. He had already lived longer than any of the Buckkeep healers had expected.

Old Chade is acting dead, he conveyed to me anxiously.

We'll do what we can to wake him, I assured the little man.

Steady, half-brother to my Nettle and part of the king's Skill-coterie now, stood at Thick's side. I nodded a quick greeting to him. I had pushed my way through hovering healers and their various assistants to reach Chade's bedside. The room was thick with the smells of anxious people; they pressed on my Wit-sense as if I were wading through a pen of beasts awaiting slaughter.

I did not hesitate. "Open those curtains and the windows as well. Get some light and air in here!"

One of the healers spoke. "We have judged that dark and quiet may best encourage—"

"Open them!" I snapped, for a sudden rush of memories of my first king, King Shrewd, in a stuffy room full of tonics and medicines and the smoke of drugs filled me with fear.

The healers stared at me, hostile and unmoving. Who was this stranger to enter Lord Chade's chamber, drink from his cup, and then order them about? Resentment simmered.

"Open them," Dutiful echoed as he entered the chamber, and the healers and their assistants leapt to obey.

I turned to him and asked, "Can you get them all out of here?"

Someone gasped. "My king, if you please," I hastily added. In the pressure of the moment, I had forgotten that they saw me merely as Tom Badgerlock, Holder for Withywoods. Quite possibly, they had no idea as to why I might be called in to consult on Chade's health. I tried to compose myself and saw a wry and weary smile twitch the corner of Dutiful's mouth as he issued the orders that would clear the room of the clustering healers. As light and air refreshed the room and the number of folk diminished, the pressure on my senses eased. I asked no permission as I dragged the hangings on the bed wide open. Nettle helped me. The last light of sunset fell across the bed and the features of my old mentor, my old friend, my great-uncle Chade Fallstar. Despair rose in me.

He looked cadaverous. His mouth had fallen open, his lower jaw hanging to one side. His closed eyes were sunken. The bruise I had glimpsed in my Skill-session with Nettle had spread and darkened half his face. I took his hand and was rewarded with a Wit-sense of his life. Not strong, but it was there. It had been masked by the huddle of mourning healers when I first entered. His lips looked parched, his tongue a grayish pad in his mouth. I found a clean cloth by the bedside, moistened it from the pitcher, and touched it to his lips, pushing his mouth closed as I did so. I dabbed it over his lined face. He had used his Skill to slow the erosion of years, but no magic could reverse time's tread or the tracks it left on his body. I tried to guess his true age. I'd thought him an old man when he first took me as his apprentice some forty years ago. I decided I didn't want to know and put my mind to more useful tasks. As I wet the cloth again and set it gently against the bruising, I asked, "Did you already try to heal this? Even if we cannot reach him with the Skill, healing his body may free his mind to return to us."

"Of course we tried." I forgave Dutiful for the irritation in his voice. It was an obvious question, and he gave me the obvious answer. "We tried to reach into him, to no avail."

I set the cloth aside and sat down on the edge of the bed. Chade's hand in mine was warm. I closed my eyes. With my fingers, I sensed the bones and the muscles and the flesh. I tried to push past my physical awareness of him to Skill-sensations I had not felt in years. I tried to enter his body with my thoughts, to be aware of what was right in the flow of his blood and the rush of his breath. I could not. I pushed, but the barriers did not yield.

Barriers. I drew back from them and opened my eyes. I spoke aloud my consternation.

"He's walled off. Deliberately sealed against the Skill. Like Chivalry did to Burrich."

Thick was rocking in the corner. I looked at him, and he hunched his blunt head closer between his shoulders. His small eyes met mine. "Yah. Yah. Closed like a box. Can't get in." He shook his head solemnly, the tip of his tongue curled over his upper lip.

I looked around the room. The king stood quietly by Chade's bed, his young wolfhound leaning comfortingly against his knee. Of the king's coterie only Nettle and Steady were there. That told me that his formal Skill-assemblage had already joined their strength and attempted to batter a way into Chade. And failed. That Nettle had resorted to calling on me and bringing Thick spoke volumes. As Skillmistress, she had decided that all conventional uses of the magic had been ineffective. Those of us gathered now were those who would, if commanded, venture into dangerous and unknown applications of Skill.

Thick, our beloved half-wit, was prodigiously strong with the magic, though not creative with it. The king himself possessed a goodly amount of ability for it, while Nettle's strongest talent was the Skill-manipulation of dreams. Her half-brother, Steady, was a reservoir of strength for her, one who could be completely trusted with any secret. But they were all looking at me, the Solo, the bastard Farseer with a wild and erratic talent, as if I were the one who would know what to do.

But I didn't. I didn't know any more about it than the last time we had attempted to use Skill to heal a sealed man. We hadn't succeeded. Burrich had died. In Burrich's youth he had been Chivalry's right-hand man and a source of strength for the king-in-waiting. And so Burrich had been sealed by his king, lest enemies of the Farseers use him as a conduit to discover Chivalry's secrets. Instead that wall had kept out the magic that might have saved him.

"Who did this?" I tried and failed to keep accusation from my voice. "Who sealed him from the Skill like this?" Treachery from within the coterie was the most likely explanation. It chilled me to think of it. Already my assassin's mind had linked the sealing with his fall. Double treachery to kill the old man. Cut him off from his magic so he could not cry for help, and then see that he was badly injured. If Chade had been the target of such treachery, was the king the next mark?

King Dutiful puffed his lips out in an exclamation of surprise and dismay. "It's the first I've heard of it, if you are right. But you can't be right. Just a few days ago, he and I conducted a small experiment with the Skill. I reached him without effort. He certainly wasn't sealed then! Even with all his practice, he's never become exceptionally strong with the Skill, though he's very competent with what talent he has. But strong enough to wall us all out? I doubt that he . . ." I saw my own suspicions take root in his mind. Dutiful drew up a chair on the other side of Chade's bed. He sat down and looked across the bed at me. "Someone did this to him?"

"What was the 'small experiment'?" I demanded. All eyes were on our king.

"Nothing dark! He had a small block of the black stone, the memory stone, brought from the ancient Elderling stronghold on Aslevjal Island. He pressed a thought into it, and then gave it to a messenger who brought it to me. I was able to retrieve his message. It was just a simple little rhyme, something about where to find violets in Buckkeep Castle. I used the Skill to confirm with him that I was correct. He was certainly able to Skill well enough to impress it into memory stone, and receive my response to it. So he wasn't sealed on that day."

A tiny motion caught my eye. It wasn't much. Steady had opened his mouth and then shut it again. It was not much of a trail but I'd pursue it. I looked at him suddenly, pointed my finger, and demanded, "What did Chade tell you not to tell anyone?"

Again his mouth opened for just that betraying moment, then snapped shut again. He shook his head mutely and set his jaw. He was Burrich's son. He couldn't lie. I drew breath to press him but his half-sister was swifter. Nettle crossed the room in two strides, reached up to grab her younger brother's shoulders, and tried to shake him. It was like watching a kitten attack a bull. Steady didn't move under her onslaught; he only sank his head down between his broad shoulders. "Tell the secret!" she demanded. "I know that look. You tell, right now, Steady!" He bowed his head and closed his eyes.

He was caught on a bridge with both ends torn free of shore. He could not lie and he could not break his promise. I calmed my voice and spoke slowly, more to Nettle than to him. "Steady won't break his promise. Don't ask him to. But let me make a guess. Steady's talent is to lend strength to someone who can Skill. To serve as a King's Man if the king should need extra strength in a time of great need for Skill-magic."

Steady bowed his head, a clear assent to what we already knew about him. Once, I had served in that capacity to King Verity. In his need and my inexperience, I had let him drain me, and he had been angry at how close he had come to doing me permanent harm. But Steady was not like me; he had been trained specifically for this task.

Laboriously I built my castle of logic from what I knew of Chade. "So Chade summoned you. And he borrowed your strength to . . . do what? Do something that burned his Skill out of him?"

Steady was very still. That wasn't it. I suddenly knew. "Chade drew on your strength to put a block on himself?"

Steady was unaware of the tiny dip of his head that was assent. Dutiful broke in, outraged at my suggestion. "That makes no sense. Chade always wanted more of the Skill, not to be blocked from the use of it."

I heaved a great sigh. "Chade loves his secrets. He lives his life in a castle of secrets. The Skill is a way into a man's mind. If a strong Skill-user catches a man unaware, he can suggest anything to him and the man will believe it. Tell him his ship faces a great storm and he will turn back to safe harbor. Persuade a war leader that his army is outnumbered and he will change his tactics. Your father, King Verity, spent many of his days using the Skill exactly that way to turn back the Red Ships from our shores. Think of all the ways we have used the Skill over the years. We all know how to raise walls against other Skill-users, for privacy in our own lives. But if you know that others are stronger in the Skill than you are . . ." I let my words dwindle away.

Dutiful groaned. "Then you would seek help to raise a more powerful wall. One that could not be breached without your consent, one only you could lower at will."

"If you were awake or aware enough to do so." I spoke the last words softly. Tears were rolling down Steady's cheeks. He looked so much like his father that my breath caught in my throat. Nettle had ceased trying to worry at her younger brother. Instead she rested her forehead on his chest. Thick's Skill-magic music surged into a storm of despair. I battered my way through it, organized my thoughts, and asked Steady a question.

"We know what happened. You haven't broken your promise not to tell. But this is a different question. If you helped a Skill-user block himself, do you know how to break through it?"

He folded his lips tightly and shook his head.

"The man who is strong enough to build a wall should be strong enough to break it," Dutiful suggested sternly.

Steady shook his head. When he spoke, his voice was deep with pain. Now that we knew the secret, he felt he could speak the details. "Lord Chade read about it in one of the old scrolls. It was a defense suggested for the coterie closest to the king or queen, so that the coterie could never be corrupted. It makes a wall that only the Skill-user himself can open. Or the king or queen, or whoever knows the keyword."

My gaze shot to Dutiful. He spoke immediately. "I don't know it! Chade never spoke to me of such a thing!" He set his elbow to his knee and his forehead to his hand, looking suddenly very much like an anxious boy again. It wasn't reassuring.

Nettle spoke. "If he didn't tell Dutiful, then you have to know it, Fitz. You were always closest to him. It has to be one of you two. Who else would he entrust it to?"

"Not me," I said brusquely. I didn't add that we hadn't spoken to each other in several months, not even via the Skill. It was a rift not of anger, but only of time. We'd slowly grown apart over the last few years. Oh, in times of extreme turmoil he would not hesitate to reach into my mind and demand my opinion or even my aid. But over the years he'd had to accept that I would not be drawn back into the intricate dance that was life at Buckkeep Castle. Now I regretted our distance.

I rubbed my brow and turned to Thick. "Did Lord Chade tell you a special word, Thick? One to remember?" I focused on him, trying to smile reassuringly. Behind me I heard the door to the room open, but I kept my attention on Thick.

He scratched one of his tiny ears. His tongue stuck out of his mouth as he pondered. I forced myself to be patient. Then he smiled and straightened up. He leaned forward and smiled at me. "Please. He told me to remember 'please.' And 'thank you.' Words to get what you want from people. You don't just grab. Say 'please' before you take something."

"Could it be that simple?" Nettle asked in wonder.

Kettricken spoke from behind me. "Does it involve Chade? Then simple? Absolutely not. That man never makes anything simple." I turned to regard my erstwhile queen and despite the gravity of our situation, I could not help but smile at her. She stood straight and regal as ever. As always, the king's mother was dressed with a simplicity that would have looked more appropriate on a serving girl, save that she wore it with such dignity. And power. Her fair hair, gone to early silver, flowed unbound down her back, past the shoulders of her Buckkeep-blue robe. Another anomaly. She had encouraged the Six Duchies to reach out in trade, and in my lifetime I had seen our kingdom embrace all that the wider world had to offer. Exotic foods and seasoning from the Spice Islands, peculiar styles of dress from Jamaillia and the lands beyond, and foreign techniques for working with glass, iron, and pottery had altered every aspect of life in Buckkeep Castle. The Six Duchies shipped out wheat and oats, iron ore and ingots, Sandsedge brandy and the fine wines from the inland duchies. Timber from the Mountain Kingdom became lumber that in turn we shipped to Jamaillia. We prospered and embraced change. Yet here was my former queen, immune to the changes she had encouraged, dressed as simply and old-fashioned as a servant from my childhood, without even a diadem in her hair to mark her rank as the king's mother.

She crossed to me, and I rose to accept her firm embrace. "Fitz," she said by my ear. "Thank you. Thank you for coming, and for taking great risk by coming so swiftly. When I heard that Dutiful had conveyed to Nettle that you must come at once, I was horrified. And full of hope. How selfish we are, to tear you from your well-earned peace and demand that you once more come to our aid."

"You are always welcome to any help I can bring you." Any lingering irritation I had felt for how I had been pressed to use the stone pillar vanished at her words. It was her gift. Queen Kettricken had always acknowledged the sacrifices people made in service to the Farseer throne. In exchange she had always been willing to surrender her own comfort and safety for those loyal to her. In that moment her gratitude seemed a fair exchange for the danger I had faced.

She released me and stepped back. "So. Do you think you can help him?"

I shook my head regretfully. "Chade has put a block on himself, similar to the way that Chivalry sealed Burrich off from the Skill. He drew on Steady's Skill-strength to do it. If we could break through it, we might be able to use our joined Skill-magic to aid his body in healing itself. But he has locked us out, and lacks the awareness to either permit us in or to heal himself."

"I see. And how is he?"

"Losing strength. I feel an ebbing in his vitality even in the short time I've been here."

She flinched at my words, but I knew she prized honesty. She opened her hands and gestured to all of us. "What can we do?"

King Dutiful spoke. "Little to nothing. We can call the healers back, but they only seem to squabble with one another. One says to cool him with wet cloths, another to light the hearth and cover him with blankets. One wanted to bleed him. I do not think any of them truly has a remedy for this type of injury. If we do nothing, I suspect he will die before two more nights go by." He lifted off his crown, ran his hands through his hair, and set it back on his head slightly ajar. "Oh, Chade," he said, a combination of rebuke and plea in his voice. He turned to me. "Fitz, are you sure you've had no message from him, either on paper or by the Skill, that would hint at what key will open him to us?"

"Nothing. Not for months."

Kettricken looked around the room. "One of us knows." She spoke slowly and precisely. She considered each of us with another slow, sweeping gaze, and then said, "I think it is most likely you, Fitz."

She was probably right. I looked at Steady. "How does one use this keyword, if one knows it?"

The young man looked uncertain. "He didn't instruct me in that, but I suspect it is something you Skill to him, and it is what permits you in."

My heart sank. Had Burrich had a keyword, something that would have allowed me to reach him? A key that Chivalry had taken to his grave after his riding "accident"? I suddenly felt ill to know that I might have saved Burrich from death if I'd known his key. Well, it wasn't going to happen again. Kettricken was correct. Chade was far too clever a man to have closed a lock without entrusting one of us with a key.

I took Chade's hand in both of mine. I looked at his sunken face, at his lips puffing slightly with every expelled breath. I focused on him and reached again with the Skill. My mental grip on him slid and slipped, as if I tried to grasp a glass orb with soapy hands. I set my teeth and did a thing he had always decried. I found him with my Wit, focused on the animal life that I felt ebbing through his body, and then I needled my Skill at him. I began with a list of names. *Chivalry. Verity. Shrewd. Fallstar. Farseer. Burrich. Kettricken.* I went through everyone dear to us, hoping for a twitch of response. There was nothing. I finished with *Lady Thyme. Lord Golden. Slink.*

I gave up on that list and opened my eyes. The room was quiet around me. King Dutiful still sat on the other side of the bed. In the window behind him, the sun was foundering on the horizon. "I sent the others away," he said quietly.

"I had no luck."

"I know. I was listening."

I studied my king in that unguarded moment. He and Nettle were nearly of an age and resembled each other in small ways, if one knew to look for them. They had the dark curly hair typical of the Farseer line. She had a straight nose and a determined mouth, as did he. But Dutiful had grown taller than I while Nettle was not much taller than her mother. Dutiful sat now, his hands steepled with the fingertips touching his mouth and his eyes grave. My king. The third Farseer king I had served.

Dutiful rose, groaning as he stretched his back. His hound imitated him, rising and then bowing low to the floor. Dutiful walked to the door, opened it, and said, "Food, please. And a dish of water for Courser. And some of the good brandy. Two cups. Let my lady mother know that as of yet we've had no success." He shut the door and turned back to me. "What? Why are you smiling?"

"Such a king you became, Dutiful! Verity would be proud of you. He was the same way, able to say 'please' to the lowliest servant with no trace of irony. So. We have not spoken in months. How sits the crown?"

In response, he took it off and gave his head a shake, and then ran his fingers through his hair. He set it on Chade's bedside table and said, "Heavy, sometimes. Even this one, and the formal one I must wear when I sit in judgment is worse. But it has to be borne."

I knew he was not speaking of the actual weight of it. "And your queen, and the princes?"

"They are well." He sighed. "She misses her home, and the freedom of being the Narcheska rather than the Queen of the Six Duchies. She has taken the boys to visit her mothershouse yet again. I know it is the way of her folk, that the maternal lineage is the one that counts. But both my mother and Chade believe I am foolish to risk both sons on the sea so often." He smiled ruefully. "Yet it is still hard for me to deny her anything she wants. And, as she points out, they are as much her sons as mine. After Prosper took a bad fall in a hunt last winter, she compared me doing that with them to her taking them across the water. And she frets that as yet she has not borne a daughter for her mothershouse. While for me, it has almost been a relief that we have only sons. If I never have to confront the issue of where my daughter would be raised, I would count it a blessing. But she frets that she has gone four years now with no pregnancy. Well." He sighed.

"She's young yet," I said boldly. "You are, what, barely thirty? And she is younger still. You have time."

"But there have been two miscarriages . . ." His words trickled away, and he stared at a shadow in the corner. The dog at his feet whined and looked at me accusingly. Dutiful stooped to set a hand to him. For a moment, we all were quiet. Then, plainly changing the direction of our conversation, he tipped his head toward Chade. "He's sinking, Fitz. What do we do now?"

A knock at the door interrupted us. This time I rose and went to open it. A page came in bearing a tray with food. Three others followed, one with a carafe of warmed water, a basin, and cloths, and the other with the brandy and cups. The girl came in last, carrying a small table and puffing a bit with the effort. Dutiful and I were silent as our repast and washwater were set out for us. The pages lined up, bowed in unison, and waited to receive Dutiful's thanks before retiring. When the door was shut, I gestured at the table. Courser was already at his bowl of water, lapping noisily.

"We eat. We drink. And we try again," I told him.

And we did.

In the deeps of night, by candlelight, I damped a cloth and moistened Chade's lips. I felt I was keeping a death watch now. I had given up on specific words long ago, and simply begun a long conversation with him about all the things I recalled doing with him during my apprenticeship to be an assassin. I had wandered from a time of him teaching me the mixing of poisons to our wild ride to Forge. I had recited a number of learning poems about the healing properties of herbs. I had recalled our quarrels as well as the moments when we had been closest, all in the hope that a random word might be the key. Nothing had worked. Dutiful had kept the vigil with me. The others had come and gone during the night, entering and leaving the room like shadows moving with the sun's passage. Thick had sat with us for a time, unhelpfully offering words we'd already tried. Nettle had visited Chade's old study and rummaged through the scrolls and other items left on his table. She had brought them down to us to inspect. None of them had given us a clue. Hope had been peeled away from us like a sodden bandage covering a festering wound. I had moved from feeble optimism to wishing it were all over.

"Did we try names of herbs?"

"Yes. Remember?"

"No," Dutiful admitted. "I'm too tired. I can't think of what we have tried and what we haven't."

I set Chade's hand down on his slowly rising and falling chest and moved to the table that now held the litter of items from his workbench. The half-spent candles showed me the Skill-scroll about imbuing stone with a message, a scroll about cheesemaking, and an old vellum about scrying the future in a bowl of water. In addition there was a block of memory stone with nothing stored in it, a broken knife blade, and a wineglass with some withered flowers in it. Dutiful drifted over to join me. "The broken blade?" he asked.

I shook my head. "Not significant. He was always getting in a hurry and trying to pry things open with a knife blade." I nudged the block of memory stone. "Where did this come from? Aslevjal?"

Dutiful nodded. "He has made a few trips there over the last five years. He was intensely curious about all you had told him of Kebal Rawbread's stronghold, and the Elderlings who created it and occupied it ages ago. None of us approved of his adventuring, but you know Chade. He needs no one's approval except his own. Then, abruptly, he stopped going. I suspect something happened to frighten him into good sense, but he's never spoken about it. Too proud, I think, and he didn't want any of us to have the satisfaction of saying, *We warned you.* On one journey to the island he found a room with scattered blocks of memory stone and brought back a small bag of cubes of the stuff. Some held memories, mostly poetry and songs. Others were empty."

"And he put something on one of them, and sent it to you recently."

"Yes."

I stared at Dutiful. He straightened slowly, dismay vying with relief.

"Oh. It's the key, isn't it?"

"Do you remember what it said?"

"Absolutely." He walked to Chade's side, sat down, and took his hand to make the Skill-contact easier. He spoke aloud. "Where violets bloom in a lady's lap, the wise old spider spun his trap."

We were both smiling. But as the smile faded from Dutiful's face, I asked him, "What's wrong?"

"No response. He's as invisible to my Skill as he has been all day."

I crossed the room quickly, sat, and took Chade's hand. I focused myself at him, and used both voice and Skill. "*Where violets bloom in a lady's lap, the wise old spider spun his trap.*"

There was nothing. Only Chade's hand lax in mine.

"Maybe he's too weak to respond," Dutiful suggested.

"Hush." I leaned back, not speaking. Violets in a lady's lap. Violets in a lady's lap. There was something, something from long ago. Then I had it. A statue in the Women's Garden. It was in the back corner of the garden, overhung by a plum thicket. There, where the shadows were deep and cool even in the height of summer, was a statue of Eda. She was seated with her hands loose in her lap. She had been there a long time. I recalled tiny ferns growing in the mossy folds of her gown. And yes, violets in her lap.

"I need a torch. I know where he hid the key. I have to go to the Women's Garden and the statue of Eda."

Chade took a sudden gasp of air. For an instant I feared it was his final breath. Then Dutiful said fiercely, "That was the key. The old spider is Chade. Eda, in the Women's Garden."

As he said the goddess's name, it was as if heavy draperies were parted and Chade opened to the Skill. Dutiful sent out a Skill-summoning for Nettle, Thick, and Steady, but he did not wait for the rest of the king's coterie to arrive.

"Does he have the strength for this?" I demanded, knowing well that a forced healing burns the reserves of a man's body without mercy. The magic itself does not heal; it but forces the body to speed the process.

"We can let what remains of his strength be slowly consumed by his dying, or we can burn it up trying to heal him. If you were Chade, which would you prefer?"

I set my teeth against my reply. I did not know. I did know that Chade and Dutiful had once made that decision for me and that I still lived with the consequences: a body that aggressively repaired every ill done to it, whether I would or no. But surely I could keep that fate from befalling Chade; I would know when to stop the heal-ing. I made that resolution and refused to wonder if that was the choice Chade would have made for himself.

I secured my Skill-link with Dutiful and together we sank into Chade. Dimly I was aware of Nettle coming to join us, and then Thick, bewildered with sleepiness but obedient to the call, and fi-nally Steady surging in to add his strength to our melded effort.

I led. I was not the strongest of the Skilled there. That would be Thick, his natural talent disguised by the façade of his simple-mindedness. Steady was next, a well of strength for a Skill-user even if he seemed unable to reach within himself and use it on his own. Dutiful was better taught in the varied uses of the Skill than I was, and Nettle, my daughter, more intuitive in how she wielded it. But I led by virtue of my years and my hard-won knowledge of how a man's body is put together. Chade himself had taught me those things—not as a healer, but as an assassin's apprentice, to know where a pressed finger can choke a man, or a small blade make a gout of blood leap out with every beat of his heart.

Even so, I did not "see" within Chade's body with my Skill. Rather, I listened to his body, and felt where it struggled to repair itself. I lent strength and purpose to that effort, and used my knowledge to apply it where the need was greatest. Pain is not always the best indicator of damage. The greater pain can confuse the mind into thinking that is the place of most damage. And so, Skill-linked as we were to Chade, we swam against the tide of his pain and fear to see the hidden damages behind the bone of his skull, a place of constriction where once blood had rushed freely, and a pocket of pooled blood that had gone toxic.

I had the collected strength of a trained coterie behind me, something I had never experienced before. It was a heady sensation. I drew their attention to what I wished repaired and they united their strength to persuade Chade's body to focus its energy there. It was so easy. The tempting possibilities of what I could do unfurled before me in a lush tapestry. What I could do! I could remake the man, restore him to youth! But the coins of Chade's flesh were not mine to spend. We had strength and to spare for our task, but Chade did not. And so, when I felt that we had lent his body as much of our strength as it could use and directed it effectively, I drew the coterie back, shepherding them out of Chade's flesh as if they were a well-meaning flock of chickens trespassing in a garden.

I opened my eyes to the darkened room and a circle of anxious candlelit faces. Trickles of perspiration lined Steady's face; the collar of his shirt was wet with it. He was breathing like a messenger who had just delivered his baton. Nettle's chin was propped in both her hands, her fingers splayed across her face. Thick's mouth hung ajar, and my king's hair was sweated flat to his brow. I blinked and felt the distant drumbeat of a headache to come. I smiled at them. "We've done what we can. Now we must leave him alone and let his body take its time." I stood slowly. "Go. Go rest now. Go on. There's no more to do here just now." I shooed them out of the room, ignoring their reluctance to leave.

Steady now leaned on his sister's arm. "Feed him," I whispered as they passed. My daughter nodded. "Yah," Thick agreed heartily and followed them. Only Dutiful dared defy me, resuming his seat by Chade's bed. His dog sighed and dropped to the floor at his feet. I shook my head at them, took my place, and ignored my own orders to them as I reached for Chade's awareness.

Chade?

What has happened? What happened to me? His mind touch was muzzy and confused. ▬

You fell and struck your head. You were unconscious. And because you had sealed yourself to the Skill, we found it hard to reach you and heal you.

I felt his instant of panic. He reached out to his body like a man patting his pockets to be sure a cutpurse had not robbed him. I knew he found the tracks we had left and that they were extensive. *I'm so weak. I nearly died, didn't I? Give me water, please. Why did you let me sink so low?*

At his rebuke, I felt a flash of anger. I counseled myself that now was not the time. I held the cup to his lips, propping his head as I did so. Eyes closed, he lipped feebly at the edge of the cup and sucked water in noisily. I refilled the cup and this time he drank more slowly. When he turned away from it as a sign he had had enough, I set it aside and asked him, "Why were you so obtuse? You didn't even let any of us know that you'd sealed yourself against the Skill. And why do it at all?"

He was still too weak to speak. I took his hand again, and his thoughts touched mine.

Protect the king. I know too many of his secrets. Too many Farseer secrets. Cannot leave such a chink in armor. All coteries should be sealed.

Then how could we reach one another?

Shielded only when asleep. Awake, I would sense who was reaching for me.

You were not asleep. You were unconscious and you needed us.

Unlikely. Just . . . a bit of bad luck. And if it did . . . you came. You understood the riddle.

His thoughts were fading. I knew how weary he was. My own body had begun to clamor at me for rest. Skilling was serious work. As draining as hunting. Or fighting. It had been a fight, hadn't it? An invasion of Chade's private territory . . .

I twitched awake. I still held Chade's hand, but he was deeply asleep now. Dutiful sprawled in his chair on the other side of the bed, snoring softly. His dog lifted his head to stare at me for a moment, and then dropped it back to his forepaws. We were all exhausted. By the last flames on the candle stubs, I studied Chade's ravaged face. He looked as if he had fasted for days. The pads of flesh on his cheeks were gone, and I saw the shape of his skull. The hand I still held was a bundle of bones in a sack of skin. He would live now, but he would be days rebuilding his body and his strength. Tomorrow he would be ravenous.

I leaned back with a sigh. My back ached from sleeping in the chair. The rugs on the floor of the chamber were thick and inviting. I stretched out on the floor by his bedside like a faithful dog. I slept.

I came awake to Thick stepping on my hand. I sat up with a curse, nearly knocking the tray from his hands. "You should not sleep on the floor!" he rebuked me.

I sat up, trapping my bruised fingers under my arm. It was hard to argue with Thick's remark. I clambered to my feet and then dropped back into my familiar chair. In the bed Chade was partially propped up. The old man was skeletal, and his grin at my discomfort was frightening in his wasted face. Dutiful's chair was empty. Thick was arranging the tray on Chade's lap. I smelled tea and biscuits and warmed jam. A bowl on the tray held soft-cooked eggs mashed up with a little butter, salt, and pepper next to a rank of thick rashers of bacon. I wanted to fall on it and devour it all. I think it must have showed on my face, for Chade's bony grin wid-ened. He didn't speak, but flapped a hand, dismissing me.

Once I would have gone directly to the kitchens. As a boy, I'd been Cook's pet there. As a youngster and then a young man, I'd eaten with the guardsmen in their noisy and untidy dining hall. Now I Skilled to King Dutiful, asking if he'd eaten yet. I was imme-diately invited to join him and his mother in a private chamber. I went, anticipating food and the good conversation that would go with it.

Kettricken and Dutiful were both waiting for me. Kettricken, true to her Mountain heritage, had arisen early and eaten lightly. Still she shared a table with us, a delicate cup of pale tea steaming before her. Dutiful was as hungry as I was, and even wearier, for he had gotten up early to share details about Chade's healing with her. A small caravan of pages arrived with food and arranged it for us on the table. Dutiful dismissed them, and the door closed to leave us in relative privacy. Other than a morning greeting, Kettricken held her silence while we filled our plates and then our bellies.

After we had emptied our first plates, Dutiful talked, sometimes through a mouthful of food, while I ate. The healers had visited Lord Chade while I slept. They had been horrified at how wasted he was, but his appetite and short temper had convinced them he would mend. Steady had been royally forbidden to lend strength to Chade in any attempt to seal himself again. Dutiful hoped that would be enough to prevent future mishaps. Privately I suspected that Chade could always find a way to either bribe or deceive Thick into helping him.

When our eating had slowed, and Kettricken had filled our cups with tea for the third time, she spoke softly. "Once again, FitzChiv-alry, you have answered our desperate call. You can see how much we still need you. I know you enjoy your quiet life now, and I will not dispute that you have earned it. But I will ask you to consider spending perhaps one month of every season here at Buckkeep Castle with us. I am sure that Lady Molly would enjoy being closer to both Nettle and Steady for those times. Swift also comes and goes frequently. She must miss her sons, and I know that we would love to have you here."

It was an old discussion. I had been proffered this invitation any number of times, in all sorts of forms. We had been offered chambers in the keep, a lovely house atop the cliffs with an amazing view of the waters below, a cozy cottage on the edge of the sheep meadows, and now the offer of coming and going as guests four times a year. I smiled at both of them. They read the answer in my eyes.

For me, it was not a question of where I lived. It was that I did not want a day-to-day intimacy with the politics of being a Farseer. Dutiful had previously opined that enough time had passed that few people would even care if FitzChivalry Farseer were miraculously resurrected from the dead, no matter how much disgrace had once been attached to me. I doubted that. But even as the humbler Holder Tom Badgerlock, even Lord Badgerlock, as they had offered, I did not wish to navigate those waters again. It was inevitable that their currents would drag me down and away from Molly and drown me in Farseer politics. They knew that as clearly as I did.

So now I said only, "If you have urgent need of me, I will always come. I think I've demonstrated that, over and over. And having used the stones once to get here swiftly, if need drives me hard, I would probably do it again. But I do not think I will ever again live within the keep walls, or be advisor to the throne."

Kettricken drew breath as if to speak and Dutiful said quietly, "Mother." It was not a rebuke. Perhaps a reminder that we had trodden this path before. Kettricken looked at me and smiled.

"It's kind of you to invite me," I told her. "Truly it is. If you didn't, I'd fear that you thought me useless now."

She returned my smile, and we finished our meal. As we rose, I said, "I'm going to visit Chade, and if he seems strong enough that I'm not fearful for him, I will want to return to Withywoods today."

"Via the stones?" Kettricken asked me.

I wanted, badly, to be at home. Was that why the thought tempted me? Or was it the lure of the Skill-current that flowed so deep and swift behind those graven surfaces? They were both watching me closely. Dutiful spoke softly. "Remember what the Black Man told you. Using the stones too often in quick succession is dangerous."

I needed no reminder. The memory of losing weeks inside a pillar chilled me. I gave my head a small shake, scarce able to believe that I had even considered using the Skill portals for my return journey. "Can I borrow a horse?"

Dutiful smiled. "You can *have* any horse in the stable, Fitz. You know that. Choose a good one to add to your stock."

I did know that. But it wasn't a thing I would ever take for granted.

It was mid-afternoon when I went to see the old man. Chade was propped up by a multitude of pillows in all shades of green velvet. The drapes of his bed were pulled back and secured with heavy cords of twisted silk. The bell pull had been placed within his reach, as had a bedside table with a bowl of hothouse fruit. There were fruits and nuts that I did not recognize, evidence of our lively trade with new partners to the south. His hair had been freshly brushed and bound back in a warrior's tail. It had been shot with gray when first I met him, and now it gleamed an even silver. The purpled swelling and bruise had vanished, leaving only a yellowish-brown shadow where they had been. His green eyes were as bright as polished jade. But those signs of health could not restore the flesh he had lost to our forced healing. He was, I thought, a very vital skeleton. As I entered the room, he set aside a scroll he had been reading.

"What is that you are wearing?" I demanded curiously.

He glanced down at himself without the slightest shadow of self-consciousness. "A bed jacket, I think it is called. A gift from a Jamaillian noblewoman who arrived with a trade envoy a few months ago." He smoothed his fingers down the heavily embroidered sleeve. "It's quite comfortable, really. It's meant to keep the shoulders and back warm if one decides to stay in bed and read."

I drew a stool up beside his bed and sat down. "It seems to be a very specialized garment."

"In that, it is very Jamaillian. Did you know that they have a special robe to wear while they are praying to their two-faced god? You put it on one direction if you're begging something of the male aspect, or turn it round if you're praying to the female aspect. And . . ." He sat up straighter in bed, his face becoming more animated as it always did when he fastened on to one of his fascinations. "If a woman is pregnant, she wears one sort of garment to ensure a boy child, and another for a daughter."

"Does that work?" I was incredulous.

"It's supposed to be helpful, but not absolute. Why? Are you and Molly still trying for a child?"

Chade had never regarded any part of my life as private since he'd learned of my existence. And he never would. It was easier to tell him than to rebuke him for his prying. "No. We've had no real hope left for some time. She's long past her bearing years now. Nettle will be our only daughter."

His face softened. "I'm sorry, Fitz. I've been told that nothing completes a man's life in quite the way that children do. I know that you wanted—"

I interrupted. "I had the raising of Hap. I flatter myself that I did well enough for a man handed an eight-year-old orphan at short notice. He keeps in touch with me still, when his travels and minstrel duties allow it. And Nettle turned out well, and Molly has shared all her younger children with me. I watched Hearth and Just grow to manhood, and we watched them ride off together. Those were good years, Chade. There's no good to be had from pining after lost chances. I have Molly. And truly, she's enough for me. She's my home."

And there, I'd successfully cut him off before he could importune me to stay awhile, or move back to Buckkeep Castle just for a season or a year or two. His litany was as familiar as Kettricken's, but flavored more with guilt than duty. He was an old man, and had so much more to teach me. I had always been his most promising student. Dutiful still had need of an accomplished assassin, and I was a unique weapon in that the young king could converse silently with me via the Skill. And there was the Skill itself. There were so many mysteries yet to unravel. So much translating left to do, so many secrets and techniques to be mined from the trove of scrolls we had retrieved from Aslevjal.

I knew all his arguments and persuasions. Over the years I had heard them all. And resisted them all. Repeatedly. Yet the game had to be played. It had become our farewell ritual. As had his assigning of tasks.

"Well, if you will not stay and do the work with me," he said, just as if we had already discussed it all, "then will you at least take some of the burden with you?"

"As always," I assured him.

He smiled. "Lady Rosemary has packed a selection of scrolls for you, and arranged a mule from the stables to bear them. She was going to put them in a pack but I told her you would be traveling by horseback."

I nodded silently. Years ago Rosemary had taken my place as his apprentice. She had served him now for a score of years, doing the "quiet work" of an assassin and spy for the royal family. No. Longer than that. Idly I wondered if she had yet taken an apprentice of her own.

But Chade's voice called me back to the present as he listed off some herbs and roots he wished me to obtain discreetly for him. He brought up again his idea that the crown should station an apprentice Skill-user at Withywoods to provide swift communication with Buckkeep Castle. I reminded him that as a Skill-user, I could facilitate that myself without welcoming another of his spies into my household. He smiled at that and diverted me to a discussion as to how often the stones could be used and how safely. As the only living person who had been lost in the stones and survived, I tended to be more conservative than Chade the experimenter. This time, at least, he did not challenge my opinion.

I cleared my throat. "The secret keyword is a bad idea, Chade. If you must have one, let it be written down and put into the king's care."

"Anything written can be read. Anything hidden can be found."

"That's true. Here is something else that is true. Dead is dead."

"I've been loyal to the Farseers all my life, Fitz. My death is preferable to being used as a weapon against the king."

Painful to realize that I agreed. Still, "Then by your logic, every member of his coterie should be Skill-locked. Each with a separate word that can only be discovered by answering a riddle."

His hands, large and agile still, spidered bonily along the edge of his coverlet. "That would probably be best, yes. But until I can persuade the rest of the coterie that it's needed, I will take steps to protect the most valuable member of the coterie from corruption."

His opinion of himself had never been small. "And that would be you."

"Of course."

I looked at him. He bridled. "What? Do you not agree with that assessment? Do you know how many secrets I hold in trust for our family? How much family history and lineage, how much knowledge of the Skill, now resides only in my mind and on a few moldering scrolls, most of them nearly unreadable? Imagine me falling into someone else's control. Imagine someone plundering my thoughts of those secrets and using them against the Farseer reign."

It chilled me to discover that he was absolutely correct. I hunched over my knees and thought. "Can you simply tell me the word you will use for your lock, and trust me to keep it secret?" I already accepted that he would find a way to do it again.

He leaned slightly forward. "Will you consent to Skill-locking your mind?"

I hesitated. I didn't want to do it. I recalled too vividly how Burrich had died, sealed off from the help that could have saved him. And how Chade had nearly died. I had always believed that given a choice between a Skill-healing and death, I'd now choose death. His question made me confront the truth. No. I'd want the option available. And it would be more available if my mind wasn't locked against those who could help me.

Chade cleared his throat. "Well, until you are ready, I'll do as I think best. As you will, too, I'm sure."

I nodded. "Chade, I—"

He waved a dismissive hand at me. His voice was gruff. "I already know that, boy. And I'll be a bit more careful. Get to work on those scrolls as soon as you can, would you? The translations will be tricky, but not beyond your abilities. And now I need to rest. Or eat. I can't decide if I'm hungrier or more tired. That Skill healing—" He shook his head.

"I know," I reminded him. "I'll return each scroll as it's translated. And keep a copy secreted at Withywoods. You should rest."

"I will," he promised.

He leaned back on his multitude of pillows and closed his eyes, exhausted. I slipped quietly from the room. And before the sun had set, I was well on my way home.

Chapter 4

PRESERVATION

I did not know who my father was until I arrived at Buckkeep Castle. My mother was a foot soldier in the Farseer army in the two years that the Six Duchies forces were massed on the border of Farrow and Chalced. Her name was Hyacinth Fallstar. Her parents had been farmers. In the year of the choking sickness they both died. My mother was unable to keep up the farm by herself, so she leased the land to her cousins and went to Byslough to seek her fortune. There she became a soldier for Duchess Able of Farrow. She was instructed in swordplay and showed an affinity for it. When war broke out along the borderlands and the King of the Six Duchies himself came to lead his troops into battle, she was there. She remained with the forces on the Chalcedean border until the invaders' army was pushed back into their own territory and a new boundary established.

She returned to her farm in Farrow and there gave birth to me. A man named Rogan Hardhands followed her back to her farm, and she took him to husband. He had soldiered alongside her. He loved her. Toward me, her bastard son and not his at all, he did not feel so kindly, and I returned his sentiments with vigor. Yet we both loved my mother and were loved by her, and so I will speak fairly of him. He knew nothing of farming, but he tried. He was the father I knew until the day my mother died, and though he was a callous man who found me an unwelcome nuisance, I have seen far worse fathering. He did what he thought a father should do with a boy: He taught me to obey, to work hard, and not to question those in authority. Moreover, he toiled alongside my mother to find coin that I might go to a local scribe and be taught to read and figure, skills he did not possess, but my mother thought vital. I do not think he ever considered whether or not he loved me. He did right by me. I hated him, of course.

Yet in those final days of my mother's life, we were united in our grieving. Her death shocked us both for it was so useless and foolish a fate to befall a strong woman. Climbing up to the loft in the cow byre, she slipped on the old ladder and took a deep splinter in her wrist. She pulled it out and it scarcely bled. But the next day, her whole arm was swollen and on the third day, she died. It was that swift. Together we buried her. The following morning, he put me on the mule with a satchel that held late apples, biscuits, and twelve strips of dried meat. Two silvers he gave me also, and told me not to leave the king's highway and eventually I would get to Buckkeep Castle. Into my hands he put a scroll, much battered, for me to deliver to the King of the Six Duchies. I have never seen that scroll since the day I gave it over, hand-to-hand, to the king. I know that Rogan Hardhands had no letters. It must have been written by my mother. I read only the one line on the outside of it: "To be opened only by the King of the Six Duchies."

MY EARLY DAYS, CHADE FALLSTAR

Chade's intrusion was like a whisper by my ear. Except that I could have slept through a whisper. A Skill-intrusion cannot be ignored.

Do you ever regret writing it all down, Fitz?

Chade never slept. Not when I was a lad, and it seemed to me that the older he got, the less sleep he needed. As a result, he assumed that I never slept, and if I dozed off after a hard day of physical labor without my wards set tight around my mind, he was prone to intrude into my sleeping thoughts with no greater sense of my privacy than he had had about entering my bedchamber when I lived at Buckkeep Castle. When I was a boy, he had simply triggered the secret door to my room and come down the hidden staircase from his concealed tower room to my chamber in the keep. Now, a lifetime later and days away, he could step into my thoughts. *The Skill,* I thought to myself, *is truly a wonderful magic, and an incredible nuisance in the hands of an old man.*

I rolled over in my bed, disoriented. His voice always echoed in my thoughts with the same command and urgency as it had when I was a boy and he was a much younger man and my mentor. But it wasn't just the force of his words. It was that his Skill-contact with my mind brought with it the imprint of his impression of me. Just as Nettle had once seen me as more wolf than man, and her sense that I was a wild and wary beast still tinged our Skill-conversations, so with Chade I would always be twelve years old and an apprentice completely at his disposal.

I mustered my Skill-strength and reached back to him. *I was asleep.*

Surely it's not that late! I became aware of his surroundings. A comfortable room. He leaned back on a cushioned chair, staring into a small hearth fire. A table was at his elbow, and I smelled the rich red wine that he lifted in a delicate glass and the applewood burning on his hearth. All so different from his assassin's workroom above my boyhood bedroom at Buckkeep Castle. The secret spy who had served the royal Farseer family was now a respected elder statesman, advisor to King Dutiful. I wondered sometimes if his new respectability bored him. Certainly it did not seem to tire him!

Not so late at night for you, old man. But I spent hours on the record keeping for Withywoods tonight, and tomorrow I have to be up at dawn to go to the market at Oaksbywater to speak to a wool buyer.

Ridiculous. What do you know of wool and sheep? Send one of your sheep tenders to speak to him.

I can't. It's my task, not theirs. And actually, I've learned a great deal about sheep and wool in my time here. I drew my body carefully away from Molly's before I eased out from under our blankets and groped with a foot for the robe I had discarded on the floor. I found it, kicked it up, caught it, and pulled it on over my head. I crossed the darkened room on soundless feet.

Even if I wasn't speaking aloud, I did not want to take the chance of disturbing Molly. She had not been sleeping well of late, and several times I had caught her regarding me with a speculative smile on her face. Something occupied her thoughts by day and left her restless at night. I longed to know her secret, but knew better than to press her. When she was ready, she would share it with me. Tonight, at least, she slept deeply and I was grateful. Life was harder for my Molly than it was for me; the aches and pains of aging took a toll on her that I did not have to pay. *Unfair,* I thought to myself and then, as I slipped from our bedroom into the corridor, I banished the thought.

Too late.

Molly is not well?

She isn't ill. Just our years catching up with us.

Chade seemed surprised. *She need not feel those pains. The coterie would be glad to assist with a small reordering of her body. Not a major change, just . . .*

She would not welcome that sort of interference, Chade. We've spoken of it and that was her decision. She deals with aging on her own terms.

As you wish. I could feel that he thought I was foolish for not intervening.

No. As she wishes. The Skill could indeed have banished a lot of her aches. I knew that I went to bed with twinges that were gone by morning. The price of those tiny healings was that I ate like a longshoreman, with impunity. No cost at all, really. *But Molly's health is not why you woke me out of a sound sleep. Are you well?*

Well enough. Still regaining flesh since my Skill-healing. But as that healing seems to have set right a host of other small ailments, I judge it a good bargain.

I padded through the wood-paneled corridors in the dark, leaving our comfortable chambers in the main house and making my way to the little-used west wing. With the shrinking of our household, Molly and I felt that the main house and the north wing were more than ample space for the two of us and our rare guests. The west wing was the oldest part of the house, chilly in winter and cool in summer. Since we had closed most of it, it had become a last refuge for creaking chairs and wobbly tables and anything else that Revel considered too worn for daily use but still too good to discard. I shivered as I hurried down a dark corridor. I opened a narrow door and in the blackness descended one flight of servant stairs. Down a much narrower hall I went, my fingertips lightly brushing the wall, and then I opened the door to my private study. A few embers still winked on the hearth. I wended my way through the scroll racks and knelt by the fire to light a candle from it. I carried the flame to my desk and one after another lit some half-spent tapers in their holders. My last evening's translation work was still spread on my desk. I sat down in my chair and yawned hugely. *Come to the point, old man!*

No, I didn't wake you to discuss Molly, though I do care for her health as it affects your happiness and Nettle's focus. I woke you to ask you a question. All your journals and diaries, written through the years . . . have you ever regretted all the writing you've done?

I pondered it very briefly. The light from the flickering candles danced teasingly along the edges of the laden scroll racks behind me. Many of the spindled scrolls were old, some almost ancient. Their edges were tattered, the vellum stained. My copies of them were made onto fine paper these days, often bound together with my translations. Preserving what was written on the tattering vellums was a work I enjoyed and, according to Chade, still my duty to him.

But those were not the writings that Chade referred to. He meant my numerous attempts to chronicle the days of my own life. I had

seen many changes in the Six Duchies since I had come to Buckkeep Castle as a royal bastard. I had seen us change from an isolated
and, some would say, backward kingdom to a powerful trading destination. In the years between, I had witnessed treachery born of
evil, and loyalty paid for in blood. I had seen a king assassinated,
and as an assassin I had sought my own vengeance. I sacrificed my
life and my death for my family, more than once. I had seen friends
die.

At intervals throughout my life, I had tried to record all I had
seen and done. And often enough I'd had to hastily destroy those
accounts when I feared they would fall into the wrong hands. I
winced as I thought of it. *I only regret the time I spent writing them
when I had to burn them. I think of all the time I spent carefully writing,
only to have it burn to ash in a matter of minutes.*

But you always began again. Writing it down.

I almost laughed aloud. *I did. And each time I've done so, I've found
that the story changed as my perspective on life changed. There were a
few years where I fancied myself quite the hero, and other times when I
saw myself as star-crossed and unjustly oppressed by my life.* My thoughts
wandered for a moment. Before the whole court I had chased my
king's killers through Buckkeep Castle. Brave. Foolish. Stupid.
Necessary. I could not count the ways I had thought of that incident through the years.

Young, Chade suggested. *Young and full of righteous fury.*

Hurt and heartbroken, I suggested. *So tired of being thwarted. Tired
of being bound by rules that no one else had to follow.*

That, too, he agreed.

Abruptly, I didn't want to think about that day, not who I had
been or what I had done, and most of all not why I had done it. It
was from a different life, one that could no longer touch me. Old
pain could not hurt me now. Could it? I turned the question back
on him. *Why do you ask? Are you thinking of writing down your life's
memories?*

*Perhaps. It is something to do during my recovery time. I think I under-
stand a bit better now why you have warned us about the judicious use of
Skill-healings. El's balls, but it has taken me far too long to feel like my-*

self. My clothing hangs on me so that I am almost shamed to be seen. I totter about like a man made of sticks. I felt him suddenly shift the conversation away from himself, almost as if he had turned his back on me. He never cared to admit any weakness. *When you wrote things down, why did you begin it? You were always writing things down.*

An easy question. *It was Fedwren. And Lady Patience.* The scribe who had taught me and the woman who had longed to be my mother. *Both of them said often that someone should write an orderly history of the Six Duchies. I took their words to mean that I should do it. But every time I tried to write about the kingdom, I ended up writing about myself.*

Who did you think would read it? Your daughter?

Another old bruise. I answered honestly. *At first I didn't think about who might read it. I wrote it for myself, as if by doing so I could make sense of it. All the old tales I had ever heard made sense; good triumphed, or perhaps the hero died tragically, but he accomplished something with his death. So I wrote down my life as if it were a tale, and I searched for the happy ending. Or the sense of it.*

My mind wandered for a time. Back through the years I went, back to the boy who had been apprenticed to an assassin so that he might serve the family who would never acknowledge him as a son. Back to the warrior, fighting with an axe, against ships full of invaders. Back to the spy, to a man serving his missing king while all descended into chaos around him. Was that me? I wondered. So many lives lived. So many names I'd borne. And always, always, I had longed for a different life.

I reached toward Chade again. *For all the years when I couldn't speak to Nettle or Molly, I sometimes told myself that someday they might read it and understand why I had not been with them. Even if I never came back to them, perhaps one day they would know that I had always wanted to. So at first, yes, it was like a long letter to them, explaining all that had kept me from them.* I tightened my walls, not wanting Chade to sense my private thought that perhaps I had not been as honest in those early attempts as I might have been. I had been young, I excused myself, and who does not put himself in the best possible light when he presents his tale to someone he loves? Or his excuses to someone he has wronged. I thrust that thought away and pushed a question back at Chade.

Who would you write your memoir for?

His answer shocked me. *Perhaps it's the same for me.* He paused, and when he spoke again, I felt he had changed his mind about telling me something. *Perhaps I write for you. You're as close to being my son as makes no difference to me. Perhaps I want you to know who I was when I was a young man. Perhaps I want to explain to you why I shaped your life as I did. Maybe I want to justify to you decisions that I've made.*

The idea shocked me, and not that he would speak of me as a son. Did he sincerely believe that I did not know and understand his motives for what he had taught me, for all he had asked of me? Did I want him to explain himself? I thought not. I warded my thoughts, trying to think of a response. Then I felt his amusement. Gentle amusement. Had it been an object lesson?

You think I underestimate Nettle. That she would not need or want me to reveal myself completely to her.

I do. But I also understand the urge to explain yourself. What is harder for me to understand is how you make yourself sit down and do it. I've tried, because I think it's something I need to do, more for myself than anyone else who might come after me. Perhaps, as you say, to impose some sort of order or sense on my past. But it's hard. What do I put in, what do I leave out? Where does my tale begin? What should come first?

I smiled and leaned back in my chair. *I usually start trying to write about something else, and end up writing about myself.* A sudden insight came to me. *Chade, I would like it if you wrote it down. Not to explain it, but just because there is so much I've always wondered about you. You've told me some bits of your life. But . . . who decided you'd become a royal assassin? Who taught you?*

A cold wind blew through me, and for a moment, I felt as if I were being choked mercilessly. As abruptly as it had begun, it stopped, but I felt the wall that Chade had quickly erected. There were dark, harsh memories back there. Was it possible he'd had a tutor whom he had dreaded and feared as much as I had Galen?

Galen had been more interested in trying to kill me quietly than teaching me how to Skill. And the so-called Skillmaster had almost succeeded. Under the guise of creating a new Skill-coterie to aid King Verity in his efforts against the Red-Ship Raiders, Galen had battered and humiliated me and almost extinguished my talent for the magic. And he had corrupted the coterie's loyalty to the true Farseer monarch. Galen had been Queen Desire's tool and then Prince Regal's as they had tried to rid themselves of the Farseer bastard and put Regal upon the throne. Dark days. I knew Chade could tell where my thoughts had gone. I admitted it to him, hoping to draw him out a bit. *Well. There's an "old friend" I hadn't thought about in years.*

Scarcely a friend. But speaking of old friends, have you heard from your old companion lately? The Fool?

Did he deliberately change the topic so abruptly, to try to catch me off guard? It worked. As I blocked him from my reaction, I knew that my defensive impulse told him just as much as all I tried to hide from him. The Fool. I had not heard from the Fool in years.

I found I was staring at the Fool's last gift to me, the carving of the three of us, him, me, and my wolf, Nighteyes. I lifted a hand toward it, and then pulled it back. I never again wanted to see his expression change from that half-quirked smile it wore. Let me remember him that way. We had journeyed through life together for many years, endured hardships and near-death together. More than one death, I thought to myself. My wolf had died, and my friend had parted from me without a farewell, and with never a message since. I wondered if he thought I was dead. I refused to wonder if he was dead. He couldn't be. Often he'd told me that he was far older than I knew, and expected to live much longer than I would. He had cited that as one reason for leaving. He had warned me before we last parted that he was going away. He had believed he was freeing me of bond and obligation, setting me loose finally to pursue my own inclinations. But the unfinished parting had left a wound, and over the years the wound had become the sort of scar that ached at the change of the seasons. Where was he now? Why had he never sent as much as a missive? If he had believed me dead, why had he left a gift for me? If he had believed I would appear again, why had he never contacted me? I pulled my eyes away from the carving.

I haven't seen him or received a message from him since I left Aslevjal. That's been, what, fourteen years? Fifteen? Why do you ask now?

I thought as much. You will recall that I was interested in the tales of the White Prophet long before the Fool declared himself as such.

I do. I first heard the term from you. I kept my curiosity on a tight leash, refusing to ask any more questions. When Chade had first begun to show me writings about the White Prophet, I had regarded them as yet another odd religion from a faraway place. Eda and El I understood well enough. El, the sea god, was a god best left alone, merciless and demanding. Eda, the goddess of the farmlands and the pastures, was generous and maternal. But even for those Six Duchies gods, Chade had taught me small reverence, and even less for Sa, the two-faced and double-gendered god of Jamaillia. So his fascination with the legends of the White Prophet had mystified me. The scrolls foretold that to every generation was born a colorless child who would be gifted with prescience and the ability to influence the course of the world by the manipulation of events great and small. Chade had been intrigued by the idea, and with the legendary accounts of White Prophets who had prevented wars or toppled kings by triggering tiny events that cascaded into great ones. One account claimed a White Prophet had lived thirty years by a river simply so he could warn a single traveler on a certain night that the bridge would give way if he tried to cross it during a storm. The traveler, it revealed, went on to be the father of a great general who was instrumental in winning a battle in some distant country. I had believed it all charming nonsense until I met the Fool.

When he had declared himself a White Prophet, I had been skeptical, and even more so when he declared that I would be his Catalyst who would change the course of history. And yet undoubtedly we had done so. Had he not been at Buckkeep during my lifetime, I would have died. More than once, some intervention of his had preserved my life. In the Mountains, when I lay fevered and dying in the snow, he had carried me to his cottage there and nursed me back to health. He had kept me alive so that dragons might be restored to their rightful place in the world. I was still not sure that was beneficial to humanity, but there was no denying that without him, it would not have happened.

I only realized how deeply I had retreated into my memories when Chade's thoughts jolted me back to awareness of him.

Well, we had some odd folk come through Buckkeep Town recently. About twenty days ago. I did not hear of them until after they had departed, or I would have found a way to learn more about them. The fellow who told me about them said they claimed to be traveling merchants, but the only wares they had were cheap gewgaws and very common bartering items, glass jewelry, brass bracelets, that sort of thing. Nothing of any real value, and though they claimed to have come a long way, my fellow said that it all looked to him as if it were the sort of common wares that a city merchant might take to a village fair, to be sure he had something for a lad or lass with only a half-copper to spend. No spices from a distant land or unique gemstones. Just tinker's trash.

So your spy thought they were only pretending to be merchants. I tried not to be impatient. Chade believed in thorough reporting, for the truth could only be found in details. I knew he was right but wished he would jump to the heart of the matter and embroider it later.

He thought they were actually hoping to buy rather than to sell, or better yet to hear information for free. They were asking if anyone had encountered a friend of theirs, a very pale person. But the odd part was that there were several descriptions of the "pale friend." Some said a young man, traveling alone. Another said she was a woman grown, pale of face and hair, traveling with a young man with red hair and freckles. Yet another was asking after two young men, one very blond and the other dark-haired but white-skinned. As if the only description they had was that they were seeking a traveler who was unnaturally pale, who might be traveling alone or with a companion.

Or they were looking for people who might be traveling in disguise. It sounds as if they were looking for a White Prophet. But why in Buckkeep?

They never used the term "White Prophet," and they did not seem like

*devout pilgrims on a quest. He paused. My fellow seemed to think they
were hirelings sent on a mission, or perhaps mercenary hunters, promised
a reward for their prey. One of them got drunk one night, and when his
fellows came to the tavern to haul him away, he cursed them. In Chalcedean.*

*Interesting. I did not think the White Prophecies had any followers in
Chalced. In any case, the Fool has not lived in Buckkeep for decades.
And when last he was there, he was more tawny than pale. He masquer-
aded as Lord Golden.*

*Well, of course! I know all that! He took my musings to be a prod
to his aging memory and was irritated by it. But few others do. Even
so, their questions provoked some old tales of King Shrewd's pale jester.
But the merchants were not interested in such old news. They sought news
of someone who had passed through Buckkeep recently.*

And so you thought perhaps the Fool had returned?

*It occurred to me to wonder. And I thought that if he had, he would
have sought you out first. But if you have not heard from him, well, then
it's a mystery with few clues.*

Where did these merchants go?

*I sensed his frustration. The report reached me late. My fellow had
not realized how much it would interest me. The rumor is that they followed the River Road inland.*

*Toward Withy. You said twenty days ago. And there are no more tid-
ings of them?*

They seem to have vanished quite effectively.

Not merchants, then.

No.

We both fell silent for a time, pondering the few bits of information we had. If their destination had been Withywoods, they should
have arrived. Perhaps they had, and then passed through the town
to a more distant destination. There were not enough facts to make
even a puzzle, let alone a solution.

*Here is another interesting bit for you. When my spies reported back to
me that they had no news of either a pale traveler or those merchants, one
asked if I had interest in tales of other strangely pale folk. When I replied
that I did, he told me of a murder along the King's Road four years ago.*

Two bodies were found, both in foreign garb. They were discovered by the King's Guard during a routine patrol. One fellow had been bludgeoned to death. Beside him was found another body, described as a young girl, pale as a fish's belly with hair the color of an icicle. She, too, was dead, but there was no sign of violence done to her. Instead she appeared to have been dying of some wasting disease. She was near-skeletal but had died after the man, for she had torn strips from her cloak to try to bandage his wound. Perhaps her companion had been tending her, and when he was slain she had died as well. She was found a short distance from his corpse, near a small campfire. If they had had supplies or mounts, they were stolen. No one ever came to ask after them. It seemed a strange murder to my spy. They killed the man, but left the sickly woman alive and untouched. What sort of highwaymen would do that?

I felt oddly chilled by the tale. *Perhaps she was hiding when they were attacked. It could be nothing.*

Or, it could be something. Chade's considering tone invited me to speculate. *A small bit of information. She wore yellow boots. As did your messenger.*

Unease prickled my scalp. That Winterfest night flooded back into my mind. How had Revel described the messenger? Hands as white as ice. I had thought them bloodless with cold. What if she had been a White? But Chade's news of a murder was four years old. My messenger had come three winters ago. And his spies had brought him news of another messenger, or perhaps two, only twenty days ago. So possibly a succession of messengers, possibly Whites. Possibly from the Fool? I wanted to think about it alone. I wanted none of it to be so. The thought of a missed message from him tore my heart. I denied it. *And it could be something that has absolutely nothing to do with either of us.*

Somehow, I doubt that. But I shall let you go back to your bed now. Lack of sleep always made you irritable.

You saw to that often enough, I retorted, and he annoyed me even further by laughing. He vanished from my mind.

One of the candles was guttering. I pinched it out. Morning was not far away now; might as well light another taper, for there would be no more sleep for me. Why had Chade Skilled to me? To ask me about writing, or to tease me with a bit of news about foreign travelers who might or might not be connected to the Fool? I didn't have enough information to ponder it, only enough to keep me awake. Perhaps I should remain at my desk and resume that translation; I certainly wasn't going to find peace again tonight, thanks to Chade. I stood slowly and looked around me. The room was untidy. There was an empty brandy cup on the desk, and the two quills I'd botched cutting the night before. I should tidy the place. I didn't allow the servants in here; indeed I would have been surprised to find that any of the servants other than Revel were aware of how much I used this chamber. I seldom came here during daylight hours or in the long evenings that Molly and I shared. No. This place was my refuge from restless nights, from the times when sleep forsook me or nightmares relentlessly assaulted me. And always I came here alone. Chade had inculcated in me a habit of stealth that had never left me. I was the sole custodian of this chamber in a little-used wing of the house. I brought the firewood in, and took the ashes out. I swept and tidied . . . well, sometimes I swept and tidied. The room was in sore need of such attention now, but somehow I could not muster that sort of energy.

Instead I stretched where I stood, and then halted, my hands reached up over my head, my eyes fixed on Verity's sword over the mantel. Hod had made it for him, and she had been the finest swordsmith that Buckkeep had ever known. She'd died defending King Verity. Then Verity had surrendered his human life for his people as he entered into his dragon. Now he slept in stone, beyond my reach forever. My sudden pang of loss was almost physical. Abruptly, I had to get out of the room. There was too much within those walls that connected me to the past. I allowed myself one more slow sweep of the space. Yes. Here was where I stored my past and all the confusing emotions it engendered in me. This was where I came to try to make sense of my history. And it was also where I could barricade it behind a latched door, and go back to my life with Molly.

And for the first time, it came to me to wonder why. Why had I gathered it here in mimicry of Chade's old chambers in Buckkeep

Castle, and why did I come here, alone and sleepless, to dwell on tragedies and disasters that could never be undone? Why didn't I leave this room, close the door behind me, and never return? I felt a stab of guilt, and seized that dagger to study it. Why? Why was it my duty to recall those I had lost, and mourn them still? I had fought so hard to win a life of my own, and I had triumphed. It was mine now; it was in my hands. Here I stood, in a room littered with dusty scrolls, spoiled quills, and reminders of the past while upstairs a warm woman who loved me slumbered alone.

My gaze fell on the Fool's last gift to me. The three-faced memory-stone carving rested on the mantel over the fireplace. Whenever I looked up from my work at the desk, the Fool's gaze met mine. I challenged myself; slowly I picked it up. I had not handled it since that Winterfest night three winters ago when I had heard the scream. Now I cradled it in my hands and stared into his carved eyes. A tremor of dread went through me, but I set my thumb to his brow. I "heard" the words it always spoke to me. "*I have never been wise.*" That was all. Just those parting words, in his voice. Healing and tearing in the same moment. Carefully, I put the carving back on the mantel.

I walked to one of the two tall narrow windows, pushed aside the heavy drape, and looked down onto the kitchen garden of Withywoods. It was a humble view, fit for a scribe's room, but lovely all the same. There was a moon, and the pearly light laced the leaves and buds of the growing herbs. White-pebbled paths ran between the beds and gathered the light to themselves. I lifted my eyes and looked beyond the gardens. Behind the grand manor that was Withywoods were rolling meadows and in the distance the forested flanks of mountains.

On this fine summer night and in this tamed valley, the sheep had been left out in the pasture. The ewes were larger blots, with the half-grown lambs clustered beside them. Above all, in the black sky, the stars glittered like a different sort of scattered flock. I could not see the vineyards on the hills behind the sheep pasture, nor the Withy River that wound through the holdings to eventually join with Buck River. To call it a river was something of a conceit, for in most places a horse could easily splash across it, and yet it never ran dry in the summer. Its generous and noisy flow fed the rich little valley. Withywoods was a placid and gentle holding, a place where even an assassin could mellow when pastured. I might tell Chade that I must go to town to discuss wool prices, but in truth he had the right of it. The old shepherd Lin and his three sons more toler-ated than relied on me; I had learned a great deal from them but my insisting on visiting Withy to speak with the wool buyer was mostly for my own pride. Lin would accompany me and two of his sons, and though my handshake might seal whatever agreement we reached, Lin's nod would tell me when to extend that clasp.

It was a very good life I had. When melancholy overtook me, I knew it was not for anything in my present, but only darkness from the past. And those bleak regrets were only memories, powerless to hurt me. I thought of that, and yawned suddenly. I could sleep now, I decided.

I let the drape fall back into place and then sneezed at the cloud of dust it released. Truly the room needed a good cleaning. But not tonight. Perhaps not any night. Maybe I would leave it tonight, let the door close behind me, and allow the past to keep its own com-pany. I toyed with that notion as some men toy with the ambition of giving up drink. It would be good for me. It might be better for Molly and me. I knew I would not do it. I couldn't say why. Slowly, I pinched out the remaining candle flames. *Someday*, I promised my-self, and knew I lied.

When I shut the door behind me, the cool darkness of the cor-ridor engulfed me. The floor was cold. An errant draft wandered the hallways; I sighed. Withywoods was a rambling place that re-quired constant upkeep and repair. There was always something to do, something to busy Holder Badgerlock. I smiled to myself. What, did I wish that Chade's midnight summons had been an order for me to assassinate someone? Better far that tomorrow's project was consulting with Revel about a blocked chimney in the parlor.

I padded hastily along as I backtracked through the sleeping house. When I reached my bedchamber, I eased the door open silently and as quietly closed it behind me. My robe fell to the floor again as I slid under the coverlets. Molly's warm flesh and sweet scent beckoned me. I shivered, waiting for the blankets to warm the chill from me and trying not to wake her. Instead she rolled to face me and drew me into her embrace. Her small warm feet perched on top of my icy ones, and she nestled her head under my chin and on my chest.

"I didn't mean to wake you," I whispered.

"You didn't. I woke up and you weren't here. I was waiting for you." She spoke quietly but not in a whisper.

"Sorry," I said. She waited. "It was Chade Skilling to me."

I felt but did not hear her sigh. "All is well?" she asked me quietly.

"Nothing wrong," I assured her. "Just a sleepless old man looking for some company."

"Mm." She made a soft sound of agreement. "I can understand that well. I do not sleep as well as I did when I was young."

"As true for me. We're all getting older."

She sighed and melted into me. I put my arms around her and closed my eyes.

She cleared her throat softly. "As long as you're not asleep . . . if you're not too tired." She moved suggestively against me, and as always my breath caught in my throat. I smiled into the darkness. This was my Molly, as I knew her of old. Lately she had been so pensive and quiet that I had feared I had somehow hurt her feelings. But when I had asked her, she had shaken her head, looking down and smiling to herself. "I'm not ready to tell you yet," she had teased me. Earlier in the day, I had walked into the room where she processed her honey and made the candles she created for our personal use. I had caught her standing motionless, the long taper she had been dipping dangling forgotten from her fingers as she stared off into the distance.

She cleared her throat, and I realized I was the one who was woolgathering now. I kissed the side of her throat, and she made a sound almost like a purr.

I gathered her closer. "I am not too tired. And I hope never to be that old."

For a time, in that room, we were as young as we had ever been, save that with the experience of years of each other, there was no awkwardness, no hesitation. I once knew of a minstrel who bragged of having had a thousand women, one time each. He would never know what I knew, that to have one woman a thousand times, and each time find in her a different delight, is far better. I knew now what gleamed in the eyes of old couples when they saw each other across a room. More than once I had met Molly's glance at a crowded family gathering, and known from the bend of her smile and her fingers touching her mouth exactly what she had in mind for us once we were alone. My familiarity with her was a more potent love elixir than any potion sold by a hedge-witch in the market.

Simple and good was our lovemaking, and very thorough. Afterward, her hair was netted across my chest, her breasts pressed warm against my side. I drifted, warm and content. She spoke softly by my ear, the breath of her words tickling.

"My love?"

"Um?"

"We're going to have a baby."

My eyes flew open. Not with the joy I had once hoped to feel, but with the shock of dismay. I took three slow breaths, trying to find words, trying to find thoughts. I felt as if I had stepped from the warm lapping of water at a river's edge into the cold deep current. Tumbled and drowning. I said nothing.

"Are you awake?" she persisted.

"I am. Are you? Are you talking in your sleep, my dear?" I wondered if she had slipped off into a dream, and was perhaps recalling another man and another time when she had whispered such momentous words and they had been true.

"I'm awake." And sounding slightly irritated with me, she added, "Did you hear what I told you?"

"I did." I steeled myself. "Molly. You know that can't be so. You yourself told me that your days of bearing were past now. It has been years since—"

"And I was wrong!" There was no mistaking the annoyance in her voice now. She seized my wrist and set my hand to her belly. "You must have seen that I'm getting larger. I've felt the baby move, Fitz. I didn't want to say anything until I was absolutely certain. And now I am. I know it's peculiar, I know it must seem impossible for me to be pregnant so many years after my courses have stopped flowing. But I know I am not mistaken. I've felt the quickening. I carry your child, Fitz. Before this winter is out, we will have a baby."

"Oh, Molly," I said. My voice shook and, as I gathered her closer, my hands were shaking. I held her, kissed her brow and her eyes.

She slipped her arms around me. "I knew you would be pleased. And astonished," she said happily. She settled against me. "I'll have the servants move the cradle from the attic. I went looking for it a few days ago. It's still there. It's fine old oak, with not a joint loose in it. Finally, it will be filled! Patience would have been so thrilled to know that finally there will be a Farseer's child at Withywoods. But I won't use her nursery. It's too far from our bedchamber. I think I will make one of the rooms on the ground floor into a special nursery for me and for our child. Perhaps the Sparrow Chamber. I know that as I get heavier, I will not want to climb the stairs too often . . ."

She went on, breathlessly detailing her plans, speaking of the screens she would move from Patience's old sewing room, and how the tapestries and rugs must be cleaned well, and the lamb's wool she wished spun fine and dyed especially for our child. I listened to her, speechless with terror. She was drifting away from me, her mind gone to a place where mine could not follow. I had seen her aging in the last few years. I'd noticed the swelling of her knuckles, and how she sometimes paused on the stairs to catch her breath. I'd heard her, more than once, call Tavia the kitchenmaid by her mother's name. Lately Molly would begin a task and then wander off, leaving it half-done. Or she would enter a room, look around, and ask me, "Now, what was it I came here to get?"

We had laughed about such lapses. But there was nothing funny about this slipping of her mind. I held her close as she prattled on about the plans she had obviously been making for months. My arms wrapped her and held her, but I feared I was losing her.

And then I would be alone.

Chapter 5

ARRIVAL

It is common knowledge that once a woman has passed her child-bearing years, she becomes more vulnerable to all sorts of ailments of the flesh. As her monthly courses dwindle and then cease, many women experience sudden flushes of heat or bouts of heavy sweating, often in the night. Sleep may flee from them and a general weariness possess them. The skin of her hands and feet becomes thinner, making cuts and wounds to these extremities more common. Desire commonly wanes, and some women may actually assume a more mannish demeanor, with shrinking breasts and increased facial hair. Even the strongest of farm women will be less able than they were in the heavy tasks that they once accomplished with ease. Bones will break more easily, from a simple slip in the kitchen. She may lose teeth as well. Some begin to develop a hump on the back of the neck and to walk with a peering glance. All of these are common parts of a woman aging.

Less well known is that women may become more prone to fits of melancholy, anger, or foolish impulses. In a vain grasping at lost youth, even the steadiest of women can give way to fripperies and wasteful practices. Usually these storms pass in less than a year, and the woman will resume her dignity and calm as she accepts her own aging.

Sometimes, however, these symptoms can precede the downfall of her mind. If she becomes forgetful, calling people by the wrong names, leaving ordinary tasks incomplete, and in extreme cases losing recognition of her own family members, then her family must recognize that she can no longer be considered reliable. Small children should not be entrusted to her care. Forgotten cooking may lead to a kitchen blaze, or the livestock left unwatered and unfed on a hot day. Remonstrances and rebukes will not change these behaviors. Pity is a more appropriate response than anger.

Let such a woman be given work that is of less consequence. Let her sit by the fire and wind wool or do some such task that will endanger no one. Soon enough, the body's decline will follow the mind's absence. The family will experience less grief at her death if she has been treated with patience and kindness during her decline.

If she becomes exceedingly troublesome, opening doors in the night, wandering off in rainstorms, or exhibiting flashes of fury when she can no longer comprehend her surroundings, then administer to her a strong tea of valerian, one that puts her into a manageable state. This remedy may bring peace both to the old woman and to the family weary of caretaking for her.

ON THE AGING OF THE FLESH, HEALER MOLINGAL

Molly's madness was all the harder to bear in that she remained so pragmatic and sensible in all other parts of her life.

Molly's courses had stopped flowing some years ago. She had told me then that she would not ever conceive again. I had tried to comfort her and myself, pointing out that we had a daughter we shared, even if I had missed her childhood. It was foolish to ask more of fate than what we'd been gifted with already. I told her that I accepted there would be no last child for us, and I truly thought she had accepted it as well. We had a full and comfortable life at Withywoods. Hardships that had complicated her early life were a thing of the past, and I had separated myself from the politics and machinations of the court at Buckkeep Castle. We finally had time enough for each other. We could entertain traveling minstrels, afford whatever we desired, and celebrate the passing holidays as lavishly as we wished. We went out riding together, surveying the flocks of sheep, the blossoming orchard, the hayfields, and the vineyards in idle pleasure at such a serene landscape. We returned when we were weary, dined as we would, and slept late when it pleased us.

Our house steward, Revel, had become so competent as to make me nearly irrelevant. Riddle had chosen him well, even if he had never become the door soldier that Riddle had hoped for. The steward met weekly with Molly to talk of meals and supplies, and he worried me as often as he dared with lists of things he thought needed repairing or updating or, I swear to Eda, changed simply because the man delighted in change. I listened to him, allocated funds, and left it mostly in his capable hands. The estates generated enough income to more than compensate for their upkeep. Still, I watched the accounts carefully and set aside as much as I could for Nettle's future needs. Several times Molly rebuked me for spending my own funds on repairs the estate could have paid for. But the crown had allocated me a generous allotment in return for my years of service to Prince Dutiful. Truly, we had plenty and to spare. I had believed that we were in the quiet backwater of our days, a time of peace for both of us. Molly's collapse at that Winterfest had alarmed me, but I had refused to accept that it was a foreshadowing of what was to come.

In the year after Patience died, Molly grew more pensive. She often seemed distracted and absentminded. Twice she had dizzy spells, and once she spent three days in bed before she felt fully recovered. She lost flesh and slowed down. When the last of her sons decided it was time to make their own ways in the world, she let them go with a smile for them, and quiet tears with me in the evening. "I am happy for them. This is their beginning time. But for me it is an ending, and a difficult one." She began to spend more time at quiet pursuits, was very thoughtful of me, and showed more of her gentle side than she had in previous years.

The next year she recovered a bit. When spring came, she cleaned the beehives she had neglected, and even went out and captured a new swarm. Her grown children came and went, always full of news of their busy lives, bringing her grandchildren to visit. They were happy to see that their mother had recaptured some of her old energy and spirit. Desire came back to her, to my delight. It was a good year for both of us. I dared to hope that whatever had caused her fainting spells was past. We grew closer, as two trees planted apart from each other finally find that their branches reach and intertwine. It was not that her children had been a barrier between us so much as that she had always given her first thought and time to them. I will shamelessly admit that I enjoyed becoming the center of her world, and did all I could to show her, in every way, that she had always held that place in my life.

More recently, she had begun to put on flesh again. Her appetite seemed endless, and as her belly rounded out I teased her a bit. I stopped the day she looked at me and said, almost sadly, "I cannot be ageless as you seem to be, my love. I will grow older and fatter perhaps, and slower. My years of being a girl are long gone, as are my years of childbearing. I am become an old woman, Fitz. I only hope that my body gives out before my mind. I have no desire to linger on past a time when I don't recall who you are or I am."

So when she announced her "pregnancy" to me, I began to fear that her worst dreads and mine were coming true.

When a few weeks had passed and she persisted in believing she was pregnant, I tried again to make her see reason. We had retired to our bed, and she was in my arms. She had spoken, again, of a child to come. "Molly. How can this be so? You told me yourself . . ."

And with a flash of her old temper, she lifted her hand and covered my mouth. "I know what I said. And now I know something different. Fitz, I'm carrying your child. I know how strange that must seem to you, for I myself find it more than passing odd. For months I've suspected it, and I kept silent, not wanting you to think me foolish. But it's true. I felt the baby move inside me. For as many children as I've had, it's not a thing I would mistake. I'm going to have a baby."

"Molly," I said. I still held her, but I wondered if she was truly with me. I could think of nothing more to say to her. Coward that I am, I did not challenge her. But she sensed my doubt. I felt her stiffen in my arms, and I thought she would thrust herself away from me.

Then I felt her anger die. She eased out the deep breath she had taken to rebuke me, leaned her head against my shoulder, and spoke. "You think I'm mad, and I suppose I can hardly blame you. For years, I thought I was a dried-up husk, never to bear again. I did my best to accept it. But I'm not. This is the baby we've hoped for, our baby, yours and mine, to rear together. And I don't really care how it's happened, or if you think I'm mad right now. Because, soon enough, when the child is born, you will know that I was right. And until then, you may think me as mad or as feebleminded as you please, but I intend to be happy."

She relaxed in my arms, and in the darkness I saw her smile at me. I tried to smile back. She spoke gently as she settled into the bed beside me. "You've always been such a stubborn man, always sure that you know what is really happening far better than anyone else. And perhaps, a time or two, that has been true. But this is woman's knowing that I'm talking about now, and in this I know better than you do."

I tried a last time. "When you want a thing so badly for so long, and then it comes time to face that you cannot have it, sometimes—"

"Sometimes you can't believe it when it comes to you. Sometimes you're afraid to believe it. I understand your hesitation." She smiled into the darkness, pleased at turning my own words against me.

"Sometimes wanting what you can't have can turn your mind," I said hoarsely, for I felt compelled to say the terrible words aloud.

She sighed a little sigh, but she smiled as she did so. "Loving you should have turned my mind long ago, then. But it didn't. So you can be as stubborn as you want. You can even think me mad. But this is what is true. I'm going to have your baby, Fitz. Before winter ends, there's going to be a baby in this house. So tomorrow you had best have the servants bring the cradle down out of the attic. I want to arrange his room before I get too heavy."

And so Molly stayed in my home and my bed, and yet she left me, departing on a path where I could not follow.

The very next day she announced her condition to several of the maidservants. She ordered the Sparrow Chamber transformed into a nursery and parlor for herself and her imaginary child. I did not contradict her, but I saw the faces of the women as they left the room. Later I saw two of them, heads together and tongues clucking. But when they looked up and saw me, they stilled their talk and earnestly wished me good day, never meeting my eyes.

Molly pursued her illusion with energy I thought long lost to her. She made small gowns and little bonnets. She supervised the cleaning of the Sparrow Chamber from top to bottom. The chimney was freshly swept and new draperies ordered for the windows. She insisted that I Skill the news to Nettle, and ask her to come and spend the dark months of winter with us, to help us welcome our child.

And so Nettle came, even though in our Skill-discussions we had agreed that Molly was deceiving herself. She celebrated Winterfest with us, and stayed until the snow started to slump and the bare paths to show. No baby arrived. I thought Molly would be forced to admit her delusion then, but she steadfastly insisted that she had but been mistaken as to how pregnant she was.

Spring came into full blossom. In the evenings we spent together she would sometimes drop her needlework and exclaim, "Here! Here, he's moving, come feel!" But every time I obediently set my hand to her belly, I felt nothing. "He's stopped," she would insist, and I would nod gravely. What else could I do?

"Summer will bring him," she assured us both, and the little garments she crocheted now were light rather than warm and woolly. As the hot days of summer ticked by to the chirping of grasshoppers, they became another layer of garments in the chest of clothing she had made for her imaginary child.

Autumn went out in a blaze of glory. Withywoods was lovely as it ever was in fall, with scarlet sprays of alder and golden birch leaves like coins and thin yellow willow leaves in curls, drifting down for the wind to push into deep banks at the edges of the carefully tended grounds. We no longer went out riding together, for Molly insisted she might lose the child if she did so, but we went for walks. I gathered hickory nuts with her, and listened to her plan to move screens into her nursery to make an enclosed area for the cradle. As the days passed, the river that threaded the valley grew swift with rain. Snow arrived and Molly again knit warmer things for our phantom baby, sure now that it would be a winter child, in need of soft blankets and woolly boots and caps. And just as the ice covered and hid the river, so did I strive to conceal from her the growing despair I felt.

But I am sure she knew it.

She had courage. Against the current of doubt that all others pressed her way, she swam. She was aware of the talk of the servants. They thought her daft or senile, and wondered that so sensible a woman as she had been could so foolishly assemble a nursery for an imaginary child. She kept her dignity and restraint before them and by that forced them to treat her with respect. But she also withdrew from them. Once she had socialized with the local gentry. Now she planned no dinners and never went out to the crossroads market. She asked no one to weave or sew for her baby.

Her imaginary child consumed her. She had little time for me or the other things that had once interested her. She spent her evenings and sometimes her nights in her nursery-parlor. I missed her in my bed but did not press her to climb the stairs and join me there. Sometimes of an evening I would join her in her cozy room, bringing whatever translation I was working on. She always welcomed me. Tavia would bring us a tray with cups and herbs, set a kettle to boil on the hearth, and leave us to our own devices. Molly would sit in a cushioned chair, her swollen feet propped up on a small hassock. I had a small table in the corner for my work, and

Molly kept her hands busy with knitting or tatting. Sometimes I would hear the ticking of her needles cease. Then I would look up and see her staring into the fire, her hands on her belly and her face wistful. At such times I longed with all my heart that her self-deception were true. Despite our ages, I thought she and I could manage an infant. I even asked her, once, what she thought of us taking in a foundling. She sighed softly and said, "Be patient, Fitz. Your child grows within me." So I said no more of it to her. I told myself her fancy brought her happiness, and truly, what harm did it do? I let her go.

In high summer of that year, I received the news that King Eyod of the Mountains had died. It was not unexpected, but it created a delicate situation. Kettricken, the former Queen of the Six Duchies, was Eyod's heir; her son King Dutiful was in line after her. Some in the Mountains would hope that she would return to them, to reign there, even though she had often and clearly stated that she expected Dutiful to bring the Mountains under his rule as a sort of seventh duchy in our monarchy. Eyod's death marked a transition that the Six Duchies must observe with gravity and respect. Kettricken would of course travel there, but also King Dutiful and Queen Elliania, the Princes Prosper and Integrity, Skillmistress Nettle, and several of the coterie, Lord Chade, Lord Civil . . . the list of those who must attend seemed endless, and many minor nobles attached themselves to the party as a way to curry favor. And my name was appended to it. Go I must, as Holder Badgerlock, a minor officer in Kettricken's guard. Chade insisted, Kettricken requested, Dutiful all but ordered me, and Nettle pleaded. I packed my kit and chose a mount.

Over the year, Molly's obsession had ground me down to a weary acceptance. I was not surprised when she declined to accompany me as she felt her "time was very close now." A part of me did not wish to leave her when her mind was so unsettled, and another part of me longed for a respite from indulging her delusion. I called Revel aside and asked that he pay special attention to her requests while I was gone. He looked almost offended that I thought such a command necessary. "As ever, sir," he said, and added his stiff little bow that meant, *You idiot.*

And so I left her and rode away from Withywoods alone and quietly joined the procession of noble folk from the Six Duchies going north to the Mountains for the funeral rites. It was passing strange for me to relive a journey I had once made when I was not yet twenty, and had traveled to the Mountain Kingdom to claim Kettricken as bride for King-in-Waiting Verity. In my second journey to the Mountains, I had often avoided the roads and traveled cross-country with my wolf.

I had known that Buck had changed. Now I saw that the changes had happened all through the Six Duchies. The roads were wider than I recalled, and the lands more settled. Fields of grain grew where there had once been open pasturage. Towns sprawled along the road, so that sometimes it seemed one scarcely ended before the next began. There were more inns and towns along the way, though the size of our party sometimes overwhelmed the accommodations. The wild lands were being tamed, brought under the plow, and fenced for pasture. I wondered where the wolves hunted now.

As one of Kettricken's guardsmen, clad in her white and purple, I rode close to the royal party. Kettricken had never been one to stand upon formality, and her request that I ride at her stirrup was simply accepted by those who knew her. We spoke quietly, the jingling and clopping of the other travelers granting us a strange privacy. I told her stories of my first journey to the Mountains. She spoke of her childhood and of Eyod, not as king but as her loving father. I said nothing of Molly's disorder to Kettricken. Her sorrow at the death of her father was enough for her to bear.

My position as a member of her guard meant that I was accommodated at the same inns where Kettricken stayed. Often that meant Nettle was there as well, and sometimes we were able to find a quiet place and time for conversation. It was good to see her and a relief to discuss frankly with her how her mother's illusion persisted. When Steady joined us, we were not as blunt, but that reticence was Nettle's choice. I could not decide if she thought her younger brother was too young for such tidings or if she thought it too much of a woman's matter. Burrich had named his son well. Of all his boys, Steady wore most of Burrich's features and his sturdy build, and shared, too, his deliberate way of moving and unflinching devotion to both honor and duty. When he was with us, it was as if his father sat at the table. I marked Nettle's easy dependence on her brother's strength, and not just for the Skill. I was glad he was so often at her side, and yet wistful. I wished he could have been my son, even as I was glad to see his father live on in him. I think he sensed how I felt. He was deferential to me, and yet there were times when his black eyes bore into mine as if he could see my soul. And at those times, I missed Burrich with a cutting sorrow.

In more private times Nettle shared with me her mother's monthly letters detailing the progress of a pregnancy that had now seemingly stretched over two years. It broke my heart to hear Molly's words as Nettle read aloud of her mulling on names, and progress on her sewing projects for a baby that would never exist. Yet neither one of us had any solution other than to take a small comfort in the sharing of our worry.

When we arrived in the Mountains, we were given a warm welcome. The bright structures that made up Jhaampe, the Mountain capital, still reminded me of the bells of flowers. The older structures were as I recalled them, incorporating the trees they were built among. But even to the Mountains change had come, and the outskirts of that city were more like the towns of Farrow and Tilth, buildings of stone and plank. It made me sad for I felt that the change was not a good one, as if such structures were a canker growing over the forest.

For three days we mourned a king whom I had respected deeply, not with wild wailing and oceans of tears, but with quietly shared stories of who he had been and how well he had ruled. His people grieved for their fallen king but in equal measure they welcomed his daughter home. They were happy to see King Dutiful and the Narcheska and the two princes. Several times I heard people mention with quiet pride that young Integrity greatly resembled

Kettricken's brother and his late uncle, Prince Rurisk. I had not seen that resemblance until I heard it spoken, and then I could not forget it.

At the end of the time of mourning, Kettricken stood before them and reminded them that her father and King-in-Waiting Chivalry had begun the process of peace between the Six Duchies and the Mountains. She spoke of how wisely they had secured that peace with her marriage to Verity. She asked that they look at her son King Dutiful as their future monarch and recall that the peace they now enjoyed should be viewed as King Eyod's greatest triumph.

With the formalities of King Eyod's funeral over, the true work of the visit commenced. Daily there were meetings with Eyod's advisors, and there were lengthy discussions on the orderly handing over of the governance of the Mountains. I was present for some of it, sometimes standing at the side of the room, as Chade and Dutiful's extra eyes and ears, and sometimes sitting outside in the sun, my eyes closed but Skill-linked to both of them in the higher-level meetings. But in the evenings I was sometimes released to have time on my own.

And so it was that I found myself standing outside an elaborately carved and painted door, looking wistfully at the work of the Fool's hands. Here was the house where he had lived when he thought he had failed to fulfill his fate as the White Prophet. On the night King Shrewd had died, Kettricken had fled Buckkeep and the Fool had gone with her. Together they had made the arduous journey to the Mountain Kingdom, where she believed she and her unborn child would be safe in her father's home. But there fate dealt the Fool two blows. Kettricken's child did not live, and news of my death in Regal's dungeons reached him. He had failed in his quest to ensure there was an heir to the Farseer line. He had failed in his quest to bring about his prophecy. His life as a White Prophet was over.

When he believed me dead, he had stayed in the Mountains with Kettricken, lived in this small house, and tried to make a little life for himself as a wood carver and toy maker. Then he had found me, broken and dying, and brought me here to the dwelling he shared with Jofron. When he took me in, she had moved out. Once I was recovered, the Fool and I accompanied Kettricken on a hopeless quest to follow her husband's cold trail into the mountains. The Fool had left the little house and all his tools for Jofron. By the colorfully painted marionettes dangling in the window, I suspected she still lived there and still made toys.

I did not knock on the door but stood in the long summer evening and studied the carved imps and pecksies that frolicked on the trim of the shutters. Like many of the old-fashioned Mountain dwellings, this structure was painted with bright colors and details, as if it were a child's treasure box. An emptied treasure box, my friend long gone from it.

The door opened and yellow lamplight spilled out. A tall, pale lad of about fifteen, fair hair falling to his shoulders, stood framed there. "Stranger, if you seek shelter, you need but knock and ask. You are in the Mountains now." He smiled as he spoke and opened wide the door, stepping aside to gesture me in.

I walked slowly toward him. His features were vaguely familiar. "Does Jofron still live here?"

His smiled widened. "Lives and works. Grandmother, you have a visitor!"

I moved slowly into the room. She sat at a workbench by the window, a lamp at her elbow. She was painting something with a small brush, even strokes of goldenrod yellow. "A moment," she begged without looking up from her task. "If I let this dry between strokes, the color will be uneven."

I said nothing but stood and waited. Jofron's long blond hair was streaked with silver now. Four braids trapped it away from her face. The cuffs of a brightly embroidered blouse were folded back to her elbows. Her arms were sinewy and flecked with paint, yellow, blue, and a pale green. It was much longer than a moment before she set down her brush and leaned back and turned to me. Her eyes were just as blue as I recalled them. She smiled easily at me. "Welcome, guest. A Buckman, by the look of you. Come to honor our king's final rest, I take it."

"That is true," I said.

When I spoke, recognition flickered and then caught fire in her eyes. She sighed and shook her head slowly. "You. His Catalyst. He stole my heart and lifted my spirit to search for wisdom. Then you came and stole him from me. As was right." She lifted a mottled cloth from her work desk and wiped vainly at her fingers. "I never thought to see you under this roof again." There was no enmity in her voice, but there was loss. Old loss.

I spoke words that might comfort her. "When he thought our time together was over, he left me as well, Jofron. Close to seventeen years ago we parted company, and never a word or a visit have I had from him since."

She cocked her head at that. Her grandson closed the door softly. He ventured to the edge of our conversation and cleared his throat. "Stranger, may we offer you tea? Bread? A chair to sit on or a bed for the night?" Plainly the lad longed to know what connection I had to his grandmother, and hoped to lure me to stay.

"Please bring him a chair and tea," Jofron told him without consulting me. The lad scuttled off and returned with a straight-backed chair for me. When her blue eyes came back to me, they were full of sympathy. "Truly? Not a word, not a visit?"

I shook my head. I spoke to her, thinking here was one of the few people in my life who might understand my words. "He said he had lost his sight of the future. That our tasks together were done, and that if we stayed together, we might unwittingly undo some of what we had accomplished."

She received the information without blinking. Then, very slowly, she nodded.

I stood, uncertain of myself. Old memories of Jofron's voice as I lay on the floor before that hearth came to me. "I do not think I ever thanked you for helping me when the Fool first brought me here, all those years ago."

She nodded again, gravely, but corrected me, saying, "I helped the White Prophet. I was called to do so and have never regretted it."

Again the silence stretched between us. It was like trying to converse with a cat. I resorted to banality. "I hope you and your family
are well."

And like a cat, her eyes narrowed for just an instant. Then she
said, "My son is not here."

"Oh."

She took up her rag again, wiping her fingers very carefully. The
grandson returned with a small tray. A little cup, smaller than my
closed fist, held one of the aromatic tisanes of the Mountains. I
was grateful for the distraction. I thanked him and then sipped
from it, tasting wild currant and a certain spice from a Mountain
tree bark that I had not tasted in years. It was delicious. I said so.

Jofron rose from her workbench. She walked across the room,
her back very straight. One wall of the room had been shaped in a
bas-relief of a tree. It must have been her work, for it had not been
that way the last time I had stayed here. Leaves and fruit of all sorts
projected from its carved branches. She reached over her head to a
large leaf, gently eased it aside to reveal a small cubby, and brought
out a little box.

She returned and showed it to me. It was not the Fool's work,
but I recognized the hands curved protectively to form a lid over
the box's contents. Jofron had carved his hands as a lid for her box.
I nodded at her that I understood. She moved her fingers and I
heard a distinctive *snick*, as if a hidden catch had given way. When
she opened the little box, a fragrance came from it, unfamiliar but
enticing. She was not trying to hide its contents from me. I saw
small scrolls, at least four and possibly more concealed under them.
She took one from the box and closed the lid.

"This was his most recent message to me," she said.

Most recent. I knew a moment of the sharpest, greenest envy I
had ever felt. He had not sent me as much as a bird message, but
Jofron had a small casket of scrolls! The soft brown paper was tied
closed with a slender orange ribbon. She tugged at it and it gave
way. Very gently she unrolled it. Her eyes moved over it. I thought
she would read it aloud to me. Instead she lifted her blue gaze and
met my eyes in an uncompromising stare. "This one is short. No

news of his life. No fond greeting, no wish for my continued health. Only a warning."

"A warning?"

There was no hostility in her face, only determination. "A warning that I should protect my son. That I should say nothing of him to strangers who might ask."

"I don't understand."

She lifted one shoulder. "Nor do I. But understanding completely is not necessary for me to take heed of his warning. And so I tell you, my son is not here. And that is all I will say about him."

Did she think me a danger? "I did not even know you had a son. Nor a grandson." My thoughts rattled like seeds in a dry pod. "And I did not ask after him. Nor am I a stranger to you."

She nodded agreeably to each of my statements. Then she asked, "Did you enjoy your tea?"

"Yes. Thank you."

"My eyes tire easily these day. I find sleeping helps, for then I wake refreshed, to do my best work in the early dawn light." She spindled the little brown paper, and looped the orange ribbon round it. As I watched she returned it to the box. And shut the lid.

The Mountain folk were so courteous. She would not tell me to get out of her house. But it would have been the worst of manners for me to attempt to stay. I rose immediately. Perhaps if I left right away, I could come back tomorrow and try again to ask more about the Fool. I should go now, quietly. I knew I should not ask. I did. "How did the messages reach you, please?"

"By many hands and a long way." She almost smiled. "The one who put this last one into my hands is long gone from here."

I looked at her face and knew that this was my final chance for words with her. She would not see me tomorrow. "Jofron, I am not a danger to you or your family. I came to bid farewell to a wise king who treated me well. Thank you for letting me know that the Fool sent you messages. At least I know that he still lives. I shall keep that comfort as your kindness to me." I stood up and bowed deep to her.

I think I saw a tiny crack in her façade, the smallest offer of sympathy when she said, "The last message arrived two years ago. And it had taken at least a year to reach me. So as to the White Prophet's fate, neither of us can be certain."

Her words brought cold to my heart. Her grandson had gone to the door and opened it, holding it for me. "I thank you for your hospitality," I said to both of them. I set the tiny cup on the corner of her worktable, bowed again, and left. I did not try to return the next day.

Two days later, King Dutiful and his retinue departed from the Mountains. Kettricken remained behind to have more time with her extended family and her people and to assure them that she would more often visit there as they began the long transition to becoming the seventh duchy under King Dutiful.

Unnoticed, I remained behind as well, lingering until the last of the king's company was out of sight, and then waiting until late afternoon before I departed. I wanted to ride alone and think. I left Jhaampe with no care or thought as to where I would sleep that night or how.

I had believed I would find some sort of serenity in the Mountains. I had witnessed how gracefully they surrendered their king to death and made room for life to continue. But when I departed, I took more envy than serenity with me. They had lost their king after a lifetime of his wisdom. He had died with his dignity and his mind intact. I was losing my beloved Molly, and I knew with dread that it would only get worse, much worse, before the end. I had lost the Fool, the best friend I had ever had, years ago. I thought I had accepted it, become immune to missing him. But the deeper Molly ventured into madness, the more I missed him. Always he had been the one I turned to for counsel. Chade did his best, but he was ever my elder and mentor. When I had visited the Fool's old home, I had thought only to look at it for a time and touch the stone that once I had had a friend who had known me that well and still loved me.

Instead I had discovered that perhaps I had not known him as well as I had thought. Had his friendship with Jofron meant so much more to him than what we had shared? A startling thought

pricked me. Had she been more to him than a friend or follower of
the White Prophet?

*Would you have begrudged him that? That for a time, he lived in the
now and had something that was good when all hope had left him?*

I lifted my eyes. I wished with all my heart to see a gray shape
flitting through the trees and brush beside the road. But of course
I did not. My wolf was gone these many years, gone longer than the
Fool had been gone. He lived only in me now, in the way his wolf-
ness could suddenly intrude into my thoughts. At least I still had
that of him. It was thin soup.

"I would not have begrudged him that," I said aloud, and wondered if I lied so that I need not be ashamed of myself. I shook my
head and tried to put my mind into the now. It was a beautiful day,
the road was good, and while problems might await me when I returned home, they were not here with me now. And truly, my missing the Fool today was no different from how I had missed him on
any of the yesterdays I'd spent without him. So he had sent missives to Jofron and not to me? That had been true for years, apparently. Now I knew of it. That was the only difference.

I was trying to persuade myself that knowing that small fact
made no difference when I heard hoofbeats on the road behind me.
Someone was riding a horse at a gallop. Perhaps a messenger. Well,
the road was wide enough that he could pass me effortlessly. Nonetheless, I reined my mount more to one side and glanced back to
watch him come.

A black horse. A rider. And in three strides, I knew it was Nettle
on Inky. I thought she had gone on with the others, and then realized she must be hurrying to catch up with them after being delayed
for some reason. I pulled in my horse and waited for her, fully expecting her to pass me with a wave.

But as soon as she saw I had halted, she slowed her mount; by the
time she reached me Inky had reduced her pace to a trot. "Ho!"
Nettle called to her, and Inky halted neatly beside us.

"I thought you were going to stay another night, and then when
I realized you were gone I had to race to catch up with you," she
announced breathlessly.

"Why aren't you with the king? Where are your guards?"

She gave me a look. "I told Dutiful I'd be with you and needed no other guard. He and Chade both agreed."

"Why?"

She stared at me. "Well, among them, you do have a certain reputation as a very competent assassin."

That silenced me for a moment. They still thought of me that way when I did not? I put my thoughts back in order. "No, I meant, why did you stay to travel with me? Not that I'm not glad to see you, I'm just surprised." I added the last as her glance at me darkened. "I had not even realized anyone had noticed that I did not remain with the main party."

She cocked her head at me. "Would you have noticed if I were not there?"

"Well, of course!"

"Everyone noticed when you quietly withdrew. Dutiful spoke to me several days ago, saying that you seemed even more morose than one might expect you to be at a funeral and perhaps it was best if you were not left alone. Kettricken was a party to his words, and she added that this visit might have stirred old memories for you. Sad ones. So. Here I am."

And indeed, there she was. I was almost annoyed at her for spoiling my perfectly good sulk. And that was when I realized that was what I had been doing. I'd been sulking because the Fool had sent letters to Jofron and not to me. And like a child, I'd been testing the people who loved me, pulling away from them almost for the sole reason of seeing if anyone would come after me.

And she had. I felt thwarted in my petulance, and as foolish as I knew that to be, it still stung when Nettle laughed at me. "I wish you could see the look on your face!" she exclaimed. "Come. Will it be so terrible that after all these years, you and I finally will have a few days and nights of being able to talk to each other, without disasters or small boys interrupting us?"

"It would be good," I conceded, and just that simply my mood lifted. And our homeward journey together began.

I had never traveled in such indulgence. I had brought few supplies, thinking I would live rough on the way home. Nettle was like-wise traveling light, save for a wallet full of silvers. The first time I proposed that if we were going to camp for the night, we should begin to look for a likely place, she stood up in her stirrups, looked all around, and then pointed to smoke rising. "That's a house at the least, and more likely a village with an inn, however humble. And that is where I intend to stop tonight, and if there is a hot bath to be had, it will be mine. And a good meal!"

And she was right. There were all three of those things, in fact, and she put silver out for me as well as herself, saying, "Chade told me not to let you do anything to punish yourself for being sad."

For a few quiet moments, I handled her words, trying to see if they truly applied to me. They didn't, I was sure, but I could think of no defense. She cleared her throat. "Let's talk about Hap, shall we? Did you know that there is rumor that despite being a minstrel, and a wandering one at that, he has a sweetheart at Daratkeep, and he is true to her? She is a weaver in the town there."

I had not known that, or much of the other gossip she shared with me. That evening, although there were several other minor no-bles occupying the same inn, Nettle kept company with me. And we remained long by the hearth fire in the central room after the others had sought their beds. From her, I learned that Buckkeep politics were as tangled and the intimate royal gossip as thorny as ever. She had quarreled with King Dutiful, for she feared for the safety of the adolescent princes, too often off to the Out Islands with their mother. He had dared to tell her it was none of her busi-ness, and she had replied that if it was his business that she could not wed because he consistently exposed his heirs to danger, then she had a right to add her thoughts on it. Queen Elliania had re-cently suffered a miscarriage: It had been a girl child, the child she had dreamed of; it was a terrible loss as well as a bad omen to her mothershouse. When they had departed so hastily for Buckkeep, it was so that Elliania could take the princes for yet another long visit to her homeland. Some of the dukes had begun to grumble about how often the lads were away. King Dutiful was caught between his dukes and his queen, and seemed able to find no compromise.

When I asked after Riddle, Nettle said he was well the last time she had seen him and then decisively steered our conversation away from that. She seemed to have given up all hope of ever gaining King Dutiful's permission to wed, and yet I had never seen her evince interest in another man. I longed to know what was in her heart, and wished she were more inclined to confide in me as she once had in her mother.

Instead she turned our talk to other problems brewing along our border.

Dragons were ranging over Chalced, preying where they pleased, and they had begun sometimes to cross the border and ravage the herds of Shoaks and even Farrow. The Six Duchies folk expected the Skill-coterie of the king to turn back the dragons or at least negotiate with them. But the concepts of diplomacy and compromise were laughable to dragons. If dragons laughed, which both Nettle and I doubted.

We pondered if one could negotiate with dragons, and what the repercussions would be of slaying a dragon, and if paying tribute to dragons with slaughter herds was cowardly or simply pragmatic.

Some of her news was not political but of family. Swift and Web had recently visited Buckkeep. Swift's bird partner was healthy and strong. But Web's gull was so poorly that Web had taken a room in Buckkeep Town that overlooked the water. The bird mostly lived on his windowsill; he fed her, for she flew little now. The end was coming and they were both awaiting it. While Nettle herself was not Witted, through me and her brother Swift she understood what it was to lose a Wit-partner.

But it was not only gossip we shared. We talked of food, and music we enjoyed, and which old tales were our favorites. She told me stories of her childhood, mostly of the mischief she and her brothers had perpetrated. In turn, I spoke of my days as a boy in Buckkeep, and how different both castle and town had been then. Burrich figured much in all our tales.

On our last evening together, before we left the River Road to follow the narrower road that led to Withywoods, she asked me about Lord Golden. Had he truly once been a jester for King Shrewd? Yes, he had. And he and I had been . . . very close? "Nettle," I said, as she rode looking straight ahead. I waited until she turned to look at me. Her tanned cheeks were a bit more flushed than usual. "I loved that man as I have loved no one else. I do not say I loved him more than I love your mother. But that the way I loved him was different. If you have heard there was anything improper in our bond, there was not. That was not what we were to each other. What we had went beyond that."

She did not meet my eyes, but she nodded. "And what became of him?" she asked in a softer voice.

"I do not know. He left Buckkeep while I was still lost in the stones. I never heard from him again."

I think my voice told her far more than my words did. "I am so sorry, Da," she said quietly.

Did she know that it was the first time she had honored me with that title? I held a very careful silence, savoring the moment. And then we crested a slight rise, and the village of Withy was before us, cupped in a gentle valley beside a river. And I knew we would reach Withywoods before the afternoon was old. I found I suddenly regretted how soon our journey together must end. Even more, I dreaded what she would think of her mother and how far her delusions had carried her away from us.

And yet the visit began well. When we arrived, Molly hugged me warmly and then turned delightedly to her eldest child. She had not expected me to return so soon, and had not expected to see Nettle at all. We had arrived shortly after noon and were both ravenous. All three of us retired to the kitchen where we merrily dismayed the household staff by insisting on raiding the pantry for a simple feast of bread, cheese, sausage, and ale instead of waiting for them to prepare something more elaborate for us. When Cook Nutmeg put her foot down and chased us out of her kitchen, we picnicked at one end of the great dining table. We told Molly all about our journey, the simple but moving ceremonies that had preceded the king's interment, and Kettricken's decision to stay for a time in the Mountains. And as there is from any journey, no matter how solemn the destination, there were humorous stories to tell that set us all laughing.

Molly had stories of her own to share with us. Some goats had managed to get into the vineyards and had done damage to some of the oldest vines there. They would recover, but most of this year's grapes from that section of the vineyard were lost. We'd had several major incursions of wild pigs into the hayfield; the major damage they did was trampling the hay to where it was almost impossible to harvest it. Lozum from the village had brought his dogs and gone after them. He'd killed one big boar, but one of his dogs had been badly ripped in the process. I sighed to myself. I was sure that would be one of the first problems I'd have to tackle. I'd never enjoyed boar hunts, but it would be necessary now. And Tallman would once again renew his plea for hounds of our own.

And somehow, while I was silently woolgathering on boars and dogs and hunting, the topic changed, and then Molly was tugging at my sleeve and asking me, "Don't you want to see what we've done?"

"Of course," I replied, and arose from the pitiful remains of our haphazard meal to follow my wife and my daughter.

My heart sank when I realized she was leading us to her nursery. Nettle glanced back at me over her shoulder, but I kept my expression bland. Nettle had not seen the room since Molly had taken it over. And when she opened the door, I realized I hadn't, either.

The room had originally been a parlor intended for greeting important guests. In my absence it had become a carefully appointed nursery, rich with every luxury that a gravid woman could wish for her child to come.

The cradle in the center of it was of fine mellow oak, cunningly fashioned so that if one stepped on a lever, it would gently rock the child. A carved Farseer buck watched over the head of the cradle. I believe Lady Patience had had it built in her early days at Withywoods, when she still hoped to conceive a child. It had waited, empty, for decades. Now the cradle was heaped with soft bedding, and netted with lace so that no insect might sting the occupant. The low couch now boasted fat cushions where a mother might recline to feed her child, and there were thick rugs underfoot. The deep windows looked out onto a garden cloaked in the first fall of autumn leaves. The thick glass was curtained first with lace, and then translucent silk, and finally with a tightly woven curtain that would keep out both bright sunlight and cold. There was a painted glass enclosure Molly could put around the lamp to dim its light as well. Behind a fanciful screen of flowers and bees wrought in iron, the low fire danced for her in the large hearth.

She smiled at our amazement. "Isn't it lovely?" she asked quietly.

"It's . . . beautiful. Such a peaceful room," Nettle managed to say.

I tried to find my tongue. I'd been holding Molly's fancy at a distance; now I had stepped into her delusion. The stupid wanting that I thought I had smothered roared up like a fire through charred twigs. A baby. How sweet would it have been, to have our own little baby here, where I could watch him grow, where I could see Molly be mother to our child? I feigned a cough and rubbed my face. I walked to the lamp and examined the painted flowers on the screen with a scrutiny they didn't merit.

Molly went on talking to Nettle. "When Patience was alive, she showed me this cradle. It was up in the attic. She'd had it made in the years when she and Chivalry lived here, when she dreamed it was still possible she might conceive. All those years, it has waited. It was far too heavy for me to move by myself, but I called Revel and showed it to him. And he had it carried down here for me, and once the wood was polished it was such a lovely thing that we decided we really needed to make the whole room as fine a nursery as the cradle deserved.

"Oh, and come here, just look at these trunks. Revel found them in a different attic, but isn't it wonderful how close a match the wood is? He thought that perhaps the oak was grown right here at Withywoods, which could explain why the color is so close to the cradle. This one has blankets, some of wool for winter months and some lighter, for the spring. And this entire trunk, I'm shocked to say, is all clothing for the baby. I had not realized how much I'd actually sewn for him until Revel suggested we put it all in one place.

There are different sizes, of course. I wasn't as foolish as that, as to make all the little gowns for a newborn."

And on. The words poured out of Molly, as if she had longed for months to be able to speak openly about her hopes for her child. And Nettle looked at her mother and smiled and nodded. They sat on the couch and took clothing from the trunk and laid it out to look at it. I stood and watched them. I think that for a moment, Nettle was caught in her mother's dream. Or perhaps, I thought to myself, it was the same longing they shared, Molly for a child she was long past bearing and Nettle for a child she was forbidden to bear. I saw Nettle take up a little gown and lay it across her breast as she exclaimed, "So tiny! I had forgotten how small babies were; it has been years since Hearth was born."

"Oh, Hearth, he was almost the biggest of my babies. Only Just was larger. The things I'd made for Hearth, he outgrew within a few months."

"I remember that!" Nettle exclaimed. "His little feet hung out the bottoms of his gown and we'd cover him, only to have him kick all his blankets off a moment later."

Purest envy choked me. They were gone, both of them, back to a time when I hadn't existed in either of their lives, back to a cozy, noisy home full of children. I did not begrudge Molly her years of marriage to Burrich. He had been a good man for her. But this was like a slow knife turning in me, to watch them recollect an experience I would never have. I stared at them, the outsider again. And then, as if a curtain had lifted or a door opened, I realized that I excluded myself. I went over and sat down beside them. Molly lifted a tiny pair of knit boots from the chest. She smiled and offered them to me. Without a word, I took them. They scarcely filled the palm of my hand. I tried to imagine the tiny foot that would go into one, and could not.

I looked over at Molly. There were lines at the corners of her eyes and lines framing her mouth. Her rosy full lips had faded to pale-pink arcs. I suddenly saw her not as Molly, but as a woman of some fifty-odd years. Her lush, dark hair had thinned, and gray streaked it. But she looked at me with such hope and love, her head turned just slightly to one side. And I saw something else in her eyes, something that had not been there ten years ago. Confidence in my love. The wariness that had tinged our relationship was gone, worn to nothing by our last decade together. She finally knew that I loved her, that I would always put her first. I had finally earned her trust.

I looked down at the little booties in my hand and slipped my two fingers inside them. I stood them up on my palm. I danced them a couple of steps on my hand. She reached to still my fingers, and slid the soft gray boots away. "Soon enough," she told me, and leaned against me. Nettle looked up at me and such gratitude shone in her eyes that I felt I had suddenly won a battle I had not even known I was fighting.

I cleared my throat and managed to speak without huskiness. "I want a hot cup of tea," I told them, and Molly sat up, exclaiming, "You know, that would be exactly what I want right now, myself."

And despite our weariness from travel, the afternoon passed pleasantly. Much later that night, we shared a dinner that met Cook Nutmeg's standards, and a jot of brandy that exceeded mine. We had retired to the estate study, where Nettle had refused to look at my careful bookkeeping, saying she was certain all was well. Nettle had insisted she must leave in the morning. Molly had tried to dissuade her to no avail. I was nearly dozing in a chair by the fire when Nettle spoke softly from her corner of a settee. "Seeing it is much worse than hearing about it." She sighed heavily. "It's real. We are losing her."

I opened my eyes. Molly had left us, saying she wished to see if there was any of that pale sharp cheese left in the larder, as she suddenly fancied it. She'd put her desire for it down to her pregnancy and, Molly-like, had disdained the idea of ringing for a servant at such a late hour. She was beloved by our servants simply because she spared them such thoughtless abuse.

I looked at the place where Molly had been sitting. The imprint of her body was still on the cushions, and her scent lingered in the air. I spoke softly. "She's slowly sliding away from me. Today was not too bad. There are days when she is so focused on this 'baby' that she speaks of nothing else."

"She makes it seem so real," Nettle said, her words faltering away between wistfulness and dread.

"I know. It's hard. I've tried to tell her it's impossible. And when I do, I feel like I'm being cruel. But today, playing along . . . that feels crueler now. As if I've given up on her." I stared at the dying fire. "I've had to ask the maidservants to indulge her. I'd seen them rolling their eyes after she'd passed by. I rebuked them for it, but I think it only—"

Angry sparks sprang in Nettle's eyes. She sat up straight. "I don't care if my mother is mad as a hatter! They must be made to treat her with respect. You can't indulge them in any smirking 'tolerance'! She is my mother and your wife. Lady Molly!"

"I'm not sure how to deal with it without making it worse," I confided to her. "Molly has always taken care of the running of the household. If I step in and start disciplining the servants, she may resent me usurping her authority. And what can I say to them? We both know your mother's not pregnant! How long must I order them to maintain this pretense? Where does it end? With the birth of an imaginary child?"

Nettle's face went pale at my words. For a moment the planes of her face were white and stark like the frozen flanks of a mountain under snow. Then she abruptly dropped her face into her hands. I looked at the pale parting in her gleaming dark hair. She spoke through her fingers. "We're losing her. It's only going to get worse. We know that. What will you do when she no longer knows you? When she cannot take care of herself anymore? What will become of her?"

She lifted her face. Silent tears gleamed in streaks down her cheeks.

I crossed the room and took her hand. "I promise this. I will take care of her. Always. I will love her. Always." I steeled my will. "And I will speak to the servants privately, and tell them that regardless of how long they have worked here, if they value their positions, they will treat Lady Molly as befits the mistress of this household. No matter what they may think of her requests."

Nettle sniffed and drew her hands free of mine, to wipe the backs of her wrists across her eyes. "I know I'm not a child anymore. But just the thought of losing her . . ."

She let her words trail away, her voice stilling before she uttered the words we both knew welled up in her. She still mourned Burrich, the only real father she'd ever known. She did not want to lose her mother as well, and even worse would be to have Molly look at her and not know her.

"I'll take care of her," I promised again. *And you,* I thought to myself. And wondered if she would ever let me step into that role. "Even if it means pretending for her that I believe she has a child growing inside her. Though it makes me feel false to her when I do so. Today . . ." I faltered, guilt welling up in me. I had behaved as if Molly were truly pregnant, indulging her as if she were a fanciful child. Or a madwoman.

"You were being kind," Nettle said quietly. "I know my mother. You won't convince her to give up this delusion. Her mind is unsettled. You may as well be—"

Molly set down the tray with a solid clack on the table. We both jumped guiltily. Molly stared at me, her eyes black. She folded her lips tightly, and at first I thought she would yet again ignore our disagreement. But Nettle was right. She stood her ground and spoke plainly. "You both think me mad. Well. This is fine, then. But I will tell you plainly that I feel the child move within me and my breasts have begun to swell with milk. The time is not far when you will both have to beg my pardon."

Nettle and I, caught in our secret worrying, sat dumbstruck. Nettle had no reply for her mother, and Molly turned and stalked from the room. We looked at each other, guilt-stricken. But neither of us went after her; we soon sought our beds. I had looked forward, on my ride home, to a sweet reunion with my wife and a shared night. Instead Molly had sought out the couch in her nursery. I went alone to our bedchamber, and it seemed a cold and empty place.

The very next day, Nettle left before noon to return to Buckkeep

Castle. She said she had been long away from her Skill-apprentices and that there would be all sorts of neglected work awaiting her. I didn't doubt her, but neither did I believe that was her prime reason for leaving. Molly hugged her farewell, and a stranger might have thought all was well between mother and daughter. But Molly had not mentioned the baby since she had left us the evening before, nor asked if Nettle would return for the birth.

And in the days that followed, she no longer spoke of her phantom child to me. We ate breakfast together; we spoke of the matters of the estate, and over dinner shared the events of our days. And each of us slept alone. Or, in my case, did not sleep. I did more translation work for Chade in the late-night hours than I had in the previous six months. Ten days after the incident, one late evening, I made bold to seek her in her nursery. The door was closed. I stood before it for several long moments before deciding that I should knock rather than walk in. I tapped, waited, and then knocked more loudly.

"Who is it?" Molly's voice sounded surprised.

"It's me." I opened the door a crack. "May I come in?"

"I never said you couldn't," she replied tartly. The words stung, and yet a smile tugged at my face. I turned slightly away from her lest she see it. Now, there was the Molly Redskirts I knew.

"That's true," I said quietly. "But I know that I hurt your feelings, badly, and if you wanted to avoid me for a time, I thought I should not intrude."

" 'Not intrude,' " she said quietly. "Fitz, are you certain you are not the one who has been avoiding me? For how many years have I wakened at night to find your side of the bed cool and empty? Slipping out of our bed in the dead of night to hide away in your dusty little scroll hole, scribbling until your fingers are all ink?"

I bowed my head to that. I had not realized she was aware of those times. I had been tempted to point out that she had left our bed for this nursery. I put that barb down. It was not time to begin a battle. I was inside her door now, and felt like the wolf the first time he had ventured inside a house. I wasn't sure where I should stand or if I could sit. She sighed, and sat up on the divan where she had been reclining. She was in her nightrobe, but she moved a half-finished bit of embroidery to make room for me. "I suppose I do spend too many hours there," I apologized. I sat down beside her. Her scent reached me and I suddenly said, "Whenever I smell you, I always want to kiss you."

She stared at me in astonishment, laughed, and then said sadly, "Of late, I wondered if you even wanted to be near me at all anymore. Old and wrinkly, and now you think me mad . . ."

I gathered her close before she could say more. I kissed her, the top of her head, the side of her face, and then her mouth. "I will always want to kiss you," I said into her hair.

"You don't believe I'm pregnant."

I didn't let go of her. "You've been telling me for over two years that you are pregnant. What am I to think, Molly?"

"I don't understand it myself," she said. "But all I can tell you is that I must have somehow been mistaken at first. I must have thought I was pregnant before I was. Perhaps I knew, somehow, that I was going to be pregnant." She leaned her brow on my shoulder. "It has been hard for me, to have you gone for days at a time. I know that the maidservants giggle about me behind their hands. They know so little of us. They think it scandalous for a man as young and hale as you to be married to an old woman like me. They gossip that you married me for my money and position! They make me feel an old fool. Who do I have who understands who we are and what we have been to each other? Only you. And when you abandon me, when you think me as foolish as they do, then . . . Oh, Fitz, I know it's hard for you to believe it. But I have believed much harder things for your sake and with only your word to go on."

I felt as if the whole world went still around me. Yes. She had. I'd never stopped to see it from that perspective. I bent my head and kissed her salt-teared cheek. "You have." I took a breath. "I will believe you, Molly."

She choked on a laugh. "Oh, Fitz. Please. No, you won't. But I'm going to ask you to pretend that you do. Only when we are in here, together. And in return, when I am not in this room, I will pretend I am not pregnant, as best I can." She shook her head, her hair rubbing against my cheek. "I am sure that will be much easier for the servants. Except for Revel. Our steward seemed absolutely delighted to help me construct this nest."

I thought of Revel, tall, almost gaunt in his thinness, always grave and correct with me. "Was he?" It didn't seem believable.

"Oh, yes. He found the screens with the pansies on them, and had them cleaned before he even told me. I came in here one day, and they were set up around the cradle. And the lace over it, to keep insects away."

Pansies. From Patience, I knew they were sometimes called heart's ease. I owed Revel.

She stood, pulling herself out of my arms. She stepped away from me, and I looked at her. Her long nightgown was scarcely revealing, and she had always been a woman of curves. She went to the hearth, and I saw that there was a tray set on a stand with tea things on it. I studied her profile. She looked little different to me than she had five years ago. Surely if she were pregnant, I'd be able to tell. I measured the slight swell of her belly, her ample hips and generous breasts, and suddenly I was not thinking of babies at all.

She glanced over at me, asking, teapot in hand, "Would you like some?" Then, as I stared at her, her eyes slowly widened and a wicked smile curved her mouth. It was a smile worthy of a naked girl wearing only a holly crown.

"Oh, indeed I would," I replied. As I rose and went to her, she came to meet me. We were gentle and slow with each other, and that night we both slept in her bed in the nursery.

Winter found Withywoods the next day, with a fall of wet snow that brought down the remaining leaves on the birches and lined their graceful branches with white. The stillness that the first snowfall always brings settled like a mantle over the land. Within Withywoods Manor it suddenly seemed a time for wood fires and hot soup and fresh bread at noon. I had returned to the manor's study and a clear-flamed fire of applewood was crackling on the hearth when there was a tap at the door.

"Yes," I called, looking up from a missive from Web.

The door opened slowly and Revel entered. His fitted coat hugged his wide shoulders and narrow waist. He was always impeccably attired and correct in his manners. Decades younger than me, he had a bearing that made me feel like a boy with dirty hands and a stained tunic when he looked down at me. "You sent for me, Holder Badgerlock?"

"I did." I set Web's letter to one side. "I wanted to speak to you about Lady Molly's chamber. The screens with the pansies on them . . ."

The expectation of my disapproval flickered in his eyes. He drew himself up to his full height and looked down on me with the dignity that a truly good house steward always radiates. "Sir. If you please. The screens have not seen use in decades, and yet they are lovely things worthy of display. I know I acted without direct authorization, but Lady Molly has seemed . . . dispirited of late. Before you departed, you had directed me to see to her needs. I did. As for the cradle, I came upon her sitting at the top of the stairs, all out of breath and near weeping. It is a heavy cradle, sir, and yet she had managed to move it that far on her own. I felt shamed that she had not come to me and simply told me what she wished me to do. And so, with the screens, I tried to anticipate what she would wish. She has always been kind to me."

He stopped talking. Plainly he felt there was much more he could have said to someone as thick-witted and rock-hearted as I apparently was. I met his gaze and then spoke quietly.

"As she has to me. I am grateful for your service to her and to the estate. Thank you." I had called him in to tell him that I had decided to double his wages. While the gesture still seemed correct, speaking aloud of it suddenly seemed a mercenary thing to do. He had not done this for money. He had repaid a kindness with a kindness. He would discover our largesse when he received his month's wages, and he would know what it was for. But money was not what would matter to this man. I spoke quietly. "You're an excellent steward, Revel, and we value you highly. I want to be sure you know that."

He inclined his head slightly. It wasn't a bow, it was an acceptance. "I do now, sir."

"Thank you, Revel."

"I'm sure you're welcome, sir."

And he left the room as quietly as he'd come.

Winter deepened around Withywoods. The days shortened, the snow piled up, and the nights were black and frosty. Molly and I had made our truce and we both kept it. It made life simpler for both of us. I truly think peace was what we most desired. Most early evenings I spent in the room I had come to think of as Molly's study. She tended to fall asleep there, and I would cover her well and then creep away to my own disorderly den and my work there. So it was very late one night as we were drawing close to midwinter. Chade had sent me a very intriguing set of scrolls, in a language that was almost Outislander. There were three illustrations in them, and they seemed to be of standing stones, with small notations at the side that could have been glyphs. This was the sort of puzzle that I dreaded, for I did not have enough clues to solve it and yet I could not leave it alone. I was working on the scrolls, creating a page beside the first one that duplicated the faded illustrations, substituting the words I could translate and leaving room for the others. I was trying to gain a general idea of what the scroll was about, but was totally mystified by the apparent use of the word "porridge" in its title.

It was late, and I believed myself the only one awake in the house. Wet snow was falling thickly outside, and I had closed the dusty curtains against the night. When the wind blew, the snow splatted against the glass. I was half-wondering if we'd be snowed in by morning and if the wet snow would put an ice glaze on the grapevines. I looked up abruptly, my Wit-sense stirred, and a moment later the door eased open. Molly peered around.

"What is it?" I asked, sudden anxiety making my query sharper than I intended. I could not recall the last time she had sought me out in my study.

She clutched at the door frame. For an instant she was quiet, and I feared I had injured her feelings. Then she spoke through a held breath. "I'm here to break my word."

"What?"

"I can't pretend I'm not pregnant anymore. Fitz, I'm in labor. The baby will come tonight." A faint smile framed her gritted teeth. An instant later she took a sudden deep breath.

I stared at her.

"I'm certain," she replied to my unasked question. "I felt the first pangs hours ago. I've waited until they were strong and closer together, to be sure. The baby is coming, Fitz." She waited.

"Could it be bad food?" I asked her. "The sauce on the mutton at dinner seemed very spicy to me and perhaps—"

"I'm not sick. And I didn't eat dinner, not that you noticed. I'm in labor. Eda bless us all, Fitz, I've had seven children that were born alive, and two miscarriages in my life. Don't you think I know what I'm feeling now?"

I stood slowly. There was a faint sheen of sweat on her face. A fever, leading her delusion to deepen? "I'll send for Tavia. She can go for the healer while I help you lie down."

"No." She spoke the word bluntly. "I'm not sick. So I don't need a healer. And the midwife won't come. She and Tavia think me just as daft as you do." She took a breath and held it. She closed her eyes, folded her lips, and her grip on the door's edge grew white-knuckled. After a long moment, she spoke. "I can do this alone. Burrich always helped me with my other births, but I can do this alone if I must."

Did she mean that to sting as much as it did? "Let me help you to your nursery," I said. I half-expected her to swat at me as I took her arm, but instead she leaned on me heavily. We walked slowly through the darkened halls, pausing three times, and I thought I might have to carry her. Something was deeply wrong with her. The wolf in me, so long dormant, was alarmed at her scent. "Have you vomited?" I asked her. And "Do you have fever?" She didn't answer either question.

It took forever to reach her chamber. Inside, a fire burned on the hearth. It was almost too warm in the room. When she sat down on the low couch and groaned with the cramp that took her, I said quietly, "I can bring you a tea that would purge you. I really think—"

"I labor to bring forth your child. If you won't be any help, then leave me," she told me savagely.

I couldn't stand it. I rose from my seat beside her, turned, and walked as far as the door. There I halted. I will never know why. Perhaps I felt that joining her in madness would be better than letting her go there alone. Or perhaps that joining her would be better than remaining in a rational world without her. I changed my voice, letting my love rule it. "Molly. Tell me what you need. I've never done this. What should I bring, what should I do? Should I call some of the women to attend you?"

Her muscles were tight when I asked; it was a moment before she answered. "No. I want none of them. They would only titter and simper at the foolish old woman. So only you would I have here. If you can find the will to believe me. At least within this room, Fitz, keep your word to me. Pretend to believe me." Her breath caught again and she leaned forward over her belly. A time passed, and then she told me, "Bring a basin of warmed water to bathe the child when he comes. And a clean cloth to dry him. A bit of twine to tie the cord tight. A pitcher of cool water and a cup for me." And then she curled forward again, and let out a long, low moan.

And so I went. In the kitchen I filled a pitcher with hot water from the simmering kettle always kept near the hearth. Around me was the comfortable, familiar clutter of the kitchen at night. The fire muttered to itself, crocks of dough were slowly rising for the next day's bread; a pot of brown beef stock gave off its fragrant aroma near the back of the hearth. I found a basin and filled a large mug with cold water. I took a clean cloth from a stack there, found a big tray to put it all on, and loaded it. I stood for a long moment, breathing in the serenity, the sanity of an organized kitchen in a quiet moment. "Oh, Molly," I said to the silent walls. Then I bared my courage as if I were drawing a heavy blade, hefted the tray, balanced it, and set off through the quiet halls of Withywoods.

I shouldered the unlatched door open, set the tray down on a table, and walked around to the divan by the fireside. The room smelled of sweat. Molly was silent; her head drooped forward on her chest. After all this, had she fallen asleep sitting in front of the fire?

She sat spraddled on the edge of the couch, her nightrobe hiked to her hips. Her cupped hands were between her knees and the tiniest child I had ever seen rested in her hands. I staggered, nearly fell, and then dropped to my knees, staring. Such a small being, streaked with blood and wax. The baby's eyes were open. My voice shook as I asked, "It's a baby?"

She lifted her eyes and stared at me with the tolerance of years. Stupid, beloved man. Even in her exhaustion, she smiled at me. Triumph in that look and love I did not deserve. No rebuke for my doubts. She spoke softly. "Yes. She's our baby. Here at last." The tiny thing was a deep red, with a pale thick umbilical cord coiling from her belly to the afterbirth on the floor at Molly's feet.

I choked as I tried to take in a breath. Utter joy collided with deepest shame. I had doubted her. I didn't deserve this miracle. Life would punish me, I was sure of it. My voice sounded childish to me as I begged, against all odds, "Is she alive?"

Molly sounded exhausted. "She is, but so small. Half the size of a barn cat! Oh, Fitz, how can this be? So long a pregnancy and so small a child." She took in a shaky breath, refusing tears for practicality. "Bring me the basin of warm water and the soft towels. And something to cut the cord."

"Right away!"

I brought them to her and set them at her feet. The baby still rested in her mother's hands, looking up at her. Molly ran her fingertip across the baby's small mouth, patted her cheek. "You're so still," she said, and her fingers moved to the child's chest. I saw her press them and feel for a heart beating there. Molly looked up at me. "Like a bird's heart," she said.

The infant stirred slightly and took a deeper breath. Suddenly she shivered and Molly held her close to her breast. She looked into the little face as she said, "So tiny. We've waited for you so long, we've waited years. And now you've come, and I doubt that you will stay a day."

I wanted to reassure her, but I knew she was right. Molly had begun to tremble with the fatigue of her labor. Still, she was the one to tie the cord and cut it. She leaned down to test the warm water, and then to slide the baby into it. Gently her hands smoothed the blood away. The tiny skull was coated with downy pale hair.

"Her eyes are blue!"

"All babies are born with blue eyes. They'll change." Molly lifted the baby and, with an easy knack I envied, transferred her from towel to soft white blanket and swaddled her into a tidy bundle, smooth as a moth's cocoon. Molly looked up at me and shook her head at my numb astonishment. "Take her, please. I need to see to myself now."

"I might drop her!" I was terrified.

Molly's solemn gaze met mine. "Take her. Do not put her down. I do not know how long we may have her. Hold her while you can. If she leaves us, she will leave as we are holding her, not alone in her cradle."

Her words made the tears course down my cheeks. But I obeyed her, completely meek now in the knowledge of how wrong I had been. I moved to the end of her couch, sat down, and held my new little daughter and looked into her face. Her blue eyes met mine unflinchingly. She did not wail, as I had always believed newborns did. She was utterly calm. And so very still.

I met her gaze; she looked to me as if she knew the answer to every mystery. I leaned in closer, taking in her scent, and the wolf in me leapt high. *Mine.* Suddenly she was obviously mine in every way. My cub, to protect. Mine. From this moment, I would die rather than see harm come to her. Mine. The Wit told me that this little spark of life burned strong. Tiny as she was, she would never be prey.

I glanced at Molly. She was washing herself. I set a forefinger to my child's brow and very carefully extended my Skill toward her. I was not certain of the morality of what I did but I pushed away all compunction about it. She was too young to ask her permission. I knew clearly what I intended. If I found something wrong with the baby, something physical, I would do whatever I could to mend it, even though it might task my abilities to their limit and might use all the small reserves of strength she had. The child was calm, her blue eyes meeting mine as I probed her. Such a tiny body. I felt her heart pumping her blood, her lungs taking in air. She was tiny, but if there was aught else wrong with her, I could not find it. She squirmed feebly, puckering her tiny mouth as if she would cry, but I was firm.

A shadow fell between us. I looked up guiltily. Molly stood over us in a clean, soft robe, already reaching to take the child back from me. As I handed her over, I said quietly, "She's perfect, Molly. Inside and out." The baby settled into her embrace, visibly relaxing. Had she resented my Skill-probe? I looked aside from Molly, ashamed of my ignorance as I asked, "Is she truly so small for a newborn?"

Her words struck me like arrows. "My love, I've never seen a baby this small survive more than an hour." Molly had opened the baby's wrappings and was looking at her. She unfolded the tiny hand and looked at her fingers, stroked the small skull, and then looked at her little red feet. She counted each toe. "But maybe . . . she didn't come early, that's for certain! And every part of her is formed well; she even has hair, though it's so blond you can barely see it. All my other children were dark. Even Nettle."

The last she added as if she needed to remind me that I had fathered her first daughter, even if I had not been there to see her born or watch her grow. I needed no such reminder. I nodded and reached out to touch the baby's fist. She pulled it in close to her chest and closed her eyes. I spoke quietly. "My mother was Mountain-born," I said quietly. "Both she and my grandmother were fair-haired and blue-eyed. Many of the folk from that region are so. Perhaps I've passed it on to our child."

Molly looked startled. I thought it was because I seldom spoke of the mother who had given me up when I was a small child. I no longer denied to myself that I could recall her. She'd kept her fair hair bound in a single long braid down her back. Her eyes had been blue, her cheekbones high, and her chin narrow. There had never been any rings on her hands. "Keppet," she had named me. When I thought of that distant Mountain childhood, it seemed more like a tale I had heard than something that belonged to me.

Molly broke into my wandering thoughts. "You say she is perfect, 'inside and out.' Did you use the Skill-magic to know that?"

I looked at her, guiltily aware of how uneasy that magic made her. I lowered my eyes and admitted, "Not only the Skill but the Wit tells me that we have a very small but otherwise healthy child here, my love. The Wit tells me the life spark in her is strong and bright. Tiny as she is, I find no reason that she will not live and thrive. And grow." A light kindled in Molly's face as if I had given her a treasure of inestimable value. I leaned over and traced a soft circle on the babe's cheek. She startled me by turning her face toward my touch, her little lips puckering.

"She's hungry," Molly said and laughed aloud, weakly but gratefully. She arranged herself in a chair, opened her robe, and set the babe to her bared breast. I stared at what I had never seen before, moved far past tears. I edged closer to her, knelt beside them on the floor, carefully set my arm around my wife, and looked down at the suckling infant.

"I've been such an idiot," I said. "I should have believed you from the start."

"Yes. You should have," she agreed, and then she assured me, "No harm done," and leaned into my embrace. And that quarrel was ever done between us.

Chapter 6

THE SECRET CHILD

The hunger for using the Skill does not diminish with use or with age. Curiosity disguises itself as a legitimate desire for wisdom and adds its temptation. Only discipline can keep it in check. For this reason, it is best that members of a coterie are kept in proximity to one another throughout the span of their lives, so that they can reinforce with one another the proper use of the Skill. It is also vital that journeymen coteries monitor the apprentices and that Masters monitor both journeymen and apprentice coteries. With your Solos, be most vigilant of all. Often Solos exhibit an adventurous and arrogant nature, and this is what keeps them from successfully joining a coterie. It is absolutely essential that the Skillmaster be vigilant in overseeing every Solo. If a Solo becomes secretive and excessively private in his habits, it may be necessary for all Masters of the Skill to convene and discuss containing his magic, lest it gain control of the Solo and he hurt himself or others.

But who shall watch over the shepherd?

This question presents the problem neatly. The Skillmaster, at his elevated level, can be disciplined only by himself. This is why the position must never be political, nor granted as an honor, but only bestowed to the most learned, the most powerful, and the most disciplined of Skill-users. When we convened to discuss the abuse of the Skill, the horrific damage inflicted on Cowshell Village, and the fall of Skillmaster Clarity, we had to confront what the politicization of this title had done to us all. Unchecked, Skillmaster Clarity entered dreams, influenced thinking, passed judgment on those he considered evil, rewarded his "good" with advantages in trading, and arranged marriages in this small community, all in an ill-considered attempt "to create a harmonious town where jealousy, envy, and excessive ambition were checked for the good of all." Yet we have witnessed what this lofty goal actually created: a village where folk were compelled to act against their own natures, where their emotions could not be expressed, and where ultimately, in a single season, suicides and murders took the lives of more than half the population.

In considering the magnitude of the suffering that was created, we can only find fault with ourselves that the Master level of Skill-users remained ignorant of what Skillmaster Clarity was doing until the damage had been done. In order to avoid such a disastrous misuse of the Skill in the future, the following actions have been taken.

Skillmaster Clarity is to be sealed from use of the Skill in any form henceforth. The selection of a new Skillmaster will be made by a process in which the queen or king suggests three candidates from among the Masters and a vote of the Masters chooses the new Skillmaster. The vote will be done in secrecy, the ballots counted publicly, and the results announced by three randomly chosen minstrels dedicated to the truth.

This gathering of the Masters concludes that no Solo must ever hold the rank of Skillmaster again. If Clarity had had a coterie of his own, he would have been unable to conceal his actions.

Henceforth, the Skillmaster shall submit himself to a review of

all the Masters at least once a year. If he is found incompetent by a
vote of the Masters, he will be replaced. In extreme cases of abuse
or poor judgment, he will be sealed.

Compensation and care will be provided to the survivors of the
Cowshell Village Tragedy. While it cannot be revealed to any of
them that the Skill was the source of the madness that overtook their
village that night, all amends that can be made to them must be
made, with openhanded generosity and no cessation of such repara-
tion until their natural deaths.

RESOLUTION OF THE MASTERS FOLLOWING
THE COWSHELL VILLAGE TRAGEDY

That first evening that the baby existed outside of Molly's body, I
was dazed by her. Long after Molly fell asleep with the baby cradled
against her, I sat by the fire and watched them both. I invented a
hundred futures for her, all of them bright with promise. Molly
had told me she was small; I dismissed that concern. All babies
were small! She would be fine, and more than fine. She would be
clever, this little girl of mine, and lovely. She would dance like thistledown on the wind, and ride as if she were part of her mount.
Molly would teach her of bees and to know the names and properties of every herb in the garden; I would teach her to read and to
figure. She would be a prodigy. I imagined her little hands stained
with ink as she helped with a transcription, or copied over the illustrations that would never go right for me. I imagined her on the
floor of the ballroom of Buckkeep Castle, twirling in a scarlet
gown. My heart was full of her and I wanted the world to celebrate
with me.

I laughed aloud, ruefully, at how astounded everyone would be
to hear of her. Nettle and I had not noised about Molly's claim to
be pregnant. We had thought it a sorrow we should keep to ourselves. And now, how foolish we would both look when the word
went out that I had a child, a little daughter, fair as a daisy. I imagined a gathering to welcome her to the world. Her brothers would
come, with their families, and Hap. Oh, that I could somehow send
word to the Fool of the joy that had come into my life! I smiled to

think of it and longed that it could be so. There would be music and feasting on her naming day. Kettricken, and Dutiful and his queen, and the princes, even Chade would make the journey to Withywoods.

And with that thought, my elation began to unravel. A child imagined is not the same as a child sleeping in her mother's arms. What would Kettricken and Chade see when they looked at her? I could imagine Chade's skepticism that such a fair-haired child could be of Farseer lineage. And Kettricken? If she recognized that my own Mountain mother had likely been fair and acknowledged the babe as the daughter of FitzChivalry Farseer, what then? What would she think she had the right to ask of my daughter? Would this infant, like Nettle, be seen as a secret reserve of Farseer blood, an heir that could be produced if the recognized line should somehow fail?

Trepidation rose in me, a cold tide that drowned my heart in fear. How could I have longed for this child and never considered the dangers that would surround her, simply by virtue of her being my daughter? Chade would want to test her for the Skill. Kettricken would believe that the Farseer throne had the right to select a husband for her.

I rose and soundlessly paced the room, a wolf guarding his den. Molly slept on, the sleep of exhaustion. The swaddled babe next to her stirred softly and then subsided. I had to protect them, to give the child a future she could determine for herself. My mind swirled with ideas. Flight. We would pack tomorrow and flee; we'd travel to where we could settle as simply Molly and Tom and our baby . . . no. Molly would never consent to breaking off contact with her other children; nor could I just walk away from those I loved, no matter what threat they might seem to present right now.

So what could I do? I looked at them, sleeping so peacefully, so vulnerable. I would keep them safe, I vowed to myself. It suddenly came to me that the child's fair hair and blue eyes might be in our favor. No one would look at her and assume that she was the natural child of Molly or me. We could claim she was a foundling, taken in. The falsehood blossomed in my mind. So easy to claim! Not even Nettle need know; once I had shown Molly the threat to the child, perhaps she would agree to the deception. Nettle would believe we had adopted the babe to placate her mother's longing for an infant. No one need know that she was truly a Farseer. One simple lie could keep her safe.

If I could get Molly to agree to it.

That night I went to our room for bedding and took it back down to the nursery. I slept across the door, on the floor, like a wolf guarding his den and cub. It felt right.

The next day was filled with both sweetness and trepidation. By the light of dawn, I saw my plans for denying my child as the foolishness it was. The servants in a great house know all, and Revel would immediately know that no foundling had been delivered to us the night before. I could not possibly conceal from the staff that Molly had borne her child, so I warned them that the babe was small, and her mother weary. I am sure they considered me quite as mad as they had Molly as I insisted that I would take Molly's meals in to her and that she must absolutely not be disturbed. Not only my veracity as to there being a baby in the house but my authority as a male in such a female area was instantly dismissed. By ones and twos and threes, the women of the Withywoods staff each found some pressing errand that demanded entrance to the nursery. First it was Cook Nutmeg, insisting that she must speak with Molly to know exactly what her mistress would wish to have for her luncheon and supper on such a momentous day. Her daughter Mild slipped in behind her, a slender shadow to her mother's generous figure. Molly had been unaware of my efforts to keep her undisturbed. I could not blame her for a certain starchy smugness as she presented the baby to Cook and her daughter.

Molly, I think, was aware only that she was proving them wrong: She had been pregnant, and all their snide dismissal of her insistence that a nursery be prepared was now answered. She was regal as a queen as they advanced to look at the tiny bundle she held so protectively. Cook kept control of herself, smiling at what a "dear little thing" our baby was. Mild was less schooled to decorum. "She's so tiny!" the girl exclaimed. "Like a doll! And pale as milk! Such blue eyes! Is she blind?"

"Of course not," Molly replied, gazing at her child adoringly. Cook swatted her daughter and hissed, "Manners!"

"My mother was fair. With blue eyes," I asserted.

"Well, then, that explains it," Cook Nutmeg asserted with an unnatural amount of relief. She bobbed a curtsy to Molly. "Mistress, shall it be the river fish or the salt cod, then? For all know fish is best for a woman who has just delivered a child."

"River fish, please," Molly replied, and with that vast decision settled, Cook whisked herself and her child from the room.

Scarcely had enough time elapsed for Cook to return to her duties before two housemaids presented themselves, asking if the baby or her mother required fresh linens. Each bore an armful and they all but trampled me as they overran my position in the door, insisting, "Well, if not now, then soon, for all know how quickly a baby will soil her crib."

And again I witnessed the unnerving spectacle of women barely controlling their shock and then expressing admiration for my daughter. Molly seemed blind to it, but every instinct I had alarmed me. Well I knew how small creatures that were too different were treated. I'd seen crippled chicks pecked to death, witnessed cows that nudged away a weak calf, the runt piglet pushed away from a nipple. I had no reason to think that people were any better than animals in that regard. I would keep watch.

Even Revel presented himself, bearing a tray with low vases of flowers on it. "Winter pansies. So hardy that they bloom through most of the winter in Lady Patience's hothouses. Not that they are truly hot anymore. They are not as well tended as they once were." He rolled a look in my direction, one I steadfastly ignored. And then Molly honored him as she had none of the others. Into his gangly arms she gave over the tiny bundle of child. I watched him catch his breath as he took her. His long-fingered hand spanned her chest, and a doting smile made foolish his usually somber face. He looked up at Molly, their eyes met, and I was as close to jealous as a man could feel to see them share their mutual delight in her. He spoke not a word as he held her, and only gave her back when a housemaid tapped at the door and requested his expertise. Before he left, he carefully arranged each vase of little flowers, so that the flowers and the screens echoed one another charmingly. It made Molly smile.

That first day of her life, I kept up with the bare minimum of the supervision and work of running the estate. Every moment I could spare, I was in the nursery. I watched Molly and our child, and as I did my trepidation changed to wonder. The infant was such a tiny entity. Each glimpse of her seemed a wonder. Her tiny fingers, the whorl of pale hair at the back of her neck, the delicate pink of her ears: To me it seemed amazing that such a collection of wondrous parts could simply have grown so secretly inside my lady wife. Surely she was the dedicated work of some magical artist rather than the chance product of love. When Molly left to bathe, I stayed by her cradle. I watched her breathe.

I had no desire to pick her up. She seemed too delicate a creature for me to have in my hands. *Like a butterfly*, I thought. I feared that with a touch I might damage the shimmer of life that kept her moving. Instead I watched her sleep, the minuscule rise and fall of the blanket that covered her. Her pink lips moved in and out in sleepy mimicry of nursing. When her mother returned, I observed them more intently than if she and Molly were players acting out a tale. Molly was as I had never seen her, so calm and competent and focused as a mother. It healed something in me, a gulf I had never known existed until she filled it. So this was what a mother was! My child was so safe and cared for in her embrace. That she had been a mother seven times before made it seem no less wondrous to me. I wondered, as I must, about the woman who had held and watched me so. A wistful sorrow rose in me as I wondered if that woman still lived, if she knew what had become of me. Did my little daughter's features mirror hers at all? But when I looked at her sleeping profile, I saw only how unique she was.

That night Molly climbed the stairs with me to our bedchamber. She lay down with the swaddled child in the center of the bed, and when I joined them there, I felt as if I formed the other half of a shell around a precious seed. Molly dropped off to sleep immediately, one of her hands resting lightly on our slumbering baby. I lay perfectly still on the edge of the bed, preternaturally aware of the tiny life that rested between us. Slowly I moved my hand until I could stretch out one of my fingers and touch Molly's hand. Then I closed my eyes and skimmed sleep. I woke when the baby stirred and whimpered. Even without light in the room, I felt how Molly shifted her to put her to the breast. I listened to the small sounds the babe made as she suckled and Molly's deep slow breathing. Again, I dipped down into sleep.

I dreamed.

I was a boy again, at Buckkeep Castle, and I walked along the top of a stone wall near the herb gardens. It was a warm and sunny spring day. Bees were busy in the fragrant blossoms of a heavy-laden cherry tree that leaned over the wall. I slowed my balancing act as I stepped through the reaching embrace of the pink-petaled branches. Half-concealed there, I froze at the sound of voices. Children were shouting excitedly, obviously in the grip of some competitive game. A longing to join them filled me.

But even in the grip of the dream, I knew that was impossible. Within Buckkeep Castle I was neither meat nor fish. I was too common to seek friends among the well-born, and my illegitimate blood was too noble to allow me to play with the children of the servants. So I listened, keenly envious, and in a moment a small, lithe figure came eeling through the gate to the herb garden, pushing it almost closed behind him. He was a scrawny child, clad all in black save for his white sleeves. A close-fitting black cap confined all but the ends of his pale hair. He went skipping lightly across the garden, hurtling over the herb beds without breaking a leaf to land on a stone path with a near-soundless scuff before flinging himself over the next bed. He moved almost in silence, yet his noisy pursuers were not far behind. They flung the gate open with a shout just as he slid behind a climbing rose on a trellis.

I held my breath for him. His hiding place was not perfect. Spring was young, and he was a black shadow behind the slender branches and unfurling green leaves of the espaliered rose. A smile bent my mouth as I wondered who would win this game. Other children were spilling into the garden, half a dozen of them. Two girls and four boys, all probably within three years of my own age. Their dress revealed them as the children of servants. Two of the older boys were already clad in Buckkeep-blue tunics and hose, and probably were truant from lesser tasks about the keep.

"Did he come in here?" one of the girls cried in a shrill voice.

"He had to!" a boy shouted, but there was a note of uncertainty in his voice. The pursuers spread out quickly, each competing to see who should first spot their quarry. I stood very still, heart beating fast, wondering if they might see me and suddenly include me in their game. Even knowing where the boy hid, I could only just make out his silhouette. His pale fingers gripped the trellis. I could see the very slight rise and fall of his chest that betrayed how long he had been running.

"He went past the gate! Come on!" one of the elder boys decided, and like a pack of dogs whipped off a fox the children surged back, milling about him as he led the way back to the gate. Behind them, their prey had turned and was already seeking handholds in the sun-warmed stone wall behind the trellis. I saw him take a step up it, and then a shout from one of the seekers betrayed that someone had glanced back and caught that motion.

"He's there!" a girl shouted, and the pack raced back into the garden. As the black-clad boy spidered up the tall wall, the children hastily stooped. In an instant the air was full of flung earth clods and rocks. They hit the rosebush, the trellis, the wall, and I heard the hollow thuds as they hammered against the slim youth's back. I heard his hoarse gasp of pain, but he kept his grip on the wall and climbed.

The game was suddenly not a game at all, but a cruel hunt. Splayed on the wall he could not seek cover, and as he climbed the hunters stooped for more rocks and clods. I could have cried out to them to stop. But I knew that if I did, it would not save him. I would simply become an extra target for them.

One of the stones hit the back of his head hard enough to snap his head forward against the wall. I heard the slap of flesh on stone, and saw how he halted, half-stunned, fingers slipping. But he did not cry out again. He shuddered, and then began to move more swiftly. His feet slipped, gained purchase, slipped, and then he had a hand on the top of the wall. As if gaining that goal had changed the game, the other children surged forward. He reached the top of the wall, clung there for the bare instant that it took his eyes to meet mine, and then tipped over onto the other side. The blood running down his chin had been shockingly red against his pasty face.

"Go round, go round!" one of the girls was shrieking, and yelping like hounds the other children turned and poured back out of the garden. I heard the harsh clang of the gate as they flung it closed behind them, and the wild pattering of their feet on the path. They were laughing as they ran. A moment later I heard a shrill and desperate scream.

I woke. I was breathing as harshly as if I'd just fought a bout. My nightshirt was sweated to my chest and twisted about me. Disoriented, I sat up and fought free of the blanket.

"Fitz!" Molly rebuked me as she flung a sheltering arm over our child. "What are you thinking?"

Abruptly I was myself again, a grown man, not a horrified child. I crouched in our bed, next to Molly, next to our tiny baby that I might have crushed in my thrashing. "Did I hurt her?" I cried out in horror, and in response the baby began a thin wailing.

Molly reached across and seized my wrist. "Fitz. It's all right. You just woke her, that's all. Lie down. It was just a dream."

After all our years together she was familiar with my nightmares. She knew, to my chagrin, that it could be hazardous to wake me from one. Now I felt shamed as a whipped dog. Did she think me a danger to our child? "I think I'd best sleep somewhere else," I offered.

Molly did not let go of my wrist. She rolled onto her side, snugging the baby closer to her. In response, the infant gave a small hiccup and immediately began to root for a nipple. "You will sleep right here beside us," Molly declared. Before I could say anything else, she laughed softly and said, "She thinks she's hungry again." She released her grip on me to free her breast for the child. I lay very still as she arranged herself and then listened to the small, contented sounds of a young creature filling her belly. They both smelled so good, the baby with her infant smell and Molly's female-ness. I suddenly felt large and brutal and male, an intruder in the safety and peace of domesticity.

I began to ease away from them. "I should—"

"You should stay right where you are." She caught my wrist again, and tugged on it, pulling me nearer to both of them. She was not content until I was close enough that she could reach up and run her fingers through my hair. Her touch was light, lulling, as she lifted the sweaty curls from my brow. I closed my eyes to her touch, and after a few moments my awareness drifted.

The dream that had faded into obscurity when I woke painted itself into my mind again. I had to force myself to breathe gently and slowly despite how my chest constricted. A dream, I told my-self. Not a memory. I had never hidden and watched as the other children of the keep tormented the Fool. Never.

But I might have, my conscience insisted. *If I had been in such a place and time, I might have. Any child would.* As one does at such an hour and after such a dream, I sieved my memories for connec-tions, trying to discover why such an unsettling dream had invaded my sleep. There were none.

None except the memories of how the children of the keep had spoken of King Shrewd's pale jester. The Fool was there, in my childhood memories, as far back as the day I had arrived at Buck-keep. He had been there before I was, and if he was to be believed he had been waiting for me all that time. Yet it had been years be-fore our encounters in Buckkeep Castle had progressed beyond a rude gesture from him in the hallway or unflattering imitations of me as he followed me down a corridor. I had avoided him as assid-uously as the other children had. I had not, I thought as I granted myself an exemption from guilt, treated him with cruelty. I had never mocked him or even expressed abhorrence of him in any way. No. I had merely avoided him. I had believed him a nimble and silly fellow, a tumbler who delighted the king with his antics but was, for all that, rather simpleminded. If anything, I had pitied him, I told myself. Because he was so different.

Just as my daughter would be so different from all her playmates.

Not all children in Buck were dark-eyed and dark-haired and warm-skinned, but the preponderance of playmates she would find would be so. And if she did not grow quickly to match them in size, if she remained tiny and pale, what then? What sort of a childhood would she have?

Cold began in my belly and radiated up to my heart. I moved even closer to Molly and my child. They both slept now, but I did not. Vigilant as a watching wolf, I put my arm lightly across both of them. I would protect her, I promised myself and Molly. No one would mock her or torment her in any way. Even if I had to keep her secret from the entire outside world, I would keep her safe.

Chapter 7

THE PRESENTATION

Once upon a time there was a good man and his wife. They had both worked hard all their lives, and slowly fortune had favored them with everything that they could desire save one. They had no child.

One day as the wife was walking in her garden and weeping that she had no child, a pecksie came out of the lavender bush and said to her, "Woman, why do you weep?"

"I weep that I have no babe of my own," the woman said.

"Oh, as to that, how foolish you are," said the pecksie. "If you but say the word, I can tell you how a babe can be in your arms before the year is out."

"Tell me, then!" the woman implored.

The pecksie smiled. "As to that, it is easily done. Tonight, just as the sun kisses the horizon, set out on the ground a square of silk,

*taking care that it rests flat on the ground with never a wrinkle in it.
And tomorrow, whatever is under the silk is yours."*

*The woman hastened to do as she was bid. As the sun touched
the horizon, she set the silk flat to the ground, with never a wrinkle.
But as the garden darkened and she hurried back to her house, a
curious mouse came to the silk, sniffed it, and scampered across it,
leaving a tiny wrinkle at the edge.*

*In the earliest light of dawn, the woman hastened to the garden.
She heard small sounds and saw the silk moving. And when she
lifted the square of silk, she found a perfect child with bright black
eyes. But the babe was no bigger than the palm of her hand . . .*

OLD BUCKKEEP TALE

Ten days after our baby's birth I finally resolved that I must make
confession to Molly. I dreaded it, but there was no avoiding it, and
delaying it any longer was not going to make it easier.

Since both Nettle and I had doubted Molly's pregnancy, we had
not shared the news with anyone outside our immediate family.
Nettle had informed her brothers, but only in the context that their
mother was aging and her mind had begun to wander. The lads all
had busy lives of their own, and in Chivalry's case that meant three
youngsters as well as a wife and a holding to tend to. They were far
too caught up in their own lives and wives and children to give
more than a passing worry that their mother might be losing her
mind. Nettle and Tom, they were sure, would handle any crisis in
that area, and in any case what could they do about their mother's
increasing senility? It is the way of the young to accept the debilita-
tions of old age very gracefully on behalf of their elderly parents.
And now there was a baby to explain to them. And not just to them,
but to the whole rest of the world.

I had confronted this difficulty by ignoring it. No one beyond
Withywoods had been told. Not even to Nettle had I passed the
news.

But now I had to admit that to Molly.

I armed myself for the task. I had requested from the kitchen a tray of the little sweet biscuits Molly loved, along with a dish of thick sweetened cream and raspberry preserves. A large pot of freshly brewed black tea joined it on my tray. I assured Tavia that I was perfectly capable of carrying a tray and set out for Molly's nursery. On the way, I arrayed my reasons as if I were facing a battle and setting my weapons to hand. First, Molly had been weary and I had not wanted any guests to trouble her. Second, there was the baby herself, so tiny and possibly frail. Molly herself had told me she might not survive, and surely keeping her undisturbed had been for the best. Third, I never wanted anyone to put any obligations on our baby beyond her need to be herself . . . No. That was not a reason to share with Molly. Not right now, at least.

I managed to open the door of the room without dropping the tray. I set it down carefully on a low table and then managed to move the small table with the tray on it next to Molly's seat without oversetting anything. She had the baby on her shoulder and was humming as she patted her back. The soft gown hung far past our daughter's feet, and her arms and hands were lost in the sleeves.

Molly had a honeysuckle candle lit; it lent a sharp sweet scent to the room. There was an applewood fire burning in the small hearth, and no other light; it made the room as cozy as a cottage. She enjoyed the luxury of not worrying constantly about money, but she had never become completely comfortable with the life of a noble lady. "I like to do for myself," she had told me more than once when I had suggested that a personal maid was entirely appropriate to her new station. The larger work of the manor, the scrubbing and dusting, cooking and laundering—that, the servants might do. But Molly was the one who dusted and swept our bedchamber, who spread fresh sun-dried linens on our bed or warmed the featherbed before the hearth on a cold night. In that chamber, at least, we remained Molly and Fitz.

The pansy screens had been moved to catch and hold the warmth of the fire. The burning logs crackled softly, and shadows danced in the room. The baby was close to sleep in her mother's arms when I set down the table and the tray.

"What's this?" Molly asked with a startled smile.

"I just thought we might have some quiet time, and perhaps a bite of something sweet."

Her smile widened. "I can't think of anything I'd like better!"

"And true for me as well." I sat down beside them, careful not to jostle her. I leaned around her to look into my daughter's tiny face. She was red, her pale brows drawn together in concentration. Her hair was only wisps, her fingernails smaller than a fish's scale and as delicate. For a time, I just looked at her.

Molly had taken a biscuit and dipped it in the raspberry preserves and then scooped a small amount of cream onto it. "It smells and tastes like summer," she said after a moment. I poured tea for both of us, and the fragrance of it mingled with the scent from the raspberries. I took a biscuit for myself, and was more generous with both jam and cream than she had been.

"It does," I agreed. For a short time, we simply shared food and tea and the warmth of the fire. Outside a light snow was falling. We were here, inside, safe and warm as a den. Perhaps tomorrow would be a better time to tell her.

"What is it?"

I turned startled eyes to her. She shook her head at me. "You've sighed twice and shifted about as if you have fleas but aren't allowed to scratch. Out with it."

It was like ripping a bandage off a wound. *Do it quickly.* "I didn't tell Nettle the baby was born. Or send your letters to the boys."

She stiffened slightly, and the baby opened her eyes. I felt the effort Molly made to relax and be calm for the infant's sake. "Fitz. Why ever not?"

I hesitated. I didn't want to anger her, but I desperately wanted my own way about this. I finally spoke, my words awkward. "I thought we might keep her a secret for a time. Until she was bigger."

Molly shifted her hand on the baby. I saw how she measured the tiny chest, less than the span of her fingers. "You've realized how different she is," she said quietly. "How small." Her voice was husky.

I nodded at her. "I heard the maids talking. I wish they hadn't seen her. Molly, they were frightened of her. 'Like a doll come to life, so tiny and with those pale-blue eyes always staring. Like she ought to be blind but instead she's looking right through you.' That's what Tavia said to Mild. And Mild said she 'wasn't natural.' That no child that tiny and young should seem as alert as she is."

It was as if I had hissed at a cat. Molly's eyes narrowed and her shoulders tightened. "They came in here to tidy yesterday. I'd told them I didn't need their help, but that's why they came in, I'm sure. To see her. Because yesterday I took her to the kitchen with me, and Cook Nutmeg saw her. She said, 'The little mite hasn't grown a bit yet, has she?' She has, of course. But not enough for Cook to notice." She clenched her teeth. "Let them go. All of them. The maids and Cook. Send them all away." There was as much pain as anger in her voice.

"Molly." I kept my voice calm as I called her back to reason. "They've been here for years. Mild's cradle was in that kitchen, and only last year she took employment with us as a scullery girl. She's scarcely more than a child, and this has always been her home. Patience hired Cook Nutmeg, all those years ago. Tavia has been with us sixteen years, and her mother, Salin, before her. Her husband works in the vineyards. It will cause hard feelings among the whole staff if we let them go! And it would cause talk. And rumors that there was something about our babe that we needed to hide. And we'd know nothing of those we hired to replace them." I rubbed my face, then added more quietly, "They need to stay. And perhaps we need to pay them well to be sure of their loyalty."

"We already pay them well," Molly snapped. "We've always been generous with them. We've always hired their children as they came of age to be useful. When Tavia's husband broke his leg and had to sit out the harvest that year, we kept him on. And Cook Nutmeg spends more time sitting than cooking these days, but we've never spoken of letting her go. We simply hired more help. Fitz, are you seriously saying that I need to bribe them not to think ill of my baby? Do you think they're a danger to her? Because if they are, I'll kill them both."

"If I thought they were a danger, I'd already have killed them," I retorted. The words horrified me as they came out of my mouth, because I recognized they were absolutely true.

Any other woman might have been alarmed by what I had said. But I saw Molly relax, comforted. "Then you love her?" she asked quietly. "You aren't ashamed of her? Appalled that I've given you such a peculiar child?"

"Of course I love her!" The question jolted me. How could she doubt me? "She's my daughter, the child we hoped for all those years! How could you think I wouldn't love her?"

"Because some men wouldn't," she said simply. She turned the child and held her on her knees for my inspection. It woke her, but she didn't cry. She looked up at both of us with her wide blue eyes. She was nearly lost in the soft gown. Even the neck opening was too large for her, baring a small shoulder. Molly tugged it closed. "Fitz. Let's say aloud what we both know. She's a strange little thing. I was pregnant so long; I know, you doubt that, but trust me in this. I carried her inside me for over two years. Perhaps even longer than that. And yet she was born so tiny. Look at her now. She seldom cries, but she watches, just as Tavia said. Still too young to even hold her head up, but she looks so knowing. She watches, and her eyes go from you to me as we speak, as if she listens and already knows every word we say."

"Maybe she does," I said with a smile, but I didn't give any credence to her words. Molly folded her close in her arms again and forced out words. She didn't look at me as she spoke them. "Any other man would look at her and call me a whore. Hair pale as a spring lamb and such blue eyes. Any other man would doubt that this was your child."

I laughed out loud. "Well, I don't! She is mine. Mine and yours. Given to us as miraculously as any child bestowed by the pecksies in an old tale. Molly, you know I have the Wit. And I tell you plainly, from the first time I scented her, I knew her as mine. And yours. Ours. I have never doubted that." I drew one of Molly's hands free from the baby, unfolded her clenched fingers, and kissed her palm. "And I have never doubted you."

Gently I pulled her closer to lean on me. I found a curl of her hair and twined it about my finger. It took a bit of waiting, but I felt her clenched muscles ease. She relaxed. For a short time there was peace. The fire muttered softly to itself, and outside the wind wound through the ancient willows that gave the place its name. We were a simple family for a few heartbeats. Then I girded up my courage and spoke again.

"But I'd like to keep her a secret awhile longer. Not because I doubt she is mine or fear her strangeness."

Molly shook her head, a tiny movement. Her opinion of my utter stupidity radiated from her. I felt it but I did not release her from my embrace; nor did she pull away from me. She spoke with her brow resting on my chest, asking in a cheery voice, "How long, my dear? A year? Two? Perhaps we will reveal her to the world on her sixteenth birthday, like a princess in an old tale?"

"I know it sounds foolish but—"

"It *is* foolish. That's why it sounds foolish. It's too late to keep her a secret. The servants know we have a child, so the village knows, and doubtless all their cousins up and down the river know. Fitz, dear, you should have sent those letters. Now Nettle and the boys will wonder why they were delayed. Keeping this a secret will have old Lord Chade sniffing about like a hound with a fox in a tree. To say nothing of what the old queen will wonder. And the longer we wait to announce her, the more questions folks will ask themselves about her. Is she truly ours? Is she the child of some poor girl who had to give her up? Did we find her in a hollow tree in the forest or is she some changeling child that the pecksies left on our doorstep?"

"That's ridiculous! No one would believe such a thing!"

"They might find it easier to believe than the idea that a parent concealed a lawfully born child from even her brothers and sister. That's already difficult for me to believe."

"Very well." I was beaten. "I'll send the letters tomorrow."

She didn't let me get away with it. She leaned slightly away to look at me. "You should let Nettle know right away. Now. She is closer to her brothers and can send messengers more swiftly. Oh, Fitz." She closed her eyes and shook her head at me.

Total defeat. "Very well." I stood and retreated a little from her.

Once it had been a secret that Nettle shared the Skill-magic with me. But now she was the leader of the King's Own Coterie, the Skill-users who were the Six Duchies' magical line of defense against all dangers. All had to guess she was a bastard Farseer though most had the political sense not to utter those words aloud. Molly was not always comfortable with the magical bond that Nettle shared with me, but had come to accept it. Just as she had accepted that Swift possessed the Wit. It had been even stranger when we discovered that Steady possessed an aptitude for Skill-magic as well. I did not speak what we both wondered now. Would the child she held inherit either of those magics from me?

"See. She almost looks like she's smiling," her mother whispered.

I opened my eyes. I had reached Nettle and conveyed the news. I had a half-wall in place now, almost blocking her outraged response that she had not been informed sooner and her flood of questions about how her mother could have possibly borne a child and her frantic reorganizing of her schedule to come to see us as soon as she practically could. Nettle's flood of information threatened to overwhelm my own thoughts. I closed my eyes, conveyed to her that we would be delighted to see her whenever she could come, and the same for any of her brothers who chose to visit, and would she please send those messages on for us. Then I hastily retreated from her mind, walling myself into my own thoughts again.

I knew that I would pay for it when my elder daughter and I were in the same room and I could not so easily retreat from her tongue-lashing. I was content to wait for that experience. I settled my shoulders. "Nettle knows now, and will pass on the word to the boys. She will soon be coming to visit," I told Molly. I wandered back to her, but sat down on the floor at her feet. I leaned lightly on her legs and picked up my cup of tea.

"Will she travel by the stones?" Her dread was in her question.

"No. I have prevailed there, and the pillars will only be used in matters of great urgency, and in secrecy. She will come as soon as she can arrange it, by horseback, and with an escort."

Molly had been busy with thoughts of her own. "Is it the queen you fear?" she asked in a low voice.

I raised my brows at her. "Scarcely. She pays no attention to my existence at all. She and Dutiful have taken both the princes and gone to visit Bearns Duchy for ten days. He is finally listening to Chade, I believe. The plan is that the royal family will visit all Six Duchies and the Mountain Kingdom, staying at least ten days with each duke. I confess, I wonder if the dukes are already showing their daughters to the princes in the hope of early arrangements for—"

"Don't try to distract me. You know very well which queen I am talking about."

I had and did. I lowered my eyes at her scowl. "Kettricken is on her way home from the Mountains right now. Dutiful Skilled the news to me some days ago. She has reached an agreement with both the Mountain people and the Six Duchies dukes. She will be spending much more time there now, maybe even half of each year. She will not be called queen there, but will consult with Dutiful frequently. When she reaches Buckkeep, they intend to choose one of the Skill-apprentices to be a companion to her whenever she travels there, to make communication between the Mountains and the Six Duchies far more swift. I think both she and Dutiful will find it a relief. There, she is still a queen, even if they do not name her so. And Queen Elliania will have much more room to adjust the court and the castle to her liking. I think it was a wise compromise they reached."

Molly shook her head. "It will be, if Dutiful lives up to his share of it and stands up to the Narcheska. The boys were supposed to be sent to the Mountains for two months of every year, to better learn the language and ways of that duchy. If he does not undertake that, when Queen Kettricken dies, he may find that his beloved seventh duchy rises against the idea of becoming a full part of the Six Duchies."

I nodded, taking relief in the change of topic. "You have put your finger exactly on what worries me. The two queens have always chafed against each other and—"

Molly was relentless. "But that does not answer *my* question.

Regarding our little one and your ridiculous idea to raise her in secrecy, who were you hoping to conceal her from? I wonder this, and the only answer I can think of is Queen Kettricken. And perhaps Lord Chade?"

I shifted uncomfortably and then leaned my head against her knee. She moved her hand and stirred her fingers through my hair. She spoke softly. "I've never been stupid, you know."

"Far from it. I know that you've pieced it all together over the years, even if we seldom speak of it aloud. But when we talk of it, the memory of how I lied to you and deceived you for so many years is like a sword in my chest. Molly, I am so—"

"Evasive," she filled in for me in a deliberately light voice. "Fitz, you have apologized a thousand times for those days, and I have forgiven you. So, please, do not make me angry by trying to distract me now. Who and what do you fear?"

Silence hovered. Then, "I fear everyone," I admitted in a low voice. I acknowledged it to myself as much as her. "You and I see a baby we have longed for, and a child who is so different that others may despise her for that reason alone. But others might see her as a secret princess or a potential Skill-user or a political pawn, a future woman to be wedded where she is most useful to the throne. I know they must see her that way. Just as they saw me as a royal bastard and a very useful tool. An assassin or a disposable diplomat. Just as they saw Nettle as a potential broodmare for a royal heir should Dutiful's seed somehow fail to thrive. When Chade and Kettricken blocked Nettle's engagement to Riddle—"

"Please, Fitz. Not again! Done is done, and there is no need to stir up old pains."

"How can I consider it 'done' while Nettle still moves through life alone?" The old outrage I had felt on my daughter's behalf roared through me. I would never, never understand how she had accepted that secret edict from the throne, and still continued to serve them. I had come very near to sundering my ties with Buckkeep over it. Only Nettle's request that I remain calm and allow her to "handle my own life decisions" had prevented me from doing so. Every time I thought of it—

"Oh, Fitz." Molly sighed. She sensed my mood and her hand moved soothingly on the back of my neck. She kneaded at the tight muscles with her still-strong hands and spoke quietly. "Nettle has always been a private person. She appears to be alone, and to have resigned herself to the throne forbidding her marriage to Riddle. But appearances can be deceiving."

I sat up straight and twisted to look up at her. "Nettle would defy the Farseer throne?"

She shook her head. "Defy? Probably not. Ignore? Yes. Just as we ignored what Lady Patience and King Shrewd decreed for us. Your daughter is very like you, Fitz. She keeps her own counsel and follows her own will. I am sure that if she still wants to be with Riddle, then she is."

"Sweet Eda, what if she gets pregnant?" Anxiety twisted my voice tight.

Molly gave a brittle caw of laughter. "Fitz! Must you always leap from one imagined disaster to another? Listen to what I'm actually saying, which is that I don't know what path Nettle chose for herself. But if she is alone now, it is because she chose to be alone, not because someone decreed it for her. Her life is hers to live, not yours to repair."

"Then you do not think that she and Riddle are together?"

She sighed again. "I think nothing about that. Deliberately. But I will point out to you that Riddle left our employ to take work in Buckkeep Town, and that Nettle shows no sign of encouraging anyone to court her. In any case, she is a woman grown for many years now. It isn't up to me to worry her worries for her, any more than it is your place to decide her decisions. My love, we have all we can deal with within these four walls. The other children have grown up and gone on with their lives. Even Hearth has a sweetheart now and an apprenticeship of his own to serve in Rivertown. Let Nettle and Riddle live their own lives, so that we can have a bit of peace. If you are so anxious to have a child to worry about, well, there is one right here. Look. Hold her for a bit."

She leaned down and set the babe into my hands. As always, I received her with reluctance. It had nothing to do with how I felt

about her and a great deal to do with my terror that I would somehow hold her wrong and damage her. Puppies and foals did not fill
me with that fear, but she did. She was so tiny and so naked, so
weak compared with any other infant creature I'd ever tended. A
foal could stand within the day of its birth. Pups could whine and
shuffle their way to their mother's teats. My infant could not even
hold her head up. Yet as I settled her into my lap, the spark of life
in her burned incredibly bright to my Wit. And to my Skill? I
touched her little hand, skin-to-skin, and felt something there.

Molly rose, groaning a little as she straightened her back. "I've
been sitting still too long. I'm going to get more hot tea. I'll take the
pot and just be a moment."

"Shall I ring for a servant?"

"Oh, no. I could do with a stroll to the kitchen and back. I'll be
but a moment." She was at the door as she spoke.

"Very well," I responded distractedly. I gazed into my child's
face, but she stared past my shoulder. I heard Molly's slippers scuff
softly away. I was alone with my daughter. No reason to be nervous.
How many young things had I cared for in my days in the Buckkeep
stables? A baby could not be so different. I'd won over spooky foals
and wary pups.

"Hey. Baby. Look at me. Look at Da." I moved my face into her
view. She shifted her eyes, and her hand flailed away from my touch.
I tried again.

"So, baby, you're going to live and stay with us awhile, are you?"
I spoke not in the higher-pitched tone that so many would use when
speaking to an infant, but in a low deliberate cadence. As one spoke
to a puppy or a horse. Soothing. I clicked my tongue at her. "Hey.
Over here. Look at me."

She didn't. I hadn't really expected her to.

Patience. Just keep talking. "You are such a tiny thing. I hope you
start growing soon. What are we going to call you? It's time we gave
you a name. A good name, one that is strong. Let's think of a strong
name for you. But a pretty one. Lacey? Do you like that name?
Lacey?"

No response at all. It seemed to me that the spark I had felt went dimmer, as if she shifted her attention away from me. Was that possible?

My finger traced a figure on her chest. "Maybe a flower name? Your sister is Nettle. What about . . . Fern?" I could not be mistaken. She had definitely put her attention elsewhere. I considered for a moment, and tried again. "Myrtle? Foxglove? Thyme?"

She seemed to be listening. Why wouldn't she look at me? I touched her cheek with my finger, trying to make her look at me. She turned her face toward the touch but avoided my eyes. I suddenly recalled that Nighteyes had seldom met my gaze in a steady look, but the wolf had loved me all the same. *Don't force her to meet your eyes. Let the cub come to you, as you let me come to you.* I nodded to the wolf-wisdom and did not try to meet her eyes.

Unfolding her tiny hand, I put my little finger in her palm. Even my smallest finger was still too large for her to grip. She let go of it and coiled her hand into her chest. I lifted her to hold her closer and inhaled deeply, taking her scent. In that moment I was my wolf, and I recalled my bond with Nighteyes so vividly that I ached with the loss. I looked at my cub and knew how sharply sweet her birth would have been for him. *Oh, Nighteyes. Would that you could be beside me for this.* Tears stung my eyes. I stared in amazement as I saw the infant blink away newly formed tears. They ventured onto her little cheeks.

I swallowed against the old pain of losing my wolf. Could she be sharing my feelings? I stared at her and dared myself. I opened myself to her, Skill and Wit.

The baby suddenly waved her arms helplessly and thrashed her feet, as if she were trying to swim away from me. Then, to my horror, she opened her mouth wide and wailed aloud, a sound that seemed far too loud and shrill to come out of such a small being. "Shh! Shh!" I begged her, dreading that Molly would hear. I placed her on my lap and lifted my hands away. Surely she could not be that open to me. I'd done something wrong in how I held her. Had I pinched her somehow, or held her too tightly? I could only look down at her in utter dismay.

I heard the hasty whisper of slippers against the flagged floors and then Molly was suddenly in the room, a dripping teapot in her hand. She hastily clacked it onto the tray and leaned over us, her hands reaching to take her baby back. "What happened? Did you drop her? She's never cried aloud like this before!"

I leaned back, well clear of the baby, and let Molly take her. Almost immediately her wails ceased. Her face was bright red and as her mother patted her, she panted still with the effort it had taken her to scream so loudly.

"I don't know what I did. I was just holding her and looking at her and suddenly she began to scream. Wait! I put my finger in her hand! Did I hurt her fingers? I don't know what I did to upset her! Did I hurt her hand? Is she all right?"

"Shush. Let me see." Molly took the baby's hand softly and very gently unfolded her fingers. The infant didn't flinch or wail. Instead she looked up into her mother's face, and I can only describe her expression as relief. Molly gathered her to her shoulder and began her gentle rocking walk. "She's fine, she's fine," Molly singsonged as she made a slow circuit of the room. When she came back to me, she said gently, "She seems fine now. Perhaps it was just a little air stuck in her gut. Oh, Fitz, it gave me such a turn to hear her cry like that. But, you know"—here she startled me by smiling—"it was such a relief as well. She has been so silent, so calm that I wondered if she could cry. Or if she was too simple to make such a sound." She gave a short laugh. "With the boys, I always wished for them to be quieter, to be easier to put down to sleep. But with her, it has been the opposite. I've worried at how placid she is. Would she be simple? But she's fine. Whatever you did, you've proven she has your temper."

"My temper?" I dared to ask.

She mock-scowled at me. "Of course your temper! Who else could she have inherited it from?" She took her seat again, and I nodded at the puddle around the pot on the tray.

"Looks like you were interrupted. Shall I take it back to the kitchen for more hot water?"

"I'm sure there's enough tea left for us."

She settled in her chair. The room grew quieter as peace flowed back into it. Molly spoke to our baby. "Once, I saw a black-and-white horse with one eye blue, just the same color as yours. The man who owned him said it was his 'wild eye' and not to stand on that side of him." She fell silent for a time, considering her babe. She rocked her gently, calming all of us.

It took me a few moments to realize she was asking to be reassured that our baby was all right. I didn't know. My words were cautious. "I don't think Burrich ever brought a blue-eyed horse into the stables. Or a dog with one odd eye. Did he tell you something about it?"

"Oh, no. Let's not be silly, Fitz. She's a girl, not a horse or a puppy. And blue-eyed Queen Kettricken seems to have your trust."

"That's so," I agreed. I poured a tiny bit of tea from the pot. Too pale. I put it down to let it brew some more. "I don't think she likes me," I ventured softly.

Molly blew out an annoyed breath. "My love, must you ever and always find something to worry about? She hardly knows you yet. Babies cry. That's all. She's fine now."

"She won't look at me."

"Fitz, I'm not going to indulge you in this! So stop. Besides, we have more important things to think about. She needs a name."

"I was just thinking the same thing myself." I edged over to sit more closely to them, and reached for the teapot again.

Molly stopped me. "Patience! It needs to brew a bit longer."

I halted and raised my brows at her. "Patience?"

"I've considered it. But she's so tiny . . ."

"So . . . she needs a small name?" I was completely confused.

"Well, her name has to fit her. I had thought . . ." She hesitated, but I waited to hear what she would say. She spoke at last. "Bee. Because she's so small."

"Bee?" I asked her. I had to smile. Bee. Of course. "It's a lovely name."

"Bee," she asserted firmly. Her next question surprised me. "Will you seal her name to her?" Molly was referring to the old custom of the royal family. When a Farseer prince or princess was named, there was a public ceremony with all the nobility called to witness.

The custom was to pass the child through flame, sprinkle him with soil, and then plunge the infant into water to seal the name to the babe by fire, earth, and water. But such babies were given names such as Verity or Chivalry or Regal. Or Dutiful. And when the name was sealed to the child, it was hoped that he would develop an affinity for the virtue.

"I think not," I said quietly, reflecting that such a ceremony would draw to her the very sort of Farseer attention I sought to avoid. Even then, I was still hoping to keep her existence quiet.

Such hopes vanished when Nettle arrived five days later. She had left Buckkeep as quickly as she could make arrangements and ridden horseback to make the trip as swiftly as possible. Two of her guardsmen had ridden with her, the minimum escort expected for the king's Skillmistress. One was a gray-haired old man, the other a willowy girl, but both looked more exhausted than my daughter did. I had only a glimpse of them from my study window when I pushed aside the drapes and peered out after I heard horses whinnying outside.

I took a deep breath to steel myself. I let the curtain fall and left my study, striding hastily through the manor to intersect with her. Before I had reached the front entrance, I heard the door open, the sound of her clear voice lifted in a hasty greeting to Revel, and then the clatter of her boots as she ran down the hall. I stepped from the connecting corridor and she nearly caromed into me. I caught her by the shoulders and looked down into her face.

Nettle's dark curling hair had pulled free of its tie to fall to her shoulders. Her cheeks and brow were reddened from chill. She still wore her cloak and had been pulling off her gloves as she ran. "Tom!" she greeted me, and then, "Where is my mother?"

I pointed down the hall to the door of the nursery; she shrugged free of me and was gone. I glanced back. In the entrance Revel was greeting her retinue. Our steward had things well in hand. The guardsmen who had ridden with her looked weary and cold and desirous of nothing so much as rest; Revel could deal with them. I turned and followed Nettle.

By the time I caught up with her, she stood in the open door of the nursery. She gripped the door frame and seemed frozen there. "You really had a baby? A baby?" she demanded of her mother. Molly laughed. I halted where I was. As Nettle stepped cautiously into the room, I ghosted up and stood where I could watch them but not be seen. Nettle had halted by the empty cradle set near the fire. Abject penitence was in her voice as she cried out, "Mother, I'm so sorry I doubted you. Where is she? Are you well?"

Molly sat, an image of calm, but I felt her anxiety. Did Nettle see, as I did, how carefully she had arranged herself to meet her elder daughter? Molly's hair looked recently smoothed, and her shawl was evenly spread on her shoulders. The baby was swaddled in a soft cover of palest pink; a matching cap hid her tiny face. Molly did not waste time or effort in answering Nettle but offered the child to her. I could not see Nettle's face but I saw the set of her shoulders change. The bundle her mother offered was too small to be a baby, even a newborn. She crossed the room as cautiously as a wolf walking into unknown territory. She still feared madness. When she accepted the baby, I saw her muscles adjust for the lightness of the infant. She looked into Bee's face, startled to find her really there and even more shocked at her blue gaze, and then she lifted her eyes to look at her mother. "She's blind, isn't she? Oh, Ma, I'm so sorry. Will she live long, do you think?" In her words I heard all I had feared— that not only the world but even her sister would perceive our Bee as peculiar.

Molly took Bee swiftly back from her, sheltering her in her arms as if Nettle's words were an evil wish on the child. "The baby's not blind," her mother said. "Fitz thinks it likely his Mountain mother had blue eyes and that is where she gets them. And though she is tiny, she is perfect in every other way. Ten toes, ten fingers, she eats well and sleeps well, and almost never fusses. Her name is Bee."

"Bee?" Nettle was puzzled but then smiled. "She is such a little thing. But I wonder what the old queen will think of her."

"Queen Kettricken?" Molly's voice was between alarmed and confused.

"She comes, not far behind me. She arrived home at Buckkeep just as I was leaving. I gave her the news before I left, and she was full of joy for you both. She won't be more than a day behind me. I was glad I won Dutiful's permission to leave right away; she clearly wished me to wait for her." She paused, and then her loyalty to her mother prevailed. "And I know that Fitz knew she was coming because I Skilled the knowledge to him myself! And he has said nothing to you! I can tell by the look on your face. Which means that the servants probably haven't been put to airing the rooms or otherwise preparing for guests. Oh, Mother, that man of yours—"

"That man is your father," she reminded Nettle, and as always Nettle looked aside and made no response. For if a child can inherit a trait from a fostering parent, then Nettle had inherited Burrich's stubbornness. She swiftly changed the subject to a more immediate concern. "I'll have the servants open the rooms right away, and freshen them and make sure that there is wood for the hearths. And I'll let the kitchen staff know as well. Don't worry!"

"I don't worry," her mother replied. "The Mountain Queen has never been a difficult guest for us, in that way." But in other ways, she had, Molly's unspoken words said. "Nettle." Her tone stopped her daughter before she could escape. "Why does she come here? What does she want?"

Nettle met her mother's gaze directly. "What you know she wants. She wishes to see FitzChivalry Farseer's younger daughter. To witness her name sealed to her and make a claim to her. A minstrel will ride with her party. She will show him only what she wants him to see, but once he has seen, he will never deny the truth. He is a man that she trusts not to sing until he's told to, and then to sing only the truth."

It was Molly's turn to cast her eyes aside and say nothing. My heart chilled to know that Nettle, too, had seen clearly the reason for Kettricken's visit.

There remained between Molly and Kettricken a strange bond that was both affection and jealousy. Queen Kettricken had always treated Molly and Burrich and their children with impeccable fairness. But Molly had never forgotten nor forgiven that she had been left to believe that I was dead, first to mourn me and then to accept another man in my place, and all the while the queen knew that the Farseer Bastard lived. It was as much my doing as Kettricken's, but I believe Molly found it harder to forgive a woman. Especially a woman who knew what it was to live in the painful belief that her lover was dead.

And so the rift remained, acknowledged by both women as a gap that could never be closed. Kettricken was the sort of woman who would believe she deserved that bitter twist to her friendship with my wife.

Nettle gave a curt nod and left the room, already calling for Tavia to give her a hand to get some guest rooms into order for Lady Kettricken of the Mountains, who would be arriving perhaps before the day was out. Nettle set as little stock by formality with the servants as her mother did. She passed me in the hall and gave me a glance full of rebuke before shouting for Revel as well. I slipped past her and into the nursery. "She'll be opening the windows and shaking out the comforters herself," Molly said to me, and I knew she was proud of her pragmatic daughter.

"Sometimes she reminds me of Verity." I smiled as I entered. "She doesn't ask anyone to do anything that she'd hesitate to do herself. And if she thinks a task needs doing, she doesn't wait."

"You knew Kettricken was coming and you didn't tell me," Molly greeted me.

I looked at her silently. I had told myself that not telling her something was different from lying to her. She didn't agree. Her anger was frozen fire in her voice as she said quietly, "It doesn't make it easier for me when I don't have time to prepare."

"I thought it through carefully. There is nothing we can do to prepare for this, except meet it head-on today. I saw no use in worrying you ahead of time. The servants are adept at quickly readying the rooms."

Her voice was low. "I wasn't speaking of readying the rooms. I was talking of preparing myself. My thoughts. My bearing." She shook her head at me and then spoke more clearly. "Fitz, Fitz. All goes well between us, until your Farseer legacy intrudes. Then you return to the close-mouthed, deceitful ways that doomed us once before. Will you ever be free of that? Ever reach a time when your first impulse is not to conceal what you know?"

Her words struck me like arrows, and I shuddered with their impact. "I'm sorry," I said, and hated the words. Truly I regretted that I had hidden information from her and wondered, as she did, why I always fell prey to the drive to keep knowledge to myself. There echoed through me a warning I had received long ago, from Chade. The old man had cautioned me that I could wear out the words "I'm sorry," could apologize so often that it meant nothing to anyone, not even myself. I wondered if I had reached that point with Molly. "Molly," I began.

"Fitz," she said firmly. "Just stop."

I fell silent. She gathered our baby closer to her. "Listen to me. I share your worries. This is not a time for us to be at odds. Later, we will speak of it. After Kettricken has left. But not before then, and certainly not in front of Nettle. If the old queen comes to look at our child, then we must be ready to face that together. And insist to her that we will know what is best for Bee as she grows."

I knew her anger was not vanquished but restrained. And I knew that I deserved it. "Thank you," I said quietly, and that lit the sparks again in her eyes. Then, almost sadly, she shook her head and smiled at me. "They took that piece of you away from me, long before I even claimed you as my own. Not your fault, Fitz. Not your fault. Though sometimes I think that you could take it back, if you tried hard enough." She settled our baby against her shoulder and then looked at me as if she had banished anger to the Out Islands.

The rest of that day, Nettle had the staff in an uproar. Only Revel seemed to delight in the challenge of entertaining royalty at a moment's notice. No less than eight times he came to consult with me on menus and bedchambers. When he appeared at my door again, to ask if he might hire some musicians from Withy for evening entertainment, I heartlessly referred him to Nettle.

But the end result was that we had one quiet evening as a family, a time for all three adults to share a meal and stay up late talking. Between Nettle and Revel, everything that could be arranged or planned had been done. When evening deepened, we gathered in the nursery and had our food brought to us there. We ate and talked, and ate and talked. Nettle held the baby and studied Bee's face as she stared past her shoulder.

Nettle gave us news from Buckkeep, but Molly was most hungry to hear of her boys. Nettle gave us fresh news of her brothers. Steady had been not at Buckkeep but visiting Hearth. She had sent him word. Swift was traveling with Web; she'd sent a message but had no idea when it would find them. Chivalry was prospering. He'd built on the fine foundation of horseflesh that Burrich had left to him. Recently he had acquired the holding next to his, increasing his pasture and giving himself room to build a larger stable. And so on, naming each brother, all scattered across the Six Duchies now. Molly listened and rocked Bee as she held her close. I watched her and thought I guessed her heart: This was her last child, the one who would be at her side as she grew old. I watched Nettle's gaze travel from me to her mother and then to Bee. Pity, I read in her face. Pity for all of us, for in her estimation, Bee would either die soon or live the life of a stunted thing, limited in both mind and body. She did not speak the thought aloud but Burrich had raised her well, to look at a young thing and judge its chances. Still, I thought to myself, I had the advantage of experience. Bee might well and truly be a runt but she had the spark to survive. She would live. What sort of a life, none could yet tell, but Bee would live.

In the morning a herald arrived to announce that Kettricken would soon be there. By the time the old queen arrived that afternoon, the guest rooms were ready, a simple meal of good food was simmering and baking, and Bee was freshly attired in garments hastily taken in to fit her. Nettle came herself to tell Molly and me of the arrival of Kettricken and her guard. She found us in the nursery. Molly had dressed Bee twice, and changed her own garments three times. Each time, I had assured her that she looked lovely to me, but she had decided that the first dress was too youthful, and the second "made me look like a doddering granny." The third try was something I had never seen her wear before. She wore long loose trousers, so full that they appeared at first to be a skirt. A garment like a knee-length vest was worn over a loose-sleeved white blouse; a wide belt sashed her waist. The vest, trousers, and sash were all in different shades of blue, and Molly netted her hair back into a sack made of blue ribbons. "How do I look?" she asked me when she returned to the nursery, and I was not sure what to reply.

"I like the slippers," I said cautiously. They were red, with black bead embroidery and very pointed toes.

Molly laughed. "Nettle brought these clothes for me. It's a Jamaillian style, now favored at Buckkeep." She turned slowly, inviting me to admire the garments. "It's very comfortable. Nettle begged me to wear it, so I would not look too provincial. And you know, Fitz, I think I shall."

I myself wore a simple jerkin of brown over a shirt of Buckkeep blue, brown trousers, and black knee-boots. The fox pin that Kettricken had given me still sparkled at my collar. For a moment I wondered if I looked provincial, then decided I did not care.

Nettle came into the room, smiled, and lifted her brows at her mother, well pleased with her appearance. She was similarly garbed in rich browns and amber yellow. Then she glanced down into Bee's cradle and visibly startled. Blunt as she ever was, she said, "Even though the other clothes were too big, they made her look larger. Mother, she is so tiny, she's almost . . . grotesque." Despite her words, she picked up her sister and held Bee in her arms, looking into her face. The baby gazed past her shoulder. Yet as Nettle studied her, Bee suddenly began to toss her little hands. Then her mouth opened wide, she drew a deep breath, and she began a shrill wail of protest.

At her first wail, Molly went to take her. "What's wrong, my little Bee? What's wrong?" The moment Molly took her from Nettle, the child went limp in her hands and her wailing became a snuffling sobbing. Molly held her and patted her and she quickly quieted. She looked at Nettle apologetically. "Don't be hurt. She does the same thing to her father. I think she's just old enough to realize I'm her mother and to think that I should always be holding her."

I gave Nettle a small, rueful smile. "I'm almost relieved. I was beginning to think it was just me she disliked."

Molly and Nettle shot me twin looks of outrage. "Bee does not dislike Nettle!" Molly insisted. "She just . . ." Her words dwindled away and her eyes widened slightly. Then, as direct as Nettle herself, she looked at her elder daughter and asked, "Did you do something to her? With your mind?"

"I . . . no! Well, not intentionally. Sometimes . . ." She let her words trail off. "It's hard to explain to someone who doesn't have it. I touch people when I'm close to them. Not always on purpose. It's like . . ." She groped for a comparison. "Like smelling someone. Even if it might seem rude, I can't really help it. I've become aware of people in that way."

Molly weighed her words as she began the slow shifting of her weight from foot to foot that she always affected when she held the child. "Then your sister is Skilled? As you are?"

Nettle laughed and shook her head. "I couldn't tell something like that just from holding her. Besides, she's a baby." Her words trailed off slightly as she reflected on her own talent for Skill and how early it had wakened in her. She glanced over at me, and I felt her send a seeking tendril of Skill toward the baby. I caught my breath. Should I stop her? I watched as Bee curled more tightly against her mother and buried her face in Molly's neck. Did she sense her sister reaching for her? I watched Nettle's face. Puzzlement and then resignation. She didn't sense any Skill in the baby.

My curiosity piqued, I sent a thread of Skill toward Bee, moving with utmost caution, but all I found was Molly. She had no Skill at all, but reaching toward her filled my senses with her. I found myself smiling fondly at her.

Then Nettle cleared her throat and I became aware of the room and my daughters and wife again. Molly drew a deeper breath and squared her shoulders. "Well. I will go to meet Kettricken and welcome her. Do you think I should bring Bee with me?"

Nettle shook her head hastily. "No. No, I think it is best that you choose the moment for the Mountain Queen to meet her, and that it be private at first. Can her wet nurse stay with her while we—" And then her voice ran down. She laughed. "I've been too long at court, haven't I? A whole day here and of course I've seen no one tend her except you. Does she have a wet nurse? Or a nurse or a caretaker of any kind?"

Molly made an amused sound in her throat and shook her head. "No more than you had," she replied.

"Could you ask one of the kitchen girls? Or one of the maids?" Nettle was well aware that her mother kept no personal servant. "I'd never have enough tasks to keep her busy," she had always told her daughter.

Molly shook her head. "They are busy with their proper tasks. No. She will be fine here in her nursery. She's a placid child." She returned Bee to her cradle and covered her warmly.

"It feels odd to leave her here alone," Nettle objected uncomfortably as Molly drew a lacy covering over the cradle.

"Not really," Molly replied calmly. She moved about the room, letting down layer after layer of curtains. It became twilight, the warm firelight the only illumination. And as she turned to look at her elder daughter, she sighed and said, "You *have* been too long at court. You should find a way to have time to yourself. Come here, or go visit one of your brothers. Get away from the suspicions and that careful dance you always seem to be treading. Look. She's already dozing off. She'll be fine here."

"I'm certain she'll be fine here alone, Nettle," I lied agreeably. I ventured closer and looked down into the cradle. Bee's eyes were almost completely closed.

"Come," Molly said, taking my hand. "We'd best go meet the queen." I let her lead me from the room.

Steward Revel did a far better job of being the lord of the manor than I could ever attempt. We did not go to the entrance hall, where I was sure he was sorting our guests into levels of importance. The guards and lesser servants would be bustled off to simple but clean rooms and offered an immediate opportunity either to visit the Withywoods steams or to warm their faces and hands with hot water before descending to a casual and hearty meal of soups, bread, butter, cheese, ale, and wine. Revel had nothing but sympathy for frequently hard-used servants. While they visited Withywoods, they would be treated as the guests of our own servants. I was sure they would welcome his hospitality after the morning's chilly ride through the freshly fallen snow.

With the expertise of a general marshaling his troops, he had recruited temporary help from the village. Any lesser nobility would be entrusted to these willing but less experienced hands as luggage was carried to rooms, washwater fetched, fires built up, and any other small chores accomplished. To our experienced staff would go the honor of waiting on the highest echelon of guests, with Revel putting himself and his right hand, Dixon, at the full service of Lady Kettricken. All of these arrangements had been tediously explained to me the day before. I had nodded endlessly and authorized everything he suggested.

Molly, Nettle, and I hurried to the Great Hall where Revel had decreed we would welcome our guests. I entered to find that the room had been transformed overnight. The paneled walls gleamed with a fresh wiping of some fragrant oil, a large and welcoming fire burned in the hearth, and a long table had been brought in and decorated with vases of flowers. My ladies peremptorily stationed me there to await our refreshed guests, as they made a final dash to the kitchens to be sure all was in readiness. I waited until I could no longer hear their slippers pattering hastily down the hallway. Then I stepped out into the hall and heartlessly detained one of our temporary serving boys.

"Lad, I've forgotten something in my rooms. Just stay here for me, and if anyone arrives, assure them that Lady Molly and Nettle will both return very shortly, and that I shall be down soon."

His eyes widened. "Sir, mayn't I fetch whatever it is you've forgotten? I don't know how to talk to a queen, sir, even if she isn't the queen anymore."

I smiled ruthlessly at him. "And that, my lad, is exactly why you are the perfect person for this task. If you greet her with the same warmth and respect you'd accord your own grandmother, that will be more than sufficient."

"But, sir!" I didn't realize he had freckles until he went so pale they stood out on his face.

I laughed genially and pitied him in my heart. "Only a moment, only a moment." And I left him, striding off down the hall with a fine clacking of boots.

The moment I turned the corner of the corridor, I stooped, removed my boots, and then ran as light-footedly as if I were the serving boy himself. This would be the time I would choose, were it my mission. Was I being foolish? Had I, like Nettle, lived too long at Buckkeep among the multiple layers of intrigue there? There was only one way to find out. I swung the door of the nursery open just wide enough for me to enter. I slid into the room and froze beside the door. I eased it shut behind me. My Wit told me I was alone in here except for my daughter. Nonetheless, no board shifted under my tread, and my shadow never crossed the firelight as I carried my boots to the corner and concealed them there. A quick glance into the cradle as I passed it. She was there, but I did not think she was asleep. *Quiet,* I begged her. *Stay quiet.* I ghosted into the most shadowy corner behind the two pansy screens and composed myself, setting my feet and finding my balance. Not a sigh of breath, not a shift of weight on the old floor timbers. I raised all my walls, blocking my Skill and my Wit into my own mind. I became an empty place in the darkness.

The fire spat sap. A log settled with a soft *thud.* Outside, wind-driven snowflakes kissed the glass panes of the window. I could not hear my own breathing. I waited. I waited. I was a suspicious fool. A slave to old fears. I waited. The guests would be there. I'd be missed. Nettle and Molly would be furious with me. I waited.

The door eased open; someone weaseled inside and then pushed the door silently closed again. I couldn't see him. I smelled perfumed oil and heard the rustle of rich fabrics. Then a slight figure detached itself from the shadows and flowed toward my child's cradle. He did not touch it nor lift the veil, but leaned closer to peer at my baby.

The youngster was well dressed in a silk shirt with an embroidered vest. He wore a silver necklace and two silver rings in each ear. The perfume was his hair pomade: His black curls glistened in the firelight. He stared down at Bee. I imagined her looking up at him, wondering if he meant her harm. He was completely absorbed in his scrutiny of her. I moved. When he lifted his hand to move the lace that veiled her, my shining blade swooped in on his throat. I pressed the flat of it hard against his flesh.

"Step back," I advised him softly, "and I'll let you live. At least for a little while."

The boy's intake of breath sounded like a sob. He held his hands open and pleading before him as the pressure of my slender knife moved him away from the cradle. I guided him backward. One step, two, three. His voice shook as he said, "Lord Chade said you would catch me. But Lady Rosemary insisted on sending me."

I cocked my head like a listening wolf, trying to decide if I heard truth. "An interesting gambit. Those names could be seen as chinks in my armor. Another man might laugh and release you, send you back to your masters with a warning that you need more training."

"I've only been with them three months." There was relief in his voice.

"I said, 'another man,'" I reminded him in a deadly voice. "Not me." I put myself between the assassin and my baby's cradle. "Strip," I ordered him. "Down to skin. Now."

"I—" The boy choked. His eyes flew wide open and he all but crossed his arms over himself. His voice went a notch higher. "Sir! This is unbecoming of you. No. I will not."

"You will," I informed him. "For I won't be satisfied until you do. And I have no reason not to raise an alarm and then take affront at your being here. The Farseer throne sends an assassin-spy not only into my house, but into my child's room? Tell me, boy, what do I have to lose? And what will Lady Kettricken have to do to erase this embarrassment? Will Lord Chade and Lady Rosemary admit you are theirs? Or did they warn you that they would distance themselves if you were caught?"

The youngster was breathing raggedly. His hands were shaking, I was certain, and he struggled with an endless row of tiny pearl buttons. Pearls! On their newest assassin! What was Chade thinking these days? If he had not been in my child's room, I might have found such foolishness amusing. But nothing was humorous in this attempt. My blood moved cold in my veins.

I heard the rustle of silk and then a soft thud as he dropped his shirt to the floor. "An interesting sound for a shirt to make as it falls," I observed. "The rest, please. Without delay. I'm sure we would both like to have this over with as soon as possible." He had to bend down to peel his trousers and stockings off. A trick of the firelight caught the gleam of tears on his cheeks. Better his tears than Molly's or mine, I thought. "To the skin," I reminded him, and his smallclothes joined the heap on the floor. A short time later, I added, "You look chilly. Go stand by the fire. And don't move."

The lad followed my instructions with alacrity. He turned his back to me, and then twisted around to watch me. He was hugging himself despite the fire behind him while I systematically went through his garments. Tiny pocket seams gave way with small ripping sounds. My blade made a *shush* as it slid though fine silk. I was proud of that. It takes a sharp blade to part silk. Then I was finished.

"Only seven?" I asked him. I lifted my eyes to watch him as I let my hands check each garment and boot again. I set my plunder out in a short row on the floor before me. "Let's see. Two poisons to mix with liquid, one toxic dust, a sleeping powder, and an emetic. So much for the hidden pockets. A tiny shoe-knife, scarcely worthy of the name, a set of lock picks, and a block of soft wax . . . for what? Ah, impressions of keys. Of course. Now, what's this?"

"That is what I was to leave in her crib." His voice was stiff, thickened with tears. "For you to find. As a proof that I'd been here."

Ice encased my heart. I gestured at the assassin with my knife, ordering him farther away from the cradle. I moved with him, keeping the same distance. Whatever was in the packet, I would not chance opening it near Bee. I brought it to a small table touched by firelight.

It was a little packet of good paper. I sliced the side carefully with my blade, then tipped it. A very fine chain slid out of it first. I tapped it and the rest emerged. "A very pretty necklace. And expensive, I'd hazard." I held up the chain. Firelight glinted red from it. "It's the Farseer buck, in silver. But he has his head lowered to charge. Interesting." I watched the boy's face as it dangled from my hand. Did he know what it was? The sigil of FitzChivalry Farseer, the long-dead bastard of the royal family.

He didn't. "It's a gift for her. From Lord Chade Fallstar."

"Of course it is." My voice was flat. I returned to his garments, hooked my toe under the heap, and kicked them to him. "You can get dressed."

"And my things?" the youngster asked sullenly. He spoke over his shoulder as he tugged on his underthings. I stooped to the floor, and the tools of his trade disappeared up my sleeve. I heard the rustle of fabric as he pulled on his shirt and trousers.

"What things?" I asked pleasantly. "Your boots and stockings? There on the floor. Put them on. Then get out of this room. And stay out of this wing of my home. Or I'll kill you."

"I wasn't sent to do the baby harm. Only to see it, to leave the gift, and to report back what I'd seen. Lord Chade warned her that you'd catch me but Lady Rosemary insisted. It was a test. One I've failed."

"Failed twice, I assume. I doubt they gave you permission to name their names to anyone."

The boy was quiet. "They said it was just a test." His voice broke on the words. "And I've failed it. Twice."

"You're assuming that *you* were the one they were testing. Dressed? Good. Get out. No. Wait. What's your name?"

He held his tongue. I sighed and took a step toward him.

"Lant."

I waited.

The boy took a breath that was half a sob. "FitzVigilant."

I pondered a moment, sifting names of minor nobility. "Of Farrow?"

"Yes, sir."

"And how old are you?"

The boy drew himself up straighter. "Twelve, sir."

"Twelve? Eleven, I might have believed. But ten is more likely, isn't it?"

The lad's dark eyes flashed fury. The tears were running freely down his cheeks. *Oh, Chade. Is this your future assassin?* He looked down and said simply, "Sir."

I sighed. Had I ever been that young? "Go, boy. Now."

The spy fled with no pretense at stealth. He did not quite slam the door behind him, but he shut it quite firmly. I listened to the sound of his pattering steps as he fled. When they became softer, I stepped to the door, listened, opened it, and stepped out. Then I closed the door again, retrieved my boots, and came to Bee's cradle. "For now, he's gone," I told my child and shook my head. "Chade, you old spider, what are you playing at? Was that truly the best you could send my way? Or was he the decoy?"

I moved efficiently about the room, checking the window latch and looking everywhere an assassin might conceivably hide. When I had made that round, I returned to the cradle and lifted the lacy drapery away. I found a lamp, lit it, and moved it to the stand by the cradle. I worked as if my staring baby were made of spun sugar as I lifted each blanket away and carefully shook it. Her garments looked untouched. Would I chance that? I had begun removing her clothing to check for anything that this spy or a previous one might have been able to put on her when Molly entered the room.

"There you are! I've half a dozen serving boys scouring Withywoods for you. Our guests are waiting to go in for a meal. You've missed their minstrel singing a very long song to thank us for our welcome."

"Glad of that," I admitted. The tiny ribbons on Bee's gown were defying me.

"Fitz?" Molly swept into the room. "What are you doing? Didn't you hear me? The meal is nearly ready."

I lied to her. Again. "I came in to be sure she was fine and she was crying. I thought she might be wet."

"Crying? And I didn't hear her?"

"It wasn't loud. I wouldn't have heard her except that I was passing the door."

Molly immediately took charge of her. I clenched my teeth, fearing that there might still be something hidden in her garments that could hurt either her or her mother. Molly expertly opened her clothes, checked her napkin, and then looked at me in consternation. "She's fine." I watched intently as Molly refastened the ribbon ties I had loosened.

"I don't want to leave her here alone," I said abruptly.

Molly stared at me. Then she shook her head. "Nor I," she admitted. "But I didn't want to take her with us to greet our guests. I want to choose when and how Queen Kettricken first sees her."

"Lady Kettricken," I reminded her. "Queen of the Six Duchies no more."

"Only in name," my wife harrumphed. "The Narcheska is in Buckkeep Castle only a few months of every year. And King Dutiful spends too much time away from the throne. She rules the Six Duchies, Fitz, and the Mountain Kingdom."

"Well. Someone must hold the reins of power when King Dutiful is not there. Better Kettricken than Chade unchecked," I replied. Could she hear the divided loyalties in my voice? Hear my unspoken thought that if Kettricken had not assumed those duties, they might have fallen on me? Certainly Chade had hoped to harness me for that role, and Kettricken and King Dutiful would have been happy to allow it. I had known Kettricken since I was a youth, and once we had been as close as only conspirators could be. But tonight she had brought a spy into my house, one that had come in stealth to my daughter's cradle. Did she know of young FitzVigilant's mission? Or had Chade and Lady Rosemary acted alone, out of concern for the Farseer throne and lineage? Well did I know that to Chade, the best interests of the throne came far ahead of the best interests of any individual Farseer. That I had learned at the old assassin's knee.

Molly broke into my thoughts. "Nettle will be leading our guests into the dining room soon. We have to be there."

I made a decision. "Let's take her with us. Cradle and all."

"Fitz, I don't think . . ."

But I had already stooped and lifted the cradle. It was not large, but neither was it light. I tried to make it look easy as I edged out the door with it and started down the hall. Behind me, Molly followed with Bee clasped to her breast.

The dining hall was not often used. The ceilings were high, and the two hearths at either end of the room struggled to warm such a large space. Molly and I had formed the habit of taking most of our meals in a much smaller room, but tonight the fires had been set and the chandeliers lit. The long table, prepared for fifteen, could easily have seated forty. The dark wooden table had an embroidered runner down the center, and silver candelabra holding graceful white tapers, the work of Molly's own hands. Carved wooden bowls in the shape of Eda's cupped hands held red and yellow apples, fat grapes in bunches, and gleaming brown nuts. The candles cast a warm glow over the table, but their light could not reach the distant ceiling or the far corners of the room.

We arrived simultaneously with the guests. Molly and I stood and greeted them as they filed past. I put more effort into making holding the cradle look effortless, and was grateful finally to follow them into the room. I made no comment as I set the cradle where the hearth would warm it but it would not be more than six paces from my chair. Molly swiftly settled Bee inside it and then draped the lace hanger above her that would keep away drafts and casual glances. We moved to the head of the table, once more acknowledged our guests, and took our places.

Lady Kettricken was to my right. Nettle occupied the other seat of honor at Molly's left hand. If any thought the seating arrangement odd, no one spoke of it. I located the young spy seated on the left side of the table and as far from me as possible. He had changed his garments, which was not surprising, as I had not been excessively careful when I was slitting open seams and pockets. He appeared fascinated by the edge of the table. The captain of Kettricken's guard had accompanied her on this visit and he was seated with us, attired in his purple and white. She had brought a healer with her, one of noble blood, Lady Solace, and her husband, Lord Diggery. Kettricken's other followers were unknown to me except by name. Lord Stoutheart was a bluff and hearty man, white-haired and red-nosed. Lady Hope was plump and pleasant, a chatty woman who laughed frequently.

Kettricken lifted her hand and set it on mine. I turned to her with a smile, and as always I knew that brief moment of surprise. To me she was always a young woman, golden-haired and blue-eyed, with an open mien and a tranquil air about her. I saw a woman with silver hair, her brow lined with care. Her eyes were as blue as Bee's. Her spine was straight, her head upright. She was like a graceful glass vessel that brimmed with power and certainty. She was no longer the foreign Mountain Princess struggling to negotiate the currents of power at a strange court. She had become the current of power that others must navigate. She spoke for Molly and me alone. "I am so glad for you."

I nodded, and gestured to Revel to begin serving. I made no comment on Bee or how we had brought her into the dining room. Kettricken understood and did not broach the topic. The meal commenced. It was served with considerably less formality than a dinner at Buckkeep Castle, yet more pomp than we usually observed at Withywoods. Nettle had instructed Revel to keep the visit simple, and though he had chafed at this, he had almost complied. So dishes were passed and I served the wine, and the conversation was casual and sometimes merry. We learned that Lady Solace often traveled with Kettricken now, for the old queen had begun to have problems with her joints. At the end of the day she welcomed her handmaid's oil rubs as well as the hot drinks she concocted. Lord Stoutheart and Lady Hope had joined them simply because they were bound for their own homes for the winter after a pleasant visit at Buckkeep Castle. Withywoods was on the route that they must travel. Indeed, the bulk of the servants and guards accompanying Kettricken were not her own people but Lord Stoutheart's.

The smells of the food and the pleasant clatter of eating might have lulled another man. I took this time as my opportunity to study my guests. I considered Lady Solace's presence as genuinely the product of Kettricken's wish, but reserved judgment on Lord Stoutheart and Lady Hope. I wondered if the youthful assassin had come as part of Kettricken's retinue. If he had, did Kettricken know the full of what he was or had the royal assassins added him as an anonymous member of her party? Perhaps he had been slipped in by Lady Rosemary as a stable boy for the traveling party. I had often served in that capacity when Chade wanted eyes or ears somewhere he himself could not go. Yet the lad had been well dressed, not in a stable hand's leathers but in silk and linen. I watched Lant as he picked at his food and wondered again if he was a lure to distract me. I was glad we had not left Bee alone in the room, and decided I would inspect the entire nursery before I put her to bed there tonight. No, I abruptly decided. I would put the cradle by my bed and watch over Bee myself.

The relief I felt at that decision was palpable. I found my tongue and became more talkative and jocular, and Molly, Nettle, and Kettricken all smiled to see me so. The conversation was lively, ranging from the late apple crop, to the hunting prospects near Withywoods and Buckkeep Castle, to news of old friends who lived in the Mountain Kingdom. Kettricken asked after Molly's children, and relayed the latest news from the princes. The minstrel and his two assistants arrived, with their small drums and pipes, and added music to our enjoyment. The meal lasted long and the hour was late when the last dish was finally cleared from the table.

"Shall we move to a cozier room?" Molly suggested, for the large dining hall was inevitably drafty and cool on a stormy night.

"Let's," I agreed, and Kettricken replied, "A warmer room will be a pleasanter place for me to meet your little daughter."

She did not ask, she assumed. I smiled at that. We were old partners at this sort of gaming. She had recognized my gambit, respected it, and now advanced her own. Nonetheless, I resolved that I would win this round against her for Bee as I had not won for Nettle. As Molly and I and our guests rose, I smiled but did not verbally respond to Kettricken's words. I reached the cradle quickly and held the gauzy drapery aside to allow Molly to gather Bee up. She draped a blanket around the baby as she did so, and then waited confidently for me to once more lift the cradle. I managed it without a groan. A quick glance told me that Nettle had detained the former queen with some minor conversation, and that she then motioned for her to precede her out of the room. Molly and I came last, following our guests as Nettle led the way to a sitting room.

A stranger might have assumed this room was my den. In addition to comfortable seating and a roaring fire in the hearth, the walls were lined with shelves and held many books bound in the Jamaillian style. Above them, on racks, were older scrolls and vellums. There was a desk in the corner near the heavily draped window, and on it was an inkpot and blank paper. It was all for show. On these shelves a spy might find a journal of the birds I had seen in the last four years, or notes on the operation of Withywoods. There were enough estate records and papers in this room to make at least a casual thief believe he had found my lair. But he would find no sign here of FitzChivalry Farseer or of the work I did for Chade.

Once again the cradle was carefully placed but as Molly moved to install Bee in it, Kettricken swept past Nettle to her side. "May I hold her?" she asked, and there was such simple warmth in her request that no one could have refused it. Perhaps only I saw how Molly's smile stiffened as she offered our bundled child to the former queen. As she took Bee into her arms, blanket and all, Kettricken's brows lifted in subtle surprise. Nettle moved closer; I felt my older daughter's Skill thrumming wariness. I think it was a pack instinct to protect the smallest that operated on a level so profoundly deep she was scarcely aware of how she joined her Skill to mine. The moment could not be avoided. Molly lifted the light covering that had hidden our baby's face.

I watched Kettricken's expression as she looked down into Bee's answering stare. For the baby was silent but awake, meeting her gaze with eyes as blue as her own. Kettricken gave so tiny a gasp that perhaps no one else remarked it. Her smile did not fade, but it grew stiffer. She took two steps to a chair and sank into it. Then, as if determined to prove something to herself, she loosened the blanket that wrapped Bee.

My daughter was dressed in a confection of silk and lace such as none of Molly's other children had ever worn. Even taken in to fit our tiny babe—for Molly had sewn it months before the birth—it only emphasized how tiny she was. Bee's hands were curled onto her chest, and Kettricken stared at the fingers as small as a bird's toes. As if daring herself, she touched Bee's left hand with her forefinger.

The other guests had drawn closer, expecting that they, too, would be allowed to see her. Kettricken glanced up, not at me, but at Lady Solace, her healer. The woman had moved to the old queen's shoulder to look at the child, and now as her gaze met Kettricken's I knew what her resigned countenance conveyed. I had seen it in the eyes of our household women. In her healer's opinion, Bee was not a child who would remain long in this world. Whatever Kettricken thought of her pale hair and blue eyes, she said nothing of it. The old queen gently folded the blankets around her and covered her face again. The action chilled me, for her fingers were as gentle as if she were shrouding a dead child. "She's so tiny," she said as she offered Bee back to her mother. She offered sympathy. Somehow her words conveyed that she understood why Bee had not been announced to a world where she would stay only briefly.

As I watched Molly's arms enfold her, I sensed her relief to have Bee safely back in her embrace. Molly's back was straight as a guardsman's, her eyes calm, and her voice level as she added, "But perfect."

"And she's growing every day," I lied heartily.

Silence followed my words and I wished I could call them back. Every woman worked out their import in her own mind, but only the healer spoke. "How tiny was she when she was born? Did she come early?" The room stilled, awaiting a response.

But Molly only gathered Bee to her and walked over to stand by the fireplace. She rocked and patted her as she stood silently, and as if rebuked the guests receded to take chairs. Even Kettricken found a comfortable seat; only Lady Solace remained standing. She studied Molly and suddenly observed, "You seem to have recovered very swiftly from your confinement, Lady Molly." An unspoken question. *Is the baby truly yours?*

"I had an easy time of it," Molly replied modestly, and glanced aside from the men present in the room. I could feel how avid Lady Solace was to ask more questions; she had the healer's drive to know every root of a problem and then apply her skills to solving it. Molly sensed that, too, and it made her uneasy. When she looked at our child, she saw nothing amiss, save that Bee was much smaller than all her other babies had been. But in the healer's inquisitive glance, Molly read that the woman saw Bee as damaged or sickly. Were she given over into that woman's care, she would attempt to fix our babe as if Bee were a broken toy. I felt a rush of antipathy toward the woman; how dare she see my Bee as less than perfect! And beneath that, a cold river of trepidation that she might, somehow, be right. The urge to get her safely away from the healer's anxious eyes raced through me. I did not wish to hear anything the woman might say about Bee. My glance met Molly's. She held our baby closer and then smiled.

"You are so kind to be concerned for me. It is so thoughtful of you, for of course I do tire easily. It is not easy to be a new mother at my age." Molly smiled round at her guests. "Thank you kindly for understanding that my daughter will take up my duties as hostess, for I know you will understand my need to retire early. But please, do not feel you must emulate me. I know that my husband has longed for company, and seldom gets a chance to spend hours in conversation with old friends. I shall trouble him only to move Bee's cradle for me, and then I shall send him right back to you."

I hoped I covered my surprise. It was not just that she had made such a sudden decision, but the imperious way in which Molly informed all gathered that she had done so. I had a glimpse of Nettle's face; she was already calculating how to repair the social damage. In the set of her mouth I saw two things: She shared her mother's fear that Lady Solace might find something wrong with Bee, and shared her cold tide of certainty that the healer would be right.

But I had a cradle to lift. Again. And a long flight of stairs before me. I stitched a smile to my face and took up my load. Our guests treated us to a chorus of swift good nights. Molly preceded me and I came behind, my pride creaking as much as my back. As soon as the door closed behind us, Molly whispered, "She sleeps in our room tonight, by my bedside."

"My thoughts exactly."

"I don't like how that woman looked at Bee."

"Lady Solace?"

Molly was silent, seething now. She knew I wanted to be assured that she had taken no offense at Kettricken's comment, but she would not give me that. She had been offended by Lady Solace, and as Kettricken had brought her into our home, she extended her affront to the former queen. She knew it divided my loyalty, but offered me no relief. She walked briskly down the hall and then up the wide steps to our bedchamber on the next floor. I followed her more slowly, the cradle weighing more with every step. By the time I set it down in our bedchamber, Molly had settled Bee in the center of our bed, and I knew she would sleep between us. Ah, just as well. I moved swiftly around the room, pretending to close the hangings tighter and build the fire higher, but actually checking alcoves and draperies for intruders. I kept my peace while she freed Bee of her finery and clothed her in a soft little nightshirt. It dwarfed her. As Molly folded the excess length around her feet, I asked her quietly, "You'll be all right here if I go back down to our guests?"

"I'm latching the door behind you," she told me.

I met her gaze. My mate's stare assured me that our cub would be safe with her. "That would be wise," I agreed. "I'll knock and speak through the door when I come up to bed."

"Well. That's reassuring," she said quietly, and then, despite ourselves, we both laughed.

"I'm sure I'm being silly to worry so," I lied to her.

"I'm sure you're being silly to think I'd believe you," she responded, and followed me to the door. After it closed behind me, I heard Molly struggle a moment with a stiff, seldom-used bolt. Then I heard it slide home, metal against metal. It was a good sound.

Kettricken and her companions stayed only a night. We did not bring Bee in to breakfast the next morning, and no one asked to see her. The minstrel was never summoned to look on her, in public or in private. Kettricken never mentioned that Bee should be documented as the true child of FitzChivalry Farseer. She was never entered into the formal lineage of possible heirs to the throne. Her life would not be like her sister's; that was clear enough. Kettricken had evaluated my child and found her wanting. I could not decide if I felt angered by her dismissal of Bee or deeply grateful.

For there was another side to that coin. If Kettricken had acknowledged my child, even privately, it would have been a veil of protection around her. That she had not claimed Bee as part of the Farseer dynasty put her outside the circle and left her as I had been left for so many years: a Farseer who was both an asset and a liability to the throne.

Kettricken announced that she must leave shortly after noon, and that her friends were also traveling on to their home. The looks she gave me were deeply sympathetic. I think she assumed Molly and I wished to be left in privacy with our dwindling baby, to have what time we could with her before she was gone. It would have been a kind gesture, if Bee were truly failing. As it was, it was hard to bid her a fond farewell, for her departure almost seemed as if she were wishing a swift death on my daughter.

Nettle stayed on for a week. She saw Bee daily, and I think she slowly realized that although Bee was not thriving and growing, neither was she dwindling. She stayed as she was, eating and drinking, her blue eyes taking in everything, her Wit-spark strong in my awareness. At last, Nettle announced she must return to Buckkeep and her duties there. Before she left, she found a quiet moment to berate me for not telling her sooner of Bee's birth, and to plead that if there was any change in the health of the child or Molly, I Skill to her immediately. I promised her that without difficulty.

I did not Skill to Chade about his failed spy. I needed time to think. Bee was safe. Jest or test or threat, whatever it was, it was over. I had seen little of young Lant during Kettricken's stay, but I did stand outside to be sure he was with her when she rode away. In the days that followed, I heard nothing from Chade about him.

In the weeks that followed, Molly's sons came and went in ones and twos, some with wife and children, others alone. They inspected Bee with the fond and accepting equanimity of much older siblings. There she was, another baby, very small, but their mother seemed happy and Tom Badgerlock seemed content with his lot, so there was nothing for them to fret about here, and a great deal to worry about at their respective homes. The house seemed to grow quieter after the company had left, as if winter had truly settled into the bones of the land.

I enjoyed my lady wife and my child.

And I pondered my next move.

Chapter 8

THE SPIDER'S LAIR

And so, as I always have, I turn to you for counsel. Fool that you are, you always gave me the wisest advice. Even as I know how impossible it is, I yearn once more to sit down and take thought with you. You always had the mind to look at the tangled knot of court politics and tell me where each thread was wound and trapped, to trace each strand in the hangman's noose back to its instigator. I miss your insights sorely, as much as I miss your companionship. No warrior you, and yet, with you at my back, I felt guarded as with no other.

But I will also admit that you have wounded me as few others could. You wrote to Jofron? But not to me? If there had been but one note from you, in all these years, at least I would have a place to send these useless musings. By messenger or bird, I could send them on their way to you and imagine that in some distant time or place, they reached you, and you spared a thought for me. You know my nature. I take the bits and clues and puzzle them into an image in *which you deliberately do not write to me, so that I cannot reach out to you in any way. Why? What can I think except that you fear I will somehow undo your work? From that foundation, I must wonder if that was always what I was to you. Only the Catalyst? The weapon that must be wielded without mercy, and then set aside, lest somehow it do an injury to you or your work?*

I need a friend, and I have none to whom I can admit my weakness, my fear, my errors. I have Molly's love and Bee's need for my strength. I dare not admit to either of them that my heart breaks to see Bee remain a passive infant. As my dreams for her evaporate and I fear a future in which she remains forever infantile and stunted, to whom can I confide my pain? To Molly, who dotes on her and fiercely insists that time will give her what she lacks? She does not seem to recognize that our child appears less intelligent than a two-day-old chick. Fool, my child will not meet my eyes. When I touch her, she draws away from me as much as she can. Which is not far, for she does not roll herself over, nor lift her head at all. She makes not a sound, save when she wails. Even that is not often. She does not reach for her mother's finger. She is passive, Fool, more plant than child, and my heart breaks daily over her. I want to love her, and instead I find I have lost my heart to the child that is not here, the child I imagined she would be. And so I look at my Bee and long for her to be that which she is not. Which, perhaps, she never shall be.

Ah, I do not know what comfort anyone could offer me, save to let me say these things aloud and not recoil in horror from my heartlessness.

Instead I write these words and consign them to the flames or the litter of other useless musings that nightly I obsessively write.

I waited four months before I went to Buckkeep Castle to confront Chade and Lady Rosemary.

During those days the household was quiet, but busy in the routine way that life was always busy. My baby daughter nursed well and slept as little as any newborn did, according to Molly, which seemed an impossibly small amount to me. Yet she did not disturb our nights with crying. Instead she lay still and silent, eyes open and staring into the corner of the darkened room. She slept still sheltered between Molly and me, and all hours of the day she was in her mother's care.

Bee grew, but so slowly. She remained healthy, but Molly confided to me that she did not do what other babes of her age could do. At first I ignored this worrying. Bee was small but perfect in my eyes. When I looked down on her in her crib, she stared at the ceiling with a blue gaze that pierced my heart with love. "Give her time," I told Molly. "She'll get there. I've fed up many a weakling, and seen them become the sharpest hounds in the pack. She'll do."

"She isn't a puppy!" Molly rebuked me, but she smiled and added, "She was long in the womb, and emerged small. Perhaps it will take her more time to grow outside me as well."

I do not think she believed my words, but she took comfort all the same. As the days passed, however, I could not ignore that my baby was not changing. At a month, she was little bigger than when she had been born. At first the maids would remark on what a "good baby" she was, so calm and placid. But soon they stopped saying such things, and pity grew in their faces. The fear rose in me that our child was an idiot. She had none of the features of a half-wit child that all parents know. Her tongue fit her mouth, her eyes and ears were proportional to her little face. She was as pretty as a doll, and as small and unresponsive.

I did not face it, then.

Instead I focused on the spy that Chade had sent into my home. In quiet, my anger grew. Perhaps I fed it with the fear and dread that I did not admit to myself. I thought long about it. I did not want to confront Chade by way of the Skill. I told myself that I needed to stand before him and make him recognize that I was not a man to be toyed with, not when it concerned my child.

At the end of four months, satisfied that all had remained quiet at home, I invented an excuse to visit Brushbanks. My tale was that I wished to look at a stud horse I'd heard was there. I promised Molly to return as soon as I possibly could, packed warmly for a chilly journey, and chose an unremarkable chestnut mare named

Sally from the stable. She was a rangy mount with an easy gait that ate up the miles and no ambition to challenge her rider. I thought her the perfect mount for my journey to Buckkeep Town.

I could have used the standing stones to make the journey, but I would have had to stable the horse somewhere. I told myself I did not wish to invite curiosity, and while my business with Chade was urgent, it was not an emergency. And I could admit to myself that I was afraid to do so. Since I had used the stones to travel to Chade's sickbed, I had felt drawn to repeat the experiment. Had I been younger and less experienced with the Skill, I would have put it down to curiosity and a desire for knowledge. But I had felt that yearning before: It was the Skill-hunger, an urge to use the magic simply for the sake of feeling it thrill through me. No. I would not risk a Skill-pillar journey again. Especially since I suspected Chade now monitored them and would be aware of my coming.

I intended to surprise the old spider. Let him recall how it felt to discover that someone had penetrated his defenses.

I rode from early morning to late at night, eating dried meat or oatcakes as I rode, and sleeping well off the side of the road. I had not traveled so rough in years, and my aching back each morning reminded me that even when I was a young man, it had been un-comfortable. Nonetheless, I did not stop at any inns nor pause in any of the small towns I passed. A day away from Withywoods, I had donned the humbler garb of a tradesman. I did all I could to keep anyone from remarking on the passage of a lone traveler, let alone recognizing me as Tom Badgerlock.

I timed my journey so that I arrived at Buckkeep late in the evening. I found a tidy little inn among the outskirts of Buckkeep Town and bought myself a room for the night and stabling for my horse. I ate a fine meal of roast pork, stewed dried apples, and dark bread, and went up to my room.

When night was full and dark, I left the inn quietly and took a long walk up to Buckkeep Castle. I did not go to any of the gates, but to a very secret entrance that I had discovered as Chade's ap-prentice. What had been a fault in the wall had been "repaired" to allow a covert route in and out of the keep. The masking thorn bushes around it were as thick as ever, and both my skin and my jerkin were torn before I reached the actual stone of the wall and squeezed though the deceptively narrow gap there, gaining entrance to Buckkeep.

But penetrating the outer wall was just the first step. I was inside the walls of the keep but not in the castle itself. This section of the keep's grounds was reserved for protecting stock should we ever be besieged. During the Red-Ship War some animals had always been kept here, but I doubted it had seen much use in recent times. In the darkness behind some empty sheep pens I shed my homespun blouse and loose trousers, and concealed the garments in an unused wooden trough. Beneath them I was dressed in Buckkeep blue, in my old blue Buck guardsman's uniform. It was a bit snugger about the middle than I recalled it being, and smelled of fleabane and cedar from the chest where I had stored it, but I trusted it would get me past any casual glance.

Head down and walking slowly as if I were weary or perhaps a bit drunk, I wandered across the yards and in through the kitchen door that led to the guardsmen's dining area. I felt a strange mixture of emotions at this secretive homecoming. Buckkeep Castle would always be home to me, and the kitchens especially so. So many boyhood memories surged back on the wave of aromas that welcomed me. Ale and smoked meats and fat cheeses, bread baking and hot soup bubbling and beckoning. I nearly yielded to the temptation to go in and sit down and eat. Not for hunger's sake, but just to taste again the flavors of home.

Instead I wandered down the stone-flagged corridor, past two storage rooms; just short of the steps to the cellar I entered a certain pantry. There I let my self-discipline slip and helped myself to a short rope of linked sausage before triggering the panel of shelves that accessed the castle's spy-ways. I pulled it closed behind me and stood for a moment in the utter darkness of those passages.

I ate a link of the sausage and idly wished there had been time for a tankard of Buckkeep ale to go with it. Then with a sigh I let my feet lead the way through the twisting corridors and narrow stairs that threaded the interior walls of Buckkeep Castle. This was a lab-

yrinth I had known since my childhood. The only surprises I encountered were the few spiderwebs that were a familiar hazard of
this maze.

I did not go to the secret chambers where Chade had first taught
me the assassin's trade. I knew he no longer lived and slept in that
space as he once had. Instead I wormed my way through the narrow passage behind the walls on the same level as the king's bedchamber. I swiftly gained access to Chade's grand bedchamber via
a mirrored panel in his water closet and was a bit surprised that he
had not blocked it in some way. I crept silently in, dreading that
he would be waiting for me, having somehow divined my plan, but
his room was empty and chill, the fire banked low on the hearth.
Moving swiftly, I took a gleaming brown acorn from my pocket and
left it in the center of his pillow. Then I retreated once more to the
spy-labyrinth and sought his old murder laboratory.

Ah, but how it had changed since my childhood. The floors were
swept and mopped clean of dirt and dust. The scarred stone table
where we had conducted our experiments when I was a boy was
immaculately clear of ingredients and apparatus. All was neatly
stowed on shelves. The bowls and glassware had been cleaned and
sorted by category. There was a specific place for each mortar and
pestle, and for each spoon of wood and iron and brass. There were
far fewer scroll racks than I recalled, and the ones that were there
were neatly stocked. Another rack held the tools of my erstwhile
trade. Small knives with grooved blades, some sheathed and some
bare, rested beside neatly packaged and labeled powders and pel-
lets, some soporific and some toxic. Gleaming needles of silver and
brass were safely thrust through strips of soft leather. Coiled gar-
rotes slumbered like deadly little snakes. Someone with a very me-
thodical mind was in charge of this now. Not Chade. Brilliant and
precise as the man was, he had never been tidy. Nor did I see signs
of his ongoing scholarship; no tattered old manuscripts awaited
translation or recopying. There were no scatters of spoiled pens, no
open containers of ink. A sumptuous featherbed covered the old
wooden bedstead, and the small fire in the neatly swept hearth
burned cleanly. The bed looked as if it was for show rather than

something that was regularly used. I wondered who tended these chambers now. Certainly not Thick. The simple little man was old for one of his kind, and he had never cared for his housekeeping tasks. He would not have supplied a rack of wax tapers, standing tall and straight as ranked soldiers, ready to take their places in the candleholders. I lit two to replace the ones that had almost guttered out in the brass holders on the table.

I deduced this was Lady Rosemary's domain now. I settled in her cushioned chair by the hearth after adding two logs to the fire. Little sweet biscuits in a covered bowl and a decanter of wine were on a small table close at hand. I helped myself and then kicked out my feet toward her fire and leaned back. I didn't care which of them found me here. I had words for both of them. My gaze wandered over the mantel and I almost smiled to see that King Shrewd's fruit knife was still embedded in the center of it. I wondered if Lady Rosemary knew the tale of how it had come to be there. I wondered if Chade recalled how coldly angry I had been when I drove the blade into the wood. The anger that burned in me now was colder and far more controlled. I'd have my say, and when I had finished, we would come to terms. My terms.

Chade had always been a night owl. I was resigned to a long wait before he would find my message on his pillow. The watch passed and I dozed in the chair, lightly. But when I heard the light scuff of slippers on the steps, I knew it was not his stride. I lifted my head and turned my gaze to the concealed stairway. A heavy tapestry draped it to keep out the draft from the maze. I was only mildly surprised when it lifted to reveal the countenance of young FitzVigilant. He was dressed far more simply than the last time I had seen him, in a simple white shirt, blue vest, and black trousers. His soft low shoes whispered his approach. The large silver earrings in his ear had been replaced by two much smaller ones of gold. His tousled hair hinted that perhaps he had risen from his bed to perform his duties here.

I watched him startle at the sight of the freshly lit tapers. I was very still, and it took a moment for his eyes to pick me out. Then he gaped at the sight of a humble guardsman in such a special and secret place before he recognized me. "You!" he gasped and took a step back.

"Me," I affirmed. "Well, I see they kept you on. But you've still much to learn of caution, I think." He stared at me wordlessly. "I suspect that Lady Rosemary or Lord Chade will soon be arriving, for a late-night lesson with you. Am I correct?"

He opened his mouth to speak, then clapped it shut. So. Perhaps he had learned a bit of caution since last we had met. He assayed a sideways shift toward the weapons rack. I smiled and cautioned him with a wag of my finger. Then, a flip of my wrist and a knife sprang into my hand. Some tricks one never forgets. He gaped at it and lifted wide eyes to stare at me.

It was very gratifying. I suddenly wondered if I had ever looked at Chade with such puppyish awe. I made a decision. "Neither one of us needs to be armed," I told him pleasantly. I bent my hand and the knife was gone. It was enough that he knew how quickly it could reappear. I leaned back in my chair and appeared to relax, and saw his shoulders lower in response. I sighed to myself. The lad had so much to learn.

For now, however, his naïveté served my purpose well. I looked at him for a moment, reading as much as I could of him without making my gaze into a stare. He'd have his guard up against direct questions. But he was already beginning to be uncomfortable with my silence. I sighed, letting my body appear to relax even more as I reached for the wine again. I poured another glass. He shifted his feet uncomfortably. "That's Lady Rosemary's favorite wine," he objected mildly.

"Is it? Well. She has good taste, then. And I know she wouldn't mind sharing some with me. We've known each other a long time . . . she was just a child when I first met her."

That piqued his interest. I wondered how much he had been told of me when they'd sent him on his mission to Bee's cradle. Not too much, I judged. Chade valued caution as a virtue surpassing almost all others. I smiled at him. He took my bait.

"Is that who showed you how to get here? Lady Rosemary?" Furrows appeared in his brow as he tried to piece it together and see where I belonged.

"Who are you talking to, Lant?" Lady Rosemary's voice reached us before she had entered the room. The lad spun toward her. I remained where I was, wineglass in hand.

"Oh." She halted, holding the curtain aside, and looked at me. I had told the apprentice the truth. I had known her when she was a child, though we'd had little to do with each other since then. Prince Regal had recruited her when she was a chubby little maid, even younger than FitzVigilant. Regal had arranged a position for her, serving the Mountain-born princess who had wedded King-in-Waiting Verity. She had been Regal's little spy on his brother's wife, and quite likely had been the one who greased the tower steps and caused the pregnant Kettricken to take a bad fall. That had never been proven. When Regal had tumbled from power, all of his minions had descended into disgrace as well, the child Rosemary among them.

Only Kettricken's forgiving nature had saved her. When all else shunned her, Kettricken had seen her as a confused child, torn between loyalties, and quite possibly guilty only of trying to please the man who had been so kind to her mother. Queen Kettricken had taken her back into her court and seen to her education. And Chade, never one to waste anything, had seen her as a partially trained tool for spying and assassination, and quickly made her his own.

Now she stood before me, a woman in the middle of her life, a lady of the court, and a trained assassin. We regarded each other. She knew me. I wondered if she clearly recalled how she had pretended to drowse on the steps of the queen-in-waiting's throne while I reported to Kettricken. Even after all those years, I felt both horror and resentment that a mere child had so easily deceived me. She stepped into the room, lowered her eyes before my gaze, and then dropped into a deep curtsy.

"Lord FitzChivalry Farseer. You honor us. Welcome."

And as neatly as that, she had foxed me again. I did not know if she tried to convey respect to me, or if she was conveying information to her apprentice as quickly as she could. The boy's swift intake of breath told me that he'd had no idea of my true identity, but that he now guessed the full import of my visit. And perhaps he understood more of his original errand at Withywoods. I looked at her coolly. "Has no one ever warned you what you may conjure up when you give welcome and name a ghost?"

"Welcome? And honor? I'd call it an extreme annoyance, dropping in at this hour, unannounced." Chade pushed into the room from behind the same tapestry that had admitted Rosemary. Lady Rosemary was attired in a simple morning dress, and I suspected that after whatever lesson she'd planned with FitzVigilant, she had intended to begin her day. In contrast, Chade was nattily attired in a snug-fitting green shirt with voluminous white sleeves. The shirt was belted with black and silver, and the skirts of it fell almost to his knees. His leggings were black, his slippers likewise but worked with silver beads. His silver-gray hair was bound back in a severe warrior's tail. Obviously he was at the end of a very long night's entertainment rather than the beginning of a day's work.

He was blunt. "What brings you here?"

I met his gaze. "That's the same question I asked young FitzVigilant, about four months ago. His answer did not satisfy me, so I thought I might come here and get a better one. From you."

Chade gave a huff of disdain. "Well. There was a time when you were not so severe when a prank had been played upon you." He crossed the room, his carriage a bit stiff. I suspected a binding beneath that shirt, helping him look fit and easing his old back. He reached the hearth and looked about distractedly. "Where has my chair gotten to?"

Rosemary gave a small sigh of exasperation. "It has been months since you've been up here, and you told me I might arrange things to suit myself."

He scowled. "That doesn't mean that you can arrange things to discomfort me."

She pursed her lips and shook her head, but motioned at Fitz-

Vigilant. "The old chair is in the corner, with the other rubbish that hasn't gone out yet. Fetch it, please."

"Rubbish?" Chade repeated indignantly. "What rubbish? I had no rubbish up here!"

She crossed her arms on her chest. "Cracked bowls and chipped cups. A small cauldron with a broken bail. Flasks of old oil, gone nearly to shellac. And all the rest of the litter you had pushed to the end of the table."

Chade's scowl deepened but he only grunted in response. Fitz-Vigilant brought his old chair back to its place by the hearth. Without rising, I slid Rosemary's chair over to make room for it. For the first time in decades, I looked at Chade's seat. The scrolled wood-work was scarred. The joints were loose, and the cushion still showed where I had mended it after Slink the ferret had had a tremendous battle with it one night. I looked around the room. "No ferret?" I asked.

"And no ferret droppings," Rosemary replied acerbically.

Chade rolled his eyes at me. With a sigh, he lowered himself into the chair. It creaked under him. He looked at me. "Well, Fitz. How have you been?"

I would not allow him to dismiss my mission so lightly. "Annoyed. Offended. And wary, ever since I found an assassin creeping about my baby's cradle."

Chade gave a dismissive snort of laughter. "An assassin? Scarcely. He's barely even a spy yet."

"Well, that's so comforting," I responded.

"Ah, Fitz, where else should I send him to cut his teeth? It's not like when you were a boy and we had a simmering war and a treacherous little pretender to the throne simpering and plotting at Buck-keep. I had a dozen ways to measure your progress right here within the castle walls. But FitzVigilant isn't so fortunate. I have to send him farther afield to test him. I try to choose his tasks carefully. I knew you wouldn't hurt him. And I thought it might be a good way to test his mettle."

"Not to test me, then?"

He lifted his hand from the chair's arm and waved it vaguely. "Perhaps a bit. It never hurts to be sure a man hasn't lost his edge." He looked around. "Is that wine?"

"Yes." I refilled my glass and offered it to him. He received it, took a sip, and set it down. When he did, I asked, "So. Why do I need an edge still?"

He stared at me, his green eyes piercing. "You bring another Farseer into the world, and ask me that?"

I kept my temper. "No Farseer. Bee Badgerlock is her name." I bit back that my little girl would never be a danger to anyone.

Elbow on the arm of his chair, he rested his chin in his hand. "You have lost your edge if you think a shield that thin can protect her."

"Protect her from what?" I glanced past him to where Rosemary and FitzVigilant were standing. "The only danger I've seen has come from people I should be able to trust. People I thought would protect her."

"It wasn't danger. It was a reminder that you need to be watchful. From the beginning. By the time you discover there's a danger it's too late to put your wards in place." He bristled his eyebrows at me. "Tell me, Fitz, what have you planned for this child? What education, what training? What will you dower her with, and where do you hope she will wed?"

I stared at him. "She's a baby, Chade!" And probably ever would be. Even if she began to grow and show a clever mind, there was plenty of time for me to think of such things. Still, it smote me that I had given no thought to any of that. What would become of her when Molly and I were gone? Especially if she was an idiot?

Chade turned in his chair, and the outline of his binding showed briefly beneath his shirt. He glared at our audience. "Haven't you two some lessons to complete?"

"Yes, but . . ."

"Somewhere else," he added authoritatively.

Rosemary folded her lips for a moment. "Tomorrow," she said to FitzVigilant, and the boy's eyes grew round to be so hastily dismissed. He sketched a bow to her, then turned to us and halted, plainly confused as to how to bid us farewell.

I nodded to him pleasantly. "I hope not to see you again soon, FitzVigilant."

"Likewise, sir," he responded and then froze, wondering if he had been rude. Chade chuckled. The boy whisked himself from the room, and with a final exasperated sigh Lady Rosemary followed him at a more dignified pace. Chade did not speak, giving them time to be well down the hidden staircase before he turned to me.

"Admit it. You've given no thought at all to her future."

"I haven't. Because I didn't even realize Molly was truly pregnant. But now that Bee is here . . ."

"Bee. Such a name! Is she going to live? Does she thrive?" He cut in relentlessly.

That gave me pause. "She is tiny, Chade. And Molly says that she is not doing the things she should be doing by now. But she eats well, and sleeps and sometimes cries. Other than how small she is and that she does not lift her head or roll over yet, I see nothing wrong . . ."

My words ran out. Chade was looking at me with sympathy. He spoke kindly. "Fitz. You have to imagine every possible future for her. What will you do if she is simple, or if she can never care for herself? Or what if she grows to be beautiful and intelligent and people recognize her as a Farseer? Or if she is ordinary and plain and not very bright? At the very least, all will know she is the sister of the king's Skillmistress. That is enough power to be courted right there. Or to make her a valuable hostage."

He gave me no time to gather my thoughts as he added, "Nettle was educated well enough for a country girl whose prospects were little better than to marry a landed farmer. Talk to her, sometime, about where she feels that lack. Burrich taught her to read and write and tally. Molly taught her beekeeping and gardening, and she's a good hand around a horse. But history? The shape of the world? Languages? She got little of that, and has spent years trying to mend those gaps. I've met Molly's other children, and they are good enough men. But you are not raising a farmer's daughter, Fitz. If the bones had rolled differently, she might expect to wear the coronet of a Farseer princess. She won't. But you should educate her as if she would."

If she could be educated. I pushed the thought away. *Follow Chade's reasoning.* "Why?"

"Because one never knows what fate will bring." He gestured expansively with one hand as he lifted the wineglass in the other. "If she tests for the Skill and has it, would you have her come to Buckkeep Castle with no knowledge of her heritage? Would you have her struggle, as Nettle did, to learn to navigate the waters of society? Tell me, Fitz. If you raise her as Bee Badgerlock, will you be content to marry her off to a farmer and let her toil all her days?"

"If she loves him and he loves her, that is not a terrible fate."

"Well, if a wealthy nobleman fell in love with her, and she had been raised to be an eligible match for him, and she loved him, that might be a better one, would not you say?"

I was still trying to think of a response when Chade added, "Fitz-Vigilant had no prospects. Lord Vigilant's young wife has less than no use for the bastard, and resents that he is older than the legitimate heirs she has borne her lord. She is raising his two younger brothers to hate him. Word came to me that she was looking for a quiet death for the boy. Instead of that, I brought him here. To make him yet another useful bastard."

"He seems bright enough," I said carefully.

"Bright, yes. But he has no edge. I'll do what I can with him. But in seven or eight years, I'll need to put him somewhere else. Lord Vigilant's wife regards him as a usurper. She already mutters against him being at court. She is the worst sort of jealous woman, one who puts her ill will into action. Better for all if he is gone from Buckkeep when she presents her two sons here."

"Seven or eight years from now?"

"Unlike you, I plan ahead for those I take under my wing."

"And you will ask me to take him." I frowned and tried to see his plan. "As a possible match for Bee when she's older?"

"Gods, no! Let's not mingle those bloodlines! We'll find her a lordling from Buck, I think. But yes, I'd like you to be ready to take him in. When he's ready."

"Ready to be a killer and a spy? Why?"

Chade shook his head. He seemed oddly disappointed. "No. There's no assassin in him. I'm certain of that, though Rosemary remains to be convinced. And so I will take his training in a different direction. One useful to both of us. The boy has a bright mind. He learns almost as quickly as you did. And he has a loyal heart. Give him a good master, and he would be true as a hound. And very protective."

"Of Bee."

Chade was watching the dying fire. He nodded slowly. "He's quick with languages, and has almost the memory of a minstrel. In the guise of a tutor, he could be placed in your household, to the benefit of both of them."

The pieces were beginning to fit together. *Oh, Chade. Why is it so hard for you to ask a direct favor?* I put it into words for him. "You like the boy. But if you keep him here, sooner or later, when his legitimate younger brothers come to Buckkeep, it will cause problems. Especially if he has made friends among the nobility here."

Chade nodded. "He's very charismatic. He likes people. He likes to be around them, and they like him. He quickly becomes too visible to be a good spy. And he doesn't have . . . whatever it is that we have that makes us able to kill." He drew a breath as if he would say more and then sighed it out. We were both silent, thinking. I wondered if that ability was something we both had, or if we both lacked something, and thereby could do the sorts of things we had done. The silence was not a comfortable one. Yet it wasn't guilt we shared. I'm not sure a word exists for whatever it was.

"I'd have to talk to Molly about it."

He sent me a quick sideways glance. "You'd tell her . . . what?"

I bit my lip. "The truth. That he's a bastard like me, that he will eventually have difficulties because of it, possibly life-threatening difficulties. That he's well educated, and would be a good tutor for a little girl."

"The truth with holes in it," Chade amended for me.

"What holes?" I demanded.

"Indeed. What holes?" Chade agreed dryly. "And you need not talk to her yet. We have years, I suspect, before I must send him off to you. I'll educate him in all he must know to be a tutor. And a bodyguard. Until he is ready, I know a nursemaid I could send you for the child. Face like a hare and the arm of a smith. Not the brightest of servants, but formidable as a guard."

"No. Thank you. I think that, for now, I can protect my daughter."

"Oh, Fitz. I don't agree but I know when it's useless to argue with you. Riddle and I have agreed that you need door soldiers, but you won't listen. How many times have I suggested that you should host one of our Skill-journeymen at Withywoods so that even in your absence messages could be swiftly passed? You should have a man of your own, to watch your back and mingle with the servants and bring you the news that you otherwise would not hear about your holdings." He shifted in his chair, the old wood creaking under him. His gaze met my stubborn look. I prevailed. "Well. It's late. Or it's early, depending on what part of the day you work in. Either way, I'm off to bed." Furtively he tugged at the top edge of the girdle. I suspected it was cutting into him. He pulled himself to his feet. With one hand he made a vague gesture at the bed. "You can sleep here, if you wish. I don't think Rosemary ever uses that bed. She just likes to make things pretty, when she can."

"I may." To my surprise, I realized my anger had vanished. I knew Chade. He'd meant no harm to Bee. Perhaps his whole aim had been to provoke this visit from me. Perhaps he missed me more than I'd realized. And perhaps I should have taken under advisement some of his suggestions . . .

He nodded. "I'll have FitzVigilant bring some food up for you. Get to know him, Fitz. He's a good lad. Tractable and anxious to please. Not like you were."

I cleared my throat and asked, "Are you getting softhearted in your old age?"

He shook his head. "No. Practical. I need to set him aside so Rosemary and I can find a more fitting apprentice. He knows too much of our inner workings for us to just let him go. I have to put him somewhere that will keep him safe."

"Keep him safe or keep you safe?"

He cracked a smile. "It's the same thing, don't you see? People who are dangerous to me seldom flourish for long." The smile he gave me was crooked with sadness. I saw his dilemma more clearly as he handed the half-emptied glass to me.

I made my suggestion quietly. "Start to move him out of your circle, Chade. Less time with you or Rosemary, more time with the scribes and minstrels. You can't make him forget what he has seen and what he knows, but you can lessen its importance. Make him grateful. And when you can no longer keep him here, send him to me. I'll keep him for you." I tried not to realize what I had just agreed to do. This was not a promise that would last a year or two. So long as FitzVigilant lived and remembered the secret ways of Buckkeep Castle, I would be responsible for seeing that he remained loyal to the Farseers. Loyal. Or dead. Chade had just handed me a dirty task that he did not want to do. I sipped the wine, covering the bitterness of that knowledge with the too-sweet vintage.

"Are you certain when you say, 'You can't make him forget'?"

That jerked my attention back to the old man. "What are you thinking?" I countered.

"That we are still deciphering the old Skill-scrolls. They hint that you can make a man, well, change his mind about things."

He shocked me into an appalled silence. To be able to make a man forget something: what a horrifying power. I found breath. "And that worked so very well when my father decided to make Skillmaster Galen forget his dislike of him and love him. His hate didn't vanish; it just found another target. As I recall, it was me." He'd nearly managed to kill me.

"Your father did not have the benefit of complete instruction in the Skill. I doubt that Galen did. So much was lost, Fitz! So much. I work on the scrolls almost every evening, but it's not the same as being instructed by a knowledgeable Skillmaster. Deducing what they mean is laborious. It doesn't go as fast as I wish it would. Nettle has no time to help me. The information they contain is not to be shared with just anyone, and the fragility of the scrolls themselves is another consideration. I myself have far less time for late-night studies than I used to. So the scrolls are neglected, and with them, who knows what secrets?"

Another favor couched as a question. "Select the ones you consider most interesting. I'll take them back to Withywoods with me."

He scowled. "Couldn't you come here to work on them? One week out of each month? I'm loath to send them away from Buck-keep Castle."

"Chade, I've a wife and a child and a manor to take care of. I can't spend my time gallivanting back and forth to Buckkeep Castle."

"The Skill-pillars would make your 'gallivant' the matter of a few moments."

"I won't do it, and you know why."

"I know that years ago, against all advice, you used the pillars repeatedly over a very short period. I'm not talking about your coming and going each day. I'm suggesting that once a month you could come to take some scrolls and drop off what you had translated. From what I've read, there were Skilled messengers who used the pillars at least that frequently, and possibly more often."

"No." I put finality in the word.

He cocked his head to the other side. "Then why don't you and Molly come live in Buckkeep, and bring the baby? Easy enough for us to find a competent manager for Withywoods. And Bee would have all the advantages that we earlier spoke about. You could help me with the translations and other tasks, get to know young Lant, and I'm sure Molly would enjoy seeing Nettle more frequently and—"

"No." I said it again, firmly. I had no desire to take up the "other tasks" he might pass back to me. Nor for him to see my simple child. "I'm happy where I am, Chade. I'm at peace, and I intend to remain so."

He sighed noisily. "Very well, then. Very well." He suddenly sounded elderly and petulant. It was unnerving when he added, "I miss you, my boy. There is no one left with whom I can speak as freely as I do with you. I suspect we are a dying breed."

"I suspect you are right," I agreed, and did not add that perhaps that was a good thing.

Chade and I left our discussion there. I think he finally accepted that I had stepped away from the inner politics of Buckkeep Court. I would come when there was urgent need, but I would never again live in the castle and be a party to his inner counsels. Rosemary would have to step up to that role, and behind her must come whatever apprentice they chose. It would not be FitzVigilant. I wondered if the lad would be disappointed or relieved.

In the time that followed, I both dreaded and expected that Chade would try again to draw me back. He did not. Scrolls were delivered for translation and my work was carried away from me five or six times a year. Twice his couriers were journeymen Skill-students who arrived and departed through the pillars. I refused to allow him to provoke me. The second time it happened, I confirmed with Nettle that she knew of it. She said little, but after that his messengers arrived on horseback.

Although Nettle often touched minds with me, and Dutiful sometimes, Chade seemed to have decided to set me free. And sometimes, at odd wakeful moments, I wondered if I was disappointed or relieved to be finally clear of the darker side of Farseer politics.

Chapter 9

A CHILDHOOD

It is as I feared for young Lant. He is completely unsuitable for quiet work. When I first told him that I would be ending his apprenticeship and finding him a more suitable post, I was unprepared for how dramatically upset he would be. He begged both Rosemary and me to give him a second chance. Against my own better judgment, I agreed. I must be becoming both softer of heart and feebler of mind, for of course it was not a kindness. We continued to train him in the physical skills and the requisite knowledge. He is very nimble of finger and hand, excellent at sleight, but not as quick to remember the recipes that one must master for use in an instant. Still, I confess I had hope that the lad would follow in my footsteps.

Rosemary had less doubt of him and proposed that we give him a challenge. I set him a theft, and he accomplished it. Rosemary proposed a minor poisoning. His target was but a guardsman. We told him the man had taken bribes and was actively spying for a

Chalcedean nobleman. Nonetheless, over the course of three days and ample opportunities, Lant was unable to achieve his task. He returned to us shamed and despondent. He simply could not bring himself to end a life. I refrained from telling him that the "poison" was merely a finely ground spice and would have done the man no harm. I am glad we tested him on a subject that was not truly a threat to anyone.

The result is that Lant now realizes he is unsuited to this profession. He has, to my surprise, said that he does not mind if he cannot be my apprentice so long as he does not lose my friendship! And so, to ease his transition, I think I shall keep him here in Buckkeep for a time longer. I will see that he receives sufficient education to be a tutor, and weapons training that will fit him as a bodyguard as well.

Only to you will I admit that I am sadly disappointed in him. I was so certain I had found a worthy successor. Fortunately, a second candidate has been located and her training begun. She seems to show an aptitude, but then, so did Lant. We shall see. I tell you all this, of course, in the greatest confidence in your discretion. Strange, where once I taught you never to entrust such things to paper, now it is the only way I can be certain that no one else in our coterie shall be privy to my thoughts. How times change.

UNSIGNED AND UNADDRESSED SCROLL

Oh, the things we discover and the things we learn, much too late. Worse are the secrets that are not secrets, the sorrows we live with but do not admit to one another.

Bee was not the child we had both hoped for. I hid my disappointment from Molly, and I think she did the same for me. The slow months and then the year ticked past, and I saw little change in our daughter's abilities. It aged Molly, taking a toll on both her body and her spirit as she allowed no one else to care for the child, and silently contained her growing sorrow. I wanted to help her, but the child clearly avoided my touch. For a time I sank into a darkness of spirit, losing appetite and the will to do anything. My days always seemed to end with thunderous headaches and a sour belly. I woke at night and could not find sleep again, only anxiety over the child. Our baby remained a baby, small and passive. Chade's eagerness to plan for her education and eventual marriage became a sour-sweet memory. Once, there had been a time when we could hope for such things. But the passing year stole all such dreams from us.

I do not recall how old Bee was the first time Molly broke down and wept in my arms. "I'm sorry, I'm so so sorry," she said, and it took me some time to understand that she blamed herself for our simple child. "I was too old," she told me through her tears. "And she will never be right. Never, never, never."

"Let's not be hasty," I told her, with a calmness I did not feel. Why had we hidden our fears from each other? Perhaps because sharing them, as we did now, made them more real. I tried to deny them. "She's healthy," I told my Molly as she sobbed in my arms. I bent to whisper the words by her ear. "She eats well. She sleeps. Her skin is smooth, her eyes are clear. She's small and perhaps slow to do things, but she will grow and—"

"Stop," she begged me in a dull little voice. "Stop, Fitz." She pulled a little away and looked up at me. Her hair clung to her wet face like a widow's veil. She sniffed once. "Pretending won't change it. She's simple. And not just simple, but weak in her body. She doesn't roll over, or hold her head strongly. She doesn't even try. She just lies in her cradle and stares. She hardly even cries."

And what was there for me to say to that? She was a woman who had birthed seven healthy children. Bee was the first baby I'd ever experienced.

"Is she truly so different from what she should be?" I asked helplessly.

Molly nodded slowly. "And ever will be."

"But she's ours," I objected softly. "She's our Bee. Perhaps she is what she's meant to be."

I don't recall how I intended her to hear those words. I knew I did not deserve it when she gave a sudden sob and then hugged me tightly, asking my chest, "Then you are not bitterly disappointed and shamed by her? You can still love her? You still love me?"

"Of course," I said. "Of course and always." And even though I had comforted her by chance rather than by intent, I was glad I had done so.

Yet we had opened a door that could not be closed. Once we had admitted that our little girl would likely be always as she was now, we had to talk about it. Yet we did not speak of it before the servants, nor in the light of day, but at night, in our bed, with the child that had so wounded us sleeping nearby in a cradle. For though we could admit it, we could not accept it. Molly faulted her milk, and tried to coax the tiny thing to sip cow's milk and then goat's milk, with very little success.

Our baby's health baffled me. Many a young creature had I tended in my life, and yet I had never known one that ate with an appetite, slept well, appeared full of good health, and yet did not grow. I tried to encourage her to move her limbs, but I quickly learned that she did not seem to want me to handle her at all. Placid and calm when left to herself, she would not meet my gaze when I bent over her crib. If I picked her up, she would lean away from me and then with her feeble strength try to fling herself from my arms. If I insisted on holding her and flexing her legs and moving her arms, she rapidly went from wails to angry screams. After a time Molly begged me not to try, for she feared that somehow I was causing her pain. And I gave way to her wishes, though my Wit showed me no sense of pain from her, only alarm. Alarm that her father would try to hold her. Is it possible to express how painful that was for me?

The servants were at first curious about her, and then pitying. Molly all but hissed at them, and kept all care of the child to herself. To them, she would never admit anything was wrong. But late at night her worries and fears for her child grew darker. "What will become of her after I am gone?" she asked me one evening.

"We will make provision for her," I said.

Molly shook her head. "People are cruel," she said. "Who could we trust that much?"

"Nettle?" I suggested.

Molly shook her head again. "Must I sacrifice one daughter's life to be caretaker for the other?" she asked me, and to that I had no answer.

When one has been disappointed for so long, hope becomes the enemy. One cannot be dashed to the earth unless one is lifted first, and I learned to avoid hope. When, midway through Bee's second year of life, Molly began to tell me that she was getting stronger and could hold her head more steadily, I nodded and smiled but did little more than that. But at the end of her second year, she could roll over, and shortly after that she began to sit without support. She grew, but remained tiny for her age. In her third year she began to crawl, and then to pull herself to a stand. In her fourth year she toddled about the room, a peculiar sight to see a child so tiny walking. At five, she trotted behind her mother everywhere. She began to have teeth, and she made garbled noises that only Molly could interpret.

The oddest things seemed to excite her. The texture of a piece of weaving, or the wind stirring a cobweb, would catch her attention. Then the little thing would shake her hands wildly and gabble out nonsense. Every now and then a word would burst from her lips embedded in a stream of burbled sound. It was both maddening and sweet to hear Molly talk to her child, keeping up her half of an imaginary conversation.

We kept Bee mostly to ourselves. Her older siblings did not visit as often as they once had, for growing families and the demands of their occupations kept them busy at their homes. They visited when they could, which was not often. They treated Bee kindly, but they realized that pitying her was useless. She would be what she would be. They saw that Molly seemed content with her, and possibly gave no more thought to the child that comforted their mother as she aged.

Hap, my fostered son, came and went on his minstrel wanderings. He most often arrived in the coldest months, to spend a moon with us. He sang and played pipes, and Bee was the most avid listener that any minstrel could ask for. She would focus her pale-blue eyes on him, and her little mouth would hang ajar as she listened. She would not willingly go to bed while Hap was there unless he followed her to her room and played her a soft, slow tune until she slept. Perhaps that was why he accepted Bee as she was, and when he visited, he always brought her a simple present such as a string of bright beads or a soft scarf figured with roses.

Of all her brothers and sisters, Nettle came most often in those early years. I could tell she longed to hold her sister, but Bee reacted to her touch much as she did to mine, and so Nettle had to be content with being beside her sister but unable to tend to her needs.

Very late one night as I left my private study, my route took me past the door of Bee's nursery. I saw a light burning through the half-open door and paused, thinking perhaps Bee had taken sick and Molly was sitting up with her. But as I peered in I saw not Molly but Nettle sitting by her sister's bed, looking down at her with a face of tragic wistfulness. She was speaking softly. "For years, I imagined a sister. Someone to share dreams with, to braid each other's hair and tease about boys and take long walks with me. I thought I would teach you to dance and we would have secrets and cook together late at night when everyone else was asleep. And here you are, at last. But we will have none of that, will we? Yet this I will promise you, little Bee. No matter what happens to our parents, I will always care for you." And then my Nettle lowered her face into her hands and wept. I knew then that she mourned for the sister she had imagined, just as I still longed for the perfect little girl I had dreamed we would have. I had no comfort for either of us, and I left that scene silently.

Since her birth, Bee had accompanied Molly everywhere, in a sling or riding on Molly's hip or tottering along behind her. Sometimes I wondered if she feared to leave the child alone. When Molly went about her regular tasks at Withywoods, from supervising the servants to managing her own hives, honey, and candlemaking, tasks she still seemed to enjoy, Bee was with her, watching and listening. Now that the babe had discovered she could make sounds, Molly redoubled her efforts with her. She did not speak in the babyish singsong I'd hear the servants use on the rare occasions when they spoke to Bee. Instead Molly earnestly explained every aspect of her work as if Bee might one day need to know how to smoke a hive or strain hot wax for candles or polish silver or make a bed. And Bee, in her simple way, mirrored Molly's earnestness, peering at what she was shown and gabbling back at her. My most unnerving experience was when I went to seek Molly one summer day and found her tending her hives. Over our years I'd become accustomed to Molly's calm acceptance that her bees might blanket her arms in the course of her beekeeping. What I did not expect was to see small Bee standing beside her mother, holding a bucket and cloaked in bees. The child was smiling beatifically, her eyes almost closed. Every now and then she would giggle and give a tiny wiggle as if the fuzzy creatures had tickled her. "Molly," I said in a soft warning voice, for my lady was so intent on her tasks that I was not sure she had seen what was happening to our child.

She turned slowly, ever mindful of her buzzing charges.

"The baby," I said with quiet urgency. "The bees have her."

Molly looked down and behind her. A slow smile appeared on her face. "Bee! Are you tending the hives with me?"

Our little daughter looked up and babbled something to her. Molly laughed. "She's fine, dear. Not scared at all."

But I was. "Bee. Come away. Come to Papa," I coaxed her. She turned and looked past me. She never willingly met my eyes. She babbled at her mother again.

"She's fine, dear. She says you are worried because you don't know the bees like she and I do. Go on. We'll be along presently."

And so I'd left them, and spent an anxious hour in my study. I wondered if my child was Witted, and if it was possible for a Witted child to bond to a hive of bees. *Don't be ridiculous,* the wolf in me snorted. And insisted that if it were true, he would have sensed it. I could only hope so.

Another year passed and Bee slowly grew. Our lives changed, for Molly centered her days on our daughter and I circled the two of them, marveling at what they shared. By the time Bee was seven, she was a genuine help to her mother, in her simple way. I could see

Molly was slowing and feeling the burden of her years. Bee could pick up what Molly had dropped, could harvest the herbs that Molly pointed out or bring her items from the lowest shelves in the sewing room.

She looked like a little pecksie as she followed her mother and assisted in her small ways. Molly had the softest wool dyed in the brightest colors she could create, as much to make Bee happy as to make her easy to see in the deep grass of the meadows. She was no taller than waist-high on Molly when she was seven. Her pale-blue eyes and blond brows lent her a perpetually startled expression, and her wildly curly hair added to it. Her hair flew into stubborn knots at the slightest breeze and grew so slowly that Molly despaired of her ever looking like a girl. Then, when it did reach her shoulders in a wild cloud of ringlets, it was so fine that Molly resorted to wetting it, combing it, and braiding it in a long tail down her back. They came to show me, with my little girl dressed in a simple yellow tunic and green leggings of the sort that Molly and I had worn as children. I smiled to see her and told Molly, "That's the smallest warrior I've ever seen!"—for so the soldiers of Buck had always worn their hair tailed back. Bee surprised me by crowing with delight at my comment.

And so our days passed, and Molly took great pleasure in our peculiar child and I took satisfaction in her pleasure. Despite her years, Molly would romp like a child with our Bee, seizing her and tossing her high, or chasing her recklessly around and sometimes through the manicured flower and herb beds of Patience's garden. Round and round they would go until Molly was wheezing and coughing for breath. Bee would halt as soon as Molly did and go to stand close to her mother and look up at her with fond concern. There were times when I longed to join in, to spring out and pounce on my cub and roll her on the grass to hear her laugh. But I knew that would not be the response I would get from her.

For despite Molly's assurance that our child did not dislike me, Bee remained distant from me. She rarely came closer than arm's length, and if I sat down near her to see her little bit of needlework, she would always hunch her shoulders and turn slightly away from me. She seldom met my eyes. On a few occasions, when she fell asleep beside Molly in her chair, I would pick her up and try to carry her off to her bed. But at my touch, awake or asleep, she would stiffen and then arch like a fighting fish, flinging herself away from me. It would be a struggle for me to set her safely down, and after a number of efforts I gave up trying to touch her. I think Molly was relieved when I surrendered to Bee's will in this.

So Molly tended to all Bee's personal needs. She taught our child to keep herself clean, and to tidy her room as much as such a small person was able. Molly had a little bed built for her, and bedding of a matching size. She was required to keep her playthings in order and to do all things for herself as if she were a peasant child. Of this, I approved.

Molly taught her to gather from the woods mushrooms, berries, and herbs that we could not easily grow in our gardens. In the gardens and hothouses, I would find them together, picking caterpillars from leaves or gathering herbs to dry. I would pass Molly's wax room and see small Bee standing on the table, holding a wick straight as Molly carefully poured hot wax. There they strained the golden honey from the combs and packed it into fat little pots for our winter sweetness.

They made a perfect unit, Molly and Bee. It came to me that though Bee was not the child I had dreamed we would have, she was perfect for Molly. She was utterly devoted to her mother, intent on every shift of the expression on her face. If, in their closeness, they closed me out, I tried not to resent it. Molly deserved the joy she took in this child.

So I was content to hover at the edges of their world, a moth at a window, looking in at warmth and light. Slowly I began to forsake my private study, and instead to take my translation work to the room where Bee had been born. By the time Bee was seven, I spent almost every evening in that warmly lit room. Molly's softly flickering candles scented it with heather and lavender, or sage or rose, depending on her mood. She and Bee would do simple stitching together, while Molly softly sang the old learning songs about herbs and bees and mushrooms and flowers.

I was at my work one evening, the fire crackling softly and Molly humming over some embroidery she was working onto the neck of a little red nightgown for Bee, when I became aware that my daughter had left off sorting skeins of thread for her mother and had approached my table. I was careful not to look at her. It was as if a hummingbird hovered near me. I could not recall that she had ever voluntarily come so close to me. I feared that if I turned, she would flee. And so I painstakingly continued to copy the old illustration on a scroll about the properties of nightshade and its relatives. It asserted that one branch of the family that grew in desert regions bore red fruit that could be eaten. I was skeptical of such a claim for a toxic plant, but nonetheless I copied the text and did my best to reproduce the illustrations of leaves, starry flowers, and hanging fruit. I had begun to ink the flowers in with yellow. This, I surmised, was what had brought Bee to my shoulder. I listened to her open-mouthed breathing and became aware that Molly was no longer humming. I did not need to turn my head to know she was watching our child with as much curiosity as I felt.

A small hand touched the edge of my table and spidered slowly to the edge of the page I was working on. I pretended not to notice. I dipped my brush again and added another yellow petal. As softly as a pot bubbling on the hearth, Bee murmured something. "Yellow," I said, as if I were Molly pretending to know her thoughts. "I'm painting the little flower yellow."

Again, the bubbling mutter, this time a bit louder with more of a plea in it.

"Green," I told her. I lifted the vial of ink and showed it to her. "The leaves will be this green at the edges. And I will mix green and yellow for the center, and green and black for the veins of the leaves."

The little hand fumbled at the corner of my page. Her fingers lifted it and tugged. "Careful!" I cautioned her and received a cascade of bubbling muttering in a pleading tone.

"Fitz," Molly gently rebuked me. "She's asking you for paper. And a quill and ink."

I transferred my gaze to Molly. She met my eyes steadily, her brows raised that I could be either so stupid or so unreasonable. The happily affirmative note in Bee's babbling seemed to confirm that she was right. I looked down at Bee. She lifted her face and looked past me, but did not retreat. "Paper," I said, and did not hesitate as I took a sheet of the best-quality paper that Chade had sent to me. "A quill." It was one I had just cut. "And ink." I slid a small well of black ink across the table. I set the paper and the quill on the edge of my desk. Bee stood silent for a moment. Her mouth worked and then she pointed a small finger and trilled at me.

"Colored ink," Molly specified and Bee gave a wriggle of delight. I surrendered.

"We'll have to share, then," I told her. I moved a chair to the other side of my table, set a cushion on it, and then arranged Bee's supplies where she could reach them. She surprised me with the alacrity with which she mounted to this throne.

"You dip just the pointed end of the quill into the inkpot . . ." I began. I stopped. I had ceased to exist in Bee's world. Her entire focus was on the pen that she carefully inked and then set to her page. I froze and watched the child. Obviously she had been ob- serving me for some time. I had expected her to dunk the quill and smear ink across the page. Instead her little hand moved with preci- sion.

Her effort was not without blotches and drips. No one uses a pen correctly the very first time. But the image that emerged onto the page was intricately and intimately drawn. In silence, she filched my pen wipe, cleaned the quill. She blew on the black ink to dry it and claimed the yellow and then the orange ink. I watched in rapt si- lence, scarce aware when Molly drew near. A bee, exactly the scale of a live one, emerged from the pen onto the paper. There came a moment when our Bee heaved a huge sigh of satisfaction, as if she had consumed the perfect meal, and stood back from her work. I examined it without moving closer to her, the delicate antennae, the panes of the wings, and the bright bands of yellow shaded to or- ange.

"It's her name, isn't it?" I said quietly to Molly.

Bee shot me a rare look that met my eyes and then skated away.

Her annoyance with me was plain. She drew the paper closer as if to protect it from me and hunched over it. The pen once more visited the black well and then scratched carefully over the paper. I glanced at Molly, who wore a proud and secretive smile. I watched in growing suspense until Bee leaned back from the page. There, in careful characters that mirrored Molly's hand, was lettered "Bee."

I was not aware my mouth was hanging open until Molly put her fingers under my chin and pushed it shut. Tears welled in my eyes. "She can write?"

"Yes."

I took a breath and carefully capped my excitement. "But only her name. Does she understand they are letters? That they mean something?"

Molly made a small sound of exasperation. "Of course she does. Fitz, did you think I would neglect her education as mine was? She reads along with me. So she recognizes the letters. But this is the first time she has taken pen in hand and written." Her smile trembled a little. "In truth, I am almost as surprised as you to see her do so. To know the shape of a letter on the page is so different from reproducing it on paper. Truly, I did not do as well as she has the first time I tried to write."

Bee was now ignoring both of us as a twining vine of honeysuckle began to emerge from her pen.

I wrote no more that night. I ceded all my inks and my best quills to my little daughter, and allowed her to fill page after page of my best paper with illustrations of flowers, herbs, butterflies, and insects. I would have needed to study the live plant to capture it well; she drew it forth from her memory and captured it on the page.

I went to bed that night a grateful man. I was not at all convinced that Bee understood the concepts of letters or writing or reading. What I had seen was someone who could duplicate on paper what she had seen, even if she did not have the model before her. It was a rare enough talent that it gave me hope for her. It put me in mind of Thick, a man prodigiously strong in the Skill even if he could not fully grasp the concept of what he was doing when he used it.

That night, in bed with Molly warm beside me, I had the rare pleasure of reaching out with the Skill and rousing Chade from a sound sleep. *What?* he demanded of me in a tone of reproach.

Do you remember the herbal scrolls from that Spice Island trader that we set aside as beyond my skill to copy? The tattered ones that might be of Elderling origin?

Of course. What of them?

Send them to me. With a good supply of paper. Oh, and a set of rabbit-hair brushes. And have you any of that purple ink from the Spice Islands?

Do you know how much that costs, boy?

Yes. And I know that you can afford it, if it's used well. Send me two bottles of that as well.

I smiled as I closed my mind to his hailstorm of questions. They were still rattling against my walls as I sank into sleep.

Chapter 10

MY OWN VOICE

*This is the dream I love the best. I had it once. I've tried to make it
come back, but it does not.*

Two wolves are running.

*That is all. They run by moonlight across an open hillside and
then into an oak forest. There is little underbrush and they do not
slow. They are not even hunting. They are just running, taking joy in
the stretch of their muscles and the cool air flowing into their open
jaws. They owe nothing to no one. They have no decisions, no duties, and no king. They have the night and the running, and it is
enough for them.*

I long to be that complete.

DREAM JOURNAL OF BEE FARSEER

I freed my tongue when I was eight years old. I remember the day
very clearly.

My fostered brother Hap, more like an uncle to me, had paid us a brief visit the day before. His gift to me was not a little pipe or a string of beads or such simple things as he had brought me on previous visits. This time he had a soft packet wrapped in a rough brown fabric. He put it on my lap and when I sat looking at it, unsure of what to do next, my mother took out her small belt-knife, cut the string that bound it, and unfolded the wrappings.

Within were a pink blouse, a vest of lace, and a set of layered pink skirts! I had never seen such garments. They were from Bingtown, he told my mother as she gently touched the intricate lace. The sleeves were long and full, and the skirts rested on a pillow of petticoats and were overlaid with pink lace. My mother held them up to me and for a wonder, they seemed to be the right size.

The next morning she helped me put them on and caught her breath to see me when the final sash was tied. Then she made me stand still for a weary time while she worried my hair into reluctant order. When we went down to breakfast, she opened the door and ushered me in as if I were the queen. My father lifted his brows in astonishment, and Hap gave a whoop of pleasure to see me. I ate breakfast so carefully, enduring the chafing of the lace and keeping the sleeves from dragging through my plate. I bore the weight of the garments bravely as we stood in front of the manor and wished Hap a pleasant journey. And mindful of my glory, I walked carefully through the kitchen gardens and seated myself on a bench there. I felt very grand. I arranged my pink skirts and tried to smooth my hair, and when Elm and Lea came out of the kitchens with buckets of vegetable parings to take down to the chicken house, I smiled at them both.

Lea looked away uneasily and Elm stuck her tongue out. My heart sank. I had supposed, foolishly, that such extravagant garments might win me their regard. Several times I had heard, as Elm intended I should, that I was "dressed like a butcher's boy" when I wore my usual tunic and leggings. After they had passed me by I sat a time longer, trying to think it through. Then the sun went behind a bank of low clouds and I suddenly could not stand any more chafing from the high lace collar.

I sought out my mother and found her straining wax. I stood before her, lifting my pink skirts and petticoats. "Too heavy." She understood my garbled words as she always did. She took me to my room and helped me change into leggings of dark green, a tunic of lighter green, and my soft boots. I had reached a decision. I had come to understand what I must do.

I had always been aware there were other children at Withy-woods. For the first five years of my life, I was so bonded to my mother, and so small, that I had very little to do with them. I saw them, in passing, as my mother carried me through the kitchens or as I trotted at her heels through the corridors. They were the sons and daughters of the servants, born to be part of Withywoods and growing up alongside me, even if they sprouted up taller much more swiftly than I did. Some were old enough to have tasks of their own, such as the scullery girls Elm and Lea and the kitchen lad Taffy. I knew there were children who helped with the poultry and sheep and the stables, but those I seldom saw. There were also little ones, infants and small children who were both too small to be given work and too young to be separated from their mothers. Some of them were of a size with me, but far too babyish to hold my interest. Elm was a year older than I was, and Lea a year younger, but both of them were taller than I was by a head. Both had grown up in the pantries and kitchens of Withywoods, and shared their mothers' opinions of me. When I was five, they had shown a pity-ing tolerance for me.

But both pity and tolerance were gone by the time I was seven. Smaller in stature than they were, I was still more competent at the tasks my mother entrusted to me. Yet because I did not speak, they considered me stupid. I had learned to keep my silence with every-one except my mother. Not only the children, but even the grown servants would mock my gabbling and pointing when they thought I was not near. I was certain it was from their parents that the chil-dren learned their dislike of me. As young as I was then, I still un-derstood instinctively that they feared that if their children were near me, somehow they would become tainted with my oddness.

Unlike their elders, the children avoided me without bothering to pretend it was anything but dislike for me. I would watch their play from a distance, longing to join in, but the moment I approached they would gather their simple dolls, scatter the acorn-and-flower picnic they'd been sharing, and race off. Even if I gave chase, they easily outran me. They could climb trees whose lower branches I could not reach. If I dogged their steps too much, they simply retreated to the kitchen. I was often shooed out of that room with a kindly voiced, "Now, Mistress Bee, run along and play where it's safe. Here you'll be trodden upon, or scalded. Off you go." And all the while Elm and Lea would make simpering faces and shooing motions from behind their mothers' skirts.

Taffy I feared. He was nine, bigger and heavier than Elm and Lea. He was the meat boy for the kitchen, bringing a freshly slaughtered chicken or lugging a butchered and skinned lamb. To me, he seemed massive. He was boyishly blunt and direct in his dislike of me. Once, when I followed the kitchen children down to the creek where they intended to sail some walnut-shell boats, Taffy turned on me and pelted me with pebbles until I fled. He had a way of saying "Bee-ee" that made my name an insult and a synonym for "stupid." The two girls did not dare join in his mockery of me, but oh, how they enjoyed it.

If I had told my mother, she would have told my father, and I am certain that all the children would have been banned from Withy-woods. So I did not. As much as they disliked and scorned me, all the more I longed for their company. It was true I could not play with them, but I could watch them and learn how to play. Climbing trees, setting walnut boats with leaf sails afloat, contests of jumping and skipping and tumbling, little mocking songs, how to catch a frog . . . all of these things children learn from other children. I watched Taffy walk on his hands, and in the privacy of my bedroom bruised myself in a hundred places until I could cross the room without falling. I did not know to beg for a spinning top from the market until I had spied Taffy's red one. From a distance, I learned to whistle with my lips or with a blade of grass between my thumbs. I hid and waited until they had departed before I tried to swing on a rope tied to a tree branch or venture into a secret bower built from fallen branches.

I think my father suspected how I spent my time. When my mother told him of my desire, he bought me not just the spinning top but a jumping jack, a little tumbler fastened to two sticks with a twist of string suspending him. Of an evening, when I would sit by the hearth and play with those simple toys, he would watch me from lowered eyes. I felt in his gaze the same hunger I felt when I watched the other children play.

I felt I stole from them when I spied on them. And they felt the same, for whenever they discovered me watching them, they would drive me away with their shouts and name-calling. Taffy was the only one who dared pelt me with pinecones and acorns, but the others shouted and cheered when he hit me. My silence and timidity made them bold in their attacks.

Such a mistake. Or not. When I could not join them, I followed, and played where they had played after they had left. There was a place by a creek where slender willows grew thick. In early spring they wove the little trees together, and by summer the trees had grown into a shady arch of leafy branches. It became their playhouse, where they brought bread and butter from the kitchen and ate it on plates of big leaves. Their cups were leaves, too, spindled to hold a bit of water from the stream. And Taffy was Lord Taffy there, and the girls were ladies with necklaces of golden dandelions and white daisies.

How I longed to join them at that game! I had thought that a lacy pink dress might win me admittance to their circle. It had not. So that day I followed them stealthily and I waited until they were called away to their chores before I ventured in. I sat on their mounded moss chairs. I fanned myself with a fan of fern fronds that Elm had made and left there. They had built a little bed of pine boughs in the corner, and on a warm and sunny day I lay upon it. The sun beat down but the bent branches of the shelter let in only a dappling of it. I closed my eyes and watched the light on my eyelids and smelled the fragrance of the broken boughs and sweet

smell of the earth itself. I must have dozed. When I opened my
eyes, it was too late. All three of them stood in the entrance, looking down at me. I sat up slowly. Against the sunshine outside, they
were silhouettes. I tried to find a smile and could not. I sat very
still, looking up at them. Then, as if the sun had come out from
behind clouds, I remembered this day. I had dreamed it, and all of
the many paths that could diverge from it. I could not remember
when I had dreamed it, and then it seemed that perhaps it was a
dream I was going to have. Or a dream of . . . something. A dream
of a crossroads, a place not of two roads intersecting but of thou-
sands. I folded my legs under me and stood up slowly.

I could not see the children for the overlay of dreams and shadows around them. I tried to study the myriad paths. One, I felt, led
to something I desperately wanted. But which one? What must I do
to put my feet on that path? If I went along another path, I died.
There, they mocked me. There, my mother came running when I
screamed. And there . . .

I could not make it happen. I had to allow it. I had to let the path
form around me from the words I tried to say and the taunts they
flung at me. The moment came when I could have fled but I was
both too afraid to move and aware that only this path led to where
I longed to go. The girls held me, their fingers biting into my thin
wrists until the flesh stood up in ridges that were red, and then
white. They shook me, and my head snapped back and forth on my
neck, so hard that I saw flashes of light behind my eyes. I tried to
speak, and it came out as gobbling. They shrieked with laughter,
and gobbled back at me. Tears sprang into my eyes.

"Do it again, Bee-ee. Make the turkey noise." Taffy stood over
me, so tall he had to crouch inside the bower. I looked up at him
and shook my head.

Then Taffy slapped me. Hard. Once and it rocked my head one
direction, and then again almost instantly, from the other side, and
I knew this was how his mother slapped him sometimes, rocking
his head back and forth so that his ears rang. When the blood
flooded salt into my mouth, I knew it was done. I was on the path.
And now it was time to twist free of them and run, run, run, be-

cause from that point there were so many paths that led to my lying on the earth, broken in ways that could never be mended. And so I snapped my wrists from their grips and pushed through the willow trunks and out through a gap none of them could negotiate. I fled, not toward the manor, but into the wild part of the woods. In a moment they were after me. They chased me, but a small person can run doubled over and use the trails made by rabbits and foxes. And when the trail led into a thick and prickly bramble, I went where they were far too large to follow me without tearing their clothes and skin.

In the middle of a briar patch, I found a hollow, a place where soft grass grew and the brambles shielded me all around. I hunkered down in it and froze there, shaking with fright and pain. I'd done it, but oh, the cost. I heard them shouting and beating the edges of the bramble with branches. As if I would be foolish enough to leave its shelter! They called me vile names but could not see me, nor tell for certain that I still hid there. I made no sound as I opened my mouth and tipped my face down to let the blood run out. Something in my mouth had torn, a piece that went from the underside of my tongue to the bottom of my mouth. It hurt. It bled a lot.

Later, when they were gone, and I tried to spit out the blood, it hurt even more. My tongue moved in my mouth now, flapping like a piece of leather on an old shoe. When the afternoon was ending and the shadows deepening, I crawled out of my briar bower. I went back to the manor by a long and winding way. I stopped at the creek and washed the blood from my mouth. When I went in to the evening meal, both my parents were horrified at the spreading blue bruises on my cheeks and my blackened left eye. My mother asked me how it had happened, but I only shook my head and did not even try to speak. I ate little. My free-flopping tongue got in the way. Twice I bit myself before I gave up and sat staring at the food I longed for. For the next five days, it was hard to eat, and my tongue felt like a strange object that flapped in my mouth.

And yet, and yet, it was the path I had chosen. And when the pain lessened, I was shocked at how freely I could move my tongue. Alone in my room, after my mother thought me asleep, I practiced my words aloud. The sounds that had eluded me before, the sudden starts and sharp endings of words, I now could make. I still did not converse, but now it was because I chose not to, not because I could not. To my mother, I began to speak more clearly, but only in a very soft voice. Why? Because I feared the change I had wrought in myself. Already my father looked at me differently since he had seen I could hold a pen. And dimly I knew that the girls had dared to attack me because I had worn the pink dress that declared a status higher than theirs, one they felt I did not deserve. If I began to speak, would all the servants retreat from me, kindly Cook Nutmeg and our grave steward? I feared that speech would only make me more of a pariah than I already was. I longed so for companionship of some kind. It was to be my downfall.

I should have learned my lesson from what had befallen me. I did not. I was lonely, and the lonely heart has hungers that can overpower both common sense and dignity. Summer advanced, my mouth healed, and I began again to spy on the other children. At first I kept my distance, but it was too frustrating to view them from afar where I could not hear what they said or see what they did. So I learned to go ahead of them and shinny up a tree to look down on their games. I thought myself very clever.

It had to end badly, and it did. That day is as vivid as a dream to me still. They had caught me watching them when I sneezed. For a time they had me treed, and I was fortunate that acorns and pinecones were the best ammunition that Taffy could find. At last I thought of climbing higher up the tree, out of his range. But a tree slender enough for a small child to shinny up is thin enough for three hearty children to shake. For a time I rode the whipping top, and then I fell, flung in a wide arc to land flat on my back. Airless and stunned, I lay helpless. They were silenced and awestruck as they crept up on me.

"Did we kill her?" Elm asked. I heard Lea suck in a terrified breath and then Taffy shouted boldly, "Let's be sure of it, then!"

That brought me out of my daze. I staggered to my feet and ran. They stared after me, and I thought they would let me go. Then, with a roar from Taffy of "Get her!" they came after me, as eager as rabbit-hounds on a trail. My legs were short, my fall had dazed me, and they came close behind me, yammering and shrieking. I ran blindly, my head down, my hands clasped over it to shield myself from the rocks that Taffy scooped up and flung with ever-increasing accuracy. I did not plan to flee toward the lambing shelter. I ran silent as a hare, but when a large body suddenly stepped in front of me and snatched me up high, I shrieked as if I were being killed.

"Quiet, girl!" Lin the shepherd barked at me. As quickly as he'd picked me up, he dropped me, and his dog came up to block my pursuers as Lin turned on them. They had been close on my heels; if he had not been there, they would have caught me that day, and I still wonder if they would have left me alive.

Lin seized Taffy by the back of his collar and swung him up, one-handed, while delivering such a powerful smack to his bottom with his free hand that Taffy's whole body arched to the blow. Lin dropped him and spun on the little girls. They had not been as close, and they nearly managed to get away, but Lin caught one by the pigtail and the other by the edge of her skirts. Both crumpled before his wrath, as he demanded of them, "What be you doing, chasing a tiny child, you great bullies? Shall I teach you what it is to have someone larger than you give you a thrashing?"

Both girls began to wail. Taffy's chin quivered, but he stood up and clenched his fists at his side. I sat flat where Lin had dropped me. It was only when he stooped to help me to my feet that he exclaimed, "Oh, by Eda and El, it's worse than fools you are! This is the little mistress, sister to Lady Nettle herself! Do you think she'll forget what you've done to her this day? Do you imagine that when you are men and women grown, you'll work in the kitchens or fields as your parents have done for generations before you? Or your children after you? If Holder Badgerlock or Lady Molly does not send your parents and you packing from their lands this very day, I'll be shocked!"

"She spied on us!" wailed Lea.

"She follows us about!" Elm accused me.

"She's witless, a moron, and she stares at us with ghost eyes!" This last from Taffy. It was the first time I knew that he feared me.

Lin only shook his head. "She is the daughter of the house, you ninnies! She can go where she will and do as she wishes. Poor little mite! What else is she to do? She only wants to play."

"She can't talk!" Elm objected, and Taffy added, "She's dumb as a post and simple as a stone. Who can play with an idiot? They should keep her tethered inside, they should, and out from underfoot." I knew he repeated something overheard from adults.

Lin looked from them to me. After my first shriek, I hadn't made a sound. His dog came back to me, and I put an arm across her shaggy back. My fingers sank deep into her silky coat, and I felt her comfort flow up into me. She sat down beside me, and our heads were on a level. The shepherd looked from his dog back to the children. "Well. Whatever she be, it costs you nothing to be kind to her. Now you've put me in a bind here. I should tell the Holder, that I should, but I've no desire to see your folks turned out of the places they've held for years. I *will* speak to your parents. You've all three of you too much time on your hands if this is what you get up to. Now, little mistress, let's look at you. Have they hurt you?"

"We didn't touch her!" they shouted.

"Don't tell the Holder! I swear, we'll never chase her again," Taffy bargained.

Lin had gone down on one knee. He picked a dried leaf and a burr from my tunic, and dared to smooth back my tangle of curls. "Well, she's not weeping. Maybe not much hurt, then. Maybe? Not hurt, little one?"

I drew myself up straight and met his eyes. I put my hands behind me and tightened them into fists, my nails biting hard into my palms to give me courage. I found my voice. With my newly loosened tongue, I formed each word as if it was a gift. "Thank you kindly, Shepherd Lin. I am not injured." His eyes grew round. Then I shifted my stare to the gaping children. I fought to keep my new voice steady, speaking each word precisely. "I will not tell my father or my mother. Nor do you need to do so, I think. These children have realized their error."

They stared. I focused my gaze on Taffy and tried to burn holes in him with my eyes. He glared back at me sullenly. Slowly, very slowly, I cocked my head at him. Hatred met hatred in our gazes, but his was greater than mine. What would he fear, if not my hate? I knew. I had to remember each muscle in my face, but slowly I constructed and then let blossom a fawning smile upon my face. I spoke in a gentle whisper. "Dear Taffy."

His eyes bulged at my fond gaze. Then Taffy screamed, more shrilly than I had, and turned and fled. The little girls ran after him. I glanced up at Lin. His eyes were measuring me, but I did not see disapproval. He turned to watch the fleeing children. I think he was speaking more to the dog than to me as he said, "They'll beat you and mistreat you if they think you're a dumb brute. Doesn't matter if you're a mule, or a dog, or a child. And when they find out there's a mind beneath the flesh they've been battering, they fear you. And leave you alone. Sometimes." He took a deeper breath and turned an appraising eye on me. "You'll need to watch your back now, mistress. Time ye had a dog, is what I'm thinking. You speak to your da about that. Daisy and I, we could find a good pup for you. A smart pup."

I shook my head and he shrugged in response. I stood, staring after the wailing children until they rounded the corner of the herb-garden wall. As soon as they were out of sight I turned to the dog and buried my face in her coat. I did not cry. But I shook and held tight to her. She stood steady under my grip, and turned her head to whine and then nuzzle my ear.

"You take care of her, Daisy." Lin's voice was deep, and perhaps something more passed between him and the dog than what I heard. I only knew that she was warm and unthreatening and seemed to have no desire to move away from my desperate hug.

When finally I lifted my face from her coat, Lin was gone. I will never know what he made of that encounter. I gave Daisy a final hug and she licked my hand. Then, seeing that I no longer needed her, she trotted off to find her owner. And I made my way back to the house and up to my chamber. I thought of what I had done. None of the children would dare speak of it to their parents: They would have to explain why I said what I said. Shepherd Lin would, I decided, keep it to himself. How did I know? He had told me to watch my own back, and advised me to get a dog. He expected me to handle this myself. And I would.

I considered his advice about the dog. No. My father would want to know why I wanted one. I could not tell him, not even through my mother.

After my encounter with the children, I took Lin's advice. I stopped following them and avoided them when I could. Instead I began to shadow my father, to see what he did all day while my mother was about her familiar routine. I flattered myself that he did not notice his small shadow, but later I would discover he had been aware of me. His long hikes about the estate to check on things were taxing for my small legs. If he took a horse, I gave up at once. I feared horses, with their long knobby legs and sudden snorting breaths. Years ago, when I was five, he had put me on one, to teach me to ride. In my terror and distress at his invasive touch and at the height of the animal's back, I had snapped myself out of his grip and vaulted over the animal and onto the hard-packed earth. My father had been terrified he had injured me, and had never attempted the experiment again. In my garbled way, I had made excuse to my mother that it had felt rude to sit on someone and expect her to carry me about. And when my mother gave my father that explanation, he had become even more pensive and reluctant to expose me to horses. As I followed him now, I began to regret that. While I dreaded my father's touch and the overwhelming surge of his thoughts into my mind, I still wished to know more of him. If I had been able to ride a horse, I could have followed him. But letting him know that presented difficulties.

Since discovering I could draw, he had begun to spend more time with me. Of an evening he would bring his work to my mother's sitting room. I had my own little table there, with my own inks and pens and paper now. Several times he had shown me moldering old scrolls with faded illustrations of plants and flowers and letters I did not recognize. He had conveyed to me that I should try to copy what I saw, but this was something I had no desire to do. There was so much already stored in my mind, flowers and mushrooms and plants I had seen that I wished to capture on the paper. I did not share his obsession for writing again what had already been written; I knew that disappointed him, and yet it was so.

My father had never understood my mumbling tongue, and even now I did not speak to him much. I hesitated to draw his attention to me. Even to be in the room with him challenged me. When he looked at me or focused his attention on me, the sheer power of his drenching thoughts terrified me. I dared not let him touch me, and even to meet his eyes was to feel the pull of that whirlpool. And so I avoided him, as much as I was able, even though I know it hurt him and grieved my mother.

Despite that, he began to try to play with me. He came one night to the fireside with no scrolls to copy. He sat down on the floor near my little table and patted the hearth next to him. "Come see what I have," he invited me. Curiosity overcame my dread and I left my inks and ventured to stand near him.

"Here's a game," he told me, and lifted a kerchief that covered a tray. On it were a flower, a white pebble, and a strawberry. I looked at it, mystified. Abruptly, he covered it. "Tell me what you saw," he challenged me. I looked at my mother for explanation. She was in her chair on the other side of the hearth, her hands busy with some needlework.

She raised her brows in puzzlement, but prompted me, "What was on the tray, Bee?"

I stared at her. She lifted a rebuking finger and raised her brows at me. I spoke softly without looking at him. "Flowa."

"What else, Bee?"

"Ro-ock."

My mother cleared her throat, bidding me try harder. "Bewwry," I added softly.

"What color flower?" My father prompted me patiently.

"Pink."

"What color rock?"

"White."

"What kind of berry?"

"Stwawbewwy."

"Strawberry," my mother corrected me softly. I looked at her.

Did she know I could say it correctly? I was not sure if I wanted to speak that clearly for my father. Not yet.

My father smiled at me. "Good. Good, Bee. You got them all. Shall we play again?"

I scooted closer to my mother's feet. I looked up at her, pleading with her to rescue me.

"It's an odd game," she ventured, sensing my unease.

My father made an amused sound. "I suppose it is. I used to play it with Chade. He'd add more and more things to the tray, or he'd add something and take something away, and I had to say what was missing. He was training my eyes." He gave a small sigh. Elbow on knee, he cupped his jaw in his hand. "I don't know any real games. I didn't have much chance to play with other children." He looked at me and lifted a helpless hand. "I just wanted to . . ." He sighed away the rest of his words.

"It's a good game," my mother said decisively. She stood, and then surprised me by sitting down on the floor next to him. She drew me close to her side and put her arm around me. "Let's play again," she said, and I knew she sat by me to give me courage, because she wanted me to play with my father. And so I did. We took turns, my mother and I, as my father added more and more items from a leather bag behind him. At nine items, my mother threw up her hands. I played on, forgetting to fear him, my focus only on the tray.

There came a moment when my father said, not to me but my mother, "That's all I have."

I lifted my eyes and looked around. My parents seemed hazy, as if I saw them through a fog or at a great distance. "How many was that?" my mother asked.

"Twenty-seven," my father said quietly.

"How many could you do, as a child?" my mother asked softly. There was trepidation in her voice.

My father took a breath. "Not twenty-seven," he admitted. "Not on my first try."

They looked at each other. Then they returned their focus to me. I blinked and felt myself sway slightly. "I think we are past her time to bed," my mother announced in an odd voice. My father nodded mutely. Slowly he began to return his items to his bag. With a groan for her aching joints, my mother clambered to her feet. She led me away to my bed, and that night she sat beside me until I fell asleep.

On a day of wide blue skies studded with fat white clouds, with a soft wind blowing the scents of lavender and heather, my mother and I puttered in her garden together. The sun was past noon, the flowers breathing gentle fragrance all around us. We were both on our hands and knees. I was working with my little wooden trowel, carved by my father to fit my hand, loosening the earth around the oldest beds of lavender. My mother had her shears and was pruning the runaway sprawl of lavender plants. She would stop now and then to catch her breath and rub her shoulder and the side of her neck. "Oh, I am so tired of getting old," she said once. But then she smiled at me and said, "Look at the fat bee on this blossom! I've cut the stem and he still won't get off. Well, he can just ride along for a while."

She had a large basket to save the trimmings in and this we dragged behind us as we crawled through the lavender bed. It was pleasant, sweet-smelling work, and I was happy. So was she. I know that. She spoke of the odd bits of ribbon she had in her sewing basket, and told me that she was going to show me how to make lavender bottles that would hold the fragrance and could be stored in my clothing chest and hers. "We need to cut the stems long, because we'll fold the stems over the blossoms, and then we'll lace the ribbons through the stems to hold it all together. They'll be pretty, fragrant, and useful. Just like you."

I laughed and she did, too. Then she halted in her work and took a deeper breath. She rocked back on her heels and smiled at me even as she complained, "I've such a stitch in my side," rubbing her ribs and then moving her hand up to her shoulder. "And my left arm aches so. You would think it would be my right, for that's the hand that's doing all the work." She took hold of the edge of the basket and pushed on it, intending to stand. But the basket overturned and she lost her balance and sprawled into the lavender, crushing the bushes under her. A sweet fragrance rose around her. She rolled herself over on her back, and frowned, small lines crinkling her brow. She reached with her right hand and lifted her left and looked at it in wonder. When she let go of it, it fell back to her side. "Well, this is so silly." Her voice was mumbly and soft. She paused and took a deeper breath. With her right hand, she patted my leg. "I'm just going to catch my breath for a moment," she murmured to me, the edges of her words gone rounded. She took a ragged breath and closed her eyes.

Then she died.

I crawled into the heather alongside her and touched her face. I leaned down and put my head on her chest. I heard the last beat of her heart. Then her breath sighed out and all went still inside her. Around us, the wind blew softly and her bees busied themselves in the blossoms. Her body was still warm and she still smelled like my mother. I put my arms around her and closed my eyes. I rested my head on her breast and wondered what would become of me now that the woman who had loved me so was gone.

The day was just cooling when my father came looking for us. He had been to the sheep fields, I knew, for he carried on his arm a big bouquet of the little white roses that grew along the path. He came to the wooden gate in the low stone wall that surrounded the garden, looked in at us, and knew. He knew she was dead before he opened the gate. Still he ran to us, as if he could run back to a time when it wasn't already too late. He dropped to his knees by her body and set his hands to her. He breathed hard and flung his heart into her, searching her flesh for some sign of life. He dragged me with him, and I knew what he knew. She was irrevocably gone.

He gathered us both up to him, threw back his head, and howled. His jaws stretched wide, his face turned up to the sky, and the ridges of muscle in his neck stood out.

He made no sound. Yet the grief that poured through him and up to the sky soaked me and choked me. I drowned in his sorrow. I put my hands against his chest and tried to lever away from him, but could not. From impossibly far away, I felt my sister. She battered at him, demanding to know what was wrong. There were others, ones I had never met, shouting into his mind, offering to send soldiers, to lend strength, to do anything for him that could possibly be done. But he could not even verbalize his pain.

It's my mother! my sister suddenly grasped. And, *Leave him alone. Leave us alone!* she commanded them all, and they receded like a tide.

But still his grief roared on, a storm that battered me with tempest winds that I could not escape. I squirmed wildly, knowing that I was fighting for my sanity and possibly my life. I do not think he even knew he held me trapped between his thundering heart and my mother's cooling body. I wriggled out from under his arm and fell back to the earth and lay there, gasping like a fish out of water.

The slight distance I had gained from him was not enough. I was plunged into a maelstrom of memories. A kiss stolen on a stairway. The first time she had touched his hand and it was no accident. I saw my mother running down a beach of black sand and stone. I recognized the ocean that I had never seen. Her red skirts and blue scarves flapped in the wind and she was laughing over her shoulder as my father chased her. His heart had pounded with joy at the thought that he might catch her, might playfully hold her in his arms, for just a moment. They were children, I suddenly saw, children at play, only a handful of years older than I was now. They had never grown older, neither one of them, not really. All their lives she had remained that girl to him, that wondrous girl just a few years older than he was, but so worldly wise, so female to all that was so male in his life.

"Molly!" he cried out, the word suddenly breaking from him. But he had no breath to shout it; he gasped it out. He crumpled over her body, weeping. His voice came in a whisper. "I'm all alone. I'm all alone. Molly. You can't be gone. I can't be this alone."

I didn't speak to him. I did not remind him that he still had me, for that was not what he was talking about. He still had Nettle, too, and Chade and Dutiful and Thick. But I knew his heart then; could not help but know it as the feelings gushed out of him like blood from a killing wound. His grief mirrored mine exactly. There would never again be anyone like her. Never anyone who would love us so completely, with so little reason. I gave myself over to his grief. I sprawled on my back on the earth and watched the sky darken and the summer stars begin to appear in the deep-blue sky.

A kitchenmaid found us there, shrieked in horror, and then ran back to the house to fetch help. The servants came back with lanterns, half-afraid of the master in his wild grief. But they had no need to be cautious. All strength had gone out of him. He could not even rise from his knees, not even when they tugged her body from his arms to carry her back to the house.

It was only when they reached for me that he roused himself. "No," he said, and in that moment he claimed me as his. "No. She is mine now. Cub, come here, to me. I will take you in."

I set my teeth to his touch as he picked me up. I kept my body stiff and straight as I always did whenever he held me and looked away from his face. I could not bear him, could not bear his feelings. But the truth was on me and I had to speak it. I caught my breath and whispered by his ear the poem from my dream. "When the bee to the earth does fall, the butterfly comes back to change all."

Chapter 11

THE LAST CHANCE

You are correct in your surmise. I haven't told everything I know about that event but in some ways I have shared as much as I believe is safe to share with Chade. Hence, what I will repeat here is for the eyes of the Skillmistress only. Fond as we both are of the old man, we know that he is inclined to risk himself in the pursuit of knowledge.

The first thing to remember is that I was never truly there, myself. I dreamed, and in that dream I Skill-walked. But as one highly gifted in Skill-dreams, you of all people will know that what I saw there, I saw through the eyes of King Verity.

In my dream, we were in a broken city. It held its memories still, as we now understand that some Elderling cities do. I saw it as it had been, full of delicate soaring towers and graceful bridges and thronged by exotic people in bright clothing. And I saw it as Verity experienced it, cold and dark, the streets uneven and every fallen wall a hazard he must negotiate. Sand blew in a vicious wind; he bowed his head to it and trudged toward a river.

As a river I perceived it. But it was not water. It was Skill, as a liquid, as molten gold or even running red iron. To me, it seemed to have a black luminescence then. But in my dream, it was night and winter. Did it have a color at all? I cannot tell you.

I do recall how my king, wasted to a scarecrow of a man, knelt on that bank and relentlessly plunged his hands and arms into the stuff. I shared his pain, for I swear it ate the flesh and muscles from his bones. But when he pulled back from that current, his hands and arms were silvered with pure Skill, with magic in its strongest and most powerful form.

I will also tell you that I helped him refrain from throwing himself into that flow. I lent him the strength to step back from it. Had I truly been there, in my own flesh, I do not think I would have had the strength of will to resist the temptation to drown myself in it.

So, for myself, I am grateful that I do not know the way to that place. I do not know how Verity got there; I do not know how he went from there to the quarry. I suspect he used Skill-pillars, but which ones and what emblem they bore, I do not know and I do not wish to know. A number of years ago, Chade asked me to travel through pillars with him, to go back to the Stone Dragons and from there to the quarry, to discover what pillars King Verity might have used. I refused him then, and I have continued to refuse him.

For the safety of all, I beg that you keep this knowledge only to yourself. Destroy this scroll, if you will, or conceal it where only you can find it. I truly hope that the site is far, far away, reached only by a series of pillar journeys that none of us ever undertakes. The small amount of Skill-magic that we have learned to manipulate should be enough for us. Let us not seek power that exceeds our wisdom to use it.

UNSENT SCROLL FROM FITZCHIVALRY FARSEER
TO SKILLMISTRESS NETTLE

There are endings. There are beginnings. Sometimes they coincide, with the ending of one thing marking the beginning of another. But sometimes there is simply a long space after an ending, a time when it seems everything has ended and nothing else can ever begin. When my Molly, the keeper of my heart since I was a boy, died it was like that. She ended, but nothing else began. There was nothing to take my mind from that void, nothing to redeem my pain, nothing that made sense of her death. Instead her death made every other ending I had ever known a fresh wound.

In the days that followed, I was useless. Nettle came quickly, arriving before the first night had passed, bringing Steady and Riddle with her. I am sure she traveled by the stones, and they as well. Molly and Burrich's sons and their wives and children were there as swiftly as they might come. Other mourners arrived, people I should have greeted, people I should have thanked for their thoughtfulness. Perhaps I did. I've no idea what I did in those long days. Time did not seem to pass, but dragged on and on. The house was full of people, talking and eating together, eating and talking together, weeping and laughing and sharing memories of times when I had not been part of Molly's life, until my only solitude was to retreat to my bedchamber and bolt the door. Yet Molly's absence was greater than anyone's presence. Each of her grown children mourned her. Chivalry wept unashamed. Swift went about with his eyes blank while Nimble simply sat. Steady and Hearth seemed to drink a great deal, something that would have grieved Molly to see. Just had become a solemn young man, and a dark aura of aloneness, very reminiscent of Burrich, hung about him. Nonetheless, he was the one who busied himself taking care of his brothers and sister. Riddle was there as well, ghosting about in the background. We spoke once, late at night, and with good intention he tried to say that my sorrow would pass eventually and my life begin again. I wanted to strike him and I think it showed on my face. After that, we avoided each other.

Dutiful, Elliania, the princes, and Kettricken were in the Mountain Kingdom, so I was spared their presence. Chade never came to funerals, nor did I expect him to visit. Almost every evening I felt him at the edge of my mind, inviting but not intruding. It reminded me of how he would open the secret door to his tower and wait for me when I was a boy. I did not reach back to him, but he knew I was aware of him and grateful for his discretion.

But listing who came and who did not makes it seem as if I noticed or cared. I did not. I lived my grief; I slept mourning and ate sorrow and drank tears. I ignored all else. Nettle stepped into her mother's place, managing it all with seeming effortlessness, as she consulted with Revel to assure that arriving folk had a place to sleep and coordinated meals and supplies with Cook Nutmeg. She undertook that everyone who should be notified of Molly's death was told. Just became the man of the house, directing the stable hands and servants, giving greetings and making farewells. All that they did not command but needed doing, Revel and Riddle managed. I let them. I could not help them with their mourning. I could do nothing for anyone, not even myself.

Somehow, all needful things were done. I cut my hair for mourning, and someone must have cut the child's. Bee looked like a brush for hoof oil when I saw her, a little stick all swathed in black with fuzzy pale stubble standing up on her little head. Her blank blue eyes were dead. Nettle and the boys insisted that their mother had wanted to be buried. Like Patience before her, she wished not to be burned, but to return as quickly as possible to the earth that nurtured all things that she had loved. Buried in the ground. It made me cold. I had not known. I had never spoken to her of such things, had never thought of or imagined a time when she would not be there. Wives always outlive their husbands. Everyone knows that. I had known that and counted on it. And fate had cheated me.

Burying her was hard for me. It would have been easier for me to watch her burn on a pyre, to know she was gone, gone completely and untouchable, than to think of her wrapped only in a shroud and put under the weight of damp soil. Day after day I went back to her grave, wishing that I had touched her cheek one more time before they put her into the dark earth. Nettle set the plants that would define her mother's resting place. Daily, when I visited, I saw the prints of Bee's small feet. Not a weed dared show itself.

I saw little more of Bee than her footprints. We avoided each other. At first I felt guilt that in the depths of my grief, I had deserted my child. I went seeking her. But as I entered a room, she would leave it. Or place herself as far from me as possible. Even when she sought me in my private den late at night, it was not me she sought, but the isolation that room granted us both. She entered that sanctuary like a tiny ghost in a scarlet nightgown. We did not speak. I did not bid her go back to her sleepless bed, nor offer her empty promises that all would eventually be well. In my den, we huddled as separately as scalded cubs. I knew I could no longer bear to be in Molly's study. I suspect she felt the same. Her mother's absence was stronger in that room than anywhere else in the house. Why did we avoid each other? The best explanation I can offer is a comparison. When you hold your burned hand near the fire, the pain flares anew. The closer I came to Bee, the more acute my pain became. I believe that in the crumpling of her little face and the trembling of her lower lip, I read that she felt the same.

Five days after we buried Molly most of the mourners packed up and left Withywoods. Hap had not come. He had a minstrel's summer post far away in Furrow. I don't know how he received word so quickly, but he sent me back a note by bird. It came to the Buckkeep cotes, and from there a runner brought it to me. It was good to hear from him, but I was just as glad that he had not come. There were other notes that came in various ways. One was from Kettricken in the Mountain Kingdom, a simple note on plain paper, written in her own hand. Dutiful had touched minds with me and knew there was nothing to say. From Lady Fisher, once Starling, came a letter elegantly written on fine paper, with heartfelt words. I had a rougher missive from Web. They said what such notes always say. Perhaps words are helpful to others when they mourn; to me they were only words.

Molly's boys had farms and work and families and animals to tend. Summer does not allow anyone who makes a living from the land any time to stand still. There had been much weeping, but also fond recollections and the gentle laughter they brought with them. Nettle had quietly asked me to sort some keepsakes that each of her brothers could take. I asked her to do it, saying I was not up to such a task and that without the woman, her possessions meant little to me. Only later would I realize how selfish a decision that was, to put that weight on my elder daughter's shoulders.

But at the time I was numb and stunned, thoughtless of anyone except myself. Molly had been my safety, my home, my center. With her gone I felt flung to pieces, as if my core had exploded and chunks of me were strewn to the wind. For almost all of my life, there had been Molly. Even when I could not be with her, even the agony of watching her from afar as she gave her life and love to another man, even that pain was infinitely preferable to her total absence from my world. In our years apart, I had always been able to dream "one day." Now all dreams were over.

Some days after her death, when the house had emptied of guests and the extra staff Revel had called in had also departed, Nettle came into my private study. Her duties at Buckkeep were calling her. She had to return, and I did not blame her, for I knew there was nothing she could do here that would improve anything. When Nettle entered, I lifted my eyes from my paper and set my pen carefully aside. Writing down my thoughts has always been my retreat. That night, I had written page after page, burning each one almost as soon as it was finished. Rituals do not have to make sense. On the hearth, on a folded blanket, Bee was curled into a kitten ball. She was dressed in her little red robe and fur slippers. Her curved back was to me, her face turned toward the fire. Night was deep, and we had not spoken a single word to each other.

Nettle looked as if she should have gone to her rest hours ago. Weeping had left her eyes red-rimmed, and her glorious mane of black waves had been reduced to a curly cap. It made the circles under her eyes darker and the thinness of her face bony. The simple blue robe she wore hung on her, and I realized how much flesh she had lost.

Her voice was hoarse. "I have to return to Buckkeep tomorrow. Riddle will escort me."

"I know," I said at last. I did not tell her it would be a relief to be alone where I could mourn as savagely as I needed and no one would witness it. I did not tell her that I felt suspended, restrained by civility in a place where I could not express the anguish I felt.

Instead I said, "I know you must wonder. You know I brought the Fool back from the other side of death. You must wonder why I let your mother go."

I had thought my words would trigger her hidden anger. Instead she looked horrified. "That would have been the last thing I wished for! Or that she would have wanted! To every creature is given both a place and a time, and when that time is over, we have to let them go. Mother and I spoke plainly of that, once. I had come to her about Thick. You know how he is, how his joints hurt him. I asked her for a liniment that Burrich used to make for the boys when they had strained muscles, and she mixed some up for me. Sweet Eda, that is another thing gone! Why did I never write that down? So much she knew, so much he knew, and they took it to their graves with them."

I did not tell her, then, that I knew that recipe as well as anyone could. Doubtless Burrich had passed his lore on to his sons as well. It was not a time to speak of those things. I noticed there was ink on the little finger of my right hand. I always managed to get ink on myself when I wrote. I took up my pen wipe and smeared it away. "What did Molly say about Thick?" I dared to ask.

Nettle came back to herself as if she had walked a far and darkening path. "Only that there was mercy in making pain bearable, but not in forcing someone to remain in this life when their body's work was done. She was cautioning me about using the Skill on him. I told her that Thick was far stronger in that area than I was, and that he was more than capable of turning that talent on himself as he desired it. He hasn't. So I'll respect his choice. But I know that Chade has availed himself of that magic. He keeps himself as spry as he was when I first met him."

Her voice trailed away, but I thought I heard her unasked question. "I don't," I told her bluntly. "I never desired to stay young and watch your mother age away from me. No. If I could have aged with her, Nettle, I would have. I am still bearing the consequences of that mad Skill-healing that our coterie did on me. Could I stop it, I would. It renews me when I wish it would not. I strain a shoulder doing some task, and that night I lose flesh as my body burns me up repairing itself. I wake ravenous and am tired for a week. But my shoulder will have healed." I tossed my latest sheet of writing onto the fire, and shoved it deeper into the flames with the poker. "There. Now you know."

"I knew already," she told me tartly. "Do you think my mother didn't know? Fitz, stop it. No one blames you for her death; nor should you feel guilty for not following her. She would not have wanted that. I love you for the life you gave her. After my father . . . after Burrich died, I thought she would never smile again. And when she discovered you were still alive, after she had so long mourned you as dead, I thought she would never stop being furious. But you came back to her and were patient enough to win her back. You were good for her, and she has lived her last years exactly as I wished all her life could have been."

I wheezed in a breath past my constricted throat. I wanted to thank her but could not find words. I didn't need to. She sighed and reached out to pat my arm. "So. We'll be gone in the morning, then. I was a bit surprised to find that Bee does not have a pony, and seemed completely unfamiliar with the concept of riding. Nine years old and she can't ride! Burrich put me on a horse when I was . . . well, I simply can't remember a time when I couldn't ride. When I tried to put Bee up on a horse, she struggled against me and clambered down the other side of the beast as swiftly as she could. So I think our journey to Buckkeep will be an interesting one for me. She is small enough that I think I can fit her into a pannier on a pack animal and balance her with her clothes and toys. Or some of them. I was totally astonished that one small child could possess so many toys and so much clothing!"

I felt as if I were running along behind her. "Bee?" I asked. "Why would you take Bee to Buckkeep?"

She gave me an exasperated look. "Where else can I take her? Both Chivalry and Nimble offered to have her, even though Nimble does not have a wife to help him with her. I said no to both of them. They've no idea of what they would be taking on. At least I've my experience of Thick. I think in time, I will be able to reach through her fog and get some understanding of her."

"Her fog," I said stupidly.

My elder daughter just stared at me. "She's nine. She should be speaking by now. And she can't. She used to babble at Mother, but I haven't even heard her do that lately. With Mother gone, who will be able to understand the poor little thing? I wonder if she knows that Mother has died. I've tried to speak to her about it, but she just turns away from me." Nettle sighed heavily. "I wish I knew how much of anything she grasps." She cocked her head at me and spoke hesitantly. "I know Mother would not have approved, but I have to ask. Have you ever used the Skill to try to touch her mind?"

I shook my head slowly. I wasn't following her trail of thought. I tried to make a connection. "Molly did not wish me to do that, and so I did not. I discovered the dangers of letting Skill touch children years ago. Don't you recall?"

That wrung a bit of a smile from her. "Both Dutiful and I recall that well. But I thought that after years of silence from your daughter, you'd at least have tried to see if she had a mind."

"Of course she does! She's a clever little creature. Sometimes alarmingly so! And she talks when she pleases. It's just not very clear. Or as often as one might expect." I had not stopped to think that Nettle had never seen her little sister sewing a sampler at their mother's knee, or standing on a table to take candles from their molds. All she had ever seen of Bee in her comings and goings was a shy and elfin child, quiet and watchful. And now she was a mute child, curled in a tight ball. I rose, paced around the room, and then stooped by my younger daughter. "Come here, Bee," I said impulsively, but the moment I set my hand on the child's back, she stiffened straight as a sun-dried fish, then scooted away from my touch and curled again, her face away from me.

"Leave her be," Nettle said firmly. "Fitz, let us speak plainly to each other. You are a man in deep grief and you cannot think outside yourself right now. Even before this happened, you were not . . . well, focused on your daughter. You cannot care for her. Did I not know you better, I would say she fears you. I do know it is not in you to be cruel to a child. So I will plainly say only that she does not want to be touched by you. How could you possibly take care of her? She will have to go with me tomorrow. There are many nurses at Buckkeep, and as I have seen in the last few days she actually takes little tending. Once dressed, she feeds herself, she knows not to soil herself, and left alone she seems content to sit and stare into a fire. One of the women who used to tend Thick would be a good choice, I think, especially one who is older now and looking for a simple position." Nettle drew a chair closer to the fire and sat down. She leaned down to touch her sister. The child wriggled away from her, and Nettle let her go. Bee found her favorite spot on the hearth and folded her legs up inside her robe. I watched her little body relax as she folded her hands and lost herself in the dancing flames. Safe there. Safe as she would not be in Buckkeep. I thought of letting her go with her sister. I didn't like the idea. Was it selfish to keep her with me? I wasn't sure.

"They'll be cruel to her there." The words bled slowly from me.

"I would not hire a woman who would be cruel! Do you think so little of my judgment?" Nettle was outraged.

"Not her nurse. The children of the keep. When she goes for her lessons, they will peck her for being small and pale. Pinch her at meals. Take her sweets away, chase her down the corridors. Mock her. For being different."

"The other children? Her lessons?" Nettle was incredulous. "Open your eyes, Fitz. Lessons in what? I love her as dearly as anyone can, but a comfortable and safe life is the best we can do for her. I would not send her to lessons, nor put her at a table where she might be mocked or pinched. I'll keep her safe in her own chamber, near my own. Fed, dressed, and clean, with her simple little toys. It is the best we can offer her and all she knows to want from life."

I stared at her, baffled by her words. How could she see Bee that way? "You think her a simpleton?"

She looked jolted that I would deny it. Then she reached into herself and found steel. "It happens. It's not her fault. It's not your fault. It's something we cannot hide from. She was born to my mother late in her life, and she was born tiny. Such children seldom have a . . . a growing mind. They stay children. And for the rest of her life, be it short or long, someone must look after her. So it would be best if—"

"No. She'll stay here." I was adamant, shocked that Nettle could suggest otherwise. "Regardless of what you may think, despite her strange ways, she has a bright little mind. And even if she were simple, my answer would be the same. Withywoods is all she has ever known. She knows her way about the house and grounds, and the servants accept her. She isn't stupid, Nettle, nor slow. She's small, and yes, she's different. She may not speak often, but she does talk. And she does things. Sewing, tending the hives, weeding the gardens, writing in her little book. She loves to be outdoors. She loves being free to do as she will. She followed Molly everywhere."

My elder daughter just stared at me. She tipped her head toward Bee and asked skeptically, "This tiny child sews? And can tend a hive?"

"Surely your mother wrote to you . . ." My words dwindled away. Writing was a task for Molly. And it was only in the last year that I myself had seen the bright spark of intellect in my child. Why should I think Nettle had known of it? I had not shared the knowledge of it with her, or Chade or anyone at Buckkeep. At first I had feared to rejoice too soon. And after our remembering game, I had been wary of sharing knowledge of the child's talents with Chade. I was still certain he would quickly find ways to exploit her.

Nettle was shaking her head. "My mother was overly fond of her youngest. She bragged to me of things that seemed . . . well. It was plain that she longed desperately for Bee to be . . ." Her voice sank as she could not bring herself to say the words.

"She's a capable little girl. Ask the servants," I advised her, and then wondered how much of Bee's abilities they had seen. I walked back to my desk and dropped into my chair. None of it mattered. "In any case, she's not going with you, Nettle. She's my daughter. It's only right that she stay with me."

Such words for me to say to her. She stared at me, her mouth slowly flattening. She could have said something cruel then. I saw her choose not to do so. I would have called my words back if I could, would have found another way to state that thought. Instead I added frankly, "I failed at that duty once, with you. This will be my last chance to do it right. She stays."

Nettle was silent for a short time and then said gently, "I know you mean well. You intend to do right by her. But Fitz, I just doubt that you can. It's as you say; you've never had the care of such a small child as she is—"

"Hap was younger than she when I took him in!"

"Hap was normal." I do not think she meant for the word to come out so harshly.

I stood. I spoke firmly to my elder daughter. "Bee is normal, too. Normal for who and what she is. She's going to stay here, Nettle, and keep her little life as it is. Here, where her memories of her mother are."

Nettle had begun to weep. Not for sorrow but because she was so weary and still knew she was going to defy me and that it would hurt me. Tears slid down her face. She did not sob. I saw her set jaw and knew she would not back down from her decision. Just as I knew I would not allow her to take Bee from me. Someone was going to break; we could not both win this.

"I have to do right by my baby sister. My mother would expect that of me. And I can't allow her to stay here," she said. She looked at me, and in her eyes I read a hard sympathy for what she knew I was feeling. Sympathy but no mercy. "Perhaps if I find a good nurse for her at Buckkeep, she could sometimes accompany Bee to come back here and visit," she offered doubtfully.

I could feel my anger start to build. Who was she to question my competence in this? The answer that came to me was a dash of cold water in my face. She was the daughter I had abandoned so that I might serve my king. The daughter raised by another man. More than anyone else in the world, she had the right to believe me an incompetent parent. I looked away from both my daughters.

"If you take her, I'll be alone here." The words sounded so self-pitying that I instantly regretted them.

Nettle spoke softly and more gently than such a selfish statement deserved. "Then the answer is clear. Close up Withywoods. Leave the staff to run it. Pack up your things. Come back with me to Buckkeep Castle."

I opened my mouth to speak and could think of nothing to say. I'd never even considered the idea that I might return to Buckkeep Castle one day. Part of my heart leapt up at the thought. No need to face this gulf of loneliness. I could run from it. At Buckkeep, I'd see old friends again, the halls of the keep, the kitchens, the steams, the stables, the steep streets of Buckkeep Town . . .

As abruptly, my enthusiasm died. Empty. No Molly, no Burrich, no Verity, no Shrewd. No Nighteyes. The yawning cavern of emptiness gaped wider as each remembered death slashed at me.

No Fool.

"No," I said. "I can't. There's nothing for me there. Only politics and intrigue."

The sympathy I had seen in her face faded. "Nothing." She said the word stiffly. "Only me." She cleared her throat. "And Chade and Dutiful and Kettricken and Thick."

"That's not what I meant." Suddenly I was too tired to explain. I tried anyway. "The Buckkeep Castle I knew is long gone. And life there has gone on without me for too long. I don't know how I'd fit in there now. Not as FitzChivalry Farseer, certainly. Not as the assassin and spy for the royal family. Nor as Tom Badgerlock, the serving man. One day I'll come to visit for a week or even a month, and see everyone then. But not to stay, my dear. Never again to stay there. And not now. The thought of going somewhere now, of meeting old friends, eating and drinking, laughing and talking . . . no. I have no heart for it."

She rose and came to me. She stood behind my chair and set her hands to my shoulders. "I understand," she said. There was forgiveness in her voice for my thoughtless remark. She had that in her, that ability to forgive easily. I had no idea where she had learned it. It humbled me: I knew I didn't deserve it. She spoke on. "I had hoped it might be otherwise, but I understand. And maybe in the spring you will feel differently. Maybe by then you'll be ready to come and spend some time with us."

She sighed, squeezed my shoulders a final time, and then yawned like a cat. "Oh. It's gotten late somehow. I should have put Bee to bed hours ago. We've an early start to make, and I still need to find a way to make her comfortable in a pannier. I should go to bed now."

I made no reply. Let her go to bed and get some sleep. In the morning, when she tried to take Bee, I'd simply say no. But for tonight, I could let it go. A coward's way out.

Bee was still sitting cross-legged, still staring into the flames. "Come, Bee, bedtime," Nettle said, and stooped to pick up her sister. Bee rolled her little shoulders in a way I knew well, moving herself just outside Nettle's grip. Nettle tried again, and again the child shrugged her away. "Bee!" Nettle objected.

Bee turned her face up and looked somewhere between Nettle and me. "No. I'm staying with Papa."

Never had I heard her speak so clearly. It shocked me, and I fought to keep that from my face and from my Skill.

Nettle froze. Then slowly she crouched down next to her sister to peer into her face. "Staying with Papa?" She spoke each word slowly and carefully.

Bee turned her head sharply aside and said nothing. She looked away from both of us, into the shadowy corners of the room. Nettle shot me an incredulous look. I realized that it might be the first time she had ever heard her sister speak a full sentence. Nettle put her attention back on the child.

"Bee, it's time to go to bed. In the morning we must get up very early. You're going for a ride with me, a long ride to a place called Buckkeep Castle. It will be so much fun to see a new place! So come to me so I can take you to your bed and tuck you in."

I saw Bee's shoulders tighten. She bent her head down, tucking her chin to her chest.

"Bee," Nettle warned her and then tried again to pick her up. Again Bee squirmed out of her grip.

She had moved closer to me, but I knew better than to try to pick her up. Instead I addressed her directly.

"Bee. Do you want to stay here with me?"

No words came from her, only a single sharp nod of her head.

"Let her stay," I told Nettle, and with a sigh my elder daughter rose.

She rolled her shoulders, stretched, and added with a sigh, "Perhaps it's better this way. Let her wear herself out and fall asleep. Once she's bundled up tomorrow, she can catch up on her rest for part of the journey."

Nettle had not accepted her sister's response. I had to make it clear for her. I leaned down toward my younger daughter.

"Bee? Do you want to go on a journey with Nettle tomorrow, to Buckkeep Castle? Or do you want to stay here at Withywoods with me?"

Bee turned her head, and her pale glance slipped past both of us. She looked up into the dark recesses of the ceiling. Her eyes darted to me once and then away. She took a long slow breath. She spoke each word distinctly. "I do not wish to go to Buckkeep Castle. Thank you, Nettle, for your kind offer. But I will be staying home here, at Withywoods."

I looked at Nettle and turned a hand up. "She says she wants to stay here."

"I heard her," she replied sharply. She looked jolted at hearing her sister speak, but I maintained a calm façade. I would not betray that this was more talking than she usually did in a week, let alone that her enunciation was unusually clear. Bee and I were in this together, I sensed. Allies. So I looked at Nettle calmly as if I were not startled at all.

For a moment Nettle resembled her mother right before she would fly into a temper. I looked at her and my heart smote me. Why had I so often provoked that look from Molly when she had been alive? Couldn't I have been kinder, gentler? Couldn't I have let her have her way more often? Black and utter loneliness rose in me. I felt sick with it, as if the emptiness were something I needed to vomit out of my body.

Nettle spoke in a low voice. "It's not a decision that she is competent to make for herself. Think of the days ahead. How are you going to take care of her, when you've barely taken care of yourself these last two weeks? Do you think she can go without eating, as you have? Do you think she can stay up until dawn, sleep a few hours, and then drag herself through the day as you do? She's a child, Tom. She needs regular meals, and a routine and discipline. And, yes, you are right, she does need lessons. And her first lessons need to be in how not to be strange! If she can speak, as she just so clearly did, then she needs to be taught to speak more often, so that people know she has a mind. She needs to be taught all that is needful for her to know. And she needs to be encouraged to speak, not let everyone think she is a mute or an idiot! She needs to be cared for, not just day-to-day food and clothing, but month to month and year to year, learning and growing. She can't run about Withywoods like a stray kitten while you soak yourself in old books and brandy."

"I can teach her," I asserted, and wondered if I could. I remembered the hours I had spent with Fedwren and the other children of Buckkeep. I wondered if I could find the patience and tenacity he had possessed in teaching us. Well, as I must, I would, I decided silently. I had taught Hap, hadn't I? My mind leapt sideways to Chade's offer. He had said he would send me FitzVigilant. He had not told me yet that it was time, but certainly it must be soon.

Nettle was shaking her head. Her eyes were pink from both tears and weariness. "There is another thing you are ignoring. She looks like a six-year-old, but she is nine. When she is fifteen, will she still look like a much younger child? How will that affect her life? And how will you tell her about what it is to be a woman?"

How, indeed? "That is years away," I asserted with a calmness I did not feel. I realized that my Skill-walls were up and tight, keeping Nettle from feeling any doubts that I had. Yet by the very impenetrability of my walls, she would know I was keeping something from her. That could not be changed. She and I shared the Skill-magic and had been able to reach each other since she was a little girl. That unforgiving access to each other's dreams and experiences was one reason I had refrained from using the Skill to know Bee's mind. I glanced at her now, and to my shock she was staring directly at me. For a moment our gazes met and held, as they had not for years.

My instinctive response surprised me. I dropped my eyes. From somewhere in my heart, an old wolf warned me, "Staring into someone's eyes is rude. Don't provoke a challenge."

An instant later I looked back at Bee, but she, too, had cast her gaze aside. I watched her and thought I saw her sneak a glance at me from the corner of her eye. She reminded me so much of a wild creature that I knew a lurch of fear. Had she inherited the Wit from me? I had left her mind untouched by mine, but in many ways that meant I had left it unguarded as well. In her innocence, had she already bonded with an animal? One of the kitchen cats, perhaps? Yet her mannerisms did not mirror a cat's. No. If anything, she mimicked the behavior of a wolf cub, and it was impossible that she would have bonded to one of those. Yet another mystery from my peculiar child.

"Are you listening?" Nettle demanded, and I startled. Her dark eyes could flash fire just as her mother's had.

"No. I'm sorry, I wasn't. I was thinking of all the things I'd need to teach her, and it distracted me." And gave me more reason than ever to keep her safely at Withywoods with me. I recalled an incident with a horse and felt cold. If Bee was Witted, then home was the safest place for her. Feeling against the Witted was not as publicly hostile as it had been, but old habits of thinking died hard. There would still be plenty of folk at Buckkeep who would think even a Witted child was best served by hanging, burning, and being cut into pieces.

"And are you listening now?" Nettle persisted. With an effort I pulled my gaze from Bee and met her eyes.

"I am."

She folded her lower lip into her mouth and chewed on it, thinking hard. She was going to offer me a bargain, one she didn't much like. "I'm coming back here in three months. If she looks neglected in any way, I'm taking her with me. And that's the end of it." Her tone softened as she added, "But if anytime before then you realize you've bitten off more than you can chew, let me know and I'll send for her immediately. Or you can bring her to Buckkeep Castle yourself. And I promise I will not say, *I warned you*. I'll just take her over."

I wanted to tell her, *That is never going to happen*. But over the years I've learned not to tempt fate, for it has always seemed to me that the very things I swore I would never do are the ones that I ended up doing. So I nodded to my formidable daughter and replied mildly, "That seems fair. And you should go to bed and get some sleep if you're making an early start."

"I should," she agreed. She held out a hand to the child. "Come, Bee. Now it's bedtime for us both, and no argument."

Bee hung her head, her reluctance obvious. I intervened.

"I'll put her to bed. I've said I can take care of her in all ways. It's fitting that I begin now."

Nettle rocked, hesitant. "I know what you'll do. You intend to let her stay there until she falls asleep on the hearth, and then just trundle her into her bed as she is."

I looked at her, knowing what we were both remembering. More than once I had fallen asleep on Burrich's hearth in the stables, some bit of harness or simple toy in my hands. Always, I woke under a woolen blanket on my pallet near his bed. I suspected he had done the same for Nettle when she was small. "Neither of us took any harm from that," I told her. She gave a quick nod, her eyes filling with tears, and turned and left.

I watched her go through misted eyes. Her shoulders were rounded and slumped. She was defeated. And orphaned. She was a woman grown, but her mother had died just as abruptly as the man who had raised her had. And though her father stood before her, she felt alone in the world.

Her loneliness amplified my own. Burrich. My heart yearned for him suddenly. He was the man I would have gone to, the one whose advice I would have trusted in dealing with my grief. Kettricken was too contained, Chade too pragmatic, Dutiful too young. The Fool was too gone.

I reined my heart away from exploring those losses. It was one of my faults, one that Molly had sometimes rebuked me for indulging. If one bad thing befell me, I immediately linked it to every bad thing that had happened in the last week or might happen in the coming week. And when I became sad, I was prone to wallow in grief, piling up my woes and sprawling on them like a dragon on a hoard. I needed to focus on what I had, not what I had lost. I needed to remember there was a tomorrow, and I had just committed myself to someone else's tomorrow as well.

I looked at Bee, and she immediately looked away. Despite my aching heart, I smiled. "We two, we need to talk," I told her.

She stared into the fire, still as stone. Then she nodded slowly. Her voice was small and high, but clear. Her diction was not a child's. "You and I *do* need to talk." She flickered a glance in my direction. "But I never needed to talk to Mama. She just understood."

I truly had not expected any response from her. With her nod and earlier brief words, she had already exceeded most of her previous communication directed at me. She had spoken to me before, simple requests when she wanted more paper or needed me to cut a pen for her. But this, this was different. This time, looking at my small daughter, a cold realization filled me. She was profoundly different from what I had always assumed her to be. It was a very strange sensation as the familiar tipped away and I spilled into the unknown. This was my child, I reminded myself. The daughter Molly and I had dreamed of for so long. Since Molly's strange pregnancy and Bee's birth, I had been trying to reconcile myself to what I thought she was. In one night nine years ago, I had gone from fearing my beloved wife was delusional to being the father of a tiny but perfect infant. For the first few months of her life, I had allowed myself the wild dreams that any parent has for a child. She would be clever and kind and pretty. She would want to learn all Molly and I had to teach her. She would have a sense of humor and be curious and lively. She would be company for us as she grew, and, yes, that trite concept, a comfort to us in our old age.

Then, as week after month and then years passed, and she did not catch up her growth, nor speak, I had been forced to confront her differences. Like a worm slowly eating into an apple, the knowledge burrowed in and hollowed my heart. She did not grow, or laugh or smile. Bee would never be the child I had imagined.

The worst part was that I had already given my heart to that imaginary child, and it was so terribly hard to forgive Bee for not being her. Her existence turned my life into a gamut of emotions. It was hard to kill my hope. As she slowly developed skills that other children would have had years ago, my hope that somehow, now, she was getting better would flare up in me. Each crash of that vain hope was harder than the previous one. Deep sorrow and disappointment sometimes gave way to cold anger at fate. Through it all, I flattered myself that Molly was unaware of my ambivalence toward our child. To cover how hard it was to accept her as she was, I became fiercely protective of her. I would tolerate no one else speaking of her differences as shortcomings. Anything she desired, I got for her. I never expected her to attempt anything she was reluctant to try. Molly had been serenely unaware that Bee suffered in comparison with the imaginary child I had created. She had seemed content with our daughter, doting, even. I had never had the heart to ask her if she ever looked at Bee and wished for another child. I had refused to consider if I ever looked at her and wished that she had never been.

I had wondered what would become of her as she grew and we aged. I had thought that her sparse words meant she was simple in some way, and I had treated her as such, until the evening when she had astonished me at the memory game. Only in the last year had I found the wisdom to enjoy what she was. I had finally relaxed and taken pleasure in the joy she brought to her mother. The terrible storms of disappointment had given way to calm resignation. Bee was what she was.

But now Bee spoke clearly to me, and it woke shame in me. Before she had given me simple sentences, as sparing of her mumbled words as if they were gold coins. Tonight I had felt such a leap of relief when she spoke that first simple request to stay with me. Small she might be, but she could talk. Why shame? It shamed me that it was suddenly so much easier to love her than it had been when she was mute.

I thought of the old fable and decided I had no choice. I would grasp the nettle. Nonetheless, I approached it cautiously. "Do you dislike speaking?"

She gave a short shake of her head.

"So you held silent with me because . . . ?"

Again a flash of her pale-blue glance. "No need to talk to you. I had Mama. We were together so much. She listened. Even when I could not speak plainly, she could make out what I meant. She understood without all the words you need."

"And now?"

Her little shoulders twisted away from me, a squirming discomfort in this conversation. "When I have to. To stay safe. But before, it was safer to be quiet. To be what the servants are accustomed to me being. Mostly they treat me well. But if I suddenly spoke to them as I am speaking to you, if they overheard me speaking to you like this, they would fear me. And then they would consider me a threat. I would be in danger from the grown-ups, too."

Too? I thought. I made the leap. "As you are from the children."

A nod. No more than that, and of course that must be so. Of course.

She was so precocious. So adult. That tiny voice speaking such grown-up words. And so chilling to hear her assess the situation as if she were Chade rather than my little girl. I had hoped to hear her speak to me in simple sentences; I would have welcomed the uncomplicated logic of a child. Instead the pendulum swung the other way: From resignation that my daughter was mute and simple I suddenly felt dread that she was unnaturally complex and perhaps deceitful.

She looked at my feet. "You're a little bit afraid of me now." She bowed her head and folded her little hands on her crossed legs and waited for me to lie.

"Uneasy. Not afraid," I admitted unwillingly. I tried to find the right words but could not. I settled on, "I am . . . amazed. And a bit unsettled that you can speak so well, and I never guessed you were capable of such thought. It is unnerving, Bee. Still, I love you a lot more than I fear you. And with time, I'll get used to . . . how you really are."

The little pink head with its haze of blond hair nodded slowly. "I think you can. I'm not sure Nettle could."

I found I shared her reservations about that but felt obliged to defend my older daughter. "Well, but it's not fair that you expect she could. Or even that I could! Why did you hold back? Why not begin talking as you learned to speak rather than keep silent?"

Head still lowered, she lifted one shoulder and shook her head mutely. I had not expected any answer. In truth, I understood the keeping of such secrets. For years in my own childhood, I had hidden the secret of my bastardy from Molly, pretending I was no more than the scribe's errand boy. Not to deceive her but because I had longed to be so unremarkable. I knew too well that the longer that sort of secret is kept, the harder it is to expose it without seeming deceitful. How could I not have seen this? How could I keep her from the mistakes I had made? I tried to speak to her as a father should.

"Well, it's an odd secret you've kept. And I advise you to surrender it now. You should begin to speak to other people. Not like we are talking now, but with a few words here and there. Naming things you want when you point at them. Then moving on to simple requests."

"You want me to practice a new sort of deception," she said slowly. "You want me to pretend I'm just now learning to speak."

And I realized I had sounded more like an assassin's mentor than a loving father. I was giving her the sort of advice Chade would have given me. I felt uncomfortable at that thought and spoke more firmly because of it. "Well. Yes. I suppose I am. But I think it's a necessary deception, based on the first one you chose. Why on earth would you pretend that you can barely speak at all? Why did you keep your words so hidden?"

She pulled her knees tighter to her chest, clasped her arms round them, and held herself tight and small. Holding her secret close, I guessed. Doubt dropped the floor of my belly. There was more here that I did not know. I consciously took my eyes off her. *Don't stare at her. She is only nine.* How large a secret could such a tiny person conceal? I thought of myself at nine and grew still inside.

She didn't answer my question. Instead she asked, "How did you do that?"

"Do what?"

She rocked slightly, chewing on her lip. "You are holding it in now. Not spilling out everywhere."

I rubbed my face and decided to let her lead the conversation, even if she carried me onto painful ground. Let her become accustomed to talking to me . . . and me to listening to her. "You mean, how sad I've been? That I'm not weeping today?"

An impatient shake of her head. "No. I mean everything." Again that tilt of her little head and a look from the corners of her eyes.

I considered my words and spoke gently. "You're going to have to explain better than that."

"You . . . boil. Like the big kettle in the kitchen. When you come near, ideas and images and what you think come out of you like the steam from the pot. I feel your heat and smell what seethes inside you. I try to hold back but it drenches me and scalds me. And then, when my sister was here, suddenly you put a lid on. I could still feel the heat but you kept in the steam and the smells . . . There! Just now! You made the lid tighter and cooled the heat."

She was right. I had. As she had spoken, dread had risen in me. She did not think of the Skill as I did, but the images she used could not apply to anything else. And the moment I realized that she had been privy to my thoughts and emotions, I had slammed my Skill-walls tighter, sealing myself behind them as Verity had taught me so many years ago. Verity had pleaded with me to learn to hold my walls tight because my adolescent dreams of Molly were spilling over into his sleep and infiltrating his own dreams and destroying his rest. And now I walled out my little daughter. I cast my thoughts back over not just that evening, but all the days and nights of the past nine years, wondering what she had heard and seen in her father's thoughts. I recalled how she had always stiffened when I touched her, and how she averted her eyes from my glance. Even as she did now. I had suspected she disliked me, and it had grieved me. Never had I stopped to think that if she knew all my thoughts about her she had every right to dislike me, the man who had never been content with her, who had always wished his daughter to be someone else.

But now she looked up at me cautiously. For less than a wink, our gazes met. "It's so much better," she said quietly. "So much more peaceful when you are contained."

"I wasn't aware that you were . . . so beset by my—my thinking. I shall try to keep my walls closed when I am around you."

"Oh, could you?" she begged, relief evident in her voice. "And Nettle? Can you ask her, also, to close her walls when she comes near me?"

No. I could not. To tell her sister that she must keep her Skill-walls tight when she was around Bee would betray to her how sensitive her sister was to that magic. And I was not prepared for Nettle to wonder, as I did now, just how much ability Bee would have for that Farseer magic. How "useful" might she be? I was suddenly Chade, seeing before me a child, apparently a very young child, but actually years older and Skilled. Rosemary had been an excellent child-spy. But Bee would outshine her as the sun outshines a candle. Walls tight, I did not betray that thought to her. Senseless to make her worry about such things just yet. I would do all the worrying for both of us. I made my voice calm.

"I will speak to Nettle about it, but not just now. Next time she comes to visit us, perhaps. I will have to think how to phrase the request." I had no intention of conveying this to Nettle, not until I myself had decided how best to handle it. I was rummaging in my thoughts, trying to decide how best to push my question of why she had concealed her intellect and speaking abilities, when she suddenly stood up. She looked up at me, all big blue eyes, with her little red nightrobe falling down to her slippered feet. My child. My little girl, sleepy and innocent-eyed. My heart swelled with love for her. She was my last vestige of Molly, the vessel that held all the love Molly had poured into her. She was a strange child, and no mistake.

But Molly had always been a keen judge of people. I suddenly knew that if she had seen fit to trust her heart to Bee then I need not fear to emulate her. I smiled down at her.

Her eyes widened in surprise. Then she cast her gaze aside from mine, but an answering smile blossomed on her face. "I'm sleepy now," she said quietly. "I'm going to bed." She looked toward the darkened doorway outside the circle of firelight and lamplight. She squared her little shoulders, resolving to face the dark.

I lifted the lamp from my desk. "I'll take you to your bed," I told her. It suddenly seemed very strange to me that in all nine years of her life, it had always been Molly who put her to bed at night. Molly would bring her to me as I was at my books or writing, and I would say good night, and she would whisk the child away. Often Molly, too, had gone to bed without me, knowing I would join her as soon as I had trapped my thoughts on paper. Why, I suddenly wondered, had I wasted all those hours I could have spent with her? Why hadn't I gone with them, to listen to a bedtime story or nursery song? To hold Molly as she fell asleep in my arms?

Grief choked me so I could not speak. Without a word, I followed my daughter as she led the way through the paneled halls of her grandparents' home. We passed portraits of our ancestors, and tapestries, and mounted arms. Her small slippers whispered on the grand stair as we mounted to the second floor. These corridors were chill and she wrapped her little arms around herself and shivered as she walked, bereft of a mother's embrace now.

She had to reach for the door handle, standing on tiptoes, and then she pushed it open to a room lit only by the fading fire on the hearth. The servants had prepared her bedchamber hours ago. The candles they had lit for her had guttered out.

I set my lamp on a table by her canopied bed and went to the hearth to build her fire up again for her. She stood silently watching me. When I was sure the logs were catching well, I turned back to her. She nodded grave thanks and then stepped on a low stool and clambered up onto the tall bed. She had finally outgrown the small one we'd had made for her. But this one was still far larger than she needed. She pulled off her slippers and let them fall over the side of the bed. I saw her shiver as she crawled between the chill white sheets. She reminded me of a small puppy trying to find comfort in a big dog's kennel. I moved to her bedside and tucked the blankets in well around her.

"It will warm up soon enough," I comforted her.

"I know." Her blue gaze roamed the room, and for the first time it struck me how strange this world might look to her. The room was immense in comparison with her, everything sized for the benefit of a grown man. Could she even see out of her windows when she stood by them? Open the heavy cedar lid of her blanket chest? I suddenly remembered my first night in my bedchamber at Buckkeep Castle after years of sleeping cozy in Burrich's chamber in the lofts above the stables. At least the tapestries here were all of flowers and birds, with no golden-eyed Elderlings staring down at an awestruck child who was trying to fall asleep. Still, I saw a dozen changes that needed to be made in the room, changes that would have been wrought years ago by a father with any sensitivity. Shame flooded me. It felt wrong to leave her alone in such a large and empty space.

I stood over her in the darkness. I promised myself I would do better. I reached to smooth the pale stubble on her skull. She curled away from my touch. "No, please," she whispered into the darkness, looking away from me. It was a knife to my heart, a stab I well deserved. I drew back my hand, did not stoop for the kiss I had intended to bestow on her. I held back my sigh.

"Very well. Good night, Bee."

I took up my lamp and was halfway to the door when she asked timidly, "Can you leave a short candle burning? Mama always left me one candle."

I immediately knew what she meant. Molly often lit a small fat candle by our bedside, one that scented the room as she drifted off to sleep. I could not recall how many times I had come to our bed to find her deep in slumber and the last bit of flame dancing on the foundering wick. A pottery saucer on Bee's bedside table awaited such a candle. I opened the cupboard beneath the table and found ranks and rows of such candles. Their sweet fragrances drifted out to me as if Molly herself had entered the room. I chose lavender for its restfulness. I lit the candle from my lamp and set it in its place. I drew the bed's draperies closed, imagining how the dancing candlelight would seep through the hangings to softly illuminate the enclosed space.

"Good night," I said again, taking up my lamp.

I started for the door, and her whisper reached me softly as blown thistledown. "Mama always sang a song."

"A song?" I asked stupidly.

"You don't know any," she surmised. I heard her turn away from me.

I spoke to the curtains. "Actually, I do." Obtusely, it was "Cross-fire's Coterie" that leapt to the forefront of my mind, a martial and tragic tale completely inappropriate for a child's bedtime. I thought of others I knew, the learning tunes and rhymes I had acquired growing up. "The Poisoner's Prayer," a list of deadly herbs. "Blood Points," a musical recitation of where to stab a man to make the blood leap. Perhaps not for bedtime.

She whispered again, "Do you know 'The Twelve Healing Herbs'?"

"I do." Burrich had taught it to me, as well as Lady Patience hammering it into my head. I cleared my throat. When had I last sung a song when mine was the only lifted voice? A lifetime ago. I drew a breath and suddenly changed my mind. "Here's a song I learned when I was much younger than you are now. It's about horses, and choosing a good one." I cleared my throat again and found the note.

"One white hoof, buy him.

"Two white hooves, try him.

"Three white hooves, think for a day.

"Four white hooves, turn him away."

A brief silence greeted my effort. Then, "That seems cruel. Because his hooves are white, you turn him away?"

I smiled into darkness, and remembered Burrich's answer. "Because his hooves are soft. Sometimes. White hooves can be softer than black hooves. You don't want to buy a horse whose hooves will split easily. The rule isn't always true, but it reminds you to check the hooves of a horse you are thinking of buying."

"Oh." A pause. "Sing it again, please."

And I did. Four more times, until my listener did not request an encore. I took my lamp and walked softly to the door. The fragrance of lavender and soft candlelight remained as I stepped out into the corridor. I looked back at the draped bed, so large compared to the very small person who slept there. So small, with only me to protect her. Then I eased the door closed behind me and sought my own chill and empty bedchamber.

The next morning I woke at dawn. I lay still, looking up at the shadowy corners of the bedchamber ceiling. I had slept but a few hours, and yet sleep had deserted me. There was something.

The cub.

I took in a sudden breath. It happened, not often, that I heard my wolf speak in my mind as clearly as if he still lived. It was a Wit phenomenon, something that happened to people who had been so long partnered with an animal that when it died, some influence lingered. It was close to a score of years since I had lost Nighteyes, and yet in that instant he was at my side, and I felt the nudge as clearly as if it were a cold nose intruding under the blankets. I sat up. "It's barely dawn," I grumbled, but I swung my legs over the edge of the bed.

I found a clean tunic and leggings and dressed. The view from my window showed me a beautiful summer day. I let the curtains drop back into place and then took a deep breath. Life wasn't about me anymore, I discovered. It surprised me to realize that it had been so. *Molly*, I thought to myself. I had believed that I spoiled her with my attentions and gifts. Actually, she was the one who had spoiled me, allowing me to wake in the morning and think first of what I needed to do that day, rather than what someone else needed done.

The wolf in me had been correct. When I tapped softly on Bee's door and then entered at her muffled invitation, I found her awake and considering a variety of garments she had taken from her little clothing chest. Her blond hair stuck up in tufts. "Do you need any help with that?" I asked her.

She shook her head. "Not with clothes. But Mama always stood on the other side of the bed as we made it each morning. I've tried, but it doesn't go straight for me."

I looked at her effort. It had probably been like trying to raise canvas on a ship by herself. "Well, I know how to do that," I told her. "I'll make the bed for you."

"We are supposed to do it together," she rebuked me. She took a deep breath and squared her little shoulders. "Mama told me that I must always be able to take care of myself, for few in this world will make allowances that I am small."

Yes. Molly would have thought of that.

"Then let's make it together," I offered, and followed her very precise directions to do so. I did not tell her that I could simply tell one of the housemaids that this was now her task. What Molly had carefully built in our small daughter, I would not tear down.

She shooed me out of the room while she dressed herself. I was standing outside her door, waiting for her, when I heard the tap of Nettle's boots on the stone-flagged floor. She halted in front of me, and it was not flattering that she was obviously startled to see me there. "Good morning," I greeted her, and before she could respond the door swung open to reveal Bee dressed and ready to meet the day.

"I did brush my hair," she told me as if I had asked. "But it's too short to lie flat."

"Mine, too," I assured her. Not that I had even attempted to make it do so.

She looked up at me and asked, "Does it make it hard to trim your beard, too?"

Nettle laughed, as much to hear her sister speak as to see me uncomfortable.

"No. It does not," I admitted gravely. "I've just neglected it."

"I'll help you before I go," Nettle offered, and I wondered how she knew it was a task Molly had often undertaken.

Bee looked up at me solemnly. She shook her head slowly. "There's no reason for your beard anymore. You should just shave it off."

That gave me a twinge. How had she known? Had Molly told her that I had grown it in an attempt to look closer to my true years? "Perhaps later. But now, we should go down to breakfast, for your sister wishes to make an early start."

Bee walked between us, and at table she essayed a few words to the staff, but mostly muttered to her plate. Still, it was a start, and I think even Nettle saw the wisdom of letting her reveal herself slowly.

The farewell was hard for all of us. Bee endured a hug from Nettle, but I would have held my elder daughter longer in my arms if she would have allowed it. Her eyes were bright as she bid us farewell, and I promised that she would hear from me regularly. She looked down at Bee and charged her to "Learn some letters, and write to me, little Bee. I expect you to try as hard as your papa to make this work." It was well for me that Nettle did not see the guilty look Bee and I exchanged behind her back.

Riddle had stood silent and watched us make our partings. He approached me then with a grave face, and I thought he would offer me awkward words. Instead he suddenly engulfed me in a hug that nearly cracked my ribs. "Be brave," he said by my ear, and then released me, walked to his horse, and mounted, and they all rode away.

We stood in the carriageway of Withywoods and watched until Nettle and her party were out of sight. A time longer we stood there. Steward Revel and several of the other servants had turned out to bid Nettle farewell. They ebbed away from us until only Bee and I were left standing there. Birds called from the woodland. A light morning breeze stirred the leaves of the white paper birches that lined the carriageway. After a time Bee ventured a single word. "Well."

"Yes." I looked down at her. What was I to do with this tiny girl? I cleared my throat. "I usually begin my rounds with a walk through the stables."

She looked up at me and then quickly away. I knew she feared the large animals of the manor. Would she go with me? I could scarcely blame her if she refused. But I waited. After a moment, the small blond head nodded once.

And so we began a new pattern that day. I wished I could carry her but knew that she dreaded my touch, and why. And so she trotted at my heels and I walked more sedately so she could keep up with me. We walked the stables and conferred with Tallerman. He was visibly relieved to see the guests departed and his workload returned to normal. Lin the shepherd glanced once at my small follower and then spoke to me while his dog gravely poked Bee under the chin with her nose until Bee petted her.

The vineyard required a horseback trip. When I told Bee this, she seemed to consider it for a longer time before informing me, "I have not checked on my mother's beehives for some days. I do have tasks of my own, you know."

"I don't know how to help you with the hives," I told her.

She lifted her head and again squared her small shoulders. "I know what must be done. And I'm stronger than I look," she told me.

And so we parted, but came back together for a noon meal. I reported to her that the grapes had an excellent set, and that I had seen many of her bees busy at their work. She nodded gravely to that and said all had appeared well with the hives.

After our meal I retreated to the Withywoods study to go over the long-neglected accounts. There was a list from Steward Revel there of maintenance projects for Withywoods that he judged too important to ignore. There were small notes next to some of the suggestions, in Molly's handwriting. I couldn't bear to look at it. She'd put it there at least two months ago, and I had promised her, promised her that we'd get the most pressing work under way this summer. But I hadn't. I'd set it aside, confident that she would nag me into action when it became urgent.

Well, she wouldn't. Not ever again.

There were other messages on my desk, accounts that needed to be paid for supplies brought in from the outlying farms. There was a lot of tallying to do for men who had worked the hayfields in ex-change for a share. Here was a note that we'd have to hire more workers for the grape harvest, and if we wanted good ones, we'd best secure them now. Everything needed to be done now.

And another list, poorly written and spelled worse, of various foodstuffs. I stared at it for a time. I must have looked perplexed because Bee wandered over to peer past my elbow at it. "Oh. Cook Nutmeg wrote that, I think. She always asked Mama what meals she would like for the week to come, so Cook could be sure she had all she needed on hand for them. Mama used to write the list for her to send to town."

"I see. And this?"

She scowled at it for a minute. "I'm not sure. I think that word is meant to be 'wool.' And that might be 'cobbler.' Mama was talking of winter woolens for the help, and new boots for you and me."

"But it's summer!"

She cocked her head at me. "It's like the garden, Papa. You have to plan now what you want to have three months from now."

"I suppose." I stared at the unintelligible scribbling, wondering if I could somehow persuade Revel to translate and assume com-mand of whatever this was. It was suddenly all too much. I set it down and pushed away from the desk. "We should go look at the apple trees."

And so we did, until evening.

Day by aching day, we groped toward a routine. We made our needless daily inspection of the stables, the sheep pens, and the grapes. I did not throw myself into the work; I did not have the focus—but the accounts did not go too late, and Revel seemed al-most relieved to take up the meal planning. I didn't care what he put before me; eating had become a task to accomplish. Sleep evaded me, only to ambush me at my desk in the middle of the af-ternoon. More and more often Bee followed me to my private study in the evenings, where she amused herself by pretending to read my discarded papers before drawing lavish illustrations on the backs of them. We talked little, even when we played games to-gether. Most evenings ended with her asleep on the floor. I would carry her back to her bed, tumble her into it, and then return to my study. I let go of far too many things. I felt sometimes as if we were both waiting for something.

The evening that I realized I was waiting for Molly to come back, I put my head down on my arms and wept useless bitter tears. I only came back to myself when I felt a soft hand patting my shoulder and heard her voice saying, "It can't be changed, dear. It can't be changed. You must let go of the past."

I lifted my head and looked at my little daughter. I had thought her asleep on the hearth. It was the first time she had touched me of her own volition. Her eyes were such a pale blue, like Kettricken's, and sometimes she did seem—not blind, but as if she looked past me into another place. Her words were not ones I would have expected from a child. They were Molly's words, the words she would have spoken to me to comfort me. My little child, trying to be strong for me. I blinked my eyes clear of tears, cleared my throat, and asked her, "Would you like to learn how to play Stones?"

"Of course," she said, and even though I knew she didn't mean it, I taught her that night and we played until it was almost morning. We both slept in until nearly noon the next day.

The message came, delivered in the usual way, as autumn was winding to a close. When I sat down at the breakfast table with Bee, there was a fat brown acorn with two oak leaves still attached to it on the table. Once, I had carved such a motif on the top of a little box where I kept my poisons, the kit of my trade as an assassin. The box was long gone, but the meaning was the same. Chade wished to meet with me. I scowled at the acorn. For as long as I'd lived at Withywoods, he'd been able to do this. No one on the staff would admit to putting the acorn on the table, nor to leaving a door unbarred or a window unlatched. Yet there it was, a reminder from my old mentor that no matter how clever and wary I thought myself, he could still steal through my defenses if he wished to. He'd be waiting for me by evening at an inn called the Oaken Staff at a crossroads near Gallows Hill. That was a two-hour ride away.

Which meant that if I kept the rendezvous, I would be very late returning, perhaps not getting back until dawn if this was one of Chade's convoluted discussions. Whatever it was, he was not going to Skill to me about it. That meant no one in the coterie knew of it. It was another of his damned secrets, then.

Bee watched me handling the acorn. When I set it back on the table, she picked it up to examine it. She had begun to use small phrases to the staff: "Please, more bread." Or a simple "Good morning." Her childish lisp was not entirely pretense, but I was not sure if I felt pride or dismay at how polished an actress she was. In the last few evenings, we had played our memory game as well as Stones, and at both she seemed incredibly gifted. I tutted at my fatherly pride, reminding myself that every parent must think his child the cleverest and prettiest. She had shown me a page from an herbal that she had copied out with painstaking care at my urgent request. She had her mother's gift for illustration. And she had written a brief note to Nettle, scarcely blotched at all and in a hand so like my own that I wondered if her sister would deem it counterfeit. Our last few weeks together had been like balm on a wound. Briefly, it eased the aching.

But Chade's summons I could not ignore. The only times when he went back to the cryptic communications of my boyhood were when he had something of the utmost delicacy to broach to me. Was it private to him, or too dangerous to share? My heart sank at the thought. Now what? What was happening at Buckkeep Castle that was worthy of this secret liaison? What was he trying to drag me into?

And what arrangements could I make for Bee that evening? If I went to meet Chade, I would not be there to see her to bed that night. We had begun to build something, we two, and I did not want to neglect it. As Nettle had warned me, caring for the child full-time was not as easy as one might think it, but neither was it as hard as she had painted it. I was enjoying my daughter, even when we both were in the same room but quiet and busy at our own tasks. Her latest fancy was a set of brushes and some paints. Her copies of illustrations were painstaking and accurate. She sighed over them, but since I had suggested that Nettle needed to see her abilities, she did them. I was more charmed by the peculiar and childish images she created when left alone with brushes and inks. She had painted a small man with his cheeks puffed as if blowing, and told me that he breathed out fog. She had never seen the ocean or a ship, but had drawn a little boat towed through the waves by water snakes. Another was a row of flowers with tiny faces. She showed me such work shyly, and I sensed she was letting me into her world. I didn't want to leave her for a housemaid to tuck into bed. Nor would I drag her out and into the night with me. An autumn storm was threatening.

Bee was looking at me curiously as I pondered my lack of choices. "What's this?" she piped in her childish voice, and held up the acorn.

"An acorn. A seed from an oak tree."

"I know that!" she said, as if amazed I could think her so ignorant. She silenced herself hastily. Tavia had come out of the kitchen with a steaming kettle of porridge. She set it down on the table and ladled two generous servings into our bowls. A pitcher of cream and a pot of honey were already on the table, beside a loaf of freshly baked dark bread. One of the younger kitchen girls, Elm, followed her with a bowl of butter and a dish of stewed prunes. She did not look at Bee, I noticed. I marked, too, how Bee stiffened slightly and did not breathe as the girl passed behind her chair. I nodded my thanks to Tavia and waited until she had whisked herself and her daughter back to the kitchen before I spoke.

"I have to go on a brief trip this evening. I may be gone all night."

I felt Bee's eyes flicker over my face, trying to read what I was thinking. It was a new habit she had. She still did not meet my gaze, but sometimes I felt her looking at me. She was relieved that I now attempted to keep my Skill contained at all times, but I think it also made me more mysterious to her. I had to wonder how much she had read from me in the first nine years of her life. The thought was so saddening that I pushed it aside. She had not spoken. "Shall I ask Tavia to put you to bed tonight?"

She shook her head briskly.

"Mild, then?" The other kitchenmaid was younger, in her twenties. Perhaps she would suit Bee better.

Bee lowered her eyes to her porridge and shook her head more slowly. Well, that canceled both of my easy solutions, unless I simply told her she'd have to endure whatever arrangements I could make. I wasn't ready to be so firm with her yet. I wondered if I ever would be, and then chided myself to think that I might be the sort of father who spoiled a child by indulging her will. I would think of something, I promised myself, and pushed the matter from my mind for the time being.

Despite Chade's visit looming before me, I went about my regular tasks for the day. The needs of a manor stop for nothing, not even a death. I was swiftly discovering just how many unseen parts there were to managing a household, even with Revel stepping up to much of it. Molly had always been the one to coordinate with him. Together they had discussed meals and seasonal tasks, routine maintenance, hiring of help. It had all been invisible to me, and now the man and his insistence that we meet each afternoon to discuss the day's needs nearly drove me mad. He was a pleasant enough fellow and good at what he did, but every time he tapped at my study door it was a reminder that Molly was not there to intercept him. Twice he had brought up maintenance that should be done before winter. The carefully detailed notes he gave me, with suggestions as to tradesmen and material and dates, overwhelmed me. It was all stacked on top of my ordinary work. Today I was already late paying the staff, and though they had seemed understanding of my grief, I knew that their lives went on. How to manage? Hire yet another person to nag me through the day? I dreaded trying to find someone trustworthy, and my heart sank even deeper as I realized that I still needed to find a nanny or tutor for Bee as well. I wondered if FitzVigilant was ready yet, and then realized that for a little girl, a woman would be more appropriate. Someone who could sleep in the unused servant's chamber adjacent to her own. Someone who would move from being a nanny to a maid as Bee grew. My woe deepened at the thought of bringing a woman into her life who would do some of what her mother had done for her. I knew

I must. Although Chade's visit would be the first task to take me from her side, it would not be the last.

I had no idea where to begin looking for a servant who could fulfill such a demanding role.

I was silent as I ate, pondering my dilemma, and silent when I rose. For neither the first nor the last time I considered the strange isolation my peculiar station in life had conferred on me. To the landholders and gentry around Buckkeep, Molly and I had been neither aristocracy nor common folk, but creatures trapped between classes. The men who worked for me as groundskeepers and ostlers spoke of me well and appreciated my firsthand knowledge of their tasks, but they did not consider me a friend. And those nobles with holdings within an easy ride had known us as Holder Tom Badgerlock and Lady Molly. To their eyes Molly had been elevated only as recognition from the crown for Burrich's services. They had been pleasant enough when we encountered them, but none had extended invitations to socialize and Molly had wisely held back from pressing the matter. We'd had each other for daily company, and the irregular invasions of our relatives to inject both chaos and merriment into our lives. It had been enough for us both.

But now that she was gone I looked around myself and perceived how solitary my life at Withywoods was without her. Our children had gone back to their own lives and left me here alone. All save one. I glanced down at her. It wasn't right for a child to grow up so alone.

Bee's little slippers were close to silent as she ghosted along behind me through the house. I glanced back at her and said, "I have to go out to the stables. And a storm is waiting. Let's get you into some warm clothes."

"I can do that myself," she insisted softly.

"Can you reach everything?" I frowned. Were her winter things still stored in a chest somewhere? Would they still fit her?

She thought about it for a moment, and then nodded consideringly. She tilted her head up, and I felt her gaze brush across me. "I'm not as little as I look. I'm nine."

"Very well. I'll wait for you in my private study."

She bobbed her head in grave acknowledgment and I watched her hasten up the stairs. It was a climb for her, a reach for every step. I tried to imagine being so small in a world scaled for adults, and could not. She was a very capable child, I thought to myself, and wondered if I was underestimating her. There was a danger in asking too much of a child, but the danger of asking too little was almost equal. Nonetheless, provision should be made for her, lest she need me and I not be there to protect her. I reached a decision.

When she came into my study, she was wearing her boots and warm leggings, with her winter cloak slung over her arm. Her hair was pulled back into a stubby tail. I could tell she had done it herself and did not criticize it. She looked around the room, obviously wondering why we were there so early in the day. The room was smaller than the formal study, but pleasant enough. The walls were rich dark wood, and the hearth was built of big flat river stones. It was a comfortable room, a man's retreat, but that was not why I had chosen it for my den. I considered and hesitated. But she was nine. The same age I had been when Buckkeep Castle's secret had been shared with me.

"Please close the door behind you," I told her as she came in.

She did so, and then looked past my shoulder, wondering at my odd request. "I thought we were going out."

"We are. But not right away. I want to show you something. And see if you can do it. But first I have to explain it. Sit down, please."

She climbed up to sit on one of the cushioned chairs and perched there, watching me but not meeting my eyes. "This is a secret," I warned her. "It's a secret only for you and me. Patience showed it to your mother and me when we first came here. Patience is gone, and now Molly is gone, too." I waited, swallowed, and went on. "So only I know about this now. And soon you will, too. It's not written down anywhere, and it must never be put on paper. You cannot show it to anyone else. Do you understand?"

For a time she was very still. Then she nodded slowly.

I got up from my seat behind the desk, went to the door, and made sure it was latched. "This door has to be shut completely," I told her. I touched the hinges of the massive door. "Look here. This door has four hinges. Two at the top, and two closer to the bottom. They all look just the same."

I waited and again she nodded gravely.

"This one, not the lowest one, but this one above it is false. When you pull the pin out of the top of this hinge, it becomes a handle. See? Then you can do this." I pulled the brass pin out, took hold of the false hinge, and pulled on it. A tall narrow door disguised as a wood wall panel swung open. Spiderwebs stretched and broke as I pulled it open. Darkness breathed out. I glanced back at Bee. Her attention was absolute, her lower lip caught between her small perfect teeth. "It's a secret passageway."

"Yes?" she queried, and I realized I was telling her the obvious. I scratched my cheek and felt how deep my beard had grown. I'd still not trimmed it, I suddenly realized, and Molly had not rebuked me. All thoughts fled my mind for a moment as a wave of loss drenched and drowned me again.

"Papa?" Bee tugged at my shirt cuff.

"I'm sorry," I said, and drew breath again.

"I'm sorry, too," she said. She did not take my hand, but held on to my cuff. I had not even been aware of her getting down from the chair or crossing the room to me. She cleared her little throat, and I became aware of the glistening tracks on her cheeks. I tightened my Skill-walls, and she nodded a silent thanks to me. In a low voice she asked me, "Where does it go?"

And so, together, we crested that wave of sorrow and pushed on.

"It goes to a little room above and to the left of the hearth. There's a tiny peephole there, so someone could sit there and watch people come and go and talk in this room." I rubbed my eyes. "And from that little room, there is a narrow stair that goes to a very low crawlway. And it goes to other little spy-rooms in other parts of the house." I swallowed and my voice became almost normal as I added, "I think it's a Farseer obsession. We seem to like spyholes and secret places in our homes."

She nodded, staring past me at the door. The broken cobwebs

stirred in a slight draft. A smile dawned on her face and she actually clasped her little hands together under her chin. "I love it! Is it for me?"

It was the last reaction I could have predicted from her. I found my smile answering hers. "It is now," I told her. "There are two other ways to get into it. One from my bedroom. And another from a pantry. Those are both difficult to open, mostly because they haven't been used in a very, very long time. This one is easier. But it, too, hasn't been used in a long time. So it will be full of cobwebs and dust, and mice and spiders."

She had advanced to the edge of the passageway. She flapped a hand through the dangling webs and then shook her fingers free of the rags, undaunted by small things with many legs. A glance back in my direction. "Can I go in now? Can I take a lamp?"

"I suppose so." Her enthusiasm had caught me off guard. I had thought only to seed an idea with her today, to show her a place to retreat to if she was ever in danger and I was not around to protect her. I shot the concealed bolts on the study doors so that no one could enter. I took the lamp from my desk. Then I shut the door to the passage and dropped the hinge pin back into its place. "You try to open it."

The pin was stubborn and it took some tugging before she freed it. "We can oil that," she said breathlessly, and then stood up to pull the panel open. She glanced back at me. "Can I take the lamp and go first?"

If she fell and dropped the lamp, the spilled oil and flame would set all of Withywoods afire. "Be careful," I told her as I handed it to her. "Use both hands. And don't fall."

"I won't," she replied, but as soon as it was in her hands, I doubted my wisdom in entrusting it to her. She was so obviously excited and focused only on exploring. She walked unhesitatingly into the narrow dark corridor. I stooped and followed her.

The spy-passages of Withywoods were not nearly as elaborate as the ones that threaded Buckkeep Castle. I think if they had been my father's handiwork, he would have made them for a taller man.

I suspected they dated back to the first rebuilding of the house, when they had added the south wing. I'd often wondered if there were more of them, the secret of opening the doors lost in the process of the house changing inhabitants.

The passage had a short landing and then a steep stair. At the top of the stair there was a landing and a sharp turn to the left. There the passage became slightly wider. It went up six more steps and then was flat until it reached the area beside the hearth. I could not stand straight in the little compartment, but someone had been comfortable there once. There was a short sturdy stool for him to perch on while he did his spying, a little cabinet of dark wood, its doors securely closed, and a small shelf where Bee set down her lamp. Her instinct was correct. I noticed now the little guard around the peephole that would keep the lamplight from being visible. She sat down on the stool without dusting it off, leaned forward to peer into my study, then leaned back and proclaimed, "I love it. It fits me perfectly. Oh, Papa, thank you!"

She stood up and went to the little cupboard, reaching the handle easily. She peered inside. "Look! Here's an inkpot! It's all dried up, but I could put ink in it. And here's an old quill pen, all eaten away to its spine. I'll need a fresh one. Look! The shelf folds down and now it's a little table for writing! How clever! Is it truly all for me?"

What had probably been a rather cramped space even for a small spy did fit her perfectly. The space I had thought of as an emergency retreat for her, she saw as a refuge, perhaps even a playroom.

"It's a safe place for you. A place to come and hide if you feel you are in danger and you can't get to me. Or if I tell you there is danger and you must run and hide."

She looked at me earnestly, not meeting my eyes, but her pale gaze wandering over my face. "I see. Of course. Well, then, I shall need candles, and a tinderbox. And something to keep water in, and something with a tight lid for keeping hard bread. So that I shall not be hungry if I have to hide for quite a long time. And a cushion and a blanket against the chill. And perhaps a few books."

I stared at her, aghast. "No! No, Bee, I'd never leave you hidden here for days at a time! Wait . . . a few books? Do you truly read that well?"

The expression on her face would not have been as surprised if I'd asked her if she could breathe. "Of course. Can't everyone?"

"No. Generally, one has to be taught to read. I know your mother showed you letters, but I didn't think . . ." I stared at her in amazement. I had watched her at play with her pen and her book, thinking that she did no more than practice random letters. The note she had written to her sister had been a simple one, just a few lines. I now recalled she had asked for paper so she could write down her dreams; I thought she had meant her odd drawings. I quelled my sudden desire to know what she wrote, to see what she dreamed. I would wait until she offered to share it with me.

"Mama read to me. Her big beautiful book about herbs and flowers, the one Lady Patience gave her. She read it very slowly, pointing at each word. She had told me the letters and the sounds. So I learned."

Molly had come to reading late, and mastered it with great difficulty. And I knew immediately the book she had read to Bee, one that had not pages of paper, but narrow slabs of wood with the words and the illustrations engraved in them, and the herbs and flowers carved and then painted in their correct colors. Patience had treasured that gift from me. And Molly had taught our daughter to read from it.

"Papa?"

I had been woolgathering. I looked down at her.

"What happened to Lady Patience? Mama told me many stories about her, but never the end of her story."

"The end of her story." I had been there the day my stepmother's story had ended. I thought of it now, and it suddenly took on a completely different significance to me. I cleared my throat. "Well. It was a day in early spring. The plum trees had begun to waken from the winter, and Lady Patience wanted them pruned before the buds burst into flowers. She was quite an old lady by then, but still very fussy about her gardens. So she insisted on leaning out an upper window and shouting instructions to the workers pruning her trees."

I had to smile at the memory. Bee was almost looking at me, her face intent with interest, her brow wrinkled. "Did she fall out the window?"

"No. For a wonder, no, she didn't fall. But she wasn't happy with how they were doing the pruning. So she declared that she was going out to make them do it as she wished, and to bring back some of the trimmings to force into bloom for the table. I offered to go fetch her some, but no, she was off to her room and then came clumping back down in her boots and a heavy wool cloak and out she went." I paused. I remembered it all so clearly. The blue sky, the blustery wind, and Patience's eyes snapping with indignation that the orchard crew was ignoring her.

"Then what?"

"She was gone for a little while. I was in the morning room when I heard the door slam. She was calling for me to come and take some of the cuttings. I stepped out in the hall, and here she came with a great armful of them, dropping twigs and bits of moss as she went. I was going to take them from her when she suddenly stopped where she was. She stared, and her mouth fell open, and her cheeks that were pink with cold went even pinker. Then she shouted, 'Chivalry! There you are!' And she flung up her arms, and the branches went everywhere. She opened her arms wide and took two running steps past me. And then she fell."

Tears suddenly prickled my eyes. I blinked but could not stop them.

"And she was dead," Bee whispered.

"Yes," I said hoarsely. I recalled the loose weight of her as I gathered her and turned her faceup in my arms. She was dead and staring, but smiling still. Smiling.

"She thought you were her dead husband when she saw you."

"No." I shook my head. "She didn't look at me. She was looking past me, down the hallway behind me. I don't know what she saw."

"She saw him," Bee decided with great satisfaction. She nodded to herself. "He came to get her at last. It's a good end to her story. May I keep her book up here, the one of herbs?"

I wondered if Molly would come to get me someday. A fluttering of hope rose in me. Then I came back to myself, to the little room and my daughter sitting at the folded-down desktop. "You could keep books up here if you wish. You may keep anything here that you want. You may have candles and a tinderbox, if you promise to be very careful with them. But you must remember, this room and its entrance are a secret, one that is not to be shared with anyone. Only you and I know that it exists. It's important that it stays our secret."

She nodded gravely. "Can you show me where the other passage goes, the one we passed, and how to open the other doors?"

"Perhaps tomorrow. Right now, we must close it up snug, and then go see the man who takes care of the sheep."

"Lin," she reminded me casually. "Shepherd Lin takes care of the sheep."

"Yes. Lin. We need to talk to him." An idea blossomed in my mind. "He has a son named Boj, who has a wife and a little girl at his house. Perhaps you would like to meet them?"

"No. Thank you."

Her crisp reply killed that hope. I knew there would be more to that story. I waited in patient silence as she took up our lamp and led us down the narrow stair. She paused hopefully at the intersection to the other passage, lifting her lamp to peer into the darkness, but then with a short sigh led us back down to my study. I held the lamp as she closed the panel and secured it. Then I blew out the lamp and drew open the heavy curtains to let in the gray light. It was raining. I blinked as my eyes adjusted and realized we must have had a frost in the night. The leaves had begun to change, with the edges and veins of the birch leaves turning gold. Winter was drawing closer. I still hadn't spoken.

"Other children don't like me. I make them uncomfortable. They think I'm a tiny child dressed up as a girl, and then, when I can do things, like pare apples with a sharp knife, they think . . . I don't know what they think. But when I go into the kitchen, Tavia's sons go out. They used to come to work with her every day. They don't anymore." She looked away from me. "Elm and Lea, the kitchen girls, hate me."

"Oh, Bee, they don't hate you! They hardly know you. And Tavia's sons are of an age where they go with their father now, to learn what he does all day. It's not you, Bee." I was looking down at my small daughter with a sympathetic smile. She glanced up at me and, for the instant that our eyes met, the blue anger in hers burned me.

She looked down at the floor, her whole body stiff. "Perhaps I shall stay in out of the rain today," she said in an icy little voice. "It might be a good day to stay by myself."

"Bee," I said, but before I could go on that fury was flashed at me again.

"I hate it when you lie. You know that other children will fear me. And I know when they hate me. It's not something I pretend. It's real. Don't lie to me to make me think that I'm the one who is judging them badly. Lies are bad, no matter who tells them. Mama put up with it from you, but I shan't." She folded her arms across her chest and stood staring defiantly at my knees.

"Bee! I am your father. You cannot speak to me like that!"

"If I cannot be honest with you, I shall not speak to you at all." All the force of her will was behind her words. I knew that she was completely capable of resuming her long silence. The thought of being deprived of the only companionship I'd found since Molly's death struck me so deep a blow that I immediately recognized how close a bond I was forming with my daughter. The second bolt of lightning was how dangerous it would be to both of us if I let my need for her company overcome my duty to be her parent.

"You can be honest with me and still respect me. As I can with you. You are different, Bee. It will make some parts of your life very difficult. But if you always fall back on your differences to explain everything you dislike about the world, you will fall into self-pity. I've no doubt that you did make Tavia's boys uneasy. But I also know that neither one of them liked working in the kitchens, and so their father took them down to the mill, to see if that suited them better. It is not always all about you. Sometimes you are just one factor."

She lowered her eyes to the floor. She did not uncross her arms.

"Get your cloak on. We're going down to see Lin." I gave the order confidently, holding in my anguish over what I would do if she refused to obey. When Starling had given Hap to me he'd led such a life of privation that he was pathetically grateful to sleep inside and be given food. He'd been well past ten before we'd had any confrontations about my authority. The thought of physically disciplining a creature as small as Bee filled me with revulsion. Yet I knew I had to win this battle.

I concealed my relief when she retrieved her cloak and put it on. I didn't say anything to nettle her pride as we left the study and went out onto the grounds. I did shorten my stride as we walked out to the pastures and the sheds. She still had to trot to keep up with me.

Lin was waiting for me. He showed me three sheep that he'd isolated from the flock after they'd developed a rash that had them rubbing themselves raw on trees and fence posts. I knew little of sheep, but Lin had been tending them since he was a youth, and his hair was now as gray as most of his woolly charges. So I listened, and nodded, and asked him to keep me informed if any more of the ewes became infected. As we spoke, his eyes wandered from me to my small charge and then back again. Bee, perhaps still smarting from being corrected, stood small and stiff and silent throughout our conversation. Lin's dog Daisy wandered over to inspect her. When Bee stepped back at her approach, she wagged her tail appreciatively and her tongue lolled with dog laughter. *So easy to herd.* I chose to ignore them as Daisy backed my daughter into a corner and then prodded her with a nose, her tail wagging all the while. Lin glanced at them apprehensively, but I walked over to a ewe and asked Lin how old she was. Distracted, he came to me. I asked if mites might be causing the irritation, making Lin furrow his brow and go down to part the sheep's wool and look for insects.

Out of the corner of my eye I saw Bee reach out to fondle one of the dog's silky little ears. Daisy sat down and leaned against her. Bee buried her chilled hands into the herd dog's thick golden ruff and I saw suddenly that she and the dog were easy and familiar with each other. Her earlier backing away from the dog had not been apprehension, but an invitation to their game. I listened to Lin recount the ewe's earlier symptoms with only half my attention.

When Lin was satisfied that I'd heard his worries and had confidence in what he was doing, our meeting was over. I'd never enjoyed sheep, and had little to do with their care when I was growing up at Buckkeep Castle, so I did with Lin what Burrich had done with the hawk tenders at Buckkeep. I'd found a good man who knew more about the woolly knot-heads than I'd ever care to learn and entrusted Nettle's flocks to him. But hearing him out did take a time and I felt my morning fleeing.

When I turned around to look for Bee, she was not there. Daisy was sitting calmly. My reaction was instinctive. I reached out to both dog and man as I asked, "*Where is she? Where did my daughter go?*"

"*Kittens,*" they responded as one. If Lin was Witted and Daisy his beast-partner, he had never told me, and now was not a time to ask. He would not be the first unWitted man I'd met who behaved as if he and his partner could speak to each other. But my concern now was not with them but Bee.

"Kittens?"

"There's a litter back there under one of the mangers. Got their eyes open two weeks ago and now they've started to explore."

Indeed they had. And the litter of four kits was exploring my daughter as she lay on her belly in the damp straw and let them climb on her. An orange-and-white one sat on her back and pulled her hair, his pin teeth set in her scruffy hair and his small feet braced. Two calicos were in the curve of her arms under her chin. At a short distance a black-and-white kit with a kink in his tail glared at her as she stared back at him. "Bee, it's time to go," I warned her.

She moved slowly, reluctantly. I reached down to unfasten the orange kitten from her hair. It smacked me experimentally. I set it on the straw beside her. "We need to go now," I prodded her.

She sighed. "I like the kittens. I've never held one before. These ones are nice, but that one won't let me touch him."

Lin spoke. "Oh, that blackie is like his father. Full of piss and vinegar already. He'll be a good ratter, but I wouldn't choose him, Mistress Bee."

"We're not choosing any of them," I corrected him. "She just wanted to hold one."

Lin cocked his head at me. At his side, his dog mimicked him. "Well, I'm just saying she's welcome to one if you want him. They're the right age to find a new home. Their mother is tired of them and they've started to hunt. And a little friend might be a comfort to the little girl, sir. A warm little bit of company." He cleared his throat and added, "Though I think a pup would be better for her."

I knew a moment of impatience. A kitten or puppy would not cure her grief over her mother's death. Then a sharp memory of a pup named Nosy intruded into my mind. But another young creature to be her friend could help. A lot. And perhaps in all the wrong ways. I spoke firmly.

"Thank you, but no, Lin. Perhaps when she's a bit older, but not now. Come, Bee. We need to get back to the house."

I expected a plea from her. Instead she sat up, gently letting the pair of calicos slide back into the straw. A moment longer she stared at the black kitten. She pointed one finger at him, as if to warn him, but then stood up the rest of the way and followed obediently as I left the sheep sheds. I slowed my pace even more on our walk back to the house. "So. What did you hear?" I asked Bee.

She was silent for a long time. I was on the point of pushing for a response when she admitted, "I wasn't really paying attention. It was just about sheep. It wasn't about me. And there were the kittens."

"We talked about sheep that belong to your sister, with a man who makes his living taking care of those sheep. Someday you may have to walk down there to talk to him, or to his daughter or grand-child, about those sheep. Next time, you listen." I paused to give her a moment to mull that, and then asked, "So you didn't hear this time. What did you see?"

She surprised me in what she had heard me say. My question had not entered her mind at all. She spoke hesitantly in a voice full of trepidation. "So. Withywoods does not belong to you, or to me. It's Nettle's house and they are Nettle's sheep. They'll never be mine. Or the grapes or the orchards. None of it is really mine. Nettle was Mama's eldest, and she now owns it all. But someday I may have to take care of all of it for her, just as you do." She pondered a moment. "Papa, when I am grown and you are dead, what *will* belong to me?"

An arrow to my heart. What would belong to this odd child of mine? Even if I set aside a good marriage portion for her, would she grow to be a woman that a man would wish to wed? A good man? How would I find him, or know him when I had? When I was dead and gone, what would befall her? Years ago, Chade had asked me the same thing, and I had replied she was but a baby, and it was too soon to worry. Nine years had passed since then. Another nine and she would be eligible for marriage.

And I was a procrastinating idiot. I spoke quickly to fill my long silence. "I am sure that your sister and brothers would never allow you to live in want," I told her, and I was confident that I spoke truth to her.

"That's not the same as knowing there would be something that was mine," she said quietly.

I knew she was right. Before I could assure her that I would do my best to see that she was provided for, she spoke again. "This is what I saw. I saw sheep, and sheep dung, and straw. I saw lots of wool on the lower rungs of the fence, and lots of little spiders, red and black, on the bottom sides of the rungs. I saw one ewe lying down, and she had rubbed all the wool and some of her skin off her rump. Another ewe was rubbing her hip on a fence post and licking her lips while she did it." I was nodding, pleased at her observation.

She gave me a glance, looked aside, and added, "And I saw Lin looking at me and then looking away, as if I was something he'd rather not see."

"He was," I agreed. "But not in dislike. He's sad for you. He liked you enough to think you should have a kitten or a puppy of your own. Look at how he is with his own dog, and you'll see that isn't something he'd suggest for a child he disliked."

She made a skeptical noise in her throat.

"When I was a boy," I told her calmly, "I hated being a bastard. I thought that whenever anyone looked at me, that was the first thought he had. So I made being a bastard the most important thing about me. And whenever I met anyone, the first thing I thought of was how he was thinking about meeting a bastard."

We walked for a time in silence. I could tell she was already tired. I caught myself thinking that I'd have to build her endurance with regular challenges and then reminded myself that she was not a dog nor a horse, but my child.

"Sometimes," I added carefully, "I decided that people didn't like me before they had had a chance to decide for themselves. So I didn't speak to them or make any effort to have them like me."

"Being a bastard is something that doesn't show unless you make it show," she said. She gestured at herself. "I can't hide this. Being small and looking younger than I am. Being pale where most folk are dark. Being able to talk as if I am older than I am is something I can hide. But you said I shouldn't do that."

"No. Some of your differences you can't hide. Little by little, you can let people see that you are a lot more intelligent than most children of your age. And that will make you less frightening to them."

Again that sound of disdain.

"Were you scared of Daisy?" I asked her.

"Daisy?"

"The herd dog. Did she scare you?"

"No. Of course not! She does like to poke me with her nose. But Daisy's nice."

"How do you know?"

A hesitation before she replied. "She wagged her tail. And she wasn't afraid of me." A pause. "May I have a puppy?"

Not where I'd wanted the conversation to go, but again it was inevitable. "It would be hard for me to let you have a dog just now." Not while my heart was so desperately lonely still. Not while I reached out, whether I would or not, to any creature that looked at me with sympathetic eyes. Even if I did not bond, the dog would be drawn to me, not her. No. "Perhaps in the future we can talk about it again. But what I wanted you to see . . . Are you tired? Shall I carry you?"

Her walk had slowed to a trudge, and her cheeks were bright red with effort and the chill wind's kiss.

She straightened her spine. "I'm nearly ten. I'm too old to be carried," she said with great dignity.

"Not by your father," I said, and swooped her up. She went stiff in my arms, as she always did, but I was relentless. I set her up high on my left shoulder and lengthened my stride. She perched there, speechless and stiff as a stick. I thought I perceived her problem. I took a breath and walled myself in tighter. It wasn't easy. For a moment I was as disoriented as if I had suddenly discarded my sense of smell or sight. When one has the Wit, to use it is instinctive, and the Skill wells over and out of the untrained. But I was rewarded by her relaxing a trifle, and then exclaiming, "I can see so far! Can you see this far all the time? Well, I suppose you can! How wonderful it is!"

She was so pleased and excited that I hadn't the heart to drag her back to my lecture. Another time would be soon enough, I promised myself. She had just lost her mother, and she and I were only now discovering how to reach out to each other. Tomorrow I would talk with her again about how to put others at ease. For now I would enjoy a moment when she seemed an ordinary child and I could simply be her father.

Chapter 12

EXPLORATIONS

Once there was an old woman who lived all alone in the middle of a busy city. She made her living as a washerwoman for several wealthy merchant families. Each day she would go to one of their homes, gather the dirty clothing, and take it to her own home where she would scrub and pound it clean, spread it to dry on her thatched roof, and do whatever mending might be required. It did not afford her a good livelihood, but she liked her work because she could do it by herself.

She had not always been alone. Once she had had a dog. The dog had been her Wit-beast and her friend. But no dog lives forever, and few live as long as a human, and so the sad day came when the woman found herself alone. And alone she had been ever since then. Or so she thought.

Early one morning as she clambered from her bed, she slipped and fell. And when she tried to stand up, she could not, for she had *broken her leg high at the hip. She called for help, but no one heard her and no one came. All that day, and the night, and the next day she lay on the floor. She grew faint with hunger, and thirst took her voice away. Her mind began to wander and she ran the streets of the city as her dog once had. Now as a dog and in her dream, she met a young man and said to him, "My mistress has need of your aid. Follow me, please, I beg of you."*

She woke to a man holding a cup of cool water to her lips. "I dreamed a dog and he brought me here," he told her. He saved her life, and though she mended but slowly and always walked with a stick and a hitch, ever after that they were friends.

BADGERLOCK'S OLD BLOOD TALES

When I was sure my father was well and truly on his way, I slid out of my bed, took one of my mother's scented candles from the supply in the bedside table, and kindled it at the fire. I put it into a holder and set it on the floor while I got a warm woolen robe from my winter clothing chest. I didn't like the big storage chest. The lid was beautifully carved, with birds and flowers, but it was heavy. I was not tall enough to open it all the way, so I had to hold it up with one hand while I rummaged in the depths with the other. Fortunately there was a robe close to the top, and the prickly touch of the wool against my fingers told me it was the one I wanted. I fished it up and leapt back, letting the lid of the chest fall with a *thump.* Tomorrow, I decided, I would ask my father to prop the chest open for me so that I could move warm clothing from it to the smaller chest he had made for me. The night's storm surely meant winter was on its way. It was time to make the changes.

I pulled the robe on over my nightdress, and then put on my warm stockings. I didn't bother with shoes. My house shoes were too tight to go over the thick wool and my old boots too heavy for what I had in mind. I picked up my candle, opened the door, and peered out into the corridor. All was quiet. I slipped out, letting the door shut softly behind me. Finally I would have the leisure to explore the secret passageway as thoroughly as I wished. Ever since I had glimpsed it, I had thought of nothing else. I had wanted to return there directly as soon as we came back from the sheep pens, but there had been a meal to eat, and then my father had kept me by his side as he worried and fretted that he would have to leave me alone that night. So silly. Was not I alone every night when he sat in his study or slept in his bed? What difference did it make that he was far from our home?

The banked embers of the hearth fire in my father's study had burned low. I added another log, as much for light as warmth. I took two tall candles from the drawer of his desk. Then I carefully did as he had done earlier, making sure that the drapery at the window was tightly closed, latching the study doors, and working the secret catch on the false hinge. When the narrow door opened, the house breathed out at me, a chill breath of old secrets. I breathed it in and felt them fill me. Candleholder in hand, I started up the narrow way.

I went first to the small room my father had shown me. I investigated it more carefully, but found little that I hadn't seen before. It was pleasant to sit there alone, the candle making a yellow pool of light around me while I thought of how I would put my book on the little shelf and my ink pot and pen beside them. I had never realized how much I had longed for a space of my very own. My bedroom had always seemed a vast and chilly space to me, little different from trying to sleep in the middle of the table in the dining hall. Here I felt cozy and sheltered. I resolved that the next time I came here, I would bring a duster to sweep away cobwebs and make it all tidy, and a cushion and blanket to make it cozy. I would make pictures to go on the walls. It was very satisfying to imagine the space made over to suit me exactly, and I lingered so long at that pursuit that my scented candle burned low. I kindled one of the tapers I had taken from my father's desk. I quickly resolved that a supply of them must be kept here. No time like the present. I put my extra taper onto the little shelf and turned to pinch out the small flame on what was left of the scented candle. A tiny wisp of fragrant smoke rose from it, scenting the air. I set the stub on my desk and put the lit taper in the holder. I should bring some of the sachets my mother and I had made, some of the rose and honeysuckle ones. I would fill the little cabinet with all the things I wished to keep here. Dried apricots and raisins. The hard little sausages that I loved to chew. It would be cozy and comfortable, a place to read or draw or write. My own tiny room.

The fresh candle reminded me of the passing time. I wanted to explore the other passageway that I had only glimpsed earlier. I recalled that my father said it led to two other entrances, one in his bedroom and one in the pantry. The pantry was on the lower floor behind the kitchens, while my parent's chamber was in the main part of the house and upstairs. So at some point there must be stairs, I reasoned, and immediately decided that I would explore that passage.

I returned to the intersection that I had earlier glimpsed and this time instead of going back to the study, I followed the other passage. I noticed that the passageway was walled with dark-planked wood here, and wondered if it was older than the first section I had explored. As my father had warned me, it had not been used in quite some time. Draping cobwebs sizzled and twitched as they met my candle's flame. The passage bent first one way and then another as it followed the walls of the chambers. At one point, the wall of the passage was brick and mortar and very cold. Drafts made the flame of my candle dance and I shielded it with my hand. I felt that perhaps I was now in the main part of the house. I hurried along, passing the bared bones of a mouse, dead so long there was no stink to him. I found two more peepholes, each shuttered with a tiny lid. I set my candle down and endeavored to see where I was, but try as I might, I could see nothing of the darkened rooms they spied on. Indeed, I had only a hazy idea of where I was in the house, and could not tell if I passed bedchambers or sitting rooms.

I came to a place where the passage diverged into not two but three possible paths. So perhaps there were more entrances to the spy-tunnels than my father had told me. The first one I chose was a disappointment. It did not go far before it came to a peephole and another little bench beneath it. Again I set my candle down and after a short struggle, I managed to push the stubborn cover to one side. I was astonished to find I was looking into my own bedchamber. The fire was burning low but it still cast enough light for me to see by. I was on the hearth-wall of my room, where I could look down on the bed. I wondered if there was a secret entrance to my bedroom, and carefully felt all along the nearby wall for some catch or hinge. But if there was one, I did not find it, which was very disappointing—I had become quite excited at the idea of being able to access my new refuge from my bedroom.

I returned to the intersection of the tunnels, resolving not to dawdle, for my candle was almost half gone. A lamp was what I needed for future exploration. I was certain that my father would allow me neither to possess my own lamp, nor to wander through the walls of Withywoods with a borrowed one. I wondered if he would notice it if I took the one from my mother's sewing room. He had avoided that room since her death. I felt a pang of conscience at the thought of going behind his back to get what I needed, but not a large one. I was quite certain that he considered me far less capable than I was. Did that mean I should limit myself to what he thought I could do? I didn't think so.

I chose a path at random and followed it. It wound for quite a way through the walls, and twice I negotiated what would have been very tight corners for an adult. I went down some crude steps, then up, and a short time later down a longer slant. I encountered more evidence of vermin and halted once when I heard small feet scampering away from me. I do not care for rats and mice. Rats do not stink as badly as mice do, but I do not like their beady eyes. The droppings along the wall edges grew thicker and the urine stink stronger. I found two gnawed holes in the passage: Obviously the rodents had discovered this safe and easy passage and had been using it, by which I deduced that this one would lead to the pantry.

And it did. My candle was now just a quarter of its length, and I resolved that I should exit the passage here before it guttered out and left me in darkness. The lever to open the panel was obvious, and though it was stiff, I heaved on it until I heard a click in the wall. I pushed at what I judged was the door, but it moved only a handspan. It was designed to swing out, and when I put my hand out through the opening, I clearly felt that sacks of something, peas or beans, had been stacked against it. I pushed against them, but they were heavy and unyielding. I would not get out that way.

It was time to leave my warren. I closed the secret panel to the pantry and headed back the way I had come, feeling both chilled and sleepy. I walked into a heavy cobweb and had to stop to clear it from my eyes. My robe, I noticed, was now very dusty and coated in webbing. I wondered if I could clean it myself and avoid the questions, for I was certain my father would not approve of this solo exploration.

I reached the intersection and turned to go back to my father's study. My feet were chilled, and cold was starting to creep up my legs. I felt a tickling on my neck and nearly dropped my candle. I set it down, and with my fingers combed spiderweb from my hair. I did not find the spider despite several moments of futile searching. I took up my candle and walked on. The dimness of the passage seemed to make my eyelids feel heavier. It would be good to be back in my room and under my blankets.

I set my candle down again to clear more cobwebs from my path. I continued down the corridor and turned a corner before it occurred to me that there should no longer be spiderwebs in my way if I were retracing my steps. I halted where I was, lifted my candle, and peered ahead down the narrow way. No. There was no sign that I had passed this way earlier. The cobwebs were undisturbed, as was the dust on the floor. I turned back, pleased to note that my footprints and the drag of my robe were obvious here. Finding my way back was no trick at all now, and I stepped up my pace.

The candle was down to a stub in the holder when I reached the intersection. I thought angrily of how I had left my other candle at my little desk in the first spyhole. Well, it was not so far to go, and soon I would be back in my father's study. I thought longingly of the fireplace and hoped that the log I had put on the hearth was still burning. I hurried along, following my own tracks. The dark-planked walls seemed to lean in closer as my candle faltered. I tipped it a little to allow some of the wax to run off in the holder. Now the wick stood taller and the flame longer, but I could also see the bottom of the melted wax. A wandering draft from the masonry wall nearly blew it out. I set my hand to shelter the flame and then stood stock-still, wondering. Had I turned the wrong way? Wasn't the masonry wall on the way to the pantry entrance? Or had it been along the passageway that led to the peephole in my bedroom? I blinked my weary eyes and suddenly could not remember. My tracks in the corridor were no help. The mouse skeleton! Where had I seen the mouse skeleton?

I stood staring at my dying flame. "Next time," I said to the gathering darkness. "Next time I shall bring chalk and mark where each passage goes." The draft from the masonry wall was fingering its way through my robe. I turned back the way I had come. I could not hurry now, for the flame was a dancing mite on the last bit of wick. Once I reached that first intersection, I promised myself, I would be fine. Even if my candle went out, I could find my way back to the secret cubby by touch. Couldn't I? I banished from my thoughts any fear of rats. My light had chased them away, and surely they never ventured this far from the kitchens. Rats stayed where there was food.

Unless they were hungry and looking for more food.

Something touched my foot.

I leapt, ran two steps, and then fell, splattering hot wax as my candle snuffed out. Darkness rushed in to drown me. It filled the space where my candlelight had held it back. For a moment I could not breathe, for there was darkness instead of air. I pulled my feet up into my robe, terrified that rats might leap onto them and bite my toes off. My heart was beating so hard, it shook my whole body. In the dark I sat up, shaking my burned hand and clawing the gobbets of wax from it. I looked all round but the blackness was absolute. The darkness pressed on me, a substance that I could not breathe or push away. Terror rose in me.

"Mama!" I shrieked and then suddenly the reality of her death was all around me as thick and choking as the darkness. She was gone and there was no one, no one who could rescue me. Darkness and death became the same thing to me.

"Mama! Mama, Mama, Mama!" Over and over I screamed her

name because if I was in the darkness and it was death, then she must be able to come to me.

I screamed myself hoarse, and beyond hoarse into abject shaking silent terror. No one came. If anyone woke and exclaimed at my muffled cries, I did not hear it. After the initial fit passed, I huddled in a ball in the darkness, panting. At least I had warmed myself: My hair was plastered to my scalp with sweat. Only my feet and hands were still cold. I hugged my knees and then pulled my hands into my sleeves. The thudding of my own heart filled my ears. I longed to be able to better hear, for though I dreaded that I might hear the scuffling of rats I feared even more to have one come on me suddenly. Little sounds of helpless fear bubbled in my throat. With my forehead resting on the gritty floor and my chest still heaving, I shut my eyes to keep out the pressing dark.

Chapter 13

CHADE

There are many legends and customs associated with the standing stones found throughout the Six Duchies and beyond their borders. Even when the true purposes of those monoliths were forgotten, the significance remained, and thus people told tales about them and revered them. Most common were tales of careless folk, often young lovers in the tales, who wandered into those circles, leaned against the stones, and vanished. In some of the stories they return a hundred years later, to find every familiar thing vanished while they themselves are aged not a day. As part of my studies of the Skill, I have often wondered if hapless folk with a wild talent for the magic and no knowledge of how to master it had not accidentally triggered a portal and been lost forever within them. I know that I shudder when I recall my misadventure involving Skill-pillar travel between Aslevjal and Buck. I know you have read my account of it. Did no one pay heed to this warning?

And again, King Dutiful himself has had some experience of the dangers of such travel. In one instance, we emerged from a pillar that was submerged by the tide. What if it had fallen facedown on the earth? We have no idea if we would have been permanently trapped within the pillars or pushed out to suffocate underground.

Even with the recovery of many scrolls relating to the Skill, our knowledge of the pillars is incomplete. Under Chade's leadership, maps have been drawn of standing stones within the Six Duchies, the ancient markings on those stones noted, and the condition of the stones documented. More than a few have fallen, and the markings on some of them have either weathered away or been deliberately obliterated by vandals.

So, with all respect, I advise caution on this project. I think only experienced members of a coterie should attempt these explorations. We do not know where some of those portals lead, for we do not know what location the marking corresponds to. For the ones where we do know, I think that an exploratory party should first travel by conventional methods to each location to confirm that the receiving pillars are still standing and in good condition.

As for experiments regarding the pillars on which the markings have faded or been defaced, I question why we would attempt to use any of them. Is it worth risking a Skilled one's life to send someone we know not where?

LETTER FROM FITZCHIVALRY FARSEER
TO SKILLMISTRESS NETTLE

From my earliest recollections of Chade, he had enjoyed any opportunity to inject drama into his life. From Lady Thyme to the Pocked Man, he had savored the roles he had played. Age had not decreased his love of subterfuge and disguise; instead he relished them more than ever now that he had time and resources to indulge in them fully.

Thus I never knew who I would be encountering when he sent me one of his messages to meet him. Once he had been an old peddler with a sack of gourds to sell. Another time I had entered the inn to find a singularly unattractive female minstrel mangling a

tragic and romantic song, to the uproarious mockery of the inn
patrons. The passage of years had, if anything, only increased his
pleasure in such mummery. I knew that he would travel from Buckkeep Castle by the stone, reducing a journey of several days to a
snap of the fingers. He would enter the Witness Stones not far from
Buckkeep Castle and step out on top of Gallows Hill. From Gallows Hill to the taproom of the Oaken Staff was a pleasant stroll on
a warm summer's evening. Unfortunately for Chade, that night he
would step out from the pillar into a sleety rain that threatened to
be snow by morning.

I sat near the big hearth, my drenched cloak saving a place for
him on the bench nearest the flames. The Oaken Staff was a crossroads inn used mostly by merchants and travelers. I did not frequent it, and expected to encounter no one who knew me.
Nonetheless, for this rendezvous, I had grayed my beard with chalk
and donned a plowman's coarse tunic. My worn boots were muddy,
and I sat with my woolen cap pulled down over my brow and ears.
The only time I came to the Oaken Staff was when Chade demanded
a meeting. Yet it would not do for any neighbor of Tom Badgerlock's to see me in the common room and wonder why I was there.
So I drank mulled wine with hunched shoulders and a sullen air
that I hoped would put off anyone trying to strike up conversation.

The door of the inn swung open, admitting wind, rain, and a
drenched stable boy followed by two sodden merchants. Beyond
him, the evening sky was darkening to night. I growled to myself. I
had hoped that Chade would arrive early and conclude his business
swiftly. I had not been happy to leave Bee alone at Withywoods.
She had assured me that she would be fine, that she would paint
pictures in her room by the fire and go to bed as soon as she was
sleepy. I had tried in vain to convince her that she might enjoy an
evening spent with Lin and his wife. She had looked both horrified
and terrified at the idea. And so I had left her, promising her that I
would look in on her as soon as I returned. I sipped my mulled
wine and tried to decide between worrying about Bee alone at home
or worrying about Chade somewhere out in the storm.

The second time the woman bumped me from behind, I swiveled

on my bench and stared up at her. My first thought was that it was Chade in one of his more outlandish incorporations. But she was too short to be the rangy old man I knew. Seated on my bench as I was, my turning had put my eyes exactly on a level with her breasts. Unmistakably real. When my gaze traveled up, she was grinning at me. She had a slight gap between her front teeth and long-lashed green eyes. Her hair was a very dark auburn. "Hello," she said.

So, not Chade. His messenger, an overly friendly tavern girl, or a whore? So many possible ways for this evening to go very wrong. I lifted my mug, drained it, and held it out to her. "Another, please." I put no friendliness in my voice.

She raised one brow at me. "I don't fetch beer." The disdain in her voice was not feigned. My hackles lifted slightly. *Be wary.*

I leaned closer, pretending to struggle to bring her face into focus. I knew this girl. I'd seen her somewhere, and it was frustrating and alarming that I could not recall when I had met her or under what circumstances. Someone in the market? A daughter of one of our shepherds, grown and out on her own? Well, she hadn't called me by name; nor had her pupils reacted as if she recognized me. Play drunk. I reached up and scratched my nose, and tested her. "Not beer," I told her. "Mulled wine. It's cold out there."

"I don't fetch wine, either," she told me. A trace of an accent in her voice. She hadn't spent her childhood in Buck.

"That's a pity." I turned back to the fire.

She pushed my wet cloak to one side and boldly sat down next to me. That narrowed her roles to whore or messenger. She leaned close to me. "You look cold."

"No. Got myself a good spot by the fire. Had some mulled wine. Just waiting for an old friend."

She smiled. "I could be your friend."

I shook my head in drunken confusion. "No. No, you couldn't. My friend is much taller and older and he's a man. You can't be my friend."

"Well, maybe I'm your friend's friend. That would make you my friend, wouldn't it?"

I let my head wobble slightly on my neck. "Maybe," I said. I fingered my pouch at my hip and frowned. Then I smiled. "Hey. If you're my friend's friend, and you're my friend, then maybe you could buy the next round?" I held up my mug hopefully with a vacuous grin and watched her face. Any whore worth her salt wouldn't bother with a man who didn't have enough coin to buy himself another drink.

Uncertainty rippled over her face. I hadn't said what she expected. I suddenly felt very old. At one time I would have enjoyed this sort of intrigue. I'd always taken great pleasure in mastering the little tests that Chade had constantly set for me. I'd participated in more than one of his dramas for the benefit of befuddling others. But tonight I suddenly just wanted to meet with my old master, find out what he wanted, and then go home. Was any of this subterfuge truly necessary any longer? We were at peace and politically stable. Why did he need to employ spies and set tests for people? It was time for me to cut through the fog and move the play along. But not so brazenly that Chade would be offended. So I peered at her again and asked, "Which do you think is best? Mulled wine by a warm hearth on a cold day, or having a tankard while sitting in the shade?"

She cocked her head at me, and she was much younger than I'd thought. I was suddenly sure she hadn't seen twenty summers. Where did I know her from? "Beer in the shade," she said without hesitation. "Though shade can be hard to find when the sun hasn't been out for days."

I nodded and gathered up my wet cloak. "Why don't we look for Chade?" I suggested, and she smiled.

I stood and she took my arm. She led the way as we threaded our way through the inn's customers toward the base of the wooden stairs that led to the rooms above. The storm outside had grown stronger. A gust of wind buffeted the inn; the interior shutters lunged with it. An instant later the door blew wide open and stood thus, wind and rain gusting in. Amid cries from all tables for someone to shut the door, two men staggered in, leaning on each other. One of the men reached an empty table, put both hands flat on it, and stood there, just breathing. Riddle turned back to the door and slammed it shut against the storm. In the next moment I recognized

Chade leaning on the table. "And there he is," I said to my companion in a quiet voice.

"Who?" she asked me, and I knew a moment of chagrin.

"My friend. The one I was waiting for." I slurred the words slightly, tugged free of her grip on my arm, and went to meet Chade and Riddle. I turned my head just enough that, from the corner of my eye, I was aware of her backward glance at me as she ascended the stairs. A man descending the stairs met her eyes and gave her a barely perceptible nod. A whore, then?

Well, that had been peculiar. It was not the first time that Chade and his machinations had left me in an awkward position.

"Are you all right?" I asked quietly when I reached his side. He was breathing as if he'd just run a race. I offered him my arm and he took it, a distressing sign of how battered he felt. Without a word, Riddle took his other arm. We exchanged concerned looks.

"Terrible storm. Let's get a place by the fire," Chade suggested. His lips were dark, and he breathed noisily through his nose. His "disguise" was limited to soberly colored garb of an excellent weave and a plain cut. His steel-gray hair hinted at his age, but his face and bearing did not betray it. He had outlived his brother and all three of his nephews and I suspected he would outlast me, his grandnephew. But tonight the journey had taken a toll on him and he needed rest. The Skill could maintain his body but it could not make him a young man again.

I surveyed the crowded room. The place I had saved near the hearth had closed up as soon as I vacated it. "Unlikely," I told him. "But two of the upstairs rooms have hearths in them. I'll ask if either is empty."

"Arrangements were made. Riddle, please make sure my requests were granted," Chade told me. Riddle nodded, dismissed for now. He and I exchanged a look. Riddle and I had a long history, longer than his friendship with Nettle. Long before he had met and courted my daughter, he had been my brother-in-arms. In our little war with the Pale Woman on Aslevjal Island, I had left him as worse than dead. He'd forgiven me for that. I'd forgiven him for being Chade's spy upon me. We understood each other, perhaps better than

Chade realized. And so the nod we shared was that of old fellow-ship. He was a typical Buckman, dark-haired and dark-eyed, and garbed tonight to blend in with the tavern's crowd. He moved off, effortlessly eeling through the crowd without anyone scowling at being displaced. It was a talent I envied him.

"Let's sit down until Riddle comes back," I suggested and set an example. The table was an undesirable one, placed near the draft of the door, and away from both the hearth and the kitchen. It was as private a place to chat as we could wish for in such a busy place. Chade sank ungracefully into a chair across the table from mine. His eyes wandered the room; he glanced up the stairs and nodded slightly to himself. I wondered if he was looking for someone, or if it was merely an old assassin's habit to be aware of anyone who might be a danger. I waited for him to broach his business.

"Why so busy in here?" he asked me.

"A caravan of horse and cattle traders passing through, is what the talk at the fire was about. Three merchants, six hands. They'd expected to make the next town before they stopped for the night, but the weather forced them in here. I hear they're not too pleased with leaving their stock in open corrals for the night, but it was the best this place could offer them. The working hands will be sleep-ing in the barn lofts tonight. The merchants claim to have some top-quality stock and say they're worried about thieves, but I heard two stable boys referring to their horses as used-up hacks. One merchant doesn't say much, but the tack on his riding horse is Chalcedean style. And his personal horse is a pretty good one."

He nodded and despite his weariness, his mouth twisted with wry amusement. "I taught you that," he said with satisfaction. His eyes met mine, and the fondness in them startled me. Was he be-coming sentimental in his old age?

"Reporting to you, correctly and completely, was one of the first things you taught me," I agreed. We were both silent for a moment, thinking of all else he had taught me.

I had rebelled and escaped the fate of being the king's assassin. Chade had never wished to. He might no longer live like a hidden spider in the secret passageways of Buckkeep Castle, he might be hailed as Lord Chade now and openly advise King Dutiful, but I had no doubt that if King Dutiful thought a man needed killing, Chade could still rise to the occasion.

He was breathing more easily now. A tavern boy appeared, thunked down two heavy mugs of hot buttered rum, and waited. Chade smiled at me. I tipped my head at him, shook my head, and then with a faked show of reluctance found coins inside my belt and paid for our drinks. As the lad moved away, I asked Chade, "Was it harder than you expected to bring Riddle through the pillar with you?"

He didn't deny it. "He took it better than I did," Chade admitted. "Even if I did borrow strength from him to do it." He lifted his steaming mug, drank, and sighed. His eyes above the rim roved the room again.

I nodded, and then had to ask, "How did you do it? He's not Skilled."

"No. But Nettle has taught him to lend strength to her when she needs it, and that creates a sort of opening . . . well, that's not the right word. A handle? I'm not sure what to call it. Rather like a horse with a halter always on, there's a place to clip a lead when he's needed. He serves her in that capacity, as a source of strength. And in a few others as well."

Bait I would not take. I took a sip of my rum. Nasty stuff, but warming all the same. "How can he lend Skill-strength if he's not Skilled himself?"

He coughed and spoke hoarsely. "The same way Burrich loaned strength to your father. There was a deep personal bond and, like Riddle, he had a great reserve of physical strength. The Skill would help, of course, if he had it. But having served one person in that capacity, he was able to trust enough to allow another to tap him."

I mulled that over. "Had you tried this experiment before?" I asked curiously.

He drew a deeper breath and shuddered abruptly. He was still chilled, but his body was starting to warm in the still air of the tavern. "No. I thought this a good opportunity. The weather was fine at Buckkeep. I've used the stones to travel here often. I don't know why it was so taxing."

I refrained from saying anything about his age. "Did you read of this in a scroll or tablet?" And was he about to propose a more extended and regular use of the Skill-pillars? I braced myself to dissuade him.

He nodded. His eyes weren't on me but on Riddle, who was threading his way back to us, his own mug of rum held high. In his wake was a serving lad with a sling of firewood and a supply of extra candles. "He'll prepare the room," Riddle greeted us as he sat down and the boy headed up the stairs with his bucket. "Give him a few minutes to build up the fire, and then we'll go up." He transferred his gaze to me. "Tom. You look a bit better than the last time I saw you."

"A bit," I agreed. I reached across the table to grip wrists with him. I felt an odd little tingle when my hand touched his skin. He was Nettle's. It was a strange sensation to recognize her touch on him, as intimate as if I had smelled her perfume on his clothing. The wolf in me sat up, alert. I wondered if Chade sensed it as clearly as I did. A thought uncoiled in the back of my mind, and I suspected I knew why the trip through the stones had been so arduous. Was Nettle riding with Riddle, hearing with his ears and seeing all he saw? It was an intuitive leap that made me believe her presence would complicate their journey. I kept the theory to myself. I looked into his eyes, wondering if I could glimpse my daughter there. I saw nothing, but his smile broadened. All in the space of a moment. "So. A taxing journey, in this storm and all," I said.

I released Riddle's grip and turned back to Chade. "Well, what brings you so far on such a foul night?"

"We'll wait for the room with the fire," he said to that, and picked up his mug again. Riddle's glance caught mine and he lifted one eyebrow. He intended some sort of message for me, but I didn't know what.

We sat in relative silence, letting the rum warm us while we waited. When the boy came down to the table and let us know the fire was burning well, Riddle tossed him a cut coin and we went upstairs. The room was at the end of the hall, sharing a chimney with the downstairs hearth. I was surprised that the horse traders hadn't claimed it, but perhaps their purses were flatter than Chade's. Riddle opened the door, and with a startling swiftness a little knife appeared in his hand. Seated on the end of one of the beds in the room was the girl who had earlier confused me. I took my cue from Chade, who did not seem startled at all. Nor did the girl seem alarmed at our sudden entrance. Head slightly lowered, she looked at us warily from the corner of her jade-green eyes.

Something I knew but could not bring to the front of my mind uncurled in the back of my thoughts. I was staring at the girl. Her lips curled in a cat smile.

Chade paused, then walked in and seated himself at the table. It was a well-appointed room designed to accommodate traveling parties, with a table and four chairs, four narrow beds, and heavy curtains at the window. There was a trunk in the corner, the new leather straps barely scuffed. The girl might not have been there for all the attention Chade paid to her. Instead he spoke to Riddle. "See if you can find hot food for everyone. And perhaps another drink. Tom, one for you?"

I shook my head slowly. I'd had enough and suddenly I didn't want my wits to be muzzy. "Food would be good. They were roasting a nice beef joint earlier. A carve off that and some bread, perhaps."

Riddle looked at me a moment longer. He knew he was once more being dismissed, and like me he could not imagine why. Also like me, he did not like it. Chade had said nothing about the strange girl.

I looked directly at her. "I think we had a misunderstanding earlier. Perhaps you should go now."

She looked at Chade and he spoke. "No. She needs to stay here." He didn't look at anyone as he said, "Riddle, please. Food. And another hot drink." He looked at the girl. "For you?" She gave the tiniest nod. "For all of us," he confirmed for Riddle.

Riddle's glance met mine, and I knew what he asked. I spoke it aloud. "I have his back, Riddle. You can go."

Chade started to speak, then nodded instead. Riddle left with one more baleful glance at me. I moved around the room, making no pretenses as I looked under the beds for other intruders, checked that the sole window was tightly closed and latched, and then inspected the strapped trunk. "That's not really necessary," Chade said in a low voice.

"That's not what you taught me," I said, and finished my tasks. I came back to the table and sat down.

The girl still hadn't moved from her perch on the foot of the bed, but now she spoke. "Looks to me like you've forgotten a lot of what he taught you. Checking under the beds now is too little and too late." She cocked her head at me. "I can see why he might need me."

Chade spoke softly. "Please join us at the table." He cleared his throat and transferred his gaze to me. "I wish I had not been delayed. But here we all are, so we may as well discuss this together." It was as close as he would come to an apology for not preparing me for this. Whatever "this" was. Something he had not wanted to discuss via the Skill. Yet if Riddle knew, then Nettle would know. But not King Dutiful, perhaps. I pushed those thoughts aside. *Focus on the here and now.*

I watched the girl as she rose to accept his invitation. She moved like a cat, save for the sway of her hips as she sauntered to the table. If she'd been wearing bells on them, they'd have rung at each step. I tried to catch Chade's gaze. He evaded me. So I studied her as she crossed the room. She did not look dangerous; nor did she appear innocuous in the way that the most dangerous people I have known appeared. She looked ordinary, but contained. No. Not contained. Ready to burst with pride in herself. She walked like a cat with a bird in her mouth, one that wasn't quite dead. In a moment she'd release her prey for the joy of pouncing on it again.

I suddenly recognized what made her familiar. Her heritage was unmistakably Farseer. I was accustomed to seeing those features echoed in the males of my lineage. Nettle now resembled her mother more than she had ever resembled me. But this girl, despite the femininity of her features, echoed Verity and, eerily, me. My mind was assembling bits of knowledge into theory as fast as it could. A Farseer born. Younger than Dutiful, but too old to be his get. Certainly not mine. So whose? I felt as if the room had suddenly tilted. Whence had come this sprout on the family tree?

I waited for one of them to speak. I wondered at her slow stroll to the table. Chade would have interpreted that as insolence if I'd ever tried it, and a rap on the skull would have been the least reminder I would have received. But in her, he tolerated it. Something to mull.

As soon as she sat down, he said, "Report."

She cast me one glance and then focused her attention on Chade. "He's careless," she said offhandedly. "His 'disguise' is pathetic. I bumped him twice before he noticed me. It was stupidly easy to get next to him. All he was thinking about was watching for you." She swung her eyes to look at me, daring me to respond. "I could have killed him three times over, drugged him, or picked his pocket."

That stung. "I very much doubt that. And I think that is the poorest excuse for a report that I've ever heard."

She raised her brows at me. "All necessary information was conveyed." She cocked her head at my old mentor and asserted, "If Lord Chade had needed more detail, he'd have asked me for it." As she spoke, she rose and came around to my side of the table. I twisted my head to look up at her. She spoke to Chade in a very confident tone. "Tell him that he should let me touch him."

Chade met my gaze then. "It's safe. She's one of ours."

"In more ways than one, obviously," I retorted. I heard a small exhalation of breath from her, but I couldn't tell if I'd hit my target or she was amused by me. I sat still, but somewhere a wolf lifted his hackles and growled low.

I felt her light touch on the back of my collar, then the shoulder of my shirt. She leaned down to touch my hip, and then I felt her hand brush my ribs. As she drew her fingers away, my shirt followed them briefly. Then she set the pins out on the table. There were six of them, not four, each less than half a finger's length. The heads were shaped like tiny green spiders.

"If I had nudged any one of them a bit harder, they would have pierced your skin." She leaned closer, over my shoulder, and spoke by my ear. "Any of them could have been tipped with poison, or a sleeping dose. You'd have keeled over in front of the fire, just another drunk passing out, until no one could wake you again."

"I've told you," Chade said sternly. "Those spiders are a vanity that no assassin can afford. *Never* leave a mark that anyone might associate with you. I'm disappointed in you."

Her voice tightened at his rebuke. "I merely used them in this instance to prove that I was the one who set them, not some other spy or assassin sent in before me. I would never use them on a task that was confidential or important. I only used them today to prove what I told you. He's careless." Her disdain burned me. She stood behind me, slightly to my left, and added, "Sloppy. Anyone could kill him. Or his child."

I hadn't known I was going to do it. My chair overturned as I moved. I wasn't as fast as I once was, but I was still faster than she was. She hit the floor on her back. My left hand gripped her right wrist with the small knife she'd pulled as she fell beneath me. My right thumb was in the hollow of her throat, pressing firm and deep, my fingers biting into the back of her neck. Her teeth were bared and her eyes bulging at me when I became aware of Chade on his feet over us.

"Stop it! Both of you! This is not why I brought you together. If I wanted either one of you dead, I could do it a lot more efficiently than setting you on each other."

I lifted my thumb from her throat at the same time I throttled the knife from her hand. I came back to my feet with a backward leap that put me out of easy reach. Another step back and I had the wall behind me and both of them in full view. I hoped neither of them could see what it had cost me. I breathed slowly and steadily despite my hammering heart and desperate need for more air. I pointed a finger at the girl. "Never threaten my child."

"I didn't!" Her angry retort was strangled as she used a chair to come to her feet. I ignored her and focused my anger on my old mentor. "Why did you set your assassin on me?" I demanded of Chade.

"I didn't set an assassin on you," he objected with great disgust. He moved around the table to resume his chair.

"I wasn't told to kill you, only probe your weakness. It was a small test," the girl interjected. She wheezed in another breath and added vindictively, "One that you failed." She levered herself to her feet and sat down.

Much as I wished to deny that, I couldn't. I spoke only to Chade. "Like the one you sent before. When Bee was only days old."

Chade didn't flinch. "Somewhat. Except that he was just a boy. And, as I suspected, not suited to the training. It was one of the things we wished to discover about him. I moved him in a different direction, as you suggested. My own fault. He really wasn't prepared for you."

"But I was," the girl said with quiet satisfaction.

"Stop gloating," Chade told her. "Your tongue runs away with you. You're taunting a man who could have quickly killed you a minute ago. To no purpose. You're getting completely on his wrong side, and then you'll never be able to work with him."

I didn't move from my position. "I don't do that sort of 'work' anymore," I told the old man coldly. "Nor do I currently need to live as if every stranger might be out to kill me. Unless you've done something to set those sorts of threats in motion again."

He crossed his arms on his chest and leaned back in his chair. "Fitz. Stop being an ass and come back to the table. Those threats never went away. You of all people should know that. You put yourself out of harm's way, and it's worked for you. Most of the folk who have deduced who you are either have no ill will toward you, or haven't had much reason of late to wish you dead. But when you produced a child, that changed things. I thought surely you had recognized that and were taking precautions. The first time I tested your boundaries, you seemed well aware of the danger.

"But when Nettle told me how mired you are in grief, and that the child may well need special protection for the rest of her life, I resolved to offer you help, if you needed it. Especially when she mentioned that you might send the child to Buckkeep. Or come back there yourself."

"I've no intention of coming back to Buckkeep. And I don't need anyone to help me protect myself or Bee!" I hated that he had called me Fitz in front of her. A lapse or deliberate? "The only threats I've encountered of late seem to come from those I thought I could trust."

Chade gave me a look. It appealed to me for something. I wasn't sure what he was asking. His words contradicted his expression. "That's exactly how I expected you to respond. Which was why I charged Shun with first determining if you did or not. And you obviously do."

Riddle warned us with a knock before he shouldered open the door and entered with a tray of plates and mugs. His dark eyes flickered over the room, taking in my stance, the overturned chair, and the girl's sullen face. I saw his brows lift slightly. But he made no comment. As he slid the heavy tray onto the table, he noted, "I brought plenty for all of us. I assume she's our guest?" He stooped and righted the chair, gestured courteously at it for the girl.

"Let's eat before we talk more," Chade suggested.

I came to the table reluctantly. My pride was chafed. I didn't like Chade sharing so much about me with this girl when I knew so little about her, save what I'd surmised. He'd spoken my name before her! All I knew of her was that she was related to us. How old was she, who was her mother, and how long had Chade been training her? Was she nobly born, with all the political strings that would attach to her? And why did he suddenly want to place her with me?

For that was obviously his intent, that he'd put her in my house-hold, ostensibly as Bee's bodyguard. A laudable idea, in some ways, if my child had truly needed guarding. Patience had had Lacey at her side, and no one had questioned that Prince Chivalry's wife would be accompanied everywhere by her servant. Nor had they thought it odd that Lacey had always had her tatting and her long needles for working lace with her. Lacey had watched over Patience, keeping her safe even after assassins had managed to kill her hus-band. In their old age the roles had reversed, and Patience had lov-ingly tended her failing "serving woman" to the end of her days.

But I doubted this girl had the temperament for such a role. She looked of an age to be a nurse or nanny for a small child, but she had shown me no signs that she could adopt such an identity. Her stealth skills were impressive, but in a physical fight she had no muscle or weight to draw on. Her Farseer features would draw too much attention at Buckkeep; she'd be useless as a spy there.

I doubted even more that we would get along well enough for me to trust her with my daughter. And I didn't like that Riddle had looked surprised and still seemed to regard her with caution. Obviously, he had known as little of Chade's plan as I had. He hadn't recognized her. I couldn't tell if he had realized she was related to the royal family or not.

I seated myself opposite her. Riddle served her first, setting a laden plate in front of her. For short notice, he'd done well by us. Thick slabs of steaming meat fresh carved from the spit, the crackling fat nicely browned, potatoes popping white and mealy from crispy baked skins, and dark-brown gravy. There was a loaf of warm bread and a pot of pale butter beside it. It was simple but there was plenty of it and Shun swallowed audibly as he set it in front of her. She had a healthy appetite and made no pretense of waiting for the rest of us, but seized a fork and knife and began eating. Riddle raised his brows at such childish manners but said nothing as he set out plates for Chade and me and then himself. He'd brought up a pot of tea and four cups as well.

Riddle went back to the door, latched it, and then returned to join us at table. He ate with an appetite. Chade sorted through his food like an old man. As for me, I recognized that the food was of good quality but could not concentrate on it enough to enjoy it. I drank hot tea and watched them. Chade was quiet, his gaze moving between me and the girl as he ate. At the end of the meal, he looked much the better for having eaten. Shun ate with obvious and focused enjoyment. She seized the teapot and refilled her own cup without asking if any of us would care for more. She did not hesitate to take the last potato in the dish, and when she was finished she leaned back in her chair and breathed a loud sigh of satiation. When Riddle began gathering and stacking the emptied plates back on the tray, I spoke bluntly to the old assassin.

"You trained me to report well to you, to give you the whole of what I learned. After we had all the facts laid out, then we'd build our assumptions. Yet you've sprung this on me with no warning and less explanation, and expect me to humbly accept it without questions. What are you about, old man? What do you want? And don't pretend that this youngster becoming my daughter's protector is the sum of this."

"Very well." He leaned back in his chair and looked from me to Shun, and then at Riddle.

Riddle returned his gaze. "Am I supposed to leave now?" he asked. There was a chill edge to his voice.

Chade considered it so quickly that it seemed as if he answered without a pause. "Little point to that. I've seen that you've put it together."

Riddle flicked a glance at me and hazarded an interpretation. "You'd like to put this girl with Tom, so he can protect her for you."

The muscles at the corner of Chade's mouth twitched. "That's a fairly accurate summation."

I looked at Shun. She was dismayed. Evidently she hadn't seen things from that vantage, and had been preening herself that she was being sent out on her first real assignment, only to discover that actually she was being banished from Buckkeep, possibly because she had grown into a phase where it would be next to impossible for anyone to miss that she was a Farseer. No. Not Buckkeep. If she'd been anywhere in the castle, Riddle would have known of her. Then where? I watched her straighten in her chair. Little sparks of anger lit in her gaze. She opened her mouth to speak but I was quicker.

"I'd like to know who she is before I take her on," I said bluntly.

"You've seen her lineage. I saw you recognize it."

"How did it happen?" I demanded, baffled.

"The usual way," Chade muttered; he looked uncomfortable. That triggered the girl.

She shook her head, making her auburn curls dance. A chill note, almost accusatory, came into her voice. "My mother was nineteen when she visited Buckkeep Castle with her parents for a Springfest. She went home, where it was discovered she was with child. She had me. A couple of years after I was born, her parents managed to find her a husband. My grandparents kept me to raise. Which they did, until my grandfather died two years ago, and my grandmother died six months later. At which time I went to live with my mother for the first time in my life. Except that her husband did not feel in a fatherly fashion toward me. And instead of being furious with him for his wandering eyes and grasping hands on her child, my mother became angry and jealous. She packed me off with a sealed note to the old queen at Buckkeep."

"And she gave you over into Lord Chade's keeping?" That didn't sound like Kettricken to me.

"No." She cast a glance at Chade. He had steepled his hands. His firmly pinched lips indicated he did not enjoy her accounting, but realized that any attempt to interrupt it would be futile.

Shun leaned one elbow on the table, feigning a casualness she did not feel. I saw her tension in the muscles of her throat and in how one hand gripped the table's edge. "I and my note were intercepted very shortly after I left my mother's home. Both were delivered to Lord Chade. He took charge of me and placed me in a supposedly safe haven. And he has been my protector ever since." There was resentment, but for what? I made note of her use of "supposedly." Were we getting closer to the bone of why she was here? Yet I was no closer to knowing her parentage. Did her Farseer looks come from her mother's side? Or her father's? How many generations back was the connection?

Riddle shifted slightly in his seat. He was not the one who had intercepted the girl. Did he know who had? But I sensed that he was gathering and sorting facts as much as I was. And this was his first encounter with Shun? Where had Lord Chade been keeping her? The sour twist of Chade's mouth showed that he was not especially pleased that Shun was sharing these details.

"How old are you?" I demanded.

"Does it matter?" she retorted.

"She's nineteen now," Chade said quietly, and scowled as Riddle and I exchanged a glance. "And as you have guessed, her resemblance to her forebears means that bringing her to court is a bad idea. For now!" he added hastily as her countenance darkened. Caution flared in me. She seemed a snippy thing, arrogant for her years. I wondered whose she was, and who she thought she was. She was giving herself an air of importance that I didn't comprehend.

I wondered. *Shun.* I pointed the thought at her, Skilling strongly. She didn't even twitch. That answered at least one of my questions. Even untrained, she should have felt something. So she had no predilection for the Skill. I wondered if that disappointed Chade or if he was glad she could not be used that way. He was watching me, well aware of what I'd just done. I shifted my focus.

I have dozens of questions. Who is her mother, and who is she married to now? Does Shun know who her father is? She doesn't name him, or her mother. Why have you kept her concealed from everyone? Or have you? Has Kettricken added her to her genealogy of unacknowledged Farseers?

Not now! He didn't even glance at me as he responded. Nor did he look at Riddle. Concealed from Nettle as well? I boiled with questions and wondered if I'd ever get a chance to ask them privately. Some I would not speak in front of the girl and some were better not aired in front of Riddle. There was one I could ask.

"And you have trained her?"

He glanced at her and then met my eyes. "In some things. Not personally, but she had a suitable instructor. Not as you were trained, but as I saw fit." He cleared his throat. "Mostly so she could protect herself. Though I did wonder if she might not be brought along in my footsteps." He coughed and added, "There is much you could teach her, if you would."

I sighed. I suspected he had given me as much information as he intended to give me in this company. "Well. You still haven't told me all I need to know. And you must see that I have to prepare my household. I can't simply ride down to the inn for ale on a stormy night and come back with a girl on the back of my horse."

"That's why I brought Riddle. I sent Shun here several days ago, and now that Riddle is here, he will act as her protector until he can deliver her to your door."

Riddle's mouth quirked once. This was news to him as well.

I tried to find my feet in the rushing current of Chade's planning. "So, in a few days she will arrive at Withywoods. Where I will greet her as my distant cousin, come to help care for my child in my bereavement."

"Exactly." Chade smiled.

I wasn't amused. It was too soon for me to find strength to help anyone except myself. I'd have to tell him no. I just couldn't do this. I'd lost Molly and found our child and was fumbling my way toward knowing her. I felt a sudden sharp pang of anxiety. Was Bee safe? Was she frightened? I'd left her alone tonight and come here to this meeting, expecting it to be some brief consultation on a political situation into which he wanted my insights. Now he was asking me to take a young woman into my household, a woman I knew nothing about, and both protect her and educate her in how she must protect herself. My first impression of her was that I would not like her, nor would she enjoy my company. With terrible regret, I wished he had been able to speak to me privately. I would have told him all the reasons I had to say no. Now he had me trapped at a table with both Shun and Riddle watching, and possibly Nettle. How could I say no in these circumstances?

I drew a breath. "I'm just not sure this is the best solution, Chade. Bee is very young, and I am still in mourning." I turned to Shun. "Have you any experience with small children?"

She stared at me. Her mouth opened and closed twice. Her glance fixed on Chade. I saw both alarm and resentment build on her face as she demanded, "How small? How young? I was stuck caring for my mother's spoiled nieces when I stayed with her, despite their having a nanny and a tutor. I didn't care for it. If you think you can exile me from court and hide me at some provincial manor to play governess under the pretense that I'm protecting her, well, you can't. Nor do I accept the idea that this Tom will watch over me. I proved for myself and you that however sharp he used to be, he's grown careless and soft. He did not guard himself; how can he protect me?"

"No one said 'governess.' We are simply discussing what it might be said you are doing while Fitz continues your training. It would be excellent practice for you to protect his daughter, as her bodyguard."

I flinched. It was the second time he had called me Fitz in front of her. She did not seem mature enough to be entrusted completely with that secret. Yet it was almost insulting that she had not seemed to realize she had been handed such a secret. I felt a sudden needle to my vanity. Nineteen. Hadn't she even heard of FitzChivalry Farseer?

She crossed her arms on her chest and lifted her head high, defying Chade. "What if I say no? This is not why I thought I was coming here. I thought you had found a task for me, something significant to do with my life. I'm tired of hiding in the darkness like a rat. I've done nothing wrong. You told me that my life would be better with you. I thought I'd live in Buckkeep Castle, at court!"

Chade steepled his fingers and spoke carefully to them. "You can, of course, say no. You do have a choice, Shun." He sighed suddenly and lifted his eyes to meet hers. "No choices were given to me, so I do know that such things matter. In this regard, I will do all I can for you. I wish I could say you had many choices, but I am as constrained by fate as you are."

I watched her face as she slowly realized that he was telling her that she was limited to the choices he would offer her. I wasn't surprised. That was the life of a Farseer bastard. He and I had both known the constraints of being an unrecognized sprout of that family tree. One could be a danger to the family and be eliminated, or one could be useful to the family in a defined role. One couldn't choose not to be part of the family. Chade was loyal to his family. He would keep her safe and guide her, and in the process he would protect the throne. And I found I agreed with him. He was right. But to Shun it must have felt like a net being drawn tight around her. He read her face as he spoke. "I can well understand your bitterness toward me. I have done all I could to ameliorate it. You still have a right to be bitter toward all the people who created the situation in which you must now live. Later, perhaps, you will understand that I am doing the best I can by you. You can, if you choose, make a home at Withywoods, at least for a time. It's a lovely place in a gentle valley. It may not be Buckkeep, but neither is it a crude backwater town. You will have opportunities there for entertainment and refined socializing. You'll be treated well and given an allowance of your own." He flickered a glance at me and saw my doubts. The plea in his expression deepened, and I looked away. Sparks were kindling in Shun's eyes.

Relentlessly, he continued. "Indeed, initially, Withywoods is where you *must* go. But if you find yourself unhappy there, I will make other arrangements for you. You may choose an appropriate location beyond Buck Duchy, and I will arrange for your lodging there. You will receive an allowance sufficient for a comfortable life, with up to two servants. That allowance will continue as long as you live quietly. That is for your safety."

She lifted her head. "And if I don't? If I get up and walk out that door right now?"

Chade gave a small, defeated sigh. He shook his head. "You'd be putting yourself beyond the pale. I'd do what I could to protect you, but it wouldn't be enough. You would be penniless. Your family would regard you as a renegade and a social liability. You would be discovered." He spoke the words I knew he would. "You're like a double-edged blade with no handle, my dear. Dangerous to hold, and dangerous to set down. Someone would find you and either kill you or use you against the Farseers."

"How? What could they possibly use me to do to the king? What danger am I to him?"

I spoke before Chade could. "They could threaten Lord Chade if they had you as a hostage. Send him an ear or a lip to prove they were serious."

She lifted a hand to her face, covering her mouth. She spoke through her spread fingers, suddenly a frightened child. "Can't I just go back? You could demand they do more to protect me. I could stay where I was at—"

"No." He cut her off sharply before she could betray where he'd been keeping her. An interesting puzzle for me. Somewhere close enough to Buckkeep Castle for him to visit often, yet far enough away that Riddle had never glimpsed her. His words stopped my musing. "Use your mind, Shun." Eyes wide, she shook her head at him.

My heart sank. I knew. "Someone has already forced Chade's hand. That's why this is all happening so suddenly."

She gave me a hateful look and turned back to her mentor. Chade was watching me. "For which I'm sorry. But you can see the situation I'm in, Fitz. It was not her father's family who sought to kill her. She has enemies of her own. I need to place her somewhere safe. And the only place I have is with you." He looked at me with pleading sincerity. It was a look he had once made me practice in front of a looking glass for several hours. I did not laugh. We did not bare our tricks before others. I met it with a look of my own.

"You have not told me who she is, nor who her enemies are. How can I guard her when I do not know whence the danger comes? Who are these enemies she has?"

The mask fell from his face. The desperation in his eyes was real, now. "Please. Trust me and do this for me. Those who stand against her are ones I am not ready yet to discuss. You should know that before I ask this of you. That this favor will involve you taking a risk for me. My boy, I have no one else I can ask. Will you take her and keep her safe? For me?"

And there it was. Any thoughts of refusing melted away. This was not a mere favor he was asking of me. It was a confirmation of who we were to each other. There was no one else he could ask this favor. No one who would understand her danger as I would, no one who would know how to protect her and still keep her from harming us. No one else could sheath this double-edged sword. This was not a request I could refuse. He knew that and he hated to ask it of me. Just as Chade drew a breath, I took control of the situation.

"I will. And I will do my best by her."

Chade froze. Then he nodded weakly, relief slackening his face. I saw now how deeply he had feared I would refuse him. That shamed me.

Shun drew a breath to speak but I stopped her with an uplifted hand. "Unfortunately, I have to leave now. I will need to prepare a place for you at Withywoods," I announced.

She looked startled. Good. Keep her unbalanced until it was determined. I spoke calmly, taking it all out of Chade's hands. "You will be given enough money to stay at this inn for three days. Riddle will remain here with you, as your protector. You need have no fear of him. He is a man of honor. You don't seem to have brought much with you from your old home. So if there is something you need, just let him know. In three days he will escort you to Withywoods, where I will greet you as my cousin, come to help me manage my household." I took a breath. It was only logical, the best way to explain her arrival, and yet it still pained me to say the words aloud. "Since my wife's recent death." I cleared my throat. "I have a little girl at home. And a large holding to manage for Lady Nettle." I lifted my eyes to meet hers. "You will be welcomed there. And you may stay as long as you find it to your liking. You do need to know that I do not live grandly as a nobleman, but as a Holder, the trusted caretaker of a large estate. I am not sure what you are accustomed to, but you may find us rustic. Simple. As my 'cousin,' you will have tasks to do, but I assure you that you will not be treated as a servant by anyone, but as a family member who has come to help in troubled times."

"Tasks?" She said the word as if she could not fit her mouth around it. "But . . . I come of a noble family! On my mother's side, I am—"

"You aren't," Chade cut in decisively. "That name is a danger to you. You must leave it behind. I'll give you a new name. My own. You are a Fallstar now. I give you my surname. The one that my mother gave to me. Shun Fallstar."

She stared at him, shocked. Then, to my horror, tears formed in her eyes. Mouth ajar, she looked at Lord Chade as the drops began their slow passage down her cheeks. Chade went pale, the old pock-scars standing out against his face. Many thought them the sign of his survival of some plague. I knew them for what they were: the traces of an experiment with a mixture that had proved far more explosive than he had thought. Like him, I bore some scars from the things we had exploded together. Just as we had this girl's life.

I thought of the other life this would impact. My child, who was still just coming to know me. Bee was slowly adapting after her mother's death. I wondered how she would react to this sudden inclusion of a new family member and knew the answer. She would not welcome it, any more than I did. Well, with a great deal of luck, it would not be for long, only until Chade found a better solution for all of us. Still. I looked at Shun. "Have you *any* experience with children?"

She made a quick swipe at her tears and shook her head. "I grew up with my grandparents. My mother was their only surviving child, so there were no other youngsters in their household. Only me. The servants had children but I had little to do with them. And my mother's nieces were the children of her husband's brother, and perfect little beasts." She took a breath and exclaimed, "I told you, I can't pretend to be her governess. I won't do that!"

"No. I only wondered if you were accustomed to children. You aren't. And I have no problems with that. I suspect you thought you might guard my child for me. I don't think that will be needed at all. I can find other tasks for you, ones that have to do with running the household staff." Yet another thing I must invent. Busy-work to keep her occupied.

Given the sort of child that Bee was, perhaps it was best that Shun had no experience of other children. Bee might seem less odd to her. But the vehemence of her instant response to the thought that she might have to care for the child was a small warning to me. I would keep Bee at a safe distance from her until I had gauged her character. I stood to leave. Chade looked alarmed.

"I'd hoped to talk more with you! Can't you stay the night? The storm outside is only getting worse. Riddle, could you see if the inn has another open room?"

I shook my head. I knew he wanted to have a long, private conversation with me. He longed for a chance to explain every part of this, and to explore every possible solution. But there was someone else who needed me more. "I can't. Bee isn't accustomed to being left alone." Was Bee asleep yet? Or lying awake and wondering when her papa would be back? Shame that I had all but forgotten her in this strange business washed through me, followed by uneasiness and urgency. I needed to get home. I looked at Chade.

"Surely her nursemaid . . ."

I shook my head, irritated at the delay. "She has none. Molly and I were raising her, and before her mother died she needed no one else. Now she has only me. Chade, I have to go."

He looked at me. Then with an exasperated sigh, he flapped his hand at me. "Go, then. But we still need to talk. Privately."

"We will. Another time. And I will ask you about that tutor you recommended as well."

He nodded. He would find a way. Tonight he needed to stay in this room and convince his sullen charge that she must do as he suggested. But that was his task, not mine. I had enough tasks of my own.

As I left, Riddle followed me out into the hall. "Bad luck all round," he said. "The passage was difficult for him to manage, and then the storm delayed us, too. He had hoped to have a quiet hour or two with you before dealing with 'a problem.' I was shocked when the problem turned out to be a girl. Shun. Terrible name, eh? I'm sure it's not what her grandparents called her. I hope she doesn't decide to keep it."

I looked at him wearily, reaching for words. "Well. At least it's good to know that the Farseer talent for dramatics is being passed on."

He grinned crookedly. "I'd say you and Nettle both carry a fair share of that." When I did not answer his smile, he asked in a gentler voice, "How are you doing, Tom?"

I shrugged and shook my head. "As you see. I'm getting by. Adjusting."

He nodded and was quiet for a moment. Then he said, "Nettle is worried for her sister. I've told her that you are far more capable than she might imagine, but she has still moved forward with preparing a chamber and a caretaker for little Bee."

"Bee and I have actually been doing very well together. I think we are well suited to each other." It was difficult to be courteous. I liked Riddle but really, Bee was not his concern. She was mine and I was feeling more and more anxious, more and more certain that I needed to get home. I was suddenly weary of all of them, longing only to leave.

His mouth tightened, and then I saw him decide to speak. "Except that you've left her alone tonight to come here. No nurse, no governess, no tutor? Tom, even an ordinary child takes constant watching. And Bee is not—"

"For you to worry about," I cut in. I was stung by his words, though I was trying not to show it. Damn. Would he go straight back to Nettle as soon as he could and report to her that I was neglecting her little sister? I stared at him. Riddle met my gaze squarely. We had known each other for years, and endured several very bad things together. Once, I had left him for dead, or worse than dead. He'd never rebuked me for that. I owed him the courtesy of hearing him out. I tucked my chin and waited for him to speak.

"We worry," he said quietly, "about all sorts of things that don't necessarily belong to us. Seeing you tonight was a shock. You're not thin, you're gaunt. You drink without tasting what you put in your mouth, and you eat without looking at your food. I know you're still mourning, and that's only right. But grief can make a man overlook the obvious. Such as his child's needs."

He meant well but I was in no mood to hear it. "I don't overlook her needs. It's exactly why I'm leaving now. Give me three days to ready things before you bring Shun to my door." He was nodding and looking at me so sincerely that my anger faded. "You'll see Bee then, and talk to her. I promise you she's not neglected, Riddle. She's an unusual child. Buckkeep Castle would not be a good place for her."

He looked skeptical but had the grace to keep his doubts to himself. "I'll see you then," he replied.

I felt his gaze follow me as I walked down the hall. I descended the stairs wearily and full of regrets. I admitted my disappointment. There had been in my heart the germ of a hope that Chade had arranged this meeting because he wished to see me, to offer me some sort of comfort or sympathy at my loss. It had been years since he had been my mentor or my protector, yet my heart had still yearned to once more feel the shelter of his wisdom. When we are children, we believe that our elders know all and that even when we cannot understand the world, they can make sense of it. Even after we are grown, in moments of fear or sorrow, we still turn instinctively to the older generation, hoping to finally learn some great hidden lesson about death and pain. Only to learn instead that the only lesson is that life goes on. I had known that Chade did not deal well with death. I should not have expected it of him.

I turned my collar up, pulled my damp cloak tighter around me, and went back out into the storm.

Chapter 14

DREAMS

This is the dream from the end of my time. I have dreamed it six different ways, but I will only write what always stays the same. There is a wolf as big as a horse. He is black and stands still as stone and stares. My father is as gray as dust, and old, so old. "I'm just so tired," he says in two of the dreams. In three he says, "I'm sorry, Bee." In one of the dreams, he says nothing at all, but his silence means everything. I would like to stop having this dream. It feels so strong, as if it must happen, no matter the path I choose. Every time I wake from it, it feels as if I have taken a step closer to a cold and dangerous place.

DREAM JOURNAL OF BEE FARSEER

I refuse to believe I slept. How could such abject terror lend itself to falling asleep? Instead I huddled there, behind my closed eyelids, trembling with terror.

And Wolf-Father came. That was the first time.

I'd had dreams before, dreams that I knew were portentous, dreams that I committed to memory upon waking. I had begun writing my dreams down, the ones that I knew meant something. So I knew what dreams were.

That was not a dream.

The smells of dust and mice droppings blew away before the brisk scents of new snow and spruce needles. Then came a warm, clean smell of healthy animal. He was close. I curled my hands into the fur of his ruff and held tight, feeling my fingers warm there. His muzzle was by my ear, his breath warm there. *Stop your whining. If you are frightened, be silent. Whining is for prey. It attracts predators. And you are not prey.*

I caught my breath. My throat was sore and my mouth dry. I had been keening, without realizing it. I stopped, shamed by his disapproval.

That's better. Now, what is your problem?

"It's dark. The doors won't open and I'm trapped here. I want to get home, back to my bed."

Didn't your father tell you to stay safe in the den? Why did you leave it?

"I was curious."

And curious cubs have been getting into trouble since the world began. No, don't start whining again. Tell me. What are you afraid of?

"I want to be back in my bed."

That is what you want. And you are wise to return to the den where your father left you, and remember not to leave it again without his permission. So why don't you do that? What makes you afraid to do that?

"I'm afraid of the rats. And I can't find my way back. I'm trapped here." I tried to draw a breath. "I can't get out."

And why is that?

"It's dark. And I'm lost. I can't find my way back." I was beginning to be angry with the calm, implacable voice even as I cherished the warmth and feeling of safety he gave me. Perhaps even then I realized that I only felt irritation with him because I now felt safe. Slowly it came to me that I was no longer afraid, just perplexed.

Why can't you find your way back?

Now he was just being stupid. Or mean. "It's dark. I can't see. And even if I could see, I can't remember which way to go."

The voice never lost its patience. *You can't see, perhaps. Perhaps you can't remember because you are so frightened. But you can smell. Get up.*

Uncurling myself was hard. I was cold all over now, shaking with the chill. I stood up.

Lead the way. Follow your nose. Follow the scent of your mother's candle.

"I can't smell anything."

Blow out through your nose. Then breathe in slowly.

"All I smell is dust."

Try again. Inexorable.

I growled low.

So. You are finding your courage. Now find your wits. Sniff your way home, cub.

I wanted him to be wrong. I wanted to be justified in my fear and hopelessness. I took a breath to tell him how stupid he was and tasted my mother's scent. Loneliness welled in me and hunger for she who had loved me so. My heart drew me toward the smell, and my feet followed.

It was so faint. Twice I paused, thinking I had lost it. I must have walked in blackness but I recall that I moved slowly through the summer garden toward the honeysuckle that tangled and sprawled along a stone wall in the herb garden.

I came to a place where a draft of air touched my face. The moving air confused the scent and suddenly I was in darkness again. My heart jammed against my throat and I reached out blindly, touching nothing. A sob of terror fought with my hammering heart to see which could leap first from my mouth.

Steady. Use your nose. Fear is useless now.

I sniffled, thinking him heartless. And caught the scent again. I turned toward it, only to have it get fainter. Turned my head back the other way, more slowly. I walked toward the smell that now felt like my mother's hands on my cheeks. I leaned my face forward, breathing my mother's love. There was a slight bend in the corner and then a gradual ascent. The scent grew stronger. And then I bumped the little shelf. That jolted my eyes open; I wasn't aware I had closed them.

And there, leaking in around the peephole's cover, was a tiny gleam of flickering light, illuminating the stub of my mother's candle. The light caressed it, yellow and warm and welcoming. I knelt and took the candle and held it to my breast, breathing the fragrance that had led me to safety. I pushed the peephole cover aside and peered into the dimly lit study. "It's going to be all right," I said to Wolf-Father. I turned to look back at him, but he was gone, leaving only a cooler place in the air behind me.

"Father?" I said, but there was no reply. My heart sank and then I heard the rapping.

"Bee. Unlatch the door. Right now." His voice was low and I could not tell if he was afraid or angry.

The rapping came again, louder, and I saw the doors shake. Then they leapt at a blow.

It took me a moment to get my bearings. I seized my courage tight and left the peephole's comforting light. Dragging my fingertips on the wall as I went down the narrow corridor, around a corner, and then another sharp corner and out of the panel. The rapping and shaking were louder now. "I'm coming!" I called back as I pushed the panel closed. I had to work the catches on it, and then I went to unbolt the study door. My father pushed it open so suddenly that he knocked me off my feet.

"Bee!" he exclaimed in a breathless shout and dropped to his knees to seize me. He hugged me so tightly that I couldn't breathe. He had forgotten to hold himself in. His fear drenched me. I stiffened in his grip. Abruptly it was gone, leaving me to wonder if I had truly felt that wave of love beneath it. He released me but his dark staring eyes held me. They were full of hurt. "What were you thinking? Why aren't you in your bed?" he demanded of me.

"I wanted to—"

"You are not allowed. Do you understand me? You are *not* allowed!" He wasn't shouting. The voice he was using was more frightening than shouting would have been. It was as low and in-tense as a snarl.

"Not allowed what?" I trembled out.

He looked at me with wild eyes. "Not allowed to be gone from where I left you. Not allowed to make me think I've lost you." He gathered me in again and held me close against his cold coat. I be-came aware that his hair was dripping wet and he still wore his outer garments. He must have come in and gone straight to my room to check on me. And instantly panicked when I wasn't there. I felt an odd little lift to my heart. I was important to him. Very important.

"Next time you tell me to stay in the den, I will," I promised him.

"Good," he said fiercely. Then, "What were you doing in here with the door latched?"

"Waiting for you to come home." Not quite a lie, and I couldn't have said why I evaded his question.

"And that's how you come to be covered in cobwebs with a dirty face." He touched my cheek with a cold finger. "You've been cry-ing. There are two clean streaks on your face." He reached into his pocket, pulled out a less-than-clean kerchief, and reached for my face. I drew back from it. He looked at the cloth in his hand and laughed ruefully. "I wasn't thinking. Come. Let's go to the kitchen and see if we can get a bit of warm water and a clean cloth. And you can tell me exactly where you were waiting for me to return."

He did not put me down but carried me, as if he did not trust me beyond his arm's reach. I felt the power thrumming through him, battering to breach his walls and engulf me. It was a frightening, contained storm inside him. But I did not struggle against him. I think I decided that night that the discomfort of being close to him was preferable to standing away from the only person in the world who I knew loved me. I suspect that at some point he had made the same decision.

In the kitchen he ladled water from the warming pot always kept there and found a clean rag for me to use to wash my face. I told him that I had been curious to explore the spy-warren and had gone in, but then lost my way when my candle went out and became frightened. He didn't ask me how I had found my way out; I am sure he did not imagine how far I had traveled in the hidden corridors, and at that time I chose to keep it that way. Of Wolf-Father, I said nothing.

He took me up to my room and found me a clean nightdress. The one I had been wearing was dirtied all round the hem, and the socks were thicker with cobwebs and dust than they were with wool. He watched over me as I got into bed and then sat in silence by my bed until he believed I was asleep. Then he blew out the candle and left the room.

I had almost been asleep, but held myself back from it for two reasons. The first was to find the peephole that had looked into my room. That took longer than I had expected. It was very well concealed in the paneling of one wall, and up high, so the viewer could see almost the entire room. I felt round the nearby woodwork and paneling to see if perhaps I could find an entrance to the spy-maze, to no avail. And I was chilly, weary, and my warm bed was tempting.

Yet as I climbed into it and put my head on the pillow, I again felt the reluctance to sleep. Sleep brought dreams, and since my mother's death they seemed to come almost every night. I was tired of them, and tired of the labor of remembering them and writing them into my book each day. Some of the most frightening ones were recurrent. I hated the one with the snake boat. And the one where I had no mouth and could not close my eyes to avoid what I was seeing. I helped a rat to hide inside my heart. There was a fog, and a white rabbit and a black rabbit ran side by side from terrible ravening creatures. The white rabbit was pierced with a living arrow. The black rabbit screamed as it died.

I hated the dreams, and yet every time they came back to my sleep I added a detail, a note, a curse to my journal.

This storm of dreams was something new, but not the dreaming. I had been dreaming for longer than I had been outside my mother's womb. Sometimes I thought that the dreams went back beyond my existence, that they were the fragments of someone else's life, but were somehow bound to me. As an infant, I dreamed, and as a very small child. Some of the dreams were pleasant, others weirdly beautiful. Some frightened me. I never forgot my dreams, as some people say they do. Each was a complete and separate memory, as much a part of my life as remembering the day we took honey from the hives, or the time I slipped on the stairs and scraped all the skin off both shins. When I was small, it was almost as if I had two lives, one by day and one by night. Some dreams seemed more important than others, but none of them seemed trivial.

But after Wolf-Father came to me, that very night, I had a dream that when I woke I knew was no ordinary dream. And suddenly I realized there were two categories to my old dreams. There were dreams and then there were Dreams. And I was seized by a compulsion to begin anew and record my real Dreams in great detail and keep them safely collected. It was as if I had discovered the difference between river pebbles and gemstones, and realized that I had left jewels scattered haphazardly about for the past nine years.

I woke in my curtained bed and lay still for a time in the winter darkness, thinking of what I must do. It had been good to record all my dreams, but now that I knew the difference between them, they must be recopied. I would need ink, good pens, and decent paper. I knew where to get those. I wanted vellum, but that would be missed, and I did not think I could persuade my father that my endeavor merited vellum. Perhaps later I would be able to acquire the quality of paper that my Dreams merited. For now I would be content with recording them and keeping them safe. It suddenly seemed to me that there was only one place in the world for either of those activities. And that presented another problem.

For I was sure that after my nocturnal exploration, my father would limit my access to the spy-network in the walls of Withywoods. As I lay in bed and became convinced of this, it also became unthinkable.

I had told him little of my explorations in the corridors last night. He had deduced I had been in the spy-network, and that I had frightened myself. Perhaps he would think that enough to put an end to my explorations. But he might check for himself. He would find my cached candle, I did not doubt, and perhaps where I had dropped the end stub of the finished taper. Would he be alert enough to follow my footprints in the dusty passages to see how far I had explored? I could not know. Last night he had been extremely alarmed to discover I was not where he had left me. Perhaps my relief at his homecoming would have reassured him.

I got up and dressed myself much more quickly than usual. The room was chill; I got the lid of my winter clothing chest opened, wedged it so with my shoe, and then climbed halfway in to find woolen leggings and a quilted tunic and my belt with the bird-shaped clasp. I had grown. Both leggings and tunic were short on me. I should tell my mother . . .

When I had finished weeping, I added some kindling to the embers in my hearth. Once, I would have wakened to my mother building up the fire in my room, and she would have set out my clothing for me. She'd continued to do that for me long after I was old enough to do it for myself. I did not think she had pitied me for my small size, but had enjoyed the rituals of having a small child and prolonged them.

I'd loved that ritual as much as she did. I missed it still. But gone was gone and done was done, I told myself. And life would go on.

I resolved to locate the other entrance in the pantry and devise a way to make it accessible. Yet even that was not a satisfactory solution. I wished again that my room had access to the corridors. The spyhole had shown me that the passage passed right behind my walls. Was it possible there was an access not even my father knew about?

I moved slowly along the walls, searching again. I could see where the spyhole was, but only because I knew to look for it. One knot-hole in the paneling looked just a bit too convenient. I tapped cautiously on the wall panels, low at first and then as high as I could reach. The sounds told me only that whoever had built the corridors in the walls had done an excellent job of concealing them.

Abruptly, I was hungry. I turned the handle on my door and pushed it open and slipped out of my room. It was early and the house was quiet. I moved silently down the flagged hall and then down the wide stairways. Ever since I'd experienced that little private chamber in the spy-corridors, Withywoods had seemed even more immense to me. To descend the stair was little different to me from being outside. The ceilings seemed almost as distant as the sky, and certainly the drafts that blew through the house were almost as chill as the winds outdoors.

The table was not yet set for breakfast. I went into the kitchens, where Tavia and Mild were already at work. The week's bread was rising in a big covered crock near the hearth. As I went in, Elm went out, calling that she would look for eggs. Liar.

"Hungry, moppet?" Tavia greeted me and I nodded. "I'll toast you a bit of bread, then. Hop up to the table."

I did what I'd always done since I could climb, which was to crawl up onto a bench and then take a seat on the table's edge. Then, after a moment's thought, I moved down and sat on my feet on the bench. It made me almost tall enough to be comfortable at the board. Tavia brought me my small mug full of milk and gave me a curious glance. "Growing up, are we?"

I gave her a nod.

"Then you're old enough to talk," Mild observed. "At least say ta." As always, her comments to me had a sharper edge. I'd been in the act of picking up my mug. I stopped. I turned so I was looking only at Tavia. "Thank you, Tavia. You are always so kind to me." I enunciated each word carefully. Behind me, I head Mild drop her stirring spoon.

Tavia stared at me for a moment. "I'm sure you're very welcome, Bee."

I drank from the mug and set it carefully back on the table.

Tavia said, softly, "Well. She's certainly her father's daughter."

"Yes. I am," I agreed firmly.

"That's a certainty," muttered Mild. She breathed out through her nose and added, "And here I scolded Elm for telling tales when she said Bee could talk if she wanted to." She began to beat whatever she was stirring very hard. Tavia said nothing, but brought me a couple of slices of last week's bread, toasted to freshen it up and slathered with butter.

"So. You're talking now, eh?" Tavia asked me.

I glanced at her and suddenly felt embarrassed. I looked at the table. "Yes. I am."

I saw her curt nod out of the corner of my eye. "That would have pleased your lady mother. She told me once that you could speak a great many words, but were shy."

I looked down at the scarred tabletop, feeling uncomfortable. I resented that she had known I could speak and said nothing. But I also valued that she had kept my secret. Perhaps there was more to Tavia than I had believed.

She set a little pot of my mother's honey on the board next to my bread. I looked at it. Now that Mama was gone, who would tend the bees in the summer and harvest the honey? I knew I should do it, but doubted I'd be successful. I'd tried over the last few months, but my solo results had been uneven. I had watched my mother and helped her, and yet when I tried to harvest the honey and the wax by myself, I had made a terrible mess. The few candles I had made were lumpy and graceless, the pots of honey tainted with small bits of wax and possibly bits of bees. I hadn't had the courage to show them to anyone. Cleaning up the mess to leave the honey-and-candle room tidy had taken me hours. I found myself wondering if we would buy all our candles now. Where did one go to buy candles? And would we buy scented ones for special days? They could not be scented like my mother's had been.

I looked up as my father came into the kitchen. "I was looking for you," he said sternly. "You weren't in your bed."

"I was here, getting food. Papa, I don't want to burn Mama's candles anymore. I want to save them."

He stared at me for three heartbeats. "Save them for what?"

"Special times. Times when I want to remember how she smelled. Papa, who will do all the things she did? Who will tend the hives and put up the honey and sew my clothes and put little bags of lavender in my clothing chest? Do all those things just stop now that she's gone?"

He stood very still in the kitchen, looking at me with his dark, broken eyes. He was untidy, his curly hair growing out raggedly from his mourning cut, his beard a tattered thing, and his shirt still wrinkled from last night's rain. I could tell he hadn't shaken it out and put it neat, but had taken it off and tossed it onto a chair or the bedpost. I felt sorry for him; Mama had always reminded him to do things the right way. Then I remembered I hadn't brushed my hair before I left my room. I hadn't brushed it out last night, either. It wasn't long enough to braid. I reached up and felt it standing up in tufts all over my head. We were a pair, he and I.

Slowly, he began again, starting to move as if he were coming back to life. He walked to the table and sat down heavily across from me. "She did a lot of things around here, didn't she? So many things. You never miss the water until the well runs dry."

I looked at him. He sighed. "We'll save her scented candles. For you. And as for those other things, well. Your sister Nettle already told me that I'd best hire more help to keep the house in better order. I suppose she was right. She might be planning to visit here more often and to bring friends with her when she comes. So there will be other people coming to live here and help us do things. I've already sent for my cousin. She'll arrive in a few days. Her name is Shun. She's about twenty. I hope you'll like her."

Mild and Tavia were listening in so hard, it made a sort of silence in the kitchen. I wanted to demand how I could have a cousin I'd never heard of. Did that mean my father had a brother or sister I didn't know about? I wanted to ask but could not while they were listening so hard. I spoke bluntly. "I don't want anyone else to come and live here. Can't we just manage on our own?"

"I'd like that, too," my father replied. Tavia came to set a fat steaming pot of tea on the board. We didn't usually breakfast in the kitchen, but I knew she was hoping he'd stay where he was and keep talking. I wondered if he was aware of their keen interest as much as I was. "But that's not realistic, Bee. Not for either of us. Sometimes I have to be away from Withywoods, and you'll need someone to look after you while I'm gone. You'll need someone to teach you all the things a girl needs to know, not just how to read and figure, but how to sew and how to take care of yourself and do your hair and, well, all those things that girls know."

I stared at him anxiously, realizing that he didn't know what those things were any more than I did. I offered, "It would be a lot easier if I were a boy. Then we wouldn't need anyone else coming to live here."

That choked a brief laugh from him. Then he grew grave again. "But you aren't a boy. And even if you were, we would still need to hire on more help. Nettle and I have spoken of it, several times. I've been neglecting Withywoods. Revel has been after me for months about a blocked chimney in one room, and a leak down the side of a wall in another. I can't put it off any longer. The entire house needs a good cleaning, and then it needs to be better maintained. Your mother and I talked about it in spring, all the things we would fix over the summer." He halted again, his eyes going far. "Now winter is upon us, and none of it's done." The cup that Tavia set down at his elbow clattered slightly in its saucer. She slid it carefully toward him.

"Thank you," he said, the courtesy a reflex. Then he turned and looked at her. "I'm so sorry, Tavia. I should have given you a lot more notice. Riddle will be escorting my cousin here, and possibly staying a few days as well. We'll have to decide what rooms to give Shun and, well, I don't know exactly what else will need to be done. Her branch of my family is fairly well-to-do. She may expect to have her own maid . . ."

My father's words faltered to a halt and his brows knit together as if he had just recalled something that was not pleasant. He fell silent. Cook Nutmeg had been pounding and kneading dough when I came into the kitchen. I glanced over at her. She was squishing it quietly on the breadboard, listening with every pore of her skin. I dared to break the quiet. "I did not know I had a cousin."

He took a short breath. "My family is not close, I'm afraid, but for all that, when trouble calls, they remember that blood is thicker than water. And so Shun will come to help us, at least for a time."

"Shun?"

"Shun Fallstar is her name."

"Did her mother not like her?" I asked and I heard Mild titter nervously.

My father sat up straighter and poured tea from the pot into the waiting cup. "As a matter of fact, she did not. So, when she comes, to be kind, we will not ask her about her name nor about her home. I think she will find it as great a relief to come to us as we shall be grateful to have her. When she first arrives, she may feel awkward and may be wearied from her journey. So we shall not expect too much of her at first, shall we?"

"I suppose not," I said and felt my confusion swirl faster. Something was not right here and I could not put my finger on it. Was my father lying to me? I watched his face as he sipped his tea and could not tell. I started to ask and then bit back the question. I should not make him admit he was lying in front of Tavia and Mild and Cook. I would ask him later. Instead I said, "I had a special dream last night. I will need pen, ink, and paper to write it down."

"Oh, will you?" my father asked me indulgently. He smiled at me but I actually felt Mild and Tavia exchange startled looks behind us. They were learning too much about me too fast, but I found I didn't care. Perhaps it would make my life easier if they didn't think me simple anymore.

"Yes. I will." I said it firmly. He had spoken as if this were just a sudden fancy of mine rather than an important matter. Did he not grasp what a special dream was? I decided to explain it.

"The dream came to me all edged in black and gold. The colors of the dream were very bright and everything in it seemed very large, so that the smallest details could not be ignored. It began in my mother's garden. The lavenders were heavy with bees and the sweet scent hung in the air. I was there. Then I saw the long carriage-way that leads to the house. Four wolves were coming up the drive, trotting two by two. A white, a gray, and two red ones. But they were not wolves." I stopped a moment, struggling to name creatures I had only seen in a dream. "They were not beautiful like wolves, nor did they have the honor of wolves. They slunk with their hind haunches low and their scrawny tails down. Their ears were round and their red mouths hung open and they slavered as they came. They were wicked . . . no, that's not right. They were the servants of wickedness. And they came hunting for the one who served the right."

My father's smile had grown puzzled. "This is quite a detailed dream," he said.

I turned to Tavia. "I think the bacon is burning," I said, and she startled as if I'd poked her with a pin. She turned back to the pan where the sizzling strips had begun to smoke and pulled it away from the heat.

"So it is," she muttered, and busied herself with it.

I turned back to my father and my toast. I ate two bites of it and drank some of the milk before I said, "I told you it's a special dream. It goes on and on, and it is my duty to remember it all and keep it safe."

The smile was beginning to fade from his face. "Why?"

I shrugged. "I'm just supposed to. There's a lot more to it. After the false wolves go past, I find a butterfly wing on the ground. I pick it up, but as I do the wing becomes larger and larger and under it is a pale man, white as chalk and cold as a fish. I think he is dead, but then he opens his eyes. They have no color. He does not speak with his mouth but opens his hand to talk. He dies with rubies falling from his eyes . . ."

My father set his cup back down on the edge of his saucer. It tipped and his cup spilled, rolling across the table and leaving a trail of tea. "Damn!" he cried in a voice I didn't know, and stood suddenly, nearly overturning the bench.

"Oh, sir, never mind, I'll clean that up," Tavia exclaimed and came immediately with a rag.

My father backed away from the table, shaking hot tea from his hand. I ate the last bite of my toasted bread and butter. The dreaming had left me very hungry. "Is there going to be bacon soon?" I asked.

Mild brought the platter to the table. It was only scorched a little, and as I've always liked it crispy, I didn't mind.

"I need to go out for a bit," my father said. He had gone to the door, opened it, and was staring out at the muddy kitchen yard. He was drawing deep breaths of the chill winter air and cooling the kitchen as well.

"Sir, the bread sponge!" Tavia objected to his open door.

He said nothing but walked out with no cloak or coat. "I'll need paper!" I cried, distressed that he would dismiss my request and my dream so carelessly.

"Take what you need from my desk," he said without looking back at me, and shut the door behind him.

For the rest of that day, I saw little of my father. He was busy, I knew, and he put Withywoods into an uproar with his business. A set of rooms was chosen for my cousin, bedding taken out of the cedar chests and aired; the flues of the hearth in the room must be cleared, for it was discovered that some creature had completely blocked it with a nest. Over the next two days the chaos increased. Our steward, Revel, was completely delighted with the activity, and dashed hither and thither in the house, thinking of more and more tasks that the servants must undertake. A stream of strangers came to our door and met with my father and Revel in the manor study. They chose artisans and laborers, maids and lads from among those who came, and some of them came back the next day with their tools to begin work. And others came with handcarts full of their possessions, to move into the servants' wing of the house.

It seemed that no matter where I went the house was full of business. People were scrubbing floors and polishing woodwork and bringing furniture out of storage. A carpenter and his helpers came to repair a leaking roof in one of the plant rooms. In so much noise and activity, I went back to my silence and stealthy ways. No one noticed. Whenever I glimpsed my father, he was talking to someone or studying a paper or walking about scowling with Revel at his elbow pointing at things and complaining. When he looked at me, he smiled, but there was something sad in his eyes and sick about his mouth that made me want to go and hide.

So that was what I did. I took the paper and ink and pens from his desk, and as he had said I could use what I needed, I did that, taking good vellum and his best colored inks and pens with tips of copper. I took candles as well. I gathered many of my mother's scented candles and hid them in my room, where they perfumed my clothing chest and filled my dreams with her fragrances. I took also the tall white slow-burning tapers we had made together, and these I kept in my spy-room.

I took many things in those days of my father forgetting about me. I took hard bread and dried fruit and a nice wooden box to keep the rats away from them. I took a jug and stopper so I could have water, and a chipped cup that no one would miss. I took a woolen blanket they put out to air that Tavia said had been nibbled by mice and was good for nothing but polishing rags. The bustle at Withywoods was such that I stole with impunity, and no one noticed, for each thought someone else had moved the missing item. I found a rug figured in reds and oranges that was only slightly too large for my spyhole. I rolled it a little up the walls, making my room a nest. From my mother's stores, I took the lavender we had gathered and other fragrant herbs in suchets.

My hidey-hole became quite comfortable. I did not access it from my father's private study. Somehow I knew that he would not approve of how much time I was spending there, so I found the hidden door in the pantry and then built a wall in front of it from boxes of salt fish. I left just enough room that I could creep behind the boxes, open the concealed door, and squeeze in. I drew it shut behind me but took care that it could not latch me in. I never discovered the latch that allowed me to open it from the pantry side, so I always left it ajar a tiny crack.

I chalked my paths through my warren, and swept cobwebs and mouse droppings to one side. I hung bunches of the fragrant herbs along my path to my little chamber, so that even in full darkness I could scent the way. I quickly memorized it, but never forgot that terrifying night.

I found that the warren of paths in the walls was more extensive than my father had told me. I wondered if he knew and had lied to me, or if the openings were so small that he had dismissed them. I had to set exploring aside for another time. I had many old Dreams to record, and each writing must be as detailed as I could wring from my memory. I wrote my Dream of the flying buck and the one about the tapestry with the tall ancient kings with golden eyes. It took six pages for me to write my Dream about the fish-white boy in the boat with no oars and how he sold himself as a slave. I wrote a Dream I'd had of my father cutting open his chest and taking out his heart and pressing it into a stone until there was no blood left in it.

I did not understand the Dreams I wrote down but I thought that one day someone might, and so I recorded them. I wrote until my fingers were all colors of ink and my hands ached abominably. I stole more paper and wrote some more.

And at night, when I put myself to bed, I read. My mother had owned three books that were completely hers. One was the herbal that Patience had given her. It was one that my father had given to Patience, and I believe she had sent it to Molly when they both believed he was dead. The other was a book of flowers and the third was a book on bees. This she had written herself, and it was not a proper book or scroll but a collection of pages bound together with ribbon laced through punched holes. It was more her journal of her hives than anything else, and it was my favorite. From the first pages to the last, I watched her lettering and her spelling become more certain, and her observations more acute as she increased her knowledge of the craft. I read it over and over, and promised myself that by spring I would tend her hives better.

Patience had spent her lifetime acquiring books and manuscripts. Many had been pilfered from the library at Buckkeep Castle. Some were very expensive books, bound with covers of oak and straps of leather and silver studs, gifts given in the hope of winning influence with her when Chivalry had been king-in-waiting and everyone had presumed that one day she would be Queen Patience. There were not many of these lovely volumes. Most of them she had sold off during the dark days of the war against the Red-Ship Raiders. Those that remained were heavy and sadly boring, being mostly historical accounts of exaggerated glory of previous Farseer royalty, tales written more to curry favor than to educate. In many places Patience had written scathingly skeptical notes about the veracity of what she was reading. Often they made me giggle uncontrollably: It was a glimpse into her that no one else had shared with me. Her notes were fading, so I renewed them in black ink as I found them.

Patience's own books were a far more eclectic and battered collection. There was a book on horseshoeing and smithing, with notes in Patience's hand about her own experiments. There were books on butterflies and birds and famous highwaymen and legends of sea monsters. There was an old vellum on the managing of pecksies and how to bind them so that they must do all your housework, and a set of little scrolls on distilling and flavoring spirits. There were three old tablets, much worn, on ways a woman might make herself fecund.

But I quickly discovered that they were not the most interesting books in Withywoods. The most fascinating volumes were the ones hidden and forgotten. In Patience's disorderly old study, I found her bundled letters. The oldest, in a box with blossoms so old they had lost all color and fragrance, were tied up with a strand of leather. They were heartfelt missives from a young man of great passion and greater restraint, promising her that he would make something of himself and acquire a fortune and a reputation that might make up for his lack of noble birth. He begged her to wait until he could come to her father and claim honorably the right to court her. The last one was much crumpled and stained as if a girl had wept over it often. In it, he was chiding her for wanting to run off with him regardless of what it might do to her reputation or how it would break her father's heart. I puzzled out that they had been seen sharing a kiss and young Lady Patience was being whisked off to visit Bingtown and Jamaillia with relatives, to benefit from exposure to art and culture and to separate her from ardent young stable hands. Lady Patience would be gone the better part of two years. The young man promised her that he would wait for her, that he would continue to think of her and work hard. He had heard there was a call for soldiers, hard work but much better pay. While she was away, he would seek his fortune and acquire what they needed for him to stand proudly before her father and beg to rightfully court her.

The next set of letters were dated some four years later and were from Prince Chivalry, begging her pardon for being so presumptuous as to send her such a personal gift on such a brief acquaintanceship but that he could not help himself, the tiny gold earrings were almost as delicate and graceful as she was. And would she allow him to call on her soon?

The next five letters were equally apologetic for his continuing gifts and missives, each with an invitation for her to travel to Buckkeep Castle and join him for a feast or a hunt or a special performance by Jamaillian acrobats. I did not possess her replies but judged that she had rebuffed him over and over.

I knew the day on which her heart warmed toward him. He wrote that he saw no reason why a young lady should not be fascinated by iron smithing and that he hoped the scrolls and small anvil and tools he was sending to her would aid her in following that interest. His next letter expressed undying gratitude for the spoon she had sent him as evidence of her new skill. He declared it his treasure and said he was sending her some excellent iron ingots from Forge to further experiment with.

Their letters after that became more frequent and eventually so romantic that my interest in them waned. It was intriguing to ponder that the first set of love letters was from Burrich, who raised my father and later wed my mother, raising my sister as if she were his child and fathering six boys of his own with her. So his first love had been Lady Patience, wife to my grandfather? And later he had raised my father, before marrying my mother? The contorted branches of my family tree dizzied and fascinated me. And that fascination led to pilfering more scrolls from my father's study.

I did not begin with the intention of spying upon him. It was my quest for good paper that led me to take a dozen sheets of the precious stuff from his supply. Only after I was safely in my hidey-hole with it did I discover that the top sheet alone was blank. Evidently my father had set a clean sheet down on a stack of written ones. I gathered them up to return them to his desk but my eyes snagged on his clean, firm penmanship and I soon found myself drawn into his tale.

It was a simple account of an incident in his childhood. At the time I recall that I wondered why he had written it down. He obviously remembered it clearly; why bother to record it on paper? Only later was I to learn from my own obsessive journaling of my dreams that sometimes the best way to understand something is to write it down. His account began with him musing on friendships, on how they begin and how they end, and also on friendships that never happened or perhaps never should have happened. Then he recounted his tale.

It was a simple incident that he recorded, but in his meticulous fashion he had noted that it happened at the hour when the dew had burned off the gardens at Buckkeep but the sun had not yet warmed them. My father and his dog named Nosy were sneaking away from the castle to follow the steep wooded path that went down to Buckkeep Town. He was shirking his chores to do so, and already felt guilty, but longing to see children of his own age and have some time to play had conquered his dread of the chastisement he'd get for absenting himself.

As he was leaving the gardens he happened to look back and saw another youngster sitting on top of the wall, looking down on him. "Pale as an egg, and as fragile-looking." The boy sat cross-legged, his elbows on his knees and his cheeks in his long-fingered hands as he stared at my father. My father had felt with great certainty that the boy longed to leap down and follow them. He suspected that if he had so much as smiled or tossed his head, the boy would have joined him.

But he did not. He was still the New Boy in the gaggle of town children that he ran with, and barely sure of his acceptance there. To bring another stranger with him, especially one so pale and odd, dressed in the motley of a jester, would risk all he had gained. He feared then that he either would have been excluded along with the pale fellow or, worse, would have had to choose between defending him from a beating and joining in with fists and feet to prove he was one with his new friends. And so he had turned his back and hurried on with his dog and left the pale boy perched there.

I lifted the last sheet, expecting to find more of the story, but there were only a few smudged words there, the ink so run with water that I could not read what he had begun to write. I restacked his pages and tapped them into alignment. The ink on the pages was dark and new; this was something he had written not years ago, but days at most. And so he would probably look for it soon, perhaps to finish it, and discover it missing. That might be disastrous for me.

And yet I could not resist the urge to read it over again before I crept back to his study to return it and filch more paper. But that was not all I took.

I had always known that my father spent time almost every evening with pen and ink. I had always assumed that it had to do with the estate accounts, keeping track of wages paid and how many sheep were sheared and how many lambs born in the spring and what the grape harvest had been like. Indeed, when I later explored his ordinary study, that was what I found in his papers. But here, in his private study, was quite a different assortment of writing. I was certain it was writing that he had never expected to share with anyone.

My mother was a pragmatic reader, given only to deciphering texts that had some use to her. She had come to letters late in her life, and though she had mastered them, they had never become her good friends. So doubtless my father would have judged her unlikely to pore over his papers. Nor were most of our servants lettered folk, save Revel; my father did not employ a clerk to keep the accounts or write his correspondence, preferring to do that for himself. And his private study was not an area where the servants tidied or came and went at all. My father kept its disorder to a level he found tolerable, and no one else ventured in.

Except for me.

And so his private writings were hidden in plain sight. I did not take many, only a handful, and those from the dustiest shelves. I restored the ones I had taken by accident to his stack of papers and then absconded with this new supply of fascinating reading. I began to do this as an everyday exercise, reading, replacing, and stealing more. It opened a window onto my father's life that I otherwise would never have glimpsed.

I sensed that I had picked up his tale in the middle, for the earliest journals were musings on coming to Withywoods and taking up residence with my mother. He recounted how he presented himself as Lady Molly's husbandman, a commoner born and simply the caretaker of Lady Nettle's estate. It explained to me why they had chosen to live so simply; he was still hiding from any who might suspect that FitzChivalry Farseer had not died in Prince Regal's dungeons, but had risen from his grave and become Tom Badgerlock. That was a tale I discerned in bits and pieces from his writing. I suspected that somewhere, perhaps in Buckkeep Castle, there was a full accounting of that portion of his life. I longed to know why he had been put to death and how he had survived, and a thousand other things about him. I discovered, in bits, that Nettle was indeed my full sister. That was a revelation. My father, I quickly saw, was not the man I had thought he was. The lies and deceptions cloaked and covered him in so many layers that it woke fear in me. To discover that all I thought I knew about both my parents was based on falsehoods and deliberate deceptions shook me.

If he was FitzChivalry Farseer, firstborn son of a king who had abdicated the throne, then who was I? Princess Bee? Or simply Bee Badgerlock, daughter of the stepfather of Lady Nettle? Snatches of overheard conversations between my parents, thoughts my mother had had while pregnant with me, comments from Nettle all began to fall into order and make an astonishing sense.

I had just returned to my bedchamber late on the third day of my discovery about my father. I had exited from my little den via the entrance in the pantry and, in the dark, crept up the stairs and regained the safety of my room. I had dared to take one of my father's documents with me. He had noted on the top that it was a fresh copy of an old manuscript. It was titled *Instructing Potential Skill-Students in Guarding One's Mind*. Lately, he had had some rather strange material on his desk. There had been a written copy of a song called "Crossfire's Coterie." And a manuscript about mushrooms with lovely painted illustrations. I was trying to read the one on guarding the mind when I heard my father's tap at my door. I dived onto my bed, pushed the paper under my pillow, and burrowed hastily under my blankets. As he opened the door, I turned toward him slowly as if roused from sleep.

"I'm sorry, dear. I know it's late." He gave a small sigh and then lied, "I'm sorry I've had so little time for you in the past few days. There's been a great deal to do to get ready for our cousin, and it has made me realize how far behind I am on the upkeep of the house. But tomorrow is the day that Shun will arrive. So I wanted to talk to you tonight, to see if you had any questions."

I studied his face for a moment in the flickering light from the hearth fire. I dared myself. I spoke. "Actually, I do. I wondered what about my dream made you so angry."

For a short time, he just looked at me. His eyes weren't angry, I saw, but full of pain. Was that why he had been avoiding me? I could almost feel him thinking about whether he would lie or not. Then he said quietly, "Your dream made me think of someone I knew a long time ago. He was a very pale man, and he often had peculiar dreams. And when he was a child, he wrote his dreams down, just as you said you would do."

I watched his face, waiting. He lifted his hand, covering his mouth as he rubbed his bearded cheeks. Perhaps he was thinking, but to me he looked as if he were holding words in. He sighed again, heavily. "We were very good friends for a long, long time. We did hard things for each other. Risked our lives. Gave up our lives and faced death, and then faced life again. You might be surprised to find that facing life can be much harder than facing death." He stopped talking and was silent for a time, thinking about something. When he blinked and looked back at me, he seemed almost surprised to see me. He took a deep breath. "Well. So when you said you had a dream with a pale man in it, and that he was dead, well . . . it was alarming." He looked away from me, to a shadowy corner of the room. "I was a bit silly to take it so seriously, I admit. So. Let's talk about your cousin coming, shall we?"

I shrugged. I was still mulling over his answer. "I don't think I'll have any questions about her until I've met her. Except . . . what is she going to help you do?"

"Oh, well, that isn't quite decided yet." He smiled evasively. I think the smile would have fooled anyone who did not know him as well as I did. "We'll get to know her, and see what she's good at doing, and then give those sorts of things to her to do," he added brightly.

"Does she do beekeeping?" I asked in sudden alarm. When spring came, I did not want anyone except myself to touch my mother's dormant hives.

"No. I'm quite sure of that." My father sounded as emphatic in his response as I had been. I felt a sense of relief. He came and sat on the foot of my bed. It was a very large bed; it still felt as if he were across the room. My mother would have sat down beside me, close enough to touch me. *Gone.* The thought blew cold through me again. My father looked as if he felt that same chill wind, but he did not move closer to me.

"What happened to your pale friend?"

He flinched and then pasted a casual smile on his face. He shrugged stiffly. "He went away."

"Where?"

"Back to the place where he had first come from. A land far to the south of here. Clerres, he called it. I don't know exactly where. He never told me."

I thought for a time. "Did you send him a message to say you missed him?"

He laughed. "Moppet, you have to know where a letter must go in order to send it."

I hadn't meant a letter. I meant that other kind of reaching out that he and my sister did. Since he had started holding himself inside his own mind, I heard far less of it than I once had. And ever since I had felt it tug at me and try to shred me away into nothing,

I'd always hung back from trying to understand it. I'd felt him do it a dozen times at least in the last few days, but hadn't really known to whom he reached or what he conveyed. Not his pale friend, though.

"Will he come back someday?" I wondered out loud. Would he come and take my father away from me?

My father fell into that stillness again. Then he slowly shook his head. "I don't think so. I think if he was going to come back or send me a letter, he would have done it by now. He told me before he left that the work he and I were to do was done, and that if he stayed near me, we might accidentally undo it. And that would mean that all we had gone through would have been for naught."

I tried to put this together in my mind. "Like the puppeteers' mistake."

"What?"

"That time the puppeteers came in the storm and Mother let them in. Remember? They set up a little stage in the Great Hall and even though they were very tired, they put on a show for us."

"I do remember that. But what was the mistake?"

"At the end, when the Blue Soldier had slain the Boar with Red Tusks and freed the Rain Cloud so it could rain on the land and the crops would grow? The story was meant to stop there. But then, when they were folding the curtains, I saw the Blue Soldier dangling next to the Boar with Red Tusks, and his tusks were deep in the soldier's vitals. So I knew that in the end, the Boar came back and slew the soldier after all."

"Uh, no, Bee. That wasn't part of the story at all! It was just something that happened when the puppets were put away."

He didn't understand at all. I explained to him. "No. It was the next story. Like your friend said could happen. An accident when it was all supposed to be over."

He looked at me with his dark eyes. I could look into them to a deep place where things were still broken, never to be mended. My mother had always been able to make that broken part recede, but I didn't know how. Maybe no one did now. "Well. It's late," he said suddenly. "And I've wakened you and kept you awake longer than I intended. I just wanted to make sure that you weren't worrying about your cousin coming. I'm glad you're fine with it." He stood and stretched.

"Do I have to obey her?"

He dropped his arms suddenly. "What?"

"Must I obey Shun Fallstar when she comes?"

"Well, she's a woman grown, so she is to be respected by you. Just as you respect Tavia or Mild."

Respect. Not obey. I could do that. I nodded slowly and slid down in my bed. My mother would have come to tuck the covers more closely around me. He didn't.

He walked softly to the door, and then paused. "Did you want a story? Or a song?"

I thought about it. Did I? No. I had his stories, his real ones, to think about until I fell asleep. "Not tonight," I said, and yawned.

"Very well. Sleep, then. I'll see you in the morning." He yawned widely. "It's going to be a big day for all of us," he said, and to me it sounded more like dread than anticipation.

"Papa?"

He stopped just inside the door. "What is it?"

"You should trim your hair tonight. Or make it lie down with grease tomorrow, or however boys do that. It looks very wild now. And your beard is awful. Like, like . . ." I searched for words I had heard long ago. "Like a mountain pony with its coat half-shed."

He stood very still, and then smiled. "You heard that from Nettle."

"I think so. But it's true." I dared to add, "Please shave it off. You don't need to look older, like Mother's husband, anymore. I want you to look like my father instead of my grandfather."

He stood there, one hand touching his beard.

"No. She never liked it in the first place. You should cut it all off." I'd known what he was thinking.

"Well. Perhaps I shall, then." And he softly closed the door behind himself.

Chapter 15

A FULL HOUSE

Wildeye was ever a reluctant Catalyst to her Master, for she regarded him as more tormentor than mentor. For his part, the old White was not pleased that his Catalyst was such a homely and resentful young woman. He complained in all his writings that fate had made him wait through most of his life for her to be born, and then when he did find her and make her his companion, she made his old age a trial to him. Nonetheless, as his darkening showed, he was able to complete some of the tasks that were appointed to him by fate, and when he died it was said that he had, indeed, set the world on a better path.

WHITES AND CATALYSTS, EULEN SCREEP

Shun arrived in the afternoon. She rode a trim little sorrel mare with white stockings, and Riddle accompanied her on a rangy white gelding. Her green cloak was trimmed with fur and draped not just her but half her mount. A mule followed laden with a trunk on one side and several boxes on the other. The sorrel's tack was gleaming new, as was the trunk. So. Chade had provided the coin, and Shun had wasted no time in directing Riddle to take her to a larger market town. I suspected that the days since I had last seen her had been spent in acquiring these things. I wondered again what had precipitated such a speedy departure from wherever Chade had been keeping her that she had left her possessions behind. Had the attempt on her life been that dire? And who was her enemy that he could find her when neither Riddle nor I knew of her existence, let alone her location? There were still far more mysteries attached to this young lady than I liked.

I met them in the carriageway. My hair was brushed and my face stung from scraping the last remnants of beard off it. I'd found my last clean shirt and given my boots a hasty wipe with my dirty shirt. I needed to make time to bundle my dirty clothing and ask one of the servants to see to it. I had realized, with shame, that I'd never given a thought to such things before. Molly had seen to it that my wardrobe was kept in order. Molly . . .

I had decided my trousers were presentable and hastily left the room we once had shared. Why was I fussing over my appearance? After all, it was only Riddle and Shun.

I had hoped to have Bee at my side, but though I had called her when a boy came running to tell me that horses were coming up the drive, she had not answered me. Of late she had taken to disappearing within the house. Although she had begun talking more, I felt as if she said less to me. She still avoided meeting my eyes. I was accustomed to that, but not to the sidelong gazes she sent me, as if she was evaluating me and studying my responses. It was unnerving.

And I'd had no real time to devote to understanding it. A veritable deluge of work had drenched me in details. Winter always brings out the worst in a house. If a roof is going to leak, winter storms make it happen. Clogged chimneys filled guest rooms with smoke and stench. It seemed to me that just as I was already overwhelmed the manor turned on me and developed every imaginable problem. The crown provided Nettle with a generous allowance for her tasks as Skillmistress of Dutiful's coterie. And Queen Kettricken had bestowed a further allowance for the upkeep of Withywoods as an acknowledgment of all that Burrich had done for the Farseer monarchy during his life. So there was coin to effect the repairs, but it did not make the noisy and unsettling process of having workmen come into the manor any more palatable to me. Nor lessen my irritation with myself that I had let it go all summer.

So in the midst of workmen coming and going, and carts arriving with timber and plank and brick, and folk mixing mortar in tubs, Shun and Riddle arrived. Riddle, damn him, did not bother to conceal his amusement, while Shun's dismay was plain on her face. I called a stable lad to take their horses, and Revel appeared to direct a new housemaid to find someone to carry Shun's trunks to the guest room. He told me that he had arranged refreshments in the Mockingbird Room, a relatively quiet parlor. I thanked him and asked them to follow me there. As we arrived, the new kitchen girl was just leaving. It took me a moment to recall that her name was Opal. I thanked her. There was a fat steaming pot of tea on the table, and an assortment of little cakes. She told us that she'd be back in a moment with sausage rolls fresh from the kitchen and asked if there was anything else we would fancy. Shun studied the table and requested wine. And perhaps some cheese, and cut bread. And butter. Opal bobbed a curtsy and said she would tell Cook Nutmeg. I added to her tasks, asking her to see if anyone could find Lady Bee and send her to us. Then she was gone and I turned to Shun and Riddle.

"I'm sorry about the clatter. It seems that as soon as I discovered one thing needed repair, it led to another. I promise that the room you'll have tonight is snug and warm, and they've told me that by the end of the week, your apartments should be fully habitable. We haven't had many long-term guests here at Withywoods, and I'm afraid the house hasn't been kept up as well as it might have been."

The dismay in Shun's eyes deepened.

"Lady Bee is not here? Is she well?" Riddle intervened. Perhaps he had hoped to change the subject.

As if summoned by his words, there was a light tap on the door and Bee drifted in. There was no other word for how she moved. Her body was languid with grace, and the pupils of her eyes were so dilated that her eyes looked almost black. She stared at me, and when she spoke, her words were thick. "It's today," she said. She smiled ethereally. "The butterfly in the garden, Father. The wing is on the ground and the pale man awaits you."

She fell silent as we all stared at her. I felt heartsick; was she drugged? Sick? This was nothing like any Bee I had ever seen. Riddle looked horrified. He stared at her and then turned accusing eyes on me. Sometimes I forgot how young she appeared to folk who did not know her well. To hear such words from a nine-year-old would have been alarming enough, but most onlookers would have guessed her age at merely six. Shun spoke. "I thought you said you had a daughter? Who is this little boy? Do your servants often speak to you so?"

I scarcely heard her. "Bee, are you well?"

She tipped her head as if finding me by sound rather than sight. Her expression was beatific. "It feels so good to be right. When the circle closes. And it actually happens. You should go quickly. There isn't much time." She shook her head slowly. "The messenger has come such a long way to die at the doorstep."

I found my wits. "I fear my child is ill." I crossed the room and caught her up in my arms. At my touch, she went rigid. Hastily, I sealed myself. "Riddle, please take care of everything else." Riddle said something as I left, his voice anxious. I shut the door on his words.

I strode down the corridor, Bee in my arms. I turned to carry her toward the stairs and her bedchamber but she suddenly came alive in my arms and with a twist of her body freed herself of my grip. She landed on her feet, swayed into a near-fall, and then contorted her body the other direction to stay on her feet. For a moment she seemed a girl made of fluid. Then she sprang away from me, calling over her shoulder, "This way, FitzChivalry. This way!" Her voice was ethereal as she ran from me.

I chased her. The child ran and her slender feet seemed barely to skim the floors. She fled toward the west wing of the house, the least-used part, and thankfully one that was not infested with workmen. She turned down a corridor that led to one of Patience's gardening rooms. I thought I would catch her there, but she was as fleet as the wind as she threaded her way through urns of ferns and fat pots overflowing with vines. "Bee!" I whisper-shouted her name, but she did not pause. I hopped and twisted through the narrow way, slowed by the obstacles, and watched helplessly as she tugged open a door and dashed outside into a section of garden mazed with hedges.

I followed. My pursuit and her flight had been a silent one save for the pattering of her feet and my heavier tread. I did not call out her name or bid her stop or come back to me. I had no desire to call attention to my child's aberrant behavior and my failure to control her. What was wrong with her? And how could I explain it to Riddle to keep him from thinking me neglectful? I was certain he would report back to Nettle and that it would reinforce her insistence that Bee be surrendered to her. As for Shun, I could not think of a worse introduction to Withywoods, Bee, or me than what she had just witnessed.

The garden on this side of the house had benefited wildly from Patience's impetuous nature. If there had ever been design or intent applied to the area, either the garden had outgrown it or it was a plan only Patience could have understood. On and on Bee led me through this esoteric jungle of paths, stone walls, birdbaths, and statuary. She danced along snowy pathways in an herb knot, and then sprang over a short picket fence and ran down a pathway sheltered by leafless roses on an arched trellis. Snowy gravel pathways gave way abruptly to mounds of moss and ferns, low walls intersected one another, and in one section elevated pots allowed trailing vines to cascade over a framework above the path, converting the dim winter day to a tunnel draped with greenery. I had always loved the randomness of the garden; for me it spoke of forest, and reminded me of my journey through the Mountains to seek Verity and the dragons. But today it seemed to deliberately hold me back while allowing Bee to slip through as nimbly as a ferret. She entered the shelter of a stand of evergreens.

And then I caught up with her. She was standing motionless, staring at something on the ground. To her right, the ancient stacked-stone wall that marked the boundary of the estate gardens was thick with dark-green moss. Just beyond it there was a steep forested slope, and then the public road that led to the front entrance of Withywoods and the grand carriageway entrance. I was panting as I caught up to her, and for the first time I realized that she was very familiar with this section of the grounds. I had never thought of my little child playing so near a carriageway, even one so lightly traveled.

"Bee," I panted when I was near enough to speak to her without shouting. "You must never again . . ."

"The butterfly's wing!" she exclaimed, pointing. And halted, still as a statue. Her eyes were wide, and when she looked at me, they seemed black edged with blue. "Go," she whispered softly. "Go to him." She gestured with a slender hand and smiled as if giving me a gift.

A premonition of disaster rose in me so strongly that my heart, which had previously beat fast from my exertion, now raced even faster with dread. I stepped toward where she pointed. A small black animal burst suddenly from nowhere and streaked off into the woods. I shouted in surprise and halted. A cat. Just one of the feral cats of Withywoods, hunting for mice. Only a cat. I took two more steps and looked down.

There, on the deep bed of shaded moss still mottled with last night's frost, was a butterfly's wing the size of the palm of my hand. There were brilliant panels of red, gold, and deep blue separated by dark veins that reminded me of the leading in a stained-glass window. I halted, transfixed by it. Never had I seen a butterfly of such size or brilliance, let alone in the cold days of early winter. I stared.

"It's for you," she whispered. She had eased soundlessly to my side. "In my dream it was for you. Only you."

In a sort of daze, I dropped to one knee by the strange thing. I touched it with my forefinger; it was soft and pliable as the finest silk. Gently I pinched the tip of it between my fingers and lifted it.

As I did so, it became something entirely different. Not a butter-fly's wing, but an airy cloak of impossible lightness. It floated like a lady's veil, and suddenly the colors were revealed as a corner lining of a much larger piece of fabric. The fabric itself was exactly the shades of the moss and the shadows that dappled it, blending per-fectly with the ground under the evergreen trees. As I lifted, I re-vealed more of the gaudy butterfly-wing lining of the cloak, and then I uncovered what had been concealed beneath it.

The Fool.

Pale and slight as he had been when we were boys together, he huddled on the bare ground. His arms were drawn in tight to his body and he was curled up, chin tucked to chest. His ice-white hair was loose, some matted to his cheek and some tangled against the deep moss. I hated that his cheek was pressed against the cold earth. A beetle crawled on the moss by his lip. He was not dressed for this weather: He had come here from a much warmer place. He wore a long cotton tunic with a pattern of large rust shapes against a wheat-colored background, over simple loose trousers of a slightly darker color. He had a boot on one foot; the other was bare, dirty, and bloodied. His skin was alabaster, his eyes closed, and his lips pale pink as a fish's gills. He was still. Then my eyes resolved that the large rosettes on the back of his shirt were actually bloodstains.

There was a roaring in my ears and darkness at the edges of my vision.

"Papa?" Bee tugged at my sleeve, and I realized she had been wor-rying it for some minutes. I was on my knees by the Fool. I could not say how long I had been transfixed there.

"It will be all right, Bee," I told her, certain it would be nothing of the kind. "Run along back to the house. I'll take care of this."

Some other man took charge of my body. I set my fingers to his throat under the angle of his jaw. I waited and when I was certain there was no pulse, I felt one. He wasn't dead, not quite. His flesh, never warm to the touch, was cold as meat. I bunched the butterfly cloak around him and lifted him, heedless of his wounds. He'd carried them for some time. Delaying to be careful of them now would not save him, but keeping him longer in the cold might finish him. He did not make a sound. He was very light in my arms, but then, he had never weighed much.

Bee had not obeyed me and I found I didn't care. She trotted at my side, crackling questions like a sap log in the fire, very much my child again. I ignored them. Her peculiar fit seemed to have passed. It still concerned me, but not as much as the unconscious man in my arms. I would tend to my crises one at a time. Calmly. Dispassionately.

Abruptly, I wondered what I was feeling. The answer came to me quite clearly. Nothing. Nothing at all. He was going to die and I was determined to stop feeling anything about it before it happened. I'd had enough pain with Molly's death. I wasn't going to feel any more. He had been gone from my life for years. If he'd never come back, I wouldn't have experienced any new sense of loss. No. There was no sense in feeling anything about regaining him when it was so obvious I was about to lose him again. Wherever he had come from, he had journeyed a long way to bring agony to my door.

I wasn't having it.

I found that somehow I had retraced the whole length of my wild garden chase of Bee. She waited for me by the door to Patience's garden room. I didn't look at her. "Open the door," I said, and she did, and I carried him inside. My mind halted for an instant, fighting to decide what to do, but my body and my daughter did not. She ran ahead of me, opening doors, and I followed her without thinking.

"Put him there. On that table," she said, and I realized she had led me to the small workroom where Molly had done her hivework. It was tidy, as she always left it, but still it smelled of her and her work, the fragrant honey, the wax, even the musky scent of dead bees from when she had cleaned out a wooden hive. It was actually a good choice, for there were cloths, washed and dried and folded, and buckets and . . .

He made a small gasping sound as I lowered him to the table, and I caught his meaning. As gently as I could, I turned him, putting him on his belly. He still gave a whimper of pain, but I knew the injuries to his back would be the worst ones.

Bee had watched in silence. Now she picked up two small buckets meant for honey. "Hot water or cold?" she asked me gravely.

"Some of each," I told her.

She paused at the door. "Honey is good for infections," she told me gravely. "The butterfly man will feel more at home here, for bees are not, perhaps, so different from butterflies."

She left and I heard her small feet pattering down the hall. I wondered what Riddle thought of my sudden abandonment of him, and what he would say to Nettle and Chade. It was so rude of me. I unfastened the glorious cloak and set it aside. Strange garment; it weighed scarcely more than spider silk. It reminded me of the amazing tent that the Fool had brought with him to the Out Islands. I thrust the memory down. I hoped Shun was not feeling neglected. Would her temporary chambers please her? I thought about that carefully, and what excuses I could make for any delay, as my hands cut away his bloody tunic. I peeled his garment from his back as if I were skinning a deer. The blood-soaked fabric was stiff as a frozen hide and clung to the wounds. I gritted my teeth and tried to be gentle as I tugged it free. Two of the injuries broke open afresh, leaking watery blood. He lay very still, and only when I had stripped his clothes away did I pause to think how very gaunt he was. I could count the knobs of his spine below the nape of his neck, and his ribs pushed tight against the skin of his back.

The wounds had come from some sort of missiles, I guessed. Not arrows, but something smaller that had penetrated deeply. Darts? He'd managed to pull them out, I judged. At least, nothing projected from any of the crusted, swollen wounds.

"Water." She spoke in a strange accent, her voice so different from my Fool's voice that I knew instantaneously that I had been completely mistaken. The breath caught in my throat. Disappointment drenched me, even as buoyant joy that this dying person was not my old friend welled. What a dizzying trick my mind had played on me, taking me back to my adolescence and convincing me this was indeed the Fool! Yet she appeared almost identical to my recollection of him as he had been in those days. Relief nearly unmanned me more than my previous panic. I held to the edge of the table as my knees bent. Oh, how the years had changed me. Where was my iron resolve, my forged nerves? Would I faint? I would not. Yet I let my knees touch the floor and lowered my head, pretending I stooped to look into her face.

She was not the Fool. Only her coloring was the same. She had no scent, just as the Fool had lacked, and to my Wit she was not there at all. But her nose was more pointed, her chin more rounded than the Fool's had ever been. However had I looked at her and thought she was him?

"The water is coming," I said hoarsely. "I'll let you drink first. Then we need to clean up these wounds."

"Are you a healer?"

"No. I'm not. But years ago I had a friend like you." I halted. The Fool had always refused to go to healers. He'd resisted anyone touching his body for such a purpose. I realized that might not be true for every White. "I'll send for a healer, right away."

"No." She spoke quickly. Her voice was breathy with weakness and pain. "They don't understand. We're not like your people." She moved her head in a feeble denial.

"I'll do what I can for you, then. Clean and bind your wounds, at least."

She moved her head. I couldn't tell if she was acceding or denying me permission. She tried to clear her throat but her voice went huskier. "What did you call your friend?"

I stood quietly. My heart went to a very still place inside me. "He was a jester at King Shrewd Farseer's court. Everyone just called him the Fool."

"Not everyone." She gathered her strength. "What you called him?" She spoke in a learned tongue, without accent, only the dropped words betraying her.

I swallowed fear and regret. This was not a time to lie. "Beloved. I called him Beloved."

Her lips pulled back in what was intended as a smile. Her breath was foul with sickness. "Then, I have not failed. Not yet. Late as I am, I have done as he bid. I bring a message for you. And a warning."

I heard a voice in the corridor. "Let me carry them. You're spilling them trying to hurry."

"I don't think you should be following me." Bee's retort to Riddle was both tart and indignant. He'd followed her to track me. He was still Chade's man. Probably Nettle's as well, when it came to spying. Useless to try to avoid what was coming. But I could spare my guest a bit of humiliation. I took off my shirt and spread it lightly over her. She still gasped at the touch and then, "Oh, warm. From your body." She sounded pathetically grateful.

A moment later Bee opened the door and Riddle came in bearing the little buckets. He looked at me in my woolen undershirt and then at the table. "An injured traveler," I said. "Would you run down to the village and bring back the healer?" That would get him out of my way until I had time to wash and bind her wounds.

Riddle stepped in for a closer look. "She's so pale!" he exclaimed. He studied her face. She stayed perfectly still, eyes closed, but I didn't think she was unconscious, only feigning it. "She reminds me of someone . . ."

I didn't let myself smile. I recalled now that he'd never met the Fool when he was so obviously a White. By the time Riddle knew him, he was the aptly named Lord Golden, a tawny man indeed. But this girl was as the Fool had been in his childhood: pale with colorless eyes and fine white hair.

Riddle's gaze shifted to Bee. "And? You're talking now?"

Her gaze flashed to me and then shifted back to Riddle. She smiled artlessly up at him. "Papa said I should try not to be so shy around you."

"How long have you been able to speak so clearly?" he pressed her. She glanced at me again, seeking rescue.

"She's lost a lot of blood," I said, to hurry him away. It worked. He set the little buckets on the table and turned for the door.

"Bring Granny Wirk," I said to his back. "She lives at the crossroads just on the other side of the Withy." And she was older than most of the trees in the area and slow to move. A good healer, but it would take him time to return with her. And I hoped to be finished with my own ministrations by then.

Then the door was closing behind him, and I looked at Bee conspiratorially. "I know you couldn't have kept him from following you," I told her. "But do you think you can keep Shun occupied? Take her on a tour of the house that doesn't bring her anywhere near here?"

She stared up at me. Her blue eyes, so unlike my own or Molly's, seemed to look past my flesh and bones to the heart of me. "Why is she a secret?"

On the table, our guest stirred slightly. She almost lifted her head. Her voice was a whisper. "I'm in danger. Hunted. Please. Let no one know I'm here. The water? Please."

I had no cup but there was a honey ladle among Molly's tools. I supported her head as she drank three ladles of the cool water. As I eased her head back onto the table, I reflected that it was too late for me to call Riddle back. He knew she was here, and when he reached the crossroads, Granny Wirk would know we had an injured traveler, too. I pondered a moment.

Bee interrupted my thoughts. "We'll wait a short time. Then let's send Shaky Amos to follow Riddle and tell him that our guest felt better and left on her own. And not to bring the healer after all."

I stared at her in surprise.

"It's the best we can do," she said almost sullenly. "If Riddle has already spoken to the healer, it will put any hunters off her trail. For a short time, at least."

I nodded. "Very well. Off you go, then. After you tell Amos, then you must keep Shun busy for a while. Show her the house, then the gardens, and then take her back to the parlor and leave her there, while you go tell the kitchen to send up a nice tray for her. Then slip away here to let me know how it all went. Can you do all that?" I hoped it would keep her busy as well as keeping Shun occupied.

She gave a sharp nod. "I know where Amos takes his naps," she said. She stood suddenly taller, inflated with importance. Shaky Amos had a decade or so on me, and had come as part of the

Withywoods staff. He was, as his name suggested, afflicted with trembling, the result of a blow to the head many years before. He had been at the estate since Patience's time there and had earned his quiet days. Once he had been a sheep shearer. That task was beyond him now, but he could lean on a crook and watch the flock on fine days. He liked to be given specific tasks from time to time. He might be slow but he still had his pride. He'd do the job admirably.

At the door, she halted. "So my butterfly man is a girl?"

"So it seems," I said.

Our invalid had opened her eyes. She stared vacantly and then her gaze fastened on Bee. A slow smile curved her lips. "Where did he come from?"

"Riddle? He followed Bee here. He's an old friend, and no danger to you."

Her eyes sagged shut again.

"It's so strange. I was so sure the butterfly man was a man. Not a girl." Bee looked annoyed as she shook her head and informed me, "Dreams are not to be trusted. Not completely."

She stood still, appearing to consider that as if it were a new idea.

"Bee?" Her eyes were far. "Bee? Are you feeling well? You were so strange when you came to tell me about the butterfly man . . ."

Her eyes finally came to me and then slid away. "I'm fine now. I felt very tired. Then I fell asleep. And the dream came and told me it was time. And it brought me to you and then—" She looked puzzled. "Then the dream was over and here we were." She slipped quietly from the room.

For a time, I stared after her. Then the girl on the table gave a brief moan of pain. My mind snapped into the now and I went to work. In the cupboards there were pots of honey, sealed with wax, and slabs of cleaned wax waiting to be transformed into candles. They'd probably still be here, a decade hence. I found the cloths Molly had used for straining the honey and the wax. They were stained but very clean. I remembered how she would wash them outside in a big kettle of boiling water and then put them on the line to bleach and dry. I chose the oldest, softest rags and knew she would forgive me as I tore some into strips for bandaging.

I softened the scabs on the young White's back with the warm water and gently cleaned away the blood and ooze from her wounds. There were four of them. I did not want to probe them, but knew personally the danger of leaving anything inside them. I pressed one and she grunted in pain. "You don't have to search them," she said breathlessly. "My companion cleaned them as well as he could. What went into me, there is no taking out. They closed over, for a time, and we fled. It almost seemed they were starting to heal. Before the hunters caught up with us. They killed my friend. And I opened the wounds again when I fled. And in the days since, I haven't been able to clean them. Now it's too late." She blinked her eyes. Drops of blood like ruby tears stood at the corners of them. "It was always too late," she admitted sadly. "I just couldn't let myself believe it."

She held a long tale, I sensed. I did not think she was up to telling me all of it, but felt the urgency of knowing the Fool's message right away. "I'm going to dress these with some honey and oil. I just need to fetch the oil. When I come back, do you think you could give me my message?"

She looked at me with pale eyes so like the Fool's had been. "Useless," she said. "I'm a useless messenger. I was sent to warn you of the hunters. So you could find the sun and run before them." She sighed out, long, and I thought she had lapsed into sleep. With her eyes closed, she admitted faintly, "I fear I may have led them right to your doorstep."

Her words made small sense to me, but her anxiety was agitating her and taking all her strength. "Don't worry about that just now," I told her, but she had sagged back into unconsciousness. I took advantage of that lapse to fetch oil and dress her injuries. When I had finished, I gathered her cut clothing around her as well as I could. "I'm going to move you now," I warned her. She made no response, and I tried to be gentle as I gathered her into my arms.

I took a little-used servants' corridor and stair and went by a roundabout path to my own room. I shouldered the door open and then halted, shocked. I stared at the rucked linens and bunched blankets on my bed. The room smelled closed and sweaty, a boar's den. Discarded clothing sprawled across the top of the storage chest and dangled to the floor. Melted candle stubs littered the mantelpiece. The heavy curtains were closed, shutting out the winter's light. Not even in Chade's messiest days had his den ever looked this dismal.

After Molly's death, I had sequestered myself here and ordered the servants to let all things be in the room. I had not wanted anything to change from the last time Molly had touched them. But change they had, on their own. The wrinkles in the linens on the unmade bed had become set like ripples in the bottom of a slow river. The light perfume that had always seemed to follow Molly had been replaced with the stink of my own sweat. When had the room become so oppressive? When Molly had shared it with me there had not been wax drippings down the candelabra, nor a coating of dust on the mantelpiece. It was not that she had tidied after me, no: I had not lived so brutishly under her roof. The wolf in me curled his lip and wrinkled his nose in distaste at denning in such a fouled place.

I thought of myself as a tidy person; this room suddenly looked like the cell of a madman or a recluse. It stank of despair and loss. I could not bear to be in it and I backed out so hastily that I tapped my charge's head on the door frame. She made a small sound of distress and then was still.

Bee's room was just down the corridor. In it, a connecting door led to a small chamber designed for a nurse or nanny. I pushed that door open and went inside. It had never been used for its intended purpose, but had become a storage place for odd bits of furniture. It was not much larger than a cell, but there was a narrow bed beside a dusty stand with a ewer on top of it. An airing rack for linens leaned drunkenly in the corner next to a broken footstool. I dragged the faded coverlet off the bed and deposited my pale victim there, pillowing her head on her butterfly cloak. I built up the fire in Bee's hearth and left the door open for the heat to wander in. I made a trip back to my room and found a clean blanket in the linen chest. It smelled of cedar when I took it out and a touch of something else. Molly.

I hugged it tight to me for a moment. Then I sighed past my tight throat and hurried back to the girl. I covered her warmly and considered my options. Time was trickling swiftly past me. As I wondered if Riddle was on his way back and if I should maintain the lie once he returned to Withywoods, I heard the door behind me sigh open. I spun, going into a fighter's crouch.

My daughter was not impressed. She halted, frowned at me in puzzlement, and then nodded as I straightened. "I see why you put her here. There's water in my washstand ewer still." As she spoke, she fetched it from her room and carried it back with her cup. As I filled the cup, she spoke. "You should go down and tell Tavia I don't feel well and I need a tray of food in my room. I'll stay here and watch over her while you go find something to keep Shun busy. I confess, that's a task that is beyond me. Are you sure she has come to help us? She seems the most useless person I have ever met. Full of sniffs and sighs, as if nothing meets her approval. I wouldn't be surprised if she wanted to leave with Riddle when he goes."

"Glad to see that you're getting along so well," I said.

She looked at me and replied, "*I* didn't bring her here to help me, you know."

I heard her mother in her voice and didn't know whether to cry or laugh. "That's true," I surrendered. "You left her where?"

"I took her back to the Mockingbird Room. But there's no assurance she's still there. She does have legs, you know. And she's a nosy sort of person. She opened the door to nearly every bedchamber to see if there was one she liked better than the one Revel had prepared. She's not a bit shy."

"Indeed," I agreed. I propped the girl's head up and held the cup to her lips. She opened her eyes to white slits, but she sucked at the water and took some down. I put the cup on the stand beside her. "I think she will be all right for now. I'll tell Tavia that you need a nice warm broth. Try to get her to drink some while it's still warm. Is there anything you really want to eat?"

Bee shook her head. "Not hungry just yet."

"Very well." I hesitated. "Do you think you can give her some broth if she wakes?"

She looked offended that I would ask.

I cast a glance at the unconscious girl. She had a message for me, one from the Fool. She had warned me of danger already, hunters on her trail. And who did I trust to watch over her? A nine-year-old girl the size of a six-year-old. I'd have to do better, but for now . . . "Keep watch, and I'll be back as soon as I can."

I visited the kitchen, delivered Bee's suggested message to Tavia, asked them to send food for me to the Mockingbird Room, and then joined Shun there. As soon as I entered the room, Mild bustled in to set a fresh pot of tea. When she left the room, I apologized to Shun for neglecting her. "Riddle was called off on an errand, and I'm afraid Bee does not feel well right now. She has taken to her bed for a few hours. So." I forced a hearty smile onto my face. "What do you think of Withywoods? Do you think you can be happy here with us for a time?"

Shun looked at me incredulously. "Happy here? Who of you is happy here? I have seen only chaos since I arrived. Riddle has left me to my own devices, without a 'by your leave' or even a farewell. Your daughter . . . Well. You yourself must know what a strange little work she is! She looks like a boy! If Riddle had not informed me that was your daughter, I would have thought her part of the stable staff here. I do not know what Lord Chade was thinking to send me here!"

Somewhere in the house, a workman began sawing something. I felt as if he were cutting into my skull. I sat down heavily opposite her. "He was probably thinking you'd be safe here for a time," I said bluntly.

Mild came bustling in to set steaming bowls of mutton-and-barley soup before us, with more bread for the basket on the table. "Thank you," I told her. "This will be all I require. I desire to have some quiet conversation with Lady Shun."

"Of course, sir," she responded and hastened from the room. I waited for the door to close completely behind her before I resumed speaking. "It's not the best plan Lord Chade and I have ever cooked up, but for short notice, it's not a bad one." I lifted my spoon and stirred my soup. Chunks of carrot bobbed to the surface and sank again while steam rose in a cloud. I set down my spoon to wait for it to cool and asked her rhetorically, "Can you think of a better one?"

"Yes. Kill the people who are trying to kill me, so I can live as I wish, where I wish." Her response was so immediate that I knew she had considered it for some time.

I decided to take her suggestion seriously. "It's seldom as simple as killing one person. First, we must determine who is trying to kill you. And most often, that person is merely the tool, not the instigator. For every one person you kill, chances are you've created six new enemies. And you might want to ask yourself why that person must die so that you can live your life as you wish." I spoke severely.

"A question that perhaps you can put to whoever it is before you kill him!" she responded angrily. She pushed her bowl and plate away from her as I broke bread and spread butter thick on it. When I did not speak, she went on, "Why must I pay for the actions of others? Why cannot I live as my birth made me? What did I do that I must be hidden away? As a noble lady's firstborn, I should rightfully inherit my mother's titles and lands! But no! No, because she was not wed when I was conceived, her shame falls on me! I pay for her selfish act, condemned to be raised in a backwater hamlet by my aging grandparents, to watch them die and then to be sent off to be pawed by my mother's lecherous husband. From there, I was banished, near-kidnapped by Lord Chade, and then hidden away from all society for two years! No parties, not a ball, not one single dress from Bingtown or Jamaillia. No. Nothing for Shun, she was born on the wrong side of the blankets! And above all, the person responsible for that must be able to dodge all consequences of it. And then, even hidden away, where I daily feared that boredom would end my life, someone tried to poison me. In my very own home, someone tried to poison me!"

Her words had come faster and faster and her voice had become shriller as she spilled out her sad little tale. I should have felt sympathy for her, but her manner of telling it was too self-absorbed. Only with extreme restraint did I prevent myself from leaping up and fleeing the room. I fervently hoped she would not break down into tears.

She did.

Her face crumpled like a piece of paper written over with too many secrets. "I can't live like this!" she wailed. "I just can't!" She collapsed forward onto the table, her head pillowed on her arms as she sobbed.

A better man than I could have reached into his heart and found kind words for her. Could have seen her as a youngster suddenly cast adrift from all that was familiar. But of late her words were the very ones I wanted to roar at fate every night as I faced my cold and empty bed. I told her what I told myself. "Yes. You can. Because you have to. There is no real alternative, unless you want to cut your own throat."

She lifted her head from her folded arms. She stared at me, eyes suddenly red, face wet with tears. "Or hang myself. I don't think I could cut my own throat, but I could hang myself. I've even learned to tie that knot."

That, I think, was what made me realize how serious she was. That small bit of information, the step she had taken to be one notch closer to planning her own death. Every assassin knows what his selected exit would be. Not poison for Shun, but the jump from the stool and the snap of her neck, with no waiting, no time to repent the decision. As for me, it would be the slash, the gouting blood, and yes, those few waning moments to say farewell to my life. With a leap of intuition, I knew this was why Chade had sent her to me. Not just because others had threatened her life, but because she was a danger to herself. It incited me to horror rather than sympathy. I did not want the responsibility. I did not want to wake to a maid shrieking that her mistress was dangling from a noose, did not want to Skill such tidings to Chade. It was impossible for me to protect her. What can anyone do for a person who wishes to harm herself? My heart sank at the thought that I must soon search her room. What tools would Chade have supplied to her? Nasty little blades, a garrote . . . poisons? Had he even considered that in her state, she might use them against herself instead of in her own defense? I felt a flash of anger toward Chade at the bubbling kettle he had sent to my home. Who would be scalded when she finally boiled over?

She was still looking at me. "You must not do that," I said feebly.

"Why not?" she demanded. "It would solve all the problems. Everyone's life would be simpler. My mother would be happy that her spoiled son would inherit with no cloud on his right. My hidden father would not have to fear that I'd somehow be discovered. And you wouldn't have an inconvenient half-mad young woman invading your home!"

She dragged in a sobbing breath. "When I was fleeing to Buckkeep, despite all that had befallen me, I had hope. Hope at last! I'd get away from my life in the shadows. I thought that at last I would be at court, with other young people, with music and dancing and life. Just life! And then Lord Chade claimed me. He said I was in danger and I could not go to Buckkeep, but that in his care, once I had learned an assassin's skills, well, then I could both defend myself and perhaps the queen." Her voice shrilled higher and choking. "Imagine that! Me, at the queen's side, defending her. Standing beside her throne. Oh, I wanted that so much. And I tried to learn all Quiver had to teach me. That awful, smelly woman, and her stupid endless drills! But I tried, and I tried. She was never happy with me. And then Rono died, poisoned, and it was meant for me. And I had to flee again. Sent off I knew not where, with only that ruffian to guard me. This time, I thought, this time surely I will be taken to Buckkeep! But where does Lord Chade put me? Here. I've done no wrong, yet here I am, in this drafty place with workmen hammering and where no one cares for me. Where there is no future, nothing lovely and cultured, nothing exciting. Where I'm nothing to anyone, only a burden and a disruption!"

One always falls back on one's strongest talents in time of distress. So I lied. "You're not a disruption, Shun. I know what it is to feel that there is no place that one belongs or is welcome. So I'll tell you now that, however strange Withywoods may be to you now, you can consider it your home. You won't be turned out of here, and for as long as you are here, I'll do everything in my power to protect you. You're not a guest here, Shun. You're home. While it may not suit you now, we can make the changes you need. It can be made lovely for you. You can find comfort here. You are welcome for as long as you need to be here." I took a breath and added a small thread of the truth. "While you are here, I consider you part of my family."

She looked at me, her mouth working strangely as if she were gumming food. Then she suddenly flung herself from her chair and launched herself at me, to land against my chest, sobbing loudly. I caught her before we both fell over. Her voice shook wildly as she said, "They tried to kill me with poison. The cook's little boy stole a tart from the platter, my favorite, a little berry tart, and he died with blood and foam coming out of his mouth. That's what they wanted to do to me. To make me die that way. Poor little Rono, who'd never done anyone any harm save thieving. He died instead of me, and he died in pain. Little Rono."

She was shaking all over. I held her firmly to keep from tipping out of my chair. "It wasn't your fault," I told her. "And you are safe now. You're safe."

I wondered if that was true.

"Papa!"

I turned my head sharply. Something in Bee's tone told me that she expected me to be ashamed of myself. She stared at me holding Shun, and then crossed her arms on her chest. "Shun's very upset," I told her, but the cold glare Bee was giving me told me that, in her opinion, that excused nothing. When Shun did not try to move clear of me, I managed to stand and sat her firmly in my vacated chair. "Are you feeling better, Bee?" I asked, to build on my falsehood that she had felt ill.

"No," she replied icily. "Actually, I feel worse. Much worse. But that isn't why I came to find you." She tipped her little head at me, and I felt as if she were drawing back a bow. "I had to leave my room, just for a few minutes. When I came back . . . I came to tell you that our other guest is missing."

"Missing?"

"Other guest?" Shun demanded.

"Missing?" Riddle echoed. As he entered the room, he looked tousled, as if he had run all the way back from the village. He was still breathing hard as he looked from Bee's disapproval to Shun's tearstained face and then at me. "The message I received was that the injured traveler had left."

"Yes. She did." I felt like a weathercock as I spun from Riddle to my daughter. "It's all right. She's not missing, Bee. She felt better and wanted to go. I should have told you." With my eyes, I tried to convey to her that I was lying, and needed her help to be convincing. She glared at me.

"Injured traveler?" Shun demanded. "There was a stranger here? How do you know she wasn't an assassin?" She caged her hands over her mouth and looked at all of us with alarm. Her green eyes were huge above her tangled fingers.

"She was just an injured traveler, one we helped on her way. There's no cause for alarm, Shun." I turned back to Riddle and made a wild leap for normality. "We were just having a bite. Riddle, are you hungry?" It was all I could do to keep my voice level. Tripping over deceit, tangled by my lies. The horrid sinking feeling was all too familiar. Shun's question had shaken me more than I wanted to betray. How indeed did I know that the young White was truly a messenger, and not someone who meant me and mine harm? Her resemblance to the young Fool had led me to bring her into my home with no thought as to her presenting a danger. And then I had put her in the room adjoining my daughter's bedchamber. And now Bee said she was missing. And most likely somewhere within the rambling confines of Withywoods.

Shun had been right. I had definitely lost my edge. I was out of practice at intrigue. My mind raced. The messenger had said that she was being hunted. Had her pursuers entered Withywoods and captured her and carried her off? In the sprawling old house, it was entirely possible. I had seen her injuries; it seemed unlikely to me that she could present a real danger to anyone. And equally unlikely that she had simply decided to run away, her message undelivered.

The silence had hung long in the room. I looked at Riddle.

"I could eat," Riddle replied uncertainly. His glance moved from Bee to Shun and then fixed on me. Bewilderment that was all his.

"Excellent." I smiled like an idiot. "I'll just let the kitchen staff know while you keep Shun company. She's feeling a bit unsettled at being here. I was trying to assure her that she would be safe now. And welcome."

"Warmly welcomed," Bee said in a low and venomous voice.

I concealed my surprise and added, "I'll be taking Bee back up to her room. She's obviously not feeling well." I reached for my daughter but she sidled out of my grasp and preceded me to the door.

No sooner had it closed behind us than she spun to me. I saw her chest rise and fall, and to my horror tears welled in her blue eyes as she accused me with, "I only came to tell you she was gone, and what do I see? You hugging that woman!"

"Not here. Not now. And you are wrong. Kitchen first." This time I was able to seize her narrow shoulder and despite her effort to squirm away from me, I marched her to the kitchen. I tersely informed Tavia of Riddle's requirements, and left as abruptly as I had arrived, taking Bee with me.

"Your room," I said in a low voice. "Now. Stay close to me. And no talking until we are there."

"Is there danger?"

"Shush."

"What about Shun?"

"Riddle is with her and he is far more capable than most folks credit him. You are my first concern, always. Be quiet!"

My tone finally silenced her and she actually slunk closer to me as we wended our way along the corridors and then up the stairs. When we reached the door of her room, I took her by both shoulders and stood her with her back against the wall. "Stay here," I breathed. "Do not move unless I call you. If I do so, come quietly and immediately and stand just behind my left side. Understand?"

Her eyes were wide, her mouth hanging open as she gave a short nod. I nodded back.

I eased the door of her room open. Before I entered, I evaluated all I could see, the bed and hangings, the curtained windows, the hearth. All looked as I had left it. I stepped in silently and checked behind the door before I made a more thorough inspection of Bee's room. There was no sign of an intruder. The untouched tray was on a stand by the bed. I stepped to the connecting door. It was ajar. I stepped back.

"Bee."

In a flash she was at my side.

"Did you leave that door open?"

She was plainly terrified as she shrugged and admitted in a breathless whisper, "I don't remember. I think so. No. You did and I didn't move it."

"Stand still."

I stepped to the door and opened it the rest of the way. The small room was dim, for it had no window of its own. Nothing there but the rumpled blanket on the bed. I ducked to glance under the bed. It was the only possible hiding place in the little room. No one was there. Of our guest, there was no sign save the ewer of water and the bedding pushed into a heap on the wall side of the narrow cot. I stepped back and shut the door. "She's gone."

"That's what I told you!"

"And now I'm certain that she's not in this room. And that's all we really know." I marshaled my thoughts. "Tell me exactly how you discovered she was gone."

"I stayed in the room here. Tavia brought up the tray of food, and set it on the little table for me. I went in to the girl after Tavia was gone. She was barely awake. I tried to give her some broth, but it only seemed to make her cough. Then she closed her eyes and went back to sleep. I sat here for a time. Then I needed to use the garderobe. So I did. And when I came back here, I went to the room to check on her. But she was gone."

"Gone." I thought. "How long were you gone?"

"Only a few minutes." Her eyes were very big.

"Bee. For the rest of this day, you are at my side. And if I tell you to do something, no matter how strange, you will do it instantly. Understand?"

She bobbed a nod. Her lips were red against the pallor of her face as she breathed through a half-open mouth. The terror in her eyes was an expression I had never wanted to see on my child's face. "Why are we afraid?" she demanded.

"We don't know if we need to be wary. So, until we do, it is safer for us to be afraid."

Chapter 16

HONORED GUESTS

White as ice. Eyes the same color. Hair the same color. They come but seldom, maybe once in every third generation. Or four. But we remember them. They walk among us, and choose one of us. Not as servant or friend, but as a tool to shape a future only that one can see. If (no idea how to translate this word) *then they are all of one color.*

Of a time, they breed upon (phrase obscured by stain) *either a man or a woman, of their own kind or one of ours. But their offspring are not of a term that matches our own. So they may leave and it is years later that* (this portion of the scroll so badly holed by insects that I can add only isolated words and phrases to it) *elderly* (a large gap) *pale* (a gap of I estimate seven lines of text followed by) *older than its years.* (Another large gap of at least two lines, ending with) *more merciful to kill it.* (The rest of the scroll scorched away.)

PARTIAL TRANSLATION FROM THE DESK OF FITZCHIVALRY FARSEER

So in that one day and a night and the next, my life changed. I remember how angry I felt about all of it. So many changes, and they all affected me, yet no one asked me if I wanted any of them.

No one ever asked me anything in those days.

First there was Shun, put for now in a room but two doors away from my own and my father's, until grander chambers could be prepared for her. My father had ordered that the Yellow Suite be renovated for her. She would have a bedchamber, a small sitting room, a room for her maid, and another room "to do whatever she wanted with," as my father put it. I had always loved the Yellow rooms and had often crept in there to play. No one thought to ask me if I would have liked to have a set of rooms like those. No. A single bedchamber and a tiny adjoining room for a nonexistent nursemaid were considered enough for me. Yet a stranger came to our home, and my father brought in a whole army of carpenters and stonemasons and cleaning staff, and even a maid to wait only on Shun.

Then there was the peculiar stranger he had put into the little room that opened to mine. He did not ask if he might put her there, he had simply done it. I had told him I understood why, and thought that he might thank me for being so understanding of how rude he had been. Instead he had just nodded curtly as if he expected me to simply accept anything he did. As if I were his conspirator in some plot rather than his own daughter. Certainly he expected me to support his lies to Riddle and Shun. And to obey him precisely after he discovered that I had told him the exact truth: The butterfly girl was gone.

And I did. I obeyed him without question that evening. He worked quickly, taking a blanket from my chest and handing me an armful of my mother's scented candles. He made me walk in front of him where he could see me, and so I led him to his private study. He hurried me there, halting me twice with a grip on my shoulder to pull me aside from where a passing servant might see me.

When we reached his private study, he shut the door immediately, bolted it, and went straight to the false hinges. "What are you doing?" I asked him.

"Hiding you," he replied. He did not speak sharply but with a finality that brooked no questions. He lit one candle for me at the fading fire in the hearth. "In you go," he told me. And then he followed me in, as if to make sure no spy had penetrated our secret place. I saw his brows lift in surprise at the changes I had made. "You've been busy," he said with grudging admiration.

"You seemed to have little time for me, so I found something to do." I wanted to rebuke him for how he had ignored me, but his smile at the changes I had made warmed me too much. He was proud of me. I could not be as stiff as I wished to be.

"You're clever. All of this is well thought out." He pushed the lit candle into my holder. Some tension seemed to go out of him. "You'll be safe here until I am sure that there is no danger to you. I have to leave you here now, but I'll be back as quickly as I can."

"Will you have to check every room in Withywoods?"

His eyes darkened as he saw that I understood what he feared. "I can do it."

I doubted that was possible. "So many strangers have come in and out in the last few days. Why do you fear this one so much?"

"There's little time to talk, dear. The sooner I'm about this, the faster I can come back for you. But I fear her because I trusted her far too quickly, without thought. She might not be a danger, but danger may have followed her. I was careless. I won't be again." He left me, backing from the small chamber into the narrow corridor. "I have to latch the door behind me. But don't fear. I'll be back."

I would have feared, if I had not already prepared my own bolt-hole through the pantry. I watched him go, and then I put my eye to the peephole and saw him close the secret panel. He turned and looked right at me and gave a nod before he left his den.

So. There I was. I was glad I had thought to provision my hiding place. I sat for a time, mulling over everything that had happened. It was too much for such a short time. Shun. I didn't like her. My dream-trance. I wondered if I should have been frightened by it instead of exhilarated. Why had I felt that way? I tried to make comparisons for myself. I was like a plant that had bloomed for the first time. No. More like a baby when it first discovers it can reach out with a hand and seize something. A part of me had been growing and today it had finally worked exactly as it was meant to. I hoped it would happen again soon. I wondered why I'd had to explain it to my father. Did not all people have dreams, and thus have dream-trances? I tried to remember who had taught me that dreams were important, that they must be recorded, and that the most important dreams would seize me and hold me until they were fulfilled. I laughed aloud when I realized when I had learned that. I'd dreamed it.

I soon began to wish that I had thought to provide myself with some sort of pastime. I took out my journal and wrote a fair account of the last day, but that was done quickly enough. On the best piece of paper I had I wrote an account of the butterfly dream, a much more detailed account than I had ever written before. I set it and my journal back on its little shelf and watched my mother's candle burn. It was exceedingly boring. I thought back to what Wolf-Father had told me, and my promise. What had my father meant when he told me to stay here? Why, only that I must stay hidden in the wall labyrinth. I assured myself of that several times.

Then I took a bit of my chalk and wrote on the wall that my father should not worry, I had gone to explore the corridors a bit, and that I would take chalk and an extra candle and mark my way.

I went first to the peephole that looked into my room, hoping again to find some secret entrance. Again there was nothing I could discover. I had begun to understand the passages and how they wound their ways through the walls of the house. They were best in the oldest part of the house, as if a builder had planned them there. In other places they went only a short way and were almost impossibly narrow or so low that my father would have had to crawl. I worked my way through the one that went past my room and was disappointed to find that there was no peephole into the room that had been temporarily given to Shun. I pressed my ear to the paneling, but could hear little. Maybe someone was weeping in the room. Maybe I was imagining it. I wondered if she was even in the room right now. I had been a bit frightened when my father had first spoken of bringing someone into our home. Now I wasn't frightened.

I was angry. I didn't like her, I decided in that moment, and justified it by deciding that she didn't like me, and that she wanted my father's attention. I wasn't sure why that made me uneasy, but it did. I needed my father now, more than ever, and it wasn't right for her to come into our home and take up his time.

Locating the Yellow Suite was more difficult, but eventually I made my way there. When I judged I was near I held my candle high and was rewarded by the sight of a little door that could be swung to one side. A peephole cover. But when I moved the door, all I found was a small glob of damp plaster pressed through what had been a peephole. The most recent round of repairs to the rooms had involved some plastering. They had covered over the hole. Now, I decided, was not the time to tamper with it. The plasterers might be back the next day, and I did not wish to call their attention to the hole. I would let it dry and later I would return to cut it out like a plug.

I wandered the hidden maze a bit longer. I visited my pantry exit to be sure it was still as I had left it. While I was there, I filched some dried apples and plums for my hoard. I had climbed onto a barrel to reach the pepper sausages when one of the kitchen cats wandered in. I ignored him. Stripy Cat was not really his name, but it was how he was called. I became aware of his stare as I was trying to clamber on top of the boxes of salt fish to reach the higher shelves in the pantry. I looked down from where I teetered to find him gazing up at me with round yellow eyes. He stared hard, as if I were one of the rats he was supposed to kill. His look froze me where I was. He was a big cat, heavy-bodied and thick-limbed, a cat for the ground rather than a climbing cat. If he chose to leap on me and attack me, I would not be the winner. I imagined those sharp claws sunk into my shoulders and his hind legs ripping at my back. "What do you want?" I whispered to him.

His whiskers perked forward and his ears tipped toward me. Then he shifted his gaze to a row of bright-red sides of smoked fish hanging from a string stretched across the pantry. I knew why they were hung so high; it was so the cats could not get them.

But I could reach them.

I had to stand on my tiptoes to break one free. The flaps of salt-glazed fish had been threaded onto the string like peculiar beads. Once I had my hands on one, I bent it until it broke. When it gave way, I lost my precarious balance and fell from the top of the boxes to the pantry floor. I landed hard on my hip and side, but managed to keep from crying out. I lay for a time, clutching the stolen fish and sausage while breathing past my pain. Slowly I sat up. Bruised, but not much more than that.

Stripy Cat had retreated to a corner of the pantry but hadn't fled. He watched me—or more specifically he watched the fish that I still clutched. I caught my breath and spoke softly. "Not here. Follow me."

I stood, hissing at my hurts, and gathered up my dried fruit and pepper sausage. Then, clutching my trove, I dropped to my knees and crawled behind and under my barricade of boxes to where my secret hatch was ajar. Once inside, I moved out of the way and waited. After a few long moments, a whiskered face appeared in the dim circle of light. I moved my candle back and beckoned to him.

Some people talk to cats. Some cats talk to people. It never hurts to try. "If you will follow me in here and spend a day killing rats and mice back here, I will give you this whole slab of fish."

He lifted his striped face, opened his mouth, and turned his face from side to side, taking in the scents of my warren. I know it smelled mousy to me. He made a low noise in his throat, and I felt he approved the prospect of hunting as well as the fish.

"I'm going to put this up in my den. When you've killed the rats and mice, come tell me. I'll give you the fish and then let you out again."

His round yellow eyes met mine, and I had no doubt that he understood our bargain well. He brushed past me, head down, tail straight. Once his tail was well clear of the hatch, I pulled the small door until it was almost entirely closed. I picked up my candle and took the fish, sausage, and fruit back to my den.

But even with my explorations, I spent a long and dull afternoon behind the walls. I wished I had stolen more of my father's old writings to read. I wrote about the cat, took a nap bundled in my blanket, ate some fruit and drank some water, and then waited. And waited. When finally my father returned to open the door for me, I was stiff and sore from being still so long. I had been watching for him, and as soon as he opened the panel, I was out. "All safe?" I asked him, and he nodded wearily.

"I think so," he amended. "There is no sign of her anywhere in the house. Though, as you know, it's a big house with many rooms. None of the servants has commented on seeing her. It's as if she vanished." He cleared his throat. "So I believe the servants know nothing of the missing girl. And I've insisted to Shun and Riddle that she left."

I followed him out of the secret den and into the corridors of Withywoods. I was silent. I knew hundreds of places to hide in our house. My father could not possibly have searched them all. Surely he knew that. I walked for a time at his side. I thought carefully and then said, "I should like a knife and a sheath, please. Like my mother always wore."

He slowed his stride, and I no longer had to hurry. "Why?"

"Why did my mother always have a knife?"

"She was a practical woman, always doing things. She had a knife to cut a bit of string, or trim back a bush or cut flowers, or cut up fruit."

"I can do all those things. Or could, if I had a knife."

"I'll see about getting you one, and a belt sized for you."

"I should like to have a knife *now*."

He stopped then and looked down at me. I looked at his feet.

"Bee. I know that you are a bit afraid. But I will keep you safe. It's right that you should have a knife, for you are old enough to be sensible with it. But . . ." He halted, floundering.

"You don't want me to stab someone if they're threatening me. Neither do I. But I don't want to be threatened and not have anything at all to protect myself."

"You're so small," he said with a sigh.

"Yet another reason why I need a knife!"

"Look at me."

"I am." I looked at his knees.

"Look at my face."

Unwillingly, I shifted my gaze. My eyes wandered over his face and met his eyes for a moment; then I looked aside. He spoke gently. "Bee. I will get you a knife, and a sheath, and a belt for it that you can wear. More than that, I will teach you to use it, as a weapon. It's not going to happen tonight. But I will."

"You don't want to."

"No. I don't. I wish I could feel like it was something you didn't have to know. But I suppose you do. And perhaps I have been remiss in not teaching you before this. But I didn't want you to live that sort of a life."

"Not being prepared to defend myself doesn't mean I'd never have to fight for my life."

"Bee, I know that is true. Look. I've told you what I'll do, and I will do it. But for now, for tonight, can you trust me to protect you? And let this be?"

Something tightened in my throat. I spoke to his feet, my voice gone hoarse and strange. "How can you protect *me* when you are going to be looking after *her* and keeping *her* safe?"

He looked shocked, then hurt, and then tired. I watched out of the corner of my eye as the expressions flitted across his features. He composed himself and spoke calmly. "Bee. You have nothing to be jealous about. Or to worry about. Shun needs our help, and yes, I will protect her. But *you* are my daughter. Not Shun. Now let's go. You need to brush your hair and wash your face and hands before we go to dinner."

"Will Shun be there?"

"Yes. And Riddle." He wasn't trying to make me trot, but my legs were short. When he walked at his normal stride, I always had to hurry to keep up. I noticed that the house was quieter. I surmised that he had sent the workmen home for the evening.

"I like it when the house is quiet again."

"I do, too. These repairs will take some time, Bee, and we will have to put up with noise and dust and strangers in our house for a while. But when they have finished, things will go back to being quiet and calm."

I thought about dinner tonight. Shun and Riddle at the table with us. And breakfast the next day. I thought about walking into a room in my home and finding Shun there. Would she walk in the garden rooms? Would she read the scrolls in the library? Now that I thought of her wandering through my home it suddenly seemed as if I could never be unaware of her presence. "How long will Shun be here?" Somehow I doubted that quiet, calm, and Shun would dwell in the same house.

"As long as she needs to be here." He tried to speak firmly but now I heard the dread in his voice. Clearly he had not asked himself that question. I liked that he disliked the answer as much as I did. It made me feel better.

He escorted me to my room. I washed, and combed my hair. When I left the room to go down to dinner, he was outside the door waiting for me. I looked up at him. "I like that you shaved off your beard," I said. I had noticed it that morning, but not commented on it then. He glanced at me, nodded once, and we walked down to the dining room together. The servants had put us in the big dining hall, but had only lit a fire in the nearest hearth. The other end of the room was a dim cave. Riddle and Shun were already seated at the table, talking, but the vast space of the room devoured their words. "And here we all are," my father announced as we came in. He had good control of his voice. He sounded pleased that all of us were there.

He seated me at his right hand, as if I were my mother, drawing out my chair for me and then pushing it in when I perched on it. Shun sat to my right and Riddle to his left. Her hair was pinned up and her dress looked as if she had expected to meet the queen in our dining room. Her face was freshly scrubbed, but cold water had not bleached all the pink from her eyes. She had been crying. Riddle looked as if he wanted to cry but had a smile hooked to his cheeks instead.

As soon as we were seated and my father had rung the bell for the food to be brought in, Shun spoke. "You didn't find any other sign of the stranger?"

"I told you, Shun, she left. She was an injured traveler, no more than that. Obviously she didn't feel safe, even here, and as soon as she could move on, she did."

Two men I didn't know came into the room carrying platters. I looked at my father. He smiled at me. They served us soup and bread and then stood back. "Cor, Jet, thank you." As soon as my father spoke the words, they bowed and went back to the kitchen. I stared at him in consternation.

"I hired more staff, Bee. It's time we did things a bit more properly here. You'll soon get to know them and be comfortable with them. They are cousins to Tavia's husband, and highly recommended."

I nodded but I still felt unhappy about it. The meal went in stages, and my father was careful to speak to Riddle and to Shun, as if conversation was something he had to share evenly with everyone at the table. He asked Shun if her room suited her, for now. She replied stiffly that it would be fine. He asked Riddle what he thought of the soup, and Riddle said it was as good as that served at Buckkeep Castle. Throughout the meal, he and Riddle spoke only of very ordinary topics. Did he think it would snow more tomorrow? My father hoped the snows would not be too deep this year. Riddle said it would be good if they were not too deep this year. Did Shun enjoy riding? There were some fine riding trails at Withywoods, and my father thought her horse looked like a good one. Perhaps she would like to explore the estate of Withywoods a bit tomorrow?

Riddle asked if my father still had the gray mare he had used to ride. My father said that he did. Riddle asked if they might go look at her after dinner. He had been thinking of asking my father if she would carry a foal from a certain black stud at Buckkeep for him.

It was such a transparent excuse for getting my father alone to talk to him that I almost couldn't stand it. After dinner, we went to a little room with comfortable chairs and a nice fire in the hearth. Riddle and my father left to walk out to the stables. Shun and I sat and looked at each other. Tavia came in with tea for us. "Chamomile and sweetbreath, to ease you to sleep after your long travels today," she said to Shun with a smile.

"Thank you, Tavia," I said after the silence had fallen and Shun had made no response to her.

"You are very welcome," she replied. She poured tea for each of us, and left.

I took my teacup from the tray and went and sat on the hearth. Shun looked down at me.

"Does he always let you stay awake and be with the adults?" She obviously disapproved.

"Adults?" I asked, looking around me. I smiled at her as if puzzled.

"You should be in bed by now."

"Why?"

"It's what is done with children in the evening. They go to bed so that adults can have conversations."

I thought about that, and then looked into the fire. Would my father start sending me to bed in the evening so that he and Shun could stay awake and talk? I took up the poker and hit the burning log with it firmly, sending up a shower of sparks. Then I hit it again.

"Stop that! You'll make the fire smoke."

I hit it one more time, and then put the poker back. I didn't look at her.

"I suppose it's as well that you are not wearing skirts. You'd dirty them down there. Why are you sitting on the hearth instead of in a chair?"

The chairs were too tall. My feet dangled. I looked at the newly swept bricks. "It's not dirty here."

"Why are you dressed like a boy?"

I looked down at my tunic and leggings. I had a few spiderwebs on my ankle. I picked them free. "I'm dressed comfortably. Do you like wearing all those layers of skirts?"

Shun flounced them out around herself. They were pretty, like the spread petals of a flower. The outer skirts were a blue one shade lighter than Buckkeep blue. The petticoat beneath was an even lighter blue, and the lacy edge of it showed deliberately. It matched the pale blue of the bodice of her dress, and the lace was the same as the lace at her throat and cuffs. That dress and petticoat had not come from any crossroads market. They'd probably been made especially for her. She smoothed them with satisfaction. "They're warm. And very pretty. They were expensive, too." She lifted her hand and touched her earrings, as if I could have failed to notice them. "So were these. Pearls from Jamaillia. Lord Chade got them for me."

I wore a simple tunic, sewn by my mother and made long enough to be modest, over a long-sleeved wool shirt. My tunic was belted at my waist with a leather belt and came to my knees. Below it, I wore only my woolen leggings and slippers. No one had ever suggested before that I was dressed like a boy, but now I recalled how the stable boys dressed. Not so different from me. Even the kitchen girls wore skirts, all the time. I looked at the cuffs of my sleeves. They were soiled with cobwebs and chalk from my earlier adventure. The knees of my leggings were dirty, too. I suddenly knew that my mother would have made me change my clothes before I came down to dinner with guests, into my red skirts, perhaps. She would have put ribbons in my hair. I lifted my hand to my hair and smoothed down what was left of it.

Shun nodded. "That's a little better. It was standing up like feathers on a bird's head."

"It's too short to braid. I cut it because my mother died." I looked at her directly for one instant.

Shun met my gaze coldly. Then she said, "I can only wish my mother were dead. I think it would make my life easier."

I stared at her knees. Her words cut me and I tried to understand why. After a moment it came to me. She considered her pain more significant than mine. I felt she had said that her cruel mother's life going on was a greater tragedy than my mother's death. In that moment I hated her. But I also discovered another important thing. I could do as my father did: that is, lift my eyes and meet her gaze and let nothing of what I was thinking show in my face.

That thought surprised me. I studied her, saying nothing, and realized that she did not share my ability. Everything she felt at the moment was writ broad and plain on her face. Perhaps she thought I was too young to read her face, or that it was unimportant if I could. But she was not trying to hide anything from me. She had known her callous words would hurt me. She was miserable and resented being in my home and was irritated by being left with me. And in her misery, she was striking out at me because I was there. And because she thought I could not strike back.

I did not feel pity for her. She was too dangerous for me to pity. I suspected that in her thoughtless wretchedness she could employ cruelty such as I had never experienced from an adult. I suddenly feared that she could destroy all of us, and take whatever little peace my father and I had found. She sat there in her pretty clothes and pearl earrings and looked at me, so small and, she thought, very young, and dirty and common. Of course. She thought me the daughter of commoner Tom Badgerlock. Not the lost princess of the Farseer family! Just the daughter of Withywoods's widowed caretaker. Yet I had a home and a father who loved me and memories of a mother who had cherished me. None of that seemed fair to her.

"You've gone quiet," she observed intently. She was like a bored cat poking at a mouse to see if it was dead all the way.

"It's late, for me. I'm a child, you know. I go to bed quite early on most nights." I yawned for her, not covering my mouth. In a softer voice, I added, "And self-pitying tales of woe always bore me, which makes me sleepy."

She stared at me, her eyes going greener. She reached as if to tidy her hair and pulled out one of the long pins that secured it. She drew it between her thumb and forefinger as if to deliberately call my attention to it. Did she think to threaten me with it? She stood abruptly and I jumped to my feet. I bet I could outrun her, but dodging past her to the door might be a challenge. I heard a murmur in the hall and an instant later Riddle opened the door. My father was behind him. "Good night!" I called cheerily to them. I ran past a glowering Shun to hug my father briefly and then step back hastily. "It's been such a long day, and so full of unexpected events. I'm quite weary. I think I shall take myself to bed now."

"Well . . ." My father looked astonished. "If you're tired. Shall I see you to your room?"

"Yes," Riddle said strongly before I could reply. Shun was tidying her hair, smiling as she slid the pin back into her bound tresses. "She didn't feel well earlier. You should see that she is tucked in warmly and that a nice fire is on her hearth."

"Yes. I should," he agreed. He was smiling and nodding, as if it were perfectly normal that I seek my bed at such an hour. Usually we stayed up late together, and often I fell asleep on the hearth in his study. Now he begged his guests to excuse him briefly, promised to return, and then took my hand as we left. I did not pull it free of his grip until the door was closed behind us. "What are you up to?" he demanded as we made our way toward the stairs and my bedchamber.

"Nothing. It's night. I'm going to bed. It's what children do, I am told."

"Shun's face was flushed."

"I think she was sitting too close to the fire."

"Bee." My name was all he said, but there was rebuke in the word. I was silent. I did not feel I deserved it. Should I tell him of her hairpin? Doubtless he would think me silly.

We reached my door and I seized the door handle before he could. "I want only to go to bed tonight. Doubtless you need to hurry back to talk to the other adults."

"Bee!" he exclaimed, and now my name meant that I had struck him, hurting him and also provoking a bit of anger. I didn't care. Let him go fuss over poor pitiful Shun. She needed his sympathy, not me. His face went still. "Stay here while I check your room."

I did as he told me, waiting by the open door. But the moment he came out, I slipped in through the door and shut it behind me. I waited, holding on to the door handle, to see if he would try to come in and talk to me.

But he didn't. I knew he wouldn't. I walked across the room and put another log on the hearth fire. I wasn't sleepy.

I peeled off my clothing, bunched it up, and sniffed it. Not just dirty, but definitely a mousy smell to it, probably from the spy-corridors. I thought of Stripy patrolling for rats and mice. I thought of stealthily leaving my room and going to my father's study to see if the cat wanted to come out yet. But I would have to get dressed again, and if my father caught me wandering the halls tonight he would be angry. I'd get up very early, I decided. Both my winter nightshirts smelled a bit fusty. When my mother was alive clothing always smelled like cedar and herbs if taken right from the chest, or sunlight and lavender if freshly washed. I had suspected that the household staff had become more lax about their chores since my mother's death, but this was the first time I had realized how directly it would affect me.

I blamed my father. Then I blamed myself. How could I even begin to imagine that he could know these things? He probably had no idea that it had been weeks since I had bathed my whole body or washed my hair. True, it was winter, but my mother had always made me wash my whole body in a tub at least once a week, even in winter. I wondered if the extra servants he had hired would mean that things would go back to the way they had been. I rather thought not. I doubted they would until someone took the reins.

Perhaps Shun? The thought made steel of my spine. No. Me. This was my household, really. I was the female here, standing in my sister's stead, in my sister's house. I imagined that the servants my father had always supervised were doing their work as they always had. Revel looked over his shoulder for those ones. But my mother had overseen the household staff. Revel was good at making things fancy, but I didn't think he supervised the daily washing up and dusting and tidying. I would have to step up to that now.

I pulled on my least smelly nightshirt. I looked at my feet, and used what water was left in my ewer to wash my face, hands, and feet. I built up my fire and clambered into my bed. There was so much to think about that I thought I would never be able to fall asleep.

But I did because I woke to the colorless girl standing over my bed. Ruby tears were on her cheeks. Pink blood was frothing on her lips. She stared at me. "The message," she said, spitting blood with the words, and then she fell upon me.

I shrieked and struggled out from under her. She clutched at me but I was off the bed and heading for the door in less than a breath.

I was screaming but no sound was coming out. The door latch jig-gled in my fumbling panic and then it swung open and I raced out into the dark hall. My bare feet slapped the floor and I was making little shrieks now. What if my father's bedroom door was latched, what if he wasn't there but down in his study or somewhere else in the house?

"Pa-pa-pa-pa," I heard myself stuttering, but I could not get any volume from my voice. His door opened at my touch and to my shock he was on his feet, a knife in his hand before I could even reach his bed. He was barefoot and his shirt was half-open, as if he'd been getting ready for bed. He snatched me up in his free arm, then twisted his body so that I was almost behind him and his knife menaced the open doorway. He spoke without taking his eyes from it.

"Are you hurt? What is it, where?"

"My room. The girl." My teeth were chattering with such terror that I do not imagine I spoke clearly. He still seemed to understand. He dropped me almost gently to the floor and began to move.

"Behind me. Close behind me, Bee."

He didn't look back to see if I obeyed. He went, running, knife in hand, and I had to race after him, going back to the last place in the world I wished to be. With no knife in my hand. If I lived through tonight, I promised myself that would never happen again. I'd steal a knife for myself from the kitchen and keep it under my pillow. I would.

We reached my room and he angrily gestured me away from the door. His lips were pulled back from his teeth, and his eyes were dark and wild. Wolf-Father was in them, and his anger was a killing anger that anything would threaten his cub. He halted at the thresh-old, and stared into the room that was lit only by the dying flames of the hearth. His nostrils were flared and he moved his head from side to side. Then he went very still. He advanced so slowly on the sprawled figure on my bed that it was as if only one small part of him moved at a time. He glanced at me. "You defended yourself? You killed her?"

I shook my head. My throat was still dry with terror but I managed to say, "I ran."

A terse nod. "Good." He drew closer to my bed and stared down at her.

He stiffened suddenly, lifting his knife to the ready, and I heard her wet whisper. "The message. You must hear the message. Before I die."

His face changed. "Bee. Bring water."

There was only a bit left in my ewer. I went into the room where we had left her and found the tray with the untouched food. There was water for tea in a pot, gone cold. I brought it to my father. He had arranged her on my bed. "Drink a little," he urged her, and held the cup to her lips. She opened her mouth but could not seem to swallow what she took. It ran out of her mouth and over her chin, washing the pink even paler. "Where did you go?" my father demanded of her. "We could not find you."

Her eyes were opened to slits. The lids looked dry and crusty. "I was . . . there. In the bed. Oh." She suddenly looked even sadder. "Oh. The cloak. It was the cloak. I was cold and pulled the cloak over me. It vanished me."

I had ventured closer to the bed. I did not think she was aware of me; I thought perhaps she was blind now. My father and I exchanged skeptical looks. She moved her hand in a vague gesture. It reminded me of a slender willow leaf moving in the wind. "It takes on the colors and shadows. Don't lose it . . . very old, you know." Her chest rose slowly and then fell. She was so still I thought she was dead. Then she cried out as if pained by the words, "The message."

"I'm here. I'm listening." My father took her narrow hand in his. "Too warm," he murmured. "Much too warm."

"So hard to think. To focus. He made it . . . a pattern. Easier to remember. Not safe to write it down."

"I understand."

She sniffed in a breath. When she breathed out, little pink bubbles formed along her lips. I didn't want to look at them and couldn't look away.

"By four things, you will know I am a true messenger from him and trust me. Ratsy was on his scepter. Your mother's name was never said. You served a man behind a wall. He took his finger-prints from your wrist." She paused, breathing. We waited. I saw her swallow and she turned her face toward my father. "Satisfied?" she asked him faintly. "That I am a true messenger?" I was right. She could not see his face.

He jerked as if stuck with a pin. "Yes, yes, of course. I trust you. Are you hungry? Do you think you could drink some warmed milk or eat something?" He closed his eyes for a moment and went very still. "We would never have neglected you so if we had known you were still here. When we could not find you, we thought you had felt well enough to travel and left us."

He did not mention that we had wondered if she was hiding somewhere in the house, hoping to kill us.

Her breath made a sound on every intake. "No. No food. Too late for food." She tried to clear her throat, and the spill of blood on her lips went redder. "Not time to think of me. The message."

"I can still send for a healer."

"The message," she insisted. "The message and then you can do whatever you wish."

"The message, then," my father capitulated. "I'm listening. Go on!"

She strangled for a moment and then pink slid over her lip and down her chin. My father wiped it tenderly away with the corner of my blanket. I decided I would sleep in his bed tonight. When she could, she took in air and said on a breath, "He told you. The old dream prophecies foretold the unexpected son. The one who sent me once interpreted them to mean you. But now he thinks perhaps not. He believes there could be another one. A son, un-looked for and unexpected. A boy left somewhere along the way. He does not know where, or when, or who mothered him. But he hopes you can find him. Before the hunters do." She ran out of breath. She coughed, and spluttered out blood and spit. She closed her eyes and for a time, just tried to breathe.

"The Fool had a son?" My father was incredulous.

She gave a short, sharp nod. Then she shook her head. "His and yet not his. A half-blood White. But it's possible he appears as a full White. Like me." Her breathing steadied for a time and I thought she had finished. Then she took a deeper breath. "You must search for him. When you find the unexpected son, you must keep him safe. Tell no one you have him. Speak of your quest to no one. It's the only way to keep him safe."

"I'll find him," my father promised. She smiled faintly, her teeth showing pink. "I'll send for a healer now," my father said, but she moved her head in a feeble shake.

"No. There's more. Water, please."

He held the cup to her mouth. She didn't drink, but sloshed the water in her mouth and let it run out over her chin. He wiped her face again.

"Hunters will come. Acting friendly, maybe. Or in disguise. Making you believe they are friends." She spoke in short bursts, breathing in between. "Trust the unexpected son to no one. Even if they say they have come for him, to take him where he belongs. Wait for the one who sent me. He will come for him, if he can. So he said, when he sent me. So long ago . . . why did he not get here before me? I fear . . . no. I must believe that he's still journeying. He escaped but they will hunt him. When he is able to, he will come. But slowly. He has to evade them. It will take him time. But he will get here. Until then, you must find him and keep him safe." I was not certain she believed her own words.

"Where should I look?" my father asked her urgently.

She shook her head slightly. "I don't know. If he knew, he gave me no hints. So if they captured me and tortured me, I could not betray him." She moved her head on the pillow, her blind eyes seeking for him. "Will you find him?"

He took her hand and held it carefully. "I'll find his son and keep him safe until he gets here." I wondered if he lied to make her feel better.

Her eyes closed until only a pale-gray moon showed under the lids. "Yes. So valuable. They will want him badly. Enough to kill. If they take him . . ." Her brow wrinkled. "Like I was treated. A tool.

No choices." Her eyelids fluttered open and her queer, colorless stare seemed to meet his gaze. "I've borne three children. Never seen or held any. They take them. As they took me."

"I don't understand," my father said, but at her desperate look, he amended it to, "I understand enough. I will find him and I will keep him safe. I promise. Now we will make you comfortable and you will rest."

"Burn my body," she said insistently.

"If it comes to that, I will. But for now . . ."

"It will come to that. My companion searched the wounds. I told you. What went in won't come out."

"A poison?"

She shook her head. "Eggs. They've hatched now. They're eating me." She winced and coughed again. "Sorry. Burn bedding. With me." Her eyes opened and her blank gaze wandered over the room. "You should put me outside. They bite and burrow. And lay eggs." She coughed pink. "Punishment for traitor." She blinked, and drops of red oozed from the corners of her eyes. "Treason is unforgivable. So punished with unstoppable death. Slow. It takes weeks." She shuddered and then squirmed. She looked up at my father. "The pain is building. Again. I can't see. They're eating my eyes. Are they bloody?"

I heard the sound of my father swallowing. He sank down beside the bed until his face was on a level with the girl's. A stillness had taken his face; I could not tell if he felt anything. He asked quietly, "Are you finished, then? That was the whole message?"

She nodded. She rolled her head to meet my father's gaze but I knew she could not see him. Blood in ruby drops clung to her eyelashes. "I'm finished. Yes."

My father lurched to his feet. He turned as if he would run from the room. Instead he snatched up the empty ewer. He spoke sternly. "Bee. I need cool fresh water. And bring some vinegar in a cup. And . . ." He paused to think. "Go to Patience's garden room. Bring me two double handfuls of the mint that grows closest to the statue of the girl with the sword. Go."

I took the ewer and a candle in a holder and went. The darkness made the corridors longer. The kitchen was a place of lurking shadows. The vinegar was in a large crock, and the containers to carry it all up out of my reach. I had to push benches and climb. I left the heavy ewer of water and the vinegar and threaded my way through the sleeping house to Patience's garden room. I found the mint and tore at the plants recklessly, filling a fold of my nightshirt with the aromatic leaves. Then I trotted back to the kitchen, candle in one hand and the other holding my hiked-up nightshirt with the mint. In the kitchen I tied up the mint in a clean cloth and gripped the knot in my teeth. I abandoned my candle to clutch the heavy ewer in one arm and the vinegar in my other hand. I hurried as fast as I could, trying not to think of maggots eating me from the inside. By the time I reached the door of my room and set everything down to open the door, I was out of breath. I felt as if I had been running for the whole night.

A horrifying sight met my eyes. My featherbed was on the floor. My father knelt beside it. He had his boots on, and his heavy cloak was on the floor beside him, so he must have gone back to his room. He had torn one of my coverlets into strips and was using them to tie the bundle he was making. His face was gray when he looked up at me. "She died," he said. "I'm taking her outside to burn her." He had not paused in his feverish bundle-making. My featherbed was taking on the shape of an immense cocoon. There was a dead girl inside it. He looked away from me and added, "Strip to the skin, here. Then go to my room. You can find one of my shirts to sleep in. Leave your nightshirt here. I'm going to burn it with her."

I stared at him. I set the ewer down, and the vinegar. The bundled mint fell from my shirt to the floor as I let it drop. Whatever medicine he had intended to make, it was too late now. She was dead. Dead like my mother. He pushed another strip of blanket under the bundle, brought up both ends, and snugged it tight in a knot. My voice came out very little. "I'm not going naked through the corridors. And you can't do this all alone. Should I get Riddle to help you?"

"No." He squatted back on his heels. "Bee. Come here." I went to him. I thought he was going to hug me and tell me it would be all right. Instead he had me bend my neck, and he looked all through my shorn hair. Then he rose, crossed to my clothing chest, and opened it. He took out last year's wool robe. "I'm sorry," he said when he came back to me. "But I have to keep you safe." He took the hem of my nightshirt and stripped it off me. Then he looked at me, all over, under my arms and at my bottom and between the toes of my feet. We were both very red in the face before he was finished. Then he gave me the wool robe and took my nightshirt to add to his bundle. "Pull on your boots and a winter cloak," he told me. "You'll have to help me. And no one can ever know what we do tonight. No one can know the message she brought. Or even that we found her again. If other people know, that child will be in greater danger. The boy she spoke about. Do you understand that?"

I nodded. In that moment I missed my mother more than I ever had before.

Chapter 17

ASSASSINS

There is, in all honesty, no way to kill someone mercifully. There are those who count it no crime to drown an imperfect newborn in warm water, as if the infant will not struggle desperately to draw air into its lungs. Did it not try to breathe, it would not drown. But they do not hear the screams nor feel the darkening of the mind that the child endures, so they have been merciful. To themselves. This is true of most "mercy killings." The best an assassin can do is create a setting in which he does not have to witness the pain he causes. Ah, you will say, but what of drugs and poisons that send a man into a deep sleep from which he never emerges? Perhaps, but I doubt it. I suspect that some part of the victim knows. The body knows it is being murdered, and it keeps few secrets from the mind. The strangler, the suffocator, the exsanguinator may all claim that their victims did not suffer. They lie. All they may truly say is that the

victim's suffering was invisible to them. And no one returns to say
they were wrong.

MERJOK'S TWO HUNDRED SEVENTY-NINE WAYS TO KILL AN ADULT

As I carried her body down the stairs, my little darling trotted before me bearing a candle to light my way. For one terrible moment
I felt grateful that Molly was dead and could not witness what I was
demanding of our child. At least I had created a long enough diver-
sion that she had not witnessed me killing the messenger. I had
used the two blood points in her throat. When I first placed my
hands, she had known what I was doing. Her blind and bloody gaze
had met mine, and for a moment I read relief and permission on
her face. But then, as I applied the pressure, she had reflexively
reached up to seize my wrists. She had struggled, fighting for a few
more moments of pain-riddled life.

She was too weakened to put up much of a fight. She managed
to scratch me a bit. It had been a long, long time since I had killed
anyone. I'd never anticipated killing with arousal, as some assassins
do. I'd never made it my joy, my fulfillment, or even my cherished
goal. I'd accepted it as my task in life when I was very young, and
I'd done it, efficiently and coldly, and tried not to think too much
about it. That night, even with the messenger's initial permission,
even with the knowledge that I was saving her from a lingering and
painful death, was probably my worst experience as an assassin.

And here I was, making my small daughter a party to it, and
binding her to silence. Had I sought righteously to keep Chade and
Kettricken from dragging her into being a Farseer with all the atten-
dant history? They certainly would not have exposed her to anything like this. I had been so proud of how long it had been since
I'd killed anyone. *Oh, good work, Fitz. Don't let them put the burdens*
of being a Farseer on those thin shoulders. Make her an assassin's ap-
prentice instead.

On an estate like Withywoods there is always, somewhere, a pile
of brush and branches waiting to be burned. All end up heaped
somewhere out of the way. Ours was at the far side of the lambing
pens in a pasture. I carried the bundled messenger and led the way

through the tall, snowy grass and the winter night. Bee walked silently beside me. It was an unpleasant walk in the dark and wet. She followed in the trail I broke. We came to a snow-edged mound of brambly and twiggy branches, thorn bushes cut and thrown here, and fallen branches from the trees bordering the pasture that were too skinny to be worth cutting into firewood. It was an ample pile for my task.

There I set down my load, and the bundled body tipped unevenly onto the pile. I pulled the branches over her and made the pile more compact. Bee watched. I thought perhaps I should send her back, tell her to go to my room and sleep. I knew she wouldn't and suspected that actually witnessing what I had to do would be less horrific than imagining it. Together we went to fetch oil and coals. She watched me fling the oil over the branches and pour it generously over the wrapped body. Then we set it alight. The evergreen branches and brambles were resinous; they caught fire quickly, and their flames dried the thicker branches. I feared they would consume themselves before the body was gone, but the oily featherbed caught and burned well with a harsh stink. I brought more branches to throw on our bone fire, and Bee helped. She was always a pale little creature, and the chill black night chalked her. The red firelight dancing on her face and shock of hair made her some strange little death sprite from an old tale.

The pyre burned well, the flames reaching up higher than my head. Their light pushed the night back. Soon my face was uncomfortably warm and my back still cold. I braced myself against the heat to push the ends of branches in and to add more to the conflagration. The fire spoke, crackling and hissing when I threw on a frost-laden branch. The flames ate our secret.

Bee stood next to me, but not touching me, and we watched the messenger burn. It takes a long time to burn a body. Most of it we spent in silence. Bee had little to say, other than, "What shall we tell the others?"

I sorted my thoughts. "To Shun, we say nothing of this. She believes the girl left. We will let Riddle believe the same. To the housekeeping staff I will say that you complained of itchy bites and I found vermin in your bed when I was putting you in it and decided to burn it immediately." I gave a small sigh and admitted, "It won't be fair to them. I must pretend to be very upset with them. I will demand that every bit of your clothing be washed fresh, and new bedding brought for you."

She gave a single nod. She turned her eyes back to the fire. I gathered another armful of branches and threw them onto the blaze. The half-burned limbs gave way under this fresh weight, crumpling down on the embered remains. The featherbed whispered away as downy ash. Were those blackened bones or blackened branches? Even I could not tell. The faint smell of roasting meat sickened me.

"You are very good at this. You have thought of everything."

Not a compliment I wanted to receive from my little daughter. "I used to have to do . . . special work. For the king. I learned to think of many things at once."

"And to lie very well. And not let people see what you are thinking."

"That, too. I'm not proud of it, Bee. But the secret that we heard tonight is not mine. It belongs to my very old friend. You heard what the messenger said. He has a son, and that son is in danger." Could she hear in my voice how peculiar I found this news? The Fool had a son. I had never been absolutely certain of his masculinity. But if a child had been born, it must have come from a woman's womb. That meant that somewhere, that son had a mother. A woman whom, presumably, the Fool had loved. I thought that I had known him better than any other person ever had. And yet this was something I never would have suspected.

The woman would be my beginning point. Who was she? I racked my brains. Garetha came to mind. She had been a gardener's maid when the Fool and I were children. Even then she had been enamored of him. As a youngster he had been a lithe and playful fellow, turning handsprings and flips and doing the juggler's tricks expected of a jester. He had been quick-tongued. Often his humor had been cruel to those he felt could be well served by being taken down a notch or two. With the very young or those not treated kindly by fate he had been gentler, often turning his jests back on himself.

Garetha had not been pretty, and he had been kind to her. For some women, that is all it takes. In later years she had recalled him, recognized him in his guise of Lord Golden. Had there been more than recognition? Had that been how he had persuaded her to keep his secret? If they had had a child, the boy would be in his mid-twenties now.

Was she the only possibility? Well, there were whores, and ladies of pleasure in plenty in Buckkeep Town, but I could not imagine the Fool frequenting them. It had to be Garetha . . . Then my thoughts stepped sideways, and I suddenly saw the Fool in a different light. He had always been a very private person. He might have had a hidden lover. Or a not-so-secret one. Laurel. The Witted huntswoman had made no secret of her attraction to him. He had spent years away from Buck, in Bingtown and possibly Jamaillia. I knew next to nothing of his life there, save that he had lived in the guise of a woman.

And then the obvious fell into place and I thought myself a great dunce. Jofron. Why had he written to her? Why had he warned her to guard her son? Perhaps because he was *their* son? I reorganized my memories of Jofron and the Fool. Close to thirty-five years ago, when the Fool found me dying in the Mountains, he had taken me to his little home. He'd had a little Mountain house that he shared with Jofron. He had moved her out when he took me in. And when he had left to go with me on my quest, he had left everything he owned there for her. I thought of how she had reacted to me the last time we met. Could I interpret her ways toward me as the reaction of a lover who had been spurned for a friend? She had seemed to enjoy showing me that he had written to her while sending me no word.

I reached back to those feverish days, remembering her voice, the adoring way she spoke of her White Prophet. I had deemed it a sort of religious fervor. Perhaps it had been a different passion. But if she had borne him a child, surely he would have known for a certainty. He had sent her messages. Had she ever replied to them? If he'd left a child there, the boy would be a year younger than Nettle. Surely not a child that needed my protection? And the grandson who had been there had looked nothing like the Fool. Surely if he were the Fool's grandson, his White heritage would have shown somewhere. The Fool's grandson. For a long moment, those words seemed impossible to fit together.

I pondered it as the flames ate her bones. The messenger's words made little sense. If the Fool had fathered a child the last time he'd been in Buckkeep, his son would be a young man, not a little boy. It didn't make sense. The messenger had called him a boy. I recalled how slowly the Fool had grown, how he had claimed to be decades older than I was. There was so much I didn't know. But if it was the way of his kind to age slowly, perhaps the son he had left behind still appeared to be a child? Then it could not be Jofron's son, who had fathered a boy of his own. Had he sent her a warning because he feared the hunters would pursue any child who might remotely be the Fool's son? My mind ran in circles, trying to build a tower with too few blocks. Surely, if it was Jofron's son, he could have told me, with dozens of clues that only I would recognize. Call him the Toymaker's son, and I'd know him. But surely that was true of any son? The gardener's boy, the huntswoman's child . . . we'd known each other so well. Any child he'd left, surely he could have identified to me. If the Fool knew for sure where the child was . . . Was he sending me on a wild-goose chase to find a child reputed to exist on the basis of some obscure White prophecies? He wouldn't do that to me. No. Almost certainly he would. Because he could believe that I could find such a child. Was it even the Fool's son? I sifted the messenger's meager words again. An unexpected son. Once, he had told me, those words referred to me. And now? Was there another "unexpected son" somewhere? Could I be certain this boy was the Fool's son? Her knowledge of my language had been less than perfect . . .

"Papa?" Bee's voice was shaking, and when I turned to her, I saw that she had wrapped her arms around herself and was shivering with cold. "Have we finished?" Her nose was red at the tip.

I looked at our fire. The last load of branches I had put on it collapsed suddenly. How much would be left of the girl? The skull, the heavier thighbones, the column of spine. I stepped forward to peer into the heart of the fire. They were covered with ember and ash. Tomorrow I'd bring the bedding from the nurse's bed in the room adjacent to Bee's and burn it here. Tonight, it was enough. I hoped. I looked around us. There was a moon, but layers of clouds veiled it. An icy mist hung over the low and boggy pasturelands. What moonlight reached the ground there was claimed by the fog.

"Let's go back in."

I held out a hand to her. She looked at it, and then reached up to put her small fingers in mine. They were cold. Impulsively I scooped her up. She pushed against me. "I'm nine. Not three."

I released her and she slid to the ground. "I know that," I said apologetically. "You just looked so cold."

"I *am* cold. Let's get back inside."

I didn't try to touch her again, but contented myself that she walked along beside me. I thought of the morrow and felt heavy with dread. It would be complicated enough without dealing with Shun and Riddle also. I dreaded that I must falsely report an infestation, for I knew the scurrying and scrubbing that would follow. Revel would be beside himself; the entire staff would be chastised. The laundering would be endless. I thought of my own room and winced. I'd have to subject myself to an invasion of housekeepers, or my accusations would ring false. And I did not want even to imagine Shun's outrage and disgust at the idea that her bedding might harbor vermin. Well, there was no help for it. My excuse for burning Bee's bedding in the middle of the night must be convincing. No avoiding the lies I must tell.

Just as there had been no way to avoid exposing Bee to all this cascading debris from my old life. I shook my head at how poorly I had protected her. All I wanted to do right now was to be alone and try to think through what it all meant. The thought that the Fool had reached out to me after all these years was overwhelming. I tried to sort the emotions I was feeling and was startled to find that anger was one of them. All those years, with no word from him and no way for me to reach out to him. And then, when he needed something, this imperious and life-disrupting intrusion! Frustration vied with a terrible desire to see him after all these years. The message seemed to indicate that he was in danger, restrained from traveling or spied upon. Injured somehow? When last I had seen him, he had been so anxious to return to his old school, to share with them the end of the Pale Woman and all he had learned during his long travels. To Clerres. I knew no more of that place than its name. Had he come into conflict with the school? Why? What had become of the Black Man, his traveling companion and a fellow White Prophet? The messenger had made no mention of Prilkop at all.

The Fool had always loved riddles and puzzles, and loved his privacy even more. But this did not feel like one of his pranks. It felt more as if he had sent every bit of information he dared, inadequate as it was, and hoped that I would have the resources to find whatever else I needed to know. Did I? Was I still the person he hoped I was?

The strange part was that I actually hoped I wasn't. I'd been a sly, resourceful assassin, capable of spying, running, fighting, and killing. I didn't want to do that anymore. I could still feel the warmth of the girl's skin under my thumbs, feel the feebling grip of her hands on my wrists as her struggling gave way to unconsciousness and then death. I'd made it quick for her. Not painless, for no death is without pain. But I'd made the pain much briefer than it otherwise would have been. I'd granted her mercy.

And I'd once more felt that surge of power one gets when one kills. The thing that Chade and I never discussed with anyone, not even each other. The nasty little burst of supremacy that I continued to live when someone else had died.

I never wanted to feel that again. Truly, I didn't. Nor did I want to wonder at how quickly I had decided to grant her the mercy of a swift death. For decades now, I had insisted that I did not want to be an assassin. Tonight I doubted my sincerity.

"Papa?"

An assassin flinched and turned his scrutiny on the small girl. For a moment I didn't recognize her. I struggled to find my way

back to being her father. "Molly," I said, the word bursting from
me, aloud, making Bee's face grow pale so that her reddened cheeks
and nose stood out as if splashed with blood. Molly had kept me
safe. She had been the waymarker on a different path my life could
take. Now she was gone and I felt as if I had fallen over a cliff's edge
and was hopelessly plunging toward ruin. And I had pulled my
child over with me.

"She's dead," Bee said in a small voice, and suddenly it was real
all over again.

"I know," I said miserably.

She reached up and took my hand. "You were leading us off into
the dark and the fog, toward the pasture. Come this way." She
tugged my hand, and I realized I had been walking toward a misty
forested strip of land beside the pasture. She turned us back toward
Withywoods where lights shone dim in a few windows.

My child guided me home.

We moved silently through the darkened corridors of Withywoods. Across the flagged entrance, up the curved staircase, and
along the hallway we softly paced. I paused at the entrance to her
room and abruptly recalled that she could not sleep there. I looked
at her and hated myself. Her nose was a bright-red button. She wore
a winter cloak and boots and, under that, only a woolen nightdress.
It was now soaked to the knee. *Oh, Bee.* "Let's get you a clean nightgown. Then you'll sleep in my room tonight." I winced at the
thought, recalling the boar's nest that my room had become. No
help for it now. I wanted every scrap of bedding in her room destroyed to avoid contagion from whatever horrid creatures the messenger had carried within her. I suppressed a shudder at the thought
of the vicious judgment passed on her. So irrevocable. So their
punishment for being a traitor was lingering and painful death, one
that no apology or explanation would halt. I still was not sure who
"they" were, but already I despised them.

I kindled a candle at her hearth while Bee went to her clothing
chest. Her nightgown dragged a wet trail on the floor. She lifted the

heavy lid, wedged a shoulder under it to hold it open, and began to rummage through the contents. I glanced around the room. The stripped bed looked stark and accusing. I'd killed a woman in this room tonight. Did I ever want my child to sleep here again? She might not be haunted by what I'd done, for surely she had no idea of it. She would believe the messenger had just died of her wounds. But this killing would bother me for a long time. I didn't want my daughter sleeping in the bed where I'd killed someone. Tomorrow I'd broach the idea of moving her into a new room. For tonight—

"*Stop!* Just stop, please! Leave me alone! *Please!*" It was Shun's voice, rising to a shriek on the last word.

"Stay here!" I barked at Bee and left the room. Shun's temporary chamber was at the end of the corridor. I was only a few steps down the hall before Riddle, in his nightshirt, knife in hand and his hair standing up in wild tufts, burst out of his room and into the corridor. Shoulder to shoulder, we ran. Shun's voice rose again, ascending in terror. "I'm sorry you're dead. It wasn't my fault, it wasn't my fault! Leave me alone!"

The door to her bedchamber was abruptly flung open and a wailing Shun sprang into the dim hall. Her auburn hair was loose about the shoulders of her nightgown. She had a knife in one hand, a fine and slender blade, and even in her terror she carried it as if she would know how to use it. She shrieked louder at the sight of us running toward her. Then she recognized Riddle and, breathlessly shouting his name, ran into his arms, narrowly missing the knife he carried. She seemed not to notice when he caught her wrist and with a pinch made her drop her own blade.

"What is it, what's wrong?" We were both shouting and in response she only wailed and hugged Riddle's neck so tightly that I thought she would choke him. She had buried her face in his chest and he held his knife well clear of her in one hand while he awkwardly patted her back with the other. She was saying something over and over, but I could not understand her. I stooped and picked up her blade. I recognized the design as one favored for assassin work. Evidently she had not felt her rudimentary training would protect her against a ghost. I tucked it away in my sleeve.

"I'll check her room. Keep her safe," I said to Riddle, but as I moved past them she suddenly lifted her head and shrieked, "Don't go in there! Don't go in there! It's his ghost, crying and crying! He blames me. Rono blames me!"

I halted, feeling a sick fear spread through me. I am not a superstitious man. I do not believe in ghosts. Yet I almost heard the distant wailing of a lost child. My heart sank and I welcomed Riddle's words as he said to her, "It was only a bad dream, Shun. You've been through a lot, and you've carried a lot of fear this past fortnight. Here you are, in an unfamiliar house, wondering what shape your life is about to take. It's only to be expected that you'd have a bad dream."

She pushed away from him violently. Her voice was indignant. "It wasn't a bad dream. I wasn't able to fall asleep. I was lying in bed, thinking, and I began to hear the wailing. It's Rono. The little wretch was always crying, always whining and begging. Anything sweet or delicious that was cooked for me, he wanted some of it. And even when he was told it was for me, he would keep begging, or he would just steal some of it. And that's what got him killed!" She was suddenly angry instead of frightened. "He stole from me and ate it, and he died. How can that be my fault?"

"It wasn't," Riddle immediately replied. "Of course it wasn't. The blame falls on whoever was trying to poison you."

Her sobs changed suddenly, and I wondered how I knew she had gone from terrified to comforted. Her face was buried in his shoulder and she clung to him, her arms wrapped around his neck and her body pressed close to him. He sent me an uncomfortable look over her shoulder. I tried not to scowl. I was not sure what he and Nettle were to each other, but even in this context I did not like seeing him hold another woman. "I'll check her room. Just to be sure there's nothing amiss," I told him.

She lifted her face. Tears and snot had dismissed any beauty from her face. "I was not dreaming, as I was not asleep! Nor did I imagine it! I heard his crying!"

"I'll see to it."

As I walked past Riddle, he passed his knife to me. He quirked one eyebrow in an abbreviated shrug. It was always better to be armed than not, in any situation. "I'll put her in my room for the night," he offered.

"You cannot leave me alone!" she wailed.

There was deep resignation in his voice as he offered, "I'll sleep across your threshold, just outside your door. If anything bothers you, I'll be only steps away."

I was already moving down the hall and did not hear the words of her choked objection. I halted outside the door of her chamber and settled myself. It could be anything or nothing, I reminded myself. I pulled the door open and looked into the room. I unfurled my Wit-sense, reaching out to investigate the room. Nothing. I sensed no human or animal within the chamber. It was not an absolute assurance that Shun had imagined an intruder, but it was reassuring to me.

Firelight from the low-burning hearth coated the room in honey. The bedding had spilled from the bed and trailed her to the door. I moved inside, stepping softly and listening. What had she heard? For I suspected there would be a grain of truth at least in her complaint. Had the wind whistled through the chimney or past her window? But all was silent save for the muted crackling of the fire.

I lit a branch of candles and explored the room with them, checking behind curtains and under the bed and even in the still-empty clothing chests. They had been freshly cleaned and held only new sachets. They smelled of cedar and lavender and waited to be used. Shun had not unpacked so much as avalanched into the room. Clothing was everywhere, cascading from her baggage, draped across the foot of the bed and on top of the clothing chests. I scowled at her untidiness. Well, by tomorrow, her maid would be here to set her to rights. Still, it did not please me that a girl of her age did not even know how to be orderly in her unpacking. Her jewelry was scattered across the top of the small vanity, next to a bag of pink and yellow sweets.

Chade had obviously opened his purse for her, and she had taken full advantage of it. What sort of training had he given the girl? She clearly thought much of herself, but no trace of discipline or order did I find in her behavior. How had he looked at her and considered her a candidate to be a spy, let alone an assassin? I wondered where he had found her and why she mattered so much to him. He'd hidden her pedigree well but I was determined to know it now. I'd sniff out his secrets. In my spare time. When I was not looking for the Fool's misplaced heir. Or accusing my servants of vermin in the bedding. Or repairing the damage I'd done to my daughter. I had not been managing my old life very well. I could not imagine coping with Shun in addition.

I finished my search carefully, checking that the windows and shutters were tightly closed and that her maid's adjoining room was innocent of all intruders. There was nothing there. I retreated from her chamber, trying to set my concerns about Shun aside for tonight. Tonight, I would take care of my immediate worries. Tomorrow would be time enough to think about adapting Shun to our simpler habits. Tomorrow . . . we were well past midnight. Today.

I took the lit candles with me and went down the hall to where Riddle stood in his nightshirt, his arms crossed on his chest. I had never seen the man look so stubborn. A rumpled kitchenmaid, one of the village girls newly hired to help, stood nearby in her night-robe and shawl, looking both sleepy and alarmed. Mild stood nearby, disapproval at this uproar stamped on her face. And Shun was complaining loudly. Mentally, I was thankful that Revel had not been roused. Tomorrow would be soon enough to put the house steward in an uproar.

Shun set her hands to her hips and glared at Riddle. Her dark curling hair was wild on her shoulders and her nightdress strained against her out-thrust chest. "No. I don't want her sleeping beside me. And what could she do if the ghost came back? Riddle, you are supposed to protect me. I want you to sleep in my room!"

"Lady Shun, that would not be appropriate," Riddle replied firmly. I had the feeling he was repeating himself. "You wanted a companion for the night? Here is Pansy, ready to serve. And I assure both of you that I'll be right here, stretched across the threshold should you need any sort of assistance."

"Ghost?" Pansy broke in, her sleepiness vanishing. She turned her shock and appeal on Riddle. "Sir, I beg you, the lady is right! I would be useless should a ghost come into the room. I'm certain I should faint dead away!"

"I checked Lady Shun's room. I assure you, there is no intruder and nothing to fear there," I announced firmly.

"Of course there isn't *now!*" Shun objected. "It was Rono's little ghost, crying and accusing me! Ghosts cannot be found when you search for them. They come and go as they please!"

"Rono?" Mild laughed, and then said, "Oh, beg pardon, Lady Shun, but there is no Rono ghost in that room. The only ghost known to walk through those chambers is old Lord Pike. So his parents named him, but all the maidservants in the manor called him old Lord Peek, for he dearly loved to catch a glimpse of any woman in her shift or drawers! My own mother told me that he would hide in the—"

"No more stories tonight!" I announced firmly. I already knew from the look on Pansy's face that she would be giving her notice tomorrow. The suppressed amusement in Riddle's eyes could not lighten my mood. All I wanted was to seek my own bed. I put authority into my voice.

"Mild, if you would, help Riddle to make up a pallet outside Lady Shun's door. Lady Shun, if you wish a companion to share this chamber with you, then we are offering you Pansy. No one else. Pansy, you will be paid extra for this service tonight. And that, ladies and gentlemen, is all. I am going to my own bed now. There have been enough disruptions after a very taxing day."

"If Rono's ghost throttles me in the night in vengeance for his death, I hope you will have a good explanation for Lord Chade as to how you failed in your duty to protect me!"

She threw the stony words at my back. I continued to walk away. I knew I was leaving the burden of sorting it out on Riddle's shoulders. I knew he could handle it. And he'd had at least some sleep, and had not murdered anyone nor burned a body tonight.

I opened the door to Bee's chamber. Empty. So she'd had the sense to change her clothing and go to my room. I continued down the corridor. I opened the door to my room and stood still. I could feel that she wasn't there. The room gave me no Wit-sense of her presence, only chill and emptiness. The fire had almost burned out.

I lifted my branch of candles high, trying to tell if she had been here. So far as I could tell, nothing had changed since I'd last left the room. Habit made me cross to the hearth and add wood to the fire. "Bee?" I called softly. "Are you hiding in here?" I dragged the rucked blankets off the bed to be sure she hadn't burrowed in and fallen asleep. The ridged sheets and stink of sweaty male assured me that she would have found it an unappealing hiding spot. No. She had not been here.

I headed back to her room. All was quiet in the corridor. Riddle opened his eyes and lifted his head as I passed. "Just checking on Bee," I told him. I was reluctant to let him know that I'd misplaced my own daughter. Just the thought of what he would report back to Nettle about the disorder in my houschold made me wince. Ghosts and smoking chimneys and a half-trained staff were as nothing compared with misplacing Nettle's small sister.

Candles held high, I entered her room. "Bee?" I called softly. Obviously not on the bared bedstead. I knew a moment of fear. Had she crept into the bedding in the servant's room? I hated my self that I had not taken it and burned it immediately. "Bee?" I cried louder, and two hasty strides carried me to the door of the adjoining chamber.

Empty. I tried to remember how it had looked when I had last seen it. Had not the bedding been less on the floor and more on the bedstead? I prayed to gods I scarcely acknowledged that she had not touched it. The room was so small that it was the work of a moment to be sure she wasn't in it. I stepped out of it and then, horror-stricken, rushed to her winter clothing chest. How often had I reminded myself that she needed something smaller with a lighter lid? I knew she had fallen into it, her head smashed, and then suffocated in the dark.

But all it held was her clothing, in pushed heaps and wads. Relief warred with worry. She wasn't there. I felt a spasm of annoyance that her clothing was so ill kept. Had the servants abandoned this room when I chased them from mine? In so many ways I was failing my child, but most of all in that I had lost her tonight. My foot nudged something and I looked down at a heap of wet clothing on the floor. Bee's clothes. So she had changed here. She'd been here and now she was gone. Where could she be? Where would she go? The kitchen? Had she been hungry? No. She'd been unsettled, even scared. So where would she go?

And I knew.

I walked past Riddle, feigning a calm I didn't feel. "Good night!" I wished him wryly. He watched me pass, and then rolled to his feet in a fluid motion.

"I'll help you look for her."

I hated his perspicacity, and welcomed it. "You take the kitchens, then. I'll check my study."

He nodded and was off at a trot. Shielding my candle flames, I followed. At the bottom of the stair, we went our separate ways. I doubled back to go to my private study. All was quiet and dark as I traversed the dark passageways. When I reached the double doors of the study, they were closed. All was still.

Chapter 18

INVISIBILITY

Beloved,

Was a time when I knew peace in your presence. Though, to be truthful with myself, there were as many times when your presence plunged me into deadliest danger. Or pain. Or fear. But the peace is what I remember and long for. Were you here, I would seize you by the shoulders and shake you until your teeth rattled. What is the meaning of this truncated message you have sent me? Did you fear to entrust too much information? Did you suspect how cruelly your messenger would be hunted, or how she would suffer such a tortured death? What need could compel you to knowingly risk her to such a fate? I ask myself that, and the only answer I can find is that if you did not, she would face a worse one? What, I ask myself, could be worse? And then I wonder what sort of danger you yourself are in right now, that you did not bring this message yourself.

All I have are questions, and each one is a torment to me at a time when I am overwhelmed by other concerns. You have set me a mysterious task with few clues. I fear it is an essential one. But just as essential are those already in my hands. The raising of my daughter . . . shall I again abandon my own child, this time to go in search of yours? Too little information, old friend, and too large a sacrifice.

UNFINISHED LETTER FROM THE DESK OF FITZCHIVALRY FARSEER

I stood alone in my room and listened to Shun shrieking out in the hallway. Bitterness rose in me. After all I had gone through tonight with him, all I had done to help him, one cry from her, and my father ran off and left me standing in the semi-dark in soggy clothing. I pushed the lid of the chest up higher and strained to reach the bottom and, by touch, discover something dry and comfortable I would wear to bed. I pushed past winter socks and itchy wool shirts. My fingertips touched something, and then I got hold of it and pulled it up from the bottom of the chest.

It was a warm felted nightrobe. Red. My favorite color. I carried it closer to the fire to look at it. It was new and unworn. I turned the collar inside-out and knew the stitches. My mother had made this. For me. Made it and set it aside, as she had so often done, to be pulled out the moment I outgrew my old one.

I shed my wet garments where I stood and pulled the new nightrobe on over my head. It fit well, save that it was a bit long. I lifted it to walk. It made me feel elegant to have to catch up my skirt when I walked, even if it was only the train of my nightrobe.

The ghost cried out, a long, distant wail that lifted the hair on the back of my head. I stood frozen for an instant. Then it came again, closer and louder. Two things happened in that moment. I knew I should never have left a cat in the spy-maze, and I abruptly deduced that yes, my chamber did have an entrance to the secret corridors. It just wasn't where I had thought it would be.

I pushed open the door to the maidservant's room. The firelight barely reached inside. I went back for a candle. The pale stranger's bedding was as she had left it, crumpled on the bed. I knew better than to touch it. I edged around it, and as I did, my feet tangled in something and I nearly fell. I cried out, in fear of the infected bedding, and the ghost cried in response.

"Just a minute!" I hissed low. "I'm coming. Be quiet and I'll give you a big piece of fish."

Water. The cat wanted water. I should have known that. He'd already found and claimed his salt fish reward, and now he was thirsty. "Water, then. And sausage from the pantry. But be quiet until I can get to you. Please."

A rumbly meow of agreement and warning. If his reward was slow in coming, he was going to sing the stones down around me.

Heart thundering, I looked down at my feet, fearing to see a flood of biting insects climbing my legs. Instead I saw only the hem of my nightrobe and, when I lifted it, my bare feet against the plank floor. Holding my robe high and bringing my candle close, I stooped. I stared. I could feel that my foot was on top of something that was not the floor, but I couldn't see anything there.

I hiked my robe higher so I could grip the hem in my teeth and curled my toes. They clasped fabric. Light and soft. I reached down and pinched it between my forefinger and thumb and as I did, a flap of it fell over, revealing once more the butterfly-wing pattern on the underside. I dropped it, startled. And again, my foot was apparently bare against the floor, but half of my toes were gone. One corner of the cloak was upturned to show the delicate panes of color. As I stared in astonishment, my toes slowly formed on the fabric. I could feel that the cloth covered them but I could see them.

I pinched the butterfly-color part of the cloak up between my thumb and forefinger and stood. Now I could see it. It hung from my uplifted hand, a garment of riotous color and very little weight. This, then, was how we had not seen her in the bed. The strange words of the messenger came back to me. "It takes on the colors and shadows." No wonder she had cautioned us not to discard it. It was a treasure from an old tale! Abruptly my fear of contagion vanished, to be replaced with the certainty that if my father saw this, he would take it from me and probably destroy it to protect me.

I set my candle on the floor and, standing carefully free of the bedding's touch, shook out the cloak and folded it, butterfly-side-out. It made a surprisingly small packet. I thought to myself that such thin fabric would be delicate and of small use against wind or rain. I resolved to take great care with it.

Stripy Cat meowed again. "Hush!" I cautioned him. Then I suggested, "Dig or scratch where you see my light. I'm trying to find the door."

The faint scrabbling came from under the bed. I didn't want to touch the bed frame but I did. I seized it in both hands and with an effort pulled the heavy bed away from the wall. It seemed to me it was much heavier than it needed to be, and I suspect it had been made so just to discourage a servant from moving it.

I lifted my candle and edged past the bed frame to the wall, to peer and poke at the wooden panels. The cat clawed diligently, even frantically. I could not see an opening or trigger, but when I put my hand where he was scratching I felt a draft. And the sound, it seemed to me, was much louder than it should have been. "Be patient," I warned him again, and suddenly thought of the door in the study. I shut the door to the room and studied the hinges. No false hinges, but there was one plank of wood behind the door that was narrower than its fellows. I caught my nails in the edge of it and tugged at it till it swung out. Behind it was a lever covered in cobwebs and spotted with rust. I pulled it and it groaned. It did not travel far, but a section of wall behind the bed suddenly moved out of alignment. The cat's excited meow was louder now.

"Shush!" I warned him. I suspected I had very little time until my father returned. I needed to hide my cloak, reward and banish the cat, and be back in my room before I was missed. I returned the narrow panel to its place, gritted my teeth, and edged around the contaminated bed. When I leaned on the displaced wall panel, it swung in. I stepped inside, pushing the cat back with my foot. "Don't go out here! There's no water here," I warned him. He growled but backed away. I tucked the cloak under my arm, set down my candle, and used every bit of my strength to pull the bed back into place. That done, I stepped into the secret corridor and pushed the concealed door closed behind me.

Cat first, I decided, and he was pleased that I did so. "Take us back to the pantry," I suggested in a whisper. "To the fish!" Stripy led and I followed. Twice he stopped so abruptly that I nearly trod on him. But he knew the way and we reached the concealed door in the pantry and together emerged there. I had to pile up boxes to reach a fine string of sausages hung out of our reach. Again, I wished for a belt-knife. I had to bite two of the sausages free of their fellows. The cat called piteously, reminding me it was water he craved most.

Together we ventured into the kitchen, where I found water for him. He drank and drank while I examined my butterfly cloak. The fabric seemed to be much sturdier than its light weight would indicate. When Stripy had finished drinking, I rewarded him with the sausage and let him carry it out into the kitchen yard. He was padding away into the night when I called after him, "What about the rats? Did you kill any?"

He had killed several, and discovered and made an end of two nests of babies.

"Will you come back tomorrow?"

It wasn't likely. He hadn't liked being confined with no water. He was accustomed to coming and going as he pleased. He trotted away, tail high, into the cold night. I could scarcely blame him. I'd left him trapped and waterless for hours. But his discovery of two nests of baby rats was something I could not ignore. I would have to find a feline ally, and soon.

I heard a whisper of sound from the house and suddenly recalled that I needed to hurry. I darted back into the pantry just as I heard someone come into the kitchen. I pinched my candle out and by touch found my way into the secret corridor. I drew the door shut behind me. The dark became absolute. I promised myself that I now knew my way well enough that I needed no light. I tried not to think of any rats Stripy had not killed.

It took me a time but I groped my way back to the small cubby that looked down into my father's study. A tiny beam of light was coming in the peephole. I peered out and I saw my father move to close the study doors. In a moment, he'd open the door.

In the dark I shook out my butterfly cloak and then refolded it so that the invisible side was out. I could not see what I was doing. I hoped I had left no betraying edge of color showing. As I heard him open the panel door, I hid my cloak on the shelf behind the candle supply.

The dance of his candlelight preceded him. Light and liquid shadows flowed and spread. They came around the corner like a wave of water and engulfed me. I sat quietly, my extinguished candle in hand, until he reached me. As the light touched me and he saw me, I heard the sigh of relief he expelled.

"I thought I might find you here," he said gently. Then, as he looked at me, "Oh, my dear, did your candle go out, too? Such a night it has been for you. My poor little cub."

He had to crouch to be in my hidey-hole. When I stood, he bent deeper to kiss me where my hair parted. He was still for a moment as if he were smelling me. "Are you all right?"

I nodded.

"Is this where you want to come when you are frightened?"

That I could answer truthfully. "Yes. This place is mine, more than anywhere else in Withywoods."

He straightened and nodded back at me. "Very well." He tried to roll his shoulders but could not in the cramped space. "Come with me now. We both need to get some sleep before dawn."

He led the way and I followed him out of the secret corridors and back into his den. I watched him close the panel and open the tall doors. I followed his candle as we went back to the main part of Withywoods. At the foot of the grand staircase, he halted. He turned and looked down at me. "Your room will need to be thoroughly cleaned before you can sleep there again. And my room is too untidy. I suggest we sleep in your mother's sitting room, where you were born."

He did not wait for me to agree. I followed him as we went to the pleasant chamber that had once served as a nursery for me. It was cold and dark. My father lit a branch of candles and left me there while he went to get a scoop of coals from another hearth to start a fire. While he was gone, I brushed cobwebs from my new red nightdress. I stared about my mother's dimly lit room. We had not spent much time here since she had died. Her presence was everywhere, from the candles ready in their holders to the emptied flower vases. No. Not her presence. It was her absence that I felt. Last winter the three of us had gathered here almost every night. My mother's workbasket was still by her chair. I sat down in it and set the basket on my lap. I pulled my feet up under my nightgown and hugged the basket to me.

Chapter 19

THE BEATEN MAN

And in a time that no one expects, when hope is dead and White Prophets fled, in a place where he cannot be found, there will be discovered the Unexpected Son. He will not be known to his father, and motherless he will grow. He will be the pebble in the track that shifts the wheel from its course. Death will thirst for him, but time and again, that thirst will go unslaked. Buried and lifted, forgotten, unnamed, in isolation and disgrace, he will yet prevail in the hand of the White Prophet who wields him without compassion or mercy for the tool that must be dulled and chipped to shape a better world.

I set the scroll aside, wondering why I had bothered to take it out. I had brought it from my private den to Molly's room, where Bee lay sleeping. It was the only bit of writing I'd ever read that mentioned the prophecy of the Unexpected Son. And it was only a fragment. There were no new answers there to the question I wanted to ask him. *Why, after all these years? Why such a message, and such a messenger?*

I turned it over, studying it for the thousandth time. It was an old piece of something . . . not vellum, not paper. Neither Chade nor I knew what it was. The ink was very black, the edges of each letter sharp. The substance it was written on was pliable and the color of honey. If I held it up to the fire, I could see light through it. Neither Chade nor I could read it, but it came with a translation that Chade assured me was accurate. At the time, he had muttered something like, "At that price, it had better be accurate."

The first time I had seen it, I was still a lad, and it was one of a number of scrolls and vellums that Chade was collecting on the topic of White Prophets and their predictions. I paid no more mind to this than I did to his fascination with elderberry propagation and creating a poison from rhubarb leaves. Chade had many obsessions during those years; I think his fixations were all that had kept him sane during his decades of isolated spying. I certainly didn't connect his fascination with White Prophets to King Shrewd's peculiar jester. In those days the Fool was merely the fool to me, a pasty-faced, skinny child with colorless eyes and a double-edged tongue. I avoided him, mostly. I had seen him frolic through the tumbler's tricks that could make the court gasp. I hadn't yet heard him slice a man's pride to ribbons with his razor-sharp sarcasm and clever wordplay.

Even after fate introduced us, first as acquaintances and then as friends, I did not make the connection. Years would pass before the Fool confided to me that he thought the prophecies about the Unexpected Son were foretelling my birth. It was one of half a hundred bits of predictions that he had quilted together. And then he had come to find me, his Catalyst, the bastard son of an abdicated king in a distant northern land. And together, he had assured me, we would change the future of the world.

He believed I was the Unexpected Son. There had been times when he was so insistent on it that I almost believed it myself. Certainly death had thirsted for me, and often enough he had intervened to snatch me away from that fate at the last possible moment.

Ultimately I had done the same for him. We had achieved his goal, the restoration of dragons to the world, and in doing so had ended his days as a White Prophet.

And he had left me, severing decades of friendship and departing to return whence he had come. Clerres. A town somewhere far to the south, or perhaps it was just the name of the school where he had been raised. For all the time that we'd spent together, he'd told me precious little of his life before I'd known him. And when he thought it was time for us to part, he'd left. He'd given me no choice in that matter, and steadfastly refused my offer to go with him. He had feared, he told me, that I would continue to act as a Catalyst, and that together we might unknowingly undo all we had wrought. And so he had gone, and I had never truly said farewell to him. The knowledge that he had left me with no intent ever to return had come to me in tiny droplets of realization spread over the years. And each droplet of comprehension brought its own small measure of hurt.

In the months that had followed my return to Buckkeep, I had discovered that finally, suddenly, I had my own life. That was a giddying experience. He had wished me well in finding my own fate to follow, and I never doubted his sincerity. But it had taken me years to accept that his absence in my life was a deliberate finality, an act he had chosen, a thing completed even as some part of my soul still dangled, waiting for his return. That, I think, is the shock of any relationship ending. It is realizing that what is still an ongoing relationship to someone is, for the other person, something finished and done with. For some years I waited, like a faithful dog told to sit and stay. I had had no reason to believe that the Fool had lost affection or regard for me. Yet the ringing silence and constant absence began, over time, to feel like dislike or, worse, indifference.

There had been times, over the years, when I had dwelled on it. I tried to excuse it. I had been missing when he passed through Buckkeep Town. Many had feared me dead. Had he? My answer to that had danced back and forth. He had left me a gift, the carved statue of him, Nighteyes, and me. Would he leave a gift that he never expected to be claimed? Well, what else would he have done with it?

There were words hidden in the carved memory stone, a single sentence. "I have never been wise." Did that mean he would be foolish enough to renew our friendship, even if it meant chancing the undoing of our work? Or did it mean that in his foolishness, he would set out on a dangerous quest without me?

Did it mean he had been a fool ever to care about me beyond my role as his Catalyst? Was it an apology that he had seemed to care for me and let me come to rely so deeply on our bond? Had he ever truly cared about our friendship?

There are always those dark thoughts, I must believe, when a deep friendship ends so abruptly. But every wound becomes a scar, eventually. That one never entirely ceased being tender, but I had learned to live with it. It did not intrude on me every moment. I had a home, a family, a loving wife, and then a child to raise with her. And though Molly's death had reawakened those echoes of loss and abandonment, I did not think I had been dwelling on it.

Then the messenger arrived. And a message so poorly conveyed or badly constructed that it made little sense. She had hinted that there had been other messengers who had not reached me. A memory stirred. All those years ago. A girl messenger, and three strangers. Blood on the floor, and bloody fingerprints on the Fool's face. That scream . . .

I felt dizzied and sick. My heart hurt as if someone had squeezed it. What message had I missed, all those years ago? What death had that messenger endured that night?

The Fool had not forsaken or ignored me. Years ago, he had reached out for me. To warn me, or to beg for help? I'd missed his message, and let it go unanswered. Suddenly that hurt me more than all the years of thinking he had abandoned our friendship. The thought that he had vainly waited for years for some sort of response from me was a razor-edged pain.

But I did not know how to reach him now, or how to begin on this quest he had set for me. And I had no idea where to search for his son, or what sort of a person I would be seeking.

I pushed the thought from my mind. I needed sleep, at least a little sleep, before the dawn came.

But there was the killing. Ironic, that the one person who had understood how little I wanted to continue as an assassin had been involved in forcing my return to that profession. I did not regret my decision; I remained absolutely certain it had been the correct one. But I resented that I'd had to make such a choice, and was deeply agitated that my child had been forced to witness me disposing of a body, and to bear the burden of keeping that secret.

When Shun's ghost hysteria was settled and after I had moved my sleeping child from Molly's chair to a couch, I had fetched a blanket from my bed and the bit of writing, thinking to study it one more time. But it was worse than useless. I concealed it beneath some forgotten mending in Molly's sewing basket and looked around her placid room. The fire was down to coals; I fed it. I took a pillow from her chair, and felt guilty about putting the pretty thing on the floor. I lay down in front of the fire and flipped and kicked at the blanket until it somewhat covered me. The stitches of Molly's embroidery on the cushion pressed into my cheek. I resolved to put all questions and fears out of my head and just sleep. For now there was no immediate threat to me and mine, I had no idea what to do about the peculiar message, and there was nothing I could do about Shun's dramatics. I closed my eyes and emptied my mind. Clean snow falling on a wooded hillside. I took a deep, steadying breath and told myself there was a hint of deer scent in the crisp wind. I smiled. *Do not agonize about yesterday. Do not borrow tomorrow's trouble. Let your heart hunt. Rest in the now.* I filled my lungs slowly and as slowly let the air out. I drifted to a place, not sleeping, not waking. I was a wolf on a snowy hillside, taking in deer scent, and living only in the now.

Fitz?

No.

Fitz? I know you're awake.

I'm not, really. My mind drifted against Chade's, a boat tethered to a dock. I more than wanted to be asleep. I *needed* to be asleep, to float freely away on that current.

I felt him sigh in annoyance. *Very well. But tomorrow, remember this as more than a dream. I'm sending the lad to you. They beat him badly, and if the city guard hadn't chanced upon the scene and chased them off, it's likely they would have killed him. But he's well enough to ride, or will be in a few more days, and I think my best course is to send him away from Buckkeep as soon as possible.*

The windswept winter forest had vanished. I opened my eyes. There was the smell of smoke and burning flesh on my hands and shirt. I should have washed. And found a nightshirt instead of sleeping in my clothes. I was too tired, too tired of all of it to do any of it right. *If I'd reported to you like that when I was twelve, you'd have called me an idiot and hit me with something.*

That's probably true. But I've been trying to reach you for hours. What made you put up your walls so stoutly? I began to think you'd taken my advice and sealed yourself against the Skill whenever you were sleeping.

Probably something I should do. I hadn't even been aware I'd put my walls up, but suddenly knew when I'd done it. Keeping my walls up around Bee was a habit, but I'd always left a chink for deliberate Skilling. I suppose it had been old instinct to raise them to full resistance during the kill. I'd wanted no chance witnesses to that. Easing into sleep must have lowered them. I told him half a truth. *I was preoccupied with Shun. She believes in ghosts and thought her room was haunted by some unfortunate child from her past. Evidently he got the poison that had been meant for her. Not her fault, but when she hears a strange noise at night, it's hard to convince her of that.*

Is she all right? Anxiety thrummed in his Skilling.

Much better than the beaten lad, whoever he is.

FitzVigilant. Who else might I be sending to you to save him from being murdered?

I don't know. Anyone who it pleased you to send my way, I suspect. My weariness was making me testy. And it was coming to me now, in pieces, that this news meant I was about to have another orphan on my doorstep. Another addition to my household, one that would be underfoot for years rather than days or months. Another room to prepare. Another horse in my stable, another plate on my table, another person speaking to me when I wanted to be left alone. I tried to muster some sympathy for the poor bastard. *So his legitimate brothers have come to court, and his mother wishes to do away with their father's by-blow?*

Not exactly. She seems to be a woman who plans ahead. Her boys will not come to court until next spring and so I thought I might safely keep him here for a time longer. Evidently she decided to be rid of him sooner rather than later, and is clever enough to attempt it in a way that will not make other folk think her sons were involved. The men she set on him were common ruffians, native to Buckkeep Town. They waylaid him outside a tavern.

Are you sure then that this wasn't just a random robbery?

I'm sure. The drubbing was too thorough and too violent. He was down and they could have easily taken his purse and run. They went past knocking him down, past knocking the fight out of him. This was personal, Fitz.

Cold seethed through his voice. Personal. The lady had made it personal, attempting to kill a boy under Lord Chade's protection. There would be some sort of repercussion for her, I did not doubt. I would not ask what it would be or who would carry it out. Would she enter her bedchamber to find it ransacked and her most precious jewelry stolen? Or would it be crueler? I suspected she should keep a tight watch on her sons, or she might find out how it felt to have someone under her protection take a bad beating. Chade could be that cold. I could not. Tonight had brought back all my distaste for killing. Call it vengeance or justice; no matter how it was named, I wanted none of it. Never again.

A bit of true sympathy for FitzVigilant invaded my soul. Beaten past his ability to fight back. I didn't like to dwell on that; I had too many memories of situations of that sort. *Is anyone accompanying him? To see he gets here safely?*

He hasn't left yet. I've hidden him. And when I send him he will have to travel alone. But I would not have decided to send him if I hadn't thought he'd be well enough to ride. He had three days of convalescing out of sight of any who might wish to harm him. He has vanished to other eyes. My hope is to make his father's wife believe she has terrified him enough to make him flee from Buckkeep Castle. She may be content

with that. *But I need to keep him past the time when she might have people watching for him to flee.*

*And if she has not given up by then? If she has watchers and they
follow?*

*She will first have a task to find him. And those she sends to look may
well find something else entirely.* A pause in his thoughts and a small
hum of cat pleasure.

I filled it in for him. *And if she finds where you have sent him, she
will still have to get past me.*

Exactly. So much satisfaction. I was so tired that even the tingle
of pride I felt at his confidence in me was annoying. *Are you sure
that you have not overestimated my ability to shepherd these lost lambs
you are sending me?*

Not at all. I regard your ability as second only to my own.

I stifled the thought that Shun had nearly been poisoned and
FitzVigilant had been severely beaten in Chade's care. Second only
to his own. Oh, yes. I yawned widely enough that my jaw cracked. I
tried to keep my mind on what he was telling me. *And what does
Lord Vigilant think of this, of his lady trying to eliminate his bastard
eldest?*

There was just the briefest hesitation. *The man has no honor. He is
not as attached to the lad as the boy deserves. He would, I think, be relieved. If, indeed, he knows of his lady's plotting. If he does not, I intend
to see that he is fully informed. He will be made to care for the boy's
safety, before I have finished with either of them.*

So. Chade had that end of the situation well in hand. At least
that had not been maneuvered into my area of responsibility. *I'll let
you know when he gets here. And now I have to sleep.*

Fitz. Are you all right? The Skill conveys emotion as well as
thought when one is careless. Genuine concern. He was reading my
pain.

I pushed him gently away. I didn't want to answer the question.
I was emphatically not all right, and he was the last person I wished
to discuss that with. *I'm very tired. Houseguests. House repairs. And
it's not the time of year when we should be doing these repairs. I should
have done them last summer.*

Well, yes, that will teach you not to put things off. And the little one? How is she adapting?

Bee is fine, Chade. Just fine. And I'm going to sleep. Now.

I pushed him firmly out of my mind, forming my walls up behind him.

There was no returning to sleep, and all peace had fled. I watched the shadows from the fire on the ceiling of the room. I tried to think about Molly, without the sadness, but that wound was still too fresh. I refused to think about the messenger or puzzle any more on her message.

But refusing to think about a thing only brings it more strongly to mind. I thought of the Fool. I tried to pretend I wasn't angry at him for sending such a cryptic message. I couldn't, so I stopped thinking about him.

I rolled to my side and looked at my little girl. Her hair stuck up at all angles. She was huddled into a ball, like a sleeping cub. Her blanket had twisted away from her and I could see that even her little toes were curled in tight to her feet. Sleeping small, hoping to stay hidden. Oh, little one. So small, but not as young as anyone else thought. Especially not after tonight. I'd done that to her. Without thinking, I'd made her my accomplice. Just as Chade had done with me. Years from now, would I be reaching out to her as Chade did to me? Was I repeating yet another cycle, raising an apprentice assassin? Was it the only sort of fathering I knew how to do?

The Fool had always asserted that time moved in a great circle, but a decaying one, where at every turning humanity repeated mistakes, making them ever graver. He had believed he could use me as his Catalyst to set that great wheel into a better track. He'd had visions of the futures, and out of all the possible futures he could see there had been one, a future in which I survived and together we changed the world.

And I was back to thinking of the Fool again. I shifted, shifted again, and rose. I built up the fire, tucked the blanket more closely around Bee, and then left as silently as a stalking assassin. Amazing how adept I was at that talent.

I moved through Withywoods, carrying a branch of candles. I inspected the work that had been done so far in the Yellow Suite, and once more wondered at the temerity of a person who would come as a desperate guest to someone's home and then complain endlessly about the accommodations. But these rooms, at least, she must love. Earlier in the day, a fire of applewood and cedar had been kindled in the hearth to freshen the room. The fragrance lingered. In the candlelight the yellow walls were a warm gold. When the newly freshened hangings were restored to the bed and the curtains rehung, it would be a cozy retreat for any young woman. Surely she could not imagine a ghost in this warm and welcoming room. I shut the heavy wooden door behind me, comforted that at least this must go right tomorrow. Today, I amended. Today. Dawn was a broken dream away.

Beyond the Yellow Suite was the Green Suite. I could not recall the last time I had been in those rooms. I opened the door and looked into dimness. Draped furniture breathed dust. Shuttered windows. The hearth was swept clean and had been cold for years. The bed frame was a skeleton, the hanging stored in a cedar chest at its foot. The room had an unused air, but I saw no rodent droppings. I would put the servants to making it habitable tomorrow. By the time FitzVigilant arrived, the rooms would have warmed through. It was not as spacious as the Yellow Suite. Still, there was a little study off the bedchamber and a small room for a servant attached to it; I wondered if he would require one. Was I supposed to supply one? So much I did not know about having a scribe. I would ask Revel. Perhaps he would know. But yes, these rooms would do for FitzVigilant. One more matter solved.

Then Bee's rooms, and here I found a task I must do. Tomorrow I must feign anger about vermin, and demand that bedding be burned and the room scrubbed. That meant that tonight I must remove Bee's precious things to keep them safe from too thorough a cleansing. There were candles to gather, and her jumping jack and top, and other small items I thought might be precious to her. I took them and hid them in my own bedchamber in the trunk that locked.

For no reason except that I couldn't sleep, I went down to the kitchen. The kitchens at Withywoods were smaller and far less busy than those at Buckkeep Castle, but the smells of the bread dough rising and a broth in a covered vat barely simmering at the back of the hearth were comforting to me. I unwrapped the last of the previous week's bread and cut a chunk, and then went through to the pantry for some sharp cheese from the wheel there. I drew a mug of ale as well and sat down at the kitchen worktable. The kitchen was probably the warmest room in Withywoods. The big hearth in the corner never went cold and the heat from the baking oven in the other wall never completely left the room. I ate and drank and kept my mind on kitchens and cooks that I had known.

Then I gave up. I folded my arms on the table, put my head on them, and stared into the fire. *Why, Fool? Why after all the empty years? Why didn't you come yourself? Were you in danger as the messenger had implied? And if you were, why didn't you send a map or instructions as to how to find you? Did you think I wouldn't come to your aid?*

I woke to thudding that vibrated through my skull. Cook Nutmeg had an immense mound of bread dough on the worktable and was kneading it. Every so often, she would lift one edge of it, fold it over, and then hit it energetically with the palms of her hands. I drew a deep breath and sat up straight. For a moment I felt a boy again, watching the predawn activity of Buckkeep's great kitchen. But it was only Withywoods, and instead of a score of workers, there were only six. Tavia turned from stirring the morning's porridge and met my gaze with a raised eyebrow. "Ale a bit stronger than you expected?"

"I couldn't sleep. I came down here. And then, I suppose, I found I could sleep."

She nodded, and then respectfully but firmly informed me, "You're in our way."

I nodded back. "I'll move," I said, and stood, stifling a yawn. "It smells so good in here," I told her, and both of them gifted me with smiles.

Tavia spoke. "It will smell even better when it's brought out to table. Lady Shun seemed a bit disappointed with our rustic efforts yesterday, so I've told the help that we need to shine today. If that pleases you, sir."

"Shine?"

"As would make our Lady Molly proud. Time to lift up our heads and be a proper household again. Revel has been chewing his own teeth over how things had begun to go down. So we're all glad to see you taking more of an interest in the house, sir. And it's good to have more folk here, to work and to live. Bring life back to the place."

Life. After Molly's death. I nodded, not sure that I agreed with her, but letting her know I valued what she was telling me. She gave me a firm nod in return, emphasizing that she was right. "Breakfast done proper won't be ready for another hour or so, sir, but I can bring you some tea if you wish."

"I do wish," I assured her, and let myself be herded out of her kitchen. My back ached and my head ached and I still smelled of smoke. I rubbed my face and became aware of the growth of whiskers. One of the perils of trying to be clean-shaven for my daughter. I'd have to tend to my face every morning now. "Tavia!" I called after her. "You can wait on the tea. I'll ring when I'm ready."

Coward that I was, I found one of the little kitchenmaids and sent her to tell my steward I'd found vermin in my daughter's bed and burned her bedding in the night. I told her to tell him to address it as he thought best, and left it at that. I fled to the steams.

One of the things I missed most from my boyhood days were the steams at Buckkeep. They were a year-round comfort, warming a man through and through in the depths of winter and sweating sickness out from a body at any time of the year. They were a legacy from Buckkeep's days as a fortification, with multiple rooms and benches. There were separate chambers for the guardsmen, prone to be rowdy and pugilistic after a night's drunk, and some for the castle servants, and a different set for the nobility.

The men's steams at Withywoods paled by comparison. There was a single chamber, not much larger than my bedchamber, with benches round the walls. The great brick oven that heated it was at one end of the room, and a brick-lined pool of water was in the center. It never pulsed with heat like the steams at Buckkeep, but a determined man could do a good job of cleansing himself there. All the folk at Withywoods, great and small, used the steams. This morning Lin the shepherd was in there with two of his grown sons.

I nodded at all three, in little mood for talk, but Lin immediately asked if I had authorized the burning of the brush pile in the night. And so I had to tell the tale of biting insects in my daughter's bedding and that I had wanted it out of the house and burned immediately.

He nodded gravely and allowed that he was a man who understood dealing swiftly with such pests, but I saw the looks his sons exchanged with each other. For a short time Lin was silent, and then he asked me if I'd given leave to anyone to camp in the sheep pastures. When I told him no, he shook his head again.

"Well, it may just have been random travelers, then, and not much to worry if you were the one that set the fire. This morning, I found the top railing on one fence taken down, and the tracks of at least three horses crossing the pasture. No real harm done, and nothing taken. Looks like they left the way they came. The flocks were fine, and I didn't even hear Daisy or the other dogs bark in the night. So perhaps they were just folk stopping for a time to rest."

"Did they make a camp there? In a snowy pasture?"

He shook his head.

"I'll walk out later and take a look."

He shrugged one shoulder. "Nothing to see. Just horse tracks. I already put the fence railing back up."

I nodded, and wondered. Simple travelers or those who had hunted my messenger? I doubted they were the hunters. Folk who had killed one messenger and condemned another to a horrible death were unlikely to simply pause in a pasture on the pursuit. I would still look at the tracks, but doubted I'd find anything more than what Lin had.

Chapter 20

THE MORNING AFTER

There is a time for an assassin to kill and disappear. There is a time for public killings, and there is a time to kill in secret. For the purposes of a lesson, a killing may be public and the body left for others to deal with. Sometimes, it is better to assassinate in private, and then display the body in a way that will shock, terrify, or admonish others. Most difficult of all, perhaps, is the assassination that must be completely concealed, not just the killing but the resulting body. The purpose of this is sometimes to create uncertainty, or to avoid blame, or to make it appear that the subject has fled or abandoned his duties.

Thus it becomes clear that simply training your assassin to kill efficiently is not enough. One must instill judgment, discipline, and self-effacement to create a useful tool.

SINGAL'S LESSONS IN MURDER,
TRANSLATED FROM THE CHALCEDEAN

I woke to gray light coming in the windows. I was on the couch where my mother had birthed me, wrapped in a blanket. On my father's regular chair near the fire, a blanket was neatly folded. I could tell that the fire had recently been fed. I lay still, thinking of all the ways my life had changed in one day. Shun had arrived. And the pale messenger. My father had seen me as useful, and even intelligent as I helped him bring her in. He'd trusted me to follow his instructions. And then Shun had distracted him with her silly complaints, and we'd lost our chance with the messenger. When we had concealed her death, I had been shocked. But I'd also felt that he valued me. Yet the moment Shun was frightened, he had left my side and forgotten me completely as he ran off to see to her hysterics.

I threw my blanket off me and onto the floor and glared at my father's empty chair as I sat up. Everyone wanted him to take care of someone else besides me. Take care of Shun and protect her; the pale girl wanted him to go off and look for a lost son. Was anyone telling him to pay attention to his own daughter because otherwise there was no one else in the world who would watch over her? No.

Except maybe Nettle. And she thought I was an idiot. Well, perhaps not an idiot and perhaps that was my own fault for never letting her share my thoughts, but it still didn't bode well for my future if I went to live with her. Or would Riddle go back to Buckkeep and tell her I wasn't as feebleminded as she thought? If Riddle went back to Buckkeep Castle. He seemed very intent on protecting Shun, too. And Shun seemed very eager to keep him by her side. I scowled at that thought. I was not sure why, but I was certain that Riddle was the property of my older sister. In that moment Shun became not only the outsider but the enemy.

And my absent father was little better.

Swiftly I constructed my resentment and believed in it. Silently seething with anger at all of them, I returned to my bedchamber. I was not pleased to find it full of folk scrubbing the walls and floors. The smell of vinegar was strong. All bedding had vanished from the servant's bed frame, and when I threaded my small way among the unfamiliar servants, I found that most of my clothing chest had been emptied as well. I was pleased at the idea that my things would be returned washed and fresh, and less pleased that so little was left for me to choose from. Nor did I like how the four newly hired women and the beefy man helping them with the heavier lifting paused in their cleaning tasks to stare at me. They were the intruders here, not I!

Yet stare they did, and not one offered to help me as I struggled with the heavy lid of the chest. I contented myself with grabbing whatever garments I could reach. I carried them off with me and went back to the relative privacy of my mother's room to change out of my nightrobe.

I changed hastily there, squatting behind the screens in the corner. The tunic was from summer and a bit too small for me, shorter than my mother would have allowed me to wear. The leggings bagged at the knee and bottom. I consulted the small pieces of looking glass set in a decorative lamp cover. My shorn hair stood up like the stubble in a harvested field. I looked more like a serving boy than our serving boys did. I took a deep breath and refused to think of Shun's fine clothing and hair combs and rings and scarves.

My new red nightrobe was on the floor. I picked it up and shook it out. I gathered it in my arms and smelled it. My mother's scent had faded but was still there. I folded it and hid it behind a stool. I myself would wash it out and scent it with one of her rose sachets. I went in search of my father.

I found him, Shun, and Riddle at breakfast in the dining room. I was surprised to see the table made up so formally. There were covered serving dishes and two pots of tea on the table. An empty place setting awaited me. I wondered if it would be like this every day now that Shun was living with us. They had almost finished eating. I came into the room quietly and slipped into the empty place.

Shun was talking, some nonsense about warding off ghosts with cups of green tea. I let her finish. Before my father could speak, I observed to him, "You had breakfast without me." It hurt me deeply and I didn't try to hide that. It was a small ritual we had shared since we had been left alone after my mother's death. Whatever else happened, he woke me in the morning and we had break-fast together.

He looked very draggled and weary, even though he had shaved and his shirt was clean. But I refused to feel sorry for him as he said, "It was a late night for all of us. I thought you would want the extra sleep."

"You should have wakened me to see if I wanted to join you."

"I probably should have," my father said quietly. He spoke in a voice that told me he wasn't pleased we were having this discussion in front of Riddle and Shun. Suddenly I regretted it.

"Children need more sleep than adults. Everyone knows that," Shun informed me helpfully. She picked up her teacup and ob-served me over the rim as she sipped from it. She had the eyes of an evil cat.

I looked at her levelly. "And everyone knows that ghosts are bound to the site of their deaths. Your Rono is wherever you left him. Ghosts don't follow people about."

If she had been a cat, she would have hissed at me. Her lips pulled back from her teeth in just the same way. But if she had been a cat, she would have known the noise in the walls was just another cat. I looked at her as I asked my father, "Is there any food left for me?"

He looked at me without speaking and then rang a small bell. A servant I didn't know hurried into the room. My father directed him to bring breakfast for me. I think Riddle was trying to be sooth-ing when he asked me, "Well, Bee, and what are your plans for the day?"

Shun narrowed her eyes when he spoke to me and I knew in-stantly what I wanted to do that day. Keep Riddle so busy he would have no time for Shun. I lifted my chin and smiled at him. "Since you are here, and my father has been so busy preparing for our guest and with the repairs to the house that he has little time for me, I wondered if you would show me how to ride a horse today?"

His eyes widened with genuine pleasure. "With your father's per-mission, I would be delighted!"

My father looked stunned. My heart sank. I should have known that asking Riddle to teach me would hurt his feelings. I had aimed for Shun and struck my father instead. Not that I had missed Shun. Her narrowed eyes made her look even more like a dunked cat. My father spoke. "I thought you said that you didn't want to learn to ride; that you didn't feel comfortable with the idea of sitting on another creature's back and telling it where to go."

I had said that, when I was much smaller, and it still made perfect sense to me. But I would not have said it in front of Shun. I felt the burn rise to my cheeks.

"Such a peculiar idea!" Shun exclaimed and laughed delightedly.

I stared at my father. How could he have said that aloud and in front of a relative stranger? Had he done it on purpose, because I'd hurt his feelings? I spoke stiffly. "I still feel it is unfair, simply because we are humans and can force animals to obey us, that we should do it. But if I am ever to visit my sister at Buckkeep Castle, it is a thing I must learn."

Riddle seemed oblivious of the currents sweeping past him as he smiled and said, "And a visit from you would please your sister more than anything, I think. Especially when she sees how well you speak."

"Did she used to stutter, then? Or lisp?" If Shun was trying to disguise her disdain for me, she was doing a poor job of it.

Riddle looked at her directly, his face solemn and his voice grave. "She spoke little. That was all."

"If Bee wishes you to teach her to ride, I'm sure I'm pleased," my father said. "There is a horse in the stables, not a pony, but a small horse. I chose her for Bee when she was five, when I thought I might persuade her to try riding, but she refused. She's a mare, a dapple-gray. With one white hoof."

I looked at him but he was hidden behind his eyes. He had chosen a horse for me, all those years ago, and when I had wriggled and squirmed when he tried to put me in the saddle, he had given up that plan with no rebuke for me. Why had he kept the mare? Because he had kept the hope. I had not meant to hurt him. "One white hoof, try him," I said quietly. "I am sorry that I did not try her, all those years ago. I'm ready now."

He nodded but did not smile. "I will be pleased to see you learn, Bee, regardless of who teaches you. But there will be no visits to Buckkeep Castle just yet. Very early this morning, I received word that your new tutor will soon begin his journey to join us here. It would be peculiar indeed if he left Buckkeep Castle and arrived here to find you gone to Buckkeep."

"My new tutor? What news is this? When was this decided?" I felt as if the room tilted around me.

"Years ago." My father spoke tersely now. "His name is FitzVigilant. This has been planned for some time. He will arrive within the next ten days." He suddenly looked as if something pained him. "And a room must be readied for him as well."

"FitzVigilant," Riddle said quietly. He did not shoot my father an odd look or raise his brows, but I heard an affirming note in his voice and knew that he was informing my father that he knew more than he had been told. "I had heard that Lord Vigilant thought his younger sons were old enough to come to court."

"Indeed, that is the case," my father confirmed. "Though I am told it was more his wife's decision than his. Indeed, I have heard that Lord Vigilant was surprised to hear of it."

Lady Shun's gaze was darting from one to the other. Did she guess that more was being conveyed than she was privileged to know? In that moment I scarcely cared. I was caught in a daze.

The memories from my earliest babyhood, like the memories I have from within my mother, are floating memories. They exist, but they are not anchored to my daily life. Only when a scent or a sound or a taste wakens one does it cascade to the front of my mind. In this case it was a name.

FitzVigilant.

The name had rung in my ears like a bell, and suddenly my awareness was flooded with a memory. It came with a scent of my mother's milk and a fire of applewood and cedar logs and for a long moment I was an infant in a cradle, hearing that name spoken in a youth's sullen voice. It is one thing to have a vague memory from one's childhood. It is quite another for the aware mind to put that memory into context and offer it back. He had crept into my cradle room when I was a baby. My father had stopped him from touching me. My father had spoken of poisons. And threatened to kill him if he came near me again.

And now he was to be my tutor?

My mind boiled with questions. The new servant whisked back into the room and set before me a bowl of porridge, two boiled eggs, and a small dish of stewed apples. A touch of cinnamon on the apples fragranced the room. Had Tavia done this especially for me, or was it for everyone? I lifted my gaze. They were all looking at me. I was in a quandary. Had my father forgotten the name of the boy who had come to my cradle that night? Did he think he had changed? Why would he be my tutor? I took a spoonful of the apples and thought before I asked, "And you think FitzVigilant will teach me well?"

Shun had been sipping her tea. She clattered her cup onto the saucer. She looked at Riddle as she shook her head in consternation. In a conspiratorial voice, as if she did not intend my father and me to overhear, she opined, "Never have I heard a child question her father's decisions! Had I objected to even one of my grandmother's plans for me, I am sure she would have slapped me and dismissed me to my room."

It was neatly done. I could not defend myself without appearing more spoiled and petulant than she had already painted me. I drank some milk, looking at my father over the rim of my cup. He was angry. His face had not changed at all and perhaps, I thought, only I could tell that he had been provoked. By Shun or by me, I wondered. Even his voice was normal as he said, "My relationship with Bee is different, then, from what you had with your grandparents. I have always encouraged her to think, and to discuss with me our plans for her." He took a sip of his own tea and added, "I cannot imagine slapping her. Ever."

His gaze briefly kissed mine, and tears stung my eyes. I had been so jealous, so sure that he was favoring Shun. But that swift look offered me something that went beyond even being my father. He was my ally. When he set down the cup, he nodded to me pleasantly and added, "For a number of years, Lord Chade has especially prepared FitzVigilant to be your tutor, Bee." He tipped me a wink that no one else saw. "Try him."

"I shall," I promised. I owed my father that. I focused and summoned a smile to my face. "It will be so exciting to learn new things."

"I am very pleased to hear you say that," he replied, and I almost felt the warmth of the thoughts he sent me.

Shun spoke over my words. "The messenger announcing his coming arrived last night? From Lord Chade? But I heard nothing, and I assure you I was not asleep. I found not the least bit of rest last night. Did the messenger say anything of me? Was there word for me from him?"

"The message came quietly, and was only about the tutor," my father said. His words said one thing while his tone pointed out that it was not her business. For myself, I understood that Lord Chade had Skilled the information to him. Truly, my father had had a very busy night and had every excuse to look haggard. I kept the smile on my face from becoming smug as I realized that I obviously knew something that Shun did not, which was that my father and Lord Chade shared the Skill-magic.

That satisfied me, and I resolved that for now I would ask no more questions. I put my attention on my food and listened to Riddle and my father speak, and Shun interrupt with questions that related only to herself. The workmen would return by noon and resume the renovations of Withywoods Manor. Shun hoped they would not begin work too early; she disliked being wakened by noise. My father had informed Revel that he must prepare chambers for Scribe FitzVigilant. Shun wondered which chambers he would be given. The subject of the imaginary bedbugs came up, and Shun expressed horror and demanded that she be given entirely new bedding. My father assured her that new bedding would be part of the renovation of the Yellow Suite. She asked if the Yellow Suite must remain yellow, as she much preferred mauve or lavender.

That made me lift my eyes. I watched my father and Riddle exchange looks of consternation. My father's brow wrinkled. "But the Yellow Suite has always been the Yellow Suite," he said, as if that explained everything.

"There is a Purple Suite, at the other end of that wing, if I recall correctly," Riddle offered.

"You would be quite a distance from the rest of the household, but if you wish it—" my father began.

I tried not to smile. I ate the last of the cooling porridge as Shun objected, "But I do like the view from those windows. Cannot you simply paint the walls of my chambers and change the hangings to a more restful color? Just because it has always been the Yellow Suite does not mean it must remain so."

"But . . . it's the Yellow Suite . . ."

My father remained baffled by Shun's failure to understand this while she hammered at him to make him see that yellow might be painted mauve. While they were distracted, I slipped away from the table. My father and Riddle were, I think, peripherally aware that I had vanished. But neither of them stopped me.

My bedchamber was bare enough that I could have painted it any color and not worried about furniture or tapestries or rugs. Something meant to kill bed vermin smoldered on the hearth, giving off a thick smoke. The wooden skeletons of the beds remained. My clothing chests had been removed to the corridor. I retreated there and rummaged again for warmer clothing before I ventured outside.

The rain had paused and a wind, warm for this time of year, was moving over the land. I went first to where my father and I had made our bone fire the night before. It had burned hot: There was only white ash in the center of a ring of partially burned sticks and branches. I took up one of the sticks and stirred the white ash. Beneath it, black coals opened red spark eyes at me as I woke them. I saw no bits of bones, not even the round of a skull I had expected to find. I wondered if my father had been here before me, at the very edge of dawn. I kicked some of the ends of the branches back into the center and waited. A thin tendril of smoke began to rise and eventually the fire woke to flames again. I stood, watching it burn, recalling all that our peculiar visitor had said, and wondering if my father would act on it, or forget it now that she was gone. An unexpected son had been foretold. And someone had once believed that my father fulfilled that foretelling. Clearly, I still did not know his full tale. I wondered if I could safely be bolder about stealing his papers and reading them while he was enslaved to the repairs on Withywoods. I decided I would have to.

I walked past the sheep pens on the way back to the house. On a lichened rock in the middle of the close-cropped pasture a lean black kitten was hunched, looking down at the deeper grass. He had two white paws that I could see, and a crook in his tail. He was hunting. I stopped and stood silently. I watched his muscles tighten and tighten and then, like an arrow released from the bow, he dived down onto something in the grass. He hit it hard with both his front paws and then shot his head in to kill it with a swift bite. He looked up at me and I suddenly knew he had been aware of my scrutiny the whole time. The dark-gray mouse was limp in his jaws.

"I know where there are plenty of mice, mice fat on cheese and sausages," I called to him. He looked at me silently as if considering my words, and then turned and trotted purposefully away with his prey. He had grown up fast, I thought to myself.

Cats do. Once a cat can hunt, he can get all he needs. Then his life is his own.

The thought came so clearly to my mind that I almost believed it was my own.

"I have need of a hunter such as you!" I called after him. He did not pause as he trotted away.

I watched him go and thought that my needs meant little to anyone but me. What I needed, I would have to obtain for myself.

Chapter 21

SEARCH FOR THE SON

The first task a lady must undertake in her new home is the estab-
lishment of respect for herself. This may be more difficult than one
might expect, especially if one is moving into her new residence
after wedding, and one's husband's mother is still the mistress of the
household. But, startling as it might seem, it can be even more diffi-
cult for the lady who takes charge of her bachelor husband's resi-
dence after wedding. In a case where servants have become
accustomed to there being only a master of the house, the new lady
may find it difficult to wrest control or even gain respect from the
upper echelon of servants. Stewards and cooks are notoriously hard
to deal with in this regard. The new mistress of the house will rap-
idly tire of hearing, "But this is how it has always been done here."
Even worse is to be told by a servant, "This is how the master prefers
it be done." If it is not addressed immediately, the new lady of the

house will find herself delegated to the same status as a visiting minstrel.

Often the best course is simply to dismiss the heads of staff and begin afresh with servants of the lady's choosing. But in cases where the master is attached to older servants, the lady must be direct and firm in taking immediate control. It is a mistake simply to accede to what is first offered to her. Immediately challenge the menus, the flower arrangements, the attire of the staff—in other words, establish control of your domestic domain from the moment you step in the door.

LADY CELESTIA'S GUIDE TO MANNERS

I found Revel already busy with the workmen. He was outside the door of the rooms that were to be Shun's, berating them for the mud they had tracked in. I waited until he had finished, and then mentioned to him that perhaps Lady Shun would want a different color of room. Could the Yellow Suite be painted to accommodate her?

He looked at me as if I were daft. "But then the rainbow would be out of order."

"I beg your pardon?"

"By Lady Patience's decree, years ago, the seven suites were painted to reflect the order of colors in the rainbow. Thus it begins with red, then orange. Yellow is followed by green, then blue, and . . ."

"And purple. Is the Purple Suite in good repair?"

The crease between his eyes deepened. "As good a repair as I've been able to keep it in, given the budget you've allotted me." He looked down on me, struggling to hide his disapproval over how little consideration I'd given to the estate over the years.

I made a hasty decision. "Send for Lady Shun. Let her select the room with the color that best suits her. And prepare the Green Suite as well. No. Wait. You are right, Revel. Bring me a list of what must be done for each of the suites in the main house in order to meet your approval. Let us begin, as we should have years ago, to make them right, one after another. Oh, and there will be another guest coming to stay with us, arriving in ten days or less. FitzVigilant is to be tutor to Lady Bee. And perhaps to some of the other estate children."

That last came to me in a flash. King Shrewd had always insisted that every child at Buckkeep be afforded at least a chance for letters and numbers. Not all parents chose to take advantage of that, and many a child begged his way out of it, but every youngster at Buckkeep Castle was offered a chance to learn. It was time I stepped up to that legacy as well.

Revel breathed in deep through his nose. For a man with such a merry name, he looked very dour as he said, "Then the schoolroom must also be put to rights, sir? And the adjoining chambers for the scribe?"

Schoolroom. I recalled abruptly that Withywoods had one. My early education had happened at one of the lesser hearths in the Great Hall at Buckkeep. And Molly's boys had come to me with a good foundation in reading and reckoning from Burrich, and had mainly been educated by me and by the other folk at Withywoods. They'd learned from the arborist, the orchard man, the shepherd . . . I'd never demanded they master another language, and their knowledge of Six Duchies history and geography had mostly been passed to them during long conversations in the evenings or minstrel songs at holidays. Had I been lax in educating Burrich's sons? Neither Molly nor either of the boys had ever asked that I supply more than that. Guilt squeezed me.

"Sir?" Revel's query jolted me back to the present. I stared at him, wondering what we had been discussing.

At my questioning look, he repeated, "The schoolroom, Holder Badgerlock. It was Lady Patience's doing. Many years ago, when she still hoped that she would have babes of her own that would grow up here. There is a schoolroom. A room especially for teaching children." He spoke the last two words as if I might not be familiar with such a concept.

Of course. And, "Of course, then, Revel. Freshen the schoolroom and the scribe's chambers, and make a list for me of any more serious repairs they might need. Oh. And a list of the children, please, who might wish to learn their letters and reckoning."

Revel's eyes held a martyr's determination to excel as he asked, "And is there anything else, sir?"

I conceded. "That's as much as I can think of right now. If anything more occurs to you, please bring it to my attention."

"As it should be, sir," he agreed, and I could almost hear his thought: *As it should have been done all along.*

That evening, when the workmen were gone and Bee once more asleep in Molly's sewing room, I Skilled to my elder daughter. *I was getting ready for bed,* Nettle greeted my questing touch.

I didn't realize it was so late, I apologized. *I wished to apprise you of my latest round of renovations to Withywoods. I deem them necessary, as does Revel, but I fear it will eat into the reserves I had set aside from the income.*

I felt her sigh. *Please stop the formalities. You are not truly my Holder reporting to me. We both know that, by every right, Withywoods should have come to you. Your insistence that it is mine and you must justify every action you take there wears on me.*

But it is your inheri—

And it hurts my feelings. Do you truly think I would object to what you might do there to benefit Bee? Or yourself? I know you do not believe me so selfish. So stop, please. Do what must be done to keep it standing and in good repair, and spend the income from the lands as it must be spent. Or as you'd like to spend it. A pause. *You know that FitzVigilant will soon be on his way to you?*

I've been so informed, yes. I tried to conceal from her the reservations I felt about the arrangements.

Well, I do not think he is truly fit for travel yet. I've urged Chade to leave him in hiding for a time. When he arrives, you should have a healer see to him. He's a stiff-necked lad, and will insist he is quite all right, thank you very much. Insist on it. He took a bad beating, a very bad beating. I think Chade will finally send him away in the hope it will keep him safe. He should have been sent to you years ago. As I've told Chade re-

peatedly. He should have put the boy's best interests before his inclination to keep him near.

I'll see that he's well cared for. I was going to put him in the Green Suite, but then Revel informed me that Patience had created a school-room in the east wing and that there are living chambers for the school-master adjacent to them.

Is there? Oh, yes, I recall it now. It's a rambling old place, isn't it? But that should suit Lant well. He's private. And seems to be even more so since the beating.

Physical abuse tends to bring that out in a person, I thought. It was nothing that I needed to share with Nettle. But I well recalled what Regal's torture had done to me, and how withdrawn the Fool had been after the Pale Woman's savage attentions. We live in our bod-ies. An assault on that outside fortress of the mind leaves scars that may not show, but never heal. I would give him his privacy. And if he chose to talk, his words would remain safe with me.

Are you still awake? Nettle sounded annoyed that I might disturb her rest with my Skilling and then nod off myself.

Yes. Just mulling over the arrangements I'll make for FitzVigilant.

Treat him gently.

You're fond of him, aren't you? Again, I had the impression that he was more important than Chade had informed me.

I am. Treat him well and make him welcome. And whatever it was, Nettle was not divulging it to me, either. *I'm going to sleep now,* she informed me. *Not all of us are night wolves, Tom. Some of us prefer to sleep.*

Good night, then, my dear.

Good night.

And she was gone, fading from my awareness like perfume blown from a room by an errant breeze.

She was not the only daughter I had who was adept at avoiding me. For the next few days Bee managed always to be leaving the room as I entered it. I saw her at meals but she had renewed her si-lent ways, while Shun chattered like a hen that had just laid an egg and wished the whole chicken yard to know of it. She had, after much dithering, chosen the Purple Suite, which she called the Lavender Chambers, to be her domain. But if I had thought that was going to win me a reprieve from her demands and complaints, I was soon divested of such an idea. She found the pattern on the draperies "too busy" and thought the bed hangings faded. The looking glass was "spotty, and far too small to be of any real use." Candelabra would not do: She wanted lamps for her dressing table. I dared not refer her directly to Revel, for I feared he would not only give way to every one of her requests, but amplify them. Riddle's solemn face and merrily glinting eyes convinced me that he had well earned my compromise, which was to send him off, with Shun and a letter of credit, to the big trading market at Lakesend, a journey that would require them to overnight at the inn there and give me at least one evening of peace. Once Revel heard of their errand, he gave me a list of needed items of such magnitude that I ordered up a wagon and team to accompany them. Tavia was next, complaining of battered pans, and knives whetted away to nothing. Her list was added, and then I thought of a few items of my own that needed replacing. They departed eventually with two wagons and teams. Riddle was not smiling as they rode off. I was. I judged that the extra lists had granted me at least one more day and possibly two before they would return.

In addition to Shun's and Revel's errands, I gave Riddle one of my own. On the way he was to listen for any news of strangers seeking to find a pale girl such as the one who had visited us. I told him that I was very curious as to why she had fled so abruptly. I wanted to know what she had feared, and if those persecuting her should, in their turn, be hunted down by the King's Guard. I know Riddle suspected there was far more to the tale than he had been told, and that, I decided, would add spurs to his quest for news. And Shun would be out from under my roof for at least a hand of days. The level of relief I felt was startling.

I would not force Bee to be near me. Perhaps after what she had seen that night, she needed a distance. But quietly, and from a good distance, I informed myself of where she went and what she did. She spent a good amount of time in her hiding place, and I soon discovered the sort of reading she was doing. I was appalled, as much by my carelessness as by what she had probably learned of me. Well, that was my own fault, and I knew how to deal with it. Just as Chade had when he had discovered that I had not limited my reading to what he was putting in front of me. Over the next five days I threw myself into my work. Revel could not do it all. He was a good manager of tasks, a man who could locate the right people, hire them, and tell them what he wanted done. But he was not the best man to see that a job was being done properly. Burrich had taught me the fine art of strolling past idlers and motivating them with a single look, and I did not hesitate to employ it. I could not claim a fine knowledge of brick-and-mortar work, nor carpentry, but I could spot workers who were only pretending to labor. It was also fascinating to watch a master such as Ant taking her time on brickwork to do the best job and to let her make her own pace.

In addition to all the repairs and tidying going on, the regular work of the estate did not falter. I sensed that Bee was avoiding me, but could not blame her. She had much to think about, as did I. And perhaps I was avoiding her as well, hoping that I had not put too much on her small shoulders. If I called her to me and we sat down to discuss it, would it gain weight and importance in her mind? Could I be honest in my answers to the questions she would ask? For those days I pushed thoughts of the messenger's errand out of my mind, telling myself that if the Fool's unexpected son had been hidden for so many years, a few more days could not matter. I had visited the sheep pasture and looked at the softening horse tracks in the snow there. Lin was right. Three horses had come and gone the same night that I'd burned the messenger's body. I found the prints of one dismounted man, enough to let me know that someone had at least stretched his legs. There was no sign of a camp-fire or prolonged use of the area. I stood where the tracks were and looked toward Withywoods. There was little they could see of the house from here; the garden walls and shade trees screened it from view. They would have been able to see my bone fire. They might have stood and watched me and Bee as we burned a bundle of bed-ding. More than that, they would not have seen. That was all the

ground could tell me, and I set it out of my mind as useless information. Travelers, or poachers, or passing thieves, perhaps.

Or had they been the messenger's pursuers? I weighed what she
had told me of them, and decided not. Either they would be vicious enough to pursue her to my door, or they would have needed
to be confident of her death. I could not imagine them standing at
a distance, watching the place where she might have taken refuge,
and then moving on. No. Coincidence. Nothing more. I suspected
they might still be trying to find her. If they were about, Riddle
would hear of them. He was good at that sort of listening.

But I would keep my guard up in case they were still tracking her.
And I promised myself that I would undertake the search for this
unexpected son as soon as I could. For now I would secure my
home and my unexpected ward before I took on any other tasks.
Better to make all clean and strong at home before I had to leave. I
dreaded a trip to the Mountains in winter, but possibly I'd have to
undertake one. I doubted Jofron would respond to any message
from me. If that was where the trail led, I'd have to go there personally.

At night, before I slept, the strange mission would come into my
mind. How could I leave Bee at home to undertake such a quest? I
could not. Could I take her with me? Into danger? I could not. Send
her to Nettle? Would the tutor be any sort of a bodyguard for her,
as Chade had once suggested? How could Lant be? The beating he
had taken was a poor recommendation for his ability to protect
himself, let alone my child.

Shun as bodyguard for Bee was a bad jest. She disliked my daughter and was afraid of noises in the night. Not the sort of protector
I would choose for Bee. I'd have to find someone I could trust.
Until then, I could not go off on the Fool's errand. Yet I could not
ignore it. Anxiety vied with anger: I feared that my old friend was
in grave danger, might indeed be dead already. And I was furious
that he had sent me such a cryptic message. I knew that his presen-
timents for the future were vague now, but surely he could have
told me something of his own situation! Perhaps if his messenger
had lived longer, she would have been clearer. Some nights, I feared

I had been hasty in granting her a merciful death. Useless to think of that now, I scolded myself. Then I would try to find a more comfortable position in my bed, close my eyes, and berate myself for what I had done to my daughters. Mostly I chided myself, over and over, for letting Chade send me his problems. But how could I have said no to him?

I steeled myself to the necessity of beginning my task at least. I will admit it was a bit petty of me to wait until the middle of the night was well past before Skilling to Chade. If I had hoped to wake him, I had wasted my effort. He was immediately open to me, and even expressed pleasure at the contact. It made me realize that I was not often the one to reach out. It made it harder to keep my secrets close.

I've an odd favor to ask you. And even odder, I must refuse, for now, to tell you why.

Oh, well, this is off to an intriguing start. Ask away, then. But don't blame me if I manage to divine your intent before you share it with me. I could feel him settling back in the chair in his den, stretching his legs out to the fire.

He seemed to relish the possibility that he might outfox me and divine my goal. So. Let it become a game for him. He'd dig like a badger for my secret and perhaps uncover others in the process.

I'll expect you to try. But for now, please, don't press me for it. Here is what I need to know. I'm looking for a son born to one of these three women. The babe was possibly illegitimate. I had considered well how to ask about it. Many a woman wed in haste to cover a child's true fatherhood.

Three women, eh. Well, who are they?

One you probably know, the second possibly, and the third it's unlikely you've ever heard of.

Oh, this gets better by the moment. Well, no promises, but ask away.

You will recall Huntswoman Laurel who aided us in Dutiful's difficulty with the Piebalds. Afterward, she was very helpful in our dealings with Old Blood.

There was a bit of a silence. Did he block me from something? Then he replied heartily, *Of course I remember Laurel!*

Do you know if she married? Had children?

Again a tiny gap, as if he hesitated. *I can certainly find out. The next one?*

Garetha. She was a gardener girl when I was growing up at Buckkeep. And was still employed in the gardens when I was living at Buckkeep as Lord Golden's man.

Never heard that name, but it will be easy enough to find someone who has, and will know what's become of her. And the last one?

He was like a squirrel gathering nuts, so eager for the next one that he was stuffing the facts into his mind without trying to digest them until he had every bit of information from me. He'd soon pick out the common thread, I knew. Well, it would be all the sweeter for him if he had to work for it. I hesitated over the third woman. Any offspring she had borne to the Fool would be a man grown by now. But I would consider all possibilities.

Jofron. She lived in the Mountain Kingdom, and helped care for me when I was so badly injured. She's a woodworker, a maker of fine cabinets and toys. I know she has a son, for I met her grandson, but I need to know who her son's father was, and when he was born. I'd like a physical description of him.

I recall Jofron. Chade did not conceal that he was startled by my request. *Well, that's a few years back and quite a distance from here, but it's not impossible to make queries. I have people in Jhaampe.*

I'm sure you do. You have people everywhere, including here at Withywoods, I half-accused and half-complimented him.

That might be so. And well you know how useful a well-spread net of quick eyes and sharp ears can be. So. Jofron, Garetha, and Huntswoman Laurel. And you are looking for a child. Boy or girl?

A boy. But one who might be well past childhood by now. In the case of Jofron her son is at least thirty-six years old. I think. Could I be sure that the Fool had not visited her since then? Could I be sure of anything? *Oh, any child, of any age, that any of them have borne. If you can get me that information, I will sort it myself and be in your debt.*

You certainly will be, he promised me, and severed our Skill-connection before I could tell or ask him anything more.

I lingered in the Skill-stream, allowing myself to feel its allure.

Youngsters training in the Skill are sternly warned against its addictive attraction. It's a difficult sensation to describe. I felt complete in the Skill. Not lonely. Even in the midst of the deepest possible love, one feels apart from one's partner—separated by skin even as we are joined in the act that makes two one. Only in the Skill does that sense of separation fade. Only in the Skill have I felt that sense of oneness with the whole world. Since Molly had died, I had felt more alone than I ever had. And so I tempted myself, letting that completeness wash against me, considering just letting go and becoming one with the greater whole. Not a part joining to other parts; no. In the Skill, all boundaries dissolve, all sense of self as an individual fades.

On the surface of the Skill, one can float and hear threads of the lives of others. Many folk have a moderate amount of Skill-talent, not enough for them to employ it actively, but enough that they unwittingly reach out to the world. I heard a mother thinking of her son, gone to sea and unheard from for six months. She hoped he was well and her heart reached after him in a seeking she was not aware she did. A young man was facing his wedding day, but was thinking of a girl he had known when he was barely a man. He'd thought she might be the love of his life but they had parted and now he had another woman he cherished. Tomorrow they would wed. But even as he contemplated the joy the next day might bring, his thoughts reached out to that first lost love. I floated in the stream, privy to the longing of dozens who reached after love. There were many sending out questing thought. Some dreamed of love and wholeness, but there were others, dreaming of vengeance and wishing ill on others as they dwelt on wrongdoings and slights.

No. I wanted nothing of that. I sank myself deeper into the stronger current where all such outreaching mingled into a vast joining. Sometimes I thought it the birthplace of dreams and intuitions. At other times I thought of it as a repository of all the folk who had gone before us, and perhaps even those to come after. It was a place where sorrows and joys were equal, where life and death were just the stitches on each side of a quilt. It was nepenthe.

I drifted there, not quite allowing it to tatter me away into threads.

I could not allow myself to let go, but I could think about letting go and how wonderful it would feel. There would be no loss, no tasks to do, no loneliness, no pain. Those I left behind would pay those tolls but I would be beyond them and beyond feeling remorse or regret for them. I thought of Molly, felt that pain, and then, chiding myself as I did so, let a thread of it unravel into the Skill. It drew it out of me like a good poultice sucks foulness from a wound. The pressure lessened and—

Fitz.

I could ignore that.

Dream Wolf!

That I could not ignore. *Nettle,* I responded. I felt ashamed to be caught in such a self-indulgent action. *I was Skilling to Chade.*

You were not! You were leaking yourself away. I might expect that of a first-year Skill-student. Not you. What is the matter with you?

She had summoned me with my daughter's name for me, but this was not Nettle the Skill-dreamer but Nettle the Skillmistress. And she was angry with me.

The matter with me is that I ache for your mother. I tried to project that as a reason rather than an excuse for bad behavior. I had drifted too far, indulged too much. Pulled up short, I suddenly recognized how close I had been to letting go. And how inexcusable that would have been. I'd have been abandoning Bee, condemning any who still cared for me to caretake a living corpse as I foundered in drool, waste, and idiocy until my body died.

Me, Nettle insisted. She'd followed my thoughts unerringly. *That task would have fallen on me. Well, I wouldn't do it, nor allow anyone else to do it for you. I would have come to Withywoods, closed the estate, and taken Bee with me. I'd leave you drooling in a corner. Don't ever think you can do that to my sister and me!*

I wouldn't, Nettle. I wouldn't! I was just . . . My thought faltered away from me.

Standing on a box with a noose around your neck? Whetting a blade on your throat? Brewing up a nice thick cup of carryme tea?

I don't want to kill myself, Nettle. I don't. I haven't even thought about it. I just sometimes get so lonely . . . Sometimes, I just need it to stop hurting.

Well, it doesn't. Her reply was savagely angry. *It doesn't stop hurting. So live with it, because you are not the only one feeling that pain. And the last thing that Bee needs is to have it doubled.*

I wouldn't do that! I was starting to be angry at her. How could she think that of me?

It's a bad example to set for the apprentices. And it's not as if you are the only one who has ever been tempted to escape by that route.

That stunned me. Cold rippled down my spine. *You?*

She did something. I wasn't sure what, but suddenly I was slammed back into my own body. I was sitting in my chair in front of a dying fire. I sat up with a start, and then leaned back, my head spinning and my heart pounding, just as if she had flung me to the ground. I had the grace to be ashamed of myself. She was right. I had been teetering on the edge, looking over, daring myself to take the plunge. If I had weakened for one moment, it would have been irrevocable. And Bee would have taken the brunt of it.

I shut my eyes and lowered my face into my hands.

And another thing!

Sweet Eda, she had grown powerful. Nettle barged into my mind as strongly as if she slammed the door open and stood before my chair. She gave me no time to respond.

You need to pay more attention to Bee. Riddle says she is much alone, running about with little supervision, no chores or expectations, and that she looks neglected. Her clothing, her hair . . . He says that you seem to pay attention to her mind, but the rest of her is . . . Well. She can't be allowed to run about like a stray cat. You need to take her in hand. Would you have her grow up both useless and ignorant? Unkempt and untaught? She needs to be occupied, both her mind and her hands! He says that we have badly misjudged how intelligent she is, and that as a result she has not been educated as she should have been, from the time she was small. Bee is jealous of Shun and the attention she demands. Don't give her cause for that. You've only the one child there, Fitz. Pay attention to her.

I will, I promised, but she was gone. And I was left sitting in my chair, my head aching from the Skill as it had not in many a year. My uncle Verity had once said of my father that being Skilled by him was like being trampled by a horse. He was strong with it; he charged into his brother's mind, dumped his information, and left. I now thought I understood what he had meant. My candles had burned down to stubs before I felt completely like myself. Nettle had planted a foreign thought in my mind. Bee was jealous? I spent that time pondering why on earth Bee would feel jealous of Shun. When I thought I had the answer, I resolved to call in Revel early the next day and remedy all.

Chapter 22

PERSEVERANCE

Safely arrived at Withywoods with my charge. This Lady Shun is perhaps the most awkward task Lord Chade has ever assigned to me. Daily I am grateful that you are nothing like her. Bee is, as you warned me, a strange little girl. I do not see any signs that your father neglects her. In fact, they seem remarkably close and (blotted area). I will watch, as I have promised you, and answer true what I think is (obscured by blotch). I could write so much more to you, my dear, but there is small space for this pigeon to carry my words. And in truth, you would already know much of what I would say.

DISCARDED PIGEON MESSAGE SCROLL

Shun's constant whining to have things changed to suit her kept both my father and Riddle busy for those days. My promised lessons in riding did not materialize. By the time I had returned from my walk that morning, Riddle had driven Lady Shun to town in the two-wheeled cart so that she might see what sorts of fabric were available in the market and buy new blankets. It was small comfort to me that the cart jolted and bumped on the icy ruts in the road, and that I knew she would be disappointed in what she found. She had succeeded in snatching Riddle away and having him to herself. I found I was jealous of that, not on my own behalf, but for my sister. I knew that in some way Riddle belonged to Nettle, and I did not like to see Shun making free with his time. If anyone recalled that I had been promised riding lessons, no one mentioned it. And when Riddle and Shun returned, they were dispatched almost immediately on a much grander journey to buy so many things that my father sent two wagons with them. No one thought to ask me if I might like to go along or if there was anything I might want bought at a market town.

The following days had been filled with noise and disorder. A new wave of workmen had arrived at Withywoods. Heavy wagons drawn by immense horses came and went in the drive. Men unloaded timber and stone and carried them through the house. Rot had been discovered in a wall and what had begun as a simple repair would be anything but. Hammering and sawing and the tramping of workers and their shouted conversations to one another seemed to fill every corner of my home. I had promised my father that I would do my best to stay out of their way, and I had. I continued to sleep in my mother's sitting room. My clothing chests were moved there and refilled with my laundered clothing. There seemed far less of it than there had been. Revel must have decided to burn some of it.

I had also undertaken, on my own, to visit the stables. It was not an area I knew well. My small size had always meant that I had a proportionately greater dread of large animals. Even the shepherd's dogs seemed large to me, and many of the horses I could have walked under without even dipping my head. Nonetheless, I not only made my way there, but located the mare that my father had so long ago chosen for me. She was, as my father had told me, a dapple-gray with one white hoof. I found a stool and dragged it to her stall, and climbed up and sat on her manger to look at her.

There was no shyness in her; she came immediately to snuffle at my shoe, and then to lip at the edge of my tunic. I put out a hand to her, and she began to lick my palm. I sat still and allowed it, for it kept her head still and let me examine her face more thoroughly.

But, "Here, miss, you oughtn't to let her do that. She's just after the salt on your skin, you know. And it may teach her to bite."

"No, it won't," I asserted, even though I had no idea if it was true. The boy looking up at me was only a few years older than myself, I suspected, even if he was head and shoulders taller than I was. I rather enjoyed looking down on him. There were bits of straw in his black hair, and the coarse fabric of his shirt had been softened by many washings. His nose and cheeks were red from enduring the bite of wind and rain, and the hands that rested on the stall's edge were work-roughened. He had a straight, strong nose, and his teeth looked too big for his mouth. His dark eyes had narrowed at my defiance.

I drew my hand back from the mare's tongue. "She's my horse," I said, trying to justify myself and then hated how the words sounded. The boy's face grew bleaker.

"Yah. I guessed as much. You're Lady Bee, then."

It was my turn to narrow my eyes. "I'm Bee," I said. "That's all."

He looked at me guardedly for a moment. "I'm Per. I'm Dapple's groom and exercise boy."

"Dapple," I said. I hadn't even known the name of my own horse. Why did I feel ashamed?

"Yah. Stupid name, isn't it?"

I nodded back at him. "It could be the name of any dappled horse. Who named her so badly?"

He shrugged. "No one named her." He scratched his head, and a bit of the straw fell to his shoulder. He didn't even notice it. "She came here with no name, and we just called her the dapple, and then it started being Dapple."

That was probably my fault. I suspected my father had expected me to come here and get to know her and give her a name. I hadn't. I'd been too afraid of how big horses were. I'd feared to imagine what one might do if he didn't want me on his back.

"Per's an odd name, too."

He gave me a sideways glance. "Perseverance, miss. It's a bit too long to shout at me, so I'm Per." He looked at me and suddenly confided, "But someday I'm going to be Tallestman. My grandfather was called Tallman, and when my father grew taller than he was, all the hands started calling him Tallerman. And that's how he's known today." He pulled himself up straight. "I'm a bit short now, but I think I'm going to grow, and when I top my da, I'm going to be Tallestman. Not Perseverance." He shut his mouth firmly and thought about it for a minute. His disclosure was like a bridge he was waiting for me to cross. It was my turn to say something.

"How long have you taken care of her?"

"Two years now."

I looked away from him to the mare. "What name would you give her?" I knew something. He had named her.

"I'd call her Priss. Because she's so fussy about some things. Hates to have her hooves dirty. And her saddle has to be just so, the pad all smooth, not a rumple anywhere. She's prissy about things like that."

"Priss," I said, and the gray ears flicked forward. She knew it meant her. "It's a good name. Much better than Dapple."

"It is," he agreed easily. He scratched his head again and then frowned and finger-combed his hair, pulling straw from it. "You want me to ready her for you?"

I don't know how to ride a horse. I'm afraid of horses. I don't even know how to get on a horse. "Yes, please," I said, with no idea why I said it.

I sat on the edge of her stall and watched as he worked. He moved quickly but methodically, and I thought that Priss knew everything he would do before he did it. When he set the saddle on her back, it wafted her scent to me. Horse, and the oiled leather, and old sweat. I set my muscles against the nervous shiver that ran down my back. I could do this. She was gentle. Look how she stood so still for the saddle and how she took the bit and bridle with no fuss.

I clambered down from the top of the stall wall as he opened the door to lead her out. I looked up at her. So tall.

"There's a mounting block near the front of the stable. Here. Walk beside me, not behind her."

"Does she kick?" I asked with rising dread.

"She'll be happier if she can see you," he said, and I decided that might mean yes.

Climbing up the mounting block was not easy for me, and even when I stood on it, her back seemed high. I looked up at the sky. "Looks like it's going to rain."

"Nah. Not until evening." His gaze met mine. "Want a boost?"

I managed a stiff nod.

He came up on the mounting block beside me. "I'll lift you, and you get a leg over," he directed me. He hesitated a moment, then put his hands on my waist. He lifted me, and I felt almost anger that it seemed so easy for him to do. But I swung my leg over the mare and he set me down on her. I caught my breath as she shifted under me. She turned her head to look back at me curiously.

"She's used to me," Per excused her. "You'd be a lot lighter. She probably wonders if anyone's really in the saddle."

I bit my lip and said nothing. "Can you reach the stirrups?" he asked. There was no malice in his voice. No mockery of my size. I felt with my foot. He took my ankle and guided my foot toward the stirrup. "Too long," he said. "Let me fix that. Pull your foot up."

I did, staring between the horse's ears while he adjusted something, first on one stirrup and then on the other. "Try now," he told me, and when I could feel the stirrup under the arch of my foot, I suddenly felt safer.

He cleared his throat. "Pick up the reins," he instructed me.

I did, suddenly feeling that I was alone and far away from all safe things. She had me now, and if Priss wanted to race off with me, throw me to the earth and trample me, she could. Then Per spoke again. "I'm going to lead her," he said. "You hold the reins but don't try to guide her. Just sit in the saddle and feel how it moves. Straighten your back, though. Got to sit straight on a horse."

And that was all we did that first day. I sat on Priss and Per led her. He didn't say much. "Back straight." "Thumbs up on the reins." "Let her feel you're there." It wasn't a short time and it wasn't a long time. I remember the moment when I finally relaxed and let out the bit of air I'd been holding in the bottom of my lungs. "That's it," he said, and that was all.

He didn't help me get off her. He just led her back to the mounting block and waited. After I was off, he said, "Tomorrow will go better if you wear boots."

"Yes," I said. Not thank you. Because it didn't feel as if it was something he had done for me. It was something all three of us had done together. "Tomorrow," I added, and I went small and quiet from the stables.

To consider it, I went to my secret place. I wanted to be alone and think, and to check on my most prized possession. I no longer entered through my father's study, but came and went by the hidden door in the pantry. I still dreaded rats but at least all the hammering and noise seemed to have driven them out for a time. Visiting my cloak had become routine. Daily, I ate my breakfast and then slipped away as soon as possible to gather my cloak and play with it.

I had discovered its limitations quickly. I could not put it on and parade invisibly through the halls. It took time for the cloak to mimic the colors and shadows of the place where it lay. I was careful in my experiments, for I feared that if I ever once dropped it with the butterfly side down, I'd never find it again. And so I had tested it privately, covering a tree stump in the woods, draping it over a statue in Patience's garden room, and even spreading it flat on the floor of my mother's room. The tree stump had become a flat mossy spot in the woods. I could feel the stump, but I could not persuade my eyes it was there. The statue had likewise vanished, and the cloak had copied perfectly the pattern of the rug I had spread it on. Folded, it made a very small packet indeed, one that I could slip under my waistband and carry with me. Today, with the cloak hidden so, I took it out to the grove of birches that overlooked the carriage drive to the main doors. I climbed one and found myself a perch overlooking the drive.

Securely wrapped in the cloak with only one eye peering out, I was confident I would not be discovered. From my vantage, I could

watch the comings and goings of all the tradesfolk moving in and
out of my home. It was not my first time to do so. The cloak was
surprisingly warm for how thin it was. This meant I did not have to
bundle myself in layers of wool against the winter chill. Whenever
I saw an arrival that I wished to investigate further, I could clamber
quickly down from my hiding place, sneak back into the house,
hide my cloak, and quickly emerge dressed as if I had never left the
manor.

I was at my observation post that afternoon when I saw a morose
young man on a gleaming black horse ride up the carriageway. He
had a mule with two panniers of luggage strapped to it on a lead
line. The rider was warmly dressed for the cold day. Black boots
hugged his legs to his knee. His woolen leggings were dark green.
They matched his cloak, a heavy one trimmed with wolf fur. His
dark hair was not in a warrior's tail but fell to his shoulders in natural ringlets. He wore two silver earrings in one ear, and a sparkling
red stone dangled from the other. He passed so close under my tree
that I could smell him, or rather the fragrance he wore. Violets. I
had never thought of a man smelling like violets. I quickly decided
by his fine clothing that this must be my tutor. I stared down at
him, trying to reconcile a babyish memory of danger from a boy
with the man I saw below me. I wondered what had befallen him on
his journey, for both his eyes were blacked and his face bruised
purple and green all over the left side.

Despite his battered face, he was the handsomest person I had
ever seen. His shoulders were wide, his back straight as he rode.
The bruising could not disguise his straight nose and strong jaw.

I watched him ride up to the door, his posture very stiff. My in-
stincts warred in me. He was a handsome man, smelling of violets
and rather battered. I had been prepared to fear and hate him. Now
I wasn't sure what to make of him. He had no servant to dash ahead
of him; nor did he shout for anyone to come and take his horse.
Instead he dismounted stiffly. He gave a small grunt of pain as his
foot touched the ground, and once he had both feet down he leaned
his head against his saddle, catching his breath. When he straightened, he stood for a time, stroking his horse's neck and looking

around. Dread, I decided, was what he felt. He did not come as a man hired to tutor a girl, but as someone expelled from one life into another. I wondered if he had come of his own will. I remembered something I had read in my father's writing. "Chade, you old spider," I whispered softly, and was shocked when he flinched a look in my direction. I sat very still, my legs tucked tight to my body, peering through a tiny gap in the cloak's shelter. His gaze went right past me. Still, I held my breath and remained motionless. He turned back to look at the door of the house. And still he hesitated.

A servant emerged suddenly, to ask courteously, "May I be of service, sir?"

FitzVigilant had a boy's voice still. "I'm the new scribe," he announced uncertainly, as if he could not quite believe it himself. "I've come to be Lady Bee's tutor."

"Of course. We've been expecting you. Please, do come in. I'll call a boy to take your mount and mule, and see that your things are carried up to your room." The servant stepped aside and gestured him toward the open door. With the cautious dignity of a man in pain, my tutor carefully ascended the steps.

The door closed behind him. I sat still, watching the space where he had been. I had the feeling that something momentous had happened in my life. I had a very tiny awareness that I should hurry inside and make myself presentable. I suspected that my father would soon be summoning me to meet my new tutor. Uneasiness roiled in me. Was I afraid? Eager to meet him? Likely he would be a part of my life now for many years.

Unless he killed me.

When common sense asserted itself, I climbed down, folded my cloak carefully, stuffed it under my tunic, and dashed for the servant's entrance. I tiptoed past the kitchen door and then sped down the hall. I reached the pantry and slipped inside.

Someone was waiting for me there. I stopped dead and stared.

The mice? He was sitting in the middle of the pantry, his kinked tail curled neatly around his mismatched feet.

"How did you know to come here?" I whispered.

He stared at me, mice dancing in his green gaze.

"This way," I told him. I dropped to my knees and crawled behind the stacked crates of fish. He followed. When I turned around to shut the hatch to the secret corridor, he darted back out of it. "No. Come in," I told him. He did. I reached to shut the door. He darted out. "I can't leave it open wide."

He sat down outside the entrance and stared at me with stubborn patience. I waited. But he was content to sit there and exist until I was tired of waiting. At last I said, "Just this first time, I'll leave it open more than a crack. Until you trust me." I crawled back inside, he followed, and I left the door ajar. I seldom shut it all the way, as I'd never discovered how to open it from the other side. As I moved slowly away from it, I more felt than saw that he was following.

Much as I wanted the mice and rats banished from my domain, I wished he had not come today. I had things to do. My black-and-white shadow dogged my steps as I threaded the maze within the walls. I traveled by touch and memory now, and he seemed to have no qualms about ghosting after me in the darkness.

When we reached my den, I put my cloak in its hiding place. I had wrapped biscuits stored in a bowl on my shelf. I took them out of the bowl, and filled it with water from the stoppered bottle I now kept there. "Here is water," I told him. "Whatever you do, you must not meow, nor make much noise of any kind. And I've left the pantry door ajar, so if you wish to go back out, you'll be able to do so. But don't let Cook or any of the kitchen girls catch you in the meat pantry. They'll take a broom to you!"

He was so motionless that I wondered if he had followed me this far. Then I felt a head bump against me, and then he wound himself past my legs. I reached down, and his fur sleeked by under my touch. I crouched, and on his second pass he allowed me to stroke his sides. He was a lean barn cat, half-grown and ribby and long. He turned and suddenly pressed his bared teeth against my hand. "I'll bring you fish and meat, too," I promised him. "So you don't get tired of eating mice."

He head-bumped his agreement to my offer. I suddenly felt he had honored me somehow. I stayed crouched in the darkness, thinking. "You'll need a name," I told him.

Not really.

I nodded silently, understanding that if he decided he wanted me to give him a name, he'd let me know. Very cautiously, he set a paw on my knee. As if I were a tree that might not be sturdy enough to climb, he ventured onto my lap. I sat perfectly still. He put his front paws on my chest and then sniffed my face, particularly my mouth. I thought it was rude but I sat still for it. After a few annoying moments, he climbed down, curled into a circle, and began to purr himself to sleep.

Chapter 23

THE TUTOR

The first time I met Chade Fallstar I was but a boy. In the middle of the night, I woke to a light shining in my face and a pock-scarred old man in a cobweb-covered gray wool robe standing over my bed. A previously concealed door in the corner of my bedchamber now stood open. It yawned at me, dark and daunting, and cobwebs fluttered at the edges of it. It was so like a nightmare that for a time I simply stared at it. Yet when he commanded me to get out of bed and follow him, I did.

Sometimes I think of the momentous meetings in my life. My first encounter with Verity. Then Burrich. Discovering that the Fool was not the vapid jester I had believed, but possessed a keen intelligence and a deep desire to influence the politics of Buckkeep Castle. There are moments that change the course of one's lifetime, and often we don't realize how significant those initial meetings may be until years pass.

— JOURNAL ENTRY

My scribe arrived as expected, save that my overtasked mind did not expect him that day. When one of the newly hired serving men came running to tell me that there was a battered traveler at my door, my first impulse was to direct him to the kitchen for food and wish him well on his way. It was only when Bulen belatedly added that the stranger claimed to be the new scribe that I left off my mediation between a painter and a carpenter and turned my steps toward the front hall.

FitzVigilant awaited me there. He had grown taller, with a man's jaw and shoulders, but it was his battered face that took all the rest of my attention.

Both Chade and Nettle had said he had taken a beating. I had expected some bruises and perhaps a blackened eye. Looking at him, I knew the blows he had taken had probably loosened teeth if not knocked some out. His nose was still swollen broad, and there was a split along the top of one cheekbone. His excessively upright posture spoke of bound ribs, and his careful way of stepping betrayed his pain. Chade and Nettle were right to be concerned for him: Healing of broken bones is not promoted by the joggling of horseback riding. Clearly he had fled Buckkeep, and possibly only just in time. The beating had not been a warning, but an attempt on his life.

I had been angry at Chade for sending him to me, and had resolved to keep my guard firmly in place against either Chade's manipulation of my household or the boy's own intentions. The sight of him, gray-faced and walking like a gaffer, dispersed my resolution and left me fighting the sympathy that welled up in me. And as I gazed at him, I had the eerie sense that he reminded me of someone. I tried to see past the swelling and bruises, and I suppose I stared at him in dismay. It made him wary. He cast a gaze toward the new serving man before he spoke.

He chose to pretend we had never met before. I heard his wheeze as he forced himself to grant me a stiff bow before he introduced himself as, "FitzVigilant, sent by Lady Nettle to be tutor to her sister, Lady Bee, and to scribe as is needed for her estate."

I accepted his greeting gravely. "We've been expecting you. Our household is in a bit of disarray as long-delayed repairs are being made to Withywoods, but I think you will find your chamber comfortable. I'll let Bulen show you to your rooms. If you wish a warm bath after your travels let him know and he'll arrange for water and a tub for you in the steams. You are welcome to join us for the evening meal, but if you are too wearied from your journey, food will be sent up for you."

"I . . ."

I waited.

"I thank you," he amended, and I sensed something unsaid. I wondered if he felt insulted that I had offered him an excuse to soak his aching body and then rest, but I had learned long ago that a warm bath and deep rest were better healers than all the unguents and restorative drinks ever concocted.

He gestured vaguely toward the door. "The mule carries my possessions, and scrolls and supplies for teaching Lady Bee."

"I'll have Bulen bring them to the schoolroom and your chambers, and find a stable boy to see to your animals." I glanced at our recently hired man. He was probably of an age with FitzVigilant and was looking at him with open dismay and sympathy. The farmer's son was wearing a cut-down set of Revel's old livery. He still looked a country boy despite Revel's best efforts, but he had an open, honest face and a ready smile. I could do far worse for a servant. I nodded to myself. "Tutor FitzVigilant, consider Bulen your man in our household. Bulen, for the time being, make yourself useful and available to our new tutor." It would keep them both busy, and allow me time to quietly inspect everything FitzVigilant had on his mule.

"Sir," Bulen agreed, and turned at once to FitzVigilant. "If you would follow me, sir?"

"One moment," I interrupted them. "Scribe FitzVigilant, if you would not mind the extra duty, I would ask if you would also be willing to teach the other youngsters of Withywoods estate. There are not many at present, perhaps as few as six . . ."

"Six?" he asked faintly. His dismay was plain. Then, if it were possible, he stood even straighter and managed a tight nod. "Of course. It is what I am here to do. Teach children."

"Excellent. I imagine you will need a day or so to settle yourself in. Let me know when you think you are ready to begin. And if you find your schoolroom lacking in anything, inform Bulen and he will bring your requests to me."

"Schoolroom, sir?"

"It is adjacent to your chambers, and already has a collection of useful scrolls, maps, and perhaps even some charts. It was stocked by Lady Patience near two score years ago, so you may find it a bit dated, but I do not think the geography of the Six Duchies has much changed."

He nodded. "Thank you. I will examine what is already there before I ask for anything more from you."

And so FitzVigilant joined our household. In less than a fortnight, the size of the staff of Withywoods had tripled and my own household had doubled in size. I found Revel and informed him that I had given Bulen to the tutor. The tall man looked down on me mournfully and I had to add that if he needed to replace Bulen, he could hire another man.

"Perhaps two," he requested gravely.

I didn't even want to know why. "Two, then," I said, and added, "He has a mule outside, laden with his belongings and scribe supplies. If those things can be brought to his room immediately I am sure he will greatly appreciate it, as will I."

"Immediately, then," Revel agreed, and I hurried on my way.

When I was certain that Bulen had escorted FitzVigilant to the steams, I visited his quarters. His baggage from the mule was there, awaiting Bulen's attention. There is an art to going through a man's personal possessions and yet leaving no trace of having done so. It takes time, and a clear memory of exactly how every item had been packed. FitzVigilant's living quarters were adjacent to his schoolroom. I latched the doors and was very thorough. Most of what he had was what one would expect a young man to possess, but in a far larger quantity than I had ever found necessary at his age. All of his many shirts were of very good quality. He had earrings of both silver and gold, some with small gems, all neatly stored in a roll of soft leather. I made a note that none of his garments showed the sort of wear one would associate with physical labor; indeed, very little of it looked appropriate for an ordinary day at Withywoods teaching children or totting up accounts. I had expected to find at least one sturdy and serviceable pair of trousers, but no, all were of fabrics I would have thought more suitable to a lady's gown. Had the court at Buckkeep Castle changed that much?

Chade seemed to have weaned him from his assassin's training. I found no extra pockets in his garments, no hidden vials of poisons or sleeping drafts. He did appear to have more small knives than a young nobleman might ordinarily require. For a time, I thought I had uncovered a secret cache of poisons, only to realize that these were Chade's most common mixtures for pain relief and wound treatments. I recognized Chade's writing on several of the labels; the others I thought had been prepared by Rosemary. Interesting that FitzVigilant did not even compound his own remedies. What, then, did this young man do with his time?

His tutoring supplies were beyond what I would have expected. He had maps of an excellent quality, of every duchy, including the Mountain Kingdom. He had a copy of Shortlegs's *History of Buck*, a book of herbs with lovely illustrations, tally rods for reckoning, chalk in plenty, and a good supply of coarse paper and ink and another soft leather roll, this one containing pens with tips of copper. In short, I found nothing in his belongings to suggest that he was anything other than a tutor and scribe. And nothing to suggest he would be a competent bodyguard for Bee.

That thought made me realize that I had hoped he would be relatively skilled in that area. The pale messenger had warned us that hunters might follow her. So far, there had been no sign of any strangers in the area, but I had not relaxed my guard. They had hunted her companion to death, and condemned her to long agony. That did not speak of people who easily gave up a chase.

Well, Bee had me. I would stand between my daughter and any dangers that might come.

I surveyed the room quickly, making sure all was exactly as Bulen and FitzVigilant had left it, and quietly let myself out.

It was time to have a talk with my daughter about her new teacher.

Chapter 24

SETTLING IN

Among the first lessons for a young Skill-student to master is that of containing herself. She must be made to realize that a container not only holds that which is within it, but prevents that which is outside it from entering; that is, to put it more clearly, a wineskin not only contains wine within it but keeps out rain and dirt. So it is with the mind of the Skill-student. She must learn to keep her own thoughts to herself, and also to keep the thoughts of others from intruding. If she does not master this twofold wall of protection, she will soon fall prey to the musings of others, be they but idle thoughts or lechery or foolishness. Herewith follows an exercise that will teach the student not only to keep her thoughts to herself, but to keep from her quiet center the thoughts of others.

ON THE INSTRUCTING OF SKILL-STUDENTS,
SKILLMISTRESS SOLICITY

I held perfectly still, wondering if he knew I was there. My father had entered his den, and he now stared at my peephole. But he knew where it was, so of course if he suspected I was there, that was where he would look. I waited. If he turned and went away, it meant he didn't know.

He spoke in a conversational tone. "Bee, I've been looking for you. If you are going to seemingly vanish from the manor, you had best let me know. Please come out. I need to discuss something with you."

I sat still. The cat was asleep against me.

"Now, Bee," he warned me. He turned and shut the door of the study, observing, "When I trigger this panel, you had best be standing right there, waiting to come out."

He meant it.

I left the dozing black cat and scurried down the narrow spy-way. When he opened the door, I stepped out, brushing at cobwebs. "Are you taking me to meet my tutor?"

My father looked me up and down. "No. But I did come to talk to you about him. He has arrived, but he is not in the best of health. I think it may be several days before he is ready to teach you."

"I don't mind," I said quietly. The relief I felt clarified my mixed feelings. It had been exciting to spy upon the young man as he arrived; it had made me feel a bit more in control of the situation to know that I had seen him before he had seen me. But I found I wanted time to become accustomed to the idea of a tutor. Until I knew more about this man, I would avoid him as much as I could.

My father cocked his head at me and gave me a measuring glance. Then he asked me, "Are you afraid to meet your teacher?"

I wanted to ask him how he had known that. Instead I chose another question. "Do you think he has come here to kill me?"

For an instant my father's face went slack. It was less than a moment and he recovered quickly, looking at me with pretend consternation and asking me sharply, "Whatever put such a thing in your head?"

How should I answer that? I came as close to the truth as I could without making him think I was a freak. "I dreamed that he was coming to kill me. That he was sent to kill me, a long time ago, but you stopped him. And that now perhaps he was coming to try again."

Another silence. He was containing his Skill so tightly he felt almost as blank as Cook Nutmeg. I had found a scroll about this and read it. Now I knew that was what it was called. Containing his Skill or keeping up his walls meant that I felt like I could breathe when he was in the room. And it also meant he would try to hide something from me.

"He was sent by your sister. And by Lord Chade. To teach you. Do you think they would send someone to kill you?"

"Nettle might send him, if she didn't know he was an assassin." I said nothing of what I thought Lord Chade might do.

He sat down heavily in the chair behind his desk. "Bee, why would anyone want to kill you?"

I looked up at the sword hanging on the wall and over his head. Maybe truth from me would win truth from him. "For being a Farseer," I said slowly. "One they didn't need. Or want."

My father looked away from me. Then he turned slowly in his chair and looked up at the sword with me. I listened to more distant sounds in the house. Someone was hammering. A door opened and shut.

"I didn't think we'd be having this discussion so soon." He drummed his fingers along the edges of his desk and then looked back at me. He was so sad. So guilty for making this part of my life. "How much do you know?" he asked gently.

I came closer to his desk and set my own fingers along the edge on my side. "I know who you are. Whose son you are. And that I'm your daughter."

He closed his eyes for a moment and let out a short breath. Without opening them, he asked me, "Who told you? Not your mother."

"No. Not my mother. I put it together myself. From bits of things. You never really hid it from me. When I was little, before I was talking much, you and Mama often spoke over my head, about many things. Stories about Patience. How much she wanted a child, and why she wanted you to have Withywoods. There are bits of my family history everywhere in the manor. My grandfather's portrait is on the wall upstairs."

His fingers moved more slowly on the desktop. He opened his eyes and looked past me, staring intently at the panel of the door. I saw I would have to put it together for him.

"Mother sometimes called you Fitz. And Nettle did, too. You look like Chivalry. And in the south wing, there is an old portrait of King Shrewd and his first queen. My great-grandmother. I suppose they sent it here when he married Queen Desire and she didn't want to be reminded of the first wife. I look like Queen Constance, I think. A little bit."

"Do you?" He spoke faintly, breathing out the word.

"I think I do. My nose."

"Come here," he said, and when I went to him, he pulled me up on his lap. I was able to sit there. He was so contained, it was almost like sitting on a chair. He put his arms around me and held me close. It was odd to feel so separate and yet so close to him. Like Mother, I suddenly realized. She had been able to hold me close like this. I leaned my forehead against my father's shoulder. I felt his arm around me, a hard-muscled arm that could protect me. He spoke by my ear. "No matter what name they call us by, you will always be mine. And I am yours, Bee. And I will always do everything in my power to protect you. Do you understand that?"

I nodded my head against him.

"I will always need you. I will always want you to be part of my life. Do you understand that?"

I nodded again.

"Now, this scribe who has come to stay with us? FitzVigilant? Well. Chade sends him here to us because he needs my protection, too. He is a bastard. Like me. Unlike you, his family would like to get rid of him. They don't need him or want him. So, to keep him safe, Chade has sent him here."

"Like Shun," I suggested quietly.

I listened to my father's heart beating. "Worked that out, too, did you? Yes. Like Shun exactly. But unlike Shun he has had some training both as a, well, a protector himself, and as a tutor. Chade's thought was that he could be a guard for you as well as a teacher. And Nettle agreed."

"And he's illegitimate?"

"Yes. That's why his given name has a Fitz at the start. His father acknowledged him."

"But his father doesn't protect him?"

"He doesn't. Can't or won't, I do not know. I suppose it makes no difference. His father's wife and his brothers do not like him or want him. Sometimes things like that happen in families. But not in the family of you and me. And FitzVigilant is no danger to you. Especially now."

"Now?"

"He was badly beaten. By people sent by his own family. Probably his stepmother. He ran away to be here so they couldn't find him and kill him. It's going to take him time to recover enough to teach you."

"I see. So I'm safe for now."

"Bee. You are safe for always while I am here. He does not come to kill you, but to help keep you safe. And to teach you. Nettle knows him and speaks well of him. So does Riddle."

He was quiet then. I sat on his lap, leaning against his warm chest, listening to him breathe. I sensed a deep and thoughtful stillness within him. I thought he would ask me how much more I knew, or how I had discovered it, but he didn't. I had the strangest feeling that he knew. I had been so careful about borrowing his papers. I always tried to put them back exactly as I had found them. Had he noticed something amiss? I couldn't ask him without admitting what I'd been doing. And I suddenly felt a bit ashamed of how I had spied on him. Was it lying to spy on him and pretend I didn't know things? A hard question. I began to feel almost sleepy sitting there. Maybe because I did feel very safe. Protected.

He suddenly gave a small sigh and then set me on my feet. He looked me up and down again. "I've neglected you," he said.

"What?"

"Look at you. You're not much better than a little ragamuffin. You've outgrown your clothes when I wasn't looking. And when was the last time you combed out your hair?"

I reached up and touched my hair. It was too short to lie down and too long to be tidy. "Maybe yesterday," I said, knowing I lied. He didn't challenge me.

"It's not just your hair or your clothes, Bee. It's all of you. I can be so blind. We have to do better, little one," he told me. "You and I, we have to do better."

I could not make sense of what he was saying, yet I knew he was mostly talking to himself. "I will brush my hair every day," I promised him. I put my hands behind my back, knowing they were not especially clean.

"Good," he told me. "Good."

He was looking at me but not seeing me. "I'll go brush my hair now," I offered.

He nodded, and this time his eyes focused on me. "And I'll do what I should have been doing, beginning now," he promised in return.

I went to my mother's sitting room. I still had not been moved back into my room. A small trunk there held a limited selection of my clothes and possessions. I found my brush and smoothed my hair, and used water from the ewer there to wipe my face and clean my hands. I found clean leggings and a fresh tunic. And when I went down to dinner, it was only my father and me at the table. It was the best evening I'd had in a long time.

Riddle and Shun returned from their expedition with two wagonloads of goods. Some of it was for Revel but a lot of it was just for Shun. She had ordered new hangings for her bed and windows, and they would be delivered when they were finished. In the meanwhile she "supposed" she would have to get by with what the Purple Suite offered her. She had bought two chairs, a lampstand and a rug for her floor, a new ewer and basin, and a rack for her clothes. None of them looked much different to me from the items that had already been in her rooms. She had also added to her stock of clothing with warm woolen things and cloaks trimmed with fur, and fur slippers. There was a carved cedar chest to keep it all in. I watched my father as he saw it all unloaded and carried into her freshly restored room. When he saw me observing him, he commented quietly, "I think that's more clothing than your mother required in all of her years married to me." And I did not think he meant that my mother had had to do with less than what she wanted.

Both Riddle and Shun expressed some curiosity about my tutor when he did not join us for any meals on the second day after their return. In Shun's hearing my father said only that some people recovered from traveling more slowly than others. Did she notice the look the two men exchanged? I was certain that Riddle would call on Scribe FitzVigilant before the day was over, and longed to accompany him. I was not permitted to do that, of course.

So the intervening days were given over to the activities I had created for myself. Each day I took myself to the stables for time with Perseverance and Priss. I did not call him Per. I don't know why. I just did not like it as a name for him. I did like that we hadn't asked anyone's permission. I felt I had taken it into my own hands and that I had chosen a good teacher for myself I liked Perseverance because he hadn't seemed to think he needed to ask anyone's permission to teach me. I suspected that no one besides us even knew I had begun to learn to ride. I liked that. It seemed to me that lately everyone had been making decisions for me. This was something I had done for myself.

Then Perseverance shocked me at the end of a ride by telling me, "We might not be able to do this at the same time as we have been."

I scowled as I dismounted. I got off the horse to the mounting block without assistance. An easy accomplishment now, one I took pride in. "Why not?" I demanded.

He looked at me, surprised. "Well, you know. The scribe came and he's going to teach us."

"He's going to teach me," I corrected him, not gently.

He lifted his brows at me. "And me. And Lukor, and Ready and Oatil from the stables. And Elm and Lea from the kitchens. Maybe Taffy, though he scoffs and says no one can make him go. And the goose woman's children, and maybe some of the sheepherder's children. Holder Tom Badgerlock put the word out that anyone born to help on Withywoods can come and learn. Lots didn't want to. I didn't. But my da says that anytime a man can learn a new thing, he should. And that it's a fine thing to be able to sign your name instead of making a mark, and an even finer thing to know what you're signing without having to send to the village for a scribe. So. I have to go, at least until I can write my own name. He seems to think that by then I'll want to keep going. I'm not sure about that."

I was sure I didn't want him to go at all. I liked how he knew me here, just as Bee. The thought of Taffy being there chilled me. He hadn't dared to chase me since that day, but perhaps it was only because I'd never dared to follow and spy on them since then. I imagined Elm and Lea, giggling and mocking me. Then Perseverance would see what a mistake he had made in being my friend. No! I could not allow them to be included. I pressed my lips tightly together. "I will be speaking to my father about this," I told Perseverance.

He looked disapproving at my chill tone. "I'd be happy if you did. Sitting in a circle getting ink on my fingers isn't my idea of a good time. My father said it just proved your father was a generous-hearted man, as he's always said. Not all agree with him. Some say the Holder has a black look to his eyes sometimes, even when he's fair-spoken. None could name a time when he had mistreated someone or been unfair, but many claimed that was your mother's influence that made him kind, and they looked for things to go badly for all of us when she died. When he brought that woman here, some said she had a look to be his blood kin, and others said she had the look of a woman come to have an easy life of it with a man handling a lot of money."

I was frozen, my mouth ajar and my heart cold as I listened to his words. I think he mistook it for ardent interest rather than a heartfelt desire to hear no more. He nodded at me. "It's so. Some talk like that. There was that night when half the staff was up till dawn because that woman was shrieking about ghosts, and then Revel fell on them all the next morning like an avalanche, full of fury and shame that there had been bugs in your bedding, and your father so angry about it he was out setting fire to it in the night. 'As if he cares for her at all, the way she runs about dressed in clothes that would better suit a cobbler's boy.' " He stammered to a halt at my look of outrage. Perhaps he suddenly recalled to whom he was speaking, for he insisted, "That's what they said, not me!"

I didn't conceal my fury as I demanded, "*Who* said those things? Who is 'they' who speak such awful lies about my father and make mock of me?"

He was suddenly a servant rather than a friend. He pulled his winter cap from his head and held it before his knees, eyes and head down as he spoke. His ears were scarlet and not from the cold. There was wariness in his voice as he said, "Your pardon, Mistress Bee. I spoke above myself and out of turn, most wrong of me. It was only gossip, not fit for a lady's ears, and I've shamed myself repeating it. I'll be about my work now."

And he turned away from me, the only friend I'd ever made for myself, and took Priss's headstall. He began to lead her away. "Perseverance!" I called in my most regal voice.

"I must take care of your horse, mistress," he apologized over his shoulder. He was walking fast, head down. Priss seemed surprised to be hurried along. I stood on the mounting block, quarreling with myself. Raise my voice and order him back. Run away and never, *ever* again come to the stables. Burst into tears and crumple up in a ball.

I stood, frozen by indecision, and watched him walk away. When he and my horse had disappeared into the stables, I jumped down and ran away. I went to my mother's grave and sat for a short time on a very cold stone bench nearby. I told myself I wasn't so stupid as to think my mother was anywhere near. It was just a place to be. I'd never been so hurt, and I couldn't tell if it was what he had said or how I had reacted to it. Stupid boy. Of course I'd get angry and demand to know who had said such horrid things. Why had he told me about them if he didn't expect to tell me who had said them? And sharing my lessons with the other children of Withywoods? I would not have minded Perseverance being there, but if Taffy and Elm and Lea were there, their opinion of me would spread like poison. Surely Perseverance would rather be friends with a large boy like Taffy than with someone like me. Elm and Lea sometimes helped at the table now; it was bad enough to glimpse them in passing, and see how quickly they put their heads together, their sharp tongues wagging like blades on a whetstone. They'd mock me. As, apparently, others were already mocking me for my appearance.

I swung my feet out in front of me. I wore last year's boots, the leather cracking at the sides of my feet. My leggings were thick with burrs from taking a shortcut through the gardens. The knees were dirtied and a dead leaf clung to one shin; I must have knelt down somewhere. I stood and pulled my tunic dress out in front of me. It was not dirty, but it was stained. I'd had less clothing since that scrubbing out of my room. I felt a vague alarm that perhaps some of my clothes had been burned. Perhaps I should check on the state of my possessions. I scratched at a bit of mud on the hem of the tunic, and it popped off. I'd put this on only a day or two ago. The stain on the breast was an old one. Dirty and stained were not the same thing at all, I thought.

Unless you were looking at someone and didn't know that those were stains, not fresh soiling. I thought about it for some time. It was all distressing. Lessons with children who hated me, who would poke and pinch and mock me if they had the slightest chance. People were talking about my father and about me in ways that I didn't like. They believed things that weren't true, but it was because they looked true. It would look to someone else that my father didn't care about me. When my mother was alive, she had done all that was needed to keep me neat and clean. I hadn't given it much thought; it was just something she did for me, one of the many things she did for all of us. Now she was gone. And my father hadn't begun doing those things for me because, I decided slowly, they weren't important to him. He saw me, not that my boots were cracked at the sides or that every tunic I owned was stained. He had mentioned that we had to "do better" but then he had done nothing.

And I was just like him. Those things hadn't mattered at all to me, until someone had pointed out that perhaps they should. I stood up and brushed at the front of my tunic. I felt very grown up as I decided that the answer wasn't to mope about it or blame my father. I lifted a hand to my fraying hair. I would simply tell him what I needed, and he would get it for me. He'd done it for Shun, hadn't he?

I went directly to find him. It took me a short time but eventually I discovered him in the Yellow Suite. He was speaking to Revel. Next to them was a servant standing on a stool, hanging the cleaned bed draperies. One of the new maids, a girl named Careful, was standing by with an armful of linens. The featherbed had been put into a fresh cover and looked deep and soft. If no one had been looking, I would immediately have tried it out.

Instead I waited patiently until my father turned, saw me, smiled, and asked, "Well, Bee, what do you think of it? Can you think of anything else you'd like done to your new chambers?"

I stared, mouth ajar. Revel gave a very pleased chuckle. My father cocked his head at me. "You've caught us a bit early, but we're close enough to finished here. I knew you'd be surprised but I didn't think you'd be speechless."

"I like my own room," I said breathlessly. With the secret entrance to the spy-maze, I did not say aloud. I looked around me and saw what I hadn't before. The chest at the foot of the bed was sized down to make it easier for me to find things in it. The empty wardrobe standing open in the corner had a stool beside it for the upper shelves. The hooks inside it were placed where I could easily reach them. This was proof that my father did think of me. I knew I could not reject this misguided gift. "You did all this for me?" I asked before he could speak again.

"With some advice from Revel," my father noted. The tall steward nodded a curt agreement.

I looked slowly around the room. I recognized the small chair by

the fire. I'd seen it somewhere else in the house; now it was freshened with new varnish and yellow cushions. I didn't recognize the
footstool. It wasn't an exact match for the chair, but it was close
enough, with the cushion done in the same fabric. The window had
a box seat in it; a step had been added to make it easier for me to
take a place there, and a handful of various-sized cushions in bright
fabrics beckoned me to relax there. I glanced from it to my father.

"Lots of help from Revel," he amended sheepishly, and the steward now beamed. "You know that I know nothing of such things as
curtains and cushions. I told him after we'd found the bedbugs that
I would not put you in that room again. He said it was known
among the servants that you favored this suite of rooms, and so he
suggested that, as we'd already begun to freshen them, we finish
them especially for you. And here you are, just in time to say if you
approve."

I found my tongue. "They're very nice. Very pretty."

My father waited and I had to add, "But I do love my old room."
I could not tell him, in front of the servants, that I wanted a room
with an entrance to the spy-maze. I wasn't sure I wanted to tell him
about that entrance. I liked being the only one who knew about it.
I weighed my secret and quick access to the spyhole against a chance
to dispel some of the gossip. And what if he decided that he must
improve my old room instead? The spy-door might be found! I
cleared my throat. "But it was a baby's room, wasn't it? This is
much better. Thank you, Father. It's lovely."

It was a bit awkward, but I went to him and put my face up to be
kissed. I was probably the only one who knew he was surprised,
and certainly only he and I knew how seldom we touched in that
way. But he stooped to give me a kiss on the cheek, exactly as if it
were something we were both comfortable doing. We were allies, I
suddenly knew, holding our walls against a hostile world.

Revel was fairly wriggling with excitement. The moment I
stepped back from my father, he bowed and said, "Mistress Bee, if
you have a moment, I'd enjoy showing you the cunning drawers in
the wardrobe, and how the mirror folds down." The moment I gave
a faint nod he stretched his long legs, and in two strides he stood

before my new wardrobe cabinet. "See. There are hooks for neck-laces, and tiny drawers for other jewelry. Here is the little shelf for scents! And, to be amusing, I've already added some for you! This charming little bottle holds rose essence, and this blue one has hon-eysuckle; both are very appropriate for a young lady of your years!

"I've added a clever little stepstool for you, to allow you to reach every shelf and to see yourself in the mirror. See how it folds up or down! And here, this compartment for larger hanging items, ah, such a pleasant scent—lined with cedar, to keep those nasty little moths away!" As he spoke, he was opening empty drawers and tap-ping hooks with much more enthusiasm than I could ever have mustered for a wardrobe. I smiled as best I could and continued to smile as he assured me that the maid's chamber attached to my room would soon be ready for an occupant. He commended Care-ful to my attention as a possible lady's maid, and I had to turn and keep all dismay from my face as she presented herself. I judged her to be at least fifteen and perhaps older. She blushed as she curtsied, her arms still full of linens, and I had no idea what to say to her. A maid. What would I have her do? Would she always be near me, following me about? Suddenly I was glad I had been gracious about accepting the new room. If I had insisted on my old one, and they had put her in there, I'd have no chance to use my secret entrance. As it was, if she was sleeping adjacent to my room, would I be able to slip out unnoticed?

I turned back to Revel. Carefully, carefully. "The room is so lovely, and the wardrobe is enchanting. You have given a great deal of thought to everything. And how kind of you, to make it easier for me to reach things. So often that has been a challenge for me, and now you have solved it."

I had never seen Revel flush pink with pleasure, but he did now. His brown eyes suddenly twinkled at me, and to my shock I realized I'd made him my friend. I turned from him to my father. I had come seeking him, intending to ask him for new winter boots and some longer tunics. But I now perceived that I must not ask for those things in front of the servants. I looked round at them, Care-ful and Revel and the man installing the bed hangings. He was nearly finished now, and Careful was stepping forward and giving a final tug to make them hang straight. I had known Revel all my life, but I had lived like the feral kitten, slipping past the tall house steward without a word. What possible interest could such a dignified and important adult have in me? And yet here he was, taking absolute joy in creating this room for me.

And now Careful would obviously become part of my world. All of the enlarged ranks of folk that would populate Withywoods would now be people I must encounter and speak to every day. And there would be other children, larger than me but equal in years, in the schoolroom with me every day. So many people were becoming part of my world. How would I deal with so many people?

Part of my world, but not part of my family. My father was my family. And he and I must stand back-to-back, always, and defend ourselves against all gossip and speculation. I was not sure why that was so . . . and then I knew. They might call me Bee Badgerlock, but I knew that in truth I was Bee Farseer. That knowledge was like a brick being set in place to fill up a chink in a wall. I was a Farseer. Like my father. So I smiled and took care to speak clearly as I said, "I came to ask when the tutor might be ready to begin my lessons, Father. I am very eager to start."

I saw understanding dawn in my father's eyes, and he played to our audience as well. "He has said that he thinks he could begin in two days. He is finally feeling recovered from his journey."

His beating, I thought. Such a polite pretense we were all sharing, but enough had seen his battered face when he arrived to know why our new tutor was keeping to his rooms and bed.

"That is wonderful, then." I looked slowly around my new room, smiling large to be sure that all would see and know how pleased I was with it. "The room is finished? I may sleep here tonight?"

Revel smiled. "As soon as the bedding is smoothed on the bed, mistress."

"Thank you. I'm sure I will love being here. There are some things in my old room that I will want to bring here. I'll fetch them."

"Oh, little need, Lady Bee, I assure you!" Revel strode to the chest at the foot of my new bed and flung it open. He went down on one knee and beckoned me over as his long fingers crawled down the stack of folded fabrics. "An extra blanket of yellow and cream, for when the nights are very cold. And here, a lap rug for when you want to sit in your window. A new red shawl with a hood. Now, as we had to dispose of so much of your wardrobe, I had Seamstress Lily fashion you some new tunics. Looking at you, I fear we have made them too large, but they will suffice until we have time to get a proper fitting done. See, here is a brown one with yellow trim, and here a green one. This one is a bit plain; would you like some embroidery done round the hems? Never mind, of course you would. I'll send it to the seamstresses."

I had stopped listening. Revel was wallowing in his enjoyment. His words flowed past me. I did not know how to feel. All this new clothing, all at once, and none of it made by my mother's hands. No one had held it up against me to check the length, or asked if I would have flowers or scrolls round the hem. I knit my brow and tried to comprehend my mother's death, all over again. Every time I thought I had mastered it, some new manifestation of it would overwhelm me.

Revel had finished. I was smiling. Smiling, smiling, smiling. I looked at my father desperately and managed to stammer out, "It's all so lovely. Still, there are a few things I will bring from my other room. Thank you all so much."

Then I fled. I hoped I exited gracefully, but once I was out of the room, I ran. I skittered past two servants carrying in a rolled-up rug, turned down the hall, and found the door of my old room. I bolted inside and shut the door behind me.

The hearth was swept, empty, and cold. The stripped bed frame looked skeletal. I made myself go to the door of the maid's room and peer in. It was as bare. The heavy bedstead was still pushed into the corner, the headboard neatly obscuring the subtle joins in the woodwork that concealed my entrance. That, at least, was still safe.

I came back slowly into my room. Nothing on the mantel over the fireplace. No blue pottery candleholder. No little carving of an owl that my mother and I had bought at the Oaksbywater market. I opened my small clothing chest. Empty. The larger chest at the foot of my old bed. Empty save for a faint waft of cedar and lavender. Even the sachets had been cleared away. The blue woolen blanket, worn to thinness, was gone. Not one of my old nightgowns or tunics remained. All those stitches from my mother's hands, gone to ash to protect my father's pretense, so no one could know we had burned a body in the night. The only old clothing left to me would be what I had carried off to my mother's room where I had been sleeping. And the nightrobe I had hidden there. Unless those had already been discovered and taken, too!

I crossed my arms on my chest and held myself tightly as I cataloged what else was missing. The engraved "book" of herbs that I had always kept by my bed. The candleholder for my bed table. A terrible fear seized me and I fell to my knees by that table and opened the cupboard beneath it. Gone, all gone, every one of the fat scented candles that my mother had made. I'd never slept in this room without one burning as I drowsed off, and I could not imagine moving into a new room without their comforting fragrance. I stared into the dim emptiness of the cupboard and held myself tighter, digging my nails into my arms to keep from flying into pieces. I shut my eyes tightly. If I breathed slowly through my nose, I could catch the fading essence of the candles that had been there.

I wasn't aware of him until he sat down on the floor behind me and put his arms around me. My father spoke by my ear. "Bee. I saved them. I came back here, late that night. I took the candles and a few other things that I knew you would want. I've got them safe for you."

I opened my eyes but I didn't relax in his arms. "You should have told me," I said fiercely, suddenly furious with him. How could he have let me feel that loss, even for a few minutes? "You should have let me come here to get my important things before they were burned."

"I should have," he conceded, and then he stabbed me with, "I didn't think of it then. And it had to be done immediately. So much was happening here, so fast."

My voice was cold as I asked, "So what did you save? My can-

dles? My book on herbs? My owl figurine, my candleholder? Did
you save my blue blanket? The tunic with the daisies embroidered
around the hem?"

"I didn't save the blue blanket," he admitted hoarsely. "I didn't
know it was important."

"You should have asked me! You should have *asked* me!" I hated
the tears that suddenly flooded my eyes and how my throat closed
and choked me. I didn't want to be sad. I wanted to be angry. Angry
hurt less. I turned and did something I'd never done before. I hit
my father, as hard as I could, my fist connecting with the braced
muscles of his chest. It wasn't a little girl's slapping. I hit him with
as much force as I could muster, wanting to hurt him. I hit him
again, and again, until I realized he was allowing me to do it, that he
could have seized my arms and stopped me at any time. That perhaps he even wanted me to hurt him. That made it useless and
worse than futile. I stopped and looked up at him. His face was still.
His eyes looked at me, open, offering no defense against my anger.
He accepted it as just.

That woke no sympathy in me. It only made me angrier. This was
my pain; I had been robbed of things I had cherished. How dare he
stare at me as if he were the one who was hurt? I folded my arms
again, this time to lock him out. I bowed my head so I wouldn't
have to look at him. When he put one hand on my cheek and the
other on top of my head, I only set my muscles and curled in more
tightly. He sighed.

"I do my best, Bee, poor as it is sometimes. I saved what I thought
was important to you. When you want to, tell me, and we'll get
them and put them in your new room. I wanted it to be something
of a surprise for you; I thought you'd like having the Yellow Suite.
It was a mistake. Too great a change, too fast, and you should have
had more say in it."

I didn't loosen my muscles, but I listened.

"So. This will not be a surprise. In five days you and I are going
into Oaksbywater. Revel was clever enough to suggest that you
might want to choose some fabric from the weavers there for your
heavy winter tunics. And we will visit the cobbler instead of wait-

ing for him to make his winter visit here. I think your feet have done more than a year's growing already. Revel told me that you needed new shoes, and that you needed boots as well. For riding."

That jolted me enough to look up at him. Sorrow still filled his eyes, but he said kindly, "That was a surprise for me. A very nice one."

I looked down again. I hadn't intended it to be anything for him. Though, now that I considered it, I had looked forward to him seeing that I could ride a horse, even if neither he nor Riddle had had time to think it important enough to teach me. I realized then how deeply angry I was with both of them that they always seemed to spend more time on Shun than on me. I wanted to hold on to that anger and make it deeper and stronger. But more than that, I wanted my mother's touches in the room where I would sleep tonight.

I spoke to the floor. I hated the hitch in my voice. "I'd like to go get my things now, please. And put them safe in my room."

"Then we will," he said. He stood. I didn't offer my hand and he didn't try to take it. But I followed him out of the room that had once been mine, the room where the messenger had died.

Chapter 25

THINGS TO KEEP

It was in the time of Queen Dextrous that the head scribe at Buck-keep Castle was given the additional duty of instructing any "will-ing" child in the keep in the art of letters. It has been said that she decreed this because of her great dislike of Scribe Martin. Cer-tainly many Buckkeep scribes who came after Martin seemed to think it more punishment than honor.

ON *THE DUTIES OF SCRIBES,* SCRIBE FEDWREN

And so, again, I had erred. And badly. I walked slowly down the corridor, my little child by my side. She did not take my hand. She walked just out of my arm's reach, and I knew that was no accident. If pain can radiate as heat from a fire, then that was the cold that I felt from her stiff little form. I had been so sure that I was doing it right. That she would be delighted with her new room and furnish-ings that took her size into consideration. And in my eagerness to deceive the staff about the "guest" who had gone missing, I had destroyed precious mementos, irreplaceable pieces of her childhood.

I took her to my bedchamber. It was a different place than it had been the last time she had been there. I'd gathered all my clothing and bedding and sent for the launderer. The man had made two trips with a very large basket, disapproval pinching his narrow nose nearly closed. That evening, when I returned to my room, my featherbed had been aired and turned, all surfaces dusted, and the room otherwise tidied. I hadn't authorized it; I suspected Revel. That night I slept on linens washed clean of the sweat of grief, on pillows that had not been soaked with my tears. The tapers for my candleholders were plain white ones, unscented, and the nightshirt I donned was soft and clean against my skin. I had felt like a traveler who had been on a long and arduous journey, and arrived at a faceless inn.

I was not surprised when Bee halted just inside the door and stared in dismay. It could have been any man's room. Or no one's. She looked around the room and then back at me.

"I want my things back." She spoke clearly. There was no trace of huskiness in her voice, no strain of tears held back. I took her to a storage chest under the window, unlocked it, and opened it. She looked in and grew very still.

Inside were not only the items I had removed from her room on that cruel and frantic evening, but many another memento as well. I had the first garment Bee had ever worn, and a ribbon stolen many years ago from Molly's hair. I had her mother's brush and her looking glass, and her favorite belt, leather dyed blue with pouches laced to it. Burrich had made it for her, and the buckle was worn thin with use. She had worn it until the day she died. There was a small casket that held not only her mother's jewelry, but each of Bee's baby teeth.

Bee found her books, and her nightgowns. "The candles are in my study, kept only for you," I reminded her. She found and gathered several small figurines. She did not speak, but by her folded lips I knew there were other significant items missing.

"I'm sorry," I said, when she turned from the trunk with her arms full of her precious possessions. "I should have asked you. If I could bring back your cherished things, I would."

She turned, and fleetingly her eyes met mine. Anger and pain smoldered in a banked fire there. Abruptly, she set her armful down on my bed. "I want my mother's belt-knife," she announced.

I looked down into the chest. The little knife rode on the belt, where it had for years. It had a bone handle, and at some time Molly or perhaps Burrich had wrapped it with a strip of leather to keep it from slipping. It had a blue sheath to match the leather belt. "The belt will be too big for you for many years," I said. It was an observation, not an objection. I had never thought of it going to anyone except Bee.

"I just need the knife and sheath now," she said. She met my eyes again with that sliding glance. "To protect myself."

I drew a deep breath and took Molly's belt from the chest. I had to take several little pouches off the belt before I could slide the sheathed knife free. I held it out toward Bee, haft-first, but as she reached for it I drew it back. "Protect yourself from what?" I demanded.

"Assassins." She asserted it quietly. "And people who hate me."

Those words hit me like stones. "No one hates you!" I exclaimed.

"They do. Those children that you have decided will take lessons beside me. At least three of them hate me. Maybe more."

I sat down on the edge of the bed, Molly's knife loose in my hands. "Bee," I said rationally. "They scarcely know you, so how could they hate you? And even if they dislike you, I doubt that the children of the keep would dare to—"

"They threw stones at me. And chased me. He slapped me so hard my mouth bled."

A terrible cold anger welled in me. "Who did this? When?"

She looked away from me. She stared at the corner of the room. I think she fought tears. She spoke very quietly. "It was years ago. And I'm not going to say. Your knowing would only make it worse."

"I doubt that," I said harshly. "Tell me who chased you, who dared to stone you, and they will be gone from Withywoods this very night. They and their parents with them."

Her blue glance slid past me as a swallow skims past a cliff. "Oh, and that would make the other servants love me well, wouldn't it? A nice life I should have then, with the other children fearful of me and their parents hating me."

She was right. It made sickness well up in me. My little girl had been chased and stoned and I had not even known. Even knowing, I could not think of a way to protect her. She was right. Anything I did would only make it worse. I found myself handing her the sheathed knife. She took it from me and for a moment I think she was disappointed I had yielded to her. Did she know that I was admitting there were times when I could not protect her? As Bee tugged the short knife free of its sheath, I wondered what Molly would have said to me, or what she would have done. It was a simple blade, showing the wear of much honing. Molly had used it for everything: cutting tough stems on flowers, shaving a wormhole from a carrot, or digging a splinter from my thumb. I glanced at my hand, remembering how she had held it tight and mercilessly dug out the ragged shard of cedar.

Bee had reversed her grip on the knife, holding it as if she was going to stab downward with it. She made several passes at the air, teeth clenched.

"Not like that," I heard myself say. She scowled at me from under lowered brows. I started to take the knife from her hand, and then realized that would not do. I drew my own belt-knife. It looked like Molly's, a short, sturdy blade meant for the dozen odd chores that might demand a knife during the day. I held it loosely in my hand, palm-up, the haft resting lightly. I balanced it. "Try this."

Grudgingly, she reversed her grip on the blade. She balanced it in her hand, and then gripped it tight. She poked the air with it, then shook her head. "I'm stronger with it the other way."

"Perhaps. If you have an obliging enemy who will stand still while you stab him. But you'll have to get close to him. If I hold a knife like this, it lets me force someone to stay back from me. Or I can reach out and cut someone before he can get close to me. Or I may choose to do a wide slash." I demonstrated that for her. "The way you were holding your blade, you can't slash effectively. Nor hold off more than one attacker."

I could see in her bunched shoulders how much she wanted to be right. It irritated her that she had to recognize she was wrong. In a small, gruff voice she conceded with, "Show me." And even more grudgingly, "Please."

"Very well." I stepped well clear of her and took up a stance. "It starts with your feet. You need to be balanced and ready, your weight set so that you can sway aside, or take a sudden step forward or back without losing your balance. Knees a little bent. See how I can move my body from side to side?"

She took a stance opposite me and copied me. She was limber, my little girl, and slender as a snake.

I set my knife down and armed myself with the sheath. "Now here's our first game. Neither one of us is allowed to move our feet. Or step forward or step back. I'm going to try to touch you with the tip of this sheath. You have to move aside and not let it touch you."

She looked at the bared blade in her hand and then at me.

"For now, set that aside. Begin by avoiding my blade."

And so I danced with my daughter, swaying counterpoints to each other. At first I touched her effortlessly, tapping her upper arm, her breastbone, her belly, her shoulder. "Don't watch the knife," I suggested. "Watch all of me. By the time the knife is moving toward you, it's almost too late. Watch my whole body, and see if you can tell when I'm going to try to tap you, and where."

I was not as rough with her as Chade had been with me. Chade's jabs had left little bruises, and he had laughed at me every time he scored a hit. I was not Chade and she was not me. Bruising her or mocking her would not wring greater effort from her. As I recalled, it had provoked me to anger, and led to errors and swifter defeat. I was not, I reminded myself, trying to teach my daughter to be an assassin. I merely wanted to teach her how to avoid a knife.

She improved rapidly, and soon I was the one being poked at with a sheath. The first time I allowed her to hit me, she stopped and then stood very still. "If you don't want to teach me, then say so," she said coldly. "But don't pretend I've learned something I haven't."

"I just didn't want you to get discouraged," I said to excuse my subterfuge.

"And I just don't want to think I've learned something I haven't. If someone wants to kill me, I need to be able to kill him back."

I stood still and fought to keep a smile from forming in my face or eyes. She would not have taken it well. "Very well, then," I said, and after that I was honest with her. It meant that she did not touch me again that afternoon, but it also meant that my back ached and I was sweating before she conceded that she'd had enough instruction for one day. Her short hair was damp and stood up in spikes as she sat down on the floor to thread the knife's sheath onto her belt. When she stood up, the knife hung heavy on her child's body. I looked at her. She didn't lift her eyes to mine. She suddenly looked to me like a neglected puppy. Molly had never let her run about in such disarray.

I felt as if I were tearing a piece from my heart as I lifted Molly's silver-backed brush and horn comb from my trove. I set them with Bee's other treasures. I had to clear my throat before I spoke. "Let's take these to your new room. Then I want you to use your mother's brush to smooth your hair. It's still too short to tie back. But you can put on one of your new tunics." Her fuzzy head nodded. "I think we will keep the knife lessons private, shall we?"

"I wish you had kept all my lessons private," she muttered sullenly.

"Do we need to talk about that?"

"You do things without asking me," she complained.

I crossed my arms on my chest and looked down on her. "I'm your father," I reminded her. "I don't ask your permission to do what I think is right."

"It's not about that! It's about not knowing before it happens. It's about . . ." She faltered. Then she looked up at me and fought to keep her gaze on mine as she told me earnestly, "They *will* try to hurt me."

"I am sure your tutor will keep order among his students."

She shook her head wildly and made a noise like a cornered cat. "They don't have to hit me to hurt me. Girls can . . ." Her clenched fists suddenly opened wide into claws. She clasped her own little head in taloned hands and squinched her eyes tight. "Forget that I asked you. I will take care of this myself."

"Bee," I began warningly, but she interrupted me with, "I told you. Girls don't have to hit to hurt."

I did not let it go. "I want you to understand why I invited the other children to be taught as well."

"I do understand."

"Then tell me why."

"To show everyone that you are not a stingy man. Or hard-hearted."

"What?"

"Perse—the stable boy. He told me that some people say you have a dark look to you, and that after Mother died they feared you would become harsh with the servants. You didn't. But this will show that you are actually a good man."

"Bee. It's not about me showing anybody anything. In Buckkeep Castle any child that wishes to learn is allowed to come to lessons at the Great Hearth. I, a bastard, was allowed to come there and learn. And so I think that, in my turn, I will allow any child who wishes to learn the chance."

She wasn't looking at me. I took a deep breath and nearly added more words, but then sighed instead. If she didn't understand what I had told her, more words would only weary her. She looked aside from me when I sighed.

"It's the right thing to do."

When I didn't respond, she added, "My mother would have wanted to learn. And if she were here, I know she would have in-sisted that every child receive the chance. You are right." She began to gather up her trove. It quickly filled her arms. She didn't ask for help but just tucked her chin over it to hold it to her chest. In a very quiet voice she added, "But I wish you weren't right, and I did not have to learn alongside them." I opened the door for her and followed her out.

We had almost reached the door of her room when I heard the tapping of hard-soled slippers and looked back to see Shun bearing down on me like a ship under full sail. "Holder Badgerlock!" she hailed me imperiously. Bee's pace increased. I halted and turned to face Shun, giving my daughter an opportunity to flee.

"Good afternoon, Lady Shun," I greeted her, assuming a smile I did not feel.

"I need to speak to you," she called breathlessly, steps before she had reached a conversational distance. When she halted, she began without greeting or preambles, "So, when are my music lessons to begin? And my dance instructor should come from Buckkeep Castle itself, if not from Jamaillia. I wanted to be sure you realized that. I don't wish to be hampered by knowing only the old steps."

I kept my smile with difficulty. "Music lessons. I am not sure that Scribe FitzVigilant is prepared to teach—"

She shook her head impatiently, her auburn curls flying. The motion propelled her scent to me. Molly had always worn perfumes of flowers and herbs: ginger and cinnamon, rose and lily. The fragrance that reached me from Shun had no recollection of a garden. A headache almost immediately assaulted me. I stepped back and she stepped forward as she continued. "I've already spoken to him, three days ago. He agrees with you that he is not qualified to teach me to play an instrument or sing, but suggested that if the manor hosted some minstrels for the winter, they were often pleased to instruct young ladies in musical accomplishments for a modest stipend.

"So then I asked him about dancing and—"

"Scribe FitzVigilant is still recovering. When did you speak to him?"

"When I went to his rooms to wish him well, of course. The poor fellow, I thought, sent away from Buckkeep Castle and the pleasures of the court to this backwater! I was sure he must be lonely and bored in his convalescence so I called on him, and engaged him in conversation to cheer him. I fear he is not a skilled conversationalist, but I well know how to pose questions and draw a shy fellow out of his shell. So when I asked him if he could dance and he told me yes, well enough, I asked if he might teach me some of the newer steps and he said he feared that his health would prevent him from dancing gracefully for a time. That was when he suggested I might need an instructor. So of course I told Riddle, and . . . he didn't speak to you, did he? For a serving man, he is most forgetful! To the point of uselessness. It's a wonder to me that you keep him on at all!"

I was casting my mind back over recent conversations with Riddle, trying to scavenge a clue to what she was talking about. I was distracted to think she had bothered poor FitzVigilant with her chatter. "Riddle is actually Lady Nettle's man, only loaned to Lord Chade for your safekeeping. And to look in on young Lady Bee, her sister."

"Her 'sister.'" Shun smiled. She cocked her head at me and regarded me with a trace of sympathy. "I respect you, Holder Badgerlock. Truly, I do. Living in your stepdaughter's home, maintaining it so diligently. And offering haven to the bastards of Buckkeep. FitzVigilant and myself and Bee. Tell me. What lord fathered her that she must hide here with you? I'm thinking her father was from Farrow. I've heard that wheat hair and cornflower eyes are more common there."

Such a surge of emotions. If I had not possessed the benefit of Chade's years of training, I think that for the first time in my life I would have struck an unarmed woman. I stared at her, masking everything I felt from her empty smile. Or was it? Was she seeking to hurt me? Truly, Bee was right. A girl did not need to hit to hurt someone. I could not tell if the blow she had dealt me was intended or not. She had her head cocked, smiling at me confidentially, as if begging for a stray bit of gossip. I spoke slowly and softly. "Bee is my true daughter, the child my loving wife bore to me. No taint of bastardy touches her."

Her gaze changed, her sympathy apparently deepening. "Oh, dear. I beg your pardon. I thought that surely, as she does not resemble you at all . . . but of course, I am sure you know what is true in that regard. So there are only three bastards seeking sanctuary at Withywoods. Myself and FitzVigilant, and, of course, you."

I matched her tone perfectly. "Of course."

I heard a soft tread and looked past her to see Riddle approaching. His movements slowed as if he had seen a crouching lynx or a snake poised to strike. Uncertainty turned to dismay as he accepted that he might have to attempt to protect Shun from me. When had the man come to know me so well? I stepped back from her, putting myself beyond striking distance, and saw his shoulders relax, then tighten again as Shun shadowed my movement, putting herself back in harm's way. His eyes met mine for a moment and then he strode lightly up to join us. When he touched Shun on the shoulder, she jumped. She had been completely unaware of his approach.

"I've arranged a meeting with Revel for you," he lied quickly. "I think he is our best source for an appropriate music instructor for you. And perhaps a dancing master as well."

She bristled, perhaps offended at being touched, and while he had her attention I walked away, leaving him with the problem. Unfair, perhaps, but safer for all of us.

In the safety of my study, with the door closed, I finally allowed myself to feel everything she had roused in me. Fury was foremost. How dared she, a guest in my home, speak so of my daughter! The slur on Molly's name was equally unforgivable. But bafflement followed fury. Why? Why had Shun, who depended on my goodwill, said such things? Was she so blind to all levels of courtesy that she regarded such a question as acceptable? Had she been deliberately trying to insult or wound me, and if so, why?

Did she truly believe Molly had cuckolded me? Did others look at Bee's pale hair and blue eyes and think me a fool?

I controlled my glance as I sat down at my desk, sparing only a flicker of a look at the wall above my worktable. Across Bee's peephole, I had coaxed a thread of spider silk, and trapped a tiny bit of bird down in it. It hung motionless save when Bee was in residence.

It had given a tiny jiggle as I crossed the room. She was there now. I wondered if she had preceded me to the study, or if she had used her badly hidden pantry entrance. I hoped she was not weeping over her father's idiocy in disposing of her treasures. Her anger was hard for me to bear, but weeping would have been worse.

I looked down at the scroll on my desk. I had no real interest in it at the moment; it was written in an archaic style in faded ink, and was something Chade had sent to me to be recopied. It dealt with a Skill-exercise for new students. I doubted it would interest my daughter. The hair I had left across one corner of it was undisturbed. So. She had not thumbed through my papers today. I remained certain that she had done so previously. I was not sure when she had begun to read papers left in my study, so I could not be certain just what she had seen of my personal writing. I sighed to myself. Every time I thought I had stepped forward to being a better parent, I discovered a new failing. I had not confronted her about her investigation of her father; I had known she could read, and I had been careless. In my own youth I had read more than one missive or scroll that Chade had left carelessly lying about.

Or so I had thought. I wondered if he did then as I did now, which was to leave out only those that I thought might intrigue her mind or educate her. My private thoughts I recorded in a ledger that I now wrote in only within my bedchamber. Even if she had known of the sliding compartment in the great chest at the foot of my bed, she would not have been able to reach it.

I thought of calling her out of her hiding place and decided against it. Let her have her private place in which to sulk or mourn.

There was a tap at my door. "Riddle," I said, and he eased the door open. He peered round it, cautious as a fox, and then sidled in, closing the door softly behind him.

"I'm so sorry," he said.

"No harm done," I replied. I was not sure if he was apologizing for Shun accosting me about music lessons, or if he had overhead her remarks about bastards and was offering sympathy. In either case, "I've no desire to discuss it now."

"I'm afraid we must," he offered. "Revel was delighted with Lady

Shun's request. He thinks it would be absolutely marvelous for you to have music and dancing at Withywoods again. He says there's an old man in Oaksbywater who can no longer croak out a note, but can teach Lady Shun to coax a tune from a harp. And Revel has offered himself as a dancing master to her, 'Only, of course, until a more suitable partner can be discovered for such a lady.' I will add that Lady Shun was not greatly pleased when he eagerly suggested that Bee might also profit from instruction in dance and music."

I saw the glint in his eye and surmised, "But you accepted on her behalf."

"I'm afraid I could not resist," he admitted, and I saw the cobweb stir, as if someone had either sighed or drawn in a breath. Little spy. What was bred in the bone, I supposed, would not be beaten out of the flesh.

"Well. Doubtless it will do her no harm," I mercilessly replied, and the cobweb stirred again. "Time and past time that my daughter received the education of a lady." Better music and dancing, I thought to myself, than the lessons in blood points and poisons. Perhaps if she was put out of my influence in the area of her education, I could refrain from raising her as I had been raised. Burning bodies by moonlight, and fighting with knives. *Oh, well done, Fitz. Well done.* And yet, in a dim corner of my mind, a sage old wolf opined that the smallest cub was the one that needed the sharpest teeth.

Riddle was still watching me. "There's more, isn't there?" I asked reluctantly.

He gave a tight nod. "Yes. But from a different source. I've a message from Chade."

That piqued my interest. "You have? And how, perchance, did that message reach you?" And did I dare let him relay it with Bee listening?

He shrugged one shoulder. "Pigeon." He proffered a tiny scroll to me. "You can read it yourself, if you wish."

"He sent it to you. Did he intend we both know whatever is in it?"

"Well, it's a peculiar note, especially coming from Chade. He offers a cask of Sandsedge brandy, apricot brandy, if I can discover exactly how you deduced FitzVigilant's maternal line."

A shiver of almost-knowing ran over my skin. "I'm sure I don't know what we are discussing here." For an instant I debated shushing him, wondering if a secret was about to be shared that my little daughter had no right to know.

Riddle shrugged and uncoiled the tiny scroll. He held it close to his face to read, and then moved it out until his eyes could focus on the minute lettering. He spoke its words aloud. "'Huntswoman or gardener's girl, he surmised. And the huntswoman it was. A cask of apricot Sandsedge brandy if you can discover for me how he narrowed it to those two . . .'"

I smiled as Riddle's voice faltered. "And the rest, no doubt, for your eyes alone?"

Riddle raised his brows. "Well, perhaps he intended it that way, but how I could keep it from you, I don't know. He ardently desires to know why this is such an important piece of information to you."

I leaned on my elbows and steepled my fingers, tapping them against my lips as I considered. "It probably isn't," I told him bluntly. Would the small listener in the wall behind me have put the shards together as quickly as I had? Most likely. It was not a difficult riddle.

"I was seeking for a child born of either of those women. But not sired by Lord Vigilant. Unless . . ." It was my turn to let my words trickle away as a peculiar thought came to me. Many a bastard had been blessed with a mother deceptive enough to proclaim him the product of the rightful marriage bed. Was this a case of a mother finding a more acceptable illegitimacy for her son? Would Laurel have conceived by the Fool, and then claimed the child was the offspring of another tryst? No. Not only did I believe that the huntswoman would have cherished any babe Lord Golden fathered on her, but the age was wrong. FitzVigilant might be Laurel's son, but he could not be the Fool's. And knowing Laurel as I had, I doubt she would willingly have ceded a lovingly conceived child, no matter his bastardy, to his father's sole care. There was more of

a tale there than I had the heart to know, something dark. A rape?
A dishonest seduction? Laurel had left a child to be raised by a man
who acknowledged him but was either incapable or unwilling to
protect him as he grew. Why? And why did Chade and Nettle seem
to value him so?

I met Riddle's inquiring look. "In truth, it's entirely coincidence.
I was looking for someone else, a much older offspring. Chade
won't believe that, so he won't pay his bribe. A pity. Apricot Sandsedge brandy is hard to come by. It's been years since I've tasted it."
I drew my thoughts back from following that memory. Too late. It
had coupled with my Fool's quest. Could FitzVigilant be the unexpected son he had bade me seek? Only if, unbeknownst to me or
Chade, Lord Golden had returned to the Six Duchies, had an assig-
nation with Huntswoman Laurel, and then abandoned her. And
she had blamed the child on Lord Vigilant? No. There was no sense
to be found there.

Riddle was still regarding me speculatively. Might as well make
use of his curiosity. "That visitor we had, the one who left without
saying farewell? She brought me a message from an old friend. Lord
Golden, to be precise."

One of his eyebrows lifted slightly. If he was surprised that she
had been a messenger, he covered it well. "You and Lord Golden
were very close, as I recall."

He said it so neutrally, it meant nothing at all. Or perhaps everything. "We were close," I agreed quietly.

The silence stretched longer. I was mindful of the small listener
behind the wall. I cleared my throat. "There is more. The messenger
said she was hunted. That her pursuers were close."

"She would have been safer if she had stayed here."

"Perhaps. Perhaps she didn't think so. I know she feared that danger would follow her to my household. But she also told me that
Lord Golden was trying to return, but that he, too, had to evade
pursuers." I weighed my risks. In for a copper, in for a gold. "Lord
Golden may have fathered a child when he was in the Six Duchies.
The messenger came to tell me that this son could be in great danger. That Lord Golden wished me to find him and protect him."

Riddle was silent, organizing all I had told him. He spoke cautiously. "You think that FitzVigilant might be Lord Golden's son?"

I shook my head. "He's the wrong age. Huntswoman Laurel was one of the women I thought might be a possible mother."

"More to the point, he has the wrong father. Laurel the huntswoman was his mother, Chade now says. But Vigilant claimed him as son. Unless the lad had two fathers . . ."

"Or was claimed by someone who didn't father him," I pointed out. Then I sighed. "He's still too young. Unless Lord Golden had paid another visit to Buck."

We both fell silent. Would he have returned to Buck and not contacted me? I didn't think so. Why would he have returned?

"What do you know of Lord Vigilant?" I asked Riddle.

"Not a great deal. He's a bit of a boor, and his estates were in disorder for some years. When I first heard of FitzVigilant, I was surprised that Lord Vigilant had been able to persuade any woman to lie down beside him, let alone that he, a single man, would recognize a bastard. But perhaps that does make sense, if he thought the boy his only chance for an heir. But he did take hold and hired a good man to help him in the running of his estates, and when he began to prosper, he married. I think that was when his troubles began. What lady would want a previous bastard to take precedent over her rightfully born sons? It wasn't long after that when Fitz-Vigilant was sent to Buckkeep, and wound up in Chade's care." He thought a moment longer. "I cannot see any connection between him and a possible child conceived by the same lady many years earlier."

I shook my head. "No. Just a peculiar coincidence. I opened a poke expecting a piglet and found a cat. But it doesn't end my search for this 'son.' I think I might be wise to make inquiries of Huntswoman Laurel herself."

Riddle shook his head. "That would be difficult. She is many years gone, Fitz. I remember when she left Buckkeep Castle, much to Queen Kettricken's disappointment. She had been instrumental, until then, in dealing with the Old Blood faction. She left so suddenly there was rumor that she had quarreled with someone in a high position, but if she did, it was well hushed. And before the year was out, we had word of her death."

I pondered this. Had Laurel fled Buckkeep to keep a pregnancy private and bear a secret child? It was a mystery many years old, and far outside my concern. I was sad to know she was gone. She had been kind to me. I shook my head and let her go. "Riddle. As you are out and about, can you keep an ear open for any gossip about my messenger?"

"Of course. I've heard nothing of her pursuers. You know that. But I may do better at tracking her. You think she fled to . . . where?"

To a pile of ash in the sheep pens. "I don't know. But I am more curious as to where she came from and who pursued her. I'd be as interested in what you might discover of her and those who hunted her before she came here as after she left."

"I'll keep an ear open. I suspect she would have come up the Buck River. I'll make some inquiries on my way back to Buckkeep."

"And I take that to mean that you wish to leave here soon."

"My task is done, and then some. I delivered my package safely to you, as I was ordered. I didn't mind helping for a time, but I do have things I must get back to."

I nodded slowly, feeling hollow. I hadn't realized how much I'd slipped into depending on him until he spoke of leaving. Riddle was someone who knew the man I once had been, someone I could speak openly to; that had been a comfort. I'd miss him. My voice did not betray that. "How soon must you leave?"

"Three days from now."

I nodded again, knowing that he was allowing me time to adapt to his absence. He added, "By then Lant should be up and around, so you'll have at least one man at your back."

"He did not watch his own back very well. I doubt I shall trust him with mine."

Riddle nodded and admitted, "He does not have the edge you and I do. But that does not make him completely incompetent. He's young yet. You should get to know him better."

"I will. As soon as he feels better. I thought he might want some privacy to heal."

He cocked his head slightly. "Not everyone is as solitary as you are, Tom. Lant can be very social. Being away from Buckkeep Castle is going to be hard on him. You should know that he actually welcomed Shun's visit. And that when he is healed, if she needs a dancing partner for practice, he's excellent. He's a witty conversationalist, well educated and affable. He was very popular with the ladies of the court, despite his low birth."

"I should visit him."

"Yes, you should. He is a bit in awe of you. Whatever you did to him the first time he met you, the effect has not worn off. It took a great deal of courage for him to come here, not only to seek permission to teach your daughter, but to hope for your protection. It was a bit . . . humiliating. But Chade told him it was really his only choice."

I hadn't seen it in that light before. And it was interesting to know that Riddle knew of my first encounter with FitzVigilant. Still Chade's man, in some ways. I said nothing of that, but observed, "He thinks I'm still angry with him."

Riddle nodded. "He's well enough to come to table and move about Withywoods. But he's been behaving as if you confined him to his rooms."

"I see. I'll take care of that this afternoon."

"Tom, he's a youngster, but that doesn't mean he can't be a friend to you. Get to know him. I think you'll like him."

"I'm sure I will," I lied. Time to end this conversation. Bee had heard enough.

Riddle's ability to understand what I didn't say sometimes made me uncomfortable. He looked at me almost sadly. He spoke more quietly. "Tom. You need a friend. Lant is young, I know, and your first introduction was . . . poorly considered. Begin again. Give him a chance."

And so that afternoon I tapped on the door of FitzVigilant's chambers. Bulen opened the door immediately. I saw Revel's hand in the improved fit of his livery and tamed hair. I surveyed the tutor's room unobtrusively, and found him to be a man of tidy habits, but not overly so. The medicinal unguents that Chade had prepared for him were neatly arrayed on the mantel. The smell of arnica oil flavored the room. FitzVigilant himself was seated at a worktable, writing a letter. Two pens were at the ready, and a pot of ink and small blotter. On the other end of the table, a gaming cloth was laid out with a Stones puzzle on it. I wondered who had taught him the game. Then I reined my thoughts sharply and kept my focus on my target.

He came to his feet immediately and bowed, then stood silently, regarding me with trepidation. There is a way that a man stands when he does not wish to appear aggressive but is ready to defend himself. FitzVigilant stood like that, but when coupled with the defeated look on his face he was almost cowering. I felt sick. I recalled what it was to have lost all confidence in my body. This was a man already subdued. I wondered how broken he was, if he would ever recover enough to be any sort of a man-at-arms. I tried to keep pity from my face.

"Scribe FitzVigilant, I am pleased to see you up and about. I came to ask if you were well enough to begin joining us for meals."

He didn't meet my eyes as he bobbed his head. "If that would please you, sir, I shall begin doing so."

"We would enjoy your company. It will give not only Bee but the rest of the household staff an opportunity to know you better."

He bowed again. "If it would please you, sir—"

"It would," I interrupted. "But only if you are comfortable also."

For a time our eyes met, and he was a boy standing naked by a hearth as a trained assassin ripped through his clothes. Yes. A bit of awkwardness to the beginning of our relationship. One we would have to overcome. The silence held, and something changed in him as determination set on his face.

"Yes. I shall be there, Holder Badgerlock."

Chapter 26

LESSONS

A dream from a winter night when I was six years old.

In a market square, a blind beggar sat in his rags. No one was giving him anything, for he was more frightening than pathetic with his cruelly scarred face and crumpled hands. He took a little puppet out of his ragged clothes; it was made of sticks and string with only an acorn for a head, but he made it dance as if it were alive. A small sullen boy watched from the crowd. Slowly he was drawn forward to watch the puppet's dance. When he was close, the beggar turned his clouded eyes on the boy. They began to clear, like silt settling to the bottom of a puddle. Suddenly the beggar dropped his puppet.

This dream ends in blood and I am afraid to recall it. Does the boy become the puppet, with strings attached to his hands and feet, his knees and elbows and bobbing head? Or does the beggar seize the boy with hard and bony hands? Perhaps both things happen. It all

ends in blood and screaming. It is the dream I hate most of all the
dreams I have ever had. It is the end dream for me. Or perhaps the
beginning dream. I know that after this event, the world as I know
it is never the same.

DREAM JOURNAL OF BEE FARSEER

My first dinner with my new tutor was the worst meal of my life. I
was dressed in one of my new tunics. It itched. It had not yet been
taken in to fit me, so I felt as if I were walking about in a small
woolen tent. My new leggings were not yet finished, so my old ones
were both too short and baggy about the knees. I felt like some
peculiar wading bird, with my legs sticking out the bottom of my
ample clothes. I told myself that once I was seated at the table, no
one could tell, but my plan to be first there failed.

Shun had preceded me, sweeping into the dining room like a
queen entering her throne room. Her hair had been dressed on top
of her head; her new maid had a gift for hair, and every auburn curl
shone. Silver pins twinkled against that sleek mahogany like stars in
a night sky. She was beyond beautiful; she was striking. Even I had
to admit that. Her gown was green and some trick of the cut lifted
her breasts away from her chest as if she were offering them to us,
demanding we look at them. She had painted her lips, and dusted
her face with a pale powder so that her dark lashes and green eyes
looked at us as if from a mask. A kiss of rouge at the top of each
cheek made her appear animated and lively. I was doomed to hate
her all the more for her beauty. I followed her into the room. Before
I could reach my seat, she turned to regard me and smiled a cat's
smile.

Worse was to come. My tutor was behind me.

FitzVigilant could not take his eyes off Shun. His beautiful face
had healed, the swelling gone and the greens and purples of his
bruises faded. His skin was not weathered as were my father's and
Riddle's. He had the complexion of a court gentleman. He had
shaved his high-boned cheeks and strong chin as smooth as could
be, but the shadow of what would doubtless be a grand mustache
was showing on his upper lip. I had worried that he would scoff at

my ill-fitting clothes—a useless fear. He halted in the door, his eyes widening as he saw Shun. Both she and I saw him catch his breath. Then he came slowly to take his place at the table. He apologized to my father for being late, but as he spoke, he looked at Shun.

In that moment of his carefully worded courtesy with his court accent, I fell in love.

People make mock of a girl or boy's first love, calling it puppyish infatuation. But why should not a young person love just as wildly or deeply as any other? I looked at my tutor and knew that he must see me as just a child, small for my age and provincial, scarcely worthy of his attention. But I will not lie about what I felt. I burned to distinguish myself in his company. I longed to say something charming, or to make him laugh. I wished that something would happen that would make him see me as important.

But there was nothing about me. I was a little girl, dressed in very ordinary garb, with no exciting tale to tell. I could not even enter the conversation that Shun began and then guided so carefully to herself and her sophisticated upbringing. She spoke of her childhood in the grandparents' home, telling stories of the various well-known minstrels who had performed there, and nobles who had come to visit. Often enough, FitzVigilant would exclaim that he, too, had heard that minstrel perform, or that he knew Lady This-and-So from a visit to Buckkeep Castle. When he mentioned a minstrel named Hap, she set down her fork and exclaimed that she had heard he was the most amusing of minstrels, knowing every humorous song that one could sing. I longed to open my mouth and say he was like an elder brother to me and once had given me a doll. But they were talking to each other, not me, and if I had spoken it would have seemed I eavesdropped. In that moment, though, how I longed that Hap would suddenly drop in on one of his random visits and greet me as kin.

As if that would have increased my standing in Scribe FitzVigilant's eyes. No. For him, the only person at the table was Shun. She cocked her head and smiled at him as she took a sip of wine and he lifted his glass to her and smiled back. My father spoke with Riddle about his return to Buckkeep, when he would depart, messages he would carry to Lord Chade and Lady Nettle and even to King Dutiful. The grapes at Withywoods had done well, and there were preserves he wished to send to Lady Kettricken as well as a sampling of wine now aged five years from the Withywoods cellars that he felt showed great promise.

And I sat silent among them, cutting and eating my meat, buttering my bread, and looking away whenever Elm came into the room to put out a fresh dish or to clear plates. She was old enough now to serve at table, and her apron of Withywoods green and yellow suited her very well. Her hair was smoothed flat to her head and the length of it was pinned in a neat coiled braid on the back of her head. I wanted to lift a hand to my own head to see if my pale thatch of hair was still combed neatly or wandering on my head like torn corn silk. I put my hands under the table and clasped them tightly together.

When it was time to leave the table, my tutor moved quickly to slide Shun's chair back and offer his arm to her. She took it readily and thanked "Lant" very prettily. So. He was Lant to her, and Scribe FitzVigilant to me. My father offered his arm to me, and as I looked up at him in surprise, his dark eyes danced with amusement as he flicked a glance at the young couple. I looked at Riddle, who rolled his eyes but also looked charmed by their behavior. I found nothing amusing about it.

"I think I shall seek my own chamber now," I said quietly.

"Are you well?" my father asked me quickly, concern in his eyes.

"Quite. I've simply had a long day."

"Very well. I'll tap on your door later to say good night."

I nodded. Was he warning me to be where I said I'd be? Well, I would be. By then. I took a candle in a holder to light my way.

Lady Shun and Scribe FitzVigilant had not even noticed that we had paused. They had moved out of the dining room and were headed toward one of the cozier sitting rooms. I didn't want to see them sitting and chatting together. I turned from all of them and strode away, my hand cupped to shelter my candle's flame.

It had been a long day, truly, but not because of anything I'd done. Rather, it was the not-doing that had stretched the hours for me. I hadn't gone down to the stables. For a time, I'd been trapped in my hidey-hole while my father and Riddle talked, until I had crept away down the passage to appear stealthily in the kitchens. But I had not dared to linger there to watch Mild knead the bread or turn the spit. Lea was there always now, sweeping up spilled flour or stirring a slowly bubbling kettle of cornmeal. Her dark eyes were like knives, her flat mouth an anvil to pound me against with her brief words. So I had spent the most of my day in one of Patience's garden rooms, with a copy of *Badgerlock's Old Blood Tales*. Every time my father had seen me with it, he had offered me a different book, which had made me believe there was something in it he did not wish me to read. Yet he had not taken it away from me. And so I was intent on reading every page of it, even the boring parts. I had finished it today and still had no idea what part of it he had dreaded me reading. Then I had wandered about the plant room, pinching dead bits off the plants. As most were dormant for the winter, this was not as interesting as it might have been.

My steps slowed as I traversed the corridor to my bedchamber. And when I reached the door of my old room, I slowed and looked carefully behind me. No one was watching. I opened the door and slipped inside.

It was dark. There was no fire on the hearth. The draperies over the window were drawn. I stepped inside and let the door close behind me. I stood still, breathing quietly, waiting for my eyes to adjust. My candle could barely push the darkness back. I moved forward slowly, groping my way. I found the corner post of my bed. By touch, I moved to the emptied chest at the foot of it. Only a few steps, and my hands met the cold stonework of the hearth.

The door to the adjacent servant's chamber was closed, and suddenly that was frightening. A prickling ran up my back. The messenger had died in there. No, actually she had died right on my bed. Right behind me. For a moment I could not make myself turn to look at it, and then I simply had to. Knowing I was being silly didn't help. Or was I being silly? I had told Shun that everyone knew ghosts only lingered where the person had died. And she had died there. I turned slowly. My hands were shaking and my candle trembled, sending shadows leaping about the room.

The stripped bed was empty. I had been foolish. I would not stare at it. I would not. I turned back to the closed door. I dared myself and walked to it. I put my hand on the door handle. It was cold. Colder than was natural? Would her ghost linger where we had unwittingly abandoned her? I pushed down on the latch and then dragged the door open. The draft from the little room nearly sucked the flame from my candle. I stood still until it steadied, and peered in.

It was emptier than when I had last seen it. The old stand and ewer remained there. And the heavy bed frame was still pushed tight against my secret entrance. Somehow tonight the idle furniture crouched and the empty ewer rebuked me. I spoke to her ghost. "If I had known you were still here, I would have taken better care of you. I thought you were gone." I felt no change in the hovering darkness, but felt a bit braver that I had dared to speak to her directly.

It was harder to pull the bed frame away from the concealed entrance while holding my candle, but I managed. I clambered over it to trigger the lever, and then climbed back to go inside. I dribbled wax on the passage floor and stuck my candle in it before dragging the bed frame back into place and pushing the door shut. In my hidden labyrinth, I felt better immediately. I held my candle steady and followed the marks I scarcely needed anymore until I came to my little lair. Just outside it I stopped suddenly, puzzled. Something was different. A scent? A slight warmth in the air? I studied the little room carefully, but saw nothing amiss. Cautiously I stepped forward, tripped, and measured my length on the floor. My candle jumped from my hand, rolled in a half-circle, and only by the greatest good fortune remained lit. By bad fortune, it fetched up against a coiled scroll I had left on the floor. The edge had just begun to smolder with a stink of burning leather when I scrabbled to my knees and seized the candle. I set it upright in the holder and turned to see what had tripped me. It had felt like a mound of fabric. Warm fabric.

I felt a moment of dizziness as the floor wavered before my gaze. Then a small, scowling cat face emerged from nothing. He rose slowly out of the floor, stretched, and gave me a rebuking *Wowr.* Only the barest edge of rolled butterfly wing betrayed the cloak in a heap on the floor. I pounced on it and snatched it up, holding it to my chest. It was warm and smelled of black cat. "What were you doing?" I demanded of him.

Sleeping. Was warm.

"This is mine. You're not to take things off my shelf." I saw now that the plate I'd put on top of my bowl of hard bread had been pushed aside. With the bundled cloak under my arm, I made a quick inspection of my supplies. The bread had been chewed at the edge and rejected. I'd had half a sausage up there. Only a few scraps of casing remained. "You ate my food! And slept on my cloak."

Not yours. Hers.

I paused in mid-breath. "Well, it's mine now. She's dead."

She is. So it's mine. It was promised to me.

I stared at him. My memories of that day had an overlay of haze, not for the evening events but those from the morning. I could not remember why I had gone walking to that part of the estate grounds. They were shady and chill, uninviting during the gray and wet days. I could scarcely remember seeing the butterfly wing on the ground; I could not tell if it was a memory from that day, or a memory of my dream. But I did recall that as my father had approached, he had given a shout of surprise. And something had raced away into the brush. Something black and furry.

Yes. I was there.

"That doesn't mean the cloak belongs to you."

He sat up very straight and wrapped his black tail neatly around his white feet. He had yellow eyes, I noticed, and the candlelight danced in them as he declared. *She gave it to me. It was a fair trade.*

"For what? What does a cat have to trade?"

A gold glitter came into those yellow eyes, and I knew I had insulted him. I'd insulted a cat. Just a cat. So why did a little shiver of dread go down my back? I remembered that my mother had told me to never be afraid to apologize when I was wrong. She had said it would have saved her and my father a great deal of trouble if they had only followed that rule. Then she had sighed, and added that I must never think that an apology could completely erase what I had done or said. Still, it was worth trying.

"I beg your pardon," I said sincerely. "I do not know much of cats, having never had one of my own. I think I have misspoken to you."

Yes. You have. Twice. The idea that a human could "have a cat of her own" is equally insulting. Abruptly, he lifted one of his hind legs, pointed his foot toward the ceiling, and began to groom his bottom. I knew I was being insulted. I chose to bear it in silence. He carried on for a ridiculously long time. I began to be chilly. I surreptitiously picked up an edge of the cloak and draped it around my shoulders.

When he had finally finished, he focused his round, unblinking eyes on me again. *I gave her dreams. I lay down beside her and purred through the long cold night. She was badly hurt. Dying. She knew it. Her dreams were dark with sharp edges, full of faces of those she had failed. She dreamed of the creatures that were inside her, chewing their way through her guts. I came into her dreams and in them I was the Cat of Cats, powerful beyond imagining. I chased and slew those who had hurt her. I embraced them with my claws and tore their entrails from their bodies. Toward dawn, when the frost was coldest, I promised I would bring you to her, and she would be discovered and her message delivered. She thanked me, and I told her I had enjoyed the warmth of the cloak. That was when she said I might have it when she was gone.*

His story rang with truth. Right up until his last statement. I knew he was lying. He knew that I knew he was lying. He smiled lazily without moving his mouth at all. It was something in the set of his ears, perhaps. He was daring me to dispute his story. Deep in my heart Wolf-Father growled, a low rumbling. He did not like this cat, but his growl was to warn me as much as the feline.

"Very well. I will leave the cloak here at night for you to use."

Trade, he suggested.

Aha. I tipped my head at him. "What do I have that a cat could possibly want?"

His eyes narrowed. *The cat who is allowed to sleep by the kitchen hearth has a basket with a soft blanket in it. And herbs . . .*

"Catmint. And fleabane." I knew about that. My mother had begun that tradition.

I want the same. And if you see them chase me with a broom, you must shriek and fuss and slap them so that they never dare do so again.

"I can do that."

And you must bring me delicious things. In a clean dish. Every day.

Somehow he had come closer to me. Slowly he stepped up into my lap and arranged himself. "I can do that," I agreed.

And when I wish to be stroked, you must stroke me. But only if I wish it. He had become a black circle of cat in my lap. He lifted one front paw, extended long and very sharp white claws, and began to tug and groom them.

"Very well." Very carefully, I put my hands on him. My fingers sank into lush black fur. He was so warm! I moved one hand carefully down his side. I found two tiny burs and a nest of thorns. I combed them out with my fingers. The end of his tail became alive and lifted to wrap around my wrist. It was utterly charming. I put my fingers under his chin and gently scratched there. He lifted his face and a strange transparent eyelid lifted to cover his half-closed eyes. I moved my hand to rub his ears. His purr deepened. His eyes became slits. For a time, we sat together. Then slowly, he began to melt onto his side. I smoothed burs from his belly fur.

Abruptly as a snake striking, he wrapped his front paws around my forearm. He delivered three vicious, clawed kicks to my arm and then streaked off down the passage into darkness. Not even the ghost of a thought hung to explain why he had done it. I clutched my bleeding wrist to my chest and rocked forward, enduring the stinging pain silently. Tears stung my eyes. In my heart, Wolf-Father rumbled his assent. *Cats are cursed creatures, never to be trusted, talking to everyone and anyone. I hope you have learned something.*

I had, but I was not sure what. I stood slowly, suddenly anxious about how much time had passed. I gathered my cloak and folded it hastily. I restored it to its place on my shelf, and put the lid back on my bread bowl. Little sneaking thief.

I could learn from him.

In the morning, unbidden, Careful came to help me rise, wash, groom my wayward hair, and then dress. It was all very trying for me. No one save my mother had ever done such things, and she had done them with merry chatter and shared plans for the day. Careful, I decided, would have been better named Hasty. Or perhaps Tart, for her mouth today was pursed as if every item in my wardrobe put a sour taste in her mouth. She tugged my smock over my head and almost before it had settled on my shoulders, she was layering my tunic over it. She pulled my sleeves even and then, without asking, reached up under my tunic and pulled my smock down smooth. She asked me for things I had never possessed, such as pins for my hair or at least a pomade to hold it down. She asked where my earrings were and was shocked that I had not even holes in my ears for such adornments. She exclaimed in loud dismay over the state of my stockings and found a heavier pair and said that my shoes were a disgrace to the household.

Perhaps she intended such things to express outrage she supposed I shared. In reality they only made me feel shabby and shy. I could find no words to defend myself or my clothing. I put on my belt with my mother's knife, for courage. Careful gave a disapproving snort, and knelt before me. "That's not how you wear that," she told me. I kept my silence as she took my belt and hastily bored a new hole in it with her own little knife, and then put it on me so that it rode at my waist instead of sitting on my hips.

When she had finished tugging at my hair and pulling my tunic straight, she stood me before my mirror and we looked at the reflection. To my surprise, I did not look nearly as poorly turned out as I had feared. I smiled at my reflection and said, "I think this is the nicest I have looked in months. Thank you, Mistress Careful."

I think my words shocked her. She had been crouching beside

me. Now she rocked back on her heels and stared at me, her large brown eyes gone very wide indeed. "You wait here," she told me abruptly. "You wait right here."

I obeyed her, and before I even had time to wonder why I was doing what a servant told me to do, she had returned. "Now, I shall want these back when you are finished with them. They cost me a pretty penny, and I've worn them less than a dozen times. So keep your wrists well away from anything sticky. Do you think you can do that?"

She hadn't waited for an answer or permission. She fitted cuffs of cream lace to the wrists of my underblouse, and then added a collar that matched. They were a bit large, but she took a threaded needle from beneath the collar of her shirt and quickly took them in. She stared at me when she was finished, her brow creased. Then she gave a small sigh. "Well. I wish the daughter of the household, placed in my care, were better turned out than the kitchen girls, but this will do for today, and before the hour is out I will be letting Revel know what I think! Off you go to breakfast now, poppet. Doubtless I shall have an hour of tidying to do in Lady Shun's room. Every morning it's the same, a dozen skirts flung about the room, and as many pretty blouses. You, now, you keep your things neat as a pin. I don't think I've ever needed more than ten breaths to tidy your room."

I kept to myself that I had not even known she was supposed to tidy my room. I had accepted without question that someone took care of my washbasin, ewer, and chamber pot, just as I accepted that my bed linens were laundered once a month. "My thanks for the care you take of me," I said, as it came to me that those were not particularly pleasant tasks.

Again, her cheeks pinked. "I'm sure you're welcome, Lady Bee. And off you run now! I hope your lessons go well."

Anticipation warred with dread. I wanted to go directly to the schoolroom. I wanted to run and hide in my special place. Instead I went down to breakfast. My father was there, waiting for me. He was not seated, but wandering about the room, as if he, too, was nervous. He turned to me when I came in and his eyes widened.

Then he smiled. "Well. You certainly look ready to begin your new studies!"

"Careful helped me," I told him. I touched the lace at my neck. "The collar and cuffs are hers. She was surprised I had no earrings. And then she said she would not let the kitchen girls outshine me."

"They could not possibly do so, even if you were in rags and dirt."

I just looked at him.

"Not to say that you look ragged or dirty! No. No! I simply meant that no matter . . ." He stopped, and looked so comically woeful that I had to laugh.

"It is fine, Da. It is not as if they do not see me every day, dressed as I ordinarily am. I will fool no one."

My father looked mildly alarmed. "I do not think our aim is to trick anyone, Bee. Rather, you dress in a way that conveys respect to the scribe who teaches you." His speech slowed as he added, "And to convey your proper status in the household." He halted and I could see he was frantically considering something. I let him, for my mind was suddenly just as occupied.

A dreadful thought had come to me. Lessons were to be something I did four of every hand of days. Did that mean that I would be dressed like this every day? Did it mean that every morning Careful would invade my rooms to prepare me? Slowly I understood that it would be a full four days before I could next do as I wished with my morning. No more riding in the morning. Not that there had been any since I'd had my falling-out with Perseverance. But I thought that eventually, somehow, I would mend things with him. My mornings being taken out of my control, though, was a permanent change. Almost daily, I'd be forced to deal with people I disliked in the schoolroom. And even at the breakfast table . . .

"Well, Bee, such a surprise! You've combed your hair. You look almost like a girl this morning."

I turned at Shun's greeting. Riddle had followed her into the room. She was smiling at me. My father looked uncertain, while Riddle's eyebrows had risen nearly to his hairline. I smiled back at her and carefully curtsied. "Why, thank you, Shun. You yourself look almost like a well-bred lady this day." I kept my voice as smooth as sweet cream. It would have been almost comical to watch my father's expression switch from uncertainty to alarm, had it not been that Scribe FitzVigilant had entered just in time to hear my words. And only my words, not the comment that had provoked them. He gave me a look that a nasty and disrespectful child would merit, then greeted Shun warmly and escorted her to her chair at table as if he were rescuing her from a small, ill-tempered animal.

As I took my place at the table, I noticed that Shun did not immediately begin eating, but waited until FitzVigilant had taken his seat beside her. They were most companionable diners, greeting my father and Riddle, but sparing neither word nor glance for me. They passed food to each other, and Shun poured him more tea. For the most part I kept my eyes on my plate and ate. Whenever I did steal a glance at them, the matched beauty they presented clawed at my heart with jealous nails. Truly, they looked as if they had been struck from the same mold, created to be matches. They both possessed the same glossy curls, decided chins, and fine noses. Their gazes admired each other as if they were staring into a vanity mirror. I stared back at my plate and pretended a great interest in my sausage.

My father was offering Riddle a side of good bacon, wines from the cellar, and smoked river fish to take back to Buckkeep Castle with him. If Riddle had said yes to all of it, he could have loaded a wagon and borrowed a team. But he was insisting that he had to travel light, and that he would try to call again soon.

Then my ears caught a fragment of Shun's words. ". . . pretend it doesn't bother me. But I am so glad that you are well enough to teach. A day filled with useful pursuits is, I believe, best for children. And discipline. Will you have a strict hand, do you think?"

FitzVigilant's voice was low and soft, like a big cat's rumble. "Very strict to begin with. Better to start with a firm hand, I think, than to try to establish one later."

My heart sank.

We finished our breakfast, and our scribe bid my father have a good morning. When he looked at me, he did not smile. "I expect to see you promptly in the schoolroom, Lady Bee."

Courtesy might change his opinion of me. "I shall follow you there, Scribe FitzVigilant."

He looked at my father rather than me as he said, "I suggest that my students call me Scribe Lant. It is less of a mouthful for young folk to remember."

"As you wish," my father replied, but I know he shared my thought. The name did not brand him as a bastard each time it was spoken.

I waited quietly as my teacher bid Riddle good day, then followed him silently as he led the way to the schoolroom. He still had a slight limp, but he strove to strike a brisk pace. I followed him as quickly as I could without breaking into a trot. He said nothing to me as we hastened to the schoolroom, nor did he look back to see if I kept up with him. Foolish as it might seem, my heart was breaking while my dislike for Shun was simmering to a boil. I would put dead rats in her wardrobe. No. That would only lead to trouble for Revel, and he had been kind to me. I tried in vain to think of any nasty trick I could do that would not create trouble for anyone else. It was so unfair that, simply because she was beautiful and a woman grown, she could command the full attention of any man in the household. They were my father, my sister's companion, and the tutor sent to teach me, but with a toss of her head, it seemed that Shun could make them hers. And I was powerless to stop her.

I had fallen well behind his long-strided haste. He reached the door of the schoolroom and halted, looking back at me in mild annoyance. He was silent as he waited for me, and stood back to allow me to trot into the room ahead of him.

I halted inside the door in astonishment. I had never seen so many children gathered in one place, and they all stood as I entered. It seemed strange and threatening, as when a tree fills up with cawing crows or bees swarm before leaving the hive. I stood still with no idea of where to go. My gaze roved over them. Some I knew from past encounters, some I had glimpsed in passing, and two were complete strangers. Elm and Lea were there, neat and tidy, dressed in the green and yellow of Withywoods, their kitchen aprons set aside for now. Taffy was there, in a simple jerkin and trousers. He glowered, his arms crossed on his chest, obviously not pleased at being there. I found Perseverance in the back, his face so scrubbed it looked raw and his hair bound back in a tail. His clothing was tidy, but had plainly seen more than one owner. The lads near him would be the boys from the stables, Lukor and Ready and Oatil. There was a lad I'd seen working in the gardens, and two, a boy and a girl, that I'd seen tending geese. So many! At least a dozen faces stared at me as I stood frozen.

A disapproving voice spoke behind me. "Lady Bee, if you would please move out of the doorway so I may enter?"

I tottered a few steps out of his way and abruptly realized the children had risen for the scribe, not me. It made me feel a bit better as I edged into the room and their gazes shifted from me to FitzVigilant.

"I am pleased to see such promptness," he greeted them. I thought I detected a note of dismay in his voice. Was he as astonished as I was at how many children had assembled? He took a short breath. "You will address me as Scribe Lant. I am here to teach you. Lady Nettle has been extremely generous in sending a tutor to instruct the children of her estate. I want all of you to be aware of how rare such generosity is. I hope you will show yourself properly grateful by exhibiting excellent behavior and applying yourselves diligently to your studies. We will begin immediately. Let each of you find a place and be seated. I think my first task will be to determine how much you already know."

A bench provided seats for four of them. Elm and Lea quickly claimed two of those spots, and the goose girl and boy took the others. Taffy and another big boy and Perseverance sat down on the hearth, backs to the fire. The others glanced about and then sank to the floor to sit cross-legged. After a moment of indecision, I sat down at the edge of the group, on the carpet with them. The garden boy glanced at me, smiled shyly, and then looked away. Two of the others shifted away from me. They both smelled slightly of sheep.

Scribe FitzVigilant had moved to a worktable and he took a seat there. "I shall have to send for more tablets," he said, half to himself and half to us. "And ask Revel to bring in seating."

Then he pointed to the children seated on the bench. "I'll start with you. Please come up, one at a time, and tell me what learning you already have." His gaze swept the room. "I am sure the rest of you can wait quietly while I do this."

The children exchanged glances. He had not chosen to speak to me first. I wondered if they thought he already knew all about me or if, as I did, they knew it indicated he already disapproved of me. I had noted to myself that he ascribed the generosity to Lady Nettle, rather than my father, and that he spoke of coming to teach the children of the estate. No mention that I was sharing my tutor with them. No. He had grouped me with all the other students. As had I, I suddenly realized, when I had taken a seat on the floor with the others. An error. How could I correct it? Did I want to correct it?

Some of the children settled immediately into more comfortable positions. This was going to take some time. Taffy sat scowling. He took out his belt-knife and began to pare and dig at his nails. The gardener's children were looking about in wonder. Perseverance sat as attentively as a dog at a table's edge.

Scribe Lant called Elm up first. I folded my hands in my lap, stared at the floor, and eavesdropped with all my might. She could count, of course, and do simple sums as long as they did not go far past the fingers on her hands. She did not have any letters or reading or writing, except her name. She could name all the duchies in Buck, and knew that Chalced was dangerous to us. She was hazy on the rest of geography. Well, I knew more than that, but not so much that I felt sure of myself.

Lea had about the same level of learning as Elm, except that she could recognize the names of some spices from having to fetch the containers from the shelves. The goose girl was named Ivy. She had no reading or writing, but she and her brother played games with arithmetic to pass the time. Her brother was Spruce, and he stood as tall as his name. He, too, did not know letters but was obviously excited at the chance to learn them. He was as quick at figures as his sister, with our scribe setting him problems such as "Twelve geese were on the water, and seventeen more landed while five flew away. Then twenty-two goslings came out of the reeds. A bullfrog ate one. How many geese and goslings remain?" Spruce answered the question quickly but added, a bit pink about the cheeks, that not all numbers needed to be about geese. FitzVigilant praised his quick mind and his eagerness to learn and called Perseverance to him.

Perseverance stood, head bowed, and answered respectfully that he had no letters or reading. He could reckon "well enough to get my work done." He volunteered that it was his father's wish he learn more, and added that he respected his father's will in knowing what was best for him. "As do I," the scribe agreed. He set the stable boy some simple arithmetic problems, and I saw Perseverance's fingers move as he worked them to an answer. The tops of his cheeks and his ears were redder than when the wind kissed them, and once, when he stumbled, he glanced my way. I pretended to be straightening the hem of my tunic.

It was much the same with the other students. I noted that most seemed to have inherited whatever level of schooling their parents had. Oatil, also from the stables, sometimes helped bring in the supplies and tally them. He could read a little, and his mother wanted him to learn more reading and writing as well so that he could help her more with her tasks. The gardener's boy, to my surprise, could write his name and read simple words, but had little skill with numbers. "But I'd be willing to learn," he offered, and "Learn you shall, then," our tutor replied with a smile.

When Taffy was called to the scribe's table, he rose lazily and slouched over. The half-smile on his face did not escape FitzVigilant's attention. He glanced up at him, said, "Stand up straight, please. Your name?" He poised his pen over his paper.

"Taffy. My da works in the vineyards. My ma comes round to help with the lambing, sometimes, when she's not dropping a kid herself." He glanced round at the rest of us, smirking, and added, "Da says she's happiest with a big belly or one on the tit."

"Indeed?" Our tutor was unruffled. As Taffy had spoken for all to hear, he asked aloud, "Can you read or write, young man?"

"Nar."

"I'll assume you meant to say, 'No, Scribe Lant.' I'm sure you'll do better the next time I ask you a question. Can you reckon? On paper, or in your head?"

Taffy gave his bottom lip a swipe with his tongue. "I reckon that I don't want to be here."

"Yet here you are. And as your father wishes it, I will teach you. Return to your place."

Taffy sauntered away. It was my turn. I was last. I rose and went to stand before the scribe's table. He was still making notes about Taffy. His dark curls were formed in perfect spirals. I looked down at his handwriting. It was clean and strong, even upside-down. "Insolent and unwilling," he had noted next to Taffy's name.

He glanced up at me, and I snatched my gaze away from the paper to meet his. His eyes were a soft brown, with very long lashes. I looked hastily down again. "Well, Lady Bee, it is your turn now." He spoke softly. "It is Lady Nettle's earnest wish that you learn to read and write, at least a little. Or as much as you are able. Do you think you could try to do that, for her?" His smile tried to be kind, but it was a false kindness.

It shocked and hurt me that he spoke to me so condescendingly. It was much worse than when he had looked at me earlier with such disdain for my poor manners. I glanced up at him and then away. I did not speak loudly but I took care to form my every word as clearly as I could. I knew that sometimes my speech was still garbled and muted. I would take care that would not happen today. "I can already read and write, sir. And I can work with numbers up to twenty in my head. Beyond that, if I have tally sticks, I can get the correct answer. Most of the time. But not swiftly. I am familiar with the local geography, and can place each duchy on the map. I know 'The Twelve Healing Herbs' and other learning rhymes." That last was a gift from my mother. I had noticed that none of the children had spoken of learning rhymes or sayings.

Scribe Lant gave me a guarded look as if he suspected me of something. "Learning rhymes."

I cleared my throat. "Yes, sir. For instance, for catmint, the rhyme begins, 'If you set it, the cat will get it. If you sow it, the cat won't know it.' So the first thing to know of that herb is that if you try to start it with tiny plants in your garden, the cat will eat them. But if you plant the seeds, it will come up and the cat will not notice it so much, and the plants will be able to thrive."

He cleared his throat. "It's a clever little rhyme, but not something that we could count as learning here."

Someone giggled. I felt blood creeping up into my face. I hated my fair skin that showed my humiliation so plainly. I wished I had not chosen the simplest of my mother's rhymes to share. "I know others, sir, which are more useful, perhaps."

He gave a tiny sigh and closed his eyes for a moment. "I am sure you do, Lady Bee," he said, as if he did not wish to injure my feelings over how ignorant I was. "But I am more interested in seeing your writing now. Can you make some letters for me on this?" He pushed a piece of paper toward me and offered me a bit of chalk. Did he think I did not know what a pen was?

My humiliation boiled over in anger. I reached over his hand to take up his fine pen. In careful strokes, I inscribed, "My name is Bee Badgerlock. I live on Withywoods Estate. My sister is Lady Nettle, Skillmistress to His Majesty King Dutiful of the Six Duchies." I lifted the pen, regarded my writing critically, and then turned the paper back toward him for him to read.

He had watched me write with ill-concealed surprise. Now he regarded the paper in disbelief for a moment. Then he returned it to me. "Write this. 'Today I begin lessons with Scribe Lant.'"

I did so, more slowly, for I found I was not certain how to spell "Lant." Again I turned it back to him. He next shoved at me a black wax tablet on which he had been scribing words. I had never seen such a device before, and I ran my finger lightly over the heavy coating of wax on the wood plank. He had written with a stylus, carving the words into the wax swiftly and gracefully.

"Well. Can you read it or not?" His words were a challenge. "Aloud, please," he added.

I stared at the words. I spoke them slowly. "It is a wicked deceit to pretend to ignorance and inability." I looked back up at him, confused.

"Do you agree?"

I looked at the words again. "I don't know," I said, wondering what he intended by the words.

"Well. I know that I *would* agree. Lady Bee, you should be ashamed of yourself. Lady Nettle has been full of concern for you, believing you were both simple and near-mute. She has agonized over how you would fare in this world, over who would care for you as you grew older. And now I arrive here, thinking that my task would be to give you basic instruction in the simplest things, and I find you fully capable of reading and writing. And of being quite saucy to a lady who deserves your respect. So, Lady Bee, what am I to think?"

I had found a small knot in the wooden table. I stared at the dark whorl of the wood grain and wanted to vanish. It was all too complicated to explain it to him. All I had wanted was not to appear strange to others. Small chance of that. I was too small for my age and too intelligent for my years. The first should have been obvious; saying the second aloud would make me appear to be as conceited as he believed me rude. I felt the heat come in my face. Someone spoke behind me.

"Yah, she pretends to be a half-wit so she can spy on people. She used to follow me all the time, and then she got me in trouble. Everyone knows that about her. She likes to make trouble."

And now the blood left my face and I felt dizzy with its absence. I could hardly get my breath. I turned to stare at Taffy. "That's not true," I tried to shout. It came out as a jagged whisper. He wore a jeering smile. Elm and Lea were nodding confirmation, their eyes glittering. The goose children looked on, eyes wide with wonder. Perseverance's gaze slid past me and focused on the gray sky framed in the window. The other children just stared at me. I had no allies there. Before I could turn around and look at FitzVigilant, he ordered me tersely, "Sit down. I know where to begin your lessons now." He continued speaking as I returned to my spot on the floor.

My neighbors slid away from me, as if the tutor's disapproval was contagious. He went on speaking. "I'm afraid I did not expect so many students and so diverse a level of learning, so I did not bring enough supplies. I do have six wax tablets and six styli for writing on them. These we will have to share. Paper I have, and I am sure we can find a supply of good goose quills for pens." Here the goose children smiled and wiggled happily.

"But we shall not use pens and ink and paper until we merit them. I have written the letters out large and clear on papers, and each of you shall have one of them to take with you. Every night I wish you to trace the letters with your fingers. Today we will practice the shapes of all the letters, and the sounds of the first five." He glanced at the gardener's boy and added, "As you are already quite capable, Larkspur, I shall not bore you with these exercises. Instead there are several excellent scrolls and books here that have to do with gardening and plants. Perhaps you would like to study them while I work with the others."

Larkspur glowed with his praise and quickly rose to accept a scroll on roses. It was one I'd read several times, and I recognized that it had come from one of Patience's libraries. I pinched my lips shut. Perhaps my father had told him he could make free with the books of Withywoods. When he handed me the letter sheet, I did not protest that I, too, already knew my letters. I knew this was a punishment. I would be made to do tedious, useless exercises to demonstrate his disdain for my supposed "deceitfulness."

He walked among us as first he named each letter aloud, and then we repeated it and traced it with a finger. When we had traced all thirty-three of them, he took us back to the first five, and asked who could remember their names. When I did not volunteer, he asked me if I was still pretending to be ignorant. That had not been my intent; I had resolved to accept my punishment in silence. I did not say so, but only looked at my knees. He made a sound in the back of his throat, a noise of impatience and disgust with me. I did not look up. He pointed at Spruce, who remembered two of them. Lea knew one. One of the sheep children knew another one. When the scribe pointed at Taffy, he stared at the page, scowled, and then announced, "Pee!" with earnest mockery. Our teacher sighed. We began again to repeat each one as he said it, and this time the results were better when he called on one of the goose children to recite the letters.

It was, I think, the longest morning of my life. When he finally released us just before noon, my back ached and my legs hurt from sitting still so long. I had wasted a morning and learned nothing. No. I corrected my thought as I staggered to my feet on stiff legs and spindled my sheet of letters into a roll. I had learned that Taffy, Lea, and Elm would always hate me. I had learned that my teacher despised me and was more interested in punishing me than in teaching me. And lastly, I had learned how quickly my own feelings could change. The infatuation with FitzVigilant that I had tended and nurtured since I had seen him arrive had been abruptly replaced with something else. It wasn't hate. There was too much sadness mixed with it to be hate. I didn't have a word for it. What would I call a feeling that made me want to never encounter that person again, in any situation? I suddenly knew I had no appetite for a noon meal at the same table with him.

The pantry entrance to my lair was too close to the kitchens. I was sure both Elm and Lea would be there, sowing gossip about the morning's lessons and then waiting table. And Scribe FitzVigilant would be at the table. No. I went to my bedroom and carefully divested myself of Careful's finery. As I set the lace aside, I reflected that she had been kind to me. As had Revel. It suddenly occurred to me to wonder what I could do that would show them I appreciated that. Well, in a few days my father had promised to take me to the market. I knew that Careful had admired my little bottles of scent. I would get one for her. And Revel? For him, I was not sure. Perhaps my father would know.

I set aside my new tunic and the heavy stockings and crawled back into my short one and my old leggings. Feeling much more like myself, I slipped into my old bedchamber and from there into the labyrinth of wall tunnels. I went by feel this time, needing no light. When I came to my den, I smelled the warmth of the sleeping cat. I touched his lax form, once more bundled in our cloak. Then

I stepped over him and made my way to my father's true study. There I filched a candle, kindled it at his hearth, and chose a scroll about Taker Farseer, the first King of the Six Duchies. It was in my father's hand, probably his copy of some older writing. I wondered why he had it out on his desk. In my den I made myself comfortable with my cushions, the candle, my blanket, the cloak, and a warm cat. I had thought only to share the cloak's warmth; I had never realized how much heat a cat could generate. We were quite comfortable there, and when he woke it seemed only fair to give him a share of the hard bread and sausage that had become my noon repast.

Cheese?

"I haven't any here. But I'll get some for us. I'm surprised to find you here. I shut the pantry hatch the last time you left."

This warren is full of holes. Where a rat can go, a cat can follow.

"Really?"

Most of the time. There are many small ways in. And the hunting here is good. Mice, rats. Birds in the upper reaches.

He subsided and crept back under the cloak, where he snuggled his body against mine. I resumed reading, amusing myself by trying to sort the flattery from the facts in this account of my ancient ancestor. Taker had arrived, dispatched the savage wretches who had tried to fend off him and his men, and had, in his lifetime, transformed Buckkeep from the crude log fortification he first raised to a stone-walled fortress. The castle itself had been many years in rising, built largely from the tumbled stone so prevalent in the area. Much of it had been available as perfectly carved blocks.

My father had made some notes between the lines of that section. He seemed interested that Buckkeep Castle had evidently been raised first as a timber stronghold on top of the tumbled stone foundation of a more ancient keep. It had been rebuilt in stone, but he had inked in several questions as to who had built the original stronghold of worked stones and what had become of them. And to one side, there was a little drawing of what he believed had been standing as stone walls when Taker first arrived. I studied it. Obviously my father believed that there had been a great deal of castle there already and Taker had only rebuilt what someone else had torn down.

The cat sat up a moment before I became aware that my father was in his study. As he closed the doors and then opened the hinge-catch, the cat vanished in a furry streak. I snatched up the cloak, rolled it into a ball, and thrust it to the back of my cupboard. There was no time to hide the scroll I had taken from his study before he came down the passage, stooped over and bearing his own candle. I looked up at him and he smiled down on me. "Well, there you are!" he said.

"Yes," I agreed.

He folded his legs and, uninvited, sat on my rug beside me. He waited a moment and when I didn't say anything, began with, "I missed you at noon. You didn't come to eat with us."

"I wasn't hungry," I said.

"I see."

"And after a long morning among so many people, I wanted to be alone for a time."

He nodded to that, and something in the set of his mouth told me he understood that need. With the back of his forefinger, he tapped the scroll. "And what's this you're reading?"

Face it squarely. "I took it from your scroll rack. It's about Taker Farseer and how he first raised a fortification on the cliffs above Buckkeep Town."

"Um. Long before there was a Buckkeep Town."

"So. Who had the ruins belonged to?"

He furrowed his brow. "My guess is that it was an Elderling for-tification. The stone is the same used in the standing stones near there, the Witness Stones."

"But the Elderlings had all sorts of powerful magic. Why would they need a fort? Who were their enemies? And who destroyed the castle the first time?"

"Now, that is a very good question. Not many people have asked it, and so far as I know, no one can answer it."

The conversation lapsed, and to say something I blurted out, "One day I should like to visit Buckkeep Castle."

"Would you? Then you shall." He fell silent again, and then spoke as if words were painful. "Your tutor spoke of the morning's lesson today when we were at table."

I said nothing. Absurdly, I wished the cat were with me.

My father sighed. "He praised the goose-herder's children for their skill at arithmetic. And was very pleased to discover that Larkspur could read and write."

I waited. He gave a small cough, and added, "Lady Shun asked then what good numbers could do for a child who would grow up to manage geese. Or what a gardener might read on the earth or in leaves. She sees no sense to educating the children of servants."

"Revel can read and write and do figures," I pointed out. "Mama used to give him lists and he would take money and buy things she wanted at the market, and bring back the right amount. Even a goose girl should know enough numbers to count the eggs in a nest! And Larkspur will learn much from reading Lady Patience's scrolls on plants and gardening. Cook Nutmeg knows how to read and write, and how to keep track of how many sacks of flour or how much salt fish she needs for the winter."

"You make a good argument," my father said, approvingly. "Much the same one that I presented to Shun. And then I asked Lant how you had fared at your lessons."

Lant. My father called him Lant now, as if he were my cousin. I looked down at my blanketed feet. They had been warmer when the cat had been there. And I felt slightly ill, as if something terrible had fallen into my stomach and squatted there.

"I did not like what I heard," my father said quietly.

There was no one in the world who loved me. I swallowed hard. My words came out breathlessly. "I could not explain." I shook my head wildly and I felt tears fly from my eyes. "No. He didn't really want me to explain. He thought he knew what was true, and he did not want to be wrong."

I hugged my knees tightly to my chest, pulling them in hard, wishing I could break my own legs. Wishing I could destroy myself so I could escape these terrible feelings.

"I took your side, of course," my father said quietly. "I rebuked him for not asking me about your intellect. Or speaking with you before lessons were to start. I told him that he had deceived himself about you; you had not lied to him. And I told him he would have one more chance to instruct you at a level befitting what you had taught yourself. And that if he could not, he might continue to instruct the other children, but I would not allow you to waste your time. That I would find it a pleasure to instruct you myself in all I think you need to know."

He said the words so calmly. I stared at him, unable to breathe. He cocked his head at me. His smile looked shaky. "Did you imagine I could do otherwise, Bee?"

I coughed and then flung myself into his lap. My father caught me and held me tight. He was so contained that it did not hurt. But for all that, I felt the anger that simmered in him like hot oil inside a lidded pot. He spoke in such a growl I felt as if it were Wolf-Father speaking inside me. "I will always take your part, Bee. Right or wrong. That is why you must always take care to be right, lest you make your father a fool."

I slid off his lap and looked up at him, wondering if he was trying to make a joke of all of it. His dark eyes were serious. He read my doubt. "Bee, I will always choose to believe you first. So it is your serious responsibility to be righteous in what you do. It is the pact that must exist between us."

I could never bear his gaze for long. I looked aside from him, pondering it. Thinking of the ways I already deceived him. The cloak. The cat. My explorations of the tunnels. My stolen reading. But did not he also and already deceive me? I spoke quietly. "Does this go both ways? That if I always take your part, I will not end up a fool?"

He didn't answer immediately. In a strange way, that pleased me, because I knew it meant he was thinking it through. Could he promise me that I could always believe he was doing what was right? He cleared his throat. "I will do my best, Bee."

"As will I, then," I agreed.

"So. Will you sit down to dinner with us, then?"

"When the time comes," I said slowly.

"Child, you've been in here for hours. I suspect they are holding dinner for us now."

That was too sudden. I clenched my teeth for a moment and then asked him honestly, "Must I? I do not feel I am ready to face them yet."

He looked down at his hands, and I felt a dreadful gulf open in my belly. "You need to do this, Bee," he said softly. "I want you to think of what tidings Riddle must carry back to your sister. I do not wish Shun or FitzVigilant to see you as backward or awkward. So, young as you are, you must master yourself and your feelings and come to table tonight. I understand, far better than you can imagine, what you feel toward someone who mocked you and punished you when he was supposed to be teaching you. It will be hard for you to believe this, but I don't think he is an inherently cruel man. I think he is just very young, and prone to take the word of others before he finds out things for himself. I even dare to hope that he will prove worthy of your regard, and that you might even come to enjoy each other. Though I will add that right now it is difficult for me to pretend to enjoy his company. Something that I suspect he knows."

His voice sank to a low growl on those last words, and I realized then that my father was profoundly angry with FitzVigilant. He would observe the rules of society but it did not abate the active dislike that the scribe had wakened in him. I looked at my hands folded loosely in my lap. If my father could do so, if he could contain his anger and treat FitzVigilant in a civil fashion, then perhaps I could do so as well. I tried to imagine myself sitting at the table. I did not have to sit with my head lowered as if guilty. Nor did I have to let him know how badly he had hurt me. I could be my father's daughter. Impervious to what he had done. Sure of my own worthiness. I lifted my chin. "I think perhaps I am hungry after all."

The evening meal was not comfortable for me. I was aware that both Shun and Lant were looking at me, but I have never been good at meeting anyone's stare. So I looked at my plate or glanced just past my father or Riddle. I did not flinch when Lea or Elm passed near my chair, but neither did I accept any food from any dish they brought. I saw them once, rolling their eyes to the corners to ex-change a glance at they passed each other behind Riddle. Elm's cheeks grew very pink and I suddenly realized that Riddle, old as he was, was still a handsome man. Certainly Elm stood very close to his chair as she offered food. And Riddle, I saw as I smiled trium-phantly to myself, noticed her no more than a fly on the wall.

For the first part of the meal, I was silent. Father and Riddle were once more talking about his departure for Buckkeep. Shun and Lant immersed themselves in their own quiet conversation, frequently punctuated by her laughter. I had read a poem about a girl with "silvery laughter" but Shun's sounded to me as if some-one had fallen down a long flight of steps with a basket of cheap tin pans. After Father had spent some little time in conversation with Riddle, he turned to me and said, "So what did you think of Taker Farseer and his invasion of this land?"

"I had not thought of it that way," I responded. Truly I had not. And in the next breath, I had to ask, "Then who was here before Taker and his men came and claimed the land around the mouth of the Buck River? The scroll says that the bones of the old stone keep were deserted. Were the folk who were living here the same ones who had once had a fortification there? You said it might have orig-inally been built by Elderlings? So were they Elderlings he fought to take this land?"

"Well. They were mostly fishermen and farmers and goatherds, I believe. Lord Chade has tried to find more writings by those peo-ple, but they don't seem to have entrusted their lore to letters and scrolls. Some of the bards say that our oldest songs are actually rooted in their songs. But we can't really say 'they' and 'them' be-cause we are actually the product of Taker and his invaders and the folk that were already here."

Had he known? Did he deliberately give me that opening? "Then, in those days, people learned things from songs? Or poems?"

"Of course. The best minstrels still recite the longest genealogies from memory. They are, of course, entrusted to paper as well, now that paper is more abundant. But a minstrel learns them from the mouth of his master, not from a paper."

Riddle was listening as raptly as I, and when Father paused, he jumped in. "So that song that Hap favored us with the last time I saw him, a very old song about Eld Silverskin, the dragon's friend?"

The next lines came into my mind and were out my mouth before I paused to consider. "'Of precious things, he has no end. A stone that speaks, a drum that gleams, he's pecksie-kissed or so it seems.'"

"What is 'pecksie-kissed'?" Riddle demanded as my father simultaneously said, "Hap will be proud to know you have remembered his song so well!" Then he turned to Riddle. "'Pecksie-kissed' means lucky out in far Farrow. But I do not know if Silverskin is Hap's own song, or a much older one."

Shun interrupted abruptly. "You know Hap Gladheart? You've heard him sing?" She sounded scandalized. Or furiously jealous.

My father smiled. "Of course. I fostered Hap when he was an orphan. And I was never so glad myself as when I heard that he had taken that name for himself. Gladheart." He turned back to Riddle. "But we are getting far afield from Bee's question. Riddle, who do you think first built a fort on that cliff?"

Soon all three of us were speculating, with Riddle adding comments about things he had noticed in the lower reaches of Buckkeep Castle. He had seen what might have been runes, badly eroded, on the wall of one dungeon. My father spoke about the Witness Stones, and the Buck tradition of holding combats there, as well as weddings. Now that we knew the Witness Stones were actually portals that the highly trained Skill-user might use to cover great distances in a single stride, it was intriguing to speculate how they had come to be called the Witness Stones.

It was only when the meal was drawing to a close that I realized my father had staged our conversation as carefully as if it were a counterattack on a fortification. In talking with Riddle and him I had completely forgotten my bruised feelings. I became aware that FitzVigilant's conversation with Shun had faltered to a halt and that he was listening in on our talk. She was picking a piece of bread to pieces, her mouth pursed in displeasure. I became aware of all this only when my father shifted in his seat and casually said, "Well,

Scribe Lant, and what do you think of Riddle's theory? Have you ever been in the lower reaches of Buckkeep Castle?"

He jumped a tiny bit, as if discomfited to be discovered eaves-dropping. But he recovered and admitted that when he was younger, he had ventured into the bowels of the keep with several of his friends. It had been done as a dare, but when they ventured too close to the cells down there, a guard had turned them back with a stern warning, and he'd never gone there again. "It was a miserable place. Cold and dark and dank. It gave me the greatest fright of my young life when the guard threatened to put us in a cell and hold us until someone came looking for us. We all ran at that. Oh, doubt-less there are folk who deserve such confinement but I never even wished to look on it again."

"Doubtless," my father said in an affable voice, but Wolf-Father looked out of his eyes for a moment, and there were deep sparks of black anger in his gaze. I stared at him. Wolf-Father lived in my other father? This was a revelation to me, and I said little while I pondered it for the rest of the evening.

When the meal was over, my father offered me his arm. I man-aged not to seem surprised as I took it, and let him guide me to the sitting room where the men had brandy and Shun had red wine and, to my surprise, there was a mug of mulled cider on the tray for me. My father picked up our conversation about the Elderlings, and Scribe Lant joined in. I was surprised at how affable he was; I had expected him to be sullen or sarcastic, for my father had told me that his earlier rebuke of him had been rather sharp. Yet the scribe seemed to have accepted that correction, and twice he even spoke directly to me in a way that did not seem condescending or mocking. Very, very slowly, I decided that he had accepted that he had been mistaken in his impression and his treatment of me, and that he now wished to make up for it.

I saw that he looked at my father almost anxiously, as if his ap-proval was extremely important. *He fears him,* I thought to myself. And then I thought how silly I was not to realize that Scribe Lant was very vulnerable, not just in that he had seen what my father was capable of when he was a boy, but also in that he was relying on my father's hospitality to remain safely hidden. If my father turned him out, where could he go? How long before he would be found and killed? My feelings became very mixed. Shun's green-eyed annoyance that he was paying more attention to my father and the conversation than he was to her was very gratifying. At the same time I felt uncomfortable that his rudeness to me had had the end result of making him puppyishly subservient to my father. I fell silent, more watching and listening than speaking, and finally begged to be excused, saying I was tired.

I went to bed in my pleasant new room that night. My thoughts were complicated and troubling. Sleep was late in coming, and in the morning there was Careful again, tugging at me and fussing over my hair. I thanked her for the use of the lace but declined it that day, saying that I feared ink and chalk would mar it. I think she was relieved to rescue her collar and cuffs from such potential disaster, but suggested that when my father took me to the market, I should buy some lace I liked and have the seamstress fashion me some of my own. I agreed softly but wondered if I would. I did not feel like a lace-and-earrings sort of person, I discovered. My mother had enjoyed such finery and I had loved how it looked on her. Yet I felt more drawn to emulate my father's plain clothing and simple ways.

I took my scroll of letters with me when I descended to breakfast. I set it by my plate, greeted everyone at the table very politely, and then paid attention to my food. Despite my father's support, I felt sick as I thought of the lesson time to come. My father might have convinced FitzVigilant that I was not a deceptive little half-wit and perhaps my tutor now feared to treat me disrespectfully, but that would do me little good with the other children. I excused myself early from the table and went directly to the schoolroom.

Some of the other children had already arrived. The goose children were there, standing close to the gardener's boy. Larkspur was pointing to the letters on their scroll and naming each for them. Perseverance was waiting, wearing a stable boy's livery that fit him much better and looked almost new. I was not sure I liked him in green and yellow as much as I had in his simple leathers. He was also wearing a black eye and a swollen lower lip. It looked hideous when he smiled, the fat lip stretching painfully. But smile he did at the sight of me, as if we had never quarreled. I slowed my steps as I walked toward him, completely bewildered. Could it be that simple? Simply pretend we had never quarreled; just go back to treating each other as we had before? It didn't seem possible. But I was determined to try it. I smiled back at him, and for an instant his grin grew wider. Then he lifted the back of his hand to his bruised mouth and winced. But the smile stayed in his eyes.

"Perseverance," I greeted him when I was two steps away.

"Lady Bee," he responded gravely, and actually sketched a bow at me as if I were truly a lady grown. "Exactly who I was hoping to see before lessons began."

"Truly?" I raised my brows at him skeptically, trying to conceal how much my heart had lifted at his words. One ally. One ally was all I needed in that wretched schoolroom and I could endure it.

"Truly. Because I have completely jumbled what these two letters are, and neither my father nor my mother could help me." He spoke in a low voice as he unrolled the scroll, and I did not ask him why he had not asked Larkspur. I was the one he could ask for help without awkwardness. Just as he had been able to teach me to sit a horse. Without speaking a word about it, we drifted away from the others. We stood with our backs to the wall and both unrolled our letter scrolls as if we were comparing them.

I breathed out the names of the first five letters and just as softly, Perseverance repeated them. Under his breath, he added, "They look like hen's tracks and have names that are just sounds. Who can remember such useless things?"

I had never seen letters in such a light. But I had seen them through my mother's eyes before I was born, and had seen them for myself when I sat on her lap of an evening and she read aloud to me. When I considered Perseverance's words, I understood his frustration. I tried to make connections for him. "The first one, see, it makes the sound at the beginning of Revel's name, and it has long legs, just as he does. And this second one that makes the sound at the beginning of 'water' has a curl here, like water running over a rock." In this way we named not just the first five letters, but ten of them. So engrossed were we in this new game of looking at letters that neither of us was aware of the looks from the other children until Elm giggled in a very nasty way. We both looked up to see her roll her eyes at Lea. And there, coming down the hall toward us, was our teacher.

As he passed me, he observed in a jolly voice, "You, Lady Bee, have no need of that!" and he plucked the letter scroll from my startled fingers. Before I could react, he called all of us to assemble in the schoolroom. We entered, each resuming the same place as the day before. He was much more brisk than he had been yesterday. He organized us into groups, putting children of similar ages together with a wax tablet. He sent Larkspur and me to a different corner of the room. He gave us a scroll about the geography and crops of each of the Six Duchies, along with a map, and told us to familiarize ourselves with them. He smiled at both of us as he directed us, and it seemed a sincere expression. Now that I knew fear was the source of his kindly regard, I felt shamed for us both. Then he looked round in annoyance and demanded, "Where is Taffy? I will not tolerate tardiness!"

A silence held among the children. Several exchanged glances, and I became aware that there was a secret I didn't know. Perseverance was focused on his tablet. I watched him carefully copy a letter.

"Well?" Scribe FitzVigilant demanded of us. "Does no one know where he is?"

"He's home," Elm said.

One of the sheep-smelling boys said quietly, "He's poorly. He won't come today." He glanced at Perseverance. A very slight smile stretched the stable boy's swollen lip tight. He appeared to be very intent on his letter scroll.

FitzVigilant breathed out through his nose. The day had barely begun but he already sounded tired as he said, "Children, I have been charged with teaching you. It is not my first choice of what I would do with the days of my life, but it has been given me as a duty, and I will do it. I commend your families for seeing the wisdom of sending you to me. I am well aware that several of you wish yourselves elsewhere. Taffy made it clear to me yesterday that he regarded our lessons as a waste of his time. Today he pretends illness to avoid me. Well, I will not tolerate such malingering!"

Several children exchanged puzzled looks at the unfamiliar word, but Perseverance didn't even look up from his letter as he said softly, "Taffy's not shamming." Could everyone hear the satisfaction in his voice or was it only me? I stared at him, but he did not lift his eyes to meet mine.

Our scribe spoke. There was condemnation in his voice. "And did your fists have anything to do with his 'feeling poorly'?"

Perseverance looked up. He met the scribe's eyes. I knew he was only a few years older than me, but he sounded like a man as he said, "Sir, my fists took no action until after his mouth had said untrue things about my sister. Then I did what any man would do when his family was insulted." He looked at FitzVigilant. Perseverance's brow was unlined and his gaze open. There was no guilt in him for what he had done, only righteousness.

A silence held in the schoolroom. My feelings were mixed. I had not even known that Perseverance had a sister. She was not here, so she was either much younger than him, or much older. Or perhaps his parents did not think a girl needed to read and write. Some were like that, even in Buck.

Neither of them looked away, but the scribe spoke first. "Let us return to our lessons."

Perseverance immediately lowered his eyes to the wax tablet and resumed his careful tracing of the letter he had engraved there. I spoke under my breath, a sentence I had heard in a dream about a young bull. "Horns not grown, he swings his head in warning and still all take heed."

Chapter 27

TIME AND AGAIN

Withywoods is a feast of perfection, in all seasons. In summer, on the rounded hills of the high lands of the estate, the oaks make a pleasant shade, while down near the creek the twisted willows that give the place its name drip a soft rain that is refreshing. Trees to climb and a creek to fish in. What more could a boy wish? In autumn any child would be happy to gather acorns from the oak forest, or pick for himself ripe grapes in our own vineyards. In the winter? Deep banks of fallen leaves give way to slopes of snow, perfect for coasting, and a hearth in a hall that begs for Winterfest to be celebrated not for a night, but for a whole month. Spring brings new lambs frolicking on the hills, and kittens and puppies in the stables.

I know, I know that the boy would be happy here. I know I could win his heart and make him mine. I was so foolish to be hurt and bitter when first I heard of him. Conceived years before Chivalry *made me his, how could I rebuke him for unfaithfulness to a wife he did not have? But I did. For I wanted, so desperately, what an accident had bequeathed to a woman who did not want him, the child, the heir I would have cherished. I have begged him, even on my knees, to send for the boy, but he refuses. "He would not be safe here," he tells me. "Where safer than under his father's roof, protected by his father's sword arm?" I ask of him. It is the only serious quarrel we have ever had. He is adamant.*

LADY PATIENCE'S PRIVATE JOURNAL,
DISCOVERED BEHIND A STACK OF FLOWERPOTS

The night before we were to visit the market, I went to bed with anticipation. Sleep evaded me at first, and then it came with a hailstorm of dreams. Some were nightmarish, others so intense that I desperately tried to fight free of them. Yet I could not seem to fully wake. My room seemed full of a thick fog, and each time I thought I had wakened myself, images formed and pulled me back into a dream.

When morning came, I was still weary. The world seemed hazy and I was not convinced I was not still dreaming. Careful was there, insisting that I must arise. She shook my covers to let the cold air in and then sat me on a stool before the fire. I could barely hold my head straight. I made no resistance as she tugged a brush through the growing tangle of my curls. "You don't want to dawdle today, my little lady! Oh, how I envy you, going to market for pretty new things! Your father said as much to Revel, and he has made me a little list to give you. Here it is! He's a lettered man, is our steward, as I regret to say I am not, but he has told me what is written. Revel says you need boots and shoes, gloves of both wool and leather, stockings of wool in at least three colors, and he has dared to suggest a seamstress in town, one who knows how to sew the little frocks that girls wear nowadays rather than your jerkins and tunics! As if you were a boy! What your father is thinking I don't know! Not to criticize him, of course. The poor man, with no wife to tell him these things!"

I scarcely heard her words. I felt dull and wooden. Careful tugged and worried at my hair, desperately trying to make it look longer and more girlish. There was enough now that it had a color at least and my scalp no longer showed through. She dressed me with little help from me. I tried, but my fingers were fat, sleepy sausages and my head a heavy weight on my shoulders. She sighed over my tunic, but I was glad of its warmth atop my linen shirt. When I was as primped as she could manage with such a bland canvas, she sent me off to breakfast with the admonition that I should have fun and think of her if the trinket tables were out for Winterfest.

Winterfest! I woke slightly to that thought. I had scarcely thought of that holiday, but she was right, it was almost upon us. In my memories it was a warm and yet festive time at Withywoods. There were minstrels and puppeteers, and immense logs burning in the hearth, and sea salt to fling at the burning wood to make the flames leap up in different colors. Always on Winterfest eve, my mother came down to dinner wearing a holly crown. Once she left a winter staff leaning by my father's chair. It was as tall as he was, and decorated with ribbons, and for some reason it made all the servants roar with laughter and my father blush a deep scarlet. I had never understood the joke, but knew only that it was a reminder of something special that both of them shared. That night of all nights, they always shone with love, and it seemed to me that they were but boy and girl again.

And so I did my best to rally my spirits, for I knew that this year must be a sad reminder for my father. I tried to banish my peculiar dreams and be cheery at our breakfast of porridge and sausages and dried berries and hot tea. When Riddle came in and my father invited him to join us, I anticipated a good day. But then Riddle reminded us both that this was the day he was to set out on his return journey to Buckkeep.

"You can ride with us to Oaksbywater," my father urged him. "It's on your way, and we shall have a meal together in the tavern there before you begin the rest of your journey. I am told that the merchants will have begun to display their wares for Winterfest. Perhaps Bee and I can find a few small things to send to her sister."

It was the perfect bait for Riddle. I could almost see him thinking

that he might choose a small gift or two for her as well. At Winterfest sweethearts often exchanged tokens for the coming year. It
pleased me that he would want to get a gift for my sister. It meant
that Shun had no real hold on him. He was thinking of something
green for her, a green scarf or green gloves for her pretty little hands.
He could almost imagine slipping them onto her hands. I blinked. I
had not known my sister's favorite color was green. Riddle nodded
to my father and then said, "I can certainly delay a bit for that, as
long as I leave in time to reach Woodsedge before nightfall. I've no
wish to sleep outside with snow coming down."

"It's snowing now?" I asked stupidly. My voice sounded thick,
even to me. I tried to make my wandering mind return to the spoken conversation at the table.

Riddle was looking at me kindly, as if he thought I feared we
would cancel our trip. "A light fall of snow. Nothing that need dissuade any of us from our errands."

I reached for the conversation. "I like the snow," I said quietly.
"It makes all new. We walk where no one has ever trodden before
when we walk in fresh snow."

They both stared at me. I tried to smile, but my lips went too
wide. The steam was rising from the teapot. It curled as it rose,
twisting in on itself, becoming itself again in a new form. Coiling
like a serpent in the sea, or a dragon in flight. I tried to follow it as
it dispersed.

"She has such engaging fancies," Riddle said in the distance. He
poured tea into my cup for me. I watched how honey spun from the
spoon into my cup, and then I stirred it and the tea and the honey
swirled into one. I let my mind swirl with it. The men talked and I
simply was for a time.

"Dress warmly, Bee," my father said. I blinked. Their plates were
emptied. I recalled that we were going to ride through the snow to
Oaksbywater. The market. Winterfest. Today my father and Riddle
would see me ride Priss. I suddenly wished Perseverance could
come with us. Dared I ask for such a strange favor?

I was on the point of standing when Shun and FitzVigilant
breezed in to join us. The scribe seemed startled to see our empty

plates. "Are we late?" he asked in surprise, and I realized my father had called me early to breakfast. He smiled at them both and said heartily, "No, we were early. Enjoy your meal and a restful day. We are off to the market today, and will see you again near nightfall."

"The market! What good fortune! I was dreading a tedious day. I shall eat quickly and join you." Shun was absolutely radiant at the thought.

As if her thoughts were contagious, the scribe echoed her, "And I, if I may! I confess, in my hasty packing, I neglected to bring as many warm things as I would be happy to have here. And I wonder if the market would have any wax tablets? As my students progress, I would like each to have his own for his work."

My heart sank. This was our day, the day promised to me. Surely my father would defend it. He looked toward me but I lowered my eyes. After a moment he spoke. "Of course. If you wish, I suppose we can delay for a little."

We delayed the whole morning. Shun behaved as if she had just by chance heard of our expedition, but I was certain she had known of it by servant gossip and only chose to invite herself in such an untimely way. For one thing, she had arrived at breakfast dressed as if she were a dish for a feast table. That did not mean she was quickly ready to leave. No. She must flounce and twist her hair and try on a dozen pairs of earrings, and scold her maid for not having a certain jacket mended and ready for her to wear. These things I knew because she left the door of her chambers open and the sound of her strident displeasure carried well down the corridor to my chambers. I lay back down on my bed to await the announcement that she was ready, and dozed off. I fell right back into my discordant dreams, and when my father came to find me I felt disconnected and strange as I found my wraps and then followed him out to the ponderous wagon that would now transport us to town, for Lady Shun had chosen skirts that were certain to be ruined by riding horseback.

My father waved away a driver and climbed up to take the reins himself before gesturing that I should join him on the seat. Riddle's horse and his laden pack animal were tethered to the rear of the wagon and would follow. He climbed up next to us. So at least I had the novelty of riding beside my father and watching him manage the team, and not having to listen to Shun's vapid chatter. I glanced back at the stable in time to see Perseverance leading Prissy out on an exercise lead. He nodded to me, and I ducked my head in response. We had managed to find time for exactly one riding lesson since our other schooling had started. I had looked forward to making my father proud of me today with my riding skills. Trust Shun to spoil that!

But for all that, I enjoyed the ride to town. FitzVigilant and Shun were tucked into the back of the wagon with a mound of cushions, lap robes, and blankets. I heard her telling him some tale of a grand carriage her grandmother had owned, all leather and velvet curtains. I was warm as I sat between my father and Riddle. They spoke over my head of boring manly things. I watched the snow falling, and the tossing of the horses' manes, and listened to the music of the creaking wagon and thudding hooves. I went off into a sort of waking dream of gentle light that shone on us from the falling snow and drew us on and on. I roused from it only as we got closer to the trading town. First the woods gave way to open fields with little farmhouses in clusters. Then we began to see more houses on smaller holdings, and finally we were in the town itself, with all the merchants and fine houses and inns clustered around an open square. And over it all, a gleaming pearly haze made me want to rub my eyes. The falling snow diffused the winter light so that it seemed to me it came as much from the snowy ground as the sky overhead. I felt myself drifting. It was such a wonderful sensation. My nose and cheeks were chilled, as were my hands, but the rest of me was warm trapped between the two men and their deep cheerful voices. Garlands and lanterns on poles were set out for Winterfest to come, and the bright attire of the merchants and the folk wandering the shops added to the festive air. Evergreen garlands draped doors and windows, enlivened with branches bare but for clinging red berries, brown cones, or white berries. The wealthier establishments had tiny bells woven into the cedar fronds, and they chimed softly in the wind.

My father pulled in near a stable and tossed a boy a coin to see to our team. He lifted me down after him as Shun and FitzVigilant were scrambling from the tail of the wagon. My father took my hand, exclaiming over how cold it was. His hand was warm, and his walls were up enough that I could endure the skin-to-skin touch. I smiled up at him. The snow was falling and light surrounded us.

We came to the town commons. Oaksbywater had three great oaks in the center of their commons, and young holly trees, freshly trimmed of their prickly leaves and berries. In the open spaces of the commons, a new town seemed to have sprung up. Peddlers and tinkers had pulled up their carts and sold pans from racks and whistles and bracelets from trays and late apples and nuts from bushel baskets. There was so much to choose from, we could not look at it all. We passed people dressed in furs and bright cloaks. So many people and I knew none of them! So different from Withy-woods. Some of the girls wore holly crowns. It would not be Win-terfest for two more days, but there were garlands and music and a man cooking and selling hot chestnuts. "Chestnuts, chestnuts, pip-ing hot! Chestnuts, chestnuts, hopping in the pot!"

My father filled his glove with some for me. I hugged it in one arm and peeled the gleaming brown shells from the creamy nuts. "My favorites!" Riddle told me as he stole one. He walked beside me, talking of Winterfests he recalled from his boyhood in a small town. I think he ate as many chestnuts as I did. Two giggling young women passed wearing holly crowns. They smiled at him, and he smiled back but shook his head. They laughed aloud, joined hands, and ran off into the crowd.

We stopped first at a saddlery, where my father seemed discour-aged to hear that his new saddle was not quite finished. It was only when the man came to measure the length of my legs and then to shake his head and say he'd have to adjust his work that I realized the saddle would be for Prissy and me. He showed me the flaps, with a bee carved into each. I stared in surprise and I think that made my father as happy as if the saddle had been ready. He prom-ised we would come back next week, with the horse, and I scarce could take it in. I could not say a word until we were outside. Then

Riddle asked me what I thought of the bees, and I said honestly that they were very nice, but I would rather have had a charging buck. My father looked astonished and Riddle laughed so loudly that folk turned to stare at us.

We stopped in several shops. My father brought me a belt of leather stained red and carved with flowers, and a bracelet with flower charms carved from antler, and a little cake full of raisins and nuts. At one shop we bought three balls of white soap scented with wisteria and one with peppermint. Very softly, I told my father I wished to bring back something for Careful and something for Revel. He seemed pleased by that. He found buttons carved like acorns and asked if Careful might like them. I was not sure, but he bought them. Revel was much harder, but when I saw a woman selling embroidered pocket kerchiefs dyed saffron and pale green and sky blue, I asked if I might buy him one of each. My father was surprised that I was so certain he would be pleased with such a gift, but I had no doubt at all. I wished I had the courage to ask to buy a small gift for Perseverance but felt shy of even telling my father his name.

A boy had a tray full of tiny seashells. Some had been bored to string as beads. I lingered long, staring at them. Some were twisted cones, others tiny scoops with scalloped edges. "Bee," my father said at last. "They're only common seashells such as litter any beach."

"I've never seen the ocean or walked on a beach," I reminded him. And while he was musing on that, Riddle scooped a heaping handful of the shells and funneled them into my two cupped hands.

"To have until you can walk on a beach with your sister and pick up as many as you want," he told me. Then they both laughed at my delight and we wandered on. At a hastily constructed stall, my father bought me a market bag such as my mother used to carry. It was woven of bright-yellow straw, with a sturdy strap that went over my shoulder. I set it down and into it we carefully put all we had bought. My father wished to carry it for me, but I was happy to feel the weight of my treasures.

When we came to a little market square full of tinker and trader booths, my father gave me six coppers and said I might spend them as I wished. I bought Careful a string of gleaming black beads and a long piece of blue lace: I was certain she would delight in those gifts. For myself, I bought enough green lace for a collar and cuffs, mostly because I knew it would please Careful that I had done as she suggested. And finally, I purchased a little money pouch to add to my belt. I put the last two coppers and the half-copper the tinker had given back to me in my pouch and felt very grown-up. In the street, some men stood and sang, blending their voices, right there in the falling snow. There was a fat man who sat in the little space between the buildings, surrounded by a light so bright that most people could scarcely abide it and turned their gazes away from him as they passed. I saw a man juggling potatoes, and a girl with three tame crows who did tricks with rings.

The streets were busy for such a chilly day. In an alley between buildings, an ambitious puppeteer and his apprentices were setting up a show tent. We passed three musicians with red cheeks and redder noses playing pipes together in the shelter of one of the square's evergreens. The snow began to fall in earnest, in large fluffy clumps of flakes. It spangled my father's shoulders. Three beggars limped past us, looking as miserable as anyone could. Riddle gave each of them a copper and they wished him well in cold-cracked voices. I stared after them, and then I felt my gaze drawn to a pathetic lone beggar camped on the doorstep of a tea-and-spice shop. I hugged myself and shivered at his blind gaze.

"Are you cold?" my father asked me. It came to me that we had stopped walking and I had heard his query twice. Was I cold? I reached for words.

"Cold comes from the heart, on waves of red blood," I heard myself say. And I was cold. I looked at my fingers. They were white. As white as the beggar's eyes. Had he looked at them and made them white? No. He could not see me if I didn't look at him. I looked at my father. He seemed to move away from me without moving. Everything had stepped back at me. Why? Was I a danger to them? I reached for my father's hand. He reached for mine, but I did not think we touched. I felt Riddle's eyes on me but could not

meet his gaze. He was looking at me but I was not where he was
looking. A time passed, short or long, and then suddenly with a
lurch the world started up around me again. I heard the sounds of
the market, smelled the horse and cart that plodded past us in the
street. I gripped my father's fingers tightly.

My father spoke hastily as if to distract us from each other.
"She's just cold. That's all. We should get to the cobbler's shop and
get her some boots! And then, Bee, let's buy you a warm scarf to
wear. Riddle, do you need to be on your way soon?"

"I think I'll stay a bit longer," he said quietly. "Perhaps I'll even
stay the night in the inn. The snow is coming thickly; not the best
weather for starting a journey."

"I wonder where Shun and FitzVigilant have gone." My father
glanced about as if worried. It came to me that he hoped Riddle
would offer to find them. He was worried about me, and wished for
us to be alone.

Riddle did not take the bait. "Those two seemed pleased enough
with their own company. Perhaps we should take Bee somewhere
and get her something warm to drink."

"After the cobbler," my father replied stubbornly. He stooped
suddenly and picked me up.

"Papa?" I objected and tried to wriggle free.

"My legs are longer. And your boots are letting the snow in. Let
me carry you until we reach the cobbler's shop." He held me tight
to his chest and his thoughts even tighter. We passed a man leaning
up against the corner of a building. He looked at me with his eyes
all wrong. The fat man in the alley near him pointed at me and
smiled. Gleaming fog billowed around him. People walking past
the mouth of the alley slowed and looked puzzled. Then they hurried on. I huddled closer to my father, closing my eyes to keep out
the light and fog, and Wolf-Father growled at them. Three steps
later I opened my eyes and looked back. I could not see them.

And there was the cobbler's shop, on the next corner. My father
swung me down. We stamped snow from our boots and brushed it
from our clothes before we crowded in. The shop smelled pleasantly of leather and oil, and the cobbler had a roaring fire on his

hearth. He was a spry little man named Pacer. He had known me since I was a baby, and he had never made much of my differences, but had made my shoes to fit my peculiarly small feet. Now he exclaimed in dismay to see how his handiwork had been outgrown. He sat me down before his fire and had my boots off before I could reach for them. He measured my feet with a bit of string and his warm hands, and promised me new boots and a set of shoes within two days, and his apprentice to deliver them to Withywoods.

He would not let me put my old boots back on, but gifted me with a pair that he'd had on his shelves. They were too big for me, but he stuffed both toes with wool and promised that they'd serve me better than the old ones that were splitting at the seams. "I would feel shame to send you out into the falling snow in those old boots. I'm sure those must feel better," he said to me.

I looked down at them and tried to find words. "I feel taller to see my feet looking longer," I said. My father and Riddle laughed as if I had said the cleverest thing in the world.

Then we were out into the snow again, and at the next door we ducked into a woolmonger's, where I saw skeins of yarns dyed in every color imaginable. As I wandered past the shelves, gently touching each color and smiling to myself, I saw Riddle find a pair of green gloves and a hood that matched them. While he paid for them and had them wrapped, my father chose a thick wool shawl in bright red and soft gray. I was startled when he put it around me. It was large for me, blanketing my shoulders even when I pulled it up to cover my head. But it was so warm, not just with the wool but with his thinking of me before I had ever asked for such a thing.

I thought then that I should take out Revel's list of things he thought I needed, but my father seemed so pleased to be finding and buying things that I did not want to stop him. Out we went into the busy streets, and in and out of all sorts of little shops and stalls. Then I saw the man with the cart of puppies. A worn-out donkey was pulling the little two-wheeled cart through the crowded street, and an old brindled mother dog was trotting anxiously after it, for her pups were standing up in the cart, their front paws on the edge, yelping and whining to her. A skinny man with ginger whiskers was driving the little cart, and he made the donkey trot right up to one of the oaks in the central square of the market. He stood up on the cart's seat, and to my surprise he tossed a rope up over one of the oak's low bare branches.

"What is he doing, Papa?" I demanded, and my father and Riddle both stopped and turned to watch.

"These pups," the man shouted as he caught the descending end of the rope, "are the best bulldogs a man could own. All know a pup gets its heart from its mother, and this old bitch of mine is the doughtiest bitch a man ever owned. She's old now, and not much to look at, but she's got heart. I reckon this is the last litter she'll ever whelp for me! So if you want a dog that will face down a bull, a dog that will set its teeth in a thief's leg or a bull's nose and never let go till you say so, now is the time to get one of these pups!"

I stared at the brown-and-white puppies in the cart. Their ears were edged with red. Chopped off, I realized. Someone had cut their ears off short. One of the puppies turned suddenly as if bitten by a flea, but I knew what he was doing. Licking the shorn stump that had once been a tail. The old dog had only ragged stubs of ears and a nub of a tail. The man hauled on the rope as he spoke, and to my shock a blanket in the cart shuddered and then out from under it came a bloody bull's head. The man had tied the rope round the bull's horns, and it hung, nose-down, severed neck trailing the pale tubes of its throat. He hoisted it up until the bull's head hung as high as the man was tall. Then he tied off the rope and gave the head a push to set it swinging. It must have been something he had done before, for the old bitch fixed her eyes on it.

She was a battered old thing, with white around her muzzle and hanging dugs and torn ears. She fixed her red-rimmed eyes on the swinging bull's head and a quiver ran over her. All around the square, people were drawing nearer. Someone shouted something by the door to the tavern, and a moment later a full score of men poured out. "Set, bitch!" the man shouted, and the old dog surged forward. With a tremendous leap, she seized the bull's nose in her teeth and hung there, suspended by her grip. The men closest to the cart roared their approval. Someone ran forward and gave the dangling head a strong push. Severed head and dog swung together. The man in the cart shouted, "Nothing will break her grip! She's been gored and trampled and never let go! Get a pup from her last litter now!" The crowd about the cart was growing, to my great annoyance. "I can't see," I complained to my father. "Can we go closer?"

"No," Riddle said shortly. I looked up to see his face dark with anger. I glanced at my father, and suddenly it was Wolf-Father who stood beside me. I do not mean that he had a muzzle and hair upon his face, but that his eyes were wild with ferocity. Riddle picked me up, to carry me away, but instead it gave me a view. The cart man had pulled a great knife from under his coat. He stepped forward, seized his old dog by her scruff. She growled loudly but kept her grip. He grinned round at the crowd, and then, with a sudden swipe, he sliced one of her ears off. Her snarling took on a frenzied note, but she did not break her hold. The blood ran scarlet down her sides and melted the snow in a rain of red drops.

Then Riddle was turning and taking long strides away. "Come away, Fitz!" he called in a low rough voice, as firmly as if he ordered a dog. But no command could control Wolf-Father. A moment longer he stood still and I saw his shoulders bunch under his winter cloak as the man's knife rose, fell, and rose bloodied again. No more than that could I see, but the crowd of onlookers roared and screamed and so I knew that still the bitch gripped the bull's nose in her teeth. "Only the three pups for sale!" the man shouted. "Only the three, whelps of a bitch who will let me gut her and die hanging from her teeth! Last chance to bid on these pups!"

But he was not waiting for anyone to offer money. He would have his pick of the offers once he had delivered the bloodbath they craved. Riddle held me, and I knew he longed to carry me far away but feared to leave my father alone. "Damn, where is Shun or Fitz-Vigilant when they might be more useful than annoying!" he demanded of no one. He looked at me, his dark eyes wild. "If I set you down, Bee, will you stay . . . no. A fair chance you'd be trampled. Oh, child, what will your sister say to me?" And then my father suddenly lunged forward, as if a chain that had held him back had snapped, and Riddle surged after him, trying to catch hold of his cloak. The man's bloodied knife rose; I saw it over the heads of the onlookers as Riddle pushed and cursed his way through the crowd that had gathered to watch the dog's end.

Ahead of us, someone shouted angrily as my father bowled him over to get past. The man's knife fell and the crowd chorused a deep-throated shout. "Is this the blood I dreamed?" I asked Riddle, but he did not hear me. Something swirled wild around me. The feeling of the blood-mad crowd was like a smell I could not clear from my nostrils. I felt it would tear me loose from my body. Riddle held me to his left shoulder and with his right hand set hard he forced his way in my father's wake.

I knew when my father reached the dog butcher. I heard a loud crack, as if bone had hit bone, and then the crowd roared a different note. Riddle shouldered his way to the edge of an open space where my father held a man up. One of my father's hands clutched the man's throat. His other hand was drawn back and I saw it shoot forward like an arrow leaving a bow. His fist hit the man's face and ruined it with a single blow. Then he flung the man aside, threw him into the crowd with a snap like a wolf breaking a rabbit's neck. I had never guessed my father's strength.

Riddle tried to hold my face against his shoulder but I twisted free to stare. The bitch still hung from the bull's nose, but her entrails dangled in streamers of gray and white and red that steamed in the winter air. My father had his knife in his hand. He put an arm around her and tenderly sliced her throat. As her heart pumped the last of her life and her jaws let go, he eased her body to the ground. He didn't speak, but I heard him as he promised her that her pups would know a kinder life than she had. *Not my pups*, she told him. Then, *I never knew there were masters like you*, she told him, amazed beyond wonder that such a man could exist.

Then she was gone. There was only the dead bull's head hanging from the oak, a monstrous ornament to Winterfest, and the dog butcher rolling on the bloodied ground, clutching at his face and snorting blood and cursing. The bloodied thing in my father's arms wasn't a dog anymore. My father let the body fall and stood up slowly. When he did, the circle of men widened. Men stepped back from my father and the black look in his eyes. He walked up to the man on the ground, lifted his foot, and set it on the man's chest, pinning him to the ground. The dog butcher ceased his mewling and grew still. He looked up at my father as if he looked at Death himself.

My father said nothing. When the silence had lasted long, the man on the ground lifted his hands from his smashed nose. "You had no right," he began.

My father thrust his hands into his purse. He dropped a single coin on the man's chest. It was a large one, an uncut silver. His voice was like the sound of a sword being drawn. "For the pups." He looked at them, and then at the poor bony creature hitched to the cart. "And the cart and donkey." The circle of watchers had grown still. He looked slowly around at them, and then he pointed at a youngster almost a man tall. "You. Jeruby. You drive the cart with those pups out to Withywoods. Take them to the stables and give them to a man named Hunter. Then go to my house steward, Revel, and tell him he's to give you two silver pieces."

There was a small intake of breath at that. Two silver pieces for an afternoon's work?

He turned and pointed next at an oldster. "Rube? A silver if you get that bloody bull's head out of here, and shovel clean snow over this mess. It's not a fit part of Winterfest. Are we Chalcedeans here? Do we long to have a king's circle brought back to Oaksbywater?"

Perhaps some of them did, but in the face of my father's condemnation they would not admit it. The hooting, cheering crowd had been reminded they were men and capable of better. The spectators were already starting to disperse when the man on the ground complained hoarsely, "You're cheating me! Those pups are worth a lot more than what you flung down here!" He clutched the single coin my father had dumped on him and held it up in both hands.

My father rounded on him. "She didn't whelp those pups! She was too old. She couldn't last out a fight anymore. All she had left was the strength in her jaws. And her heart. You just thought to get money out of her death."

The man on the ground gaped at him. Then, "You can't prove that!" he cried out in a voice that proclaimed him a liar.

My father had already forgotten him. He had suddenly realized that Riddle was standing there and that I was staring at him. The old bitch's blood had drenched his cloak. He saw me staring at it, and without a word he undid the clasp and let it fall to the ground, the heavy gray wool given up without a thought save that he did not want to bloody me as he came to take me into his arms. But Riddle did not give me up. I looked at my father wordlessly. He lifted his gaze to meet Riddle's.

"I thought you would take her away from here."

"And I thought you might have a mob turn on you, and might need someone at your back."

"And bring my daughter into the middle of it?"

"From the time you decided to interfere, all my choices were bad ones. Sorry if you don't like the one I made."

I had never heard Riddle's voice so cold, nor seen him and my father staring at each other like angry strangers. I had to do something, say something. "I'm cold," I said to the air. "And I'm hungry."

Riddle looked over at me. A tight, hard moment passed. The world breathed again. "I'm starving," he said quietly.

My father looked at his feet. "So am I," he muttered. He stooped suddenly, scooped up clean snow, and used it to wipe blood from his hands. Riddle watched him.

"On your left cheek, too," he said, and there was no anger left in his voice. Only a strange weariness. My father nodded, still not looking at anyone. He walked a few paces to where clean snow still clung to the top of a bush. He gathered two handfuls and washed his face with snow. When he was finished, I wriggled out of Riddle's arms. I took my father's cold wet hand. I didn't say anything. I just looked up at him. I wanted to tell him that what I had seen hadn't hurt me. Well, it had, but not the things he had done.

"Let's get some hot food," he said to me.

We walked to a tavern, past the man in the alley who still gleamed with a light that made it hard to see. Farther down the street, sitting on a corner, there was a gray beggar. I turned to look at him as we passed. He stared at me, not seeing me, for his eyes were as blank and gray as the ragged cloak he wore. He had no begging bowl, just his hand held up on top of his knee. It was empty. He wasn't begging me for money. I knew that. I could see him and he couldn't see me. That was not how it was supposed to be. I turned sharply, hugging my face to my father's arm as he pushed open the door.

Inside the tavern, all was noise and warmth and smells. When my father walked in, the talk died suddenly. He stood, looking around the room as if he were Wolf-Father thinking about a trap. Slowly the voices took up their talk again, and we followed Riddle to a table. We were scarcely seated before a boy appeared with a tray and three heavy mugs of warmed spiced cider. He set them down, *thud, thud, thud,* and then smiled at my father. "On the house," he told him, and sketched him a bow.

My father leaned back on the bench and the landlord, who was standing by the fire with several other men, lifted his own mug to him. My father nodded back gravely. He looked at the serving boy. "What is that savory smell?"

"It's a beef shoulder, simmered until the meat fell off the bones, with three yellow onions and half a bushel of carrots, and two full measures of this year's barley. If you order the soup here, sir, you will not get a bowl of brown water with a potato bit at the bottom! And the bread has just come from the oven, and we have summer butter, kept in the cold cellar and yellow as a daisy's heart. But if you prefer mutton, there are mutton pies likewise stuffed with barley and carrot and onion, in brown crusts so flaky that we must put a plate under them, for they are so tender that otherwise you may end up wearing one! We have sliced pumpkin baked with apples and butter and cream, and . . ."

"Stop, stop," my father begged him, "or my belly will burst just listening to you. What shall we have?" He turned to Riddle and me with the question. Somehow my father was smiling and I thanked the jolly serving boy with all my heart.

I chose the beef soup and bread and butter, as did Riddle and my father. No one spoke while we waited but it was not an awkward quiet. Rather it was a careful one. It was better to leave the space empty of words than to choose the wrong ones. When the food came, it was every bit as good as the boy had said it would be. We ate, and somehow, not talking made things better between Riddle and my father. The fire on the big hearth sparked and spit when someone added a big log. The door opened and closed as people came and went, and the conversations reminded me of bees buzzing in a hive. I had not known that a chill day and buying things and watching my father save a dog's death could make me so hungry. When I could almost see the bottom of my bowl, I found the words I needed.

"Thank you, Papa. For doing what you did. It was right."

He looked at me and spoke carefully. "It is what fathers are supposed to do. We are supposed to get our children what they need. Boots and scarves, yes, but bracelets and chestnuts, too, when we can."

He didn't want to recall what he had done in the town square. But I had to make him understand that I understood. "Yes. Fathers do that. And some go right into the middle of a mob and save a poor dog from a slow death. And send puppies and a donkey to a safe place." I turned to look at Riddle. It was hard. I'd never looked directly into his face. I put my eyes on his and kept them there. "Remind my sister that our father is a very brave man, when you see her. Tell her I am learning to be brave, too."

Riddle was meeting my gaze. I tried, but I could not do it for long. I looked down at my bowl and took up my spoon as if I were still very hungry. I knew that my father and Riddle looked at each other over my bowed head, but I kept my eyes on my food.

Chapter 28

THINGS BOUGHT

*If a few students come reluctantly to their studies, then let them go.
If all students come reluctantly to their studies, then let your scribe
be dismissed and find another. For once students have been taught
that learning is tedious, difficult, and useless, they will never learn
another lesson.*

ON THE NECESSITY OF EDUCATION, SCRIBE FEDWREN

How often does a man know, without question, that he has done
well? I do not think it happens often in anyone's life, and it becomes even rarer once one has a child. Ever since I had become a
parent, I had questioned every decision I'd ever made for any child
I was responsible for, from Nettle to Hap and even Dutiful. Certainly with Bee, I seemed to stumble from one disastrous action to
another. I had never wished her to see the facet of myself that she
had seen killing the dog. I'd washed the blood from my face and

hands with the icy snow, but could not cleanse the deep shame I'd felt as we walked toward the tavern. Then my child had looked up at me and thanked me. She'd not only claimed to understand but had tried to smooth my rift with Riddle. Her words did not free me of my guilt; Riddle had been right. I'd completely disregarded that I might be putting her into danger when the waves of the dog's agony had struck me. The old bitch's utter faith that by doing exactly as her master commanded she would finally please him had been too great a cruelty for me to endure. Should I have endured it for the sake of protecting her?

Bee evidently thought not. Another time, I promised myself, I would be wiser. I tried to think of what I could have done differently and found no answers. But at least this time my daughter seemed to have taken no harm from my rashness.

The food was good, my brief clash with Riddle seemed settled, and my daughter wanted to be exactly where she was. Behind us, the inn door was opening and closing almost as regularly as if it were a bellows pumping hungry folk into the tavern. Suddenly two of them were Shun and FitzVigilant. His arms were laden with packages. He stooped and set them carefully on the floor beside us before they abruptly joined us, sitting down on either end of our bench. "I've found some green stockings I truly must have for Winterfest. We will celebrate it at Withywoods, won't we? Of course we must, and there will be dancing! There are many minstrels in town and I am sure you can hire some to come to Withywoods. But first, before we seek them out, I must go purchase the stockings. I am sure that if you loan me the coin, Lord Chade will be good for it!" Shun announced breathlessly.

Before I could even turn my head in her direction, from the other end FitzVigilant added, "And I have found wax tablets at a merchant who specializes in the newest items! He has them in hinged pairs, so that a student can close them and protect his work. Such a clever idea! He does not have many of them, but any we can purchase will help my students."

I looked at my earnest scribe in consternation. His spirits and confidence had quickly revived. I was pleased he was no longer so cowed by my presence, but a bit appalled that he seemed as avaricious for unnecessary trinkets as Shun was. I recalled my earliest writing efforts. Paper had been considered far too valuable for younger students. With a wet finger, I had formed letters on the flagstones of the great hall. Sometimes we used burned sticks. I recalled ink made from soot. I did not mention this. I knew that many marveled at how backward Buckkeep and, indeed, all the Six Duchies had been in those years. The isolation of war and several kings who had been determined to insulate us from foreign customs had kept us bound in older traditions. Kettricken had been the queen who had first introduced us to her Mountain ways of doing things, and then encouraged us to import not only goods from distant lands but their ideas and techniques as well. I was still not sure it had been an improvement. Did Lant's students truly need hinged wax tablets in order to learn their letters? I felt my resistance rising. Then I recalled that I had heard Revel muttering in dismay that I clothed Bee as children had dressed two score years ago. Perhaps I was the one who was clinging unreasonably to the old ways now. Was it time to give way to change? Time to put my little daughter into long skirts before she was a woman?

I glanced at her. I loved her in her little brown tunics and leggings, free to run and tumble. Next to me, Bee wriggled with boredom. I stifled a sigh and pulled my mind back to the present. "Tablets for the students first, and then I will come round to see these stockings that have so impressed Shun."

I lifted my bread and Shun broke out in a storm of arguments as to why I must first see what she coveted, ranging from a fear that the merchant would close his doors to someone else purchasing them and winding up with her fear that I might spend all my coin on tablets and have none left to buy her green stockings and whatever else it was that had caught her eye. I felt as if I were being relentlessly pelted with small stones, for FitzVigilant spoke at the same time, saying the tablets were not, truly, that essential and that of course I should see to Lady Shun's needs first.

I spoke firmly. "Then I shall. As soon as I've been allowed to finish my food."

"I would not mind something to eat," Shun agreed, contented now that she had her way. "But have they anything nicer than soup and bread? An apple pastry, perhaps? Chicken?"

I lifted a hand to summon a serving boy. He came and Shun interrogated him ruthlessly as to what foods were available. She badgered him into asking the cook to heat a cold fowl that was in the pantry, and to bring it with a dried apple tart. FitzVigilant was content with soup and bread. The boy mentioned that there were little gingercakes soon to come out of the oven in the kitchen. I asked for six of them, and the boy left.

"Six?" Shun exclaimed in amazement. "Six?"

"Some to eat and some to take. They were my favorites when I was a child, and I think that Bee will like them as much as I did."

I twisted to ask Bee if she would like to try some of my favorite cakes, and found she was not there. I lifted my eyes to Riddle. He tipped his head toward the rear of the tavern; the privy was out that way.

Shun seized my sleeve. "I forgot to ask for mulling spices in my cider!"

I lifted my hand to summon the boy back. He had his head hunched down, and I was almost certain he was pretending not to see me. I waved my hand wearily. The boy darted off to another table, where he was greeted with raucous cheers from six waiting men. I watched him strike his pose and begin his recitation. The men were grinning at him. "He's busy right now," I excused him to Shun.

"He's ignoring me!"

"I'll go back to the kitchen and tell them to spice your cider," FitzVigilant offered.

"Of course you shouldn't!" she exclaimed. "That boy should come back over here and do his tasks. Tom Badgerlock! Cannot you make that boy do as he should? Why should he ignore his betters to bring food to a table full of lowborn farmers? Call him back here!"

I drew a breath. Riddle stood so abruptly he nearly overset the bench. "I'll go to the kitchen. The inn is busy today. Leave the boy alone to do his work."

He swung his leg over the bench, turned, and strode across the crowded inn room as only Riddle could, sliding between the packed customers but somehow giving offense to none.

Except Shun. She stared after him, nostrils flared and mouth pinched white. Riddle's tone had left no doubt as to his opinion of her. FitzVigilant was staring after him, his mouth slightly ajar. He rolled his eyes to look at Shun and said weakly, "That's not like Riddle."

"He's had a trying day," I excused him. I pointed my chill remark at Shun but she seemed immune to my intent to shame her. I frowned after Riddle, feeling as if he rebuked me as much as Shun. Lant was right. It wasn't like Riddle. I suspected that my behavior had far more to do with Riddle's short temper than Shun's pique over her mulling spices. I closed my eyes for a moment, tasting bitterness in the back of my throat. That poor old bitch. For years I had rigorously controlled my Wit, refusing to reach out, refusing to allow anyone to reach into me. Today those barriers had fallen and I no more could have turned away than I could have ignored someone beating Bee. That sadistic butcher had not been Witted; but I had felt what radiated from the old dog toward him. It was not the aches in her damaged and aging body as she'd trotted after his cart. It wasn't even the sharp agony she'd felt as he cut her. I'd learned, over the years, to brace myself against that sort of bleed-over of pain from creatures. No. What had cracked my walls and flooded me with fury was something else she had felt for him. Loyalty. Trust that he knew what was best. For all the days of her life, she'd been his tool and his weapon, deployed however he wished. Her life had been harsh but it had been what she'd been bred for. For that man, she had baited bulls, fought other dogs, set on boars. Whatever he had commanded, she had done, and taken the joy of the weapon in doing what it was created for. When she'd done well and won for him, sometimes there had been a shout of pride over her, or a cut of the meat. Rare as those moments were, they were the best ones in her life, and always she had been ready to make any sacrifice to earn one more of them.

When he had set her on the bull's head, she had sprung to it. And when he'd sliced off her ear, she kept her teeth clenched, accepting in her dogged way that there was a reason for the pain her master dealt her.

Not so different from how I had been when Chade had first employed me. I'd become what he'd raised me and trained me to be. Just as he had. I did not fault him for what he'd made of me. If he had not taken me as his apprentice, I probably would not have lived past ten years old. He'd taken a bastard—an embarrassment and possibly a liability to the Farseer throne—and made me useful. Even essential.

And so I had lived, and like the bitch I'd done as he told me and never questioned it was for the best. I would never forget the first time I had completely realized that Chade was not infallible. For years, when I suffered from headaches after I Skilled or attempted to Skill, he had dosed me with elfbark. I had endured the bleak spirit and wildly nervous energy for the sake of banishing the pain. And he had commiserated with me and urged me to try ever harder in developing my Skill. For years, neither of us had known that the elfbark itself was actually eroding my ability for that magic. But when I discovered that, what I had felt was not devastation that my magic was damaged, but astonishment that Chade had been wrong.

I was beginning to suspect I'd fallen into the same trap again. Habits of thinking are hard to break.

A remarkable silence had fallen to either side of me. Shun was seething still, FitzVigilant torn. I suspected he and Riddle had known each other well at Buckkeep Castle, and despite the differences in their positions he had perhaps even regarded him as a friend. And now he must make a choice and declare for the lady, or defend his friend. I wondered if his need to win my approval would weigh into this at all. I waited silently, knowing that how he decided would be how I judged him.

He leaned on the table to look past me at Lady Shun. "You should not judge the serving boy too harshly," he suggested. For a

moment my heart warmed toward him. Then he ruined it by saying, "We are seated here among the commoners, and he is but a
tavern lad in a backwater town. It would be a wonder if he had
been schooled to the ability to recognize a highborn lady and grant
her the priority that she deserves."

How had Chade let him acquire such a high opinion of himself?
While Chade had never debased me for the illegitimacy we shared,
he had let me know that my birth to a common mother meant I
could never assume that the privilege of the noble class would be
accorded to me. I wondered if FitzVigilant knew his mother had
been a huntswoman, esteemed by the queen but of no great standing at court. Did he imagine himself to be lost nobility of a very
high order? Better than humble Tom Badgerlock, son of a commoner?

Better than Bee?

And in that moment I knew with great clarity that FitzVigilant
was completely unsuitable to teach my daughter. How could I have
ever believed otherwise? Once more I found myself shaking my
head over my own stupidity. FitzVigilant had failed as an assassin,
so Chade had assumed he would do better as a scribe and teacher.
And I had gone along with such a crooked piece of logic. Why? Did
either of us believe that teaching children might be easier than killing them?

What was wrong with me, that after so many years I still found
myself willing to accept unquestioningly Chade's suggestions? I
was an adult, surely, by now? But such was the power of my old
mentor over me. I had long ago learned he was fallible, yet in unguarded moments I always fell back into the default that Chade
knew better than I did. I seldom questioned his commands; even
worse, I seldom tried to pry out information he had not shared
with me. Well, that would change now. I would know, without
doubt, Lant's true parentage, and I would demand to know exactly
why Shun was worth a dedicated effort to kill her. And I'd ask why
on earth he had ever thought either of them could possibly func-
tion as a bodyguard or a tutor for my child.

So I would be both to her, teacher and guardian. She could already read, and it seemed to me that most of my education had come from either reading or helping Chade in his odd experiments. There had been my physical training, of course, but I scarcely saw the need to teach Bee how to wield an axe or a sword. It made me smile to think of how earnestly she still pursued our evening lessons with her knife. A quick lesson in handling the blade had replaced a night story or song. She was quick; I had to give her that. After she had cut my knuckles twice, I had replaced her belt-knife with a wooden blade. A few nights ago she had startled me by evading my blade with a tumbling trick worthy of the Fool himself. If I could teach her to dance to a blade, surely I could teach her all else she needed to know. I could manage a sufficient education for her. And what I did not know, I would have her taught by those who knew it best. We had an excellent healer in Withy; she could build on the foundation of herbal knowledge that Molly had given her. And yes, my daughter would learn to play an instrument, and to dance, and the thousand other things that were a woman's weapons in this world. And languages. The tongue of the Mountain Kingdom, certainly. And it came to me that there was little to anchor Bee and me at Withywoods. We could spend a year in the Mountains, for her to learn their generous ways as well as their language. And the same for the Out Islands. And for each of the Six Duchies. I suddenly resolved that, before she was sixteen, my daughter would have traveled to all of them. It was as if I had been following a narrow trail, and had suddenly realized that at any time I could leave it and strike out cross-country. I could choose what and how she was taught, and in the process shape who she became.

For Bee had had the right of it. Girls did not have to hit to hurt. But did I want her to learn that sort of fighting from Shun's example, with Lant's confirmation?

". . . your place to correct him, not mine or Lant's. Does not it bother you that he has insulted me? And Lant? Are you listening? Holder Badgerlock!"

When she uttered my name, I jolted back into the ongoing conversation. But I did not turn to her to respond but to FitzVigilant.

My mind seized on an odd bit of information I needed. "How many wax tablets were you hoping to purchase?"

Behind me, Shun made an exasperated sound at being ignored. It bothered me not at all. FitzVigilant looked startled at the turn of conversation. He hedged suddenly and I suspected he feared there would be a budget constriction. "The merchant did not have many, of course. The double ones, I am sure, could be shared easily enough by sibling students and . . ."

"We will buy what he has." I leaned back slightly from the table. I was watching the door of the inn for Bee to return. I worried suddenly about the quantity of chestnuts and sweets she had eaten. Was she all right? "I'll reserve one for Bee's use; I'll be taking over her education. I do not find you fit to teach her."

He stared at me, and it was a very young look. Humiliation and panic, dismay and shock vied to control his face. None of them triumphed and so he simply stared. If it had not been Bee at stake, I might have felt sorry for having to do this to him. It took a few moments for him to find his tongue. He spoke very carefully and precisely. "If I have given offense somehow, or failed in your estimation, sir, I do—"

"You have," I cut in. I refused to feel any pity or remorse. Had he pitied Bee when he'd rebuked and humiliated her in front of the other children?

His lower lip actually quivered. Then his face went stony. He sat up very straight. "When we return tonight, I will immediately pack my things and leave Withywoods."

His posturing wearied me. "No. Much as you both annoy me, I cannot allow that. No matter how little I wish it, you must remain at Withywoods. I have seen that neither of you is ready to teach nor protect my child. How, then, do you imagine I find you ready to protect yourself? FitzVigilant, you can continue to attempt to teach the other children. And I will be your instructor in both the axe and the sword, and in how to respect any man who can meet your eyes honestly." More of my time claimed, but at least it might eventually make him able to fend for himself. And Shun? I looked at her regal outrage. "I will ask Steward Revel to see you instructed in whatever is most likely to win you a husband. I judge that not to be dancing or singing, but the management of a household within a budget."

She stared at me coldly. "Lord Chade will hear of this!"

"Indeed, he will. And from me before your message reaches him."

She narrowed her eyes to a cat's squint. "I will not return to Withywoods. I will, this very night, take a room here in Oaksbywater and abide here, alone. And to Lord Chade you will answer for my leaving."

I sighed. "Shun. It's nearly Winterfest. The inns are full. And you will return this evening to my home, where we will prepare to celebrate it for the sake of my little daughter. I will not hear, from either of you, any more threats of leaving. You will not, for I have given my word to someone I respect that I will watch over you." I looked from Lant to Shun.

Her mouth actually dropped open. She shut it with a snap and then abruptly demanded, "Badgerlock, how dare you assume any authority over me! Lord Chade put you at my disposal, for my convenience and protection. Send your message however and whenever you will. I will see that he corrects any misconceptions you have about our positions."

And there it was, exposed in that single sentence. Despite Chade's careless dropping of my name, she had not put the pieces together. She was glaring at me as if she expected me to stumble back from her, bowing and apologizing. While she might be illegitimate, she was confident of her superiority to me. Lant, though a bastard, had been acknowledged by a noble father, and was hence her equal.

But not the serving boy. Nor me, nor Riddle. Because in her eyes, I was as lowborn as my daughter.

"Shun. That's enough." That was all I said. Her eyes narrowed and grew cold with fury. I almost wanted to laugh as she decided to exercise her authority.

"You are not permitted to speak to me like that," she warned me in a low voice.

I had almost thought of what I would reply when Riddle arrived at the table. He came bearing their dishes of food, cleverly balanced up one arm, and their mugs of cider in the other hand. With two thunks and a flourish, he set it all out before me. There was a glint in his eyes, his determination to put the events of the day behind him and be merry. Then his determined smile was suddenly replaced with a worried look and the question, "Where's Bee?"

Alarm pierced me. I stood in the tight space between the bench and table. "She hasn't come back. It's been too long. I'll go find her."

"My cider's barely warm!" I heard Shun exclaim as I stepped over the bench and away.

Chapter 29

MIST AND LIGHT

Then, from the gleaming mists that surrounded us, there burst a
wolf, all black and silver. He was covered in scars and death clung
to him like water clings to a dog's coat after he has plunged through
a river. My father was with him and in him and around him, and
never had I realized him as he was. He bled from dozens of unheal-
able wounds and yet at the core of him, life burned like molten gold
in a furnace.

DREAM JOURNAL OF BEE FARSEER

It had all been ruined when the door of the tavern opened and
banged shut again, and suddenly Shun and FitzVigilant were there.
The way FitzVigilant looked at my father, I knew he had already
heard the tale of what had happened in the town commons. I did
not want him to speak of it to my father. We were past it now, and
if he brought it up Riddle would have to think about it again.

Riddle and my father were behaving as if all were well now, but I knew that my father's actions would gnaw at Riddle's heart like a worm. My father was his friend, but he gave his ultimate loyalty to Nettle, and he dreaded telling her this story and revealing to her his part in it.

But Shun, if she knew of it, made nothing of it, but only began to natter on about she-must-have-this and she-must-have-that, and if my father had coin, perhaps they could go get it right now, or perhaps she would eat first. She sat down beside my father and FitzVigilant sat on the other side of Riddle, and they reminded me of red-mouthed fledglings squawking in a nest as they spoke of needing this and wanting that. My father turned away from me to speak to Shun. I couldn't stand it. I was suddenly too warm and the press of the myriad conversations felt like hands over my ears. I tugged on Riddle's sleeve. "I need to go outside."

"What? Oh. It's behind the inn. And come right back, you hear me?" He twisted away to reply to something FitzVigilant had said to him. Odd, how I must never interrupt, but my tutor saw no reason to observe the same courtesy to me. "It's country food, Lant. Different from what you'd find in a Buckkeep Town tavern, but not bad. Try the soup."

I had to wiggle to turn on the bench and then get down from it. I do not think my father had even noticed me leaving. On my way to the door, a large woman nearly stepped on me, but I darted round her. The door was so heavy I had to wait until someone was coming in before I could slip out. The cooler air greeted me; it seemed as if the bustle of the street and merry atmosphere had increased as evening drew closer. I stepped just slightly away from the door so that I would not be hit if it opened, and then I had to move out of the way again because a man needed to unload a cart of firewood for the tavern next door. So I crossed the street and watched a man juggling three potatoes and an apple. He sang a merry little song as he juggled. When he was finished, I twisted to reach past my new market bag and dug deep into my new little pouch. In the bottom I found my half-copper. When I gave it to him, he smiled and gave me the apple to keep.

It was definitely time for me to go back to the tavern and find my father, much as I dreaded being dragged about on Shun's errands now. But perhaps my father would send Riddle with her or just give her money to waste. A wagon full of cider kegs with a team of four horses had stopped in the street, so I had to go around it. To get back to the tavern, I must walk past the gray beggar.

I stopped to look at him. He was so empty. Not just his dirty pleading hand on his knee, but all of him, as if he were a plum skin hanging on a tree after wasps had stolen all its sweet flesh and left only an empty shell. I looked at his empty hand, but I desperately wanted to keep my two coppers. So I said, "I've an apple. Would you like an apple, beggar?"

He shifted his eyes toward me as if he could see me. They were terrible, dead and clouded. I did not want him to look at me with such eyes. "You are kind," he said, and I bravely stooped to set the apple in his hand.

Just then the door of the spice shop opened and the thin little woman who owned it stepped out. "You!" she exclaimed. "Are you still squatting here? Away! I told you, get away! A street full of customers and my shop is empty because no one wants to step over your smelly bones and rags. Away! Or my husband comes with his stick to teach you how to dance!"

"I go, I go," the beggar said softly. His gray hand had closed on the red apple. He tucked the fruit into the breast of his ragged tunic and began the slow struggle to rise. The woman was glaring at him. I stooped, found the staff he was groping for, and put it into his hand. "You are kind," he said again. He gripped the stick tight, one hand above the other, and levered himself to his feet. He swayed and turned his face slowly from side to side. "Is the street clear?" he asked piteously. "If I step out now, is the street clear?"

"Clear enough. Go now!" The spice woman spoke harshly as a team and wagon rounded the corner, heading our way, and I resolved never to buy anything in her store.

"Don't step out," I warned him. "You'll be crushed. Wait and I'll walk across with you."

"Well, aren't you the interfering little snippet!" She bent forward at the waist to mock me. Her heavy breasts lunged at me like chained dogs. "Does your mother know you are running wild on the street and talking to dirty beggars?"

I wanted to say something clever to her, but she turned back into her shop, calling, "Heny? Heny, that beggar is still blocking our door! See him off, as I asked you to do hours ago!"

The rumbling wagon had passed. "Come with me now," I said. He smelled very bad. I didn't want to touch him. But I knew that my father would not have left him there at the mercy of the spice woman. It was time for me to begin behaving as my father's daughter. I took hold of his staff below his grip. "I'll guide you," I told him. "Step now. Come."

It was a slow business. Even with both hands grasping his stick, he could barely stand. He took two little steps, hopped his stick forward, and took two more little steps. As I guided him out into the street and away from the door of the spice shop, I realized suddenly I did not know where to put him. There, he had been sheltered from the wind. To either side of us, the doors of the shops were busy with customers coming and going. Ahead of us was only the town commons. We hitched along slowly toward it. No one had returned to the place where the dog had died. Someone had taken her body away and the bull's head, and as my father had asked, they had spread clean snow there, but the blood had soaked up through it. Pink snow, almost pretty, if one did not know what it was. I do not know why I guided him there, except that it was an open space. The canvas that had covered the bull's head was on the ground under the tree. Perhaps he could sit on that.

I glanced back at the tavern door, knowing that if I did not return soon, my father or Riddle would come after me. Perhaps both of them.

Or perhaps neither. Shun was there and she was fully capable of keeping both of them occupied to the point at which they would forget about me. A nasty feeling smothered my heart. Jealousy. I finally named it for what it was. I was jealous.

It fueled my desire to help the blind beggar. I would not go back. They would have to come and find me, and when they did, they would see that I could be as brave and kind as my father. Helping a beggar that no one else would touch. A man by a tinker's cart was staring at us in distaste. Plainly he wanted us to move farther away from him. I steeled my resolve and shifted my bag to settle firmly on my shoulder. "Give me your arm," I said boldly. "I can help you walk better."

He hesitated, knowing how disgusting he was. Then his weariness won. "You are too kind," he said, almost sadly, and held out his stick of an arm. I took it. He lurched a little. I was shorter than he had expected. His dirty hand gripped my forearm.

The world wheeled around us. The sky rainbowed. There had been a fog, but it had been a fog I had looked through all my life. Now it parted, as if a wind of joy had torn through it. I looked in awe at a beauty that tore my heart wide open. All of them, the scowling tinker, the holly-crowned girl kissing a boy behind a tree, the inn cat under the porch, the old man bartering for a new felted hat, all of them burst forth in glorious colors I had never imagined existed. Their flaws were overcome by the potential for beauty in each of them. I made a small sound and the beggar sobbed aloud.

"I can see," he cried out. "My sight has come back to me. I can see! Oh, my light, my sun, where have you come from? Where have you been?"

He gathered me to his breast and embraced me and I was glad of it. The beauty and the possibility of glory that blossomed all around me flowed from him through me. This, this was how it was supposed to be done. Not in tiny glimpses, not as unconnected dreams. Everywhere I looked, possibilities multiplied. It reminded me of the first time my father had lifted me to his shoulder and I suddenly realized how much farther he could see from his height. But now I saw, not just from a better vantage, not just to a distance, but to all times. It was comforting to be held safe at the middle of that swirling vortex. I did not fear as I allowed my sight to follow the myriad threads. One caught my attention. The kissing girl would marry that boy, crowned with orange blossoms, and bear him nine children at a farm in a valley. Or not. She might dally with him for a time, and marry another, but her memory of this moment would add sweetness to every pie she baked, and the love she had known would be shared with chickens and cats until she died, barren, at seventy-two. But no. They would run away together, this very night, and lie together in the forest, and the next day, on the road to Buckkeep, they would both die, he of an arrow wound and she would be raped and torn and cast aside to die in a ditch. And because of that, her older brothers would band together and become the Oaksby Guard. During the time of their patrols, they would take the lives of fifty-two highwaymen and save over six hundred travelers from pain and death. The numbers were plain. It was suddenly so very simple. All I had to do was give them a tiny nudge. If I smiled at them as they strolled the village green and told them, "You shine with love. Love should not wait. Run away tonight!" they would see me as a harbinger and take my advice. His pain would last but a moment, and hers only hours. Less time than she would spend struggling in childbirth for her first child. I had the power. I had the power and the choice. I could do so much good in the world. So much good. There were so many choices I could make for the good of the world. I would start with the holly-crowned girl.

He clutched me tighter and spoke by my ear. "Stop. Stop. You must not! Not without great thought and then . . . even then . . . there is so much danger. So much danger!"

He turned my eyes, and the threads splintered into a thousand more threads. It was not as simple as I had thought. For every thread I tried to follow became a multitude, and the moment I chose one thread from that multitude, it shattered again into yet more possibilities. She might say the wrong word to him and he would murder her this afternoon. She told her father she had kissed him and her father blessed them. Or cursed them. Or drove her from her home into the storm, to die of cold in the night.

Some are far more likely than others, but each has at least one chance to be real. So each path must be studied carefully before any path is chosen. The path you observed, where they both must die? If we were dedi-

cated to this creation of the Oaksby Guard, we would look and look. There are, always, other time paths that lead to the same end. There will be some more destructive and ugly, and some less so.

I had thought he was speaking aloud to me. I became aware that his thoughts were seeping into me through the bond we shared. He poured knowledge from his mind to mine as if he were a pitcher and I the cup. Or the thirsty garden that had only been waiting, all this time, for this nourishment.

And the paths change, they change constantly. Some vanish, impossible now, and others grow more likely. That is why the training takes so many years. So many years. One studies, and one pays attention to the dreams. Because the dreams are like guideposts for the most significant moments. The most significant moments . . .

He took his attention from me, and it was as if someone had torn a warm cloak from me in the midst of an ice storm. He stared with his blind eyes, terror and joy stamped on his scarred face. "*The wolf comes,*" he recited. "*His teeth are a knife, and the flying drops of blood are his tears.*"

Then my vision faded to the same sort of sight one has in deep twilight before the last light of the day fades. The colors were muted and shadows prevailed, hiding all detail from me. I thought I would die. Every possibility was hidden, masked and limited to a single instant of time. I felt I could not move. Life was stiff and limited and slow. Time had been a limitless ocean, spreading out in every direction, and I had been a seabird, free to wheel and flit from one moment to a thousand other possibilities. Now I was mired in a tiny puddle, struggling to experience even one second fully, blinded to the future consequences of any action I might take. I stopped and stood and let life happen around me.

Chapter 30

COLLISION

My wolf taught me as much as I ever taught him. But strive as he might, he never completely succeeded in teaching me to exist in the now as he did. When we spent quiet snowy nights sprawled on the hearth before a comfortable fire, the wolf had no need of conversation or a scroll to read. He simply enjoyed the comfort of warmth and resting. When I would rise to pace the small room, or pull a burnt stick from the embers to scratch idly on the hearthstones or take up paper and pen, he would lift his head, sigh, and then put it back down and resume his enjoyment of the evening.

When we hunted together, I would move nearly as silently as he did, watching, always watching for the flick of an ear or the shift of a hoof, that tiny motion that would betray a deer standing poised in the brush, waiting for us to pass by. I would flatter myself that I was completely in the now, tuned exclusively to the hunt. And so intent would I be on that watch that I would startle when, with a pounce

and a shake, Nighteyes would kill a crouched rabbit or huddled
grouse that I had walked right past. I always envied him that. He
was open to all the information that the world offered him, a scent,
a sound, a tiny movement, or just the brush of life against his Wit-
sense. I never achieved his ability to open himself to everything, to
be aware of all that was happening, all at once.

UNSIGNED JOURNAL ENTRY

I hadn't taken more than a step before Riddle was up and beside me. He caught at my arm. His mouth was a flat line as I turned to him. He spoke quietly, almost without inflection, as if he himself had no idea how to feel about his words. "I need to say this before we go fetch Bee. Fitz, it isn't working. In fact, it's exactly what Nettle feared. You're a good man. And my friend. I hope you can remember that I'm your friend as I say this. You're not a good . . . you aren't able to be a good father. I have to take her back to Buckkeep with me. I promised Nettle that I would see how things were going for both of you. She didn't trust herself to decide; she was afraid she'd be too critical."

I pushed down my sudden flare of anger. "Riddle. Not now. And not here." Later, I'd think about his words and what they meant. I shrugged free of his hand on my arm. "I need to find Bee. She's been gone too long."

He caught at my sleeve and I had to turn back to him. "Exactly. But until I pointed it out, you hadn't noticed that. The second time today that she's been put into danger."

Shun had a fox's ears. She was eavesdropping. Behind us, she made a small sound between disgust and amusement and spoke for me to hear. "And he says you are not fit to teach his daughter," she observed to FitzVigilant snidely. I nearly turned to her but the wolf in my heart leapt to the forefront. *Find the cub. Nothing else matters.*

Riddle had also heard her. He dropped his grip on my sleeve and started toward the door. I was two steps behind him. All manner of thoughts raced through my mind. Oaksbywater was not a large town, but all sorts of folk would be converging on it for Winterfest. All sorts of people, bent on having a good time. And for some of them, a good time could involve hurting my little girl. I barked my hip on a table's edge and two men shouted as their beer leapt over the rims of their mugs. Then Shun was stupid enough to seize my sleeve. She had come after me and Lant trailed her. "Riddle can find Bee. Holder Badgerlock, we need to settle this once and for all."

I ripped my sleeve from her grip so abruptly that she cried out and clutched her hand to her chest. "Did he hurt you?" FitzVigilant exclaimed in horror.

Riddle had reached the door and was waiting for two very large patrons to come in before he could go out. He leaned to look around them. Then, "No! Stop! Put her down!" Riddle roared the words as he slammed through the two men trying to come into the tavern, and out the door. I lunged away from Shun and crossed the crowded tavern in a stumbling run. The door stood wide open and I bolted through it. I gazed wildly around the busy commons. Where had Riddle gone, what had he seen? Folk were treading calmly through the snow, a dog sat scratching itself, and the driver of the emptied wagon in front of the inn chirruped to his team. Past the wagon I caught a glimpse of Riddle, running through startled idlers toward a ragged beggar who had lifted my small daughter in his crooked dirty hands and held her tight to his breast. His mouth was by her ear. Trapped against him, she was not struggling. Instead she was very, very still, her feet dangling, her face looking up into his, her lax hands open and held wide as if begging something from the sky.

I passed Riddle and somehow my knife was in my hands. I heard a sound, a roaring like a beast and a roaring in my ears. Then my arm was around the beggar's throat, pulling his face away from my daughter's, and as I bent his head back with the crook of my elbow, I plunged my knife into his side, once, twice, three times at least. He screamed as he let go of her, and I dragged him back with me, away from my child in her red-and-gray shawl, fallen like a torn rose in the snow.

Riddle was there in an instant, wise enough to snatch my daughter from the snowy ground and fall back with her. His right arm held her to his heart while his left had his own knife at the ready. He looked all around, seeking some other foe or target. Then he glanced down at her, took two steps back, and shouted, "She's fine, Tom. A bit stunned but fine. No blood!"

Only then did I become aware of people shouting. Some were fleeing the violence, others converging in a circle around us as eager as crows at a killing. I still held the beggar in my arms. I looked down into the face of the man I had killed. His eyes were open, grayed over and blind. Row of scars lined his face in lovingly inflicted lines. His mouth was crooked. The hand that clutched still at my strangling arm was a bird's claw of crookedly healed fingers.

"Fitz," he said quietly. "You've killed me. But I understand. I deserve it. I deserved worse."

His breath was foul and his eyes like dirty windows. But his voice had not changed. The world rocked under my feet. I stumbled back, and sat down hard in the snow, the Fool in my arms. I realized where I was, under the oak, in the bloody snow where the dog had bled. Now the Fool bled. I felt the warm blood from his wounds soaking my thighs. I dropped my knife and pressed my hand to the punctures I had made. "Fool," I croaked, but I had no breath to make words.

He moved one hand, blindly groping, asking with infinite hope, "Where did he go?"

"I'm right here. Right here. And I'm sorry. Oh, Fool, don't die. Not in my arms. I could not live with that. Don't die, Fool, not at my hands!"

"He was here. My son."

"No, only me. Just me. Beloved. Don't die. Please don't die."

"Did I dream?" Tears spilled slowly from his blind eyes. They were thick and yellow. The breath of his whisper was foul. "Can I die into that dream? Please?"

"No. Don't die. Not by my hand. Not in my arms," I begged. I was curled forward over him, nearly as blind as he was as I fought the blackness at the edges of my vision. This was too terrible to live through. How could this be? How could this be? My body longed for unconsciousness, and my mind knew I had but a knife's edge of a chance. I could not survive this if he did not.

He spoke again, and blood was on his tongue and lips as he formed the words. "Dying in your arms . . . is still dying." He breathed two breaths. "And I cannot. Must not." The blood crested his lips and began to trickle over his chin. "Much as I've wished to. If you will. If you can. Keep me alive, Fitz. Whatever the cost to us. To you. Please. I need to live."

A Skill-healing, even in the best of circumstances, is a difficult thing. It's usually accomplished by a circle of Skill-users, a coterie, who are familiar with one another and are capable of loaning one another strength. The knowledge of how a man's body is put together is essential to it, for in severe instances one must decide what injuries are most deadly and deal with those first. Ideally, before the healing is attempted, all will have been done to accomplish an ordinary healing, wounds cleansed and bound, with a patient who is rested and well fed. Ideally. I knelt in the snow, the Fool in my lap, surrounded by chattering onlookers, while Riddle held my terrified daughter in his arms. I lifted my eyes to Riddle and spoke clearly. "I've made a terrible mistake. I've hurt an old friend who meant my child no harm. Care for Bee and keep these others back. I wish to say a prayer to Eda."

It was a believable excuse, and there were enough followers of Eda present that they could persuade the others to give me quiet and space. No one had shouted for the city guard: It was entirely possible that few realized I'd actually stabbed the beggar. Riddle's astonished gaze reproached me, but for a wonder he obeyed, and I suddenly knew just how deep our friendship actually went. He called out loudly for people to give me space, and then, turning, I saw him shout and beckon FitzVigilant to his side. Shun was following the scribe, walking like a cat in wet snow. I saw him speaking earnestly to both of them, taking command, and knew he would handle it all.

I closed my eyes and bent my head as if in prayer.

I plunged into the Fool's body. We no longer had a Skill-link; for an instant his boundaries opposed me. I summoned Skill-strength I scarcely knew I possessed and breached his defenses. He made a low sound, of objection or pain. I ignored it. This was a body I knew intimately, having once worn it. It was like and unlike a man's, with differences that were both subtle and crucial. To close the wounds I had caused and stem that bleeding was not a complicated feat, and I made it my first task. Undo the damage I had done to him. It took focus, and my willing his body to make that healing a priority worth burning his scanty reserves. So I stopped his bleeding, and felt him dwindle and weaken as his body accelerated that healing. For while the Skill is a powerful magic, it does not do the healing. The body does, under the Skill's direction, and there is always a cost to the body's reserves.

Almost immediately I saw my mistake. I moved through his body with his blood, finding old damage and bad repairs and places where his body had trapped poisons and sealed them off in a vain effort to control their spread. One of my knife plunges had pierced such a toxic pocket, and now it leaked blackness into his blood, and his pumping heart was carrying the poison all through his body. The wrongness was spreading; I felt his body's weary physical alarm, and then a peculiar resignation began to spread through him. It was not his mind but his body that knew his life was at an end. A strange pleasure began to spread through him, a final comforting that the flesh offered the mind. It was soon to be over; why spend your last moments in alarm? Almost that lure of peace drew me in.

"Fool. Please!" I quietly begged him to rally. I opened my own eyes to look into his face. For a long moment, the world spun around us. I could not focus; the healing had taken more from me than I had realized at the moment.

I drew a shuddering breath and widened my eyes. It had never been easy to meet his eyes when they were colorless. Even as they had acquired tint and had moved from a pale yellow to gold, it had been hard to read what was behind that gaze. Now his eyes were occluded, grayed in what I suspected had been a deliberate blinding. I could not see into his heart any more than he could see out of them. I had only his voice to go by. It was breathy and full of resignation.

"Well. A bit longer we shall have together. But at the last, we fail, my Catalyst. None have tried harder than we did." His tongue, bloodied still, moved over his chapped and peeling lips. He took breath and smiled with scarlet teeth. "Nor paid a higher price for that failure. Enjoy what good is left in your life, old friend. Evil times will soon be upon you. It was good to be near you. A last time."

"You can't die. Not like this."

A thin smile curved his lips. "Can't die? No, Fitzy, I can't live. Would that I could, but I can't." His eyelids, as dark as if they had been bruised, closed uselessly over his clouded eyes. I lifted my gaze. Time had passed. How much, I could not tell, but the light had changed. Some of the village folk had fallen back into a wondering circle, but as many had decided there was little to see; the beginnings of Winterfest beckoned, and they had gone on their ways. Riddle still stood there, a dazed Bee in his arms, flanked by Shun and FitzVigilant. Shun huddled shivering in her wraps, her face a mask of righteous anger. FitzVigilant seemed completely confused. I looked directly at Riddle and spoke heedless of who might hear or wonder.

"I must take him to Buckkeep Castle. To the Skill-coterie for healing. Through the pillars. Will you help me?"

Riddle looked down at Bee in his arms and then back at me. "She's fine," he said, and I heard his rebuke that I had not even asked about that. But surely, if she were not, he would have told me that instantly? I felt a twinge of anger at him that faded immediately. I didn't have the right to be angry at him, nor the time to be anything but desperate. I stared at him. He shook his head, denying me, but said, "I'll help you however I can. As always I have."

I gathered my feet under me and stood with little effort. The Fool weighed nothing, nothing at all. He had always been slight and limber but now he was skeletal and bound with scars and rags. The gawkers were staring at me intensely. I could not afford to care about that. I advanced toward Riddle. He stood his ground but both Shun and FitzVigilant retreated from what they thought was the body of a smelly old beggar.

I darted my eyes at FitzVigilant. "Get our team and wagon. Bring it here."

Shun began with, "But what about the green—?"

I just looked at her and she closed her lips. "Go!" I reminded FitzVigilant, and he went. When he was two steps away, Shun decided to go with him. Good.

"Bee. Bee, look at me. Please."

She had had her face buried in Riddle's neck. Now she slowly lifted it and stared at me. Blue eyes of ice in a pale face; the red in her shawl was a shocking contrast. "Bee, this man didn't mean to frighten you. I told you about him once. Remember? He's an old friend of mine, someone I have not seen in many years. Riddle knew him as Lord Golden. I knew him as the Fool when we were children together. One thing I am certain of: He would never, ever hurt a child. I know you were frightened, but he meant you no harm."

"I wasn't frightened," she said softly. "Not until you killed him."

"He's not dead, Bee." I hoped I sounded comforting. "But he is hurt, and badly. I need to take him to Buckkeep Castle right away. I think he can be healed there."

I heard the creak and rumble of the wagon, and the remaining gawkers made way for it. There were going to be some strange stories told that night in the tavern. No help for that. I carried the Fool to the tail of the wagon. Shun was already ensconced in the corner of the bed closest to the seat. "Bring some of those robes and make a pallet for him."

She stared at me, unmoving.

FitzVigilant set the brake, wrapped the reins, turned, and stepped over the back of the seat into the bed of the wagon. He gathered an armful of the unused wraps and tossed them toward me. Riddle had come to stand beside me. He set Bee down in the wagon bed, wrapped her warmly, and then arranged the other blankets. I set the Fool down as carefully as I could. He made a gasping sound. "We're taking you to get help. Just keep breathing." I left my hand on his chest as I spoke, reaching for him, trying to hold his life in his body. As always I could not sense him with my Wit, and the Skill-bond he had put on me was something he had taken back decades ago. But there was something there still, something that linked us, and I tried desperately to feed strength to him. I clambered awkwardly into the wagon bed, never breaking my touch on him. With my free hand, I reached out and pulled Bee toward me so that she leaned against me. "Riddle, you drive. The stones on Gallows Hill."

"I know them," he said briefly. He walked away, a thousand conversations in his silence. He clambered up to the seat and FitzVigilant conceded it to him, climbing into the back of the wagon to sit with Shun. They were both regarding me as if I had loaded a rabid dog into the wagon with them. I didn't care. The wagon started with a lurch, and I didn't look back at the people who stared after us. I closed my eyes and reached out for Nettle. There was no time for subtlety.

I have Lord Golden. He is grievously injured and I will need the help of the coterie to keep him alive. I'm bringing him to Buckkeep Castle through the Judgment Stone. Riddle says he will try to help me.

A long silence. Had she not sensed me? Then she responded, *Are you Skill-linked to Lord Golden, then?*

We were, once. And I have to try this, no matter how foolish.

Not foolish. Dangerous. How can you bring someone through a pillar if he has no Skill or link to you? You'll be risking Riddle as well as yourself!

I have a bond with him, Nettle. I don't understand it completely. I was able to reach into him and heal him. I think I have a strong enough connection to be able to bring him through a pillar. Riddle has no Skill, but he is able to travel with you or Chade. I would not ask this if his life were not at stake. So please, summon the others and have them ready?

Today? Tonight? But there is an important dinner this evening, with delegates from Bingtown, Jamaillia, and Kelsingra. It is to celebrate the approach of Winterfest, but also to negotiate new trading terms and . . .

Nettle. I don't want this. I need this. Please.

There was a pause that lasted an eternity. Then she said, *I will gather as many Skilled ones as can help with a healing, then.*

*Thank you. Thank you. I am in your debt. We're coming now. Meet us
at the Witness Stones. Send a wagon or sled.*

What about Bee? Who will look after her?

Who would look after her? A downward lurch in my heart. I
would have to depend on the two people I had just proclaimed unsuitable to be near her. Two people who were insulted, offended,
and, in Shun's case, without the morality to realize none of that was
Bee's fault. I knew less of FitzVigilant. Chade seemed to set great
store by him, as did Riddle. And Nettle. I'd have to give their judgment more weight than my own and hope he was a big enough man
not to take out his grudge against me on my child.

*FitzVigilant will take her back to Withywoods. Don't worry, it will be
all right. Please.* Oh, how I hoped it would be all right. Fence that
thought well with a tight Skill-wall! *Send a cart and team to meet us at
the Witness Stones,* I repeated. *Tell them my life depends on it.* An ex-
aggeration, but not much of one. Chade, at least, would understand. And Dutiful. I pulled my mind free of hers and put up my
walls. I didn't want to Skill right now. I wanted no distractions at all
from keeping the Fool alive. I looked down at Bee and felt disloyal.
This was supposed to have been our day together; well, it had been
doomed from the start. She leaned on me, and I moved her shawl,
tucking it more closely around her. We hadn't bought half the
things I'd intended to get for her. When I got back, I'd make it up
to her. I'd make a raid on the markets at Buckkeep Town and bring
her an armful of pretty things to make up for it. The Fool and I
would return together, and it would be a Winterfest to remember
for all of us.

The Fool groaned again and I turned to him. I leaned down and
spoke softly. "We're going through Skill-pillars, Fool. I'm taking
you to Buckkeep Castle for the coterie to heal. But it will be easier
for me to take you through if we are Skill-linked. So . . ."

I took his hand in mine. Years ago, in the course of tending King
Verity, the Fool had accidentally brushed his fingers against Verity's Skill-laden hands. The silver Skill had burned and soaked into
his fingertips. His touch on my wrist had once left marks, silvery
fingerprints, and a link between us. He had taken them back, right

before I made my fateful trip through the Skill-pillars and back to Buckkeep. I intended to renew that link now, press his fingers to my wrist once more and gain, I planned, enough of a Skill-link to take him through the standing stones with Riddle and me.

But when I turned his hand to look at his fingers, horror and sickness rose in me. Where once silver had outlined the delicate whorls of his fingertips, gnarled scar tissue now deadened the ends of his fingers. His nails remained as thick and yellowed nubs, but the soft pads of his fingers were gone, replaced with coarse, dead flesh. "Who did all this to you? And why? Where have you been, Fool, and how could you let this happen to yourself?" And then, the ultimate question that had haunted me for years and now sounded louder than ever in my heart. "Why didn't you send for me, send me a message, reach out somehow? I would have come. No matter what, I would have come."

I scarcely expected an answer. He might not be losing blood, but the poisons I had released into his body were spreading. I'd stolen strength from him to seal the cuts I'd made. Whatever reserves he had left, he had best marshal against the poisons within. But he stirred slightly and then spoke.

"Those who had loved me . . . tried to destroy me." He moved his blind eyes as if he tried to look into mine. "And you succeeded where they had failed. But I understand, Fitz. I understand. I deserved it."

He fell silent. His words made no sense to me. "I did not mean to hurt you. I would never hurt you. I mistook you . . . I thought you meant her harm! Fool, I am sorry. So sorry! But who tormented you, who broke you?" I pondered what little I knew. "The school that raised you . . . they did this to you?"

I watched the slight rise and fall of his chest, and rebuked myself for asking him a question. "You don't have to answer. Not now. Wait until we've healed you." If we could. My hand was on his ragged shirt. I felt ribs beneath it, ribs knotted with old breaks badly healed. How could he be alive? How could he have come so far, blind and alone and crippled? Seeking his son? I should have tried much, much harder to find the boy, if the Fool's need for him was so great. If only I'd known, had some inkling of how desperate a state he was in. I'd failed him. For now. But I'd help him. I would.

"Shame." The single word rode an exhaled breath.

I bowed my head, thinking he'd read my thoughts and rebuked me. He spoke again, very softly. "Why I didn't call on you for help. At first. Ashamed. Too shamed to ask for help. After all I did. To you. How often I plunged you into pain?" His gray tongue tried to moisten his peeling lips. I opened my mouth to speak, but he tightened his grip on my hand. He was gathering strength. I kept silent.

"How often did I watch the trap close around you? Did it truly have to be so awful for you? Did I try hard enough to find another path through time? Or did I just use you?"

He ran out of breath. I was silent. He'd used me. He'd admitted it to me, more than once. Could he have changed the path of my life? I knew that often enough a word or two from him had made me reconsider my actions. I remembered well how he had cautioned me about Galen and even suggested that I turn aside from my Skill-training. What if I had? There would never have been that beating that near-blinded me and left me with years of pounding headaches. But when would I have learned the Skill? Did he know such things? Did he know where every untaken path in my life would have led?

He gave a little gasp. "When my turn for torture came, for pain? How could I call for you to save me from it when I had not rescued you or turned you aside from it?" That speech was shattered by a series of coughs as feeble as if a bird choked. I lifted my hand from his chest. I could not bear to feel how he struggled to get his breath.

"You . . . never need to feel that way, Fool. Never. I never saw it that way."

On an indrawn gasp. "I did. In the end." Another gasp. "When I learned for myself what I'd asked of you. How a minute of de-signed pain becomes an eternity." He coughed again. I bent my face close to his and spoke very softly.

"It was long ago. And it's far too late for you to apologize, for any forgiveness was given years ago. Not that I thought there was some-thing I needed to forgive. Now stop talking. Conserve your strength. You'll need it for our journey."

Did he have enough stamina to survive a trip through a Skill-pillar? Could I take him through, unlinked to me by the Skill? But I had been able to reach into his body. Surely that meant something, that there was still some tie between us. Useless to wonder. I knew he would not survive unless I got him to Buckkeep that night. And so I would take the chance. We'd go through the pillars together, and if—

Bee spoke on my other side. Her voice was little more than a whisper. "You're going away?"

"For a little while. To take my friend to a healer." What if I didn't come back? What if neither of us survived, what would happen to her then? I couldn't think about that, and I couldn't not think about it. I still knew I must try. I felt no compunction at risking my life for the Fool. But her future? I lifted my voice slightly. "Shun and FitzVigilant will take you back to Withywoods and look after you until I come home."

Her silence was eloquent. I took her little hand in mine and said quietly, "I promise I will come back as soon as ever I can." Liar. Liar. Liar. A promise I had no right to make when I did not know if I would survive the trip.

"It would be very useful for Lady Shun and me to know exactly what is going on. Who is this beggar, why did you attack him, where are we going now, and why are you leaving Bee in our care with absolutely no warning or preparation?" FitzVigilant didn't try to suppress the edge of anger in his voice.

I supposed he had a right to his annoyance. I tried to temper my reply with patience, not to provoke him to any greater anger than he was already feeling. I had to leave my daughter in his care. At his mercy. It took me a moment to sort what I would share.

"He's an old friend. I mistook his actions, didn't recognize him, and attacked him. He needs healing, far more healing than we can do at Withywoods. I'm sure you've heard of the magic of the Skill. We intend to use the Skill to travel through a stone pillar to Buckkeep Castle. There my old friend can get the healing he needs. I must go with him. I hope I will not be gone more than a day or two."

Neither one of them said anything. I chewed my pride and swallowed it. I would have to ask this of him, at least. I looked at my Bee. For her, I would do anything. I spoke more softly. "In the tavern I told you that I doubted your abilities, not only to teach but to protect my child. Fate has given you a chance to prove me wrong. Do this, and do it well, and I will reconsider my opinion of you. I expect you to step up and assume the responsibility I'm giving you. Watch over my child." I hoped he would find the meaning in my words that I dared not say aloud. *Guard her with your life.*

Shun spoke abruptly, with the confidence born of supreme ignorance. "The Skill-magic only belongs to the royal Farseer line. How can you possibly use—"

"Be silent." Riddle spoke the command in a tone I'd never heard him use. I doubt that Shun had ever had anyone speak to her so, but for a miracle she did as she was told. With a wriggle like a nesting hen, she settled back in the robes next to FitzVigilant. I watched them exchange a look of shared outrage at how they were being treated. The team plodded on. The snow on the road was deepening, clinging to the wheels. For a moment I sensed how the horses strained, smelled their sweat in the cold air. I restrained my Wit and cleared my throat. I squeezed my daughter's hand softly.

"Bee is a capable child. I trust that you will recognize that she needs very little supervision in her daily tasks. Her lessons will go on, as I assume they will for all the children of the estate. In my absence, let her set her own routine. If she requires help from either of you, I am sure she will seek you out. If she does not, then you need not be concerned for her. She has Careful and Revel, in addition to you. Will you be comfortable with that, Bee?"

My little daughter gave me a rare direct look. "Yes. Thank you, Papa, for trusting me to mind myself. I will do my best to be responsible." Her mouth was set in a solemn line. She squeezed my hand in response. We were both putting a brave face on the situation.

"I know you will."

"Nearly there," Riddle called back to me. "Will they be ready?"

"Yes." I hoped Nettle had taken my message seriously. No. I

knew she would. I had not bothered to mask my emotions. She would have sensed my desperation. They would be waiting for us.

Again I saw Lady Shun and FitzVigilant exchange a look of mutual offense at being excluded from our cryptic exchange. I cared not at all. The track up to Gallows Hill was not well tended. The wagon jounced and slid in the ruts and I gritted my teeth at the pain it must cause the Fool. As soon as the horses halted, I was out of the wagon. I staggered sideways, the world spun, and then I found my balance. I leaned on the wagon and pointed up at FitzVigilant. "Take Bee home. And I am counting on you that she will be safe and content in my absence. Are we clear?" Even as he nodded, I knew this was not the best way to handle the man, let alone Shun. They would both be resentful and confused. It could not be helped. There was no time to do better.

I took Bee's hands in mine. With her sitting on the open tail of the wagon, we were nearly on a level. She looked up at me, her fair skin whiter in contrast with the gray-and-red shawl that now covered most of her golden hair. I spoke softly, only to her. "Listen to me. Mind FitzVigilant, and if you have any needs, make them known to him, or Lady Shun, or Revel. I am sorry, so sorry, that our day was disrupted. When I return, I promise that we will have a whole day, all to ourselves, and that things will come out well. Can you trust me for that?"

Her gaze now was tranquil and accepting, almost lethargic. "I think I will go first to Steward Revel. He knows me well. And I know that you will try your best to keep your promise," she said softly. "I see that."

"I'm glad that you do." I kissed her on top of her head. "Be brave," I whispered.

Riddle was clambering down from the wagon seat. "Where are you going?" Shun demanded of him.

"I'm going with Fitz," he told her. "Through the stone and back to Buckkeep. We are trusting Lady Nettle's small sister into your care." I more felt than saw how he turned his eyes on FitzVigilant. I was staring at my child, wondering how I could risk this and how I could not. "Lant, we've known each other a long time. I know the man you are capable of being. Never have I trusted you with more than I am entrusting you with now. Watch over Bee with kindness. Nettle and I will hold you responsible for her well-being." He spoke softly but there were teeth in his words. If FitzVigilant replied, I did not hear it.

I let go of Bee and turned to the Fool. It was as if I saw him for the first time. If not for our moment of violent intimacy, if he had not spoken as I plunged the knife into him, I never would have known him. Only his voice had identified him to me. The rags he wore were beyond dirty: They stank and dangled in hanks of rotting fabric. From his knees down, they hung in wet brown tatters. His long, narrow feet were bound in rags. All his grace and elegance were gone. The scarred skin of his face was drawn tight over his bones. He was staring sightlessly up at the overcast sky, still and resigned to whatever might befall him now.

"I'm going to pick you up," I warned him. He made the slightest nod. I tucked one of the blankets around him as if I were bundling a child. I slid my arms under him and lifted. The motion released a fresh waft of stench. I held him carefully and looked at Riddle. "How do we do this?"

He was already moving toward the stone. He glanced at me over his shoulder. "If you don't know, how do you suppose that I do?" His grin was both resigned and scared. He'd do this. He'd risk his life at my request. He'd lend me his strength to attempt something that might kill all of us. I didn't deserve such a friend. Carrying the Fool, I followed him up the snowy track toward the standing stone.

I glanced back once at the wagon. No one had moved. The driver's seat was empty. All three were watching us climb the last bit of rocky hill to the Judgment Stone. I pitched my voice lower. "How did you and Chade do it, when he brought you through the stones with him?"

"He took my arm. I thought of Nettle. When he stepped into the stone, I followed. I could feel him drawing on me. It was like, well, like someone chilled cuddling up to you in a bed. Taking your warmth. And then we stepped out. It was a lot less difficult than walking him down this hill in that snowstorm, and finding our way

to the inn. That was where he really needed my strength. Not passing through the stones." He tipped his head to indicate the Fool.
"That's really Lord Golden?"

"Yes."

He looked at him dubiously. "How can you tell?"

"I know."

He let it be, but then asked, "How will you take him through the
stone? Are you linked to him?"

"I was, long ago. I hope it will still be enough." I shook my head.
"I have to try."

Riddle's steps had slowed. "So much of you I don't know, even
after all the years. Even after all Nettle has told me." The snow had
stopped, and the light was fading from the day. "We could all get
lost, couldn't we? You and I, we've never tried this before. And
you're hoping to bring him through with us. All three of us
could . . ."

"We could all get lost." I had to finish the statement for him,
admitting what we both knew. The enormity of what I had asked
him settled on me. It was too much. I had no right. My friend, but
I now knew beyond any wondering that he was far more than a
friend to Nettle. Had I the right to gamble his life? No. "Riddle. You
don't have to do this. I can try it on my own. You could take Bee
back to Withywoods and watch over her for me. I'll send a bird as
soon as we're safely at Buckkeep Castle."

Riddle folded his arms over his chest and hugged himself as if he
were cold. Or holding his fears in tight. His dark eyes met mine
directly. No pretense. No indecision. "No. I'm going with you. I
saw your face, back there. I saw how you staggered when you got off
the wagon. I think you've spent most of your strength in trying to
heal him. You need strength, I've got it. Nettle said I could easily
have been a King's Man, if I wanted."

"You chose a queen instead," I said quietly, and he smiled, agreeing without a word.

We found ourselves facing the standing stone. I looked up at the
glyph that would take us to the Witness Stones, not far from Buckkeep Castle. I felt the terror rise in me. I stood, holding the Fool's

body to my chest, feeling the fear and the dragging weariness. Had I already spent the strength I would need for this? I looked down at his ravaged face. He was still, and slowly that same stillness filled me. I looked back once over my shoulder at Bee. She watched me motionlessly. I nodded to her. She lifted her little hand in a vague wave of farewell.

As if he knew my thoughts, Riddle grasped my arm. I took a long moment to be aware of him. My old friend. Better than I deserved, these friends. I moved my thoughts like a weaver's shuttle, from the Fool to Riddle to myself and over again. I recalled our friendships, the terrible places we had been, and how we had survived them. "Are you ready?" I asked him.

"I'm with you," he said. And I could feel that was true. It was as Chade had described it, a sort of harness to which I could cling. Rather like holding to a powerful horse while crossing a deep, cold river.

I clutched the Fool to my chest and we stepped forward into stony darkness.

Chapter 31

A TIME OF HEALING

The duties of a King's Man are simple. He must first maintain himself in excellent health of body. This will assure that when the king calls upon him to lend strength, he will have it. The King's Man must have a close affinity to the one he serves; it is best if he has a true regard for the one who will draw Skill-strength from him, rather than simple respect and a sense of duty.

This regard should ideally extend in both directions. The Skill-user who calls upon a King's Man to lend strength must keep the well-being of his partner in the forefront of his mind. For once the King's Man has surrendered control of his body's resources to the Skill-user, it will be beyond him to refuse. An experienced King's Man can let his partner know when he feels he is approaching the maximum of what he can give. It is absolutely essential to the trust that is required in this relationship that the Skill-user respond to such a reminder.

ON THE TRAINING OF A KING'S MAN, SKILLMISTRESS INKSWELL

We fell from the face of the pillar onto the snowy hilltop of the Witness Stones. The snow was deep and fresh, untracked and thigh-deep. It caught me as I stumbled, but did not fall, nor did I drop the Fool. Riddle still held to my arm as we emerged into deep dusk. I took a deep breath of cold air. "That was not near as hard as I feared it would be," I panted. I was winded, as if I'd run up a steep hill and my head pounded with a Skill-headache. But we had arrived intact. It seemed that only moments had passed and that I was wakening from a long sleep. Despite the headache, I felt rested. I had a memory of a starry blackness, in which the stars were below us as well as above, behind and before us. We stepped from that infinity to the snowy hillside near Buckkeep Castle.

Then Riddle dropped senseless into the snow beside me. He fell with terrible limpness, collapsing as if he had not a bone in his body. I held fast to the Fool as I dropped to one knee beside him. "Riddle? Riddle!" I called stupidly, as if he had only forgotten I was there and decided to fall on his face. I let the Fool's legs drop to the snowy ground as I caught at the shoulder of Riddle's shirt and tried to turn him faceup. He did not respond to my voice or my touch. "Riddle!" I shouted again, and with great relief I heard an answering shout from down the hill.

I turned and looked behind me. A boy carrying a torch waded through the snow. Behind him, a team labored to draw a sledge up the steep hill. By the wavering torchlight, I saw steam rising from their coats. A girl rode a horse behind them, and then the girl was suddenly Nettle, and at my shout she urged her mount to surge through the deep snow and pass the trudging team. She reached us before anyone else and flung herself from her horse and into the snow beside Riddle. As she put her arms around him and lifted him so that his head rested on her breast, she answered any questions I might ever have had about what he meant to her. Even in the fading light of the day, the flash of anger in her eyes was sharp as she demanded, "What did you do to him?"

I answered honestly. "I used him. And in my inexperience, more ruthlessly than I meant to, I fear. I, I thought he would stop me if I took too much." I felt like a stammering boy before her deep cold anger. I bit back my useless apology. "Let us get them both onto the sled and back to the keep and summon healers and the King's Own Coterie. Later, you can say or do whatever you wish to me."

"I shall," she warned me heartily, and then lifted her voice, giving commands. Guards rushed to obey her, several of them exclaiming in dismay as they recognized Riddle. I trusted none of them with the Fool but carried him myself to the sled, loaded him, and clambered up afterward to sit beside him.

The snow was slightly packed, and the big horses made better time going down the hill than they had coming up. Even so, it seemed an eternity in the dark and cold as we approached the lighted towers of Buckkeep Castle. Nettle had given her horse over to someone else; she rode with Riddle, and if their relationship had been a secret, it was no longer. She spoke softly and urgently to him, and when he finally stirred and managed a feeble response she bent over him to deliver a heartfelt kiss.

The sled did not even pause at the gates, but went directly to the infirmary. The healers were waiting for us. I did not object as they took Riddle first, and again I carried the Fool myself. Nettle dismissed the guards and promised them news as soon as there was any. The room was long with a low ceiling and blessedly empty of other occupants. I wondered if it was the same room where I had once recovered from my Skill-pillar mishap. There were rows of cots, not so different from a barracks. Riddle had already been stretched out on a bed, and I was horribly relieved to hear him weakly protesting at being there. I set the Fool down carefully on a bed two cots away, knowing well that Nettle would need space from me for some time. And Riddle, I thought glumly. I did not think I'd done permanent damage to him, but in my ignorance and my anxiety for the Fool, I had completely forgotten to have a care for how much of his strength I took. I'd used him roughly and I would deserve his anger. I was baffled by it. Had I needed that much from him to bring the Fool through the pillar?

At Nettle's command, the healers had clustered around Riddle's bed. I was alone with the Fool as I stripped away his outer garments and let them fall in a smelly heap by his cot. What was revealed horrified me. Someone had given great attention to inflicting pain on him. Great care and a good amount of time had been devoted to it, I judged, for here were bones with the old breaks badly healed and gashes that had been hastily or perhaps deliberately badly bandaged, so that crooked ridges of scar tissue had formed where flesh had been unevenly pushed back together. A pattern of burn scars on his left upper arm might have been a word, but in no alphabet or language that I knew. His left foot was scarcely worthy of that name. It twisted in, a lump of flesh with knobs of bone, and the toes gone dusky.

The grime was as distressing as the damage. The Fool had always been a clean man, meticulous about his garments, his hair, and his body. Dirt was ground into his skin, patterned where rain had fallen on him. Some of his clothing was so stiff with dirt that I expected it to crack as I peeled it away. He had an apple hidden in his jerkin. I let it fall to the floor with the rest. Rather than move him too much, I drew my sheath knife, cut away the worn fabric, and tugged it gently from beneath him.

The smell was nauseating. His eyes were open to cracks and I judged him to be awake, but he did not move until I tried to remove his undergarment. Then he lifted both scarred hands to the neck of the dingy linen singlet and gripped the collar. "No," he said faintly.

"Fool," I rebuked him, and tried to push his hands aside, but he gripped his garment more tightly and with greater strength than I had expected to encounter. "Please," I said softly, but he slowly shook his tattered head against the pillow. Pieces of his matted hair broke off when he did so, and I did not have the heart to challenge him. Let him take his secrets to the grave, then, if that was what he wished. I would not disrobe him in front of the healers. I drew a clean woolen blanket over him. He sighed in relief.

A healer appeared at my elbow. "How was he injured? Is he bleeding?" She was doing her best to control her distaste, but even I could barely abide his smell.

"He has been tortured, and has journeyed far in great privation. Please, bring me warm water and some cloths. Let me clean him up a bit while you find him a good beef broth."

I saw her swallow. "As an apprentice, the first cleaning of an injured man is one of my tasks."

"As his friend, it's my task. Please."

She struggled to conceal her relief. "May I remove these rags?" she asked, and I nodded. She folded her lips, stooped to pick them up, and then hastened away with them.

As she went out the door at the end of the room, Chade came in. He was dressed very finely, in several shades of green, and I knew he had made some excuse to leave the gathering. Thick was with him in Buckkeep livery, and a woman I didn't recognize. Perhaps she was a Skill-apprentice. A moment later a guardsman opened the door and King Dutiful appeared with Kettricken but a step behind him. All motion in the room ceased. The erstwhile queen waved an impatient hand and strode past Chade. She halted at Riddle's bedside. "Riddle was injured as well? I was not told of this!"

Nettle stood. Her jaw was set. Her voice was respectful when she managed to speak. "My lady, I suggest that a private Skill-healing would be the best choice for both of these men. May I dismiss the healers?"

The apprentice had just reappeared with a bucket of steaming water and several clean cloths over her shoulder. She looked about doubtfully, but I took the liberty of waving her in. She managed an awkward curtsy as she passed King Dutiful without spilling her bucket and then hurried to my side. She set the bucket down and put the folded cloths tidily across the foot of the bed. Then she looked from me to the gathering of royalty in the infirmary. It was clearly an event she had never experienced before, and she was torn between curtsying and getting on with her work.

"My king, if it please you, this is my place of both experience and expertise." The man speaking must have been the healing master. I could not tell if he objected to being dismissed because he believed he was most competent to do the required work or if he merely disliked someone usurping his place. I found I did not care, and found also that court niceties meant nothing to me. Let the healer argue with Nettle's request all he wished; I thought I knew how it would be settled. I gestured the apprentice away, and she stepped back gratefully. I ignored their genteel dispute as I set to work.

I moistened the cloth in warm water and set it gently to the Fool's face. It came away brown and gray. I rinsed it and wiped at his face again. The thick yellow tears welled in his eyes again. I stopped. "Am I hurting you?" I asked him quietly.

"It has been so long since anyone touched me with kindness."

"Close your eyes," I bade him hoarsely, for I could not bear his blind stare. I wiped his face a third time. Dirt clung in every line of his face. Dried mucus caked his eyelids. I wanted to weep with pity for him. Instead I wrung out the cloth again. Behind me, folk were wrangling in the most courteous possible way. Their very politeness seemed infuriating. I wanted to turn and bellow at them all to leave or be quiet. The hopelessness of my task was becoming clear to me. He was stronger than I had first judged him, but his body was too broken. He had no reserves to burn. I'd brought him here in the hope of a Skill-healing, but as I slowly washed first one crumpled hand and then the other, the magnitude of his ills engulfed me. Unless we could rebuild his strength before we began, he would not survive a healing. And if we did not heal him soon, he would not live long enough to rebuild his strength. My thoughts chased themselves in a circle. I'd risked all of us to bring him to a healing he could not survive.

Kettricken was suddenly at my elbow. Ever gracious, she thanked the gawking apprentice healer before sending her on her way. Behind me the room had quieted, and I sensed that Nettle had won her way. The healers had left, and her Skill-coterie was gathering around Riddle's bed. Chade was talking about having seen such things before and assuring her that Riddle would be fine, he just needed a rich meal and a few days of sleep to put him right. Chade was arguing against Skill-intervention, favoring food and rest instead. Riddle had loaned more strength than he could afford, but he was a strong man, a doughty man, and she need not fear for him.

A small part of my mind wondered just how Chade knew this. How ruthlessly had he used Thick? Or was it Steady he had drained,

and in what pursuit? Later. I would get to the bottom of that later.
I knew from my experience with King-in-Waiting Verity that he
was probably right. In my panic over the Fool, I had not given a
thought to the possibility that I might so drain Riddle as to leave
him witless and drooling. My friend and my daughter's mate. I
owed them both apologies. Later.

Because now Nettle had moved to the Fool's bedside. She ran
her eyes over him as if he were a horse she was considering buying.
She glanced once at me and then away, in a manner curiously similar to the way Bee avoided my eyes. She spoke to a young woman
who had come to stand at her side. "What do you think?" she asked
her, in the manner of a teacher to a student.

The woman took a breath, extended her hands, and moved them
slowly over the Fool's body without touching him. The Fool became very still, as if he sensed and resented her untouching of him.
The woman's hands made a second pass over him. Then she shook
her head. "I see old damage that we may or may not be able to better heal. He does not appear to have any fresh injuries that put him
in immediate danger of death. There is much that is both odd and
wrong about his body. But I do not judge him in need of immediate
Skill-intervention. In fact, thin as he is, I suspect it would do more
harm than good." She wrinkled her nose then, and sniffed, the first
sign that she felt any distaste for her patient. She stood awaiting
Nettle's judgment of her words.

"I agree," the Skillmistress said softly. "You and the others may
go now. I thank you for convening so swiftly."

"Skillmistress," the woman acknowledged her with a bow. Nettle
moved with her, returning to Riddle's bedside as the rest of the
healing coterie quietly left the infirmary.

Kettricken was regarding the ruined man on the bed with close attention. The tips of her fingers covered her mouth as she bent over
him. Then she straightened and fixed me with anxious blue eyes. "It
isn't him, is it?" she begged. "It's not the Fool."

He stirred slightly, and when he opened his sightless eyes, she flinched. He spoke in pieces. "Would that Nighteyes . . . were here to . . . vouch for me. My queen."

"Queen no longer. Oh, Fool."

There was a hint of the old mockery in his voice as he said, "My queen still. And I am still . . . a fool."

She seated herself gracefully on a low stool on the other side of the Fool's bedside. She did not look at me as she began to carefully fold back the elaborate sleeves of her gown. "What happened to them?" she demanded of me. She took a clean cloth from the foot of the bed, dipped it in the water, and with no sign of distaste lifted his hand and began to wash it. A memory long buried rose to the top of my mind. Queen Kettricken, washing the bodies of the slain Forged Ones, making them our own people again and restoring them before burial. She had never hesitated.

I spoke quietly. "I know little of what befell the Fool. Obviously he has been tortured, and he has come a long way to find us. What happened to Riddle was me. I was in haste and alarmed, and I used his strength to bring the Fool through the Skill-pillars. I have not drawn on someone for strength in such a situation before. I probably used more than he could easily spare, and I can only hope I have done no permanent harm to him."

"My fault," the Fool said quietly.

"No, mine. How could it possibly be your fault?" I spoke almost roughly.

"The strength. From him. Through you. To me." He took a breath. "I should be dead. I'm not. I feel stronger than I have in months, despite . . . what happened today. You gave me some of his life."

It made sense. Riddle had not only given me strength to bring Fool through the pillar, he had let me take life from him to give raw strength to the Fool. Gratitude warred with shame. I glanced at Riddle. He was not looking at me. Nettle sat by his bed on a low stool, holding both his hands in hers. Was there any possible way for me to repay that debt? I thought not.

I turned back to the Fool. He was blind. He could not see that as

Kettricken worked carefully to clean the crooked fingers of his hands, tears were running down her cheeks. Those clever hands with those long fingers, juggling wooden balls or wisps of silk, making a coin appear, waggling insultingly or waving expressively to illustrate some tale he was telling. Reduced now to swollen knuckles and broken stick-fingers. "Not your fault," Kettricken said quietly. "I suspect Riddle knew what he gave. He's a giving man." A long pause. "He deserves what he has earned," she said, but gave no more indication of what she meant by that. Instead she sighed. "You need more than this. You need a hot bath, Fool. Is privacy still your obsession?"

He made a small sound that might have been a laugh. "Torture strips one of all dignity. Pain can make you shriek, or beg, or soil yourself. There is no privacy when your enemies own you and have no compunction, no human compunction at all about what they will do to you. So, among my friends, yes. Privacy is still an obsession. And a gift from them. A restoration in small part of what dignity I once had." It was a long speech and it wheezed to an end.

Kettricken did not argue, or ask him if he could bathe himself. She simply asked, "Where would you be? Lord Golden's old chambers? Fitz's childhood bedroom? Chade's old lair?"

"Are all those rooms empty?" I asked, surprised.

She looked at me levelly. "For him, other people can be moved." She rested a gentle hand on his shoulder. "He got me to the Mountains. Alive. I will never forget that."

He lifted a crooked hand to cover hers. "I will choose discretion. As I seldom have before. I would have quiet to recover, if I may. In Chade's den. And be known neither as Lord Golden, nor as Fool." He turned his hazed eyes and asked, "Do I smell food?"

He did. The apprentice healer was back, a rag wrapped around the bale of a lidded pot. The lid jiggled as she walked, letting brief wafts of beefy aroma fill the room. A serving boy came behind with bowls, spoons, and a basket of bread rolls. She stopped at Riddle's bed to serve him, and I was relieved to see him recovered enough to be propped up in bed and offered hot food. He looked past Nettle, met my gaze, and gave me a crooked smile. Undeserved forgiveness. Friendship defined. I slowly nodded to him, trusting him to understand.

I knew it would be harder to win Nettle's pardon.

The apprentice girl came to fill a bowl for the Fool. "Can you sit up to eat?" I asked him.

"Probably the only thing that could make me try," he wheezed. As Kettricken and I lifted him and moved pillows to cushion him upright, he added, "I'm tougher than you think, Fitz. Dying, yes. But I'll fight it off as long as I can."

I did not reply to that until the apprentice and her assistant had finished serving the food. As they moved away, I leaned closer and suggested, "Eat as much as you can. The more strength you gain and the quicker you do it, the sooner we can attempt a Skill-healing for you. If you wish it."

Kettricken held the spoon to his lips. He tasted it, sucked the broth in noisily, near-moaned with pleasure, and then begged, "Too slow. Let me drink from the bowl. I am so hungry."

"It's hot," she warned him, but held the bowl to his mouth. His clawlike hands guided hers and he slurped the scalding soup from the edge of the bowl, trembling with his need to get nourishment inside him.

"It's him," Chade said. I looked up to see him standing at the foot of the Fool's bed.

"It is," I confirmed.

He nodded, brows drawn. "Riddle managed a partial report before Nettle chased me off. He'll be all right, Fitz, small thanks to you. This is an example of where your ignorance can hurt us. If you had returned to Buckkeep to study with the rest of the King's Own Coterie, you would have had better control of your Skill-use of him."

It was the last thing I wished to discuss just then. "You're right," I said, and in his shocked silence that followed my capitulation, I added, "The Fool would like to be lodged in our old study room. Can that be arranged? A fire built, clean linens, a fresh robe, a warm bath, and simple, hot food?"

He did not flinch at my list. "And salves. And herbs for restorative teas. Give me a bit of time. I've an evening of diplomacy and negotiation to dance through yet. And I must ask Kettricken to return with me to that. When I send a page, carry him up to Lady Thyme's old room, via the servants' stair. You'll find the wardrobe there has a false back now. Enter there. I'm afraid I must return to the welcoming festivities right away. But I'll see you either very late tonight or very early tomorrow."

"Thank you," I said. He nodded gravely.

Even in my gratitude, I knew that there would eventually be a price for Chade's favors. There always was.

Kettricken rose with a rustling of skirts. "I, too, must return to the feasting hall." I turned my head and for the first time that night, I really looked at her. She was dressed in shades of blue silk, with white lace drapery over her kirtle and skirts. Her earrings were blue and silver, and the silver coronet she wore included a network of pale topazes over her brow. My astonishment must have shown, for she smiled deprecatingly. "They are our trading partners; they are gratified to see me wearing the products of that trade, and the compliment to them makes my king's negotiations with them easier." She smiled as she added, "And I assure you, Fitz, my adornments are simple compared to what our young queen wears tonight!"

I smiled at her. "I know you favor simpler garb, but in truth, its beauty does you great justice."

The Fool spoke softly. "Would that I could see you." He clutched the empty soup bowl. Without a word, Kettricken wiped broth from the corner of his mouth.

I wanted to tell him that we would heal him and he would see again. In truth, I was wishing that I had taken Chade up on his repeated offers of learning more about the Skill. I looked at the Fool and wondered if we could straighten bones healed crooked, return light to his eyes, and lift the gray pallor from his skin. How much of his health could we restore?

"I do wish it," he said suddenly. "The Skill-healing. I do not desire it. I dread it. But I wish for it to be done. As quickly as possible."

I spoke the truth reluctantly. "Right now, we would be as likely to kill you as heal you. There is so much . . . damage. And you are weakened by all that has been done to you. Despite the strength I stole for you." Kettricken was looking at me, the question in her eyes. It was time to tell them both I didn't know the answer. "I do not know how much the Skill can restore you. It is a magic that ultimately obeys your body. It can prompt your body to repair what is wrong, much faster than your body would do if left alone. But things that your body has already repaired, a broken bone for example—well, I do not know if it will straighten an old break."

Kettricken spoke quietly. "When the coterie healed you, I understood that many old hurts were healed as well. Scars vanished."

I didn't want to remind her that such an unrestrained healing had nearly killed me. "I think we will have to take this in stages. And I don't want the Fool to lift his hopes too high."

"I need to see," he said suddenly. "Above all else, I need to see, Fitz."

"I can't promise you that," I said.

Kettricken stepped back from the bed. Her eyes were bright with tears but her voice was steady as she said, "I fear I must return to the trade negotiations." She glanced at the entrance to the infirmary. Chade awaited her there.

"I thought it was a feast, with minstrels singing, and then dancing?"

"So it might appear, but it is all a negotiation. And tonight, I am still the Queen of the Mountain Kingdom and hence a player in all the Six Duchies wishes to win. Fool, I cannot tell you how I feel. Full of joy to see you again, and full of sorrow to see all that has befallen you."

He smiled, stretching his cracked lips. "I am much the same, my queen." He pursed his smile ruefully and added, "Except for the seeing part."

It wrung a laugh from the queen that was half-sob. "I will return as soon as I may."

"But not tonight," he told her gently. "Already I am so weary I can scarce keep my eyes open. But soon, my queen. Soon, if you please."

She dropped him a curtsy, then fled in a rustling of long skirts and tapping heels. I watched her go.

"She has changed much, and not at all," he observed.

"You sound much better."

"Food. A warm bed. A clean face and hands. The company of friends. These things heal much." He yawned suddenly, and then added with trepidation, "And Riddle's strength. It is a peculiar thing, this borrowing of strength, Fitz. Not that different from how I felt when you put your own life into me. It is a buzzing, restless energy inside me, a life borrowed rather than earned. My heart does not like it, but my body yearns for more of it. If it were a cup before me, I do not think I could resist the desire to drain it dry." He took a slow breath and was quiet. But I could almost sense how he savored the sensation of extra life flowing through him. I recalled the battle madness that used to come on me, and how I would find myself fighting on, savagely and joyously, spending effort long after I knew my body was exhausted. It had been exhilarating. And the collapse that followed had been complete. That false strength, once burned, demanded repayment. I knew dread.

The Fool spoke again. "Still, I was not lying. Much as I long for a warm bath, I do not think I can remain awake much longer. I cannot recall the last time I was so warm, or my belly so full."

"Perhaps I should take you up to Lady Thyme's chamber, then."

"You'll carry me?"

"I have before. You weigh hardly anything and it seems the easiest thing to do."

He was silent for a time. Then he said, "I think I can walk. At least part of the way."

It puzzled me, but I didn't argue with him. Almost as if our words had summoned him, a page entered the infirmary. He had flakes of snow still on his hair and shoulders, and carried a lantern. He looked around and then called, "Tom Badgerlock? I've come to fetch Tom Badgerlock."

"I'm here," I told him. As I turned to him, Nettle suddenly left Riddle's bedside. She gripped my sleeve and pulled me to one side. She looked up at me, her face so like her mother's in that moment that I felt Molly had returned from the grave to reproach me. "He says I'm not to hold you accountable, that he volunteered."

"No. I asked him. He knew that if he didn't help me, I'd try it alone. And I am accountable. And I'm sorry."

"I'm sure you are."

I bowed my head to that. After a moment, she added, "People love you far more than you deserve, Tom Badgerlock. But you don't even believe that they love you at all." I was still pondering that when she added, "And I am one of those people."

"Nettle, I'm so—"

"Say it again and I'll hit you. I don't care who is watching. If I could ask one thing of you, it would be that you never say those stupid words again." She looked away from me to the Fool. "He's your friend, since childhood." Her tone said she understood that he was a rare creature.

"He was. He is."

"Well. Go take care of him, then. Riddle will be fine when he has rested." She put her hands to her temples and rubbed them. "And Bee? My sister?"

"I left her with FitzVigilant. I think she'll be fine. I don't intend to be away for long." As I said those words, I wondered how long I would be away. Would I stay here while the Fool rebuilt his strength until we could attempt a full Skill-healing? Should I try to go back in the morning, via the stones, and then return in a few days? I was torn. I longed to be in both places.

"If she's with Lant, she'll be fine." I was not at all sure I agreed with her judgment, but it seemed a very poor time to tell her that. The relief in Nettle's voice made me wonder if I had misjudged the young scribe. Then she woke guilt in me by adding, "We should send a bird to tell them that you arrived here safely."

I glanced at the Fool. He had struggled to a sitting position and draped the blanket around his shoulders. He looked pathetically feeble, and older than me by a hundred years.

"I'll do it," Nettle continued before I could ask. "Do you want me to ask a guardsman to help you move your friend?"

"I think we can manage alone," I said.

She nodded quietly. "I sensed that. You don't want many folk to know he is here. For the life of me, I don't know why. But I'll respect your love of secrecy. Well, most of the servants are busy with the feast, so if you are cautious, you should be able to get him moved without being noticed."

So I took the Fool to Lady Thyme's old chambers. It was a lengthy process, cold and wet for both of us as he insisted on hobbling across the courtyard to the door on his own. He cloaked his shoulders in the blanket, and his feet were still bound in rags. Wind and snow swept past us as we made our limping way. Using the servants' passageways meant that we had to take the long way round to everything. He grasped my arm for the climb up the narrow stairways and leaned on me more heavily with every step. The boy guiding us kept looking back at both of us in wonder and suspicion. At some point, I realized my garments were stained with the Fool's blood. I offered him no explanation.

At the door to Lady Thyme's old chambers, the page halted and offered me a large key on a heavy loop of blue cord. I took it and the small lantern he carried and told him to go. He went with alacrity. "Lady Thyme" had not existed for decades but the rumor that she haunted these chambers still had not faded. That masquerade suited Chade, and he maintained it still.

The room we entered was dim and fusty. A stand of candles on a dusty table gave off a poor light. The room smelled of disuse and ancient cloying perfume. And old woman. "I'm going to just sit down," the Fool announced and nearly missed the chair I pulled out for him. He did not sit down so much as crumple into a heap. He sat still, breathing.

I opened the wardrobe and was confronted by a packed bank of ancient gowns and shifts. They smelled as if they had never been laundered. Muttering about Chade's idiocy, I dropped to my hands and knees and crawled under the clothes to feel along the back panel. I rapped, pushed, and pried until suddenly the panel swung open. "We'll have to crawl through," I informed the Fool sourly. He didn't reply.

He had fallen asleep where he was. It was difficult to rouse him, and then I all but dragged him through the low hatch in the wardrobe. I helped him to Chade's old chair before the fire, and then crawled back to latch the door to Lady Thyme's room from the inside and extinguish the candles. By the time I had closed the entrance and returned to the Fool's side, he was nodding off again. I woke him again and asked him, "Bath or bed?"

The tub of water, still steaming slightly, was scenting the room with lavender and hyssop. A straight-backed chair was beside the tub. A low table held a towel, a pot of soft soap, a washrag, a cotton tunic and a blue wool robe in the old style of garb, and some thick stockings. They would serve. The Fool was unfolding himself like a battered jumping jack. "Bath," he muttered and turned his blind face toward me.

"It's this way." I took his stick-arm in my hand and put my other arm around him. I walked him to the straight-backed chair. He dropped into it so heavily that he nearly overset it. He sat still, breathing. Without asking, I knelt and began to unwrap the long winding of rags that bound his feet. They smelled dreadful and stuck together so that I had to peel them away. I breathed through my mouth when I spoke.

"Beside you is a table with all you need to wash yourself. And clothing for afterward."

"Clean clothing?" he asked, as if I had give him a stack of gold. He groped and his hand rose and fell like a butterfly as it touched the bounty there. He lifted the pot of soap, smelled it, and made a small heartbreaking sound. He set it down carefully. "Oh, Fitz. You cannot imagine," he said brokenly. Then his bony arm lifted, and his crooked hand shooed me away.

"Call me if you need me," I conceded. I took a candle and moved to the scroll racks at the far end of the room. He listened to my footfalls and did not look pleased when I halted at the end of the room, but that was as much privacy as I was granting him. I had no desire to discover him drowned but modest in the tub. I rummaged through the scrolls on the racks there and found one on the Rain Wilds, but when I took it to the table I found that Chade had al-

ready arranged reading material for me. Three scrolls on the proper
way to prepare and use a King's Man were set out for me. Well, and
he was right. I'd best learn it. I carried them over to Chade's old
bed, lit a branch of candles there, kicked off my boots, propped the
pillows, and settled to read.

I was a third of the way through the first one, tediously written
and overly detailed, about selecting a candidate who could share
strength before I heard the gentle splash of water as the Fool eased
into the tub. For a time, all was silent. I read my scroll, and period-
ically looked up to be sure he had not fallen asleep and sunk in the
tub to drown. After a long soak, he began the slow process of
washing himself. He made small sounds of both pain and eased
muscles. He took his time about it. I was on the third scroll, a more
useful one that gave specific symptoms that a King's Man might be
exceeding his limits, including information on how to feed strength
back into a man, should that be necessary, when I heard him heave
a great sigh and then there followed the sounds of someone exiting
a tub. I did not look toward him.

"Can you find the towels and robe?"

"I'll manage," he said shortly.

I'd finished reading the scroll and was struggling to stay awake
when I heard him say, "I've lost my bearings. Where are you?"

"Over here. On Chade's old bed."

Even freshly bathed and attired in clean garments, he still looked
terrible. He stood, the old blue robe hanging on him like slack canvas on a derelict ship as he clung to the back of the chair. What hair
he had left was still weighted with water; it scarcely reached past his
ears. His blind eyes were terrible dead things in his gaunt living face.
His breathing sounded like leaking bellows. I rose and took his arm
to guide him to the bed.

"Fed, clean, and warm. New garments. A soft bed. If I were not
so weary, I'd weep with gratitude."

"Go to sleep instead." I opened the bedding for him. He sat
down on the edge of it. His hands patted the clean linens, moved
up to the plump pillow. It was an effort for him to swing his legs up

onto the bed. When he lay back on the pillows, I did not wait, but covered him as if he were Bee. His hands gripped the top edge of the coverlet.

"Will you stay here for the night?" It was a question rather than a request.

"If you wish."

"I do. If you don't mind."

I stared at him unabashedly. Freed of grime, the lines of inflicted scars on his face were perfectly etched. "I don't mind," I said quietly.

He closed his filmed-over eyes. "Do you remember . . . a time I asked you to stay beside me for the night?"

"In the Elderling tent. On Aslevjal." I remembered. We were both quiet for a time, and then the silence stretched out longer. I thought he had fallen asleep. I was suddenly exhausted. I walked around to the other side of the bed, sat down on the edge of it, and then stretched out beside him, as carefully as if he were infant Bee. My thoughts went to her. What a day I had given her! Would she sleep well tonight or battle nightmares? Would she stay in her bed or creep off to hide herself behind the wall of my study? Strange little mite of a girl. I had to do better by her. I meant to, with every drop of my heart's blood I meant to, but it seemed things always got in the way. And here I was, days away from her, trusting her care to a man I scarcely knew. And had insulted.

"No questions?" the Fool asked of the dim room.

He was the one, I thought, who should have questions. Starting with, *Why did you stab me?* "I thought you were asleep."

"Soon." He sighed the weight of the world away. "You take me on such faith, Fitz. Years pass, I step back into your life, and you kill me. And then save me."

I didn't want to talk about how I had knifed him. "Your messenger reached me."

"Which one?"

"A pale girl."

He was silent and then spoke in a voice full of sorrow. "I sent seven pairs of messengers to you. Over eight years, I sent them to you. And only one got through?"

Seven pairs. Of fourteen messengers, one had reached me. Perhaps two. A great wave of dread rose in me. What had he fled, and did it still pursue him? "She died soon after reaching me. Those who chased her had shot some sort of parasites into her, and they were eating her from the inside."

He was silent for a long time. "They love that sort of thing. Slow pain that inevitably gets worse. They love it when those they torment hope and beg for death."

"Who loves it?" I asked quietly.

"The Servants." All life had gone from his voice.

"The servants?"

"They used to be servants. When the Whites existed, their ancestors served the Whites. The prophet folk. My ancestors."

"You're a White." There was little written of them, and what I knew, I had learned mostly from the Fool. Once, they had lived alongside and among humanity. Long-lived and gifted with prophecy and the ability to see all futures. As they had dwindled and interbred with humans, they had lost their unique characteristics, but every few generations one such as he was born. A true White, such as the Fool, was a rarity.

He made a small sound of skepticism in his throat. "So they would have you believe. And me. The truth is, Fitz, I am a creature with enough White blood in me that it manifests almost completely." He took a deep breath as if to say more and then sighed instead.

I was confused. "That wasn't what you told me years ago."

He turned his head on the pillow, as if he could look at me. "That wasn't what I believed, years ago. I didn't lie to you, Fitz. I repeated to you the lie I had been told, the lie I believed all my life."

I told myself I had never believed it anyway. But I had to ask him, "Then you are not a White Prophet? And I am not your Catalyst?"

"What? Of course I am. And you are! But I am not a full White. No full Whites have walked this world for hundreds of years."

"Then . . . the Black Man?"

"Prilkop? Far older than me, and probably of purer blood. And like the Whites of old, as he aged, he darkened."

"I thought he darkened as he was able to fulfill his mission as a White Prophet? That as much as he was successful in setting the world on a better path, so he darkened?"

"Oh, Fitz." He sounded weary and sad. After a long pause, he said, "I don't know. That's what the Servants took from me. Everything I thought I knew, every certainty. Have you ever stood on a sandy beach when the tide is coming in? Felt the waves come up around your feet and suck the sand from under you? That's my life now. With every day, I feel I sink deeper into uncertainty."

A hundred questions filled my mind. And I suddenly knew that, yes, I had believed that he was a prophet and I was his Catalyst. I had believed it, and I had endured the things he had foretold for me, and I had trusted. And if it had all been a lie, a deception practiced on him that he had perpetuated upon me in turn? No. That was what I could not believe. It was what I must not believe.

"Is there anything more to eat? Suddenly I'm hungry again."

"I'll see." I rolled off the bed and went to the hearth. Whoever Chade had dispatched had been thorough. There was a covered pot on the kettle hook, swung to the edge of the coals where it would stay warm but not burn. I hooked it over the hearth and peeked in. A chicken had been stewed down to a morass of thready flesh in a thick brown broth. Onion and celery and parsnip mingled together in a friendly sauce. "Stewed chicken," I told him. "Shall I bring you some?"

"I'll get up."

His answer surprised me. "Earlier today, when I brought you here so quickly, I thought you balanced on the knife's edge of death. Now you sound almost like yourself."

"I've always been tougher than I looked." He sat up slowly and swung his legs out, feet groping for the floor. "But don't deceive yourself. I doubted I would have survived longer than a couple more nights in the cold. I scarcely remember the last few days. Cold and hunger and pain. No difference between night and day, save that nights were colder." He stood and swayed. "I don't know where you are," he complained helplessly.

"Stand still," I bade him, as if he could do otherwise. I put a small table near Chade's old chair, and then guided the Fool to his seat. I found dishes and cutlery on a shelf; Lady Rosemary kept a much more orderly lair than Chade had. I brought him a bowl of the chicken and a spoon, and then found a bottle of brandy and some cups. "How hungry are you?" I asked, eyeing what was left in the pot. My own appetite had wakened at the smell of the food. The toil of the Skill-journey I had mostly transferred to Riddle, but it had still been a long and taxing time since I'd last eaten.

"Eat something," the Fool replied, having sensed my dilemma.

I dished out food for myself and sat down in Lady Rosemary's chair with my bowl on my knee. The Fool lifted his head. "Do I smell brandy?"

"It's to the left of your bowl."

He set down his spoon and a tremulous smile claimed his mouth. "Brandy with Fitz. By a fire. In clean clothes. With food. One last time, and almost I could die happy."

"Let's avoid the dying part, and have the rest."

His smile grew stronger. "For a time, old friend. For a time. Whatever you did to me before we entered the stones, and Riddle's sacrifice, then food and warmth and rest have pulled me back from that brink. But we shall not deceive each other. I know the rot I carry inside myself. I know you saw it." He lifted a clawlike hand to scratch his scarred cheek. "It isn't a happenstance, Fitz. They deliberately created that within me, just as they etched my face with scars and tore the Skill from my fingertips. I do not fancy that I have escaped. They set a slow death to work inside me and then pursued me as I tottered away, striving to see that I always exerted myself to exhaustion each day, always threatening those who might aid me. I fancy I traveled faster and farther than they thought I would, but even that may be a fantasy. They plot in convolutions far beyond what you or I could imagine, for they have a map of the maze of time, drawn from a hundred thousand prophecies. I do not ask why you stabbed me because I already know. They set it in motion, and waited for you to do their evil will. They sought to hurt you as much as to kill me. No one's fault but theirs. Yet you are still the Catalyst, and you turn my dying into an infusion of strength." He sighed. "But perhaps even that is their will, that you find me and bring me here. Is this a pebble, Fitz, that triggers the avalanche? I don't know. I long to see as I once did, long to pick my way through a swirling mist of possibilities. But that is gone, lost to me when you brought me back from the dead."

I could not think of anything to say to that. I had long ago learned that with both the Fool and Chade, the quickest way to provoke silence was to ask too many questions. Left alone, they always shared more with me than perhaps they intended. And so I ate a portion of the chicken and drank Chade's brandy and wondered about the Servants and his unexpected son and even the messengers he had sent who had not reached me.

He finished the chicken in the pot, clattering his spoon about inside the dish to be sure that he'd had every bite. I refilled his brandy cup. "There is broth on the left side of your mouth," I told him quietly. It had given me great pain to see him eat both so ravenously and so untidily. When I took his bowl away, I wiped the spatters and drips from the table. I had hoped not to shame him, but as he wiped his face he admitted, "I eat like a starved dog. A blind starved dog. I'm afraid I've learned to get as much food into me as quickly as I can. It's hard to unlearn something so deliberately taught to me." He sipped from his cup and leaned his head back on the chair. His eyes were closed, but it was only when his lax hand twitched and his cup nearly fell that I realized he was falling asleep where he sat.

"Back to bed," I told him. "If you eat and rest for a few days, perhaps we can begin small healings to set you back on the path to health."

He stirred and when I took his arm, he tottered to his feet. "As soon as we can, please begin. I must get stronger, Fitz. I must live and I must defeat them."

"Well. Let's begin by getting a night's sleep," I suggested to him.

I guided him back to the bed and saw him well covered. I tried to be quiet as I tidied the room and added wood to the fire. I refilled my brandy cup. It was blackberry brandy, and of a much better quality than I'd ever been able to afford when I was a youngster. Nonetheless, the lingering taste of berries and blossoms put me in mind of those days. I sank down into Chade's chair with a sigh and stretched out my feet toward the fire.

"Fitz?"

"I'm here."

"You haven't asked me why I came back. Why I came seeking you." His voice was drenched with weariness.

"The messenger said you were looking for your son. Your unexpected son."

"Without much hope, I fear. I dreamed I had found him, there in that market town." He shook his head. His voice sank low. I strained to hear his words. "He is what they want. The Servants. They thought I knew he existed. For quite a time they questioned me, trying to wring from me a secret I did not know. And when finally they told me, plainly, what they sought, I still knew nothing of him. They didn't believe that, of course. Over and over, they demanded to know where he was and who had borne him. For years, I insisted it was impossible. I even asked them, 'If such a child existed, would I leave him?' But they were so certain, I came to believe they must be right."

He fell silent. I wondered if he had fallen asleep. How could he, in the midst of such a harrowing tale? When he spoke again, his voice was thick. "They believed I lied to them. That is when they . . . took me." He stopped speaking. I heard how he fought for a steady voice as he said, "When first we returned, they honored Prilkop and me. There were long evenings of feasting and they encouraged us, over and over, to tell every moment of what we had seen and done. Scribes took it all down. It . . . it went to my head, Fitz. To be so honored and praised. Prilkop was more reserved. Then one day, he was gone. They told me he had decided to visit the place of his birth. But as months passed, I began to suspect that something was wrong." He coughed and cleared his throat. "I hope he escaped or is dead. It's terrible to imagine they have him still. But that is when their endless questioning of me began. And then, after they revealed what they sought and I still had no answers for them, they took me one night from my apartments. And the torment began. At first, it was not so bad. They insisted I knew, and that if I fasted long enough or endured cold long enough, I would remember something, a dream or an event. So I began to believe them. I tried to remember. But that was when I first sent messengers out, to warn those who might know to hide such a child until I came for him."

A mystery solved. The missive sent to Jofron and her wariness of me all made sense now.

"I thought I had been so discreet. But they found out." He sniffed. "They took me back to where they had been holding me. And they brought me food and drink and asked me nothing. But I could hear what they did to those who had aided me. Oh, Fitz. They were scarcely more than children!" He choked suddenly and then wept harshly. I wanted to go to him but I had no comfort for him. And I knew that he wanted no sympathetic words or kindly touch just then. He wanted nothing of what he had not been able to give to those victims. So I wiped the tears silently from my own cheeks and waited.

He coughed at last and said in a strained voice, "Still. There were those who stayed loyal to me. From time to time they would get a message to me, to let me know that another two had escaped and set out to warn my friends. I wanted to tell them to stop, but I had no way to respond to their messages. The Servants began on me in earnest in those years. Times of pain followed by periods of isolation. Starvation, cold, the relentless light and heat of the sun, and then such clever torture."

He stopped talking. I knew his story was not finished, but I thought he had told me as much as he could bear to now. I stayed where I was, listening to the flames, to a log settling in the fire. There were no windows in this chamber but I heard the distant howl of wind past the chimney top and knew that the storm had risen again.

The Fool began whispering. It took a short time for my hearing to sort his words from the storm wind. ". . . believed them. He existed, somewhere. They stopped asking me questions about him, but they kept on hurting me. When they stopped that . . . I sus-pected the Servants had found him. I didn't know if they would keep him to use, or destroy him to thwart him from changing the world. If they did or didn't, they'd never tell me. Funny. So many years ago, I sent to you to find my son for me. And one of those messengers was the one to get through. Too late to save my son. Years too late." His voice was running down, draining off into sleep.

I spoke softly, not wanting to wake him if he was asleep but too curious to contain my question. "Years ago, you gave up? The mes-senger took years to reach me?"

"Years," he said wearily. "Years ago, when I still had hope. When I still believed the Servants could be shown a better way. If I could get to the boy first." His voice fell silent. I stared into the flames, and Bee came into my thoughts. She'd be asleep in her bed by now. Sometime tomorrow afternoon, if the pigeons flew swiftly, Revel would let her know that a bird had arrived and that I was safe at Buckkeep. I should take paper tonight and write her a letter and send it by messenger. I needed to explain to her why I'd left her so suddenly and that I might be gone longer than I'd first expected. I toyed with the idea of sending for her. Every child should experi-ence a Winterfest at Buckkeep Castle! But then I realized she could not possibly arrive in time for that. I also could not think of any-one I'd trust enough to take her on the long winter journey from Withywoods to Buckkeep. Next year, I promised myself. Next year, we'd leave Withywoods in plenty of time and ride to Buckkeep Castle, just her and me.

The plan gave me such pleasure until I suddenly thought of the Fool and his unexpected son in that context. He had never known his child. Did that mean he had never dreamed of sharing things with him? I spoke to the fire. "The messenger couldn't tell me where to look for the child. And I had no idea of how old the boy might be."

"Nor did I. Nor where. Only that there were so many, many prophecies that seemed to speak of such a child. The Servants were so sure that such a child must exist. They asked me in every way they could imagine. They would not believe I did not know of such a child. They would not believe I could no longer see where or who such a child might be." He groaned suddenly and moved abruptly in the bed. "It has been so long . . . my belly. Oh." He coiled briefly and then rolled to the edge of the bed. "Is there a garderobe in this chamber?" he asked desperately.

His stomach made terrible noises as I guided him to the narrow door. He remained inside for so long that I began to be concerned for him. Then the door opened and he groped his way out. I took his arm and guided him back to the bed. He crawled weakly onto the bed and I covered him. For a time, he simply breathed. Then he said, "Maybe there never was such a son. That is my desperate hope. That he never existed, so they never found him, never destroyed him, never took him as their gamepiece." He groaned again and shifted restlessly on the bed. "Fitz?"

"I'm right here. Do you want anything? Brandy? Water?"

"No. Thank you."

"Go to sleep. You need rest. Tomorrow, we will both be more intelligent about what you eat. I have to build you up before the coterie can attempt a healing."

"I'm stronger than I look. Stronger now than when you found me."

"Perhaps. But I no longer take risks unless I must."

A long silence. The brandy and the food were affecting me. The weariness of the day suddenly wrapped me. I walked to the other side of the bed and kicked off my boots. I shed my outer garments and burrowed into the big bed beside the Fool. The featherbed was deep and soft. I shouldered deeper into it and closed my eyes.

"Fitz."

"What?"

"Would you kill for me?"

I didn't need to think about it. "Yes. If I had to. But you're safe here, Fool. The stout walls of Buckkeep Castle are all around you. And I am at your side. No one knows where you are. Sleep without fear."

"Would you kill for me if I asked you to?"

Was his mind wandering that he had repeated his question? I

spoke soothingly. "You wouldn't have to ask me to. If someone were threatening you, I'd kill him. Simple as that." I didn't tell him to go to sleep. It isn't that easy, after you've experienced torture. There were still nights when I woke with a jolt, thinking myself back in Regal's dungeon. The smallest thing could trigger a sudden rush of terror: the smell of a certain kind of charcoal, a creak like a rope tightening, a clang that sounded like a cell door slamming. Even just the dark. Just being alone. In the dark, I reached out and set my hand on his shoulder. "You're safe. I'll keep watch if you want me to."

"No." He reached up and put his bony hand on top of mine. The logs in the fire crackled softly and I listened to him breathe. He spoke again.

"That isn't what I meant. It's the message I sent with the last four messengers. The favor I hated to ask. I was ashamed to ask it, ashamed to ask anything of you after I had used you so mercilessly. But there was no one else I could ask, anywhere. I tried to do it myself. They'd stopped questioning me. They'd begun to leave me alone. And one day they were careless. Perhaps. I escaped. I thought I escaped. I found friends and took shelter and rested. I knew what I had to do. Knew what must be done, and I prepared for it as well as I could. And I tried. But they were expecting me. They caught me and the ones who had given me shelter and aid. They took me back and that time, they didn't bother with finesse or questions. Just brutality. Breaking my bones. Taking my sight."

"What had you done?" My breath felt short.

"I tried and botched it badly. They mocked me. They told me I'd always fail. But you wouldn't. You'd know how. You had all the training. And you were good at it."

The warmth of the bed could not dispel the chill that was building in me. I shifted away but his hand suddenly gripped mine, tight as death. "You were good at it, once. At killing people. Chade trained you and you were good at it."

"Good at killing people," I said in a wooden voice. Those words did not make sense when I said them aloud. Good at creating death. A silence thicker than darkness separated us.

He spoke again. Desperation filled his voice. "I hate to ask it. I know you have set it out of your life. But I must. When I am rested, when I explain it to you, you will understand. They have to be stopped, and only death will do it. There is only you between them and what they would do. Only you."

I did not speak. He was not himself. The Fool would never have asked this of me. He was blinded and ill and in pain. He had lived in terrible fear. He still feared. But he was safe now. As he became better, his mind would clear. He'd be himself again. He'd apologize. If he even remembered this conversation.

"Please, Fitz. Please. They must be killed. It's the only way to stop them." He took in a painful gasp of air. "Fitz, would you as-sassinate them? All of them. Put an end to them and the horrible things they are doing?" He paused and added the words I'd dreaded hearing. "Please. For me."

Chapter 32

THE RAID

According to the locals, only once in each generation is a true White Prophet born. Often enough, the child is born into a family that had no awareness that they carried such blood in their veins. If the family is in a region where the White Prophets are venerated, there is rejoicing and celebration. The wondrous child is raised at home until he or she is ten years of age. At that time, the family makes a pilgrimage to the Pale Isle, thought to have been the homeland of the White folk and now the location of the Servants of the Archives, those who dedicate themselves to the preservation of the records and prophecies of the White Prophets. There the child will be greeted with joy and taken into their custody.

It is said that every dream the child relates will be recorded there. Until his twentieth year, he is prohibited from reading any of the preserved prophecies of other White Prophets, lest their information

taint the purity of his vision. When he attains his twentieth birth-
day, his education in the Archives begins.

Then this traveler was told the sad tale of a White infant born in
a distant village where folk had no knowledge of the White Proph-
ets. When the time for a new White Prophet to be born had passed
with no such child being reported, the Servants of the Archives un-
dertook to read for themselves all prophecies that might relate to
such a lack. Their research led them to send messengers to that re-
mote region, looking for the child. They came back with a tale of a
pale child deemed a freak and an idiot, left to starve in his cradle.

SHAKERLOOM'S TRAVELS, REPPLE SHAKERLOOM

We returned to Withywoods in the dark and cold. FitzVigilant was
not as good a driver as my father or Riddle. The horses knew the
way home, but he did not keep the wheels of the wagon in the ruts
as my father did, so they rubbed up against the edges of the banked
snow and lurched or sawed along. In the darkness and with the
road hidden under the ever-deepening snow, I am sure driving the
team was more difficult than it looked. I huddled under some blankets in the back of the wagon, worrying about my father, and wondering about the beggar and wishing we were already home. I was
very tired and rather miserable at how quickly I'd been abandoned.
It did not help that all the way home, Shun and FitzVigilant huddled together on the wagon seat, well bundled in lap robes, and
conversed in low, outraged tones about all that had happened in
town. They spoke of my father and Riddle in a way that made it
seem they thought me deaf, or dismissed my feelings as unimportant.

They'd seen the incident with the dog, but had hung back to
avoid whatever sort of trouble it might bring them. Shun fervently
hoped that no gossip in Oaksbywater would connect her to the
madman that Tom Badgerlock had become over a dog. She had
been humiliated enough by how he had spoken to her in the tavern,
in front of everyone! FitzVigilant could not make sense of what my
father and Riddle had done regarding the beggar, not why nor how,
and that seemed to offend both of them most of all. That they'd

been left out of any detailed explanation seemed incredibly rude to them, yet that entire long ride back from Gallows Hill they spoke not a word to me. As we jolted slowly homeward, the cold took me in its fist and squeezed me ever tighter. I kept falling into an uncomfortable sleep and then being jolted out of it.

By the time we reached the estate, I was half-sick from the lurching and bumping. I woke a final time when FitzVigilant pulled the horses in before the tall doors of the manor house and jumped down shouting for a stable boy. He handed Shun down carefully and told her to hurry into the house and get warm. She wondered aloud why there was no servant waiting on the steps with a lantern to guide her. FitzVigilant agreed that the staff was very lax indeed and needed training. They had known we would return that night. They should have been waiting.

The falling snow had added damp weight to the blankets that had covered me. My muscles were reluctant to move from sitting still and yet not still from the wagon's lurching. I was struggling to get out from under my coverings as FitzVigilant came to the back of the wagon. "Come here, Bee," he said.

"I'm trying," I replied. He huffed impatiently, seized the edge of one wrap, and dragged them all off me, sending the mounded cold snow cascading over me. I gasped at the shock, and tried in vain not to let it become a sob. He looked appalled at what he had done to me but spoke sternly. "Now, don't be a baby. It's just snow. We're all tired and cold, but we're home. Come here, and we'll get you into the house and warmed up."

I didn't reply. The sharp motion of the blanket had overset my market bag. I felt about in the darkness, trying to gather my precious purchases from the dark wagon bed. They were scattered everywhere now, under snow and the hodgepodge of blankets he had dropped. He probably could not see what I was doing as he said, "Come now, Bee, or I'll leave you here."

I found a breath and pushed some words out. "I don't care. Please go."

"I mean it!"

I didn't respond, and after standing for a silent moment he

turned and stalked toward the house. A stable boy had come with a lantern, and was standing by to take the wagon and team on to the stables to be unharnessed. He cleared his throat.

"I'm trying to hurry," I said in a choked voice.

"You don't need to hurry," he said, and suddenly it was Perseverance. He lifted the lantern higher, and both light and shadows filled the wagon bed.

"I just need to find the things Papa bought for me," I said. Tears were trying to force a way out of me but I would not let them. He didn't say anything. He just climbed up the wheel and into the bed of the wagon, where he began to carefully lift blankets and wraps. He shook each one free of snow and folded it before he set it on the seat, and little by little our purchases were revealed. I gathered them up, putting them carefully back into my basket.

The door to Withywoods opened and closed, and then more shadows leapt and confused me as Revel came bearing a larger lantern. "Lady Bee?" he asked the air, and "A moment more, please," I replied hoarsely. I was trying. Why did they all wish to hurry me when I was so cold?

He came to the edge of the wagon and watched me finish gathering my little parcels. He looked shocked and disapproving. Yet he nodded to Perseverance in a way that promised he would not forget his service, and the stable boy ducked his head. When I had all my things, I stood slowly and hobbled stiffly to the tail of the wagon. "The big packages belong to Lady Shun and Scribe FitzVigilant," I told him as he raised his brows at the remaining baskets and sacks.

"I see," he replied gravely. "Boy, I'll send someone out to fetch those things. Then you may take the team and wagon to the stable."

"Sir," Perseverance replied. To my utter astonishment, Revel picked up my market bag and then lifted me from the tail of the wagon and carried me to the house. He was a tall man, taller than my father, and he made nothing of carrying me and my packages. I was tired and it was hard to sit straight in his arms. My brow brushed his cheek and to my astonishment, it was as smooth as my own. And he smelled wonderful, like roses but with spice added. I spoke without thinking. "You smell so wonderful!"

A smile replaced the concern on his angular face. "Such a kind thing to say, Lady Bee. I mix my fragrance oils myself. Perhaps one day you would like to help me do that?"

"I would!" I declared with heartfelt enthusiasm.

"Then you shall. Your mother taught me much of these scents when I first arrived here. It is only fitting that I pass on what she taught me to you."

I was perched on one of his arms, shaking with cold. He opened the door with his free hand and without a pause carried me through the entrance hallway and down the corridor, directly to my room. Careful had just finished building the fire, and he set me down in front of it.

"She is covered in snow! Lady Bee! Weren't you under the wraps in the wagon?"

I was too tired to explain it. Revel spoke as Careful began to divest me of my wet clothing. "She's chilled through. I'll have Cook Nutmeg send up a tray of hot food and tea. Can you see to her other needs?"

She looked up at him with anxious eyes. "Lady Shun asked me to fetch in her purchases immediately. She wants my help in— "

"I will find someone else to help her," Revel announced firmly. He strode back to the door, paused, and then said, "Lady Bee, we have not been informed as to what befell your father and Riddle, and I feel much concern that they have not returned with you."

He was aware it was not his place to ask for information, but I knew now he was my ally and I shared freely the little I could add. "There was a beggar in the marketplace who spoke to me. When he hugged me, my father feared for me and attacked him, hurting him badly. Then he realized the beggar was actually an old friend of his. So he and Riddle used the Skill-magic to take the beggar through the standing stone on Gallows Hill back to Buckkeep Castle, where perhaps he can be saved."

The two servants exchanged a look over my head, and I realized that my factual account probably sounded completely mad to them. "Fancy that!" Careful said quietly.

"Well. I'm sure your father knows what he is doing, and Riddle as well. A very practical man, that Riddle." The tone suggested that my father was not always practical. It would have been stupid to disagree with that. He whisked out the door.

By the time Careful had helped me into my nightrobe I was shaking all over. It was my red nightrobe, the one my mother had made. Someone had laundered it and brought it to my room. She took a coverlet from the bed, warmed it before the fire, and then wrapped me in it. I didn't protest but sat in the chair she pulled up to the hearth. There was a knock at the door, and a kitchen boy came in with a tray of steaming food. She thanked him and sent him on his way. As she set it out on a low table for me, I told her, "I didn't forget you. I brought you presents from town."

Her eyes lit with interest, but she said, "Tomorrow is soon enough for that, my lady. Tonight let's get hot food into you and then get you into a warm bed. Your face is all red and white with cold still." She lifted my gray-and-red shawl, hefted the heavy wool approvingly, and then set it to dry. As she put away my other things from my basket, she found the packages and the trinkets I had bought for her and immediately possessed them, thanking me over again for thinking of her. I thought of the kerchiefs I had bought for Revel. Would he truly like them? I thought of how he had smelled when he lifted me. I knew he would enjoy one of my mother's candles. My heart hurt at the thought of parting with even one, but I knew I would do it. He deserved it. Careful helped me into my bed and then moved quietly around the room, setting it to rights, humming as she did so.

I think I fell asleep before she left the room. I woke, probably hours later, to a chamber lit only by firelight. I tried to make sense of the day. So much wonder and terror packed into one day, and then to be abandoned at the end of it! I wondered why my father had not taken me with him, and who the beggar was that he was so important. My father had claimed he was his old friend. How was that possible? There was no one of whom I could ask those questions. All around me the house was very still. I slipped out of bed and went to the window, opening the shutters. The sky was black and snow was falling thickly. It was very late at night, or very early. And I was hungry and no longer sleepy at all.

I was still chilled from the long ride home, with a cold that seemed to radiate from my own bones. I went to my wardrobe to find a wrap and discovered that someone had added a new robe for me. I took it out, and found it was made of soft red wool lined with wolf fur. And below where it had hung there were soft boots made just the same, but soled with leather. The moment I put them on, I felt both warmer and safer.

I went first to my father's bedchamber, to see if perhaps he had already returned. I found no comfort there. His bed was empty and the room so rigorously tidy that it could have belonged to anyone. Or no one. "This is not his true den," I said aloud but softly. I nodded to myself, knowing now where I must go to find my answers.

I padded softly through the darkened hallways. My eyes adjusted quickly to the darkness, and I made my way to his private study without encountering another soul. The silence in the house was almost unnatural, as if I were the sole inhabitant. As I approached the study, I rebuked myself for not bringing a candle, for I would need it if I intended to search his private library for clues to my questions. But when I came round the corner I saw that the door was slightly ajar; warm firelight spilled in a sweet wedge on the floor and up the wall.

I pushed the door open and peered in. No one sat at the desk, but a large fire was burning merrily on the hearth. I stepped into the room, asking softly, "Father?"

"I'm right here," he replied. "I'm always here for you." The great gray wolf who had been sprawled on the hearth sat up slowly. He lolled his tongue out over his very white teeth as he yawned, and when he stretched, the black claws of his toes protruded and retracted. Then he looked at me with his wild brown eyes and smiled.

"Wolf-Father?"

"Yes."

I stared at him. "I don't understand," I said faintly.

"You don't have to," he replied comfortingly. "Understanding how or why is very seldom as useful as understanding that things are. I am."

His voice was deep and calm. I moved slowly toward him. He sat very tall, his ears perked, watching me come to him. When I was closer, he took in my scent and said, "You've been frightened."

"There was a dog killer in the market. My father couldn't save the dog anything except pain. Then he killed someone, and unkilled him, and then went off with him. And left me all alone."

"You're not alone when I'm with you. I'm the father that is always with you."

"How can a wolf be my father?"

"Some things just are." He stretched out in front of the fire again. "Perhaps I'm the part of your father that never stops thinking about you. Or perhaps I'm a part of a wolf that didn't end when the rest of me did." He looked up at the carved black stone on the fireplace mantel. I glanced at it. It had three faces, my father, a wolf, and . . . I stared for a long moment.

"That was him. But much older. And blind and scarred."

"The Scentless One. Then I do understand why your father went. He would have to."

"He wasn't scentless. He was a smelly old beggar, stinking of dirt and filth."

"But having no scent of his own. He and your father are pack. I spent many days in his company as well." Wolf-Father looked up at me. "Some calls you cannot ignore, no matter how it may tear your heart."

I sank slowly down to sit beside him. I looked at my feet, gray now with little black claws. The robe had changed. The wolf fur that had been on the inside of it was now on my outside. I curled up beside him and rested my chin on my paws. "He left me. The Scentless One is more important to him than I am."

"That is not so. His need must have been greater. That is all. There comes a time when every cub is left to fend for himself. You'll do well, if you don't mire in self-pity. Self-pity only gets you more of the same. Don't waste time on it. Your father will come back. He always comes back."

"Are you sure of that?" I wasn't.

"Yes," he replied firmly. "And until he does, I am here."

He closed his eyes. I watched him. The fire was warm on our backs and he smelled good, of wild clean places. I closed my eyes.

I woke deep into the morning with Careful bustling about the chamber. "I've let you sleep in, as you came home so late, and Scribe FitzVigilant said that he would begin lessons late today as well. But now you must wake up and face the day, Lady Bee!"

She wore her new beads, and a sprig of holly in her hair. "Is it Winterfest?" I asked her, and she smiled.

"Tomorrow night. But the kitchen is already cooking for it, and very late last night some minstrels arrived offering to make it merry for us. Steward Revel decided to allow them to stay until he could ask your father's permission. In your father's absence he conferred with Scribe FitzVigilant, and he said of course they must stay. And this morning Lady Shun sat down with Revel to make up the menu for the feast! Oh, such dishes as she has ordered! It will be a feast such as we haven't seen in many a year!"

I felt torn. I was excited to know there would be music and dancing and a great feast and insulted to think that it had all been arranged in my father's absence and without his permission. My reaction puzzled me. Had he been home, I was certain he would have approved it. And yet to have those two arranging it all still offended me.

I sat up in bed and asked, "What has become of my fur nightrobe?" For I was wearing my mother's red woolen nightshirt.

"A fur nightrobe? Did you buy a fur nightrobe in town? I've never heard of such a thing!" Careful hastened to my wardrobe and opened the door, only to reveal nothing of the sort.

My head was clearing of the night's fancies. "It was a dream," I admitted to her. "I dreamed I had a nightrobe of wolf fur lined with red wool."

"Fancy how warm that would make you! A bit too warm for my taste," Careful said, laughing, and she set about finding clothes for me. She was disappointed that I had not bought new garments for myself while I was in town. She shook her head as she set out one of the too-large tunics and a new set of wool leggings. I let her chatter flow past me as I tried to relegate my experience to the status of "only a dream." It was not a dream such as I had had before; it was much more like the first time I had met Wolf-Father in the passages. Who was he? What was he? He was the wolf in the carving, just as the beggar was the "Scentless One."

As soon as I was dressed I left the room, but instead of seeking breakfast I went to my father's study. I opened the door to a chill room; the hearth had been swept clean since last it had been used. I touched the cold stones and knew that there had been no blazing fire in here last night. I looked again at the carved black stone on the mantel. Well, that part of my dream had been true. The other man in the carving was definitely the beggar as a youngster. I looked at his face and thought he must have been a merry fellow back then. I studied the wolf as well; the carver had done his dark, deep eyes justice. I suddenly envied my father, having such friends when he was just a boy. Who did I have? Perseverance, I told myself. Revel. And a cat who still hadn't told me his name. For a moment I felt as if I could vomit loneliness and sadness. Then I squared my shoulders and shook my head. Self-pity would get me nothing but more of the same.

There was another carving on the mantelpiece, one of wood. It was the wolf only. I took it down. It was hard and poked me when I hugged it, but for a long, long time I held it in my arms. I wanted it very badly, but I set it back where it had been. When my father came home, I resolved, I would ask for it.

I shut the study doors, latched them, and then opened the panel to my own den. I went up to my hiding place and checked my water and bread supplies. More candles, I decided. I felt I might be spending a lot of time in here until my father got back. It would let me be undisturbed, and I doubted anyone would miss me. The cat was not there, but he had left my cloak on the floor. I found it with my foot and then, as I stooped to pick it up, I discovered he had left a half-eaten mouse on it. Wrinkling my nose in disgust, I gathered the cloak and took it back to my father's study with me. The tiny half-corpse I disposed of in the fireplace. I sniffed the cloak gingerly; it smelled of tomcat and dead mouse. I shook it out and folded it into a tiny packet. I'd have to find a private place to wash it out myself. And then, I decided, I'd find a new hiding place for it, one not shared with a cat. He had asked for a basket and a blanket, and I hadn't yet fulfilled that part of the bargain. Later today, I would. I thrust the handful of butterfly cloak into the front of my tunic, sealed up the secret panel, and left my father's den after a final glance at the wolf.

I found little left of breakfast, but the dishes hadn't been cleared, so I wrapped a bit of sausage in a piece of bread and ate it with a cup of lukewarm tea. It was enough and I was happy to slip out of the dining room as unnoticed as I'd entered.

Reluctantly, I made my way to the schoolroom. The other students were there and waiting but FitzVigilant had not yet arrived. Perseverance sidled over to stand beside me. "Pups are settling in, but one has a bad infection where his tail was lopped off. Whoever did it just whacked it off, didn't even go between the bones. Just *whack!* with a hatchet, probably. We had to pull bone splinters out of it, and he howled like to split the roof beams. The man who did it deserved what your da did to him, twice over. So Roder says, and he knows most everything about dogs. Why did your father decide he wanted dogs all of a sudden? He hasn't kept any hounds for years."

"To keep them alive, I think. Like the donkey."

"Well, we wondered about that, too. That old donkey—we'll feed him up and see his hooves get fixed, but we wondered what he was for." He looked at me. "Was what that town boy told us true?"

I moved farther down the corridor, away from the others. "A man was killing a dog in the town center when we were there. To make people want to buy her pups." Perseverance's eyes widened as I told him the whole tale. By the time I was finished, his mouth was hanging open.

"I'd heard Badgerlock had a temper, and no tolerance for cruelty. Huh." He breathed out his astonishment. "That was done well. But what's he going to do with those bulldogs?"

"What's usually done with them?"

He raised his brows as if surprised I wouldn't know such a thing. "Well, some men fight them, dog against dog. Or they do bull-baiting. You know, set them on a bull, to harry him down before slaughter. It makes the meat better, so they say. Same for pig. Hey, maybe we can use them to hunt out some of the wild pigs around here. There's a couple of big old tuskers that have been making a mess of the root fields for the last couple of years."

"Maybe," I replied. An idea touched me. "Maybe I will ask for one, to be mine."

FitzVigilant was approaching. He looked very fine today, in a blue coat with a white collar and leggings of darker blue. I realized something I hadn't before, that FitzVigilant dressed like a wealthy merchant while my father's garb was closer to that of the farmers who came to Oaksbywater to sell their wares. I looked down at myself. Yes. Closer to a farmer's daughter than to the child of a noble house. Or perhaps even a farmer's son. My tutor gave me no time to dwell on that. "Come along, then, come inside and get settled! We've lost quite a bit of the morning, so we need to be quick today with our lessons."

No one seemed inclined to remind him that he had been the last to arrive. Instead we did as we were told, settling quickly. Our teacher was distracted and almost irritable, as if we were an annoying task to accomplish and be done with rather than the reason he had been brought to Withywoods. He attempted to teach us all a long rhyme about the various kings of the Six Duchies and what each was remembered for, but instead of teaching it in bits, as my mother had taught me "The Twelve Healing Herbs," he recited all of it for us, and then went round asking each of us to attempt it. Not a one of us made it past the third king, let alone all twenty-three of them, and he professed his disappointment in detail. He recited it again, very rapidly. Larkspur managed to get through four of the verses, mostly correct. Elm broke down in sobs when Fitz-

Vigilant made her stand up and try to recite them. He had fixed his eyes on me, and I felt both determination and dread fill me as I slowly stood to recite.

I was saved by distant angry shouts followed by a booming as if someone was repeatedly slamming a door. FitzVigilant looked away from me, scowled, and went to the door of the schoolroom. He gazed in the direction of the noise, still frowning. He was starting to close the door when we all heard a long and chilling scream.

The scribe looked alarmed. "Stay here. I'll be back shortly."

And with that he left us, striding at first—and then we all heard his footsteps increase to a run. We exchanged glances. Larkspur fidgeted and then stood up. He took two steps toward the door. "He said to stay here," Perseverance reminded him. We remained as we were, listening to muffled shouts. Perseverance looked at me and then said, "I'm going to go see what's going on."

"Me, too," I insisted.

"No," he forbade me, and then as I bared my teeth at him, he added in a more conciliatory tone, "You don't want the scribe to be angry with you, Lady Bee. I'll go quickly and come right back."

I cocked my head at him and replied pleasantly, "And so shall I."

"They're going to get in trouble," Lea confided to Elm in a hopeful voice.

I gave the girls the most scathing look I could muster and then went with Perseverance to peer around the corner of the door. No one was in sight, but the sounds of men shouting was louder. There was a kitcheny sound, as of metal clashing on metal. Perseverance looked at me and mouthed, *Swords?* His expression was incredulous.

I thought him silly but could think of nothing else it might be. "Perhaps something about Winterfest?" I suggested.

His eyes lit with anticipation. "Maybe." Then a man yelled angrily. "Maybe not," he said, his smile fading.

"Stay here and be quiet," I said to the others who had gathered in the doorway behind me. We stepped out into the corridor. I felt to be sure my mother's knife was still in my belt. My heart was thundering as I followed Perseverance soft-footed down the corridor. When we reached the bend in the corridor where it joined to the halls of the main house, I felt a great rush of relief to see Revel hurrying toward us. He was carrying something clutched to his middle, something very heavy from the way it made him stagger along. As we both scurried up to him, I called out to the house steward, "Is something going on? We heard shouting and Scribe FitzVigilant left us to go see . . ."

Revel swayed to one side, his shoulder striking the wall. His knees bent and he sank down. He had lifted a hand when he hit the wall, and it left a long bloody streak as he collapsed. The object he had been carrying turned into a shaft sticking out of him. He'd been clutching at it as he lurched along. He looked at us both. His mouth moved, forming words with no breath behind them. *Run. Hide. Go!*

Then he died. Just like that, in a moment: gone. I stared at him, fully aware that he was dead and wondering why Perseverance stooped and put a hand on his shoulder and peered into his face, saying, "Steward? Steward, what happened?" He set a shaky hand on Revel's, which still clutched the shaft in his chest. He drew it back red.

"He's dead," I said, and I clutched at Perseverance's shoulder. "We've got to do as he said. We have to warn the others. We have to run and hide."

"From what?" Perseverance demanded angrily.

I was equally furious. "Revel came here, dying, to give us that message. We don't make it useless by acting stupid. We obey. Come on!"

I had hold of his shirt and I dragged on it, pulling him with me. We started at a walk and then burst into a run. I could barely keep up with him. We reached the schoolroom and dashed inside. "Run. Hide!" I told them all and they stared at me as if I were mad.

"It's something bad. The steward's dead in the hall, an arrow or something through his chest. Don't go back to the main house. We need to get out of here and away."

Lea looked at me with flat eyes. "She's just trying to get us all in trouble," she said.

"No, she's not," Perseverance half-shouted. "There's no time. Just before he died, he told us to run and hide." He thrust out his hand, scarlet with Revel's blood. Elm screamed and Larkspur sprang backward and fell over.

My mind was racing. "We go back through the south wing to the conservatory. Then out into the kitchen garden and across into the kitchens. I know a place we can hide there."

"We should get away from the house," Perseverance said.

"No. It's a good place, no one will find us there," I promised him, and Elm finished it for us by saying, "I want my mother!"

And that was that. We fled the schoolroom.

The sounds from the main house were terrifying, muffled cries and crashes and men shouting. Some of the younger children were squeaking or sobbing as we left the schoolroom. We seized hands and fled. When we reached the conservatory, I thought that perhaps we could all hide there, but decided that few if any of the others could keep still and concealed if armed men entered. No. There was only one hiding place where their sobs would go unheard, and loath as I was to share it with them, I had no other choice. I reminded myself I was my father's daughter, and in his absence I was the lady of Withywoods. When I had helped the beggar in town, I thought I had been brave. But that had been for show, for my father to see. Now I had to truly be brave.

"Outside and across to the kitchens," I told them.

"But it's snowing!" Elm wailed.

"We should get to the stables and hide there!" Perseverance insisted.

"No. The tracks in the snow would show where we'd gone. The kitchen gardens are already trampled. Our passage won't show as much. Come on. Please!" The last I flung out in despair as I saw the stubborn look on his face.

"I'll help you get them there, but then I'm going to the stables to warn my da and the fellows."

There was no arguing with him, I saw, so I jerked my head in a nod. "Come on!" I said to the others.

"And be quiet!" Perseverance ordered them.

He broke trail for us. The kitchen gardens had been idle for a month, and snow banked the mounded straw-covered beds of rhubarb and dill and fennel. Never had the garden seemed so large to me. Elm and Lea were clutching hands and making small complaints about the snow in their house shoes. As we approached the kitchen door, Perseverance waved us back fiercely. He crept to the snow-laden sill, put an ear to the door, listened, and then dragged it open against the fresh mounded snow.

A moment only I stared in at the chaos of the kitchens. Something terrible had happened here. Loaves of freshly baked bread were scattered across the floor, a joint of meat was burning over the fire, and no one was there. No one. The kitchens were never empty, not during the day. Elm gasped in horror at her mother's absence and Lea startled me by having the presence of mind to slap her hand over her friend's mouth before the scream could escape. "Follow me!" I whispered.

As I led them toward the pantry, Perseverance said softly, "That's no good! There won't be room for all of us. We should have hidden in the conservatory."

"Wait," I told him, and dropped to my knees to crawl behind the stacked boxes of salt fish. To my great relief, the hatch stood very slightly ajar as I had left it for the cat. I pushed my fingertips into the crack and pulled it open. I crawled back out. "There are secret corridors behind the walls. Go in there. Quickly."

Larkspur dropped to all fours and crawled back. I heard his muffled whisper of, "It's pitch black in there!"

"Go in! Trust me. I'll get a candle for you. We need to get inside there and hide."

"What are these places?" Elm demanded suddenly.

"Old spy-ways," I told her, and "Oh," she replied knowingly. Not even danger could curb that one's spiteful tongue.

Then, somewhere in the far chambers of Withywoods, a woman screamed. We all froze, staring round at one another. "That was my ma," Elm whispered. I thought it had sounded like Shun. We waited but no more sounds reached us. "I'll get some candles," I said. The children crouched down, and some ventured behind the stacked crates.

It took all my courage to go back to the kitchen. I knew where the extra tapers were kept. I lit one at the hearth and turned. I nearly shrieked when I found Perseverance and Spruce standing behind me. Ivy clung to a handful of her brother's sleeve. I looked at Perseverance. His face was white with determination.

"I have to go find my da. I have to warn him. Or help him. I'm sorry." He stooped and hugged me awkwardly. "Go hide, Lady Bee. I'll come back here and shout for you when it's safe to come out."

"Not yet!" I begged him. Once he left, I would have only myself to depend on. I couldn't face that. He had to help me stay and hide the others.

He wasn't listening to me. He was staring at the snow and wet we had tracked across the kitchen floor. "Oh, sweet Eda! We've left tracks everywhere. They'll find you all."

"No. They won't!" I shoved the candles at Spruce, and he took them dumbly. I stooped and snatched up loaves of bread. I pushed them into Ivy's hands. "Take these. Go behind the crates and into the wall with the others. Don't shut the door. I'll be there in a minute. Tell everyone to crawl along the passage and to be quiet. Quiet as mice. Don't light more than one candle!"

Even in the kitchen I could hear the others muttering and mewling behind the wall. Then I heard men's voices, distant but even so I recognized they were shouting to one another in a language I didn't know.

"Who are they?" Spruce demanded in an agonized voice. "Why are they here? What are they doing? Who was that screaming?"

"That doesn't matter. Living does. Go now!" I physically pushed them toward the door. As Spruce and Ivy vanished into the pantry, I seized a stack of napkins from the table and dropped to begin smearing the watery footprints. Perseverance saw my intent and did the same. In a trice we had changed the tracks to a wandering wet swath.

"Leave the door open. They may think we came in and went out again," Perseverance suggested.

I pulled it open as he suggested. "You'd better go now," I told him. I tried to keep my voice from shaking.

"First, you hide. I'll push the boxes against the wall to cover where you went."

"Thank you," I whispered. I fled to the pantry, dropped to my knees, and crawled behind the crates.

The entrance was closed. I tapped on the door, and then knocked. I put my ear to it. Not a sound. They had obeyed me and gone up the corridors. And somehow the door had latched when someone had closed it behind her.

I couldn't get in. Perseverance stuck his head around the corner. "Hurry up! Go in!"

"I can't. They shut it behind them and it latched. I can't open it from this side."

For a long moment, we stared at each other. Then he spoke softly. "We'll move the boxes to cover where they went. Then you come to the stables with me."

I nodded, trying not to let either tears or sobs break from me. More than anything, I longed to be safely hidden in the walls. It was my place, my special hiding place, and now that I needed it most it had been taken from me. Somehow my hurt at that unfairness was almost as great as my fear. Perseverance was the one who pushed the crates snug against the wall. I stood staring at them, fear strengthening in me. When I'd had a plan, a bolt-hole to flee to, I had been focused and calm. Now all I could think of was that Revel was dead and some sort of battle was going on in the house. In Withywoods. Pleasant, calm Withywoods. Where my father was not. Had blood ever been shed here before?

Then, as if I were his little sister, Perseverance took my hand in his. "Come along. My da will know what to do."

I didn't point out that it was a long run through the open to reach the stables, nor that I wore only low shoes fit for the corridors of Withywoods. I followed him as we left the kitchen door open behind us and went out into the snow. We ran across the open garden, tracing our tracks back to the conservatory but not reentering it. Instead I followed Perseverance silently as he hugged the wall of the manor. We moved behind the bushes, trying not to disturb the weight of snow that mounded upon their branches.

We could hear things out here. A man was shouting in an accent I didn't recognize, commanding someone to "Sit down, sit down, don't move!" I know Perseverance heard it and knew that he realized he was leading me closer to that voice. It seemed the worst thing we could do, but still I followed him.

We rounded the end of the wing and halted. Holly bushes grew thick there, their prickly green leaves and bright-red berries a sharp contrast with the snow. The layer of dead leaves where we crouched bit right through my thin house shoes. We huddled like rabbits and stared at the sight before us.

There were the folk of Withywoods, gathered like a flock of befuddled sheep in the open drive before the main door of the house. They stood in the snowy carriageway in their indoor clothes, hugging themselves and one another, bleating like frightened sheep. Most were people I had known all my life. Cook Nutmeg held Tavia at her side and stared defiantly at her captors. I knew the minstrels by their gaudy garb. They crouched together, staring about in astonishment. Careful hugged herself, rocking back and forth in misery. Shun's maid was there beside her, clutching the torn front of her dress closed. She was barefoot. Three burly men on horseback were looking down at the people they had herded together. I thought I had seen one of them before but I wasn't sure where. Two were not speaking at all, but all three had drawn and bloody swords in their hands. One was still shouting at everyone to sit down, sit down. Only a few were obeying him. Off to one side, two bodies lay facedown, unmoving, red melting the snow around them.

One was FitzVigilant. I knew that fine jacket, I knew those tailored trousers. I had seen them just that morning and I knew it was him, but my mind would not accept it.

"I don't see my da." Perseverance barely breathed the words. I nodded. Now I noticed a few folk from the stables, but his father was not among them. Dead or hiding, I wondered.

A woman emerged from Withywoods and walked toward the captives. She looked so ordinary, just a plump woman of middle years, dressed warmly for the snow. She had fur boots, a thick wool cape, and a fur hat pulled down over her ears. Her round face and bouncing brown curls made her look almost cheery. She walked up to the man who was shouting at people to sit down and looked at him. Her voice carried clearly when she asked him something, but it was in a language I did not know. His denial was plain in any language.

She lifted her voice and spoke to the captives. Her accent was odd but I understood what she said. "A boy was brought here, recently. Possibly within the last five years but more likely within the last few months. His skin will be as pale as snow, his hair as white. Give him to us, and we are gone. He might be as young as a child, or a man grown to middle years. We will know him when we see him. He isn't here, but you must know who we are talking about." She paused, waiting for a reply, then added reassuringly, "He isn't one of yours; he has always belonged to us, and we only want to take him home. No harm will come to him, and if you but tell us, no more harm will befall you."

Her words were measured and calm, almost kind. I saw my house people exchanging glances. Tavia shrugged free of Cook's arm and lifted her voice. "There is no one here like that. The only newcomer here was the man you killed, the scribe. Everyone else has worked here for years, or was born to us, in the village. You already seen the minstrels; they're the only strangers here!" Her words tumbled into a sob. The minstrels, already terrified, huddled closer together.

"You are lying!" the shouting man accused her. Her face crumpled with fear and she lifted her hands to cover her ears, as if his words were a threat by themselves.

The unexpected son. I knew it with a sudden certainty. These were the trackers the pale messenger had warned us about. They had followed her, and for some reason they thought to find the boy here. Perhaps they thought my father had already found him and brought him here for shelter.

"She's not lying!" Cook yelled at him, and a few others were brave enough to shout, "It's true!" "There's no one here that wasn't born here!" and similar outbursts.

"Can you stay here by yourself and hide?" Perseverance whispered next to my ear. "I need to get to the stables and find Da. If he's not there . . . I'm getting a horse and riding down to Withy for help."

"Take me with you," I begged.

"No. I have to cross all that open space to get to the stables. If they see us . . ." He shook his head. "You have to stay here, Bee. Hide." He bit his lower lip and then said, "If my da . . . if I can't find him, I'll come back for you. We'll go for help together."

I knew that was a foolish plan, for him. If he got to the stables, he should just ride like the wind for Withy. But I was terrified. I gave a sharp nod. He pushed me down lower. "Stay here," he hissed, as if I could forget to do so.

He moved to the edge of the holly bushes and waited. The round woman seemed to be arguing with the man on horseback. She pointed angrily at the bodies and gesticulated wildly. Plainly she did not like how he was conducting his search. He was gesturing with his sword and shouting. Then, out of the house came the fog man. I recognized him from my trip to town. There he had been a gleaming light in the alley that people avoided. Today he was a pearlescent mist and, in the center of it, a plump man pale as a ghost. He turned his head slowly from side to side as he walked, and either my eyes deceived me or his eyes were the color of fog. A strange chill went through me and I shrank as small as I could, pulling my awareness back into myself. Putting up my walls, my father would have called it. I felt blind but if that was the price of invisibility I was willing to pay it.

"Bee?" Perseverance whispered, but I shook my head and kept my face turned in toward my belly. I do not know what he sensed but abruptly he took my wrist in a grip like ice. "Come with me. Come on. We're going now. Together."

But he did not take me toward the stables. Rather, we crept back the way we had come, remaining behind and under the bushes that landscaped that wing of Withywoods. I did not look up but merely followed where he dragged me. "Here," he panted at last. "Stay right here. I'll go to the stables. If I can't find my da, I'll bring the horses here. I'll be moving fast and you'll have to run out and jump for Priss's back. Can you do that?"

I didn't know. "Yes," I lied.

"Stay here," he told me again, and then he was gone.

I remained where I was, behind rhododendrons whose drooping green leaves were encased in ice and snow. After a long time, I lifted my eyes and peered about. Nothing moved. I could no longer hear the huddled captives, but the angry voices still teased at the edges of my hearing.

Revel was dead. My father was gone. Riddle was not here. Fitz-Vigilant was dead. At any moment Perseverance could be dead.

And at that thought, I could not sit still. I was terrified of being killed, but even more terrified that my only ally might be dead and I would not even know it. How long would I sit here under a bush while his life was leaking out somewhere? I started panting, trying to get enough air to keep the blackness at bay. I was cold and thirsty and alone. I tried to think, to not do something stupid simply because I wanted to do something.

I took the dirtied cloak out of my jerkin front. I had not forgotten it. But I knew its limitations. It needed time to take on the colors and shadows. I could not fling it about my shoulders and run and hope to be unseen. Except that snow was white. It would not be perfect camouflage, I thought to myself as I spread it out on the snowy ground beside the bushes. I would be more like a white rabbit or a white fox; anyone with half an eye would see my movement, would see my feet and the tracks I would leave. But it would give me a better chance at reaching the stable than I'd had before.

The angry voices from the other side of the house grew louder, the man threatening, the woman unhappy but not pleading. Insistent, I thought to myself. She would have her way. I heard a scream, a man's scream this time, and I wondered who had been hurt or killed. It was followed by a woman wailing. And wailing. And all the while, the cloak lay on the snow and mutated from the color of the darkness inside my jerkin to the color of the shaded and rumpled snow. I had never before paused to think that truly, all snow was not white. Now I saw that it was gray and dirty pale blue and speckled with bird droppings and bits of fallen leaves.

I crawled under it, not wishing to pull it back under the bushes and risk it taking on the colors of leaves and branches. It was sized for an adult, so there was ample fabric to wrap round me and drape my face. I clutched it at my waist and chin, leaving a small space for my eyes. I looked all around, and saw no one on this side of the manor. I darted from my shelter to the cluster of holly bushes where we had previously sheltered, taking care not to get too close to them. I froze where I was, considering the terrain between me and the stable. Should I crawl slowly across it? Make one fast dash? Earlier, the snow had been a smooth blanket over the low sward. Now I clearly saw the tracks that meant Perseverance had managed to cross it. Suddenly I knew he had waited for them to be distracted, perhaps by the man's scream. I did not want to look at the captives. Their situation frightened me and made it hard for me to think. But I had to analyze my chances. The woman was still wailing. Was that enough of a distraction? I stood perfectly still and shifted only my eyes to look at the herded prisoners.

The wailing woman was Shun. She was bareheaded and her gown was torn from one shoulder. She stood before the angry man on his horse and wailed like a mourner. No words, no sobbing, just a high-pitched keening. The fog man was not far from her, and the plump woman seemed to be trying to ask her questions. I could not help her in any way. Much as I disliked Shun, I still would have helped her if I could, because she belonged to me, in the same way the black cat did or the goose children did. They were all the folk of Withywoods, and in the absence of my father and Nettle they were my folk. My folk, huddled and bleating in terror.

A moment before, I had been a child fleeing danger. Something changed in me. I would reach the stables, and with Perseverance I would ride for help. I needed to get there quickly, before he need-lessly exposed himself by riding a horse back toward the manor where he thought I was hiding. The fear that had been crippling me melted away and became a wolf-fierceness. I crouched and the next time the woman asked Shun a question, I ran, keeping low and following Perseverance's trail in hopes of leaving less evidence of my passage.

I reached the corner of the stable and whisked around it and crouched, breathing hard. What next, what next? Go to the back door, I decided, where the stable boys trundled out the barrows of dirty straw. That would be where Perseverance would come out with the horses. It was the door farthest from the house.

My path took me past the cote where our messenger birds had been kept. Had been. Feathers and bodies, their necks wrenched and tossed to the ground inside their fly-pen. No time to stare at all those small deaths. It was coming to me that whoever these people were, they were completely ruthless and this attack had been planned. No birds had flown to say we were being attacked. The invaders had killed them first.

When I reached the stable doors, I peered around them. A sickening sight met my eyes. Had the raiders come here first, as they had with the birds? Horses shifted uneasily in their stalls, for the smell of blood reached even my poor nose. I was grateful they had not taken the time to kill the horses. Possibly they had not wanted to risk the sound. Someone sprawled in the passageway between the stalls. He wore Withywoods colors. He was one of ours, face-down and unmoving. One of mine. I tightened my throat against a sob. No time to mourn. If anyone was to survive, Perseverance and I had to ride for help. We were my people's last hope. I was not sure how many folk there were in little Withy village but there would be messenger birds there and someone would gallop for the King's Patrol.

I was finding my nerve to step past the body when I heard a sound and looked up to see Perseverance coming my way. He was mounted bareback on a sturdy bay but had taken the time to saddle and bridle Priss for me. Tears were streaming down his cheeks but his jaw was a hard mannish jut from his boy's face. He gasped when he saw me, and I quickly let the big hood of the cloak fall back from my face. "It's me!" I whispered.

Anger flashed in his eyes. "I told you to stay where you were!"

He slid down from his horse, muffled his nostrils, and led him past the body. He gave me the reins to hold and went back for Priss, doing the same to get her past. When he stood beside me, he seized me around the waist and without ceremony flung me up on my horse. I scrabbled into place, gathering my cloak in handfuls and stuffing it once more down the front of my jerkin. I didn't want it flapping and spooking Priss. I was already dreading a hard ride.

He did not trust me with Priss's reins but kept them as he mounted his own horse. He looked at me over his shoulder and spoke quietly. "We're leaving at a gallop," he warned me. "It's our only chance. We ride at full speed and we do not stop. Not for any-thing. Do you understand me?"

"Yes."

"If someone stands before us, I will ride him down. And you will stay on Priss and follow. Do you understand?"

"Yes."

"And this time, you obey me!" he added fiercely.

I had no time to respond to that for, with a sudden lurch, we were in motion. We went out the back doors of the stable and across the open sward, keeping the stable between us and the house, heading at a gallop toward the long winding carriageway. The un-broken and drifted snow beneath the leafless trees slowed us but perhaps muffled somewhat the sound of our passage. It was not enough. As we moved from the cover of the stable and into the open, I heard a startled shout. Strange, how a wordless shout can still be in a foreign tongue. Perseverance did something, and our horses suddenly increased their pace, stretching their legs out and running as I'd never ridden before.

I hung on tight with everything I had, ankles, knees, and thighs, my hands gripping the front of my saddle as if I'd never before sat a horse. I heard myself keening and could not stop. There were shouts from behind us, and I heard something, as if a summer bee had suddenly buzzed past me. Then there were two more, and I knew that an archer was shooting at us. I shrank to a burr on my horse's back and we rode on. The carriageway curved and I felt a moment of relief that the invaders at the manor house could no longer see us. We galloped on.

Then Perseverance fell. He went down from his horse, hitting the road and then rolling into the deep snow, and the beast galloped on. He still gripped Priss's lead and she turned hard and nearly trampled him before she sidled to a sudden halt that flung me far to one side. One of my feet lost its stirrup and I hung there, half-off, before I freed my other foot and leapt clear of her to run to Perseverance. There was no arrow sticking out of him, and I thought for a moment that he had merely fallen and we could both be up and away on Priss. Then I saw the blood. The shaft had passed right through him, tearing his right shoulder. Blood was drenching him and his face was white. He rolled onto his back as I reached him and thrust Priss's lead rope at me. "Get up and ride!" he commanded me. "Run away! Get help!" Then he shuddered all over, and closed his eyes.

I stood still. I heard the hoofbeats of his fleeing horse, and other hoofbeats. They were coming. The invaders were coming. They would catch us. I knew I could not lift him, let alone get him up on Priss. Hide him. He was still breathing. Hide him and come back for him. It was the best I could do.

I tore the butterfly cloak free and spread it over him, tucking it round him. Its colors were adapting, but not fast enough. I kicked snow over him and then, as the pursuer's hoofbeats grew louder, I led Priss to the other side of the carriageway. I leapt at her, clawing my way up to the saddle as she jigged and danced in alarm. I got on her back, found the stirrups, and kicked her hard. "Go, go, go!" I shrieked at her.

And she went, lurching into a terrified lope. I leaned down, holding tight, not using my reins at all but only hoping she'd follow the road. "Please, please, please," I begged of the horse, of the world, of everything that possibly existed. And then we were galloping, galloping so fast that I was certain they could not possibly catch us.

The cold wind bit me and tears streamed from the corners of my eyes. Her mane whipped my face. I saw only the open road before me. I would get away, I would bring help, somehow it would turn out all right . . .

Then, on either side of me, two huge horses appeared. They breasted Priss, and one rider leaned down, seized her headstall, and pulled us round in a tight circle. I started to fall off her, and the other rider grabbed me by the back of my jerkin. With one hand he pulled me off my horse and dropped me. I hit the ground and rolled, nearly going under his horse's hooves, and someone shouted angrily as white lights flashed all around me.

There was a moment when I knew nothing, and then I was hanging, my mouth full of snow, my head lolling as someone gripped the front of my jerkin. I thought he was shaking me, and then it was the world shaking around me and then it was still. I blinked and blinked, and finally I could see him, a big angry bearded man. He was old, his hair between gray and white, his eyes as blue as a white gander's. He was roaring at me, furious shouts in a language I didn't know. He suddenly paused and then, in a thick accent, demanded, "Where other one? Where he go?"

I found my tongue and the wit to lie. "He left me!" I shrieked and I did not need to pretend my distress. I lifted a shaking hand and pointed where Perseverance's horse had bolted. "He ran away and left me!"

Then I heard a woman's voice. She was shouting remonstrances breathlessly as she ran down the long carriageway toward us. At a distance behind her, the fog man was coming. He was walking fast but not hurrying. They were quite a distance away. Still clutching my shirtfront, the gray-haired man began to walk back toward her, dragging me and leading his horse, while the other man followed us mounted. The bearded man held my jerkin front so tight I could scarcely breathe. We passed the spot where I had concealed Perseverance. I knew the area only by my footprints in the snow. I did not look toward the spot. I lifted all my walls and did not even think of him lest somehow they know my deceit. I was his only chance, and the only help I could give him was ignoring him. I kicked feebly and tried to shout, hoping to keep the man's attention fixed on me.

Then we were past and closing the distance between us and the hurrying woman. She called something over her shoulder to the fog man. He pointed at me and warbled back at her happily. The man dragging me shouted something at her, and she responded in a rebuke. He halted abruptly, and then shifted his grip on me so that he held me by the back of my jerkin collar. He swung me up off my feet so that I hung dangling from his hand and shook me at her. She cried out in horror and he dropped me and laughed. When I tried to scrabble away, he put his foot on me and pressed me down into the snow. He said something to her, something mocking and threatening. Her cries turned to entreaties.

I tried to breathe. It was as much as I could do with his foot pressing down on me. She reached us, and her entreaties suddenly became threats. He laughed again, and lifted his foot. She knelt in the snow beside me.

"Oh, my dear, my darling one!" she exclaimed. "Here you are at last. You poor, poor thing! How frightened you must have been! But it's all over now. We're here. You're safe now, and we've come to take you home." She helped me to sit up. She looked at me so kindly, her round face full of anxiety and fondness. She smelled like lilacs. I tried to take a breath, to say something, and instead I burst into tears.

"Oh, my poor boy!" she exclaimed. "Be calm now. You'll be fine. You're safe with us now. You're finally safe."

The fog man had drawn closer. He pointed at me and joy suffused his face. "There. That one!" His voice was high and boyish. "The unexpected son. My brother." His happiness at finding me washed over me, suffused me and filled me. I could not prevent the smile that broke out on my face. It came to me in a wave of joy. They'd come for me, the ones I belonged with. They were here and I would be safe, never lonely, never frightened again. His lolling foolish smile and his wide open arms welcomed me. I opened my arms to him, so glad to finally be gathered in.

EPILOGUE

A child is bitten by a rat. The parent rushes to comfort him. But the bite on the hand becomes septic and the child's hand must be taken to preserve his life. That day, the child's life changes forever.

Or a child is bitten by a rat. The parent rushes to comfort him. The wound heals well without a scar and all is well.

But it isn't. The memory of the bite and the rat will be carried by the child for the rest of his life. Even as a grown man, the sound of scuttling in the night will make him waken bathed in sweat. He cannot work in barns or around granaries. When his dog brings him a dead rat, he starts back in terror.

Such is the power of memory. It is fully as strong as the most feverish infection, and it lingers not just for a period of sickness but for all the days of a man's life. As dye soaks fibers, drawn into them to change their color forever, so does a memory, stinging or sweet, change the fiber of a man's character.

Years before I knew that a man's memories could be pressed into stone and waken as a dragon, I still trembled before their power, and hid from them. Oh, the memories I denied and concealed from myself, for they were too fraught with pain for me to consider, as a child or as a man. And the memories I bled away from myself into a dragon, thinking that I freed myself of a poison that would weaken me. For years I walked, dulled to my life, unaware of what I had stripped away from myself. The day the Fool restored those memories to me it was like blood pulsing through a numbed limb, wakening it, yes, but bringing with it tingling pain and debilitating cramps.

Memories of joy etch just as deeply into a man's heart as those of pain or terror. And they, too, soak and pervade his awareness of the world. And so the memories of my first day with Molly, and our first night together, and the day we vowed ourselves to each other have flavored my life and in my darkest days they gave me a light to remember. In times of sickness or sorrow or bleakness of spirit, I could recall how I ran with the wolf through the snowy twilight with no thought beyond the game we pursued. There are cherished memories of firelight, and brandy, and a friend who knew me, perhaps, better than any other could. Those are the memories from which a man builds the fortress that protects his heart. They are the touchstones that tell him he is worthy of respect, and his life has a meaning beyond mere existence. I have all those memories still, the ones of hurt and the ones of comfort and the ones of exultation. I can touch them still, even if they are faded now like a tapestry left to harsh light and dust.

But one day I will carry forward as if it were tattooed with sharp needles of both pleasure and pain into the very core of my being. There is a day I recall with colors so bright and scents so strong that I have only to close my eyes and be there again. It is a bright winter day, a day of blue sky and glistening white snow and the wrinkled gray sea beyond the roofs and roads of Buckkeep Town. Always that day will be the day before Winterfest eve. Always I will hear merry greetings and the luring calls of peddlers and tinkers and the gulls high overhead crying, crying in the wind. The crisp breeze carried the scents of hot cooked foods both sweet and savory mixed with the iodine and rot of the low tide. I walked the streets alone, buying small gifts for the daughter I had left behind at

Withywoods and necessary things for my injured friend, herbs to make the salves Burrich had taught me and clean clothing and a warm cloak and shoes for his crippled, frostbitten feet.

The gulls wheel and cry, the merchants beseech me to buy, the wind whispers of the changing tide, and below in the slight bay, the ships creak and tug restively at their lines. It is a choice day, a lapis day in a silver setting.

It is the day my life changed forever. It is the day my child was stolen, and flames and smoke and the screams of horses rose to the skies over Withywoods, unheard, unseen by me. Neither my Wit nor my Skill told me of snow melted scarlet there, of women with bruised faces and men with pierced bodies. Nothing warned me on that bright day that the darkest time of my life had begun.

ABOUT THE AUTHOR

Robin Hobb is the author of the Farseer Trilogy, the Liveship Traders Trilogy, the Tawny Man Trilogy, the Soldier Son Trilogy, and the Rain Wilds Chronicles. She has also written as Megan Lindholm. She is a native of Washington State.

robinhobb.com
Facebook.com/Robin.Hobb
@robinhobb

ABOUT THE TYPE

This book was set in Goudy Old Style, a typeface designed by Frederic William Goudy (1865–1947). Goudy began his career as a bookkeeper, but devoted the rest of his life to the pursuit of "recognized quality" in a printing type.

Goudy Old Style was produced in 1914 and was an instant bestseller for the foundry. It has generous curves and smooth, even color. It is regarded as one of Goudy's finest achievements.